THE FURTHER INVESTIGATIONS
of Joanne Kilbourn

THE FURTHER INVESTIGATIONS
of Joanne Kilbourn

GAIL
BOWEN

McCLELLAND & STEWART

Library and Archives Canada Cataloguing in Publication

Bowen, Gail, 1942-

The further investigations of Joanne Kilbourn / Gail Bowen.

Contents: A colder kind of death – A killing spring – Verdict in blood.

ISBN 13: 978-0-7710-1469-7
ISBN 10: 0-7710-1469-4

I. Title. II. Title: A colder kind of death. III. Title: Verdict in blood. IV. Title: A killing spring.

PS8553.O8995F87 2006   C813'.54   C2005-905965-6

We acknowledge the financial support of the Government of Canada through the Book Publishing Industry Development Program and that of the Government of Ontario through the Ontario Media Development Corporation's Ontario Book Initiative. We further acknowledge the support of the Canada Council for the Arts and the Ontario Arts Council for our publishing program.

Typeset in Trump Mediaeval by M&S, Toronto
Printed and bound in Canada

This book is printed on 100% post-consumer waste recycled paper.

McClelland & Stewart Ltd.
75 Sherbourne Street
Toronto, Ontario
M5A 2P9
www.mcclelland.com

1 2 3 4 5   10 09 08 07 06

CONTENTS

THE FURTHER INVESTIGATIONS
of Joanne Kilbourn

A Colder Kind of Death

CHAPTER

1

Three minutes before the Hallowe'en edition of "Canada This Week" went on the air I learned that the man who murdered my husband had been shot to death. A technician was kneeling in front of me, adjusting my mike. Her hair was smoothed under a black skull-cap, and she was wearing a black leotard and black tights. Her name was Leslie Martin, and she was dressed as a bat.

"Check the Velcro on my wing, would you, Jo?" she asked, leaning towards me.

As I smoothed the Velcro on Leslie's shoulder, I glanced at the TV monitor behind her.

At first, I didn't recognize the face on the screen. The long blond hair and the pale goat-like eyes were familiar, but I couldn't place him. Then the still photograph was gone. In its place was the scene that had played endlessly in my head during the black months after Ian's death. But these pictures weren't in my head. The images on the TV were real. The desolate stretch of highway; the snow swirling in the air; the Volvo stationwagon with the door open on the driver's side; and on the highway beside the car, my husband's body with a dark and bloody spillage where his head should have been.

The sound was turned off. My hand tightened on Leslie's shoulder. "What happened there?" I asked.

Leslie turned towards the monitor. "I just heard part of it myself, but apparently that guy with the long hair was killed. He was out in the exercise yard at the penitentiary and someone drove past and shot him. He was dead before he hit the ground."

She stood and moved out of camera range. "Two minutes to showtime," she said. Through my earpiece, I heard the voice of the host of "Canada This Week."

"Happy Hallowe'en, Regina," he said. "What'll it be: 'Trick, or Treat'?"

Beside me, Senator Sam Spiegel laughed. "Trick," he said.

"Okay," the voice from Toronto said. "We'll start with NAFTA."

Sam groaned. "Why do we always have to talk about NAFTA?"

The host's voice was amiable. "Ours is not to wonder why, Sam. Now, I'll go to you first. Is the fact that environmental regulations aren't being equally enforced by our trading partners having an impact on investor confidence up here?"

Sam looked cherubic. "Beats me," he said.

Another voice, this one young and brusque, came through the earpiece. "This is Tom Brook in Toronto. Washington, is there any sign of Keith yet?"

I looked over at the monitor. The image of my husband's body had been replaced by images of Keith Harris, the third member of the "Canada This Week" panel. Keith was late, and as he slid into his chair and clipped on his lapel mike, he grinned apologetically. "I'm here. In the flesh, if not yet in the spirit. We're in the middle of a storm, and I couldn't get a taxi. Sorry, everybody."

The sight of Keith's private face, unguarded and gentle as his public face never was, stirred something in me. Until three weeks earlier, Keith had been the man in my life. At the outset, he had seemed an unlikely choice. We had both lived lives shaped by party politics; philosophically, we were as far apart as it is possible for reasonable people to be. Somehow, after the first hour we spent together, that hadn't mattered. Keith Harris was a good man, and until he had taken a job in Nationtv's Washington bureau at the beginning of summer, we had been happy. But distance had divided us in a way politics had not. Passion became friendship, and when Keith came to Regina for Thanksgiving he told me he had met someone else. I was still trying to sort out how I felt about that news.

The monitor switched to a picture of Sam and me. Through my earpiece, I could hear Keith's puzzlement. "Sam, what are you doing in Regina?"

"I came in with the prime minister yesterday and decided to stay over. I thought it would be fun to be with Jo in person for a change."

"Wise choice," Keith said. "I wish I was with you guys. It's colder than a witch's teat down here."

"Nice seasonal image, Keith," said the voice in my earpiece. "Okay, here we go."

In our studio, the man behind the camera, sleek in a spandex skeleton costume, held up five fingers, then four, three, two, one, and the red light came on. We were live to the East Coast.

I felt as if I had turned to wood. I missed my first question, and Sam Spiegel gave me a quick, worried look, then picked up the slack. When we broke for a commercial, he touched my arm. "Are you okay, Jo?"

"I think so," I said. "I just had a shock."

On the monitor, Keith was saying, "Come on, Jo. It's starting to sound like the Sam Spiegel show out there. The only
reason I showed up tonight was to hear your voice."

"Five seconds," said the man in the spandex skeleton suit.
He held up five fingers and started to drop them again.

Sam touched my arm. "I'll set you up. Tell about that
screwup with the microphone when the P.M. was in town
yesterday. It's a great story."

The red light went on. Sam turned the discussion to the
prime minister, and I told the story of the microphone that
picked up some of the P.M.'s private and earthy musings
about the U.S. president and broadcast them province-wide.
My voice sounded odd to me, but Sam was right, it was a great
story, and as I finished, the moderator's laughter rumbled
reassuringly through my earpiece. We moved to other topics.
I could hear my voice, remote but seemingly assured, suggesting, responding. Finally, the man in the skeleton suit held
up his fingers again, and the red light on the camera in front
of me went dark. It was over.

I turned to Sam. "Thanks," I said. "I was glad you were
here tonight."

The producer, Jill Osiowy, came out of the control booth
and said, "Good show, guys." Then she looked hard at me.
"God, Jo, you look whipped. Is something wrong?"

I unclipped my microphone. "The monitor picked up the
last few minutes of the news before we went on," I said.
"Kevin Tarpley was shot today."

"And you were sitting here watching. Shit. Is there anything I can do?"

"Get them to run that tape with the sound, would you?
All I saw was the pictures."

She looked at me dubiously. "Are you sure?"

"Yeah, I'm sure."

She sighed. "I'll get Leslie to set it up."

We went into an editing room and stood behind Leslie Martin as she brought the five o'clock news up on a monitor. It was a surreal moment. The woman in the bat suit conjuring up the image of my husband's killer.

When the boy with the goat's eyes appeared on the screen, I had trouble absorbing what the news anchor was saying. His words seemed to come at me in disconnected units. "Convicted murderer Kevin Tarpley . . . twenty-five . . . assailant unknown . . ."

He was twenty-five. He had been nineteen at the trial. When he stood up for sentencing, his hands were trembling, and I was filled with pity. Then I had remembered what those hands had done, and it hadn't mattered how young he was. I wanted him dead.

I had wanted him dead, and now he was.

More words came at me from the TV screen. "Police are baffled . . . model prisoner . . . born again . . . spent days and nights reading the Bible . . ."

The goat-eyed boy vanished, and the snowy highway filled the screen again. The polished voice of the news anchor continued, and I tried to make myself focus. He was talking about my husband. "Twenty-eight when he was named to Howard Dowhanuik's cabinet . . . the country's youngest attorney general . . . believed by many to be the man who would succeed Dowhanuik . . ." The anchor's handsome face filled the screen. Leslie Martin looked up. Jill nodded and the screen went blank.

"Come on," Jill said. "I'll buy you a drink."

"I can't," I said. "I've got to get home. Taylor's waiting to go Hallowe'ening."

Jill put her arm around my shoulder and gave it a squeeze. "I'll walk you to the door."

The lobby of Nationtv is a three-storey galleria with a soaring ceiling and glass walls. In the daytime, the area is filled with natural light, and the elm trees on the lawn outside make shadowy patterns on the terrazzo floor. But that night as Jill and I came upstairs from the TV studio, the sky was darkening, and the leafless trees were black against the cold October sky.

All Hallow's Eve. Reflexively, I shuddered. A man and two women came through the entrance doors into the lobby. I knew them; they had been in the Legislature with my husband. They were all out of politics now, but it was politics that brought them to Nationtv. Politics and auld lang syne.

The year before, after ten years in the wilderness, we had won the provincial election. People were feeling good about the party again, so it was time to raise money. The following Wednesday, we were holding a roast for the former leader and one-time premier, Howard Dowhanuik. After he resigned as leader, Howard had moved to Toronto to teach constitutional law at Osgoode Hall. It was a long way from the rough and tumble of Saskatchewan politics, but Howard hadn't forgotten that even successful election campaigns have to be paid for. Despite his loathing for testimonials, he was coming home. I was emceeing the dinner, and I'd asked Jill to arrange for some of the members who'd served in the Legislature with Howard to tape a segment of a local show called "Happenings" to publicize the event. The taping was that night.

For a beat, Howard's former colleagues stood in the doorway, unbuttoning jackets, accustoming their eyes to the light. Then Craig Evanson spotted me and started across the cavernous lobby. The others followed.

Craig was fifty years old, but he still moved with the loose-limbed shamble of an adolescent. When he reached out to take my hand, his fingers grazed my shoulder.

"You saw the news report," he said.

I nodded.

"Are you okay?" he asked.

"I will be," I said.

"This is all wrong, Jo," he said. "You and Ian were so close. Julie always called you 'the legendary couple.'"

I didn't know what to say. Craig and his first wife, Julie, had been a legendary couple, too. Craig was the most uxorious of men, but Julie was poison. Before she had surprised everyone by divorcing him two years earlier, she had come close to destroying Craig's life. The day the divorce was final, it was Craig's turn for surprises. He resigned his seat in the Legislature and married one of his constituents, a twenty-five-year-old midwife named Manda Traynor, who had come to Craig's office asking him for help in organizing a campaign to legalize midwifery. Now Manda was expecting their first child, and as Craig stood holding my hand, it was obvious that it was his new wife who filled his thoughts.

"I'm just beginning to understand what you lost when you lost Ian," Craig said simply. "If anything were to happen to Manda . . ." His voice trailed off.

The woman standing behind Craig grunted with annoyance. Tess Malone looked exactly as she had on the day she'd been elected twenty years earlier: her hair was still a helmet of honey curls; the lines of her corsetted body were still bullet smooth. She looked impenetrable, like a woman who woke up every morning and prepared herself for combat. It was not a fanciful image. Tess's life was a battle.

She had run for office four times, and she had won four times. Her slogan was always the same: TRUST TESS. To an outsider, the words seemed sentimental and empty, but Tess's supporters knew the slogan was a covenant. The people who voted for Tess knew that they could trust her to be at their daughters' weddings, their babies' christenings, and their grandparents' funerals. They knew that Tess would be their champion if they needed to get their mother

an appointment at the Chiropody Clinic, their son into drug
rehabilitation, or their wife's resumé into the hands of a
bureaucrat who might actually read it.

There was one other matter on which friend and foe alike
knew they could trust Tess. Everyone who knew Tess
Malone knew she would fight the right to an abortion till
the day she drew her last breath. Ian had liked and admired
her, but when he had been attorney general, he and Tess had
fought bitterly about our government's policy on reproduc-
tive choice; after we lost, they still spent hours quarrelling
over what he called Tess's life-long love affair with the
foetus. The month after he died, Tess resigned her seat in
the house to devote herself full time to a pro-life organization called Beating Heart. She said she quit politics because
she was frustrated at our party's refusal to change its stand
on abortion. I always thought she just missed her old spar-
ring partner. As she stood looking up into Craig Evanson's
face, speaking in the rasp of an unrepentant two-pack-a-day
smoker, I felt a surge of affection.

"Don't be an ass, Craig," she said. "And don't chase
trouble. As Jo can tell you, trouble finds you soon enough.
You don't have to send up flares."

Tess turned to me. Rhinestone flowers bloomed on the
frames of her glasses, but the eyes behind the thick lenses
were clever and kind.

"What can I do to help, Jo? One thought . . . I'm sure you
already have your talk for Howard's dinner organized, but if
you don't feel like standing in front of a room full of people,
I could be the emcee . . ."

Jane O'Keefe, the other woman in the group, raked her
fingers through her short blond hair. "Not while I'm capable
of rational thought," she said. Jane was an M.D., and the past
summer she and three other doctors had opened a Women's
Health Centre in which abortions were performed. There had

been some ugly reactions in the community, and Tess had fanned the flames. She'd been on every talk show in town denouncing the Women's Centre and the women who staffed it.

"Gary can do it," Jane said. She turned and looked out the door towards the parking lot. "If he ever shows up, that is."

Tess moved towards her, "Jane, you yourself said . . ."

"I know what I said. I said I wanted a woman to emcee Howard's dinner, but if Jo backs out, you and I are the women, and I don't want you and you don't want me. That leaves Gary and Craig, and Craig is a lousy public speaker."

Craig made a little bow in Jane's direction. "Thank you, Jane."

Oblivious, Jane sailed on. "Don't be touchy, Craig. You're capable of keeping your pants zipped, which is more than I can say for my brother-in-law."

Right on cue, Jane O'Keefe's brother-in-law burst through the door of Nationtv.

In the women's magazines of the fifties there were love stories with heroes whose physical characteristics were as formulaic as those of a knight in medieval romance. With their rangy bodies and rugged features, they leapt off the pages into our female hearts. Gary Stephens had those kind of good looks, and once upon a time he had been a hero, at least to me. When I knew him first, Gary was a reformer out to transform the political landscape. Then, he changed.

It seemed to happen overnight. One day he just stopped fighting the good fight and became a jerk and a womanizer. The political world is fuelled by gossip, and for a while there was hot speculation about Gary, but the explanation most of us finally accepted was supplied by his sister-in-law. Jane O'Keefe said that, in her opinion, Gary simply lost his death struggle with the id. Whatever had happened, Gary Stephens wasn't a hero anymore, at least not in my books.

"Apologies for being late," he said. "I was . . ."

Jane smiled at him. "We understand, Gary. Everyone knows it takes a man longer after he hits forty."

Gary shrugged. "For the record, I was with a client." He turned towards me. "I heard about Kevin Tarpley on the radio coming over here. I'm sorry, babe. All those painful memories, and Ian was the best."

"I always thought so," I said, and I could hear the ice in my voice.

Jane O'Keefe looked at her watch. "We should get inside. Considering that not one of us was on time today, I don't think we should risk re-rescheduling." She touched my arm. "It was good to see you again, Jo. Hang in there."

Gary leaned forward, gave me a practised one-armed hug and kissed my cheek. The others said goodbye and headed towards the elevators. As the doors closed behind them, I reached up and brushed the place that Gary Stephens's lips had touched.

"Why would he kiss me?" I said to Jill.

She shrugged. "'Man sees the deed, but God sees the intention.'"

"That's a comforting thought," I said.

"Thomas Aquinas was a comforting kind of guy," Jill said. "You'd know these things too, if you'd had the benefit of a Catholic education."

When we stepped through the big glass doors into the night, Jill breathed deeply. The air smelled of wet leaves and wood smoke.

"Hallowe'en," she said, hugging herself against the cold. "Good times."

She grinned at me, and the years melted away. She was the shining-eyed redhead I'd met twenty years before when she showed up unannounced at Ian's office the day she graduated from the School of Journalism. She had handed him her brand new diploma and said, "My name is Jill Osiowy, and I want to make a difference." Ian always said he hadn't known whether to hire her or have her committed.

"I'm glad Ian didn't have you committed," I said.

"What?"

"Nothing," I said. "You'd better get back inside. It's freezing out here. Call me if you hear anything more about Kevin Tarpley."

When I pulled up in front of my house on Regina Avenue, Taylor and Jess Stephens were on the front porch supervising as my friend, Hilda McCourt, lit the candle in our pumpkin. Jess was Gary's son, and he and Taylor had been friends since the first day of Grade 1 when they discovered they could both roll their eyes back in their heads so the pupils seemed to disappear.

Jess was dressed as a magician, Taylor was in her butterfly costume, and Hilda was wearing black tights, a black turtleneck, silver rings on every finger and, around her neck, a silver chain with a jewelled crescent moon pendant. Her brilliant red hair was fuzzed out in a halo around her handsome face. Hilda was past eighty and counting, but she could still turn heads, and she knew it.

When she saw me coming up the walk, she called out. "Wait, I'll turn on the porch light for you. We had it off so the lighting of the pumpkin would be more dramatic."

"Don't spoil the effect," I said. "I don't need a light."

Jess waved at me.

"My mum's sick, and my dad's doing something. Taylor said I could come Hallowe'ening with you. Can I?"

"Sure," I said. "Go call your mum."

He grinned. I could see the space where his front teeth were missing. "I already did," he said. "My dad's gonna pick me up when we're through."

"Good enough," I said.

Taylor was looking at the face of the jack o'lantern, mesmerized. "Blissed out" her brother, Angus, would have said. I knelt down beside her. "T, I'm sorry I'm late," I said. "I got hung up with something at the station."

"I saw the news," Hilda said quietly.

I looked up at her. "Did the kids?"

Hilda shook her head. "No, Angus was in his room trying to decide what to wear to his dance, and tonight Taylor's concerns appear to stop at her wingtips." She leaned towards me. "How are you bearing up?"

"I think trailing along behind these guys with twenty pounds of candy in a pillowcase might be just what I need."

"In that case," said Hilda, "we'll continue with the ceremony here. I was just going to tell the magician and the butterfly the story of Jack O'Lantern."

I stood in the doorway and listened as Hilda told the kids the story of a man named Jack who was so mischievous that the devil wouldn't let him into hell because he was afraid Jack would trick him.

Hilda's voice was sombre as she finished. "And so, when Jack learned he'd have to roam the earth forever, he stole a burning coal from the underworld and placed it inside a turnip to light his way."

Jess looked puzzled. "Why didn't Jack use a pumpkin?" he asked.

"Because this was long ago, in Ireland, and they didn't have pumpkins," Hilda said.

Taylor shook her head. "Poor Jack. Carving that turnip must have taken him about twenty hours."

I touched Taylor's shoulder. "I'm going to go upstairs and check on your brother. You and Jess go in and have one last pee, and then we'll hit the streets. Okay?"

"Yeah," she said, "that'll be okay." She dropped to her knees and leaned forward so that her eyes were looking into the bright triangular eyes of the jack o'lantern. "How did Jack keep the coal lit?" she asked.

I went inside, glad it was Hilda who had to come up with an answer.

Angus was standing in the middle of his room. There were clothes thrown everywhere, but he wasn't wearing anything except a pair of boxer shorts with pigs on them.

When he saw me, he exploded. "The guys are coming by in twenty minutes and I haven't figured out a costume. Everything I try makes me look totally stupid."

"I guess this isn't the time for me to suggest that you should have started planning your costume sooner," I said.

He looked exasperated. "Mum, just give me a little help here . . . Please."

At fifteen, Angus had Ian's dark good looks. He had grown about a foot in the last six months. I looked at him and remembered.

"I have an idea," I said.

I went down into the basement and pulled out a trunk in which, against all the advice in the books for widows, I had kept some of Ian's things. I'd filled the trunk a month to the day after Ian died, but until that Hallowe'en night I hadn't had the heart to open it.

Under a pile of sweaters, I found what I was looking for: an old herringbone cape with a matching Sherlock Holmes hat and a walking stick. I took them back upstairs and handed them to my son.

"Do you remember this outfit?" I asked. "Daddy wore it every Hallowe'en."

Angus had put on a pair of jeans and a turtleneck. He threw the cape around his shoulders and pulled the cap over his dark hair. He looked so much like Ian I could feel my throat close.

"Well?" I said.

He looked at himself in the full-length mirror on his cupboard door.

"Pretty good," he said. Then his reflection in the mirror grinned at me. "Actually, Mum, the cape really rocks hard. Thanks." He started for the door.

"Hey," I said. "Aren't you going to clean up this mess?"

"Later," he said. "Chill out, Mum. It's a night to party."

When he left, the smell of the cape lingered, potent as memory. I swallowed hard and went downstairs to get my daughter and her friend.

It was a great night for Hallowe'ening. There was a three-quarter moon, and, for Taylor and Jess, every street held a surprise: doors opened by snaggle-toothed vampires and mummies swathed in white; stepladders with glowing pumpkins on every step; and on the corner of McCallum and Albert, a witch cackling in front of the cauldron that had smoked with dry ice every Hallowe'en since Angus was a baby.

When we turned onto Regina Avenue, Gary Stephens was pulling up in front of our house.

"Perfect timing," I said, as he got out of the car.

"Right," he said absently.

And then Jess ran to him, holding out his pillowcase. "Dad, look at all the stuff I got."

As he knelt beside his son, Gary's face was transformed. His charm with women might have been as false as the proverbial harlot's oath, but Gary Stephens's love for his son was the real thing. It wasn't hard to get warmth in my voice when I said goodnight.

Taylor went straight to the dining room and dumped all her candy on the table, checking for razor blades the way her

Grade 1 teacher had instructed her to. She pulled up a chair and began to arrange the candy in categories: things she liked and things she didn't like. Then she tried new categories: chocolate bars, gum, candy kisses, gross stuff. Finally, she lay her head down on her arms.

"Okay," I said. "That's it. Time for this butterfly to fold her wings."

I took her upstairs, scrubbed off her butterfly makeup, and tucked her in. When I came back, Hilda was sitting in a rocker beside the fireplace. A fire was blazing in the grate, and on the low table in front of Hilda, there was a tray with two glasses, a bottle of Jameson's, and a round loaf of fruit bread.

"I thought you'd welcome a little sustenance," Hilda said, as she poured the Irish whiskey.

"Where did the bread come from?" I asked.

"Taylor and I made it this afternoon. It's called barm brack; it's traditional in Ireland at Hallowe'en."

I cut myself a slice and bit into it. It tasted of spice and candied peel and fruit. "Good," I said.

"The children didn't think so," Hilda said drily. "They were polite, but they didn't exactly wolf it down."

"All the more for us," I said and took another bite. My teeth hit something papery and hard. I raised my hand to my mouth and took the paper out.

Hilda laughed, "I should have warned you. The barm brack is full of little charms. Of course, you've already discovered that."

I looked at the waxed paper triangle in my hand.

"Open it," Hilda said. "The charm you get is supposed to foretell your future. Angus got the gold coin."

"Good," I said, "my old age is taken care of." I opened the paper in my hand. Inside was a baby doll, no larger than my thumbnail.

"I must have someone else's fortune," I said. "I'm forty-nine years old, Hilda. I think my child-bearing days are over."

"The barm brack is never wrong," Hilda said placidly. "The baby in your future could belong to someone else, you know."

I thought of my older daughter and her husband. A grandchild. It was a nice thought. I lifted my glass of Jameson's to Hilda. "To Irish traditions," I said. "And to Irish stories. You know I'd forgotten that story about poor Jack O'Lantern with his turnip. My mother-in-law told it to me years ago."

Hilda looked thoughtful. "Your husband was Irish, wasn't he?"

"His family was. Ian was born here." I sipped my whisky. "And, as you saw on the news tonight, he died here."

"I remember the case, of course," she said. "It was before you and I met. It struck me as being a particularly brutal and senseless death."

"That about sums it up," I said. "At first, I thought the brutality was the hardest part to deal with. Isn't there a prayer where you ask God to grant you a good death?"

Hilda nodded.

"Well, Ian's death was not good. It was vicious and terrifying. He was beaten to death by a stranger. It was during the week between Christmas and New Year's. He was on the Trans-Canada, coming back from a funeral in Swift Current. There was a blizzard. A car had broken down by the side of the highway. When Ian stopped to help, Kevin Tarpley, that man who was killed today, asked Ian to take him and his girlfriend to a party. At the trial, Kevin Tarpley said that when Ian refused, he smashed Ian's head in with a crowbar."

The shadow shapes on the ceiling shifted. In the stillness I could hear the ticking of the hall clock, regular as a heartbeat.

"I had nightmares for months about what he must have gone through in those last minutes. But in the long run, it wasn't the brutality that drove me crazy; it was the lack of logic. It turned out that Kevin Tarpley's car hadn't broken down at all. When the police found it, it was fine. Kevin told them he got scared when the needle on the heat gauge went into the red zone." I leaned across the table. "Hilda, my husband died because a boy panicked. Isn't that crazy? But everything about Ian's death was senseless. Did you know he went to that funeral in Swift Current because he lost a coin toss?"

Hilda shook her head. "That particular cruelty didn't make the papers."

"We were at a Boxing Day party the Caucus Office had for families who'd stayed in town for the holidays. I guess everyone had had a couple of drinks when Howard remembered that somebody had to go to Charlie Heinbecker's funeral the next day. Charlie was . . ."

"Minister of Agriculture in Howard's first government. I remember him well," Hilda said. "He was a fine man."

"He was," I agreed, "but it's a long drive to Swift Current, and that time of year the roads can be treacherous. Nobody wanted to volunteer. Anyway, somebody decided all the M.L.A.s who knew Charlie should toss a coin. They did, and Ian lost. The next morning he drove off, and I never saw him again. Hilda, it could just as easily have been Howard or Jane or Gary or any of them on that road."

"But it wasn't."

"No," I said, "it wasn't."

The light from the fireplace struck the silver moon on Hilda's necklace and turned it to fire. When she spoke again, her voice was as old as time:

". . . this invites the occult mind,
Cancels our physics with a sneer,
And spatters all we knew of denouement
Across the expedient and wicked stones."

Suddenly, I was so tired I could barely move.

"Hilda, how can we live if the only answer is that there are no answers?"

She leaned across the table. Her eyes were as impenetrable as agate. "That's not what the poem says, Joanne. It says there always are answers. They may sicken us and they may terrify us, but that doesn't make them any less true, and it doesn't make them any less powerful."

She picked up a knife and sliced into the barm brack. "Now, let's have some bread and a little more whisky before the fire dies."

After Hilda went up to bed, I walked through the darkened house, checking, making sure we were safe. As I locked the front door, I glanced through the glass and saw our jack o'lantern on the porch, its candle guttering in the October darkness.

I opened the door and, hugging myself against the cold, I blew out the candle, picked up the pumpkin, and brought it back into the kitchen. When I moved Angus's schoolbooks along the counter to make a place for the jack o'lantern, I uncovered a small stack of mail. There wasn't much: a new *Owl* magazine for Taylor, a bill from Columbia House addressed to Angus, a pretty postcard inviting me to the opening of a visiting show of Impressionist landscapes at the Mackenzie Gallery, and an envelope, standard size, nine by twelve. My students had had essays due the day before, and my first thought was that the envelope held an essay from one of them, trying to limit the penalty for a late paper. But when I glanced at the envelope, I noticed that the letters of my name and address were oddly formed, as if the writer couldn't decide between printing and writing. I opened the envelope. There was a letter in the same curiously unformed hand.

Dear Mrs. Kilbourn,

I must be the last one you thought youd here from but this is important. WE MUST ALL APPEAR BEFORE THE JUDGEMENT SEAT OF CHRIST, THAT EVERY ONE MAY RECEIVE THE THINGS DONE IN HIS BODY, ACCORDING TO THAT HE HATH DONE, WHETHER IT BE GOOD OR BAD. (2 CORINTHIANS, 5) But the Rev. Paschal Temple says I must try to atone on this side of the grave for the wrongs I did. I'm sorry for what happened to your husband, but things are not what they seem. You may hate me, but pay attention to what I wrote on the picture because it is not My Truth. It is God's Truth.

Kevin Tarpley

Attached to the letter with a paperclip was a newspaper clipping. It was the publicity photo for Howard Dowhanuik's dinner. I was in the middle, looking slightly dazed as I always seem to in photos. On my left was Craig Evanson, and beside him was Tess Malone. On my right were Jane O'Keefe and Gary Stephens. Jane was holding the whimsical ceramic statue of Howard that the party was going to present to him the night of the roast. Kevin Tarpley had cut off the original caption of the photo and taped on a piece of scribbler paper. There was a quotation printed in block letters on the paper: "PUT NOT YOUR TRUST IN RULERS, PSALM 146."

I was standing in my own kitchen. The air was pungent with the smells of burned pumpkin meat and candle wax – good familiar smells. Upstairs my children and my friend were sleeping, safe and happy. In the hall, the clock struck twelve, and I could feel my nerves twang. Hallowe'en was over. It was All Saints' Day, the day to remember "our brethren departed," and I had just received a warning from a dead man.

CHAPTER

2

When I looked out my bedroom window at 7:00 a.m. on All Saints' Day, the world was grey, the colour of half-mourning the Victorians wore when the first black-edged grief was over. Fog blanketed everything. Rose, our golden retriever, came over to the window and nudged me hopefully.

"I don't suppose you'd forgo the walk this morning," I said. She looked anxious. "I withdraw the suggestion," I said. I pulled on my jogging pants and a sweatshirt and found my running shoes under the bed. When I was ready, I went into Angus's room. Our collie was sleeping in her usual place at the end of his bed.

"Come on, Sadie," I said, "no rest for the wicked." As I walked through the kitchen, I plugged in the coffee and took a coffee cake and a pound of bacon out of the freezer. On Sundays, I declared all the food in our house cholesterol-free.

As the dogs and I ran down the steps from Albert Street to the north shore of Wascana Lake, I was chilled by the wind off the water. It was an ugly morning. Usually, when I stood on the lakeshore, I could see the graceful lines of the Legislature that had been the focal point of so much of my adult life, but today the legislative building was just a shape, dark and foreboding in the fog, and the lake where Ian and I had canoed in summer and taught our children to skate in winter was bleak. Around the shoreline, ice was starting to form, and it pressed, swollen with garbage, against the shore. The geese in the middle of the lake seemed frozen, lifeless as decoys. Every spring Ian and I had taken the kids to the park to feed the new goslings; by midsummer the birds, wise in the ways of the park, would run at us if we forgot to bring them bread. Ian used to call them the goose-punks.

As I crossed the bridge along the parkway, Nabokov's description of a room of his childhood floated to the top of my consciousness. "Everything is as it should be. Nothing will ever change. Nobody will ever die." Numb with cold and the pain of memory, I turned south and headed for home.

I could hear Taylor the minute I walked through the door. She was in the kitchen talking on the telephone. She was still in her pajamas, and there was a half-eaten candy apple in her hand. When she saw me, she grinned and waved it. As I took the dogs off their leashes and set the table, Taylor's flutey little-girl voice was telling the person on the other end of the phone about Hallowe'en.

"At the house on the corner by the bridge, there was a Count Dracula giving out candy, and he had pointed teeth and blood on his chin, but Jess said it was fake, and next door to Count Dracula there was just an ordinary man but he gave out UNICEF money and McDonald's coupons and then there was . . ."

I turned on the oven, put in a pan of bacon and the coffee cake, then started upstairs. Angus and Hilda were in the living room, drinking orange juice and talking about Shakespeare. Hilda had taught high-school English for forty-five years, and Angus had an essay on *Othello* due the next day. I gave them the thumbs-up sign and tiptoed by. When I had showered and came back downstairs, the kitchen smelled of bacon and cinnamon, and Taylor was in mid-sentence. "Sixteen packets of Chiclets," she was saying, "thirty-two little candy bars, a lot of candy kisses, seven bags of peanuts . . ."

"Okay, T," I said, "that's enough. Time to get off the phone."

She smiled and held out the receiver. "It's for you," she said. "Long distance."

Keith Harris was on the other end of the line.

"Tell me you didn't reverse the charges," I said.

"I didn't reverse the charges," he said, "and it was worth every penny. Taylor has a nice narrative style – very thorough. It was almost like being there."

"I'll bet it was," I said, as I watched her disappear into the living room with her candy apple.

When Keith spoke again, his voice was serious. "Jo, one of the Canadian press guys just told me about Kevin Tarpley. He didn't know much. Just that Tarpley was shot, and the police were investigating."

"That's all I know too, except . . . Keith, I got a letter from Kevin Tarpley last night."

Keith swore softly.

"Apparently," I said, "when he was in prison, he was born again. Just as well, considering the events of the past twenty-four hours. Anyway, he wrote me a letter full of scriptural warnings and advice about how I should live my life."

"Is there anything I can do?"

"There's nothing anybody can do." I could hear the petulance in my voice. It was as unappealing as petulance usually is. I took a deep breath and started again. "Keith, I'm sorry. It's just that that whole time was so terrible, not just Ian dying, but the trial and our lives splashed all over the papers. I didn't want to think about any of it ever again. And now . . ."

"And now you have a chance to put an end to it once and for all." Keith's voice was strong and certain. "Jo, has it occurred to you that maybe that poor bastard Tarpley has done you a favour? Maybe now that he's dead, you really can close the door. You've got a lot to look forward to, you know: the kids, your job, the show."

"But not you, anymore," I said. "How's the lady lobbyist?"

"She's fine. Jo, I thought we'd agreed to keep her out of it."

"Sorry," I said. "Being dumped isn't any easier at forty-nine than it was at fourteen."

"You weren't dumped," he said. "It was a joint decision."

"Yes, but you made the joint decision first. Look, let's change the subject. What's happening in Washington today?"

"I'm having lunch with some Texas bankers."

"Three fingers of Jack Daniel's and a platter of ribs. You lucky duck."

"Actually, we're eating at a place in Georgetown that specializes in braised zucchini."

"Good," I said. "Being dumped is one thing. But knowing you're having great barbecue while I'm eating Spaghetti-O's would just be too much."

He laughed. "The day you eat Spaghetti-O's . . ."

"Listen, I'd better let you get rolling," I said. "The cost for this phone call must be into four digits."

"Money well spent," he said. "Take care of yourself, Jo."

"You too," I said.

The next phone call wasn't as heartening. It was a reporter from one of our local radio stations. He told me his name was Troy Smith-Windsor, and he asked me how I felt about Kevin Tarpley's death.

"Relieved," I said, and hung up.

He must have speed-dialled me back. This time his voice was low and confiding. "I know this is hard for you," he murmured. "Believe it or not, it's hard for me, too. Sometimes I hate my job, Mrs. Kilbourn, but as much as you and I value your privacy, people have a right to know. You're a well-known member of this community. People want to hear about how you're dealing with this tragic reminder of your husband's murder. Give me something to share with them."

When I answered, I tried to match Troy Smith-Windsor's tone. Unction has never been my strong suit, but I did my earnest best. "I guess I hadn't thought of it that way, Troy," I said. "But now that I have, could you tell your listeners that I appreciate their concern. And Troy, could you please tell them that, while I regret Kevin Tarpley's death as I would regret the death of any human being, I welcome the chance to put this tragedy behind me and get on with my life. Have you got that?"

"I've got it, Mrs. Kilbourn," Troy Smith-Windsor said huskily. "And thank you."

"Thank you, Troy," I said, and I hung up, proud of myself.

My self-esteem was short-lived. When I turned, Angus was standing in the kitchen doorway. He was still wearing his pig shorts; his eyes were puffy and his dark hair was tangled from sleep.

"Someone shot the man who killed Dad," he said. "The woman on the radio said it happened yesterday. You knew." A statement, not a question.

I nodded. "Angus, you've been through so much already. Last night you were excited about your party. I thought the news about Kevin Tarpley would keep till morning."

"You should have told me," he said.

I reached my arms out to embrace him. He twisted away from me.

"I'm not a kid, Mum. Last summer I went down to the library and looked up the stories about Dad. They have them on microfiche."

I closed my eyes and the scene was there: my son in the dimly lit microfiche room, surrounded by strangers as he watched the images of his father's death flicker on a screen.

"Angus, if you wanted to hear about what happened, you should have come to me."

His voice was exasperated. "Mum, don't you remember what you were like then? You weren't like you. You were like a zombie or something. I didn't want that to happen again."

"It's not going to," I said. I put my hands on his shoulders. "Now, what do you want to know?"

"Everything," he said.

He was six-foot-one, but his body was still lithe with a child's vulnerability.

"You're sure about this, Angus."

He looked at me steadily. "I'm sure, Mum."

"Okay," I said, "I'll call Jill and get her to dig out the files."

Five minutes later, it was all arranged. After church, Angus and I would go to Nationtv and look at everything the network had on the Ian Kilbourn case. Hilda had already planned to take Taylor to the art gallery, so the afternoon was free. There were no obstacles. As I poured the eggs into the frying pan, I wavered between dread and anticipation. Pandora must have been unsure, too, in that split second when her hand lingered at the edge of the box.

Few places are deader than a television station on a Sunday afternoon. A security guard watching a Mr. Fix-it show on TV waved us past the front desk. We met Jill in the corridor outside her office. She was wearing jeans and an Amnesty International sweatshirt, and she was pulling a little red wagon full of Beta tapes.

"I hope you two know you're taking a chance with these," she said. "I just brought them up from the library, and I haven't screened any of them. There may be things you'd rather not see."

"I'll be okay," Angus said. "Mum . . .?"

"Let's go," I said.

Jill started towards the elevator. "The boardroom upstairs is free. We can screen the tapes there. It's got a fridge, Angus. They usually keep it pretty well stocked."

As the elevator doors closed, I turned to Jill. "Have you heard anything more about what happened at the penitentiary?"

"Not much," she said. "The prison officials are mortified, of course. It doesn't do to have a prisoner killed inside a federal penitentiary, but the warden says their job is to make sure their inmates don't get a shot at John Q. Public; they're not set up to keep John Q. Public from getting a shot at one of their inmates. And, you know, the man has a point. Prince Albert, Saskatchewan, isn't Detroit. No one could have predicted a drive-by shooting."

"Especially not of a model prisoner," I said.

Jill looked at me sharply. "Right," she said. "And he was a model prisoner. Until six months ago, the warden said all he did was work out in the gym, watch television, and count the days till his next conjugal visit."

The elevator doors opened, and we stepped out. "With Maureen Gault," I said, remembering. "The girl who was in the car with him that night. They got married during the trial, didn't they?"

"In unseemly haste, some thought." Jill raised her eyebrows.

"That's when he changed his story." Angus's voice was tense. "I read that in the paper. After they got married, he said she tried to stop him from . . . doing what he did. That's why her fingerprints were on the . . ." For a moment he faltered again. Then he said firmly, "on the weapon."

"The Crown dropped the charges against her that afternoon," Jill said. "Just like in the movies." She stopped and pulled a key-ring out of her jeans pocket. "Here we are," she said. "Corporate heaven."

The boardroom was handsome: walls the colour of bittersweet, an oversized rectangular oak table surrounded by comfortable chairs, a big-screen TV, and, in the far corner, a refrigerator with fake wood finish. Jill opened the fridge and handed a Coke to Angus.

"Pick a chair, any chair," she said. She took out a bottle of beer, opened it, and positioned it carefully on the table. "Heads up, Jo," she said, then she slid the beer along the polished surface of the table towards me. As I caught it, she grinned. "I've always wanted to do that," she said. "Okay, it's your show. Where do you want to start?"

I bent over and took a tape out of the wagon. The label on the spine said "Kilbourn/Tarpley/Gault." The names had the resonance of the familiar, like the names of partners in a law firm or of baseball players who had executed a historic triple play. I handed the tape to Jill. When she put it in the VCR and switched off the lights, my pulse began to race. I wasn't looking forward to the show.

But the first images that filled the screen weren't of death but of life at its best. Ian was standing on the steps of the Legislature being sworn in as Attorney General. It was a sun-splashed June day; the wind tousled his dark hair and, sensitive even then about how his hair was thinning, Ian reached up quickly to smooth it. As he took the oath of office, the camera moved in for a closeup; at the sight of his father, Angus leaned forward in his chair.

And then I was there on the screen, beside Ian. My hair was shoulder-length and straight; I was wearing a flowered granny dress and holding our oldest child, Mieka, in my arms. She was three weeks old, and I was twenty-eight.

"You were so young," Angus said softly.

I felt a catch in my throat. Jill's voice from the end of the table was caustic. "And her hair was so brown, Angus. Check it out . . ."

A smile started at the corners of Angus's mouth.

"How come your hair didn't turn blond till you were forty, Jo?" Jill continued.

Angus's smile grew broader. Relieved that we'd gotten through the moment, I said. "I don't know. It seems to have happened to a lot of women my age."

"Maybe it had something to do with living through the sixties," Angus said innocently, and we all laughed.

Then the next image was on the screen, and we stopped laughing. It was the scene on the highway. Jill jabbed at the remote control and fast-forwarded the tape until the snowy highway gave way to scenes outside the Regina Courthouse. Police cars pulled up. Officers ran out of the building, then ran back in. Television people jostled one another for position. One young woman with a camera was knocked back into a snowbank. The sequences were as mindlessly predictable as a bad movie of the week.

"This is where the RCMP brought Kevin Tarpley and Maureen Gault in," I said to Angus. He seemed frozen in front of the screen. "Their luck ran out. You know that stretch of the Trans-Canada, where it happened, Angus. Normally, during a blizzard they could have counted on those hills south of Chaplin being deserted. There wasn't anything to connect the two of them to your dad, so they might have gotten away. But there was a car from Regina going back from the funeral. The driver spotted the Volvo by the side of the road and pulled over; she called the RCMP on her CB radio. Kevin and Maureen had started back to where they'd left their car on the grid road just south of the highway. The RCMP didn't have any trouble catching them."

"Good," he said.

I took a long swallow of beer. Kevin and Maureen had finally appeared on screen; the officer taking Kevin from the car put his hand on top of Kevin's head to keep him from hitting it on the doorframe. It was an oddly tender gesture. I remembered the bloody mess of my husband's head and swallowed hard. Kevin and Little Mo were wearing matching jackets from their high school; I could see their names on their sleeves. He was wearing her jacket, and she was wearing his. Kevin and Little Mo, cross-dressing killers. They disappeared inside the courthouse, and the screen went black.

"More?" asked Jill.

"I have to go to the bathroom," Angus said.

"Are you okay?" I asked. He caught the anxiety in my voice, and his eyes flashed with anger.

"I'm fifteen years old, Mum," he called over his shoulder as he walked out of the room.

"Fifteen," Jill said, "capable of handling life."

"He seems to be doing a better job of it than I am at the moment," I said. "When I saw those faces, I wanted to smash in the screen."

"I'm glad you restrained yourself," Jill said. "Smashing this set would pretty well have put an end to my rise up the Nationtv corporate ladder."

"I'm serious, Jill. I don't want to be here. I don't want to be dredging up the past. I don't know why Angus is convinced he has do this. And something else . . . I have a letter from Kevin Tarpley."

Jill's body was tense with interest. "Can I see the letter?"

"Be my guest," I said. "Come over to the house after we're through here. You can take it with you and put it in your memory book. It gives me the creeps."

"Jo, I think you'd better hold on to that letter. I have a feeling the cops are going to want to see it."

"They'd be wasting their time," I said. "There's nothing there but a warning to listen to God's truth and not to put my trust in rulers."

Jill looked thoughtful. "It could be worse," she said. "I wasn't going to mention this, but your letter wasn't the only one Kevin Tarpley sent out before he died. Apparently, there were two more. The inmate in the cell across from Tarpley's says that Kevin spent most of the last week of his life writing those letters. It was slow going for him because he was barely literate, but – get this, Jo – Kevin told his fellow inmate that he had to get the letters out to save the innocent and punish the guilty."

Suddenly, I felt cold. "Who else got letters?"

"The prison people don't know."

"Don't they keep records of the mail the inmates send out?"

"They do," Jill said, "but it seems these letters went out with a man they call 'the prison pastor.'"

"Kevin mentioned him," I said. "His name is Paschal Temple."

"Right," said Jill. "And he doesn't know who they were addressed to. He was doing God's work, Jo. He just dropped the letters in the mailbox and trusted the Lord."

Angus came back into the room. He'd been crying. His eyes were red and his hair was slicked back, wet from where he'd splashed water on his face.

"Why don't you get yourself another Coke," I said. It was as close as he would let me come at that moment, and he got the message.

He gave me a weak smile. "Thanks, Mum," he said.

Jill held up another tape. "Ready?"

Angus snapped open the tab on the pop can. "Ready."

"This is the trial," Jill said.

There were establishing shots of the street outside the courthouse. The sky was blue, and the trees on the courthouse lawn were leafing out into their first green. Two police cars pulled up: Maureen was in the first; Kevin in the second. As they stood, blinking in the pale spring sunlight, Maureen and Kevin were almost unrecognizable. She was in a navy dress with a white Peter Pan collar, and her explosion of platinum hair had been tamed into a ponytail. His long blond hair had been trimmed, and he was wearing a dark suit. Miss Chatelaine and her Saturday night date.

Spectators hurried into the courthouse. I recognized some of them: Mieka's English teacher; Tess Malone; our next-door neighbours; our minister; Gary Stephens and his wife, Sylvie; Jane O'Keefe with Andy Boychuk, who was dead now too; our dear old friend Dave Micklejohn; Craig and Julie Evanson. Then Howard Dowhanuik with his arm protectively draped around the shoulders of the woman beside him. As they started up the steps, the woman shook off his arm and turned to face the camera. Her mouth was slack and her eyes were as blank as a newborn's. I shuddered. The woman with the unseeing eyes was me. Angus was right. I had been a zombie.

I turned to Jill. "Is there another beer?" I asked.

"Help yourself," Jill said, and I did.

The reporting of the trial had its own rhythm. For four days there were shots of the key players arriving at the courthouse, then courtroom sketches of the experts as they gave their testimony. Police officers, forensic specialists, pathologists, two psychiatrists. The faces of these witnesses, skilfully drawn but static, were the perfect counterpoint to the reporter's voice droning through the endless technical details of expert testimony.

Then on the fifth day of the trial, there was real news. Kevin Tarpley had confessed he acted alone. No time now for careful sketches; just file footage of Kevin and Maureen as the news anchor's voice, high-pitched with excitement, relayed the breaking story. Kevin had lied. It hadn't been Maureen who used the crowbar. She had pleaded with him not to harm Ian Kilbourn. Her fingerprints were on the crowbar because she had tried to tear it from Kevin's hands. He was guilty; she was innocent.

The Friday before Mother's Day, Maureen Gault walked out of the courtroom for the last time, and the cameras went wild. Maureen's mother, a mountain of a woman who had been a media star from the moment of her daughter's arrest, bore down on the press.

"She's vindicated," Shirley Gault said. "Little Mo is vindicated. What more Mother's Day present could I ask?" Beside her, Maureen stood silent, smirking, her fair hair as insubstantial as dandelion fluff in the May sunshine. As her mother droned on about lawsuits and mental suffering and Little Mo's good name, Maureen looked off in the distance. Finally she'd had enough. She grabbed her mother's doughy arm, and headed down the courthouse steps. Before she got into her mother's car, she flashed the cameras a V-for-victory sign. The screen went dark.

"And so justice was done," I said.

Jill flicked off the console and turned on the lights. "Isn't it always?" she said mildly.

She picked up the tapes. "I'll leave a note with our library that you can requisition these. That way, if you want to come over some night, you can. There's a lot of stuff you and Angus might feel more comfortable looking at on your own."

"Like what?" Angus asked.

"Like the footage from the Heinbecker funeral, the one your father went to in Swift Current that last day." Jill turned to me. "Charlie's widow sent it to me last year. She's getting on, and she wanted me to have it for our archives. I almost pitched it, then I remembered that your dad had given the eulogy, Angus. People said it was terrific."

"I guess I'd like to hear that," he said. "And Jill, if you have a tape of Dad's funeral . . ." The sentence trailed off. When he spoke again, his voice was small and sad. "I'd kind of like to hear what people thought about my dad."

We went back to Jill's office and got our coats. My son and I were silent as we walked to the parking lot. There didn't seem to be much left to say.

CHAPTER

3

Taylor wouldn't let me throw out the pumpkin. When she saw me heading out to the alley with it Monday morning, she burst into tears. Normally she was easygoing, but the jack o'lantern meant a lot to her. I put it back on the picnic table. When I headed for the university the next day, I noticed that Jack's eyeholes were beginning to pucker and his smile was drooping. Apparently, when it came to aging, pumpkins weren't any luckier than humans.

In the park, city workers were putting snow fences around the broad, sloping lawns of the art gallery. Above me, the last of the migrating geese formed themselves into ragged V's and headed south. Winter was coming, and I climbed the stairs to the political science department buoyed by the energy that comes with the onset of a new season.

My nerves jangled the minute I opened the door to my office. Like Miss Clavel in Taylor's favourite book, I knew that something was not right. But, at first, it was hard to put my finger on what was wrong. My desk was as I had left it: clear except for a jar full of pencils, a notepad, and a folder of notes labelled "Populist Politics and the Saskatchewan Election of 1982."

It was never my favourite part of the course. At the top of the first page I had written "Why the Dowhanuik Government was Defeated." There were three single-spaced pages of reasons, but the explanation I liked best was the one Ian gave a reporter on election night. All of the Regina candidates and campaign workers had met at the Romanian Club for the victory party. By the time the evening was over, we had lost fifty-seven of the sixty-four seats, the temperature in the hall had climbed past thirty degrees Celsius, and everybody was either drunk or trying to get there. When the reporter doing the TV remote asked my husband if he could isolate the reason for the government's loss, Ian had looked at the man with amazement. "When you lose this badly," he said, "it pretty much means that from the day the writ was dropped, everybody everywhere fucked up everything."

Even with the expletives deleted, it had been a memorable sound bite. I leafed through the notes in the folder. A few pages in, I found a newspaper clipping: it was a picture of the survivors of the '82 election: Howard Dowhanuik, Ian, Craig Evanson, Andy Boychuk, Tess Malone, Gary Stephens, and Jane O'Keefe. The premier-elect, who considered himself the consummate cracker-barrel comic, had announced that he would call them the Seven Dwarfs.

I never thought the joke was very funny, and I didn't think what had happened to the picture on my desk was funny either. Someone had taken a felt pen and drawn X's over the faces of my husband and Andy Boychuk. I could feel my muscles tighten. Reflexively, I took a deep breath. It was then that I noticed the smell in my office, musky and sweet: perfume, not mine.

I went back out into the hall. It was empty. I walked down to the political science office. The departmental secretary was putting mail in our boxes. Rosalie Norman was a small and prickly woman, grudging with students and contemptuous of faculty.

"Did you let someone into my office this morning?" I asked.

She clenched her jaw and took a step towards me. "Hardly," she said. Then, certain the balance of power had been restored, she went back to her mail.

"I'm sorry," I said. "I didn't mean to suggest you'd been careless. It's just someone's been in there, and I need to know how they got in."

"Look in a mirror," she said. "None of you ever remember to lock your doors." Then, for the first time that morning she smiled. "Here," she said, handing me an envelope. "It's from Physical Plant. Looks like you forgot to pay a parking ticket."

The day went downhill from there. Two students told me they were going to the department head to complain that the mid-term test was too hard, and one young woman in my senior class cornered me to tell me I was the best prof she'd ever had and could she have an extension on her essay because she'd had to go to a bridal shower the night before her paper was due. She said she knew I would understand. I didn't.

It got worse. When I went to the Faculty Club to grab a quick sandwich for lunch, the first person I ran into was Craig Evanson's ex-wife, Julie. The population of Regina is 180,000, and I had managed to avoid Julie for almost four years, but, as my grandmother used to say, the bad penny always turns up, and Julie Evanson was one very bad penny.

She was standing in front of a painting of flame-red gladioli that set off her silver-blond hair and her black silk suit so brilliantly that, for a moment, even I enjoyed looking at her. Age had not withered Julie, nor, as it turned out, had time staled the infinite variety of ways in which she could upset the equilibrium of anyone who crossed her path.

When she spotted me, she smiled her enchanting dimpled smile. "Jo, I hoped I'd run into you here. It saves me a trip to your office. I'm working on the Christmas fashion show the Alumni Association is putting on, and I wanted to see if I could put you down for a table."

"I don't think so, Julie. Those events are always a bit pricey for me. Good luck with it, though." I started to move past her towards the dining room. She moved with me, blocking my escape.

"You've never concerned yourself much with fashion, have you?" she asked brightly.

"No," I said, "I guess I always thought there were other things . . ."

She looked me over with the deliberation of a professional assessor. "Of course, your life has always been so full of things," she said. Then she reached over and brushed chalk dust from the shoulder of my sweater. "I wonder why it is that some people seem to lead such messy lives? And now Kevin Tarpley's murder. Another mess for you."

"It's not a mess for me, Julie. It has nothing to do with me."

She shrugged. "I ran into a very interesting little birdy today who told me differently."

I remembered the defaced newspaper pictures in my file. "Who were you talking to?" I asked.

When she heard the tension in my voice, Julie's eyes lit up. "Oh, no, you don't," she said. "I have to protect my sources. You know about that, Joanne, now that you're such a big TV star." She looked at her watch. "I've got to fly," she said. Then she lowered her voice. "But there is one thing I feel I really do have to tell you."

I moved closer to her. "What?" I asked.

"You have a noticeable run in your panty hose," she said, and she smiled her dimpled smile and headed for the buffet.

By the time I got home, the milk of human kindness had curdled in my veins.

Taylor met me at the door. One of her braids had come undone, and her eyes were bright with conspiratorial excitement. "There's a lady here," she whispered. "She said she knew you from a long time ago. I let her in. Angus is upstairs, so it was okay."

I swore under my breath. I was certain it was Julie Evanson, back for a rematch. It took every ounce of resolve I had to walk into the living room.

The woman was standing by the fireplace; in her hands was the framed photograph of Ian that I kept on the mantel. She was dressed in black: black angora pullover, elaborately beaded; black skirt, tight and very short; black hose. When she heard my step, she looked up slowly. She wasn't disconcerted. It was as if I was the interloper.

"Hello, Joanne," Maureen Gault said. Her voice was low and husky. "I just came back from Kevin's memorial service, and I figured it was only right to bring you and your family a memento of this sad day."

She put Ian's photograph back on the mantel. "Looks like we have even more in common now," she said.

Dumbfounded, I stared at her.

"You know, both of us widows and all," she added helpfully. Little Mo had control of the scene, and she knew it. "I wish I'd had a portrait done of Kevin, so our son could remember his dad."

When I didn't respond, she shrugged, walked over to my coffee table and picked up her purse. "We couldn't have a real funeral on account of the cops haven't released the body. Anyway, Kevin's mum wants to donate his remains to science for the good of mankind. Lame, eh? But I thought there wasn't much point in waiting around." She opened her purse and took out a funeral-home program. "This has the service on it," she said, "and there's a celebration of Kevin's life. I guess all of us are a mix of bad and good. I thought your kids might want this for historical reasons. Set the record straight."

Finally, I came up with a line. It wasn't much. "Get out," I said. "Get out of my house."

She shook her head sadly. "Loss is supposed to put everybody on common ground, Joanne," she said. "I thought you would know that by now."

She took a compact and a lipstick out of her purse. She opened the lipstick and drew a careful mouth on top of her own thin lips.

"Cherries in the Snow," she said. "I love this colour." Her platinum hair had been arranged in an elaborate crown of curls. One of the curls had come loose, and she slid it back into place before she picked up her coat.

"I forgive you," she said, and her smile, sly and knowing, was the smile of the girl who had stood triumphant on the courthouse steps the day Kevin Tarpley's confession set her free. "My boy's father would want me to forgive you. He found Jesus at the end. He was saved."

"I know," I said. "He wrote to me." I felt the rush that comes with meanness. I thought my words would wound her, suggest that she wasn't the sole custodian of Kevin Tarpley's last moments on earth. But when Maureen Gault looked at me, she didn't look wounded. She looked victorious, as if I'd just handed her exactly what she'd come to my house for.

"What did he say?" she asked lazily.

"It was a private letter," I said.

"Suit yourself, Joanne," she said. She dropped the memorial-service program on the coffee table and started for the door. As she came parallel with me, she reached up and touched the scarf I was wearing. It was my favourite: an antique silk, bright as a parrot. My son-in-law, Greg, had given it to me for my forty-ninth birthday.

"I like this," she said, fingering the silk. "It just kills me how women like you always know how to wear these things. What do you do? Go to scarf school?"

She laughed at her joke and walked out of the room. I heard the front door close. She was gone, but the scent of her perfume lingered: musky and sweet. I didn't like the smell any better than I had liked it that morning in my office.

I grabbed the program from the coffee table and headed towards the back door. Out on the deck, the air was fresh and cold. I tore the program celebrating Kevin Tarpley's life into a dozen pieces and dropped them in the garbage. As I went back into the house, the jack o'lantern smirked at me from the picnic table.

CHAPTER

4

When I checked the back yard the night of Howard Dowhanuik's dinner, the pumpkin's smirk had sagged into a leer. I thought about my daughter. She was a resolute child. In the summer one of her friends had found a kitten; every day since, Taylor had asked if she could have a cat. And now we had the pumpkin. I looked at him, plumped on the picnic table, King of the Back Yard. "I'll bet you'll still be here on St. Patrick's Day, Jack," I said.

Hilda McCourt came into the kitchen as I was knotting the scarf Greg had given me. She bent to look at its intricate swirls of colour.

"Amazing," she said. "A silk for the seraglio."

She was wearing a black and gold velvet evening coat, and jewelled starbursts flashed in her ears. With her deep russet hair, the effect was stunning.

"You look as if you could be in a seraglio yourself," I said.

"I don't think I'd last," Hilda said. "I've never found it agreeable to dance on command." She smiled serenely. "I must admit, though, that the idea of having young men dance at my bidding is not without appeal."

The snow started as we turned off Albert Street onto College Avenue. By the time I drove into the parking lot behind Sacred Heart Cathedral it was coming down so hard I could barely make out the hotel across the road.

I pulled up next to an old Buick. A man was leaning over the car, brushing the snow off its windshield. I couldn't see his face, but I would have recognized the familiar bulk of his body anywhere. Howard Dowhanuik had paid his way through law school with the money he earned as a professional boxer. Age had thickened his body, but you could still sense his physical power.

I got out of the car and walked over to him. The former premier of Saskatchewan was peering so intently into the front seat of the Buick that he didn't hear me.

"Angus tells me these vintage cars are a snap to hot-wire," I said. "Want to go for a joy-ride before the big event?"

He didn't look up. "Sure," he said. "It'd bring back a lot of memories. The first time I ever got laid was in a car like this."

"When was that?" I said.

"In 1953," Hilda said. "This is a Buick Skylark, Joanne." Howard straightened and faced us.

"And you're sixty now," I said. "That would make you twenty-one. Good for you for waiting, Howard. I'll bet not many boys in law school did."

He laughed and threw an arm around my shoulder. "Same old Jo," he said. "Still a pain in the ass." He held out his other arm to Hilda. "Come on, Hilda. Let's get in there. I'll buy you a Glenfiddich before the agony begins. Did you come down from Saskatoon just to watch me squirm?"

"I'd come farther than that for a tribute to you," Hilda said simply.

Howard's old fighter's face softened. "Allow me to make that Glenfiddich a double," he said.

When we saw what was waiting for us outside the hotel, we were ready for a double. The Saskatchewan is a graceful dowager of a hotel, but that night the dowager was confronting the politics of the nineties. Demonstrators spilled from the entrance and onto the sidewalk. There seemed to be about forty of them, but they were silent and well-behaved. Around the neck of each protestor, a photograph of a foetus was suspended, locket-like, from a piece of cord. Two boys who didn't look as old as Angus were holding a scroll with the words BEATING HEART written in foot-high letters.

Beating Heart was Tess Malone's organization. The media potential of Howard's dinner must have been too tempting for her to resist. The new premier and half his cabinet were coming, and they all supported the Women's Health Centre. When the demonstrators saw Howard, there was a stir. Howard might have been only an ex-premier, but he was still the enemy. Oblivious, he took my arm and Hilda's and started up the stairs. The Beating Heart people moved closer together. Beneath the heavy material of his overcoat, I could feel Howard's body tense.

"Hang on," he said. I shuddered, remembering other demonstrations I'd had to wade through since the Women's Health Centre had opened in late summer. They were never any fun. I braced myself and moved forward. Then Hilda was in front of me, so close to the demonstrators that her trim body seemed pressed against the body of the man in front of her.

In the silence, I heard Hilda's voice, as civil and unworried as it would have sounded in the classroom. "Gerald Parker, that is you, isn't it?"

The man in front of her smiled.

"Yes, Miss McCourt," he said.

"I hear you've done well for yourself," Hilda said. "Real estate, isn't it?"

"Last year I made the Million Dollar Club for the third straight year." he said.

"Splendid," said Hilda. "You always were a hard worker. Now, Gerald, I wonder if you could let us pass. You've made your point. Nothing's to be gained by keeping us out here in the snow."

Without a word, Gerald broke his connection with the woman next to him, and Hilda walked between them. It wasn't Moses parting the Red Sea, but it was close. Before Gerald changed his mind, I followed. Then Howard. We had just reached the top of the stairs when I heard a man's voice: "She's here."

I turned. Jane O'Keefe was getting out of a taxi at the front of the hotel. Her sister, Sylvie, was with her. They glanced at the crowd, and then they turned towards one another. Their profiles were almost identical; cleanly marked jawlines, generous mouths, short strong noses, carefully arched brows. The two women had the scrubbed blond good looks you could see on the golf course of the best club in any city in North America. In fact, the O'Keefe sisters had grown up in the pleasant world of private schools and summers at the lake. As the crowd began to surge towards them, that idyllic existence must have seemed a lifetime away. The lights in front of the hotel leached the sisters' faces of colour, but Jane and Sylvie didn't hesitate. They started towards the stairs. Sylvie was carrying a camera and she hunched her body around it, protecting it the way a mother would protect a child.

The crowd surrounded the two women, cutting them off. No one moved. The only noise was the muted sound of traffic on the snowy streets. Then Howard came down the stairs towards them. This time there was force. He used his powerful shoulders as a wedge to break through the line. When he got to Jane and Sylvie, he linked hands with them and started back up the steps.

"Proverbs 11:21." A woman's voice, husky and self-important, cut through the silent night. "Though hand join in hand the wicked shall not be unpunished but the seed of the righteous shall be delivered."

I turned towards the voice. So did a lot of other people. When she saw that she was centre-stage, a smile lit Maureen Gault's thin face, and she gave me a mocking wave.

The demonstrators on the front steps had broken ranks during Little Mo's outburst, and Howard took advantage of the situation to get Sylvie and Jane into the hotel. Seconds later, the five of us were safe in the lobby, our shaken selves reflected a dozen times in the mirrors that lined the walls.

Hilda took command of the situation. She turned to Sylvie and Jane. "We were planning to have a drink before the festivities started. Will you join us?"

Jane O'Keefe smiled wearily. "As my grandfather used to say, 'Does a bear shit in the woods?' Let's go."

The Saskatchewan Lounge is a bar for genteel drinkers: the floral wallpaper is expensive; the restored woodwork gleams; the chairs, upholstered in peony-pink silk, are deep and comfortable; and the waiters don't smirk when they ask if you'll have your usual. We found a large table in the corner as far away as possible from the singing piano player. When the waiter came, I asked for a glass of vermouth, then, remembering the menace in Maureen Gault's smile, I changed my order to bourbon.

Howard raised his eyebrows. "Trying to keep pace with the guest of honour, Jo?" he asked.

"No," I said, "but Howard, didn't you see . . ."

He'd been smiling, but, as he leaned towards me, the smile vanished, and I changed my mind about telling him Maureen

Gault had been in the crowd. Howard had always been there when I needed him, and this was his night.

"Nothing," I said. "Just a case of mistaken identity."

"Sure you're okay?" he asked.

"Yeah," I said, "I'm sure."

"Fair enough," he said. Then he turned to Jane O'Keefe. "So, are you having second thoughts about the Women's Centre?"

"Not a one," she said. "And I've waded through crowds a lot loonier than that bunch out there."

Sylvie started to speak, but Jane cut her off. "My sister doesn't agree with me on this issue. But my sister hasn't had to try to salvage women who've been worked over by butchers. If you'd seen what I'd seen, Sylvie, you'd know I didn't have a choice."

"No," Hilda said, "you didn't. For sixty-five years, I've known that an enlightened society can't drive women into back alleys."

I was surprised. There were some subjects I never discussed with Hilda. The drinks came and, with them, another surprise. Hilda had never been forthcoming about her private life. She sipped her Glenfiddich and turned to Jane O'Keefe. "My sister died from a botched abortion," she said. "By the time I'd convinced her to let me take her to the hospital, she was, to use your word, Jane, unsalvageable. It's vital that women are never driven to that again." Hilda's eyes were bright with anger.

On the other side of the bar, the piano player had started to sing "Miss Otis Regrets." Jane reached over and touched Hilda's hand. "Thanks," she said. "There are times when I need a little affirmation."

Howard snorted. "Janey, you never needed affirmation. You always had bigger balls than any of us."

Jane looked at him, deadpan. "What a graceful compliment," she said, and everybody laughed.

Everybody, that is, except her sister. For as long as I'd known her Sylvie O'Keefe had been an outsider. As I watched her blue eyes sweep the table, I wondered, not for the first time, what that level gaze took in.

She had always been unknowable and, for much of her life, enviable. She was rich, she was talented, and she was beautiful. She and Gary had been a golden couple. Physically, they were both so perfect, it had been a pleasure simply to watch them as they came into a room. In the days when we were all having babies, we joked about the glorious gene pool Sylvie and Gary's child would draw from. But there was no baby, and as the months, then years, went by, Gary and Sylvie stopped being a golden couple. By the time Jess came, Gary and Sylvie had stopped being any sort of couple at all.

Jess was a miracle, but he didn't bring his parents together. Gary continued his headlong rush towards wherever he was going, and Sylvie became even more absorbed in her career. She was a gifted photographer, and her son soon became her favourite subject. Her luminous black and white photographs of him, by turns sensual and savage, were collected in a book, *The Boy in the Lens's Eye.* The collection established Sylvie's reputation in the places that counted. She was a success.

As I watched her assessing the people drifting into the hotel bar, I wondered if the time would ever come when Sylvie O'Keefe and I would be friends. Somehow, it seemed unlikely, but one thing was certain: after twenty years, fate – or the vagaries of small-city living – had brought our lives to a point of convergence again.

"Kismet," I said.

Sylvie turned reluctantly from the partygoers to me. "I don't understand."

"Sorry," I said, "just thinking out loud about how the kids' discovering each other has brought our lives together."

"Actually, I'm glad we were brought together tonight," she said. "I was going to call you about taking some pictures of Taylor. Have you ever watched her when she draws? She's so focussed and so . . . I don't know . . . tender. She has a great face."

"She looks like her mother," I said.

Sylvie looked at me quizzically.

"You know Taylor is adopted," I said. "Her mother was Sally Love."

Sylvie's eyes widened. "Of course. I'd forgotten. Sally's work was brilliant," she said.

"It was," I agreed. "That's one reason I'm happy Taylor's spending some time around you. I think being with another artist can give Taylor a link with her real mother."

Sylvie leaned towards me. "And that doesn't bother you?"

Before I had a chance to answer, there was an explosion of laughter at the other end of the table. Howard was in the middle of a story about a rancher he'd acted for in a lawsuit against a manufacturer of pressurized cylinders. The rancher's semen tank had sprung a leak. Like Onan, his seed had been wasted on the ground, but the rancher wasn't waiting for God's judgement. He hired Howard and took the case to court.

As I turned to listen, Howard was recounting his summation for the jury. It was funny, but it was crude, and at the next table a smartly dressed man with silver hair and a disapproving mouth turned to glare at him. Howard smiled at the man, then, still smiling, leaned towards me. "I make it a policy never to get into a fight with a guy whose mouth is smaller than a chicken's asshole."

The pianist segued into "Thanks for the Memories," and I stood up. Howard looked at me questioningly. "It's time to get out of here," I said. "Some cracks are starting to appear in your guest of honour persona."

We finished our drinks, and headed for the lobby. Gary Stephens was just coming up the steps from the side door, and he joined us.

"Sorry I'm late, babe," he said to Sylvie. She looked at him without interest, and I wondered how often she'd heard that entrance line. But Jane O'Keefe was interested. Her grey eyes burned the space between herself and her brother-in-law. "You're a real bastard, Gary," she said. Then she turned her back to him and started towards the cloakroom. We followed her and dropped off our coats, then we took the elevator upstairs to the ballroom.

The crowd in the upstairs hall was surprisingly young. Many of the men and women who were now deputy ministers or People on Significant Career Paths had been having their retainers adjusted and watching "The Brady Bunch" when Howard Dowhanuik became premier, but tonight that didn't seem to matter. Our party's first year back in government was going well, and there seemed to be a consensus that we had something to celebrate. In the ballroom, a string quartet played Beatles tunes, the crystal chandelier blazed with light, and silvery helium-filled balloons drifted above every table set for eight. It was party time.

Hilda looked around the room happily. "It's everything Howard deserves," she said. "Now I'd better find my place." She lowered her voice. "Joanne, I'm sitting with a man I met at the art gallery last Sunday. If we continue to enjoy one another's company, I might not go home with you. My new friend tells me he has an original Harold Town in his apartment."

"But you hate Harold Town."

Hilda raised an eyebrow. "Well, there was no need to tell my friend that."

I laughed. "Let me know if you need a ride."

"I will," she said. "Now, you'd better get over to the head table. Howard likes people to be punctual."

Manda and Craig Evanson were already in their places. Manda was wearing a blue Mexican wedding dress, scoop-necked and loose fitting to accommodate the swell of her pregnancy. Her dark hair, parted in the middle, fell loose to her shoulders. She was very beautiful.

Sylvie stopped in front of Manda, took out her camera, and began checking the light with a gauge. As always, Sylvie seemed to have dressed with no thought for what other women might be wearing, and as always she seemed to have chosen just the right thing. Tonight, it was a pinstriped suit the colour of café au lait, and a creamy silk shirt. As she moved around the table, adjusting her camera, I noticed more than one woman in iridescent sequins taking note.

"I don't usually walk around like the inquiring photographer," Sylvie said, "but I thought Howard might like some pictures of his party."

Manda smoothed the material of her dress over her stomach. "He'll be thrilled. Having Sylvie O'Keefe take your party pictures is like having Pavarotti sing 'For He's a Jolly Good Fellow' right to you."

Sylvie smiled. "Thanks," she said, "but Howard has it coming. He's a good guy." She knelt so that Manda Evanson was in her lens. "Stay exactly as you are, Manda. Don't smile. Just be. If Frida Kahlo had ever painted a Madonna, she would have looked like you."

Face glowing with love, Craig Evanson looked down at his wife. The happiest man in the world.

When Tess Malone came in, the temperature at the head table dipped ten degrees. We all knew she'd orchestrated the demonstration outside. She went straight to where Howard was sitting. That was like her: confront the problem, no matter how painful. She was wearing a satin dress in a pewter shade that made her tightly corsetted little body look more bullet-like than ever.

She sat in the empty chair beside him, lit a cigarette, inhaled deeply, and began. "I know how angry you must be, Howard, but I won't apologize. I like you and I respect you, but this dinner was a good chance for us. Never miss a chance. That's what you taught me when we were in government. If the shoe was on the other foot, you wouldn't have passed up this evening, and you know it."

For a moment, he stared at her. Then he started to laugh. "You're right," he said. "I wouldn't have passed up a chance like this. Anyway, for once, your God Squad doesn't seem to have done any harm."

Tess looked at him levelly. "In the spirit of the evening, I'll ignore that."

"Good," Howard said. "Now let me get you an ashtray before you ignite the tablecloth."

We all relaxed, and for a while it was a nice evening. The hip of beef was tender, and the wine was plentiful. Just as dessert was being served, Tess's protesters began pounding their drums in a heartbeat rhythm, and she went out and told them they'd done a terrific job and they could call it a night.

By the time the last dish was cleared away, and I stood to announce that the speeches were starting, the room was warmed by a sense of community and shared purpose. The new premier's remarks about Howard were witty and mercifully brief, and the other speakers followed his lead. Sanity all around.

And then Maureen Gault joined the party. The speeches had just finished, and there had been a spontaneous singing of "Auld Lang Syne." People were getting up from their tables to visit or to head to the bar for drinks. Our table was breaking up too. The new premier and his wife had another function to attend, and they were already headed towards the doors that would take them out of the ballroom. Manda and Craig Evanson were standing, saying their goodbyes to Tess. Howard was talking to a group that had driven in from Stewart Valley. Jane O'Keefe was leaning across her brother-in-law, saying something to her sister. I couldn't hear her words, but she didn't look as if she'd cooled off much. A waiter came with a note in Hilda's bold hand: "I think it's time to revisit Harold Town. Don't wait up. H." It seemed like a good time to do some visiting myself. I was standing, looking for familiar faces in the crowd, when I felt a hand on my shoulder. I turned and Maureen Gault was behind me. She was smiling.

"I thought I'd give you a chance to apologize," she said.

"For what?" I said.

"For being rude when I came to your house." She moved towards me. Close up, her perfume was overpowering. "Apologize, Joanne."

"Are you crazy?" I said.

People at the tables closest to us fell silent, and my words rang out, bell clear.

Maureen Gault's pale eyes seemed to grow even lighter. "You'll be sorry you said that, Joanne," she said. "I'm not crazy. But I'm powerful. I can make things happen. Just ask them," she said, and her hand swept in a half-circle that included everyone at the head table.

She leaned towards me. "Ask them," she hissed. "Ask your friends what Little Mo can do." Her spittle sprayed my mouth.

I rubbed my lips with the back of my hand. I was furious. "Get out," I said. "This is a private party. Nobody wants you here."

She drew her hand back as if she was about to hit me. Then she seemed to change her mind. She looked thought-fully at the head-table guests. "Tell Joanne I have every right to be here," she said. Her eyes were so pale they were almost colourless. "I thought it was nice the way you sang when I came in. 'Should old acquaintance be forgot,'" she laughed. "Nobody better forget me."

It was a good exit line, but she couldn't leave it alone. When she had walked the length of the dais, Maureen Gault turned towards us. "I haven't forgotten any of you, you know."

I could still feel her spittle on my lips. I took a step towards her. "I told you to leave us alone. You're not the only one who can make things happen, Maureen. If you're not out of here in thirty seconds, I'll get somebody from hotel security to throw you out."

She smiled, then left.

Howard's group from Stewart Valley were wide-eyed. Life in the big city was every bit as exciting as it was cracked up to be. Craig tightened his grip on his wife's shoulder. Sylvie looked impassively at the spot where Maureen had stood. Gary Stephens, who by all accounts should have been accustomed to strange women making public scenes, seemed thrown off base by Maureen Gault's outburst. White-faced, he poured the heel of the wine into his glass and drained it in a gulp. Jane O'Keefe left the table. Tess Malone was lighting a cigarette with shaking hands. Only Manda Evanson was immune.

"That's one flaky lady," she said mildly.

We did our best to restore the mood. But after a few nervous jokes, it was apparent the party was over. I picked up my bag and headed for the door. I wanted to go home, have a hot shower, and fall apart in peace.

There was a lineup outside the cloakroom. Regina is a government town, and the next morning was a work day. By the time I'd waded through the crush and found my coat, I was hot and irritable. My temper wasn't improved when, after I'd tied my belt, I noticed my scarf was missing. I tried to check the coat-rack and the floor, but I kept getting jostled, and after I got an elbow in the eye, I gave up and went into the hall to wait till the crowd thinned. When, finally, I went back into the cloakroom, the scarf wasn't there.

I decided to call it a night. I was tired and dispirited, and scarves were, after all, replaceable. I'd already started down the steps which lead to the side door when I remembered Greg's shy delight as he'd handed me the scarf at my birthday party. I couldn't leave without checking out all the possibilities. It was possible the scarf had fallen out when I'd taken my coat off in the bar. However, when I went back to the Saskatchewan Lounge, the scarf wasn't at our table, and the discreet waiter said no one had turned it in.

I took the elevator upstairs to the dining room. The waiters were stripping the tables, stacking the chairs. The head table had already been dismantled. It was as if the party had never been. I remembered Maureen's pale eyes and her brilliant mouth. Maybe my luck would change, and the whole evening would turn out to be a dream. I took the elevator down to the lobby. As I stepped out, I noticed the reservations clerk talking on the phone at the front desk. I went over to her and waited, but she ignored me. When I didn't go away, she put her hand over the mouthpiece. "Is there a problem?" she asked.

"Has anyone turned in a silk scarf, sort of a swirling pattern on a dark green background?"

She made a cursory pass through the paper in front of her.

"Nothing about a scarf," she said, and went back to her phone call.

I took a piece of paper from my purse, wrote my name and address on it, and shoved it across the desk towards her.

"Call me, please, if it turns up."

"Right," she said, and she waved me off.

I left through the side door. The snow had stopped, but it had been a substantial fall. Across Lorne Street, Blessed

Sacrament, fresh with snow, glowed in the moonlight. The parking lot had pretty much cleared out. Only a few cars were left. The old Buick was still there, and as I walked towards my car, I thought of Howard's prolonged virginity and smiled. I stopped smiling when I saw the body.

She was lying on her back, close to the right rear wheel of the Buick. I thought at first that someone had run her down. Then I saw the scarf. Bright as a parrot. I had always loved the way the material draped itself in a swirl of colours over the shoulder of my coat. But tonight the scarf wasn't tied right. It had been pulled so tight around Maureen Gault's neck that her head angled oddly and her eyes bulged from her head.

I felt my knees go weak. Then I took a deep breath and stumbled back through the snow towards the hotel. When I saw the cruiser turning down Lorne Street, I shouted for it to stop. The officer who jumped out of the car seemed too young to be out this late, but he knew his job. He followed me across the parking lot, but when he saw the body, he grabbed me.

"Don't go any further," he said. "Leave the area alone till the crime scene people get here. I'll call for backups." But he didn't start for his car immediately. Instead, he took a step towards the body, and looked down.

"Do you know her?" he asked.

"Her name was Maureen Gault," I said. "Little Mo," I added idiotically. The security lights glinted yellow in Maureen Gault's unseeing eyes. The crimson mouth drawn over her own thin lips seemed like a wound in her milky skin.

"Do you know of anybody who'd want her dead?" he asked.

I stared down at Little Mo's inert body and shivered. My voice seemed to come from somewhere far away. "Me," I said. "I wanted her dead."

CHAPTER

5

Half an hour later, I was sitting in police headquarters on Osler Street studying the medicine wheel on the wall behind the desk of Inspector Alex Kequahtooway. A Cree elder had told me once that the medicine wheel is a mirror that helps a person see what cannot be seen with the eyes. "Travel the four directions of the circle," she said. "Seek understanding in the four great ways."

I stared hard at the markings on the medicine wheel. At that moment, I would have given a lot to see what could not be seen with the eyes, but all I saw was cowhide and bead-work. I knew the fault was with me. A seeker must be calm and receptive. I was scared to death.

Inspector Kequahtooway was from Standing Buffalo Reserve, about a hundred kilometres east of the city. I knew this because I knew his brother. Perry Kequahtooway had been the RCMP officer in charge of investigating a tragedy which had threatened my family. During the investigation, I had counted on Perry's calm determination to discover the truth; afterwards, I had come to know his kindness, and we had become friends. But that night, in police headquarters, it didn't take Alex Kequahtooway long to let me know that my relationship with his brother didn't cut any ice with him. When he led me through the litany of what I had done and whom I had been with that evening, his face was impassive.

As I talked, he made notes in a scribbler that looked like the kind my kids used in grade school. When I'd finished, he read his notes over unhurriedly. I stared at the medicine wheel, and tried to remember the four great ways to understanding: wisdom, illumination, innocence, and something else.

Finally, satisfied that the first part of the interrogation was in order, Inspector Alex Kequahtooway turned the pad to a fresh page and looked up at me.

"Just a few more questions, Mrs. Kilbourn. You seem tired."

"I am tired," I said.

"Then let's get started. When was the last time you saw your scarf that night?"

"I left it with my coat."

"In the downstairs cloakroom. There's a coat check upstairs near the ballroom. Why didn't you use it?"

"None of us did. I came in with five other people, and we all left our coats in the cloakroom on the main floor. You have to pay to check your coat upstairs."

"Too bad you didn't pay," he said, and there was an edge to his voice. "Nobody can touch the coats upstairs without dealing with the people who work there, whereas your coat . . ."

". . . was unguarded right out there where anyone could get at it."

"Right," he sighed. "Now the next question presents even more of a problem." He looked at his notes. "Before you came in, I had a few moments to talk with Constable Andrechuk. He was the first officer on the scene after you discovered

Maureen Gault's body. Constable Andrechuk tells me he pointed to the deceased and asked you, and I quote: 'Do you know of anybody who'd want her dead?' Is that an accurate quote, Mrs. Kilbourn?"

"Yes," I said, "it is."

Inspector Kequahtooway made a check mark in the margin beside the question. "Now, listen carefully, Mrs. Kilbourn. Constable Andrechuk says that, when he asked you that question, you answered, 'Me. I wanted her dead.' Is that accurate?"

"Yes," I said, "it is."

"Why did you want her dead, Mrs. Kilbourn?"

I was silent. Images of Little Mo flashed through my mind.

Inspector Kequahtooway leaned towards me. His obsidian eyes seemed to take everything in. "Did you hate her because Kevin Tarpley had killed your husband?"

"No," I said, "I was afraid of her."

"You were afraid of her all these years?"

"No," I said. "I wasn't afraid of her after Ian died. When you see the files on his murder, you'll know that there wasn't anything . . . personal . . . about his murder."

"That's an odd word to use, Mrs. Kilbourn."

"It's the right word. Ian was killed because he was in the wrong place at the wrong time. It was Fate, like being hit by a bolt of lightning on the golf course."

Alex Kequahtooway's voice was so low I had to strain to hear it. "Something changed," he said.

"For the six years after the trial I never saw Maureen Gault. Then the day of Kevin Tarpley's memorial service, November 3, she came to my office at the university and she came to my house."

"Did she threaten you?"

"Not verbally. But, Inspector Kequahtooway, something had come loose in her. She seemed to feel she had to pursue me. I don't know why. Last night at the hotel, she told me that she could make things happen, and I'd better remember her."

"Some people who were sitting near the head table say they heard you call her crazy."

"She was crazy," I said, "and dangerous."

"And you're glad she's dead."

I looked at him. He was older than his brother, and harder. I remember Perry telling me his brother was the first Indian to make inspector on the Regina police force. I guess he'd had to be tough, but there was something about him that invited trust. I took a deep breath.

"Yes," I said. "I'm glad she's dead. But Inspector Kequahtooway, I didn't kill her."

He made a final note in his scribbler, and capped his pen. "That's good news," he said. He stood and motioned towards me. "You can go now, Mrs. Kilbourn. I guess I don't have to tell you that we'll expect you to keep us aware of any travel plans."

When I stood up, my legs were so heavy I knew I'd be lucky to make it across the room. "Travel won't be a problem," I said. "Goodnight, Inspector."

It was a little after 2:00 a.m. when I got home. I checked on Angus and Taylor, showered, put on my most comforting flannelette nightie, and climbed into bed. I was bone-tired, but I couldn't sleep. Every time I shut my eyes, I saw the red wound in Maureen Gault's white face: Cherries in the Snow.

Finally, I gave up and went down to the kitchen. Hilda was sitting at the table, drinking tea and reading a book titled *Varieties of Visual Experience.*

"Boning up on Abstract Expressionism?" I asked, and then, I began to sob.

Hilda leaped up and put her arms around me. "Good God, Joanne, what's the matter? It's not one of the children . . . ?"

"No, it's not the children," I said. "It's me. Hilda, I'm in trouble . . ."

I started to tell her about Maureen, but I guess I wasn't making much sense, because she stopped me.

"Let me get you some tea," she said. "Then you can start again. This time, tell me what happened in chronological order. Nothing calms the nerves more effectively than logic."

Hilda poured half a mug of steaming tea, then she went into the dining room and came back with a bottle of Metaxa. She added a generous shot of brandy to the tea and handed the mug to me. "Drink your tea," she said, "then we'll talk."

An hour later, when I went to bed, I slept. It was a good thing I did, because the next morning when I picked up the paper, I knew it was going to be a long day. The paper was filled with stories about Maureen Gault's murder and, whatever their starting point, by the final paragraph they all had an arrow pointing at me.

I could feel the panic rising, and when the phone rang, I froze. "Whoever you are, you'd better have good news," I said as I picked up the receiver. I was in luck. It was my daughter, Mieka, sounding as exuberant as a woman should when she was on a holiday with her new husband.

"Mum, guess where I am."

"Some place sunny and warm, I hope."

"I'm sitting at a table in a courtyard at the Richelieu Hotel in New Orleans, and I just had grits for the first time in my life."

"And you phoned to tell me," I said.

"No, I phoned to tell you that Greg and I got the same room you and Daddy had when you stayed here on your honeymoon."

A flash of memory. Lying in each other's arms, watching the overhead fan stir the soupy Louisiana air, listening to the sounds of the French Quarter drift through the open doors to our balcony.

"I hope that room's as magical for you as it was for us."

"It is," she said softly.

I could feel the lump in my throat. "I'd better let you get back to your grits while they're still hot," I said. "As I remember it, grits need all the help they can get. And, Mieka, tell Greg thanks."

"For what?"

"For making you so happy."

"I will," she said. "And you tell everybody there hello from us. We'll call on Taylor's birthday."

I'd just hung up when my oldest son, Peter, called from Saskatoon. He tried to be reassuring, but I could tell from his voice that the stories in the Saskatoon paper must have been pretty bleak.

"You know, Mum, I think I'd better come home for a while," he said.

"In the middle of term?" I said. "Don't be crazy. You know the kind of marks you need to get into veterinary medicine. Besides, by the time you get down here, this will have blown over."

"Do you really think so, Mum?"

"No, but I really do think you're better off there. Pete, if I need you, I know you can be in Regina in three hours. At the moment, that makes me feel a lot better than having you jeopardize your term by coming here to hold my hand."

"Are you sure?"

"Absolutely. Now let me tell you about what your sister and Greg are doing."

"Eating everything that's not nailed down, I'll bet," he said.

"You got it," I said. By the time I finished telling Peter about New Orleans, he sounded less scared and I felt better.

When I heard Hilda and the kids coming downstairs, I took the paper outside and shoved it into the middle of the stack in our Blue Box. Out of sight, out of mind. I made porridge and, for the next half hour, life was normal. The night before, Hilda had volunteered to stay a few days to keep my spirits up during what she called "this trying time." I turned her down flat, but as I watched her help Taylor braid her hair, I was glad Hilda had overruled me.

When Angus came to the table, it was apparent he hadn't been listening to the radio. He knocked over the juice, and as he mopped up, he grumbled about a bill that showed he owed Columbia House $72.50 plus handling charges for cassettes and CDs.

Taylor, who was turning six on Remembrance Day, chirped away about plans for her birthday. "What I want," she said, "is a cake like the one Jess had. His mum made it in a flowerpot and there were worms in it."

Angus emptied about a quarter of a bag of chocolate chips onto his porridge. "You know, T, that's really gross," he said.

I took the chocolate chip bag from him. "Speaking of gross . . . ," I said.

Taylor grinned at her brother. "They're not real worms. They're jelly-bellies. On top, Jess's mum had brown icing and flowers made out of marshmallows. Jo, do you think you could ask her how she did it?"

"Consider it done," I said.

"Probably we'll need to make two," Taylor said thoughtfully. "I have a lot of friends."

"I'll ask Jess's mum to copy out the recipe twice," I said.

Taylor shook her head. "That's another one of your jokes, isn't it, Jo?" She took her cereal bowl to the sink and trotted off upstairs.

Angus leaned towards me. "Am I supposed to be at this party?"

"Only if you expect help paying that $72.50. I hear Columbia House has goons who specialize in shattering kneecaps."

He flinched. "I'll be there," he said, and he stood up and started for the door.

"Hang on a minute," I said. "Angus, something happened last night. I think you should take a look at the paper before you go to school."

I brought the paper in, and as he read it, his eyes widened with concern. "They don't think you did it, do they?"

"I don't know what they think," I said. "But I know I didn't kill Maureen Gault." I put my arm around his shoulder. "Angus, this is going to work out. But you'd better prepare yourself for a little weirdness at school."

"I don't get it, Mum. Maureen Gault just shows up out of nowhere and all of a sudden she's dead and they think it's you. It doesn't make any sense."

"It doesn't make sense to me, either," I said. "But Angus, there isn't any logic here. Whatever else happens, hang on to that. 'This invites the occult mind,/ Cancels our physics with a sneer.'"

He furrowed his brow. "What?"

"Chill out," I said.

He gave me a small smile. "Yeah," he said. "And you stay cool, Mum. There's going to be weirdness coming at you, too."

He was right. I could hear my 10:30 class buzzing as I came down the hall, but as soon as I stepped into the classroom, there was silence. They seemed to have trouble looking at me, and I remembered a lawyer on TV saying he always knew the verdict was guilty if the jury couldn't make eye contact with the defendant. Some of my colleagues seemed to have a problem with eye contact too. As I passed them in the hall going back to my office after class, they muttered hello and hurried by.

When I opened my office door, I was glad to see Howard Dowhanuik sitting at my desk. He had shaved and he was wearing a fresh shirt, but he looked like a man who had been up all night. When he saw me, he smiled.

"First friendly face I've seen since I got here," I said.

"That bad?"

"That bad," I said. "This is a city that reads its morning paper."

"That's why they keep the morning paper at a Grade 6 reading level," Howard said.

"Whatever happened to your reverence for the common man?" I said.

"Man and woman, Jo. I'm surprised at you. And the answer is I don't have to revere them any more. I'm out of politics."

"Right," I said.

Howard looked weary. "Have you got coffee or something?"

"We can go to the Faculty Club," I said. Then, remembering the ice in the greetings I'd gotten on my way back from class, I said, "On second thought, maybe I'd better make us a pot here."

I made the coffee and plugged it in. "Howard, before we talk, let me call Taylor's school. I want to make sure someone's keeping an eye on how she's dealing with all this."

After I talked to Taylor's principal, I felt better. Taylor was the fourth of my children to go to Lakeview School, and over the years Ian MacDonald and I had come to know each other. He knew that none of the Kilbourns would ever be a Rhodes Scholar, but he also knew that my kids were decent enough, and that he could count on me when he needed an extra driver for a field trip. He said he'd talk to Taylor's teacher, then he cleared his throat and told me he knew I wasn't a murderer and he would make sure that other people knew that, too.

I'd often thought Ian MacDonald was a bit of a taskmaster with the kids, but at the moment he was a hero, and my eyes filled with tears. The tissue box in my desk drawer was empty. All I could find in my purse was a paper napkin with the Dairy Queen logo. I mopped my eyes on it. "Dammit," I said, "I'm so tired I feel like I'm going to throw up. Howard, how bad is this?"

He sipped his coffee. "At the moment it's not great, Jo. I was down at the police station after you were there. Gave them my statement, then I just kind of nosed around. I go back a long way with some of those guys."

"And . . . ?" I said.

"They've got a window for the time of death. You found Maureen Gault's body at 11:15, and the woman who works in the hotel smoke shop remembers seeing Maureen just before 11:00. She was just closing the till when Maureen came in to buy a package of LifeSavers. She said they were for her son."

For the first time since Maureen died, I felt a pang. "I'd forgotten about him," I said.

"You had a few things on your mind," Howard said drily. "You still do, Jo. The cops are still checking people's stories. Logically enough, I guess, they're starting with the head table. There are only two of us who haven't got even a sniff of an alibi. I'm one of them and you're the other."

"We should have gotten together," I said, "told the cops that we spent the hour in Blessed Sacrament praying for the justice system."

He didn't laugh. "I wish we had. Gary's okay. He went over to Tess Malone's for a nightcap. Jane and Sylvie ended up at Tess's too."

"Talk about strange bedfellows," I said.

Howard shrugged. "Apparently, Sylvie and Tess are tight as ticks. Have been for years. Anyway, the four of them were together until midnight. Craig and Manda went straight home. Their neighbour was out shovelling snow, and they talked to him at about 10:30. Around 11:00 Manda ordered pizza. It was delivered at 11:29. The pizza place they got it from is one of those 'if we're late, it's free' operations, so they keep pretty good records. Anyway there are some holes in Craig and Manda's story, but it's better than . . ."

"What I have," I said. "Howard, I don't understand this. I saw a hundred people when I was looking for Hilda. Doesn't anybody remember seeing me?"

"Lots of people remember seeing you, but nobody is willing to swear it was between 11:00 and 11:15. Jo, that's only fifteen minutes. Most people at the dinner had had a couple of drinks by then and, you know how it is, time gets kind of fuzzy." He looked as tired as I felt. "Do you want me to hang around for a couple of days? My plane leaves in an hour, but I don't have to be on it. I can get somebody to cover my classes."

"I don't need a babysitter, Howard. I just need the police to find something. And they will. They have to. For one thing, there has to be a connection with Kevin Tarpley's murder, and I'm in the clear there."

"No handgun with your initials on it at the crime scene?" Howard asked.

"No. And I wasn't anywhere near Prince Albert that day. I have witnesses, too. There was a Hallowe'en party at the art gallery. Taylor and I went to it after her lesson. There must have been thirty-five people there. After that, we picked up Angus and took him downtown to get new basketball shoes. I'll bet we went to six stores and I'm sure the sales people would remember us. Angus is a difficult customer. Howard,

I could find fifty people to verify that I was in Regina Saturday. That's probably a world record. Now come on, if we make tracks, I can get you to the airport and still get back for my next class."

As we drove along the expressway, it was like old times. We talked about politics and Howard's ongoing courtship of his ex-wife, Marty. Reassuringly ordinary conversation, but when Howard turned to say goodbye to me at the airport, I lost my nerve, and Howard, who had known me for years, saw it happen.

He reached across and covered my hand with his. "Jo, I think you're right about this thing resolving itself pretty quickly, but until it does, promise me you'll stay out of it. Whatever's going on here is ugly. This isn't a case for Nancy Drew. Go home. Enjoy your family. Teach your classes. Be safe. Trust the cops."

"I'll try," I said.

He shook his head and opened the car door. "Not good enough," he said, "but a start. I'll be in touch."

As I drove off I could feel the tension in my body. All the brave words in the world couldn't change the reality. For the time being at least, I was the prime suspect. And Howard was right. Something really ugly was happening. The only thing to do was steer a prudent course and pray that police would work their magic.

I headed back to the university. Filled with resolve, I went down to the political science office to check my mail.

Rosalie Norman was there waiting for me. "In the morning paper there was a picture of that woman who was murdered. I recognized her. She was in the hall outside your office the day you accused me of leaving your door open." Her black-berry eyes were gleaming with excitement. "What do you think I should do?"

I leaned across the desk and picked up her phone. "I think you should tell the police, Rosalie. Here, I'll dial the number for you. Put a little excitement in that life of yours."

The adrenalin was still pumping when I walked into class. I ignored the whispers and the averted eyes, and the class went well. "Don't let the bastards grind you down," I muttered as I put the keys in the ignition and started home. As I drove past Gary and Sylvie's big grey clapboard house on Albert Street, I remembered the worm cake and, on impulse, I pulled up in front of their house.

Jess answered the door. He was wearing blue jeans, a Blue Jays T-shirt, and a fireman's hat. He looked past me expectantly.

"Where's Taylor?" he said.

"At our house, I guess. I haven't been home yet, but Miss McCourt's there. I just stopped by to ask your mum if I could get the recipe for your birthday cake."

"Sure," he said. "She's out back in her darkroom. I'll go get her. You can come in."

I stepped into the entrance hall. It was a handsome area. The hardwood floor gleamed, and the patchwork quilt draped over the carpenter's bench by the door was welcoming. But my eyes were drawn to the walls. They were lined with blowups of black and white photographs. When I moved closer, I saw that the subject in all of them was the same: Jess.

I had seen Sylvie's book, *The Boy in the Lens's Eye*, and I'd been moved by the way in which she had captured the vulnerability and the toughness of her son. But nothing in the book prepared me for the power of the originals. Jess, at four, an otherworldly child, swinging naked on a tree branch, his small body surrounded by a cloud of light. Jess at two, laughing as he is engulfed by a field of sunflowers. All the fugitive moments of Jess Stephens's childhood were rivetting, but one in which he seems to swagger as he holds a brace of dead gophers out to the person behind the camera was a knockout. I was leaning close to the photograph, marvelling at the contrast between the black stiff bodies of the animals and the soft radiance of little-boy flesh, when the real Jess came up behind me.

I felt as if he had caught me trespassing, but he was nonchalant. "You can look at those anytime. Come in the living room, I've got tropical fish."

We looked at the fish, then Jess drifted off the way my kids always did when they'd fulfilled what they considered their social duty. Alone in the room, I looked around. More prints, not Sylvie's. Two Robert Mapplethorpe prints of flowers, a Diane Arbus, some I didn't recognize. Over the mantle above the fireplace was a photograph of Ansel Adams. Handwritten in its corner was a quotation, "Not everybody trusts paintings, but people believe photographs," and the signature, "Ansel Adams."

I walked over to a bookcase looking for *The Boy in the Lens's Eye*. I wanted to see if the gopher picture was there. But the book I found was Sylvie's first book, *Prairiegirl*. It had come out ten years before, and its publication had dealt a serious blow to Gary's political career. *Prairiegirl* was a collection of photographs of small-town girls from the southeast of the province. The girls were very young, mostly prepubescent, and their parents, not versed in the aesthetics of Mapplethorpe and Sally Mann, had been outraged when, instead of freezing their daughter's innocence in time, Sylvie's photographs had explored their burgeoning sexuality. I had just begun to look at the book when Sylvie came into the room.

Without a word, she strode over and took *Prairiegirl* from my hands. Her gesture was so rude that I was taken aback.

"Jess invited me in," I said. "He was a very good host till he lost interest. His social skills seem about on a level with my kids'."

She didn't respond. She was wearing blue jeans and an oversized white shirt. Her face was scrubbed free of makeup and her blond hair was brushed back. She looked weary and hostile.

"Sylvie. I just came for a recipe. Taylor's birthday is next week and she wanted me to make the same cake you made for Jess . . . He really did ask me in," I added.

She was holding *Prairiegirl* tight against her chest as if, given the chance, I would rip it from her hands. Her fear didn't make sense. Then, like Paul on the road to Damascus, the scales fell from my eyes. Sylvie thought she had a murderer in her living room. There didn't seem much point in prolonging the agony.

I walked to the entranceway. Sylvie followed me, and as I sat on the carpenter's bench pulling on my boots, she watched in silence. I put on my coat and headed for the door. When I opened it, Sylvie said, "I'll send Gary over with the recipe. I wouldn't want to spoil Taylor's birthday."

I turned. Sylvie had positioned herself in the centre of the hall, and her stance was aggressive. Behind her, Jess peeked out from the living room. "I wouldn't let you," I said, and I closed the door behind me.

When I pulled up in front of our house, there was more good news. A van from Nationtv was parked in my driveway, and there was a young woman on my front lawn talking to Taylor while the camera whirred. This time I was the one who did the grabbing. I took my daughter's hand and turned to the young woman. "Beat it," I said. "If I ever catch you bugging my kids again, I'll break your camera."

She started to argue, but I was past listening. "Count on it," I said, and I was pleased to see that she backed away.

Hilda opened the door just as Taylor and I hit the front porch. She took in the situation as soon as she saw the Nationtv van.

"Damn them," she said, her eyes flashing with anger. "I've been fending off media people on the telephone and here they were in the driveway." She looked at me. "Did they talk to . . ."

I nodded.

"No ethical sense," she said. "Ruled by expediency and the imperative to exploit."

When I picked up the telephone, my hands were shaking so badly I could barely dial Jill Osiowy's number. As the phone in her office rang, I could hear the call-waiting beep on my line. I looked out my front window. The red, white, and blue truck of another TV network was pulling up in front of my house.

Jill had to bear the brunt of my anger. "Whose decision would it be to send a news team out here to ask a six-year-old child if her mother was a murderer?"

For a moment, Jill was silent. Then she said, "It's news, Jo. I'm sorry. I know that's not the answer you want, but that's the answer there is. You're news."

"And that makes my kids fair game," I said.

"In some people's minds, yes," she said.

On the notepad beside the telephone, Hilda had carefully written the telephone numbers of all the media people who had phoned. Most had called more than once, but Troy Smith-Windsor had gone for the gold and called five times. Suddenly I was so exhausted I couldn't move.

"How long will this go on, Jill?" I asked.

"Till they find someone else."

"I'm not going to wait that long," I said.

There was silence on the other end of the line. Finally, Jill said. "What can I do to help?"

"See what you can find out about Kevin Tarpley's murder. There has to be a connection, and I'm in the clear there."

"I'll check our police sources, and I'll ask Terry Norlander from the Prince Albert affiliate to go talk to that guy in the cell across from Kevin's. The one who helped Kevin with his letters."

"Ah, yes, the letters," I said. "You know that minister – Paschal Temple – Kevin might have told him something. Jill, see if you can track him down, will you? If it sounds like he'll talk to me, I can drive up there this weekend. Hilda said she'll stay a few days, so the kids will be okay."

"You got it," Jill said. Then she laughed, "Hey, Nancy Drew, it's good to hear that you're back in business."

I winced, relieved that Howard Dowhanuik was snarled somewhere in Toronto rush-hour traffic, safely out of earshot.

Dinner was, given the circumstances, a cheerful affair. After I'd talked to Jill, I ran through the options for dinner and ordered in pizza, extra large, loaded. The kids ate like people with nothing more serious on their minds than double cheese and pepperoni. I relaxed and listened as Taylor ran through the guest list for her birthday party and Angus talked about a girl named Brie who had just moved to Regina from Los Angeles. "Talk about culture shock, eh, Mum?"

"Yeah," I said, as I opened bottles of Great Western beer for Hilda and me. "Brie's going to find it hard to keep up with the scene here in Regina."

Jill called at 6:30. "I just got off the phone with Terry Norlander. The police up there have zip on the shooting. Their ballistic people say the bullets came from a handgun. Kevin was with that inmate from the cell across from him. According to Terry, this guy is something else. Apparently, he's embraced our prison system so wholeheartedly that he prefers to be known as 49041 Rudzik. Anyway, Kevin and 49041 were shooting baskets in the exercise yard. When Kevin went down, 49041 thought he'd tripped. Then he saw the blood. Apparently the car and the driver just disappeared. Terry is going to try to see 49041 again tomorrow, but I wouldn't hold your breath about any revelations there. Speaking of revelations, we've had some luck with Paschal Temple. I called his house and got his wife. Paschal's in Regina. One of the brethren had a heart attack, and he's taken over the church down here till the guy recovers. It's Bread of Life on 13th Avenue. His wife told me they have a 7:00 service tonight, so if you hustle, you can still make it."

"I'll hustle," I said. I could hear the grimness in my voice.

Apparently, Jill did too. "Hey, Jo, guess what Mrs. Paschal Temple's name is?"

"Hepzibah," I said.

"Wrong by a country mile," said Jill. "It's Lolita."

An hour later, I was sitting in Bread of Life Tabernacle waiting for Lolita Temple's husband to begin his sermon. Bread of Life had the cheerless utilitarian look of a building that had been constructed on the cheap, but the pews were filled, and the air was electric with emotion. I sat next to a man who seemed to be about my age, but most of the congregation was in its teens. A Christian rock group with the name Joyful Noise spray-painted on its bass drum began to play.

As the music soared, some kids near the front stood up, raised their hands towards heaven, closed their eyes, and began to sway. The man beside me smiled and shook his head. I smiled back. Two middle-aged people commiserating about the excesses of youth. The music grew more intense, and the kids who were swaying began to whirl up the centre aisle towards the altar. I was absorbed in their progress when the man who had smiled at me began to howl and speak in tongues.

It was a relief when a small, sensible-looking man who appeared to be in his mid-sixties walked to the front and stood behind the lectern. He was wearing trousers, an open-necked shirt, and a red cardigan. He thanked the members of Joyful Noise and smiled with real affection at the kids who had danced in the aisle and who had collapsed, sweaty and depleted, on the floor to the left of him.

He looked out over the congregation. "I'm Paschal Temple," he said, "and I'm glad to be here." His voice was a prairie voice, flat, gentle, unhurried. He began to speak about what St. Paul had said about the gifts of the spirit in his letter to the Corinthians. I had heard the words a dozen times, but that night they struck a nerve. "Now we see only puzzling reflections in a mirror, but then we shall see face to face. My knowledge now is partial, then it will be whole . . ."

I hadn't any plan about how I would approach Paschal Temple, but he took care of the problem for me. As soon as the service was over, he came down to where I was sitting.

"Can I help, Mrs. Kilbourn?" he said.

"You know my name," I said.

He looked down, abashed. "It's been in the papers lately," he said.

"That's why I'm here," I said.

"Would you like to come to the office and talk awhile?" he asked.

The office was a small room, cheery with children's drawings of Jesus. There was a photograph on the desk of a woman holding a strawberry shortcake up to the camera. I pointed to it. "Your wife?" I asked.

"My heart," he said.

Lucky Lolita. Paschal Temple motioned me to sit down. Up close I could see the fine network of lines around his eyes. He sat back in his chair and smiled at me, patient, encouraging. I thought he had the kindest face I'd ever seen:

"I don't know where to begin," I said. "That text you used for your sermon, that's my life right now. Partial knowledge and puzzling reflections."

"That's the human condition, Mrs. Kilbourn."

"I know," I said. "But if you've been reading the papers, you know I haven't got the time to muddle through. I have to clear up some things pretty quickly. I thought one place to start was with Kevin Tarpley."

"You know about my connection with him," Paschal Temple said.

"He wrote to me." I opened my bag, took out Kevin's letter and slid it across the desk. "This came the day he died."

He read the letter and then handed it back to me. "Kevin was a very simple boy," he said sadly.

"He was a murderer," I said.

Paschal Temple touched his fingertips together and, for a few moments, he looked at them with great concentration. Then he raised his eyes to mine. "No," he said, "I don't believe Kevin was a murderer."

The room was so quiet I could hear the ticking of the wall clock. On the desk in front of me, Lolita Temple held her strawberry shortcake up to the camera. I felt as if I had turned to glass.

The Reverend Temple's voice was filled with concern. "Can I get you something Mrs. Kilbourn? Tea? Water?"

I shook my head.

"Then I'll explain myself," he said. "I guess I should start by telling you that if you hadn't come to me, I would have come to you. Until this week, I had looked upon Kevin's conversations with me as confidential, 'under the seal' as the Roman Catholics say."

"Two people are dead, and I'm in serious trouble," I said. "Surely that changes things."

"It does," he agreed. "That's why I'm talking to you now. But Mrs. Kilbourn, you mustn't get your hopes up. Kevin Tarpley never gave me a full and frank confession of wrong-doing. He was a troubled young man with some persistent questions. That's all we have to go on."

"It's better than what I have now," I said.

Paschal Temple looked at me closely. "As they say here at Bread of Life, 'Half a loaf is better than none.'"

"That's a terrible joke," I said.

"I know, but it made you smile, and that makes me feel hopeful. Let's begin at the beginning, Mrs. Kilbourn. The first time I met Kevin Tarpley was after my weekly prayer service at the penitentiary. I asked Kevin why he'd come, hoping, as you can imagine, for some indication of search-ing or need. But do you know what he said?"

I shook my head.

"He said, 'Some guy told me if I come to chapel, they'll parole me earlier.' That was Kevin. He had been in jail for six years without inquiring about the avenue to parole, but when someone he barely knew told him that going to chapel was the route to follow, he went to chapel. It would never have occurred to him to question the validity of the argu-ment or the reliability of the source. He was very limited intellectually, Mrs. Kilbourn. I had counselling sessions with him twice a week for six weeks, and I was constantly sur-prised that a fellow like that had been allowed to live on his own. He was one of those sad cases that our society allows to slip through the cracks: not so severely limited that social services could step in, but certainly not capable of making decisions for himself."

I closed my eyes, and Maureen Gault was there, derisive, boasting. "I can make people do things." That's what she'd said the night of Howard Dowhanuik's dinner. I thought of the scene on the highway. What had she made Kevin Tarpley do?

My heart was pounding. "What did he talk about in your sessions?"

"Lies," said Paschal Temple. "He agonized over a lie he had told. He asked me repeatedly how bad it was to tell a lie. And I told him repeatedly that he should ask God's forgiveness and then he should tell the truth. It wasn't enough. Finally, not long before he died, he told me what was troubling him. 'What do you do,' he asked, 'if one person is hurt by the lie, but another person is hurt by the truth?' I told him he would have to work out who was being hurt more, and then I showed him that passage about responsibility and judgement that he quoted in his letter to you. That seemed to turn the tide for him. He accepted Christ as his Saviour that night, and he told me he knew now that he had to tell the truth."

"And then he was murdered," I said. "Did he tell you the name of the person who would be hurt by the truth?"

"No," he said. "But as I remember it, there was only one other person with him on the highway the night your husband was killed."

Kevin Tarpley's letter lay on the table in front of me. The anguish even the physical act of printing had cost him was apparent in every carefully formed word.

"This wasn't the only letter," I said. "The prisoner in the cell across from him said there were two more."

Paschal Temple nodded. "Kevin told me he had three letters to write."

I pointed to the words Kevin had so laboriously printed on the bottom of the publicity picture for Howard Dowhanuik's roast.

"Did he ask you about this quote? From what you've said about Kevin Tarpley's intellectual capacity, it doesn't seem likely he would have found it on his own."

Paschal Temple read the words aloud. " 'Put not your trust in rulers. Psalm 146,' " he said. "I didn't tell him about that passage, at least not directly."

There was a battered briefcase on the floor beside him. He reached into it, pulled out a piece of paper and handed it to me. It was a photocopied sheet labelled "Biblical Character Building Chart." Beneath the title were two neat columns. The first was headed "Character Building Qualities," the second, "Character Destroying Qualities." Under "Character Building Qualities," words like "Abstinence" and "Morality" and "Thrift" were followed by a biblical reference, chapter and verse.

Paschal Temple leaned across and pointed to an entry in the column labelled "Character Destroying Qualities." "Wilful Blindness. Psalm 146." "There's your quote, Mrs. Kilbourn, and Kevin did have a copy of this sheet. I gave it to him. I give copies of this to a lot of the fellows at the penitentiary."

Unexpectedly, he grinned. "Mrs. Kilbourn, you have the same look on your face you had when the man beside you began speaking in tongues."

"I'm sorry," I said, "I guess I'm uncomfortable with this kind of thing."

"We don't all come to God in the same way," he said gently. "And whatever you may think of these little spiritual shortcuts, for some people they're just the ticket. The Reinhold Niebuhrs of this world are few and far between, you know."

"You read Reinhold Niebuhr?" I asked.

"A cat can look at a king," he said kindly, and I could feel myself redden with embarrassment.

"Well, that's neither here nor there," he said. "That passage I used as a text for the sermon tonight tells us that knowledge will 'vanish away.' It also tells us that there are three things that last forever: faith, hope, and love; but the greatest of them all is love. Maybe that passage will lead you to an understanding of what Kevin Tarpley did. And Mrs. Kilbourn, perhaps if you come to understand Kevin, you'll be able to forgive him."

I stood up. "Thank you," I said.

"I'm afraid I wasn't really very helpful," he said as he walked me to the door.

I turned and faced him. "You were," I said. "More than you know."

As I drove south on Albert Street, I tried to do what Paschal Temple had urged me to do. I tried to think about faith and hope and love. I tried to make myself understand that Kevin Tarpley had lied because he loved Maureen Gault. I tried to picture the love he felt for her. But try as I might, the only image I could summon was the image of Maureen Gault killing my husband. It blocked out everything else. Those pale eyes had looked into Ian's eyes as she raised her arm and then brought the crowbar down on the side of his skull.

I was still seeing through a glass, darkly.

CHAPTER

6

I slept badly and woke up with a headache and a sense of foreboding so acute that it took an act of will just to put on my sweats and sneakers. The run along the lakeshore with the dogs seemed endless, and by the time I got into the Volvo to drive Angus to his basketball practice and Taylor to her art class, I felt as if my nerve ends were exposed. The scene inside the car didn't help. The radio was blasting something loud and dissonant, and in the back seat Taylor was tormenting her brother about Brie, the girl who'd moved from L.A.

I turned down the sound, punched the button to change stations, then angled around towards Taylor.

"Stop it, T," I said. "I mean it."

Angus leaned over to his sister. "She means it. I can tell by her voice."

"Thank you, Angus," I said, and I snapped on my seatbelt and pulled out of the driveway.

"Top of the hour on your Rock and Roll Heaven Weekend," said the man on the radio. "Here's a celestial six-pack: Karen Carpenter, Ritchie Valens, Buddy Holly, Louis

Armstrong, Bobby Darin, and Marvin Gaye, Six Greats Whose Stars Shine Bright Even After Death!"

"I hate that station," said T.

"You can borrow my Discman," Angus said; then he hissed, "but listen, if you even breathe wrong, I'm taking it back."

At College Avenue, we had to stop for a funeral procession. As I sat and watched the hearse and the mourners go by, Karen Carpenter sang about how love had put her on the top of the world.

We dropped Angus at the Y, and Taylor hopped in the front seat with me. As we drove to the Mackenzie Gallery, she filled me in on her new art teacher.

"His name is Fil with an *F*," she said. "He wears a sleeve on his head, and he says if you understand planes, you can draw anything."

"Planes?" I said. "Planes like at the airport?"

Taylor shook her head. "Is that another one of your jokes, Jo?"

"No," I said, "it's not. I really don't understand."

"Planes like on your face." She looked at me thoughtfully. "Except," she said, "you're like me. No planes. Just chipmunk cheeks."

"Thanks, T," I said. "I needed cheering up."

She undid her seatbelt and slid across the seat towards me. "I love you, Jo."

I looked at her worried face. She'd only been with me two years, not secure yet.

"I love you, too, Taylor," I said. "Now get your seatbelt back on."

"We're almost there."

"Doesn't matter," I said. "Snap!"

Most Saturdays I used the two hours when Taylor was at her art lesson to run errands, but that morning I didn't feel

like braving the eyes of the curious in the mall. I remembered
the visiting exhibition of Impressionist landscapes at the
gallery. I decided I could use an infusion of incandescent light
and pastoral peace.

It helped. As I walked through the still rooms, I could feel
my pulse slow and my mind clear. Paschal Temple's revelation had shaken me. For six years I had lived with the fact
that Ian's death had been random, a chance occurrence in a
fatalist's tragedy. But if Maureen Gault had killed Ian, the
character of the tragedy changed. In the months after Ian's
murder I had tormented myself imagining what his death
must have been like. But as frightening as the movie in my
head was, it lacked specifics. Darkness. Shadows. A spill of
blood on the snow. I could never bring Kevin Tarpley into
focus. Maureen Gault was another matter. When I closed
my eyes, she was there, pale eyes flat with menace, thin
mouth curled in triumph, as she ended Ian's life. Oh, I could
see Maureen all right. But try as I might, what I couldn't see
was why she had killed my husband.

I checked my watch as I came out of the exhibit. Taylor
would be in her lesson for another hour. I wandered through
the lobby. In the corner was a rack of brochures for tourists.
I rejected the ones for other galleries and museums in our
city, and chose one entitled "Tips for Healthy Living." It was
full of robust good sense:

> Nutrition – Eat Right
> Physical Fitness – Exercise Regularly
> Stress – Learn to Cope
> Accident Prevention – Practise Safety
> Communicable Diseases – Practise Prevention

I put it back in the rack. Now that I had the key, Healthy
Living would be easy. I checked my watch again. I still had

almost an hour. Time enough to fight stress by coping. Jill had left me a pass for the video library at Nationtv; I could go over the tapes of Ian's death and the trial and see if there was anything I'd missed.

When I pulled into the parking lot behind the station, Janis Joplin was singing "Me and Bobby McGee." I was still humming the tune as I crossed the lobby and took the elevator upstairs. The young woman working in the video library was wearing Doc Martens, and she had a small diamond in her nose. When I asked for the Ian Kilbourn file she said, "You mean the whole thing?"

"Freedom's just another word for nothin' left to lose," I said.

She chewed her gum thoughtfully. "Is that a yes?"

I nodded. "That's a yes."

As I headed out of the library with my armload of tapes, she called me back.

"This one goes with the file, too," she said, and she balanced another tape carefully on the pile I was holding.

I looked at the name on the spine: "Heinbecker Funeral." It was the tape Jill had mentioned the afternoon Angus and I had come to Nationtv. She had said then that the eulogy Ian had given for Charlie Heinbecker had been terrific.

As soon as I got into the editing suite, I put the Heinbecker tape in the VCR. I was in the mood for something terrific.

I fast-forwarded past scenes of the mourners arriving, the choir processing, and the minister praying. Before I had a chance to prepare myself for it, Ian's image was on the screen. As I watched my husband deliver Charlie Heinbecker's eulogy, I think I stopped breathing.

It was apparent that the video had been shot by an amateur. Periodically, the camera would jerk away from Ian to focus on the members of Charlie's family in the front pews. The transitions were too abrupt, and often the images the camera captured were out of focus. None of that mattered to me. Jill had been right. Ian was terrific that day. He quoted Tennyson ("I am a part of all that I have met . . ./How dull it is to pause, to make an end/To rust unburnished, not to shine in use"), and he talked about stewardship and our obligation to others.

Good words, but it was Ian's face, not his words, that drew me closer to the screen. He had less than three hours to live, and he didn't know it. He didn't know that today was the day the dragon waited at the side of the road. In a gesture I had seen ten thousand times, Ian brushed back his hair with his hand, and I felt something inside me break. Tired of holding the pieces together, I closed the door to the editing suite and gave in.

Crying helped. By the time the monitor showed the mourners leaving the church, I had distanced myself from what was happening on the screen. As I watched for Ian, I was in control again. Finally, he came out, and the camera zoomed in for a closeup. For a moment, he stood blinking as the December light bounced off the snow. Then he started down the church steps, and the camera arced away from him and began to follow another cluster of mourners as they moved from the church to the street. I was leaning forward to punch the stop button when Ian stepped into camera range again. Blurred but recognizable, he began walking down the street. He didn't get far before a slight figure in a dark jacket came up behind him, reached out, and touched his shoulder. Ian turned. Then the camera made another of its convulsive transitions, and I was looking at the pallbearers carrying Charlie's casket out of the church.

I hit the rewind button. The first time, I rewound too far. Then I fast-forwarded past the sequence I needed to see. It took awhile, but finally my husband and his murderer were on screen. I pressed stop.

Maureen's back was to the camera, but her white-blond bouffant was unmistakable, and the baseball jacket she was wearing was the one she would be arrested in a few hours later. Ian was looking straight into her face. What did he see there?

I touched the rewind button. Ian turned from Maureen and, in the robotic walk of an actor in a silent movie, my husband and the woman who was about to kill him moved away from one another. If I kept rewinding, I could change the outcome. I could defeat death. But as I watched the mourners at Charlie's funeral walking backwards up the steps of the church, I knew I couldn't rewind the tape forever. I flicked on the lights in the editing suite. It was time to push the button marked "forward." I blew my nose, threw the Heinbecker tape into my handbag, and collected the others to take back to the library.

When Taylor and I pulled up in front of our house, Jess Stephens was standing at the front door. He handed me the worm-cake recipe.

"That's from my mum," he said.

There was no note with the recipe, but at least Sylvie had let him come over. That was a start.

"Can he stay for lunch?" Taylor asked.

"It's okay with me," I said, "but he'd better check at home."

Taylor stepped closer to Jess. She was looking at his face appraisingly. "Great planes," she said.

Jess looked baffled.

"Taylor's learning how to draw faces in her art class," I said.

"You'd be good to draw, Jess," Taylor said.

"No, thanks," he said.

I looked at him. Taylor was right. Jess would be good to draw. His cheekbones were high and well defined, and his eyes had the slightly upward tilt you sometimes see in Slovenes. Somewhere along the line, an ancestor of the O'Keefes or the Stephenses must have spent some quality time in Eastern Europe.

Taylor grabbed Jess's hand. "Go call your mum. Then we can look at Jack."

I followed them down the hall and watched through the kitchen window as they went out on the deck. Taylor immediately pressed her face against the pumpkin, peering into his right eye hole. Then she moved back to let Jess look. As I turned from the window, I thought that November had been kinder to Jack than it had to me. His rate of disintegration had slowed in the chill.

When Hilda came in, she gave me a sharp look. "I'd say 'Penny for your thoughts,' but from the look on your face, I don't think I'd be pleased with my purchase."

"I'm thinking about death and decay," I said.

Hilda picked up a knife and began buttering bread. "Not elegiacally, I take it."

"I had a lousy morning," I said. I went to the fridge and took out a block of cheddar. Everybody liked grilled cheese. As I sliced the cheddar, I told Hilda about the funeral tape. When I finished, her face was grim.

"What are you going to do?" she said.

"Take the tape to the police," I said.

"Wouldn't they have seen it already?"

"I don't think so, Hilda. It was a private taping of a family event. Old Mrs. Heinbecker had it until last year when she gave it to Jill, and Jill put it straight in the archives."

Hilda looked thoughtful: "The police have to see it, of course. That's the only ethical option you have, but, Joanne, that tape isn't going to help your case."

I shuddered. The resonance of the phrase "your case" was not pleasant.

"I don't seem to know how to help my case," I said.

"Follow the strands back to the place where they meet," Hilda said. "Find out everything you can about Kevin Tarpley and Maureen Gault." Her voice dropped. "And, Joanne, I think you're going to have to scrutinize your husband's life as well."

I could feel the rush of anger. "You're not suggesting there was a relationship between Ian and Maureen Gault, are you?"

Hilda's voice was patient, but firm. "There was a relationship. You saw it yourself on that tape. In all likelihood, the relationship was that of stalker and victim, but, if that was the case, you still need to know what it was about Ian that made Maureen hunt him down. And you need to know how long she pursued him and whether he knew about the pursuit. There are a dozen questions. Joanne."

As I plugged the parking meter outside police headquarters, I was heavy with discouragement. *A dozen questions.* I looked at the tape in my handbag. When Inspector Alex Kequahtooway saw it, a dozen questions would be just the beginning.

As I opened his office door, the first thing I noticed was that there was a Beethoven violin sonata playing softly on the CD player in the corner; the second was that Alex Kequahtooway had had his hair cut. His brother, Perry, wore his hair traditionally, in braids, but Alex's hair was very short. A "cop-cut" Angus would have called it. The night of the murder Inspector Kequahtooway had been dressed casually, but today he was wearing a navy suit, a striped shirt, and a floral silk tie.

"I like your tie," I said.

"Thanks," he said. "I was in court all morning. What can I do for you, Mrs. Kilbourn?"

He listened to my account of the tape carefully, and as I finished, he smiled thinly.

"I have to hand it to you for bringing the tape in. I can't say for certain until I see it, but it sounds as if that tape may be helpful."

"I hope it is," I said.

He nodded. "Me too," he said. Then he leaned towards me. "Mrs. Kilbourn, what were you looking for at Nationtv?"

"Answers," I said.

"Leave that to us, Mrs. Kilbourn. Don't involve yourself in this."

"I am involved. Haven't you read the papers or turned on your TV? I'm the number-one suspect."

He raised his eyebrows. "Do you believe everything you hear from the media?"

For the first time since Maureen Gault's murder, I felt a glimmer of hope.

"If you don't think I killed her, why aren't you telling the press?"

Unexpectedly, he smiled. "First, because, at least to my knowledge, there has been no flat-out assertion that you're guilty. The press has been very careful to imply rather than state. And second, because, at the moment, there are certain advantages to having the focus on you."

"Because the real killer might relax and make himself vulnerable?"

"Him or her self, Mrs. Kilbourn. And yes, that's what I'm hoping for. A lot of police work is just waiting around, you know. When I was a kid, I owned an old retriever – best squirrel dog on the reserve. He never seemed to do anything but lie in the sun. All the other dogs, soon as they spotted a squirrel, they'd start running around, yapping, going crazy till they got that squirrel into a tree. Nine times out of ten that was the end of it. The dogs would get tired and bugger off, and the squirrel would go on about his business. But that old retriever of mine would just sit and wait, and as soon as the squirrel thought it was a lovely day for a walk . . . bingo!" He smiled. "That old dog would have made a good cop."

"So you're just waiting?"

He shook his head. "No," he said.

"Then what are you doing?"

"Checking and re-checking stories," he said.

"To see if someone's lying?"

"No, just to see how everybody within earshot of the head table remembers the evening's events. People see things differently, Mrs. Kilbourn."

"Depending on where they were sitting," I said.

"Yeah, and depending on what happened to them in their lives before they walked into that room. What I'm trying to do right now is find out everything I can about the people who were sitting at the head table that night."

"Know the truth about the teller and you'll know the truth about his tale," I said.

Inspector Alex Kequahtooway's dark eyes widened with interest. "Something an elder told you?" he asked.

"Something my grandmother told me," I said.

His round face creased in a grin. "She must have been an Ojibwa."

We both laughed.

"Finding the truth about the tellers and the tales is what I'm trying to do now," he said.

"Are you getting anywhere?" I asked.

"At the moment, no. All I'm doing is mouse work." He gestured towards the medicine wheel on the wall behind him. "The other day you mentioned the Four Great Ways of Seeking Understanding. You know how Brother Mouse understands his world?"

"By sniffing things out with his nose, seeing what's up close, touching what he can with his whiskers."

He smiled. "Did your grandmother teach you that, Mrs. Kilbourn?"

"No," I said, "I learned that from my instructor in Indian Studies 232."

"Then you know that when I've got my treasure trove of facts and information, I'll try to stop seeing like a mouse and start seeing like an eagle. The big picture, Mrs. Kilbourn. That's what I'm going for."

He extended his hand to me. "Thank you for coming, Mrs. Kilbourn."

I took his hand. "You're welcome," I said. "And, Inspector, I enjoyed the Beethoven."

When I got home, Hilda was sitting at the kitchen table with the morning paper spread out in front of her and a pad and pencil beside her.

She gestured to the window when she saw me. "The children are building a snow fort. They've been remarkably persistent. It's quite impressive."

I looked into the back yard. Taylor and Jess were installing the jack o'lantern in a place of honour at the top of the snow fort. I watched as they packed snow around his base to secure him. Shrivelled but menacing, Jack surveyed the back yard. The fort and those within it were safe.

"Any word from Angus?" I asked Hilda.

"He came by with a group of friends. They admired my earrings, I admired theirs, and they left. He says he'll be home at the regular time for supper."

"Good," I said. I poured a cup of coffee and sat down opposite her. The paper was open to a story about Maureen Gault. "Anything new?" I asked.

"There might be," Hilda said. "I decided to read through all the stories about Maureen and note the significant points."

"Mouse work," I said.

She looked puzzled. When I explained, she laughed. "I like that," she said. She picked up her notepad. "Now, here's my pile of nuts and berries: Maureen Gault was born on Valentine's Day, 1968, in Chaplin."

"Kevin Tarpley was from there, too," I said. "And that's where Ian died. Funny, isn't it? For years, Chaplin was just a place I drove past on the highway, but it always gave me the creeps. It wasn't the town so much as the sodium sulphate plant on the outskirts. There were always these huge mounds of salt on the ground there. They made me think of the Valley of Ashes in *The Great Gatsby*."

Hilda raised her eyebrows. "That's certainly an ominous association."

I nodded. "It's lucky we don't know what's ahead of us, isn't it?" I said.

"Very lucky," Hilda said. She picked up her notepad again. "Maureen's father was killed in a farming accident five months after she was born. Now this next is a quotation from an interview with Maureen's mother, Shirley. 'When my husband died, I decided to devote my life to my girl. She had it all: tap, jazz, ballet, ringette. Little Mo always knew exactly what she wanted, and she knew how to get it from me. I don't know how things could have turned out so bad for her.'"

"Poor woman," I said. "Maureen was her life. I remember Shirley Gault from the time after the arrest. I think she was on the news every night. If there was a cabinet minister coming to town, she'd be at the airport, demanding justice. If there was a public meeting, she was at it, handing out leaflets, trying to get herself in front of the cameras."

"She sounds unbalanced," Hilda said.

"I thought so," I said, "but I was pretty unbalanced myself at the time, so I was no judge."

Hilda looked at me sharply. "Are you sure you want to pursue this, Joanne?"

"In for a penny, in for a pound, as my grandmother used to say."

Hilda smiled. "My grandmother used to say that, too." She took a deep breath. "Now, for Maureen's career, which to put it charitably seems somewhat chequered. She never finished high school, but in 1989 Maureen graduated from Vogue Beauty School with a degree in Cosmetology and Depilatory Esthetics. I presume that means she was licensed to apply makeup and remove body hair. At any rate, according to the paper, at the time of her death she was working at a beauty salon called Ray-elle's."

"That's not far from here," I said. "It's in the basement of that strip mall on Montague. I've seen their sign, but I've never been in there."

Hilda raised an eyebrow. "Ray-elle's may be worth looking into," she said. Then she closed her notepad. "Joanne, the most promising information I gathered isn't written down anywhere. It's just a feeling. The paper printed a number of comments about Maureen from girls she knew at school. Not much there, except a certain agreement about the fact that Maureen was a loner who always seemed to know how to get what she wanted. But the reporter from the paper also called the principal of Maureen's old high school in Chaplin for a comment."

"And . . . ?" I said.

"And the woman refused to talk to him."

"That is interesting," I said.

"There's more," Hilda said. "They printed the woman's name; it's Carolyn Atcheson. I know her. Not well, but, before she was a principal, Carolyn was an English teacher. We served on a curriculum committee together. So I called her this morning. And . . . and it was very puzzling. She was delighted to hear from me, very welcoming, full of questions about what I was doing now. But as soon as I mentioned Maureen Gault's name, there was a chill."

"Maybe she thought you were just satisfying your curiosity," I said.

Hilda shook her head. "No, I explained at the outset that my interest in Maureen Gault was not whimsical, and that a dear friend's life had been thrown into turmoil because of Maureen. Carolyn reacted oddly to that. She laughed, not a nice laugh. Then she said, 'I wonder how many lives were thrown into turmoil by that girl?'

"I thought I would press my advantage then. I asked Carolyn straight out if she believed Maureen Gault was capable of murder. There was such a long silence on the line, I wondered if she'd hung up on me. But finally Carolyn said, 'Maureen Gault was capable of anything. She was pathological.'"

"It sounds as if Carolyn's worth talking to," I said.

Hilda said, "It won't be easy. Joanne. From the minute I mentioned Maureen's name, Carolyn Atcheson sounded as if she was terrified."

"But Maureen's dead," I said. "What could Carolyn Atcheson be frightened of?"

Hilda stood up. "That's what I'm going to find out. First thing tomorrow morning, I'm driving down to Chaplin."

"What about church?" I asked. "I've never known you to miss."

Hilda folded the newspaper carefully. "I think sometimes God likes action from his foot-soldiers."

I looked at my watch. "Speaking of action, I'd better get supper started. How does spaghetti sound to you?"

"Splendid," Hilda said.

"Good," I said. For the next hour, I chopped, sautéed, stirred, simmered, and thought about the best way of finding out the truth. "Follow the strands back to the place where they meet." That's what Hilda had said. Jill was looking into Kevin's life; Hilda had taken on Maureen. That left Ian, and no one was going to follow that strand back but me.

Just as I moved the spaghetti sauce to the back burner, Jess and Taylor came in from outdoors, cheeks rosy with cold and excitement.

"It smells like Geno's in here," Taylor said.

Jess turned to her. "Do you ever go there on Kids' Night?"

Taylor shook her head. "Jo says she'd rather be pecked to death by a duck. We just go regular nights."

Jess smiled at me. I could see the edge of a permanent tooth pushing through. I bent down and looked more closely.

"Nice tooth, Jess."

"Thanks. Mrs. Kilbourn, do you have hot chocolate here?"

"Yes," I said, "I think we do."

Five minutes later, we were all sitting around the kitchen table, drinking hot chocolate and listening to Taylor talk about how, if she had a kitten, she would let it sleep on the pillow beside her so it wouldn't bother me in the night. Life in the fast lane.

When Hilda came down, she was dressed to go out.

"Want to join us?" I asked.

"Thank you, no," she said. "I'm off to Ray-elle's Beauty Salon."

"Thinking of getting a new do?" said Jess.

Hilda patted her red hair with a degree of satisfaction. "Oh, I think my old do will suffice."

"I like it," Taylor said. "In oil paints that colour is called 'raw sienna.' It's one of my favourites."

"Mine too," said Hilda.

Gary Stephens was an hour late picking up Jess. He'd called in mid-afternoon to say he'd be at our house by 5:00, but it was close to 6:00 when he pulled into the driveway.

"Sorry I'm late," he said. "The skiing was just too good." He was wearing cross-country ski clothes, and I saw his skis on the rack of his car, but he didn't radiate the sense of physical well-being of someone who'd spent the afternoon outdoors. As he stood in the hall, his handsome face was pale, and he smelled, not of fresh air, but of liquor and cologne. I wondered who the lucky woman was this time.

"It wasn't a problem," I said. "The kids had a great afternoon. They built a snow fort. Jess could have stayed for supper if he'd wanted."

"Thanks, babe, but Sylvie has something planned." He smiled his slow, lazy, practised smile. "You know how she is," he said.

You and me against the little woman. It was an ugly tactic, but before I had a chance to respond, Jess was in the hall.

"Dad, you've gotta see the fort we built. Come on. We made forty-six snowballs."

As Jess grabbed his father's hand, Gary Stephens was transformed as he had been Hallowe'en night. There was such naked love in his eyes as he looked at his son that I

felt a rush of feeling towards him. Five minutes before I'd
wanted to come down on him like a fist on a grasshopper, but
he was a complex man, and he evoked complex emotions.

Angus and I were just finishing the salad when Hilda
came in.

I checked her hair. "No new do?" I asked.

"No," she said, as she hung up her coat. "But I did come
away with some interesting new perspectives on Maureen."

"From whom?" I asked.

"From Ray-elle herself. Joanne, Maureen did not work at
Ray-elle's at the time of her death. Ray-elle had, and I quote,
'canned her' the last week in October."

"But the paper said . . ."

"Ray-elle didn't believe there was much to be gained in
giving the newspaper the complete story. She reasoned that
since Maureen was dead and Shirley Gault was suffering
enough, there was no need to dig up the past."

"I guess that makes sense," I said.

"There's more," Hilda said. "And this doesn't make
sense. At least not to me. The day after Kevin Tarpley died,
Maureen Gault came by the beauty shop and offered to buy
Ray-elle out."

"Where would Maureen get that kind of money?"

Hilda came over and took a slice of cucumber out of the
salad bowl. "I don't know, but apparently she said she could
pay cash. Joanne, the asking price for that business would be
significant. Ray-elle told me she had just finished renovat-
ing." A smile flickered at the corners of Hilda's mouth.

"What's so funny?" I asked.

Hilda shook her head. "That place. Joanne, everything in
Ray-elle's is pink. Floor, walls, chairs, uniforms, everything."

"Maybe Ray-elle had Superstar Barbie's decorator," I said.

Taylor, who was setting the table, heard a name that

interested her. "I saw a lady on TV who had nineteen operations so she could look like Barbie," she said.

"Good lord," I said, "why would she do that?"

Angus handed me the salad. "You don't want to know, Mum," he said. "How long till we eat?"

"Not long," I said. "The pasta has to cook."

"Time enough to see my snow fort," T said.

"I had to ask," said Angus, as he followed his sister out the back door.

I turned to Hilda. "How about some Chianti while you tell me what you found out."

I poured each of us a glass. Hilda took hers and raised it. "To puzzle solving," she said. "Although, to be frank, my visit to Ray-elle's has yielded more questions than answers." Hilda sipped her wine. "Joanne, let me practise what I preach and put some chronology to all this.

"When I got to the shop, Ray-elle was at the appointments desk and Cheryl, a young woman who plays a pivotal role in this story, was sweeping up. There weren't any customers. I introduced myself, and Ray-elle said she was just about to close anyway and she asked Cheryl to get me some coffee. When Ray-elle was finished, she told Cheryl she could leave, and Ray-elle and I went to a little room at the back, so she could smoke. Joanne, even her lighter was pink. It was in a kind of sheath made of pink leather, and the case she kept her cigarettes in was covered in pink leather, too."

"I used to have a cigarette case like that," I said, "except mine was white. I haven't seen a set like that in twenty-five years. I take it Ray-elle is, as the French say, 'of a certain age.'"

"She is," Hilda agreed. "And of a certain type. I liked her, Joanne. She's a school-of-hard-knocks person, physically strong and experienced. To look at her, one would think there wouldn't be much in life that would intimidate her . . ."

"But something did," I said.

"Not something, Joanne. Someone. The first thing Ray-elle said to me after we sat down was that she wasn't sorry Maureen Gault was dead because Maureen scared the shit out of her." Hilda raised an eyebrow. "You do realize I'm giving you Ray-elle's words verbatim."

"I do," I said. "Now, what did Maureen do to Ray-elle to scare her so badly?"

"It's an ugly story," Hilda said. "Cheryl, the girl who was sweeping up when I arrived at the shop, is a person with some serious limitations intellectually. She does odd jobs around the shop, sweeps up, cleans brushes and combs, that sort of thing. But Ray-elle has her wash hair, too. She says Cheryl has a gentle touch, and the customers like her." Hilda smiled. "Cheryl really did seem like a pleasant young woman. At any rate, last month, Cheryl came to Ray-elle and told her Maureen was forcing her to hand over her tips. It didn't amount to much, and when Ray-elle confronted her, Maureen said she didn't need the money."

"Why did she do it then?"

Hilda's face was grave. "Ray-elle said that Maureen seemed to get her kicks just from making the girl do her bidding."

"What did Maureen do when she was fired?" I asked.

Hilda picked up the wine bottle and filled our glasses. "She laughed in Ray-elle's face. Said she didn't need to work anyway, because she was about to come into some major money." Hilda looked hard at me. "It wasn't braggadocio, Joanne. The day after Kevin Tarpley died, Maureen paid a farewell visit to Ray-elle's. According to Ray-elle, Maureen was dressed expensively and ostentatiously. She said something cruel to Cheryl, queened it over the other women who work in the shop, then she went over to Ray-elle and offered to buy the shop. She said she could pay cash. When Ray-elle told her to get out, Maureen turned ugly. She said, 'Like I would ever want to buy a dump like this.' Then she picked up an open bottle of peroxide solution and threw it in Ray-elle's face. Ray-elle still has a nasty burn."

"Did she go to the police?"

Hilda shook her head. "She was afraid to, Joanne. She said she was afraid of what Maureen Gault would do if she crossed her."

That night I couldn't sleep. Every time I closed my eyes, Maureen Gault was there. Finally, I gave up, went downstairs, and made myself some warm milk. As I sat at the kitchen table with my mug, Rose came into the room and sat with me; in Rose's house, people didn't come down for warm milk in the middle of the night.

From the kitchen window, I could see the ice on the creek. In the November moonlight, it looked dark and sinister. A child had drowned in that creek. When they had searched for the body, the police had brought up all kinds of ugliness: stolen bicycles and grocery carts; empty whisky bottles and used condoms; a weighted gunny sack full of small skeletons that turned out to be feline.

That afternoon, when I was certain the child's body had been taken away, I had walked along the levee. The banks of the creek were still littered with the objects the police had dredged up. Until that morning, those objects had been part of the tenebrous life of the creekbed. In the pale spring light, they had looked both mean and alien and I had hurried from them.

I rinsed my mug, put it in the dishwasher, and turned out the kitchen light. I had to get some sleep. In the morning it would be my turn to dredge.

CHAPTER

7

I didn't want to remember the last hours I spent with my husband on the day of his death. The morning of December 27 was cruel in every sense: the weather was viciously cold, and, the night before, Ian had come in very late and we had quarrelled. We weren't people who fought often and, as Ian got ready to leave that morning, we were silent, stunned, I think, by the pall of bitterness that hung in the air between us. I kissed my husband as he left, but I didn't tell him I loved him, and I didn't say goodbye. I was angry at him for deciding to drive through a blizzard because he felt he had to honour the outcome of a stupid coin toss, and I was angry at him because I thought he had treated me badly at the caucus office party the night before.

That party had seemed jinxed from the beginning. The idea had been a good one: an afternoon of skating and tobogganing in Wascana Park for the families of members and staff who were in town for the holidays, then, in the evening, Boxing Day drinks in the east wing for the adults. But the wind had howled all afternoon, and most of us with children stayed away. After lunch, Ian had gone over to his office to get caught up on his mail, and he had called before dinner to say he wouldn't be home, and that I should come straight to the party and he'd see me there. As I was dressing, Angus came into our bedroom and threw up. I felt his head. He was feverish, but not worryingly so. I cleaned up, gave him a bath and some children's Tylenol, and called Ian at the office to tell him I wasn't coming. There was no answer. By the time Angus got out of the tub, he seemed better. Mieka was babysitting her brothers, and the party was only a few blocks away at the Legislature, so I decided to go after all.

It was a fine night. The wind had died down, and the air was clear and cold. The evergreens in front of the Legislature were strung, as they always were, with blue and white lights, but that year the park commission had suspended a giant illuminated snowflake over the face of the old building. It was sensational, and as I walked past the pictures of our former premiers and heard the music drifting down the marble corridors, I thought that one last Christmas party wasn't such a bad idea after all.

My merry mood didn't last long. The stately old Opposition Caucus Room was full of people, but Ian wasn't one of them. I got a drink and went over to Ian's secretary, Lorraine Bellegarde. She was wearing a red and yellow Métis ribbon shirt and a fringed leather skirt; it was a festive outfit, but Lorraine did not look cheerful. I didn't have to ask why. Lorraine was a perfectionist, and she'd been in charge of the festivities that day. I knew her well enough to know how acutely she'd be feeling the weight of the afternoon's failure. She told me she hadn't seen Ian. She also told me not to worry, but it was too late for that. I started moving around the room, asking if anyone had seen my husband. No one had, and the terrible possibilities began their assault on my consciousness: a holiday accident; a heart attack; a fatal slip on an icy step. By the time Ian walked through the door

I was half sick with worry. He looked weary and preoccupied, but I didn't pity him.

"Where were you?" I said.

"Leave it alone, Jo," he said, and there was an edge to his voice that angered me.

"It would have been nice to know where you were," I said. "Angus is sick."

A flicker of alarm passed over his face then he seemed to relax. "If it was serious, you wouldn't be here." Then he'd smiled, "Come on, relax. Angus is probably just suffering from too much Christmas."

"What if it had been serious?" I said.

"Well, it wasn't, so that's a moot point, isn't it? Look, Jo, I'm having a great time. Standing here listening to you being pissed off is exactly what I want to be doing right now. But, if you don't mind, I'd like to get a drink. Then, I'll come back and you can continue with whatever the hell it is you think you're doing."

I watched as he went to the bar and poured himself a drink. He downed it in a single gulp, poured another one, and started towards me. I was furious. I looked around for someone to talk to. Howard Dowhanuik was alone by the window. He was wearing the red plaid vest he had worn to every holiday function since I'd known him. Howard always made a point of drawing our attention to what he called the Dowhanuik tartan, but the vest had always done a pretty good job of calling attention to itself. In that evening of strange currents and jagged edges, it had been a reassuring sight.

I don't remember what Howard and I talked about, but I do remember that Ian joined us, and that, at some point, Lorraine came over and reminded Howard that the Caucus Office had to send someone to speak at Charlie Heinbecker's funeral the next day. Mellowed by good scotch, Howard had been avuncular as he gathered all our members together. I don't remember who came up with the idea of the coin toss to decide who would drive to Swift Current. Like most ideas that people come up with when they're drinking, it seemed inspired. Two people would toss, and the loser would meet a new opponent and toss again, until the outcome had been decided. When Ian lost, he had raised his glass to me. "At least I'm lucky in love," he'd said, and his voice had been heavy with irony.

I hadn't answered him. Lorraine Bellegarde had come over and told me there was a phone call. It was Mieka. Angus had thrown up again and was asking for me. I told Mieka I'd be right home. When I'd looked for Ian to tell him I was leaving, he was gone.

Three times during the evening I called the caucus office. Ian wasn't there. It must have been after 2:00 when I heard the front door, and a half-hour later than that when Ian finally came upstairs. I watched as he undressed in the moonlight, his long pale body as familiar to me as my own.

"Where were you?" I said.

His voice was infinitely tired. "Where you left me. At the party. Now I'm here, and I want to go to bed."

"Not until you tell me what's going on," I said. "Ian, you weren't at the party. I called. Nobody could find you."

"I stepped out for a while. Satisfied?"

"No," I said, "I'm not. Ian, we've never lied to each other. Where were you tonight?"

"Jo, if you'd stop badgering me, I wouldn't have to lie to you. This is my business, not yours. Now, for the last time, leave it alone."

"Go to hell," I said, and I turned my back to him. We slept fitfully, angry and apart. The next morning he showered and left. Seven hours later he was dead, and the marriage which had been the best thing that ever happened to me was over.

That was how the party had looked from my perspective, but there'd been other people there, and they would have other stories. I looked at my watch. It was too late to call anybody. All I could do was sit and watch the back yard fill up with snow until I was tired enough to sleep.

The next morning, as soon as I got in from taking the dogs for their run, I called Howard at his apartment in Toronto. He was happy to hear from me, but less happy when he heard what I was calling about.

"Jesus, Jo, I thought we agreed you'd stay out of this."

"No, Howard, you agreed. Look, the universe is not exactly unfolding as it should around here."

When I'd finished telling him about the way the arrows were pointing in the Maureen Gault case, Howard's voice was sombre.

"What can I do?"

"Tell me what you remember about the party the night before Ian died."

"You mean the one at the caucus office? Christ, Jo, that was six years ago."

"It's important, Howard. At least, I think it might be. The problem is I don't remember much about it at all. Angus was sick, and I went home early. I don't even know for sure who was there."

Howard's voice was thoughtful. "We were all there, weren't we? I remember Andy was. His mother was down for the holidays, and he brought her. Old Roma Boychuk, there was a political asset for you. She kept sniffing at the food. Finally she went up to Lorraine Bellegarde and said, 'How much you pay for all those little sausages and the crackers with the raw meat?' When Lorraine told her, Roma hit the roof. She spent the rest of the evening going around telling everybody how they'd been ripped off. 'Next time, get me. For that money I make you a five-course meal, and the meat will be cooked!'" He laughed again. "Lorraine was really steamed.

"Anyway, Roma and Andy were at the party, and Craig was there with Julie. He sure did better the second time around, didn't he? That Julie was something else . . . That night was the only time I ever remember seeing Craig stand up to her."

"What happened?"

"Julie came over to me with some hot piece of news, and Craig told her to put a lid on it."

"What was the news?"

"I don't know, but I don't imagine it was much. Julie always had a mean little story or a nasty rumour. Remember how she used to say, 'There's something I feel I have to share with you . . .'? It was always dirt.

"Let's see, if Marty and I were still together, she would have been there, but I don't remember if we were still together."

"That's probably why you're not together now," I said.

"You're probably right," he agreed.

"Jane O'Keefe was there with that fat lawyer from Saskatoon. You know, the one who dyes his hair."

"Billy Clifford?" I said. "I never knew they were an item."

"They weren't. Billy would have taken a bullet for Jane, but she was just using him as a blind."

"For what?" I said.

"For an affair she was having with another guy," he said. "Jo, let's get on to something else here. With all my nasty evasions and innuendos I'm beginning to sound like Julie Evanson."

"Howard, if that other man is somebody I know, it may be important. Was he?"

There was silence. When Howard spoke, his voice was sad. "I guess it doesn't matter any more. It's been over for years. The other guy was Gary Stephens."

"Oh, Howard, no."

"It wasn't just a fling. At least not on Jane's side. She was really in love with him. In fact, she kind of fell apart that night at the party. I don't know whether they'd had a fight or what, but Gary disappeared part way through the evening, and Jane went after him."

"Howard, I just can't believe this. Was Sylvie there?"

He laughed. "Jo, as you just discovered, I can't even remember if my own wife was at the party, but I don't think Sylvie was there."

"No," I said. "When I really think about it, Sylvie wouldn't have been there. She never had much interest in Gary's political life."

"She never had much interest in Gary," Howard said. "At least she hadn't for a while."

"I just can't believe that Jane would have an affair with Gary. She and Sylvie have always seemed so close."

"They're still close," Howard said. "Gary's the one who seems to have been frozen out."

"Howard, do you think Sylvie knew?"

"If she didn't, she was the only one. We all knew."

"I didn't," I said.

Howard sighed. "Well, now you do. Look, Jo, can I call you back? I'm supposed to be taking Marty to brunch. She divorced me once for never being there; I'm trying to get back into her good graces."

"Marty's good graces are worth getting back into," I said. "But, Howard, can I just have one more minute? Please? Did Tess Malone come that night?"

Howard's voice was testy. "I don't know, Jo." Then he added more kindly. "Tess always went to everything, didn't she? Look, I'm sorry if I'm sounding pissed off, but I've told you everything I remember."

"You left out Ian," I said. "How long was he there?"

"Off and on all evening, I think. Jo, it's been six years. People weren't punching in and punching out. I don't remember how long Ian was there."

"Try, Howard, please."

He sighed. "Well, I know he was off with that old guy at the beginning."

"What old guy?"

"I don't know who he was. Ian and I came into the building together that night. When we got to the caucus office, there was an old man waiting on the doorstep. I heard him tell Ian his name. Can't remember what it was, but it was one of the good names."

"Ukrainian?" I said.

He laughed. "Right, a good Ukrainian name like Dowhanuik. Anyway, the old man was very agitated. Ian tried to calm him down. I remember he put his arm around the old man's shoulder and walked him down to the end of the hall."

"And?"

"And nothing. I went inside and took care of a few things before the party. I never thought anything more about it. I still don't. Jo, you've been around politics long enough to know there's always some sad sack hanging around with a gripe or a problem. It comes with the territory."

"I know," I said. "Today I'm the sad sack, and I've kept you long enough. Have fun at brunch. Give Marty my love."

"I will."

"Howard, one last thing."

"Yeah?"

"Watch your language."

He sighed heavily. "Oh shit, that's right. Swearing drives Marty crazy."

I hung up. One down. Four to go.

When I walked into the kitchen, Angus was pouring juice and Taylor was eating Eggos. On my plate was a drawing of a woman: thin and glamorous, but recognizably me.

"T," I said. "This is terrific! On the best day of my life I never looked this good."

"I gave you planes," T said, smiling.

"So you did," I said. "Thanks T. You improved on God."

She shook her head. "Oh, Jo. Like I could," she said, and she went back to her Eggo.

When Hilda came down, she was dressed to travel. She made herself a plate of scrambled eggs and toast, and ate standing at the counter.

"Did you phone Carolyn Atcheson and ask if you could come?" I said.

Hilda shook her head. "It's far too easy to say 'no' on the telephone."

"If she won't see you, it's a long drive for nothing," I said.

Hilda's back was ramrod straight. "She'll see me, Joanne. I'm not a person who permits a door to be barred against her."

"Aren't you going to church?" Angus asked innocently.

"Not today," Hilda said.

Angus looked at me hopefully. "Mum . . . ?"

"Okay," I said. "We'll all backslide today. But after today . . ."

"I know, I know," Angus said, but he was already on his way to the phone to arrange a game of shinny.

I turned to Taylor. "It looks like it's you and me against the world, kiddo," I said. "How would you like to visit a pregnant lady?"

Manda Traynor sounded excited at the prospect of company. "Jo, you haven't seen our new house yet. Craig loves to show it off. And Taylor and I can play with Alex P. Kitten and Mallory."

"You have cats," I said.

"Two beautiful little Persians," Manda said.

"They have cats," I said to Taylor as I hung up.

She jumped up from the table and headed upstairs. "I'll be ready fast," she yelled over her shoulder.

Craig and Manda's new house was only about six blocks from us, so Taylor and I walked. It was a dreary November morning. The sky was overcast, and the only splashes of colour in the muted tones of the city streets came from orange Hallowe'en leaf bags leaking soddenly onto the snow.

"I'll be glad when people start putting up their Christmas decorations," I said to Taylor.

"Me too," Taylor said. "I'm going to make Jack a Santa hat and put him back out on the front porch."

"Swell," I said.

Taylor smiled up at me. "It will be swell, won't it?"

When Craig opened his front door to us, Alex P. Kitten and Mallory were waiting. Taylor was ecstatic. "Look," she said as she reached out to grab one of the ginger cats. "Their hair's the same colour as Miss McCourt's."

The cats didn't stick around long enough for me to make a comparison. They high-tailed it down the hall with Taylor in hot pursuit.

"Looks like it's going to be a long morning for Alex P. Kitten and Mallory," I said to Craig.

"They like company, and so do we," he said, and he savoured the word *we* as if it were newly coined.

"How's Manda doing?"

"She's terrific. The baby's in position now. It should be any day." He lowered his voice. "Jo, how are you doing? I've been working on the assumption that if you'd needed a lawyer, you'd have called."

"I would have," I said. "But the fact that I'm standing here doesn't mean I'm out of the woods. Craig, I need help."

"Why don't you go in and say hi to Manda? Then we can talk."

Manda was in the kitchen taking cookies out of the oven, and she was wearing a bright red apron that had CHILD- BIRTH, A LABOUR OF LOVE written on the bib. Her dark hair was tied back with a red ribbon and her face was shining. When she reached out to hug me, I could smell cloves and cinnamon.

"Jo, I'm so happy you're here."

"Me too," I said.

Somewhere in the house a cat screeched. I waited, but there was no answering howl from Taylor. "I guess Taylor's learning that loving a cat isn't easy," I said.

Manda looked serious. "Jo, loving a cat is very easy. All the same, maybe I should go and give Taylor a few tips about getting acquainted. That'll give you two a chance to get caught up."

Craig turned to me. "Why don't we go down to the family room? The chairs are more comfortable."

The family room had floor-to-ceiling windows on the wall that looked out onto the back yard. Against the window, a trestle table bloomed with plants: azalea, hydrangea, fuchsia, and a huge Christmas cactus.

"This is beautiful," I said.

"Manda and I bought the house for this room," Craig said. "We thought it would be a great place for the kids."

"Kids plural?" I asked.

He grinned. "Why not?"

"You're really happy, aren't you?" I said.

He nodded. "Happy and very humble. Not many of us get a second chance, Jo. Come here, I have something to show you."

There was a small table in the corner. It was filled with pictures from a political life – not grip-and-grin photos, just pictures of friends. Craig picked one up and handed it to me. "Here's one you'll like," he said. It was a photograph of me, as pregnant as Manda Evanson was now. I was slumped into an easy chair, asleep; propped against the wall beside the chair was a stack of VOTE KILBOURN lawn signs.

"It was fun at the beginning, wasn't it?" Craig said softly.

"Oh, yeah," I said. "It was fun."

"Ian was a terrific guy."

"He was," I agreed.

I picked up another picture. This one was of Gary, Ian, and Andy sitting around the kitchen table in our old house. As befitted men who were about to change the world, they looked very serious.

"I took that picture," Craig said. "We used to sit at the table for hours arguing about policy, remember?"

"Sure," I said. "In those days, I was the one who made the coffee."

I looked at the picture again. All that idealism and commitment. Now Ian and Andy were dead, and Gary Stephens didn't care about anything above his belt.

I turned to Craig. "What happened to Gary?" I said. "What changed him?"

Craig's eyes were sad. "I don't think you can ever point to one thing when a person changes that much. But it started with Sylvie's book."

"*The Boy in the Lens's Eye*?" I asked, surprised.

"No," he said, "the first one, *Prairiegirl*. That book was the beginning of the end of his career in politics."

"Those girls were from Gary's constituency, weren't they?"

"That didn't bother Sylvie," Craig said, and I was surprised at the asperity in his voice.

"You don't think she should have taken those pictures."

"Jo, I don't give a damn about her taking pictures, but the world is full of young girls. Why Sylvie had to photograph those particular girls is beyond me. She was one who had everything. She had the money and the talent. She must have known what those pictures would do to Gary's career. And she went right ahead. They used to love Gary out there. He grew up in those hills."

"And they stopped loving him after Sylvie's book?"

"Not everybody, but a lot of people felt betrayed. Especially the old ones. They were proud of Gary. They thought they knew him, and they thought he stood for what they believed in."

"God, the Family, and the Land," I said.

"Exactly. Have you seen the pictures, Jo? I don't know anything about art, but I do know the law, and I could have argued a case that, taken out of context, those pictures were pornography. The parents of those girls agreed to let Sylvie photograph their daughters because she was Gary's wife. For them, what she did was a breach of trust."

"And they blamed Gary because he should have kept his wife in line," I said.

Craig nodded agreement. "They're good people, Jo. But the attitudes of a lifetime aren't easily changed."

"I know that," I said. "But Gary won the next election. They might have had to hold their noses when they voted, but those people gave him a majority, Craig. If Gary had toughed it out, they would have come around."

"He was toughing it out. Then there was some more trouble. The pictures had made Gary vulnerable, and he resigned his seat."

I looked again at the photograph in my hand. "Sometimes, it seems as if there's a curse on all the Seven Dwarfs."

Craig shook his head. "This wasn't a curse. This was a problem of Gary's own making." In the yard, two chickadees were fighting at the bird feeder. Craig was silent as he watched them.

"What did he do?" I asked.

"One of his clients discovered Gary had been dipping into his funds."

"I never heard anything about this."

"It was the spring after Ian died, Jo. You were going through a pretty bad time of your own. Besides, Gary's friends took care of it, or at least we tried to. We put some money together to cover the deficit, but the client was a farmer in Gary's constituency, so, of course, word got around. *Prairiegirl* had pretty well undermined whatever loyalty Gary's constituents felt they owed him. It was only a matter of time before the rumours finished him, so he resigned."

"Craig, this doesn't make sense. Why would Gary have to steal? Sylvie's got money."

Craig moved closer to the window. The chickadees were still at it. "I guess Gary thought the problem was his. It had to do with his land. Apparently, he'd borrowed pretty heavily from the Farm Credit Corporation, and he couldn't make his payments."

"Same old story," I said. "And Ian always said Gary couldn't resist the path of least resistance."

"Well, he paid for it," said Craig. "He resigned from a job that he loved, and he's been a pretty sorry excuse for a human being ever since."

"He is that," I said, and I felt weighed down by sadness.

Craig dropped an arm around my shoulder. "Come on, let's get some tea. You look like you could use a bracing cup of camomile."

"Manda's into health food?" I said.

"With a vengeance," he said. "There are nights when I'd give five years of my life for the sight of organ meat."

The camomile tea was bracing and the cookies, molasses and whole wheat flour laced with wheat germ, were solid but tasty. Manda was as fascinated by babies and cats as Taylor was, so the table talk was lively.

After Taylor and I had said our goodbyes and started off down the sidewalk, I turned to look back at Craig and Manda. She was standing in front of him, enclosed in the circle of his arms. On the front door behind them was the wreath of dried apple slices and berries Manda had made to celebrate fertility. As they waved, I was grateful that the curse of the Seven Dwarfs seemed to have passed them by.

Taylor and I had lunch at McDonald's. While she ate, she made up a list of the names she would call her kitten, if, that is, she ever was to have a kitten. I thought of her birthday three days away and wondered how much grief Sadie and Rose's aging hearts could take.

Taylor was still talking about kittens when I pulled up in our driveway. Angus was home. I could hear the rhythmic pounding of the CD upstairs in his bedroom, but Hilda wasn't back yet. I took some chicken breasts from the freezer and made a sauce of yogurt, lime juice, and ginger to put on them after they were grilled. We could have couscous and a cucumber salad with the chicken. A nutritionally faultless meal from the woman who'd let her daughter eat two Big Macs, a large fries, and a cherry pie for lunch.

It was close to 3:00 by the time Hilda got home, and she was buoyant.

"I don't need to ask how it went," I said. "Obviously, Carolyn Atcheson didn't bar the door against you."

"At first she almost did," Hilda said, "but once she invited me in and began to talk about Maureen Gault, she was unstoppable. I think it was cathartic for her."

"Good," I said. "Let's go in where it's comfortable and you can tell me about Carolyn's catharsis."

Hilda settled back into her favourite chair in the family room. "To start with," she said, "Maureen seems to have affected Carolyn's life profoundly, but I have the sense that, until today, she hasn't discussed the girl with anyone."

"Maureen Gault was just her student," I said. "Why wouldn't Carolyn talk about her?"

Hilda shrugged. "For the same reason most of us avoid talking about a situation we've bungled."

"What did she think she'd bungled with Maureen?"

Hilda's voice was grim. "Just about everything. Joanne, Carolyn says Maureen Gault was pathological, and I trust her assessment. She's a woman who uses language carefully."

"If she knew Maureen was pathological, she must have brought in a professional," I said.

"It wasn't quite that simple. According to Carolyn, Maureen seemed normal enough when she started high school. In fact, she was quite a success socially. There was always a group of girls around anxious to do her bidding, and she thrived."

"What went wrong?"

"Maureen overplayed her hand. According to Carolyn, she had to dominate every situation and manipulate every relationship. The more she could manipulate and humiliate her little group, the better Maureen seemed to feel about herself. Of course, it didn't take long for the girls to grow weary of being props for Maureen's sell-esteem. They tried to break away and that's when the trouble began."

"Serious trouble?" I asked.

"Serious enough. There were threats. A girl opened her locker one morning and found her schoolbooks smeared with human faeces. Another girl's house was broken into, and her clothes were shredded. Another's dog was killed."

"And the school let this go on?"

"Carolyn went to Maureen's mother with the name of a psychiatrist. Of course, Mrs. Gault was furious. She kept demanding proof."

"And there was none," I said.

Hilda shook her head. "Maureen Gault was too clever to carry out the revenge herself. She kept her distance and used a confederate."

"Kevin Tarpley," I said.

Hilda nodded. "Kevin Tarpley."

"And they were never caught," I said.

"No," said Hilda. "They were never caught."

I leaned forward in my chair. "Hilda, did Carolyn Atcheson say anything about what Maureen and Kevin did to Ian?"

Hilda looked away.

"What did she say?" I asked.

Hilda's voice was low with anger. "She said she wasn't surprised. She always knew it was just a matter of time before Maureen discovered murder."

That night, as Hilda and I were finishing our after-dinner coffee, the phone rang. It was Jane O'Keefe asking if we could get together. I arranged to meet her at her office at the Women's Health Centre the next day, after classes. After I wrote the time of our meeting on my calendar, I decided I might as well fill up my dance card, and I called Tess Malone. She agreed to meet me in the Beating Heart offices at 2:00 that same day.

When I hung up, I was satisfied. The work of Sister Mouse was going well.

CHAPTER

8

The Regina Women's Medical Centre was located between a Mr. Buns Bakery and a bicycle store in a strip mall on the north side of the city. Jane had told me they chose the space because the parking was free and the rent was cheap, but there had been no penny-pinching in the reception area. Jonquil walls blazed with Georgia O'Keeffe desert prints, a brass bowl of fat copper chrysanthemums glowed on the reception desk, and the crystal clarity of a Mozart horn concerto drifted from a CD player on the antique credenza in front of the window. The Women's Medical Centre had been decorated co-operatively by a group of pro-choice women in the city, and despite what Tess Malone told the public, the Centre had ended up owing more to *Better Homes and Gardens* than to Sodom and Gomorrah.

The receptionist had just finished announcing me, when Jane came out and motioned me to follow her down the hall. My gynecologist's office was decorated with posters from pharmaceutical companies: a pictorial history of contraceptive devices, a cross section of the uterus – instructive, but not exactly *trompe-l'oeil*. Jane's walls were filled with some

serious female art: a Jane Freilicher amaryllis, so lush I
wanted to touch it; an exuberant Miriam Schapiro abstract;
an electric Faith Ringgold story quilt. On Jane's desk in a
chased silver frame was a photograph of her with Sylvie.
They looked to be in their middle teens. Tanned and grinning, they faced the camera. Life was ahead.

Jane didn't waste any time getting to the point. "Howard
called," she said.

"I thought he might," I said.

"He said he told you about Gary and me."

I nodded.

She looked at me levelly, "And . . . ?"

"And I don't understand. You're so close to Sylvie and
you're too . . . smart, I guess, is the word I'm looking for."

Jane raised her eyebrows and laughed. "Smart has
nothing to do with it, Jo. This morning I had breakfast with
a cardiologist who smokes two packs a day. Ask her about
the relationship between what we know and what we do."

"I didn't mean to sound judgemental," I said. "I know this
isn't any of my business. But, Jane, you know, don't you, that
when I talked to Howard I wasn't just digging for dirt."

Jane smiled. "You've never struck me as the logical suc-
cessor to Julie Evanson. I can read, Jo. I've seen the papers.
But can't you leave the investigating to the police?"

"No," I said, "I can't. Jane, I didn't kill Maureen Gault
and, in my more optimistic moments, I'm reasonably sure
the police are going to find that out, too. But until they do,
I'm in limbo. Every day, I just get up and go through the
motions, and it's getting to be a drag."

"I know. The sword-hanging-over-your-head syndrome.
We see it all the time in patients dealing with serious illness.
The conventional wisdom is that the best way to deal with
a hanging sword is to grab hold of it, take control."

"That's what I'm trying to do," I said.

"Fair enough," she said. "What do you need to know?"

"Could we start with the caucus office party the night before Ian died? There were all those undercurrents. Something was going on. Do you remember anything at all that might be significant?"

Jane winced. "I hardly remember anything about that party except that it was one of the worst nights of my life. For starters, it was the end of my relationship with Gary. I guess we'd been heading in that direction since Jess was born, but I loved him, Jo. I even had this fantasy about Gary and Jess and me becoming a family. Crazy stuff, but when you let your loins do your thinking, you're not always rational. Anyway, as soon as I saw Gary that night, I took him down to my office, threw my arms around him, and tried to rekindle the flame."

"And it didn't rekindle," I said.

She shook her head. "I asked him if he'd told Sylvie about us, and he looked at me as if I was insane. No, scratch that. He looked at me as if he didn't have the slightest idea what I was talking about.

"I went back to the party and did the sensible thing. I've been drunk twice in my life. Once was the night I finished exams in my last year at medical school, and the other time was that night. I was so drunk I don't even know how I got home. I didn't wake up until the next afternoon. When I remembered what had happened with Gary, I rolled over and went back to sleep. I didn't get out of bed for a day and a half. The morning I finally decided I'd better pull myself back together, I turned on the radio and heard that Ian had been killed. It seemed as if the whole world had gone to hell." Jane raked her fingers through her hair. "That was the worst winter."

"Yes," I agreed, "it was." I took a deep breath. "Jane, do you remember anything else about the party? Howard told me Ian was talking to an old Ukrainian man. Did you see them?"

Jane's eyes widened. "I saw the old Ukrainian man, but he wasn't with Ian. He was with Tess." She laughed. "It would have been funny if it hadn't been so awful. After my true love walked out on me and I was well on my way to getting pissed, I decided to step out and get some air. I wanted to get as far as possible from Gary, so I didn't go down the main stairs. I went over to the west wing and went down those stairs at the end of the hall. When I got to the landing, what to my wondering eyes should appear but Tess Malone grappling with a gentleman and making one hell of a racket. In my less than competent state, I thought they were having sex, then I noticed Tess wasn't crying out in ecstasy. She was trying to get away from him. I went over to them, and that put an end to it."

"Was he trying to rape her?" I asked.

"No, not that. I don't know what he was trying to do, but I remember he said something like, 'You stick your nose in, and now I got no more daughter.' Does that mean anything?"

"Not to me," I said. "Was that before Tess was involved with Beating Heart?"

Jane snorted. "Sometimes I think Tess has been involved with Beating Heart since she was a beating heart, but this was before she was there full time. Do you think the scene with the old man could be connected with her work there?"

"Sounds like it might, doesn't it?" I said. "Tess encourages the girl to go through with her pregnancy and something goes wrong." I picked up my coat. "I don't know, but I'm going to ask the person who will."

The offices of Beating Heart occupied the second storey of an old building on Pasqua Street. It was less upscale than the Women's Medical Centre, just a single big room with a couple of small alcoves that I guessed were used for counselling. Here, the music was chartbusters from a radio on an untended desk, and the pictures on the wall were of the graphic didactic school. Tess was standing at a table covered in boxes. On the window ledge behind her, a cigarette burned in a yellow ashtray.

She smiled when she saw me, but, for once, the smile was thin, and her manner was guarded.

"I suppose you'd like to get right to your questions," she said.

"Yeah," I said. "I would."

I looked at her. Every golden curl was shellacked into place, and she was wearing a jumpsuit that looked vaguely military. The idea of her grappling with anyone seemed ludicrous. But Jane's memory on that point, at least, had seemed clear.

I took a deep breath and began. "Tess, I need to know more about that party at the caucus office the night before Ian died. Jane O'Keefe remembers seeing you in a . . . situation . . . with an old Ukrainian man."

A flush started at Tess's neckline and moved slowly up to her face. "Jane was drunk that night. Did she tell you that?"

"Yes," I said, "she did."

Tess picked up her cigarette and drew heavily on it. "Well, she was seeing things."

"I don't think so," I said. "Howard saw the man, too."

She seemed to flinch. "With me?"

"Was he with you?" I asked.

"He had some sort of constituency problem."

"To do with his daughter," I said.

This time there was no mistaking Tess's reaction. She looked as if she'd taken a blow. "I don't remember," she said.

"Think," I said. "It could be important."

"It was six years ago, Joanne. I told you I don't remember, and I think you're out of line hectoring me like this."

"Tess, I don't mean to hector, but this isn't a tea party. I'm in a lot of trouble. Just tell me the truth. I can't promise I won't repeat what you tell me, but I can promise I won't reveal anything I don't have to."

She took another drag of her cigarette. "There's nothing to tell, Joanne. It was a man with a constituency problem."

"Do you remember his name?"

"No." She picked up a cloth from the desk, opened the box nearest her and removed a plastic foetus. Then, very gently, she began to wipe the dust from its moon-shaped skull. "I think you'd better go now," she said.

I moved closer to her. "I'm going to keep asking questions, Tess. If you remember anything, let me know."

She didn't answer me. She put the foetus she'd been dusting back in the box and picked up another. This one was larger, but still snail-like, wrapped in on itself, otherworldly.

"Tess, do you remember how, in the old days, when we got into a battle about policy, you used to invite everybody over to your house to eat?" I moved close and put my hand on her arm. "You used to say there wasn't a quarrel in the world that a pan of cabbage rolls and a bottle of rye couldn't straighten out. Do you want to find a place with cabbage rolls and see if we can straighten this out?"

She didn't answer. But when she turned to replace the foetus in the box, I saw her eyes were filled with tears. It was like seeing a general cry.

My pulse was racing when I stood on the landing outside Beating Heart. Tess knew the old man's name, and I was sure that when she had a chance to think things over, she would tell me. She was a decent person, and she would want to help. I looked at my watch. Two-thirty. Taylor wouldn't be home for another hour. I had time to find out how that last evening had looked from another seat at the head table.

Gary Stephens's office was in the same building as my dentist's. It was a cheerless cinderblock building on the corner of Broad and 12th. At the top of the stairs on the second floor was a sign with Gary's name and degree in block letters and an arrow pointing toward his law office. When I opened the door, I had two surprises. The first was that Ian's old secretary, Lorraine Bellegarde, was behind the front desk. The other was that she was obviously in the final stages of packing up the office.

When she saw me, she came over and took both my hands in hers. Lorraine was so tiny it seemed she could buy most of her clothes in the children's department, but there was nothing child-like about her organizational skills or her grasp of politics. Ian's trust in her had been absolute, and she had been a friend to us both. Lorraine and I had lost touch in the last few years, and as we stood, surrounded by packing boxes, grinning at each other, I wondered why.

"What are you doing here?" I said.

"Trying to get all this stuff out before the landlord catches me."

"Gary's moving his office?"

"Well, he's moving out of here. But this is all going into storage." She picked up a roll of masking tape and cut a length from it. "I don't know what Gary's going to do. I guess, as they say, he's exploring his options."

"I can't imagine you working for a man like him."

"Nobody's perfect, Jo. Anyway, I'm not working for him for much longer."

"It didn't work out?"

"It worked out. For a while, anyway. Gary has his faults, but I've always found him easy to get along with. And I liked the quiet around here." She placed the tape carefully along the top flaps of a packing box. "Unfortunately, it was too quiet."

"The firm was having trouble getting clients?"

She narrowed her eyes. "Look, Jo, maybe we shouldn't be talking about this. Anyway, you're the one who's got the mega-problem these days. Have the cops managed to find out who killed Maureen Gault?"

"No, that's why I'm here. I need to talk to Gary. Will he be back today?"

She shrugged. "I don't know. Gary's not exactly the poster boy for effective office practices."

"If he comes back, ask him to call me, would you? I don't want to go to his house. Sylvie thinks I'm Public Enemy Number One."

"I wouldn't let that keep you away."

"It won't," I said.

"Jo, can I tell Gary what you want to see him about?"

"Sure. Tell him I want to talk to him about the day before Ian died."

Her body tensed with interest. "They've found something, haven't they? Ian's death wasn't just lousy luck. There was a reason he was killed."

"They haven't found anything," I said, "but I think I have." As I told her about the evidence pointing to Maureen Gault, I could see the anger in Lorraine's eyes.

"You think she planned to kill him?"

"That's exactly what I think."

"But why would she want him dead?"

"I don't know, but I'm going to find out. Lorraine, could there be anything in Ian's appointment book that would shed some light on this?"

"Such as . . . ?"

"Such as the people he saw the last week. Maybe there was somebody out of the ordinary. Howard and Jane remember an old Ukrainian man who was around the night of the party. Does that ring a bell?"

She shook her head. "It's been such a long time, Jo." She smoothed the masking tape on the box in front of her. "I can tell you right now there won't be a clue in the last week's appointments. Ian wasn't there. Remember, you two took off the week before Christmas to go cross-country skiing with the kids."

"We went down to Kenosee. I'd forgotten." I said.

Lorraine picked up on the disappointment in my voice. "Don't give up on the office angle completely, Jo," she said. "Even if Ian wasn't there, I would have kept a record of his messages." She looked around the room. "I'm just about through here. I'll go over to the Legislature. I packed all Ian's stuff and sent it to the archives. It shouldn't be any problem to dig up Ian's appointment book. If anything looks interesting, I'll call you."

"Thanks, Lorraine," I said.

She came over and slid her arm around my waist. "Come on, I want to show you something." She took me over to the big plate-glass window that looked down on a parking lot. The area was a favourite for prostitutes and for the johns who sought them out.

Lorraine pointed down. "That's where Gary parks his car," she said. "All last summer one of the street girls used his car as her office: sitting on the fender, fixing her makeup in the outside mirror, even lying over the hood and working on her tan when there wasn't any action. I must have volunteered twenty times to go down and tell her to beat it, but Gary wouldn't hear of it. He said everybody needs one place where they won't get hassled."

"And the point of the story is . . . ?"

Lorraine shook her head and smiled. "I don't know. Maybe just that Gary hasn't turned into as much of a rat as you think."

I hugged her. "Let's keep in touch, Lorraine."

One more errand and I could go home. By the time I left the Humane Society I was forty dollars poorer and a kitten richer. It was windy and cold when I drove into the Nationtv parking lot. I stuck the kitten inside my coat, and as I walked into the building I could feel the sharpness of its claws through my sweater. The door to Jill's office was open. She was on the phone, and she motioned for me to come in. When I took the kitten out of my coat, she said a fast goodbye to whoever she was talking to and leapt to her feet.

"I don't believe my eyes," she said. "You with a cat."

"I don't believe my eyes either," I said. "But here she is, and I'm appealing to you as a cat person to take care of her until after Taylor's party tomorrow."

"I accept," she said. "You can always count on cat people." She took the kitten from me and began stroking under its chin. I could hear the kitten's motor-hum of satisfaction. "So Taylor was the one who finally broke you down. How many times did the other kids ask for a cat?"

"Don't remind me," I said. "But it was all Taylor wanted."

Jill held the kitten against her cheek and rubbed. "How do you think Sadie and Rose are going to feel about an interloper?"

"They'll probably put out a contract on me," I said.

She looked at her watch. "The sun's over the yardarm somewhere. Do you have time for a drink?"

"I do," I said, "but you don't." I pointed to the cat. "You have responsibilities. Jill, could you bring her over tomorrow around 3:30? I thought the adults could get together for cake and a glass of wine when the kids had wound down a bit."

"I'll be there, at 3:30. Cat people are punctual to a fault, but of course now that you're a cat person yourself, you'll be learning that."

I stopped at the mall on the way home and bought the rest of Taylor's presents. After I'd hidden them in the basement for wrapping later, I came upstairs and started dinner. I felt edgy but good. The answers seemed to be coming closer, I could feel it. I was rubbing rosemary into the lamb chops when the phone rang. It was Lorraine Bellegarde.

"I've got something," she said. "There was a stack of phone messages stuck in the appointments book. I guess after we heard about Ian, someone put them in there and forgot about them. Come to think of it, that someone was probably me. Anyway, there were the usual messages from constituents and government departments."

"How about from the Seven Dwarfs?"

"They all rang in. Do you want me to check who called when?"

"Could you?"

I wrote down the information and thanked her.

"And now for the *pièce de resistance*," she said. "There were fifteen separate messages from Henry."

"Who's Henry?"

"I'm not sure, but I think he may be your old Ukrainian man. He called and called that last week. I remember him now. A sad old guy. He was always blowing his nose. Anyway, the bad news is he wouldn't leave his last name. The good news is he left his number."

"Bingo," I said. I repeated the number and wrote it down. "Thanks, Lorraine. Ian used to say he could always count on you to come through."

"Anytime, Jo," she said softly. "Anytime."

My heart was pounding as I dialled Henry's number. There were two rings. Then the operator's voice: "Your call cannot be completed as dialled. Please check the listing again, or call your operator for assistance." I hung up and looked again at the number. It could be long distance. I dialled

"1" and tried the number again. This time I got through.

A young man answered. In the background, country music blared.

"Yeah," he said, not unfriendly.

"Could I speak to Henry?" I asked.

"There's no Henry here, lady."

I felt my heart sink. "He's an older man. Ukrainian."

He sounded kind but exasperated. "Lady, there's three of us share this house. None of us are Henry, none of us are older, and none of us are Ukrainian."

"Wait," I said. "How long have you had this number?"

"Three years." He started to hang up.

"Where are you?" I said. "Where do you live?"

"Lady . . ." His voice was edgy.

"Just tell me the name of the city, please. It's important."

He laughed. "It's no city, lady. This is Chaplin, Saskatchewan, population 400."

I felt a rush. Chaplin. I should have known.

I had one more phone call to make. I dialled Beating Heart and got the machine. "Someone would be happy to help you during regular office hours which were . . ." I hung up and opened the phone book at the M's. Tess Malone's home number wasn't listed. I dialled Beating Heart again and left Tess a message. "I need to talk to you about Henry," I said, and I left my name.

The phone rang again just as I was sliding the chops under the broiler. It was Jill.

"Did Taylor ask specifically for a female cat or was that just a whimsy of yours?"

"If I picked out a male, don't tell me," I said.

"Okay," she said, and the line was silent.

"I've changed my mind," I said. "Tell me."

"You chose a male," she said.

"How do you know?"

"I just lifted his tail and looked: three dots, not one. Next time, take me with you."

"There won't be a next time," I said, gloomily.

She laughed. "See you tomorrow."

After supper, Hilda took Taylor down to the library to return her books. I asked Angus to wrap presents while I made the birthday cake.

"What did we get her?" he asked.

"A case of cat food. A cat dish. A Garfield T-shirt and a book of cat cartoons from *The New Yorker*."

"Did we also get her a cat?" he said.

"A little ginger male. The man at the Humane Society says he's part Persian. What do you think about getting another pet?"

"I think it's amazing. Everybody knows how you are with cats. It's cool that you got one for T." He snapped his fingers. "Really cool. Okay, where's the wrapping paper?"

An hour later, when Taylor and Hilda came back, the presents were wrapped and the cakes were made. Taylor looked into the flowerpots critically.

"How did you make the dirt?"

"The way the recipe says to make it. A bag of Oreos pulverized in the food processor."

"And the mud?"

"Chocolate pudding and Dream Whip."

"And the jelly worms are in there?"

"All $5.27 worth."

She nodded. "Should I bring Jack in tonight or wait till tomorrow?"

"You're bringing Jack in?"

"For the party. For the centre of the table."

"T, he's getting pretty saggy. There are other things you could have as the centrepiece."

"Like what?"

"Angus had a clown head made out of a cabbage one year and an octopus another time. They were both pretty cute. And when Mieka was about your age, she had a doll with a cake skirt. Peter had a firehat three years in a row. You can pretty much use anything."

"Good," she said. "We'll use Jack." She leaned over and kissed me goodnight. The issue was settled.

Hilda was out with friends for the evening. After I tucked in Taylor, I made myself a pot of Earl Grey, sat down at the dining-room table, and thought of all the birthday parties that had been celebrated around it. I'd been a young mother when Mieka and Peter had had their parties. Children who had sat at this table singing "Happy Birthday" to my children were now old enough to have children themselves. And I was forty-nine. Not young.

Ian must have wasted a hundred rolls of film taking pictures of the kids' birthdays. He always managed to snap the shot at just the wrong time. We had a drawer full of photos of blurred children, of children with satanic red eyeballs, and of me, looking not maternal but menacing, as I poised the knife above the birthday cake. Memories. But there were other memories. Better ones. Memories of the times after the parties when Ian and I would clean up, pour a drink, cook a steak, and be grateful for another year of healthy kids.

When I went upstairs to get ready for bed, Rose was in Angus's room sitting on the cape he had worn Hallowe'en night. I thought of the ginger cat, and went in and sat down on the floor next to her. I put my arms around her neck. "Changes for you tomorrow, old lady," I said Full of trust, she nuzzled me. "Just remember," I said, "adversity makes us grow." She stood up expectantly. "We're not going anywhere tonight," I said. I picked up the cape. "Except down to the basement to put this back. Look, it's covered in dog hair." I brushed off the cape and headed downstairs.

The trunk I'd taken the cape from Hallowe'en night was still open. I decided to check through the clothes inside to see if there was anything Peter or Angus could wear. I found a couple of sweaters and a pair of dress slacks that looked possible. I was sorting through a stack of sport shirts when I found the wallet. It was in a small bag, like a commercial Baggie, but of heavier plastic. The boys, never inspired in their choice of gifts, had given it to Ian that last Christmas. A young constable had brought the wallet, Ian's keys, and his wedding ring back to me after the trial. The wedding ring was upstairs in my jewellery box, and I'd given the keys to Peter when he started driving. I didn't remember putting the wallet in the trunk, but there was a lot I didn't remember about those months after Ian died.

I undid the twist-tie on the bag and took out the wallet. In the upstairs hall, the grandfather clock chimed. I opened the wallet. The leather was still stiff, and the plastic photo case was pristine. Christmas afternoon Ian had made quite a show of cleaning out his old wallet and transferring everything worth transferring to the new one. The boys had been very pleased. I looked through the photo case. There wasn't much there: Ian's identification, some credit cards, the kids' school pictures, Ian's party membership, and one picture of all of us that I'd forgotten about. We'd been in Ottawa, taking turns snapping pictures of one another in front of the Parliament Buildings, when a young man asked if we'd like a family picture. It had turned out well. I looked at us, sun-tanned and smiling in our best summer clothes, and I could feel my throat tighten. I reached inside the plastic to pull the photo out. There was another picture behind it, and I slid it out too. I hadn't seen this one before. It was a Santa Claus picture from a shopping mall.

A woman, very young, very pretty, was sitting on Santa's knee, holding a baby up to the camera. On the back, in careful backhand, she had written: "He looks just like you. I love you. J."

I'd been so anxious to make the pieces fit. Maybe, at last, they'd all fallen into place. Ian's anger when I'd pressed him about what he was doing that last day. The old man who'd confronted him the night of the party. "Now I got no more daughter." And this child. Crazily, I remembered my fortune in the barm brack Hallowe'en night. The tiny baby doll.

I looked at the child the girl was holding. "He looks just like you." I tried to see the resemblance, but I couldn't. The baby didn't look like Ian; he just looked like a baby.

I put the picture into the pocket of my blue jeans. Then I slid the wallet back into its plastic bag, and carried it upstairs. I didn't stop to put on boots. I plodded across the deep snow of the back yard, to our back gate, opened it, and walked down the lane to the garbage bin. I didn't hesitate before I threw my husband's wallet into the garbage.

CHAPTER

9

The first thing I saw when I awoke the next morning was the picture on my nightstand. In the full light of morning, the woman seemed even younger and more lovely than she had the night before. I thought about the day ahead and felt the heaviness wash over me. Somehow I had to get through Taylor's party. When I'd managed that, there was just the rest of my life to muddle through.

The phone was ringing when I stepped out of the shower. I grabbed a towel, tripped over Sadie and yelled at her so viciously that she ran out of the room. My coping mechanism seemed to have short-circuited.

My caller was Inspector Alex Kequahtooway.

"I know it's early to phone, especially on a holiday," he said, "but I have news."

"Go ahead," I said, and my voice sounded dead.

"It's good news," he added quickly. "You're in the clear, Mrs. Kilbourn. The reservations clerk you talked to the night of the murder has had a chance to give her story some sober second thought. Now that she's had time to reconsider, she realizes that when you left your name and address

for the lost and found, it must have been after 11:05. not at
11:00 as she previously told us."

"It's still just her word, isn't it?" I said. "She could change
her mind again."

"I don't think so," he said. "This time she has the hotel's
telephone records to keep her memory fresh. The records say
that on the night of the murder, someone at the reservations
desk made a long-distance call to Wolf Point, Montana, at
10:47. The call was not completed until 11:05. Now, the only
connection between the Hotel Saskatchewan and Wolf Point,
Montana, seems to be the reservations clerk's boyfriend. He's
working at a western-wear store in Wolf Point."

"That still leaves ten minutes," I said dully. "I found the
body at 11:15, and that's when the police came."

I could hear the edge in Inspector Kequahtooway's voice.
"That's where we had a break, Mrs. Kilbourn. It turns out
that somebody found the body before you did."

"Who?" I asked.

"Another guest at the hotel. He's been out of the country
for a couple of weeks. When he read about the case in the
paper, he got in touch right away. A good citizen. He says
when he went to get his rental car to drive to the airport, he
saw a woman lying by that old Buick in the parking lot. He
says he remembers the time because he was in a hurry. It
was 11:00."

"Why didn't he call for help?"

Alex Kequahtooway's voice was impassive. "He had a
plane to catch. It was dark. From where he was parked he
couldn't see the woman's face. He thought she was, and I
quote, 'just another drunken Indian.'"

"I'm sorry," I said.

"For what?"

"That the world is such a shitty place," I said.

"It does have its moments, doesn't it?" He paused. "Mrs. Kilbourn, are you ill? You don't sound like yourself."

"I'm not myself, Inspector," I said. "But thanks for calling." I hung up.

I was in the clear. I could stop asking questions. I could stop trying to make the pieces fit. Life could go back to normal. I looked at the picture of the young woman. She was wearing blue jeans and a white sweater. Against the cheap red suit of the mall Santa, her blond wavy hair seemed charged with life. Her face was serene. Her eyes, slightly upturned at the outer edge, looked steadily into the camera. The curve of her breasts behind the baby suggested fullness, and the flesh on her arms was taut with abundance. The baby she held in those arms was like her, solemn, plump, and beautiful.

"Not everybody trusts paintings, but people believe photographs." That's what Ansel Adams said. I caught sight of myself in the mirror. What truth would a photograph of me convey? My hair, still wet from the shower, was slick against my skull, and my face was pale and haggard. I was forty-nine years old. It wasn't going to get any better. I pulled the towel tight around me. I wanted to vanquish that beautiful young woman with her lovely baby. I wanted to rip her picture into a dozen pieces and flush it down the toilet.

But even as I picked up the picture, I knew she couldn't be vanquished. I had to know who she was. I had to know what she had meant to Ian. I had to know whether the child she held in her arms was his, and I had to know how she was connected to his death.

I reached for my jeans and a sweatshirt, changed my mind, and chose a soft wool skirt that always made me feel attractive, and a cashmere sweater the colour of a pomegranate. After I'd dressed, I sat down in front of my mirror and brushed my hair. Then, I picked up the foundation cream and began to smooth it over my face.

A thousand years ago, Hilda had said, "Follow the strands back to the place where they join. Of course, you'll have to scrutinize your husband's life, too." Back then, *scrutinize* had seemed to suggest such a pitiless intrusion that I'd rejected the idea outright, but now I knew Hilda was right. I had to know the truth. I brushed the blush across the soft pads of my cheeks. "Chipmunk cheeks," Taylor had said. The girl in the picture had great cheekbones, high and sloping. Who was she?

"This is between you and me, Ian," I said aloud. And as soon as I heard the words, I knew they were true. No one but I should be part of this next phase of the investigation. I had to convince Hilda and Jill that, because the chase was over, life was back to normal. I dabbed the eyeshadow brush in sable brown and touched the corners of my eyelids.

If Ian hadn't been the man I thought he was, no one else was going to know. We'd been married twenty years, and whatever that marriage meant to him, I wasn't going to expose him. I picked up the mascara, leaned towards the mirror, and began darkening the ends of my eyelashes. There was something reassuring about seeing my eyes looking as they always had. I filled in my lips with colour, slid on my best gold bracelet, and put in my new gold hoop earrings.

My reflection in the mirror looked assured and in control. I hid the woman's picture under a pile of nighties in my bottom drawer and started downstairs. Before I walked into the kitchen, I took a deep breath. I wasn't an actress, and this performance had to do the job. I had to convince everybody I cared about that the nightmare was over, and happy days were here again.

Hilda and the kids were already at the breakfast table.

When she saw me, Hilda nodded approvingly. "Don't you look attractive."

"It's Taylor's birthday," I said.

Taylor jumped up. "And you said that, as soon as we were all here, I could open my presents."

"If that was the deal, then I think you'd better get started," I said, pouring myself coffee.

She didn't need to be told twice. Five minutes later, the table was covered with wrapping paper, and Taylor was beaming.

I sat down beside her. "What's your best present?" I asked.

She picked up a box of art pencils Hilda had given her. "These cost eighty-five dollars. Fil, my teacher, has some just like them, and he told me."

I knew Hilda's funds were limited. "You really shouldn't have," I said.

"An artist can always use a patron," she said tartly.

Taylor smiled at Hilda. "Thanks," she said. "Thanks a lot. And thanks for all the cat stuff, Angus. Too bad I don't have a cat."

Angus winked at me broadly, but Taylor didn't notice. She'd found something else that interested her and had run to the window. "Look, the sun came out!" she said.

I went over and stood beside her. The sun was high, the sky was blue, and the trees in the back yard sparkled theatrically with hoarfrost. I put my arm around her shoulder. "Hey, a real party day," I said.

She looked up at me. "Lucky, eh?"

"Very lucky," I said.

When I turned from the window, Hilda was watching me carefully. "You seem wound a little tightly this morning," she said.

"I'm just excited," I said. "I didn't want to take the edge off Taylor's gift opening, but I had some good news this morning." As I told Hilda about my conversation with Alex Kequahtooway, I could see the relief in her face.

"This means your life can go back to normal," she said.

"So can yours," I said. "Hilda, I can't thank you enough for being here with us when we needed you. We couldn't have made it without you."

Her eyes narrowed. "That has a distinctly valedictory tone. Am I being given my walking papers?"

I went to her. "Never. I just thought you'd be missing your life in Saskatoon."

"Well," she said, "Advent does begin in less than three weeks. The Cathedral choir will have all that splendid Christmas music to get ready."

"And you're their only true alto," I said.

She frowned. "You're sure you're all right?"

"Never better."

"If you say so," she said. "Now, if you're going to preserve that sense of well-being, you'd better eat something. Have something substantial, Joanne. We have an arduous day ahead."

After breakfast, I made some calls: to Peter, to Howard, to Keith, and finally to Jill. As the relief and congratulations swirled around me, I tried to sound like a woman whose world had just been restored to her. It wasn't easy.

Taylor's party was a success. No one got hurt; no one cried; no one got left out. The worm cakes were a hit, and the party hat I'd put on the jack o'lantern covered the dent in his skull and made him look almost festive. Taylor was as happy as I'd ever seen her, but I couldn't wait for the afternoon to end. I wanted to be alone to look at the picture and make plans.

At 3:00, the parents began to come for the kids. Sylvie and Jane came together to get Jess. The O'Keefe sisters were wearing camel-hair coats, and as they stood in the doorway with their faces flushed from the cold, laughing about something Jess had said that morning, I thought blood really must be thicker than water.

When they came inside, Jane took her boots and coat off. "I have something for the birthday girl," she said. She pulled a small, prettily wrapped package out of her bag.

"Why don't you and Sylvie stay and watch Taylor blow out her candles?" I said. "The kids had Sylvie's worm cake, but there's something a little more orthodox for the adults."

Surprisingly, Sylvie didn't hesitate. "Sounds good," she said, and she began to take off her things.

When Gary came five minutes later, it seemed churlish not to ask him to stay, too. So I did. For a woman who wanted to be alone, I was moving in the wrong direction.

At 3:30 on the dot, Jill arrived. We were still standing in the doorway when Craig and Manda Evanson pulled up in the driveway. Craig's arm was tight around Manda's shoulders as they came up the walk. Manda was holding a red wicker basket. She held it out to me. Inside was a checked blanket embroidered with the words: SHHHHH. KITTEN SLEEPING.

Craig looked at the pink balloons on the door. "We don't want to interrupt anything," he said.

"I told Craig I had to see Taylor's face when she met her cat," Manda said. She patted her belly. "At this stage, he has to indulge me, but don't worry, Jo, we'll be gone before you know it."

"Don't be silly," I said. "Come in and have some cake."

Manda grinned. "Are you sure?"

"Absolutely."

"In that case," she said, "make mine a double. I'm in a state of severe cake deficit."

The first minutes after the kitten entered our house were about as bad as I'd always imagined they would be. Sadie bared her teeth, and Angus banished her to the back yard.

Rose took one look at the interloper and ran down to hide in the basement. Angus went after her to soothe her nerves.

Taylor, of course, was transported. Manda and Jill clucked over her, showing her how to hold the cat and what to feed it. At the end of five minutes, Taylor was an experienced handler; the kitten was purring, and she handed it to me. I stroked the cat's head. The purring stopped, and the cat curled around and swiped viciously at my face. Jill glared at me disapprovingly. "Jo, when you pat a kitten on its head, you awaken its sexual feelings. Cats have very violent sex. You were lucky you didn't get your face clawed off."

I gave the kitten back to Taylor. Owning a cat was going to be even worse than I thought.

Hilda waited till there was relative peace, then she went into the kitchen and came back with two bottles of Asti Spumante.

"I thought this would be a nice accompaniment for the cake," she said.

Gary opened the Asti, Craig poured, and I turned out the lights and lit the candles on the cake. As Craig proposed the toast, Taylor held the glass with her thimbleful of wine gravely.

"To Taylor's sixth birthday," Craig said. "May there be many happy returns."

We drank and then he turned to me. "And to Jo. May there be brighter days ahead."

I looked at the faces in the circle. The candlelight made them look younger, but also less familiar and, somehow, more menacing. Now was as good a time as any to make my announcement. "Good news," I said. "The brighter days are already here. If Taylor ever blows out her candles, I'll tell you what's happened. Come on, T, make a wish."

Taylor didn't move. She was staring at the cake, paralyzed.

I dropped down beside her. "T, what is it?" I asked.

She leaned towards my ear. "I don't know what to wish for," she whispered. "I've always wished for a cat."

"Wish that your cat will learn to get along with the dogs," I said.

She nodded, closed her eyes, wished, and blew.

As soon as we had our cake and wine, I told them about Alex Kequahtooway's phone call. Gary was standing beside me and he kissed my cheek. "Great news, babe," he said.

When he moved away, I saw Jill, shaking her head and trying to suppress a smile. Gary Stephens was not one of her favourites. Craig was ebullient. "I knew it was just a matter of time," he said, and he squeezed Manda's shoulders so hard, she cried out. The O'Keefe sisters stood together, smiling but silent.

Craig picked up a bottle of Asti and refilled our glasses, and the conversation moved happily towards the inconsequential. Not surprisingly, we talked about names: a good name for Taylor's kitten; wise choices for Craig and Manda's baby.

My mind drifted. Ian and I had spent hours deciding on names for our children. Our most intense talks always seemed to come when I was in the bathtub. Ian would wander in, say something salacious about pregnant women, flip down the toilet lid, and read from a book of names he'd bought. Then we would laugh at the horrors and try out possibilities till the bath water got cold.

We had been very happy. I closed my eyes, shutting out the memories. When I opened them, Manda was leaning towards me.

"Who is Walter Winchell?" she asked.

"What?" I said, startled. "I'm sorry, Manda, I was a million miles away. What did you say?"

"I asked you who Walter Winchell was. We were talking about whether it's good to name a baby after her parents, and

Hilda said Walter Winchell named both his children after him: his son was Walter and his daughter was Walda. Everybody laughed, but I don't know who Walter Winchell is."

"You don't have to," I said. "Just don't name your baby after him."

Manda yawned and stretched lazily. "Gotcha," she said. She put her head back against her husband's chest. "I've had enough fun, Craig. Time to go."

Manda and Craig moved towards the front hall. It wasn't long before the others followed. I was almost home-free, and I felt a rush. In minutes, I would be on the phone talking to Tess Malone. Confronted with Henry's name, Tess would tell the truth, and I would be one step closer to the young woman in the picture.

As I was down on the hall floor, helping Jess find his boots, it hit me. Tess's number was unlisted. A phrase Howard Dowhanuik had used the morning after Maureen Gault's murder flashed through my mind. I'd been surprised that Sylvie and Jane had gone to Tess's for a drink after the dinner, and Howard had said, "Tess and Sylvie are tight as ticks."

I looked up at Sylvie. "Have you got Tess Malone's home number?" I asked.

"What do you want it for?" she said.

Jane smoothed over the rudeness with a smile. "More questions about Tess's old Ukrainian?"

"His name is Henry," I said.

Jane knotted her scarf with her capable surgeon's hands. "I thought you'd be out of the cops-and-robbers business now that you're in the clear."

"I am," I said. "I just wanted to ask Tess if she was free for lunch one day next week."

Without a word, Sylvie picked up a pad by the phone and wrote down the number.

"Time to leave," Jane said. "Come on, Sylvie, let's go."

Already dressed for the outdoors, Jess stood with his father. Gary Stephens's hand was resting on his son's shoulder.

"Say goodbye, Jess," Jane said, and she pushed Gary's hand from his son's shoulder and propelled the little boy towards the door.

"Bye," Jess said. And he vanished into the night, closing the door behind him.

As he stood staring at the space where his son had been, Gary Stephens's face was bleak. "Goodbye," he whispered, and his voice was so soft I could barely hear it.

After everyone had driven off, Hilda went to the kitchen to clean up, and the kids took the kitten down to the basement to start the reconciliation process with Rose. Jill and I were left alone in the front hall.

"I take it the inspector's news means I'm off duty."

"It does," I said. "You can go back to painting your nails and sticking pins in pictures of Nationtv vice-presidents."

"Speaking of Nationtv," Jill said, "Keith Harris called from Washington this morning. He sends you his love."

"Swell," I said.

"He'd like to talk about human-rights violations among some of our trading partners on Saturday's show. It's okay with Sam Spiegel if it's okay with you."

"It's okay with me," I said. "That's right up my alley."

"I'll bet that's why Keith suggested it," Jill said, then she touched my hand. "I'm glad everything worked out, Jo. I was really scared."

Her gaze was so open and her affection so palpable that I almost told her the truth. Then I remembered how Jill had revered Ian, and I steeled myself. "I'm glad everything worked out, too," I said.

It was after 9:00 when I finally managed to get into my bedroom, close the door, and dial Tess's number. Late in the afternoon, Alex Kequahtooway had told the press about the evidence clearing me. I guess he'd decided it was time for the old squirrel dog to shake things up a bit. The telephone had started ringing during dinner, and it hadn't stopped. I'd never been very good at faking, and all evening I had cringed at the falseness of my voice as I tried to sound euphoric.

There were two phone calls that didn't require acting. The first was from Peter. He had been a rock, but now the worst was over. As he relaxed into the concerns of a third-year university student – the inequities of exam timetables, gossip about friends, hints about what he wanted for Christmas – he sounded relieved to be back to normal.

Mieka and her husband, Greg, called from Galveston to wish Taylor happy birthday, and their joy in being young and in love and discovering the world together was so tonic, I almost didn't tell them about the deaths of Kevin Tarpley and Maureen Gault. But we'd always told the kids that families couldn't function without trust, so after I'd listened to Mieka's descriptions of the beauty of the old houses along the Gulf of Mexico and Greg's account of how great a bucket of crayfish tastes when you wash it down with a schooner of Lone Star, I gave them the essentials. They were shocked, but as I answered their questions, I could feel them relax. The crisis was, after all, in the past, and as we rung off, I could hear the happiness returning to their voices.

Finally, the phone grew silent, the kids were in their rooms, and I was alone. I was so tense that my hands were shaking as I dialled Tess's number. There was no answer. I couldn't believe it. I had been so certain the answers were within reach. Ten minutes later, I tried again. After that, I tried every ten minutes until, finally, exhausted, I fell into bed.

For the next two days I tried to find Tess. She wasn't at home, and she wasn't at Beating Heart. No one knew where she was. The man who answered the phone at Beating Heart told me not to worry. Tess would show up. She wasn't the kind of woman to leave town without telling anybody. I told him that's why I was worried. Have a little faith, he said, and I promised him I would try.

Friday, I took Hilda to the Faculty Club for lunch before she drove back to Saskatoon. We ate liver and onions and made plans for Christmas. I loved her, but as I watched her manoeuvre her old Chrysler Imperial out of the university parking lot, I was relieved. Hilda was a hard person to deceive, and I was certain she knew I was concealing something critical from her.

I had three students to see that afternoon. When the last one left, I pulled the picture of the young woman and her baby out of my bag and propped it against my coffee cup. I tried Tess's home number. There was no answer. I looked at the picture and I knew I was tired of waiting. It was time for action.

The receptionist at Beating Heart had a great smile, eyeglasses with bright green frames, and a sign on her desk that said, I'M MICHELLE, PLEASE BOTHER ME. But she turned her face away when I held the picture up and asked her if she knew the woman who was sitting on Santa's knee.

"We don't discuss clients," she said.

"Was this woman a client?"

Michelle pushed her chair back as if she was afraid I would force her to look at the picture. "I don't know," she said woodenly.

I moved closer to her. "This is important," I said. And then I added, "It's a matter of life and death."

It was an unfortunate choice of words. Michelle leapt up from her desk and returned with an older woman who bore a startling resemblance to the actress Colleen Dewhurst and who looked as implacable as Colleen Dewhurst had looked when she played Aunt Marilla in *Anne of Green Gables*.

"Look," I said, "I think I got off on the wrong foot here. I'm a friend of Tess Malone's. I've been trying to reach her, but I can't. I need to find this young woman."

When the two women exchanged a quick, worried glance, the penny dropped. They thought I was the enemy.

"I'm not trying to get her to change her mind about going through with her pregnancy," I said. "If you'll look at the picture, you'll see she already had her baby. It was at least six years ago. But I have to find her. It really is a matter of life and death."

For the first time, the older woman smiled. She held out her hand. "I wish you'd said at the outset you were a friend of Tess's. I think Michelle and I jumped to the wrong conclusion about you." She spoke with a slight accent, pleasant and lilting.

"My name is Joanne Kilbourn," I said.

"Irish?" she asked.

"My husband's family were," I said.

"Every last member of my family is Irish," she said. "My name is Maeve O'Byrne. Now let's look at your picture. What did you say the girl's name is?"

"I didn't say. I don't know."

Maeve O'Byrne pulled out a pair of reading glasses. As she looked at the photo, I held my breath. It didn't help. She shook her head and handed the photo back. "I don't recall her," she said.

"Don't you have files?"

When she answered, there was a hint of asperity in the lilt. "Yes, we have files, Mrs. Kilbourn. And like most organizations, we classify them by name. Since you don't know the girl's name, we have nothing to go on. At any rate, you say this was over five years ago. If there was a file, it would have been destroyed. We cull inactive files after five years."

"So I'm out of luck."

"I'm sorry."

The phone rang and Michelle answered it. "Just a minute. I'll see," she said. She put her hand over the mouthpiece and looked up at Maeve. "That's the paper," she said. "They're asking if we want to keep our ad in the personals. Tess used to check every day to make sure it was there and there weren't any typos."

Maeve sighed wearily. "Sure, tell them to keep it in. What does it say, anyway?"

Michelle asked the person on the other end of the phone, and she repeated the words for Maeve: " 'If you're pregnant and alone, we're here. Beating Heart can help.' Then there's our number."

"That sounds acceptable," Maeve said. She turned back to me. "I wish Tess were here. She's good at taking care of matters like that."

"I wish she were here, too," I said. I wrote my home and office numbers on a card. "Please, if you hear from Tess, let me know."

"I will," Maeve said.

She was as good as her word. The next Wednesday when I came in from my senior class, the phone in my office was ringing. It was Maeve O'Byrne. "Good news," she said. "Tess called."

"Where is she?" I asked.

"She didn't say."

"When will she be back?"

"She didn't say that either." I could hear the impatience in Maeve O'Byrne's voice. "The point is," she said, "Tess is all right, and I'm glad she called because I was about to phone the police."

"Maybe that's why she called," I said.

"What?"

"Nothing. Thanks, Maeve. I mean that. I know how busy you are."

"If I hear anything more, I'll be in touch," she said.

"I'd appreciate that," I said, and I hung up, more discouraged than ever. Every lead seemed to be turning into a dead end.

I spent the rest of the week teaching classes, trying to bring about a *détente* in the war between our pets, and reading up on incidences in which nations had censured trading partners for human-rights violations. Human rights had turned out to be a popular subject. The switchboards had been jammed on the call-in segment of our show, and we were revisiting the topic on Saturday night.

By the time I drove Taylor to her art class on Saturday I felt as if I was handling life again. I'd marked half a section of essays on the neo-conservatism of the eighties. I'd talked to a colleague who'd just come back from Mexico with documents that made me wonder again about the ethics of two electoral democracies entering into a trade agreement with a quasi-dictatorship. Most importantly, it seemed my peace-making efforts with the animals were paying off. The dogs no longer snarled when the kitten came into the room, and he no longer arched his small back and hissed every time he saw them. Taylor still hadn't given her cat a name, but it seemed he was here to stay.

When I walked into the gallery gift shop and found two inspired Christmas presents within five minutes, I knew I was on a streak. There was a lineup at the cash register, so I left the bronze cat I'd chosen for Taylor and the box of stained-glass tree ornaments I'd picked out for Greg and Mieka on the counter and went back to browsing.

There were several copies of *The Boy in the Lens's Eye*, but there was only one copy of *Prairiegirl*. I picked it up and began leafing through it. I was not an expert on photography, but even I knew the pictures were brilliant. Seductive, by turns naive and knowing, the prepubescent girls posed for the camera. The photographs were stunning, but they were also disquieting.

The oldest of the children in the photographs was no more than thirteen. Exulting in the changes in their young bodies, they had shown themselves to the camera. They were innocent, but what about the person behind the camera? I thought of Sylvie's cool, unwavering gaze and her blazing talent, and I knew that, for better or worse, I would never see the world as she did.

The picture of the girl lying on the dock was almost the last one in the book, and it stopped my heart. The girl had been swimming; her thin cotton panties were soaked and her hair curled wetly against her shoulders. The wood of the dock beneath her was dark and rough textured; set against it, the soft perfection of her body seemed incandescent. Technically, that contrast must have been what gave the picture its power, but I didn't care about technique. All I cared about was the girl. The ecstasy she felt that day on the dock was frozen in time, but the girl herself had grown up. She had become a mother, and she had her picture taken again. This time she was sitting on a mall Santa's knee and holding her baby. I pulled the photograph I'd found in Ian's pocket from my purse and held it against the photograph in *Prairiegirl*. Unmistakably, the face was the same.

I was shaking so badly I could barely turn the page, but I had to know if she was there again.

She was. In the last photo in the book, two young girls stood against a split-rail fence. Their arms were around each other's waists and their faces were turned toward one another. The picture was called "Friends." One of the friends was the girl from Ian's picture; the other was Maureen Gault.

CHAPTER

10

When I put the copy of *Prairiegirl* on the counter of the gallery shop, I felt dazed. The woman behind the cash register gave me poinsettia-patterned gift boxes for the bronze cat and the Christmas ornaments. After she'd rung through the book, she looked up brightly. "Shall I gift-wrap this?"

"It's mine," I said.

"The best presents are always those we give ourselves, aren't they?" she said, and she turned to the next customer.

As I waited in the lobby for Taylor, I read the introduction Sylvie had written for *Prairiegirl*. It was full of art talk about purpose and explanations of how she had used an eight-by-ten-inch view camera for the photographs. There was nothing there for me. I turned the page. In the acknowledgements, Sylvie thanked "the girls of Chaplin, Saskatchewan, whose luminous beauty was a gift to the camera." She did not thank the parents who had trusted her to preserve their daughters' innocence in their photographs.

My mind felt clearer than it had since the moment I found the photograph in Ian's jacket. The girl in the Santa photograph was from Chaplin. I sat in the lobby of the gallery assessing possibilities. My first thought was to call Sylvie. I rejected that. If Ian had been involved with this young woman, his infidelity was my private grief. Sylvie was out.

The girls were all from Chaplin. There was no doubt in my mind now that Chaplin was the key. The desolate moonscape behind the sodium sulphate plant flashed through my mind. Chaplin was a company town and a small one. Carolyn Atcheson, the teacher Hilda had visited, had known Maureen Gault. Surely, she would know at least something about her best friend. The next day was Sunday, a good day to take a long drive to visit a stranger.

By the time Taylor came from her class, full of talk about Fil and his teachings, the adrenalin was pumping. That night on "Canada This Week" I argued passionately for the need to demand stringent human-rights protections from our trading partners. When the program ended, Jill came over and paid me her highest compliment. "That worked," she said, and she offered to buy me a cup of Nationtv cafeteria coffee. Afterwards, I drove home and looked through *Prairiegirl* again. The next morning, after church, I set out for Chaplin.

It was an ugly day. The sky was heavy with snow, and the countryside looked as if it had been sculpted out of iron: iron-grey clouds and iron-grey land joined by a steel-grey sky. The only colour between Regina and Parkbeg came from the Christmas lights on Chubby's Café near Belle Plaine.

I was grateful when I left the flatness of the farmlands and hit the gentle hills of ranch country. The hills seemed to offer protection against the heaviness of the looming sky. I'd always loved this short-grass land. Ian and some of the other members of the Legislature had come here to hunt each fall. They were seldom gone for longer than three days, but three days had been enough to transform them from their everyday selves into strangers whose faces were dark with beards and who smelled of wet wool and stale liquor and something unidentifiable and primal. Boys' Night Out.

It had been six, maybe seven years since I'd been here. I hadn't driven this far west on the Trans-Canada since Ian died, and as I neared the spot on the highway where he'd been killed, I was tense.

Incredibly, I drove right by it. As the desolate mountain of sodium sulphate behind the Chaplin plant loomed up out of nowhere, I realized that somehow I'd missed the cutoff to the Vermilion Hills where my husband died. I hadn't even recognized it. As I turned off the highway into the town of Chaplin, I thought of a reservation Ian and I had driven through in Montana where each fatal accident along the road was marked by a wooden cross that had been decorated by the grieving families. At the time, we'd thought the plastic flowers and baby booties and beadwork necklaces which decorated the crosses were mawkish. Now I wasn't so sure. It would have been good if there had been something to mark the place where my husband died.

I pulled into the Petro-Can, bought a cup of coffee, and asked the mechanic for directions to Carolyn Atcheson's house. It was two blocks away. On my way into town I'd noticed the school. It was very modern: terra cotta with cobalt-blue eaves and trim. The mechanic pointed towards it.

"She lives on First Street, so she can keep an eye on that school of hers. She's got a right; it wouldn't have been built without her. She taught the whole school board."

Carolyn Atcheson's house was small, neat, and carefully kept. Her walk was shovelled, her rosebushes were wrapped in sacking for the winter, and the brown paint on her gingerbread trim and front door was fresh. The name C. ATCHESON was burned into a wooden sign nailed above her mailbox. When I saw the light inside the living room, I was relieved. It had been quixotic to drive from Regina to Chaplin without calling ahead. I knocked on the front door, and a dog somewhere in the house began to bark, but no one came out to see why. There was a large front window. I made my way between the rosebushes and stood on tiptoe to peer in. The dog, an ancient terrier, flattened his face against the window barking at me. Everything inside was shining, but no one was there.

A snowflake fell, and then another. A gust of wind came out of nowhere, rattling Carolyn Atcheson's wooden shutters. I thought of driving home through a snowstorm and shuddered. It had all been for nothing; I hadn't learned a thing. I turned to walk back to the car. "Shit," I said. "Shit. Shit. Shit. Shit. Shit."

Head bent against the wind, I didn't notice the man come out from the house next door. But he noticed me.

"That's no language for a lady," he said.

"Sorry," I said, and I kept walking.

"Wait," he said. "Are you looking for Miss Atcheson? If she isn't home, she's at the school. She leads a pretty simple life."

"Thanks," I said, and I turned and walked the half-block that took me to Chaplin School and into the not-so-simple life of Carolyn Atcheson.

She must have seen me coming, because she had the door open before I knocked. She looked like teachers I could remember from my childhood: big, over six feet, and ample, not fat, but what another generation would have called a fine figure of a woman. Her hair was salt-and-pepper grey and cropped short. She did not look pleased to see me, but she was of the old school. No matter how she felt, she would not be rude.

"Come down to my office, Mrs. Kilbourn. You'll be more comfortable there"

"You know who I am."

"I watch television," she said.

As I followed her down the empty hall, the years melted away. The principal was taking me to her office. She was not happy, and I had to think quickly.

Carolyn Atcheson's office did nothing to put me at ease. It was a no-nonsense place. Barren of photographs, plants, or personal mementoes, her oak desk gleamed. On the wall behind her was a brass plaque. KNOWLEDGE IS POWER, it said sternly.

Carolyn motioned me to the chair on the student's side of the desk; then she sat down. She didn't waste time. "I'm surprised to see you, Mrs. Kilbourn. From what I've read and heard, I thought the police had cleared you."

"They have," I said. "But I still have questions."

"About Maureen Gault," she said.

"About Maureen Gault, and about someone else, too," I said. I pulled the copy of *Prairiegirl* from my bag, found the page I was looking for, and slid the book across the desk to her.

"I need to know about this girl," I said. "What can you tell me about her?"

It had been a shot in the dark, but it found its mark. Carolyn Atcheson's face went white, and she grabbed the edge of her desk as if she needed something to hold on to. Outside in the hall, the bells announcing a class change rang and the sound echoed hollowly through the empty school. Carolyn Atcheson didn't move.

"I need to know about her," I repeated.

"She was a student here," Carolyn Atcheson said.

"And a friend of Maureen Gault's," I said. I reached across and turned to the photo on the last page of *Prairiegirl*. "Look," I said.

She turned away. "I've seen the picture," she said.

"Have you seen this one?" I asked, and I slid the Santa Claus picture across to her.

Carolyn's face seemed to grow even paler. Her dark eyes burned across the space between us. "What are you after?" she asked.

I looked at the plaque on the wall behind her. "Knowledge," I said. "I'm after knowledge. Tell me everything you know about the girl in those pictures and Maureen Gault."

She stared at me.

"Maybe your files would help," I said.

"I don't need files," she said thickly.

"Miss Atcheson, this is very important. A woman's life is at stake." As soon as I said the words, I knew they were true. The life that was at stake was my own.

What I said seemed to jolt her. She closed her eyes and rubbed her temples. Then she leaned towards me. "I assume Hilda McCourt told you something of my history with Maureen Gault."

"Yes," I said, "she did."

"In all the years I've taught, Maureen was the only truly evil student who ever crossed my path." For a moment Carolyn Atcheson seemed stunned by the enormity of what she had said, then she straightened her shoulders and continued. "My mother used to tell us that nothing is wasted. Maureen inspired me to do a great deal of reading in psychology. If I ever meet another student like her, I'll know what to do. But I didn't know what I was dealing with in that girl, and that's why I failed everyone so badly. Maureen Gault should have been stopped years ago."

"Yes," I agreed, "she should have been."

Carolyn half turned her chair so she was facing the window. As she leaned forward to watch the snow, her voice became almost dreamy. "From what I've learned, Maureen could be classified as a primary psychopath. She truly believed she was superior to everyone around her. The guiding principle of her life was to force others to recognize and acknowledge her superiority."

"Hilda told me that Maureen was very popular when she started high school."

Carolyn Atcheson seemed to find it easier to talk without facing me. "Her leadership skills were remarkable for a girl her age. I've read since that this is not atypical of her illness. At any rate, as long as everyone accepted her as leader and did her bidding, Maureen functioned. It was when the other girls got sick of being manipulated and dominated that the trouble started."

"That's when the attacks on the other students began," I said.

Carolyn's voice was sad. "Yes, and that's when she began her relationship with poor Kevin."

"He was the only one who stuck by her," I said.

"No, not the only one," Carolyn said. "That girl in the picture was Maureen's best friend. She never gave up on Maureen either."

"Who was she?" I asked.

"Her name . . ." Carolyn stopped speaking for a moment. Then, shoulders sunk in defeat, she murmured, "Her name was Jenny Rybchuk."

My heart was already pounding, but I had to know more. "What was Jenny Rybchuk like?"

Carolyn turned from the window, and I saw that there were tears in her eyes. "Innocent. Sweet. No matter what Maureen did, Jenny always forgave her, tried to understand. They'd known each other since they were babies. The families lived next door to one another. Henry was so erratic . . ."

"Henry," I repeated, remembering the man who had sought Ian out at the Legislature the night before he died.

"Henry Rybchuk," Carolyn said. "Jenny's father. When Jenny was growing up, her friends were afraid to go into the

Rybchuk house because Henry was so unpredictable. When he was sober, he was decent enough, but when he was drinking, he could be violent." She hesitated. "There were rumours that his feelings for Jenny went beyond what a father should feel for his daughter. It must have been a terrifying life for a child, and lonely. Of course, Maureen went there. That one was never afraid of anything. She spent so much time with the Rybchuks that I think Jenny came to look upon her as a kind of sister."

"How did Maureen look upon Jenny?"

Carolyn laughed bitterly. "I'm sure she thanked her lucky stars that fate had sent her a friend as compliant and as needy as Jenny. I suppose when they were children, Maureen didn't mistreat Jenny any more than any strong-willed child mistreats a more passive friend. In my experience, children are as fond of power as anyone – and as easily corrupted by it. But eventually I think Maureen's role in their relationship became more sinister than deciding which game the two of them would play . . ." Carolyn fell silent.

"Maureen used Jenny," I said.

"Oh, yes," Carolyn agreed. "Maureen used Jenny. That girl knew how to use goodness."

"How did she react to Jenny's pregnancy?"

For a beat, Carolyn was silent. Finally, she said, "Jenny didn't tell her until after the baby was born."

"If she didn't tell her best friend, whom did she tell?" I asked.

Carolyn looked away. "I don't know."

I didn't believe her. "Did Jenny tell the baby's father she was pregnant?"

Carolyn's voice was edgy. "I told you I don't know whom else she told."

"But she told you," I said gently. "Carolyn, Jenny told you she was pregnant, didn't she?"

"I was the one she came to," Carolyn said, her voice breaking. "It was such an act of trust . . ."

"She must have felt very close to you."

"She didn't have anyone else. Her mother was dead. Henry was impossible."

"Why didn't she go to Maureen?"

Carolyn shook her head. "I honestly don't know. All I do know is that she came to me. It was the day before Good Friday. The students had been dismissed for the Easter holidays. I was just getting ready to leave myself when Jenny knocked at my door."

Unexpectedly, Carolyn smiled. "Isn't it funny, the things you remember? Jenny came in and sat down in the chair you're sitting in now. I can still see her. She usually had her hair brushed back in a French braid, but that day it was loose. She was wearing a turquoise windbreaker and, on her lapel, she had a little Easter pin. It was a rabbit carrying a basket of eggs."

"And she told you she was pregnant?"

"Yes, she came straight to the point. She told me she was pregnant and that she wanted an abortion. I didn't believe her."

"You didn't believe she was pregnant?"

Carolyn shook her head impatiently. "Oh, I believed that all right. Student pregnancies are all too common in this school. What I didn't believe was that she wanted an abortion. I wouldn't have been the one Jenny'd come to if that was truly what she wanted."

"You're opposed to abortion?"

Carolyn looked at me levelly. "I'm a Roman Catholic, Mrs. Kilbourn. So was Jenny. I think her mind told her that one course of action was logical, but her heart told her differently. We talked for a long time that afternoon, but nothing I said convinced her. She was poised between two very painful alternatives, and she was eighteen years old. She needed guidance, and I wasn't adequately prepared to give her that guidance."

"So you took her to Beating Heart," I said.

Carolyn looked surprised.

"And the woman you saw there was Tess Malone."

Carolyn's eyes widened. "Yes, that was her name."

"What happened next?" I asked.

"Nothing," she said dully. "Jenny had the baby. She gave it away. She went back to school."

"Where is she now?"

"I don't know."

"As close as she became to you, she never got in touch?"

"No," Carolyn said, "she didn't."

"One last thing," I said. "Who was the baby's father?"

For a moment she was silent. Then she murmured. "That doesn't matter any more. Mrs. Kilbourn, don't persist in this. Any answer you find is just going to cause pain. You've been cleared of any suspicion of wrongdoing. Leave Jenny Rybchuk's child in peace. Please."

When I told Carolyn Atcheson I was leaving, she fluttered her hand in a vague signal of dismissal, but she didn't bother getting up. At the office doorway, I turned to say goodbye. Through the window behind her, I could see the snow falling, rhythmic, inexorable. Carolyn Atcheson didn't notice it. Sitting at her desk, back ramrod straight, hands clasped in front of her, Carolyn was the prototype for the class's most obedient student.

When I got back to my car I checked the clock on the dashboard. Three o'clock. Two hours till dark. I had time to pay one more visit. There were too many gaps in Carolyn's story. Erratic as Henry Rybchuk might be, I needed to talk to him.

When I got to the Petro-Can station, the mechanic who'd directed me to Carolyn's house was out front checking the oil in a Camaro. I pulled up next to him and rolled down my window. I noticed the name embroidered on his shirt pocket was Maurice. "I need your guiding skills again, Maurice," I said. "How can I find Henry Rybchuk?"

He smiled, revealing some missing teeth. "Maurice is long gone. My name is Bob, but there was a lot of wear left in Maurice's old shirts. Besides, I kind of like 'Maurice.' It's distinctive. Now, about Henry Rybchuk. You'll need more skills than mine to find him," he said. "Old Henry's been dead for over five years."

The driver of the Camaro went inside, and Bob and I talked a little longer. He said Henry had committed suicide. Shot himself to death in the basement of his house. He remembered Jenny, but he hadn't seen her in years either. "I'll tell you one thing," he said. "She didn't come back for the old man's funeral. After the announcement of the old man's death appeared in the obituaries in the Swift Current paper, Wrightman's Funeral Home – that's in Swift Current, too – got an envelope of cash and some instructions about the burial. It was anonymous. Most of us figured the envelope came from Jenny. Nobody tried very hard to chase her down. We figured if Jenny had managed to get away from that old bastard, she was better off."

I mentioned Maureen Gault's name, and Bob dismissed her with a one-word epithet. When the driver of the Camaro came back out and started honking his horn, I got the addresses of the Gault and Rybchuk houses, thanked Bob for his help, and doubled back through town.

Factory Road was the last street on the west side of Chaplin. It looked out on a desolate landscape of salt stockpiles and tanks for the water run-off from the sodium sulphate factory. Numbers 17 and 19 were at the end of the street, set apart from the other houses. They were small bungalows with the boxy, stripped-down look of wartime housing, but the house in which Maureen Gault had grown up had fallen on hard times. Motorcycles, in various stages of disintegration, filled the carport; the front window was covered by a tattered American flag; and a doll lay abandoned on the front steps.

I pulled up in front of the Rybchuk house. Like Carolyn Atcheson's, this house was hard-scrubbed and cared for. A young woman was out shovelling the snow, and she came over as soon as she saw me. She was wearing a leather jacket with the logo of the sodium sulphate mine on the breast pocket, and her nose was running from the cold. When I rolled down the car window, she wiped her nose on the back of her mitten and grinned.

"Gross, huh?"

"We all do it," I said.

"Right," she said. "Now what can I do for you? I'll bet you're looking for a way out of Chaplin."

"No," I said, "I'm looking for the Rybchuk house."

The young woman's face grew solemn with the importance of being forced to break bad news. "They don't live here anymore. Old Mr. Rybchuk died. I'm sorry to be the one to tell you."

"That's all right," I said.

She leaned closer to me. "You know, you're the first person who's come and asked for them since we bought the house, and that'll be six years in May."

"I think old Mr. Rybchuk was pretty reclusive," I said.

She rolled her eyes. "I'll say. Imagine nobody coming to ask about you in all that time. Listen, do you happen to know his daughter? Nobody cleaned out the house before we bought it, so there was a lot of junk. We sold most of the stuff in a garage sale, and burned the rest in the burn barrel out back, but I couldn't burn her pictures. Maybe it was an identification thing. She's like my age, and I kept thinking I wouldn't want anybody to burn my pictures and stuff." She looked at me winsomely. "Since you're here and all, could I possibly impose on you to get them to her?"

"I'd be happy to."

"Great," she said. She threw her shovel into a snowbank and ran indoors. She came back with a box which she handed through the window to me. It was bigger than a shoebox, but not much. A box for winter boots, maybe. Someone had covered it in wallpaper, white with a pattern of ballerinas in pastel tutus. There was a yellowish stain on the wallpaper, and the box smelled musty.

"Sorry about the stink," she said. "It was in the basement, and you know how they are."

I thought about Henry Rybchuk committing suicide in the basement, and I shuddered.

The girl's brow furrowed. "You will get it to her, won't you?"

"I'll do my best," I said.

It took an act of will not to open the box before I got home, but I managed. When I walked through the front door, Taylor came running, eyed the box hopefully, then held her nose.

"What's in that?" she asked.

"Just some old pictures that were in somebody's house."

"Okay," she said, then she lowered her voice. "Angus is making dinner. It's a surprise, so act surprised."

"I will," I whispered back. "What are we having?"

She pulled me down, put her mouth beside my ear, and stage-whispered, "Cinnamon buns!"

"Great," I said.

"Remember the surprise."

I gave her the thumbs-up sign, turned towards the kitchen, and said loudly. "I'd better go get dinner started."

Angus came peeling out. He was wearing a shirt that said NOBODY WITH A GREAT CAR NEEDS TO JUSTIFY HIMSELF, and he had a ring through his left nostril. It hadn't been there when I'd left him at lunchtime.

"Angus!" I said.

"I told the guys you were the coolest mother. I said my mother lived through the sixties, this won't be a problem for her."

"You were wrong," I said.

"I knew it," he said gloomily. Then he brightened. "I made cinnamon buns."

"You thought I could be bought for a cinnamon bun?"

He grinned. "I thought it was worth a shot."

That night we sat at the kitchen table, ate cinnamon buns, and watched the snow. The kids drank milk, and I drank Earl Grey tea. When I got Taylor into bed, and Angus was in his room listening to Crash Test Dummies and doing his algebra, I poured myself a glass of Jack Daniel's, picked up the box with the ballerinas on it, and went to my room.

I was glad I had the bourbon. Jenny Rybchuk's whole life was in that box. Her report cards, stacked neatly, were tied together by a thin blue ribbon. I looked at them all, and I read the teachers' comments on Jenny's development as avidly as a parent. ("Jenny is a sensible girl, whose co-operative attitude makes her a valued member of the class. She should work harder on Math." "Promoted to Grade 7 with honours. Good work, Jenny!!!") There were pictures, too. Baby pictures. School pictures. Thirteen of them. I arranged them in order on my bedspread. Kindergarten to Grade 12. The pictures were the kind a photographer who travels from school to school takes. Watch Jenny grow. Standard poses against standard backgrounds, yet something about them nagged at me. They were familiar somehow, as if I'd seen them before. Like a word on the tip of my tongue the connection was there, but I couldn't make it. I put the pictures back and closed the box.

But there was one photograph that I couldn't seem to put away. It was in black and white. Jenny looked to be about five or six, and she was wearing a flower-girl's dress. There was a blur of guests in the background, but she was alone and unsmiling. Her dress looked as if it was made of taffeta, she had a crown of flowers in her hair, and she was looking directly into the lens. There was something unsettling about those unblinking eyes. She seemed to be looking ahead into the future, collapsing the distance between past and present, seeking me out.

That night I couldn't sleep. Sometime in the early hours of morning, I turned the lights on and picked up the flower-girl picture from my nightstand. "What happened to you, Jenny?" I said. "Where are you now?" I knew I had to find her, but if I was going to find Jenny, I had to find Tess Malone.

At 5:30, I gave up on sleep and went downstairs. It was too early for the paper to be delivered, so I went out back and got an old issue out of the Blue Box. The paper's classified offices opened at 9:00. I wrote down the number. Then I turned to the classified ads and ran my finger down the column until I found what I was looking for. "If you're pregnant and alone, we're here. Beating Heart can help."

I picked up a pencil and started to write. Three minutes later, I had what I wanted: "If you're ready to talk about Henry and Jenny, I'm ready to listen. JK."

The receptionist at Beating Heart had said that Tess checked the classifieds every day to make sure its ad was there. If I was lucky, she'd keep on reading. My ad would be the one right after Beating Heart's.

CHAPTER

11

My ad in the personals column appeared for the first time on Tuesday. There was no response, and life went on. The jack o'lantern was still on the deck, and Taylor still hadn't named her cat. Angus's nose had become infected over the weekend and, by Wednesday, he had to admit defeat and take the ring out. "Temporarily," he said, but I recognized a window of opportunity when I saw one. As soon as the ring was out, I called Jill and asked her to come over and take some family pictures for our Christmas cards.

Thursday afternoon, there was a half-day holiday at Taylor's school, so she came to the university with me. She brought her sketchbook and the drawing pencils Hilda had given her for her birthday. On the way to my office, we stopped off at the cafeteria for a can of pop, a bag of chips, and box of Junior Mints; then we went to the departmental office where Rosalie Norman agreed, reluctantly, that if there was an emergency, Taylor could call her. All the bases had been covered. Still, when I picked up my notes to go to class, I was anxious.

"Are you sure you're going to be all right?" I asked.

Taylor was adjusting my desk lamp so the light fell on her sketchpad. "I'm fine," she said without looking up. "There are a couple of things I really want to work on." As I watched her choose a pencil from her case, I marvelled for the hundredth time at the metamorphosis that Taylor underwent when she was making art.

An hour later, when I came back from class, she was still at work.

"How did it go?" I asked.

She held up her sketchpad. "Take a look," she said.

She had drawn Jess Stephens, surrounded by a series of quick line drawings of her kitten. The cat sketches were fluid and funny, but the drawing of Jess was remarkable. Taylor's art teacher, Fil, had told me she still had a lot to learn about technique, but she'd captured Jess: the dreamy little boy with the great cheekbones and the eyes that tilted upwards and made him look always as if he were laughing.

I had seen Jess Stephens a hundred times, but it wasn't until I looked at Taylor's drawing that I knew why the pictures of Jenny Rybchuk had nagged at me. I tried to remember the months before Jess was born. Sylvie had gone to a fertility clinic in Vancouver. Later, because the doctors knew the pregnancy would be a difficult one, she had spent the last months of her pregnancy at the clinic and had the baby there. That had been the story. Sylvie and her baby had come back in the fall. Jess was six now. Taylor had gone to the party for his sixth birthday in September. The baby in Jenny Rybchuk's arms in the Santa picture seemed to be two or three months old. It all fit.

When I got home, there was a message from the classified department of the paper. Did I want my ad in for another three days? I called back and said I did, but I was going to change the wording. I wanted the new ad to read: "If you're ready to talk about Jenny and Jess, I'm ready to listen, JK."

Tess Malone called Saturday night. I'd just gotten back from the station after doing our show, and I was in that state that Angus calls wired but tired.

Tess just sounded wired. "I saw your ad, and you've got to take it out of the paper. You have no idea what you can bring down on yourself if you pursue this."

"Is Jess Stephens Jenny Rybchuk's son?"

"Jo, why are you meddling in this?"

"I'm not meddling," I said. "Tess, it's important that I know the truth."

"Dammit, Jo. Leave it alone."

"I can't," I said. "I need to understand what happened. Tess, you've known me for years. Give me a little credit. I'm not stirring this up just to make trouble."

She sighed. "I know you aren't." For a moment, she was silent. I hoped the silence was a good sign and it was. When she finally spoke, her voice was resigned.

"I hope you're not going to be sorry you forced this, Jo. I don't know how you found out, but you're right. Jess is Jenny Rybchuk's son."

"And you knew her," I said. "You met her when Carolyn Atcheson brought her into Beating Heart."

"Yes."

I felt a rush of excitement. "What was she like?"

"Young. Scared. Decent. Trying hard to do the right thing. I'd only been a volunteer at Beating Heart for three or four months when Jenny came in. I would have remembered her even if . . ." Her voice trailed off.

"Even if what, Tess?"

"Even if . . . if she hadn't been one of the first girls I counselled. Sometimes it's so easy to get a girl to see that having the baby is the right option. But when Jenny started to talk to me, all I could think of was how amazing it was that she was even considering going through with the pregnancy."

"Carolyn said Jenny was poised between two very painful alternatives."

"That about sums it up. Jenny was a very loyal girl, but when she talked about her home situation and what her father would do to her if he knew she was pregnant, I understood why she was considering abortion. When she came to Beating Heart, she was already three months' pregnant. High-school graduation was another three months away. All her life she'd worked towards getting that diploma. It was her ticket out of hell, Jo. I know that sounds melodramatic, but that's the way it was. Once she had her Grade 12, Jenny wouldn't be dependent on her father anymore."

"From what Carolyn said about Henry Rybchuk, that must have been a powerful argument."

"It was," Tess agreed, "but it wasn't the most powerful. Jenny's biggest concern wasn't herself. It was her baby. She was worried sick about what might happen to her baby if she gave it out for adoption. I guess she knew first-hand what an abusive parent could do to a child, and the idea that her own child would be raised by people about whom she would know nothing terrified her."

"So you convinced her to have the baby and give it to Sylvie and Gary."

"You make it sound as if I was just using Jenny to do a favour for friends. It wasn't like that. Abortion is wrong, Jo, and, in her heart, Jenny Rybchuk knew that. She knew a foetus wasn't just a collection of cells that you scrub away like dead skin. She knew she'd never forgive herself for committing murder. Sylvie and Gary offered the perfect solution. It wasn't common knowledge at the time, but before Jess came into their lives, Gary and Sylvie's marriage was in serious trouble. They'd just turned forty. There was no baby, and it didn't look as if there was ever going to be one. They were desperate.

"All I had to do was pick up the phone. I could save the marriage of two people I cared for, keep a fine young girl from making a mistake that would ruin her life, and make certain a baby came into this world. It all seemed so right."

"And so you made the call."

"Yes," she said. "I made the call, and that night Sylvie and Gary came down to Beating Heart to talk to Jenny. They were all so excited and so committed to making sure the baby had a wonderful life." She was silent for a long while, then she said, "It should have been perfect." She sounded as if she was speaking to herself, not to me.

"What went wrong?" I asked.

"Nothing," she said flatly. "Everything worked out the way it was supposed to. Jenny got her high-school graduation diploma. Carolyn Atcheson went to old Henry Rybchuk and told him she'd found his daughter a job babysitting for a family on Vancouver Island, starting in June, and that she was arranging to have Jenny write her final exams in B.C."

"And Henry Rybchuk went along with that?" I asked.

"According to Carolyn, he was relieved. He'd been laid off at the plant, and money was tight. He gave Jenny his blessing. She went to Vancouver, and, a few days later, Sylvie joined her. They stayed together until Jess was born. Sylvie didn't want to miss any part of the experience."

"They must have become very close."

Tess's voice was dead. "I guess they did." She sighed. "Jo, I don't want to talk about this anymore. I've told you everything you need to know. Goodnight."

"Don't hang up. Please, don't hang up yet. I need to know one more thing." I could feel my muscles tense. "Tess, who was the baby's father?"

"What?" she said.

"I said, do you know who Jess's father is?"

"The name's in our records," she said.

"Who was it?"

"I can't tell you that."

"Was it Ian?"

The shock in her voice seemed genuine. "Whatever made you think that?" she said.

"Then it wasn't him?"

"Of course not." For the first time that night, she sounded like the old Tess, gruff and confident, and I remembered how often that gruff confidence had got all of us through a tight spot. Now it sounded as if she was the one in a tight spot.

"Tess, are you all right?" I asked.

"It doesn't matter," she said. "Just take the ad out of the paper, Jo. Please." Then she hung up.

I went to my purse and pulled out the picture that had been in Ian's wallet. Now that I knew the truth, the photo had lost its power. It was just a picture of a shopping mall Santa, a pretty young woman, and a baby whose father was a man I didn't know. The big question had been answered, but there were others. Why had Ian been carrying the picture? What had Henry Rybchuk talked about with Ian and then with Tess the night before Ian was murdered? Why had Henry Rybchuk committed suicide? And, most naggingly, where was Jenny Rybchuk?

I opened the box of Jenny's mementoes, and put the Santa Claus picture on the top. As I replaced the lid, I thought about the girl who had pasted ballerina-covered wallpaper on to an old box to make it pretty. Jenny's Grade 6 teacher had said she was a sensible girl, and a sensible girl would know when it was time to put away the past. By now she probably had another baby and a new life.

That night I slept deeply and dreamlessly. The next morning I woke up to fresh snow and a sense of hope. It was Advent Sunday. As I made the coffee, I remembered our old minister saying that the first Sunday in Advent always reminded him of a song from *West Side Story*. When I stepped into the shower, I knew exactly how he felt. "Something's coming," I sang and, as I soaped up, I thought it was about time for something good to come whistling down my river.

Angus was the altar boy at church, and as he lit the candle, I felt my heart beat faster. To celebrate the start of the Christmas season, we went to the Copper Kettle for brunch. At the buffet, Taylor and Angus competed hotly to see who could heap the most food on their plate. As I watched them tottering back to our table, plates piled high with roast beef and ribs and perogies, I was so embarrassed I wanted to sink through the floor, but they told each other jokes all through lunch and laughed so hard that the owner of the restaurant gave them each a free dessert. "You two are good for business," he said. When we came out of the restaurant, Taylor decided to dance all the way down Scarth Street because she was so happy. As I watched her twirling around in her snowsuit and her boots, I knew my something good had already come. You could always count on Leonard Bernstein.

Monday after class, a student called asking for an appointment and, as I checked my calendar, I saw there were only twenty-four shopping days till Christmas. I made a quick list of people I was buying presents for and headed for the mall.

Inside the Cornwall Centre, it wasn't hard to feel the holiday spirit. Beside the fountain in the centre courtyard, a three-storey tree soared towards a skylight; in front of the toy store, Santa was ho-ho-ho-ing on his big red chair inside the North Pole; and every loudspeaker in the mall was blaring "Silent Night."

I was coming down the escalator in Eaton's when I saw her. She was in the accessories department, comparing two scarves. She seemed so absorbed that, for a split second, I thought I might get away unscathed. But just before the escalator got to the main floor, Julie Evanson looked up and saw me. There was no escaping her.

She was wearing her platinum hair in a new and becoming feathered cut, and her cherry-red wool coat fitted her trim figure like the proverbial glove. The look was strictly Liz Claiborne, but I knew Julie had made the coat herself. As she had told me many times over the years, she made all her own clothes. She also told me that, with a figure like mine, which must be difficult to fit, I'd find I'd look much smarter if I made my own clothes, too. That was Julie.

"Christmas shopping, Julie?" I said.

She smiled her dimpled smile. "All my shopping's done, Joanne. And wrapped."

"Mine, too," I said, crossing my fingers the way my kids did when they told a lie.

"I guess shopping kept you busy when everyone thought you'd murdered that girl."

"Not everyone thought that, Julie. The police didn't. That's why I'm standing here now."

She looked thoughtfully at the scarf in her hand. "That poor girl," she said. "Choked to death. It was good luck that you got off, wasn't it?"

"It wasn't luck," I said. "It was justice. I didn't have anything to do with Maureen Gault's death."

She shrugged. "So you say. But try as I might, I can't forget the little chat I had with Maureen the day you and I met in the Faculty Club."

"What are you talking about?"

"I just told you. I had a fascinating tête-à-tête with Maureen Gault the day before she was killed. She was coming out of the elevator in the Arts Building. You know, the building where you have your office," she added helpfully.

"I know where my office is, Julie. What did Maureen tell you?"

Julie frowned. "I'll have to make sure I remember exactly what was said. After all, Maureen isn't here to defend herself, is she? On second thought, maybe it would be better if I didn't say anything at all."

I started to leave. "Suit yourself," I said. "I'm too old for this crap."

She reached out and touched my sleeve. "I don't remember you as being profane, Joanne. But I guess I can't blame you for being anxious about what Maureen might have said to me before she died."

"Julie, please."

"All right. It was a brief encounter. I was on my way to your office to see if you'd buy some tickets to the fashion show. I was just passing the bookstore in the Arts Building when Maureen Gault got off the elevator. I recognized her, and went up and introduced myself." Julie dimpled. "I said I was a friend of yours. You're not the only one who can stretch the truth, Joanne.

"Anyway, Maureen said, 'When you see her, tell her I'm looking for her.' Of course, I asked why, and Maureen said, 'I want to ask her if she's feeling different about any of the Seven Dwarfs these days.'"

I remembered the crude X's someone had drawn over the faces of Andy Boychuk and my husband the day Julie ran into Maureen. There didn't seem to be much doubt anymore about who had wielded the felt pen. "Did she say anything more?" I asked.

"I forced her to say more," Julie said proudly. "I asked Maureen point-blank what she knew about the Seven Dwarfs. At first she seemed angry at the question, then she laughed and pointed to one of the displays in the bookstore window. They hadn't taken out the Hallowe'en decorations yet, and there was a skeleton propped up against a stack of biology books. Maureen jabbed at the window in front of it and said, 'There's your answer, blondie. I know where the Seven Dwarfs hid their skeleton.'"

Julie must have seen the fear in my eyes. "Just a figure of speech I'm sure, but in retrospect, it does seem chilling, doesn't it?" She looked at her watch. "Four o'clock, already. How the minutes fly when we're with friends."

She thrust the scarf she was holding into my hand. "Here, Joanne, you take this. All those colours. It's more the kind of thing you'd wear." She turned on her heel, and steered her way effortlessly through the other shoppers in accessories. I felt as if someone had run me over with a truck, but then Julie had always been the queen of the hit-and-run artists. The scarf she'd thrust at me was still in my hands. Julie was right. That brilliant swirl of colour was the kind of thing I liked. When it came to insights that could wound, Julie had a knack for being right. She also, much as I hated to admit it, had a knack for finding out the truth. As poisonous as she was, I had never known Julie to lie.

I put down the scarf. Christmas shopping was over for the day. I had to find out if Julie had stumbled onto some ugly truth about the Seven Dwarfs.

When I walked past the North Pole on my way out, I could hear the soft, anxious voices of the young mothers waiting with little girls in fussy velvet dresses and little boys in Christmas sweaters and new corduroy pants. "Don't forget to smile," the mothers said. "Don't forget to tell Santa what you want him to bring you. There's nothing to be afraid of . . ."

Jenny Rybchuk had stood in a line like that with her son. Where was she now? When her father said, "Now, I got no more daughter," what had he meant? As I drove up Albert Street, I could feel the anxiety beginning to gnaw.

I didn't wait to take my coat off before I dialled Howard Dowhanuik's number in Toronto.

He was furious. "A skeleton! Don't you know better than to listen to Julie? Christ, Jo, after all these years . . ."

"Howard, as awful as Julie is, I've never known her to lie."

"Maybe she's turned a corner since we knew her."

"I don't think it's that simple. Howard, Maureen Gault was murdered the day after Julie saw her. What if the skeleton Maureen was talking about wasn't figurative? What if she really did chance upon something about the Seven Dwarfs? Do you have any idea what she might have been talking about?"

"No, I don't, and to be frank I'm pissed off that you think I would. Jo, I may lack finesse and I may be a little crude, but I'm an officer of the court. We take an oath. Do you think I could know about a stiff being stashed somewhere and say, 'Oh well, one of us was responsible for that murder, so I'll overlook it'?"

"I'm sorry," I said.

"You should be," he said. Then his voice was kinder. "That goddamn Julie makes us all crazy. Just forget it, Jo."

"I'll try," I said.

But I couldn't. I dialled Craig Evanson's number. When Manda answered, I hung up. After enduring the hell of a bad marriage for twenty years, Craig had found a great wife and a great life. He didn't need to revisit his past. Besides, there was a chance Howard was right. It was possible that Julie was just making me crazy.

I went upstairs to change my clothes before dinner. I pulled on my blue jeans and a long-sleeved T-shirt Mieka had bought years ago at a concert. The Go-Go's. Another blast from the past. When I reached down to pick up my sneakers, I saw the corner of the ballerina-covered box under the bed, and I felt the panic rising.

"Where are you, Jenny," I murmured. I picked up the telephone and dialled the number of my new friends in the classified department. This time I wasn't fancy with the ad: "URGENT: I must speak to Jenny Rybchuk or anyone knowing her whereabouts. Joanne Kilbourn." I left both my office and my home numbers. I didn't want to take a chance on missing her.

The ad appeared in the late edition of Tuesday's paper. Wednesday morning as I pulled onto the parkway on my way to the university, I noticed the silver Audi behind me. When I turned into the university, the Audi stayed with me, but it sailed by when I drove into the parking lot in front of College West, and I forgot about it. Two hours later, as i started home, it was there again. The Audi's windows were tinted. Whoever was driving it had an advantage over me in our game of hide and seek. I looked for it when I stopped for groceries at the IGA, but it had disappeared. When I drove home, the Audi was behind me all the way, but it was nowhere in sight when I parked in front of our house. The first thing I saw at home was Taylor balanced on the railing on the front porch with a string of Christmas lights in her hand and a look of grim determination on her face. At that point, the Audi slipped to the back of my mind where it stayed the rest of the evening.

Peter called after supper to say he was coming home Saturday to study for his mid-term exams. Taylor, who had been standing beside me, holding her kitten and listening to my half of the conversation with Peter, looked at me expectantly when I hung up. "Now is it time to get out the Christmas stuff?" she asked.

"It's time," I said. "Come on, we'll go downstairs and dig out the decorations. But you're going to have to keep that cat out of harm's way till we're done." I looked at the animal in Taylor's arms. It wasn't a ball of ginger fluff any more; it was starting to get a rangy adolescent look. "T," I said, "when are you going to decide on a name? You're supposed to do these things when the animal is young enough to learn."

She rubbed the spot under her cat's neck thoughtfully. "I keep changing my mind. Angus says I should call him 'Dallas' after the Dallas Cowboys. What do you think?"

"Dallas? It sounds okay to me."

Taylor shook her head. "I hate it." She moved the cat into his favourite carrying position, with his body against her chest and his head looking back over her shoulder. "Come on, kitten, let's go put you in our room." As she walked out the door, I caught the cat looking at me in a defiant teenager way, and I knew he would make me pay for banishing him.

Taylor and I spent the rest of the evening decorating. We were just winding fake holly around the staircase rail when the phone rang. It was Inspector Alex Kequahtooway.

"I thought I'd call and see how you're doing, Mrs. Kilbourn."

"I'm fine," I said. "How are you?"

"Fine," he said. "Mrs. Kilbourn, I was wondering what you were doing Friday night."

I felt my heart sink. "Friday night? I don't remember. Inspector, what's happened?"

He laughed. "Nothing's happened, Mrs. Kilbourn. It's not last Friday I'm interested in. It's this Friday. I was wondering if you wanted to go to the symphony with me. They've got some hot-shot guest violinist and he's doing a Beethoven sonata. That day in my office, you said you liked Beethoven."

"I do," I said.

"Well?" he asked.

"I'd love to," I said.

"Shall I pick you up at about seven?"

"Seven would be great," I said.

The next day as I drove to school thinking about what I'd wear on Friday night, I noticed the Audi again. I'm a cautious driver, but I tried a few tricky manoeuvres to see if I was imagining that the Audi was following me. It was right with me all the way to the university turnoff. When I got to my office, I called Alex Kequahtooway. He wasn't at head-quarters, but I left a message, and when he called back a half-hour later, I told him about the Audi. He said he'd look into it. When I drove home after class, the Audi was gone, and I thought it might be handy dating a cop.

Friday night, Inspector Alex Kequahtooway was on my doorstep at the dot of 7:00. I'd had my hair cut at a new place that cost three times as much as my old place, and I was wearing a black silk dress so chic that even Julie Evanson would have approved.

Alex Kequahtooway did too. "You look great," he said, as he held out my coat for me.

"You look pretty spiffy yourself," I said.

He smiled. "I guess if the compliments are over, we can go."

The kids came down to say goodbye, and we walked out to the curb where the taxi Alex had arrived in was waiting. It was a gorgeous night, warm for December, and starry. We had the idea at the same time. "Let's walk," we said in unison. Alex sent the cabbie on her way with a Christmas tip generous enough to make her smile. I ran back to the house, put on my heavy boots, and we started for the park. As we walked through the snowy streets, we didn't talk much, but it wasn't an awkward silence. When we rounded the corner by the Legislature, Alex climbed through the snow onto a little spit of land overlooking the lake. He held his hand out to me to follow. There was a full moon, and the ice on the lake seemed to glow.

"When I was a kid, we used to walk on the lake by the reserve all winter. Christmas Eve we'd walk across to church, then we'd come back, and all my aunties would make pies. That's what I remember about Christmas. Lying in bed, smelling pies baking, and hearing my aunties laugh." He turned to me. "What do you remember?"

"Nothing that good," I said. "Come on, let's walk across the lake."

"Are you sure? It's longer."

"I don't mind," I said. "I want to start this year's store of Christmas memories off with a bang."

We jumped off the shore and walked across the ice in the moonlight. Neither of us mentioned the case that had brought us together, and neither of us mentioned the Audi. We talked about good things: Christmases and hockey and ice-fishing, and I think we were both surprised when the lights from the Centre of the Arts loomed ahead of us.

We were late. The lobby was almost empty, and we slid into our seats, laughing and out of breath, just as the orchestra struck the opening chord of the Shostakovich Fifth. My heart was pounding from the walk, and the Shostakovich kept it pounding. At intermission, I said to Alex, "I've had enough excitement, let's just stay here."

He laughed. "That's exactly what I feel like doing. I'm wearing dress shoes, and my feet haven't hurt like this since I was a beat cop."

The audience drifted off, and I picked up the program. "Which sonata are they doing?"

He shrugged.

I looked at my program. "The Kreutzer," I said. "Wouldn't you know it."

"You don't like it?" he said.

"I love it. It's just that the Kreutzer Sonata was as close as my husband and I came to having a piece of music that was 'our song.' Tonight's the first time since Kevin Tarpley was killed that I haven't spent the whole evening thinking about Ian. You and I were having such a good time . . ."

"We still are," he said. "If you want to remember, remember. Let the memories come." He leaned towards me. "You had a good marriage, didn't you?"

"Yes," I said, "I did. My friend, Jill, is a journalist, and she says, in her business, there's nothing like death to airbrush the past. I try to remember that when I think of Ian. He wasn't perfect. Neither was I. But there wasn't a day in our life together when Ian and I didn't know that being married was the best thing that had ever happened to either of us."

"Twenty years of a good marriage is about twenty years longer than most people get," Alex said.

"I know," I said, "but it still wasn't long enough for me."

He reached out, took my hand, and we settled back in our seats, holding hands till the audience came back, the lights dimmed, the musicians came onstage, and the guest violinist stepped forward and played, unaccompanied, the heart-stopping opening of the Sonata No. 9 in A Major. The piano replied, then, after a few bars of tentative approaches, piano and violin began their tempestuous pursuit of one another in the presto, and I closed my eyes and remembered the first time I'd heard the Kreutzer Sonata. Ian and I were at the University of Toronto. It was January. We'd been dating for a couple of weeks, and I was sitting in a classroom on the second floor of Victoria College waiting for my English class to begin. Suddenly, Ian was there. He wasn't wearing his jacket, and he looked half-frozen. Without a word, he grabbed my hand and led me down Vic's worn marble stairs and outside, through the snow, to a little record store around the corner on Bloor. There was a listening booth at the back. We went in. Ian's coat and books were on the floor where he'd left them, and the LP of the Kreutzer Sonata was on the turntable. Ian turned on the record player, I heard the violin's luminous entry, and my life changed for ever. We took the record back to Ian's room, and that afternoon we made love for the first time. Afterwards, as we lay in the tangle of sheets, listening to the violin and piano play their separate and confident variations on the single beautiful theme of the second movement, I knew that, whatever else happened in my life, I would have known what it was like to be happy. Four months later, Ian and I were married.

Onstage in the Centre of the Arts, the piano and violin were moving from the tarantelle to the sensuous passage before the finale. Alex Kequahtooway looked closely at me, reached into his pocket, and gave me his handkerchief. I leaned forward to listen to the final dazzling burst of virtuosity, and the movement was over. The musicians bowed to the audience, the applause swelled, and I mopped my eyes and blew my nose. When I was through, I turned to Alex. "Not many men carry a real handkerchief anymore."

He smiled. "My mother always made me carry two hankies. 'One for show. One for blow.'"

"I may need both of them," I said.

"It's a powerful piece of music," he said.

"There's a Tolstoy story where a character says the Kreutzer Sonata should never be played in a room where women are wearing low-necked dresses."

Alex Kequahtooway raised an eyebrow. "Tolstoy may have had a point there."

We walked home through the park. The temperature had risen, and the snow on the trees looked heavy and wet. Suspended from the wrought-iron lampposts along the path were globes of light that reflected red and green and white on the slick pavements.

"Do you think we'll have a green Christmas?" I said.

He shuddered. "I hope not. I can remember only one green Christmas, but it was awful. No snow for tobogganing, and the ice was too thin for skating."

A car speeded by, splashing water on us.

"Never a cop around when you need one," Alex said mildly.

I laughed. "I wouldn't say that. You were there when I needed someone to take care of that Audi. Incidentally, it seems to have decided to play hide and seek with somebody else. I didn't see it at all today."

"Good."

"I probably over-reacted," I said. "But there's been so much weirdness in my life lately."

I could see his body tense. "Such as?"

"Such as an old friend – no, not a friend, an acquaintance – telling me something disturbing."

Alex turned to me. "What did you hear?"

The decision to tell him didn't take long. I was sick of secrets. "I guess I should tell you who the acquaintance was first. It's a woman named Julie Evanson."

"Craig Evanson's first wife," he said.

I looked at him questioningly.

He shrugged. "Mouse work," he said.

"Right," I said. "You must know more about the Seven Dwarfs than we know about each other."

"Probably," he said.

"Then you know that Julie Evanson will never be anyone's candidate for humanitarian of the year," I said.

He smiled. "That seems to be the consensus."

"Nonetheless," I said, "Julie's no liar."

As I told Alex about Julie's encounter with Maureen Gault, we didn't break our stride, but when I repeated Maureen's line about knowing where the Seven Dwarfs had hidden their skeleton, Alex stopped abruptly. In the street light, I saw that his expression was all cop. "Did she elaborate?"

"No, that's not her style. Julie's the surgical-strike-and-withdraw type. She's happy just to leave you standing there bleeding. But that's not the point. The point is I think Julie really believes she knows something. Look, Alex, tell me if I'm getting into an area you can't talk about, but when you were investigating all of us, did you find anything really questionable?"

In the light his face was unreadable. "Was there something to find?"

"I don't know," I said.

"This case isn't over, Joanne. There are things I can't talk about with you." He took both my hands in his and turned me towards the light so he could see my face. "Do you understand?" he asked. "There are things you're better off not knowing."

I felt a chill. When I shivered, Alex Kequahtooway put his arm around my shoulder. We walked home that way, not talking but close. When we turned the corner onto my street, I pointed at my house. "Look," I said, "we're the only house without Christmas lights. I guess I'd better get out my ladder tomorrow."

"Do you need somebody to hold it steady?"

"Are you volunteering?"

"I guess I am."

"You're on," I said. "Is 9:00 tomorrow morning too early? My son's coming home from university around lunchtime. He puts up the lights every year; it would be great if they were blazing when he pulled in."

"Nine's fine," he said.

We were standing in front of my door. "Do you want to come in for a drink?"

"No, thanks," he said. "Nine o'clock comes early."

"I had a good time tonight," I said.

Alex Kequahtooway reached out and touched my cheek. "So did I." Then his face grew serious. "Be careful, Joanne. Don't take any chances."

I unlocked the front door. "Don't worry," I said, "I'm a very prudent person."

CHAPTER

12

Saturday morning I woke up to the radio weatherman telling us we were in for a record-warm December 5. "Get out the sunscreen, folks," he said. I looked out my bedroom window. Maybe not sunscreen weather, but there were patches of dark ground beneath the melting snow, and I could hear water dripping off the eaves. When Alex came, his windbreaker was open, and Angus refused to wear a coat at all.

"Somehow, when I envisioned this, I thought we'd all be rosy-cheeked in our toques and ski-jackets," I said.

Angus shook his head. "Dream on, Mum."

Alex and I put the lights on the house while Angus and Taylor did the trees. When we were through, Taylor brought her pumpkin out and placed it on top of the painted cream can I was going to fill with pine boughs and red velvet bows. She smiled at Alex. "Can you light him up, too?"

Alex looked at me questioningly. I nodded. "It can be done," he said, and he threaded the lights expertly through the pumpkin.

"Good job," Taylor said approvingly.

"You'd be amazed at the things they teach us at the police college," he said.

Angus ran in the house and turned on the lights, and the four of us stood on the soggy lawn assessing our handiwork. In the rotting snow, the lights looked like decorations for a used-car lot, and there was no denying that Jack was more battle-scarred than ever.

"I think my Hallmark Christmas just went down the dumper," I said.

"Let it go," Alex said. "We'll come up with something better."

I smiled at him. I liked the sound of that *we*.

We had an early lunch because Alex was on duty at noon. Peter drove up just as he was leaving. As I saw Peter pull up out front, I tried to think how his old green Volvo would look to someone who hadn't known it as long as we all had. Rust had eaten serious holes in the car's body, and the trunk was tied shut with a piece of rope, but the home-made canoe rack on top was still in A-1 shape. I turned to Alex. "As a cop, are you are obligated to do something about a car like Veronica?"

He pointed towards the Volvo. "That's Veronica?"

"Peter's pride and joy," I said.

Peter came, and after the hugs and the introductions, Alex pointed to the canoe rack.

"You enjoy the water?"

Pete grinned. "Sure, but I don't have a boat. That thing just came with the car. It seems kinda pointless to take it off."

Alex nodded in agreement. "Who knows? One day you might get a kayak or something."

Pete's grin grew even wider. "Exactly," he said, and he shot me a look of triumph. I had never been a fan of that canoe rack.

Angus and Taylor came out and hauled Pete into the house to show off the cat and see if he'd brought them anything. Alex watched their retreating backs thoughtfully. "Nice kids," he said.

"Thanks," I said. "I was afraid that between Peter's car and Taylor's superannuated pumpkin you'd be ready to write us off by now."

He shook his head. "Actually the car is pretty much like most of the cars I had when I was a kid, and Taylor's pumpkin looks like my captain." His words were casual, but when he turned to me, his dark eyes were grave. "Are you planning to stay pretty close to home today?"

"I've got our TV panel at 6:30. Till then, I hadn't planned much beyond visiting with Pete and getting ready for the show."

"Good," he said.

"Is something wrong?" I asked.

"I don't know," he said, "but it never hurts to be careful."

Our topic that night was changes in the delivery of the health-care system, and I spent the afternoon catching up on Peter's news and rereading my notes. It was a subject I was up on, but the questions viewers called in were quirky sometimes, and I wanted to be prepared. As Alex said, "it never hurts to be careful."

We ate early, and I was at Nationtv by 6:00. I had trouble finding a parking place. When I got to the entrance I remembered why. There was huge fir tree in the middle of the galleria, and the area around it was filled with people. I spotted Jill at the far end of the room, talking to a cluster of technical people who were watching a choir arrange themselves on a makeshift stage. When Jill saw me, she gave one final instruction to the camera people and came over.

She was wearing a dark green silk skirt and a matching blouse covered in Christmas roses. In her ears were gold drop earrings which, on closer inspection, turned out to be reindeers.

"You look like the spirit of Christmas," I said.

"Thank you," she said. "I'd like to find the fuckhead vice-president who came up with this community tree-lighting idea. Do you know the network's doing this all across Canada? Coast to coast, people are jumping in their cars so they can come down to their local Nationtv station, hang their trinket on our tree, and get a glass of warm apple juice and a dead doughnut. And people like me are trying to figure out where we're gonna find the money to pay all our technical people time-and-a-half. Do you know what I was doing when you came? Setting up to re-shoot a segment because a little girl in the front row of the choir peed herself in the middle of 'Frosty the Snowman.' She didn't even stop singing. The cameramen noticed it dripping off the edge of the stage."

I started to laugh.

"It's not funny, Jo," she said. Then she started to laugh, too. "Well, maybe it is funny, but a real friend wouldn't have laughed. Come on, let's go downstairs. We can run through the show when you're in makeup."

After I was made up, Jill and I walked onto the set. I sat in my place, and Leslie Martin came over and clipped my microphone on my jacket. She was wearing dark green tights, a red and white striped jerkin, and a red stocking cap with a jingle bell on the end.

"Do you get time-and-a-half for being an elf?" I asked.

"You bet your boots! And guess whose boyfriend is getting a Nordic Track for Christmas." Leslie flashed me a grin that was far too lascivious for one of Santa's helpers. "I can hardly wait to rub up against those sculptured pectorals."

Through my earpiece I could hear Jill's voice. "I was just talking to Keith," she said. "I think he and the lady lobbyist must have had a falling out. He says he's coming home for Christmas, and he wonders if you'd take it amiss if he asked you for dinner."

"I wouldn't take it amiss," I said, "but I may have other plans. I've met somebody else . . ."

"Do tell," she said.

I started. Then the monitor picked up Sam Spiegel in Ottawa, the director began counting down, and we were on the air.

It was a good show. Keith outlined the more provocative proposals for revamping the American health-care delivery system, and Sam and I talked about some of the initiatives the provinces were taking at home. There were the usual ideological flare-ups about who had the right to expect what from whom, but we were spirited rather than vicious, and when the phone-in segment started, the callers seemed, for once, to be more interested in light than heat. The questions were fair and perceptive, and I relaxed and enjoyed myself. Sixty seconds before the end of the show, I was half-listening to Sam talk about wellness models, when the moderator in Toronto said, "Time for one more quick question. Go ahead, Jenny from Vermilion Hills, Saskatchewan, you're on the air."

I heard the woman's voice. "Help me," it said. And that was all it said. I looked over to Jill in the control booth; she was rolling her eyes back in a "what next" way. In Toronto, the moderator was signing off. We all said goodnight, and the light on the camera went dark.

I unclipped my microphone and went into the control booth. "Who was that last caller?" I asked.

"Crank or prankster, take your pick." Jill said.

"Can you check with Toronto and see if they got that woman's last name?" I asked.

Jill shrugged and punched a button. "Toronto, did you get a surname on that last caller? Okay. Yeah, we do know how to grow them out here. Thanks." She looked up at me. "No surname," she said. "Just Jenny, from Vermilion Hills, Saskatchewan. Never heard of it," she added.

"I have," I said. "Can you find out who cut off the call?"

Jill asked, then turned back to me. "They cut her off in Toronto."

"Thanks," I said.

I didn't stop to take off my makeup. I grabbed my coat from the hook in the green room and ran upstairs and across the crowded lobby. On the stage, another children's choir was singing, and a group of little kids was sitting on the floor around the tree stringing popcorn and cranberries. Jenny's phone call seemed to be a cry from a different world. I was so preoccupied, I didn't notice the man at the reception desk until it was too late. I ran straight into him. When he turned, I saw that the man was Paschal Temple.

As soon as he recognized me, his face lit up with pleasure. "I was just watching you over there on the television. With all this crowd, I couldn't hear too well, but you looked very pretty. Well, this is good luck. I was just leaving something for you."

"Did you come down here just to see me?" I asked.

"No, I'm killing two birds with one stone. We brought Lolita's choir down to be on TV." He gestured to a children's choir just coming off the stage. "They're so excited. Me too. Watching how they make a TV show was fun. Anyway, I'm sure you're busy, so just let me give you my little package. It's poor Kevin's Bible. The warden gave it to me because he knew it had come from me originally." He opened the Bible and took out a folded piece of paper. "I would never have thought to give the Bible to you, but when I looked inside, I found this, and I remembered you were interested in it."

He handed me the Bible. I took it and unfolded the paper. It was a photocopy of the Biblical Character Building Chart that Paschal had shown me the night I'd gone to Bread of Life Tabernacle. Kevin had printed his name in capital letters on the top of the page and he'd printed pairs of letters beside some of the biblical passages that dealt with character-destroying qualities. The letters printed next to the notation for Wilful Blindness were my initials, JK; the biblical reference was to Psalm 146, the verse Kevin had sent me. I checked the other letters. Kevin's own initials appeared beside the entries for Cowardice and Impurity. The initials MT were printed beside Pride and Falsehood. Maureen had received a letter too. There was a final set of initials, but this one didn't have a character-destroying quality listed next to it. There was just a biblical reference.

Paschal Temple was watching me closely.

"Do you know what Exodus 20:13 is?" I asked.

His eyes were grave. "It's the sixth Commandment: Thou shalt not commit murder."

"Thank you," I said. "Look, I'm sorry. I have to leave. It's an emergency."

"Can I be of any help?"

I shook my head. Then I changed my mind. "You could add me to your prayer list," I said, and I started for the door.

There were still cars coming into the parking lot behind Nationtv. A van waited as I pulled out of my spot, and it squeezed in as soon as I was clear. When I nosed out onto the street, I saw the silver Audi in my rear-view mirror. It was coming out of the parking lot behind me, and I had a pretty good idea now who was driving it. Suddenly, I was icily calm. I drove carefully along the streets that I knew would be fully lighted. When I got home, I used the electronic eye and drove straight into the carport. I used the door between the carport and the kitchen to get inside. When I was safely in the house, I leaned against the kitchen door and closed my eyes. So far, so good. Upstairs in the family room, I could hear the sound of the television and of Taylor and the boys laughing. I dialled the number of the Regina police.

"Inspector Kequahtooway, please."

There was silence. Then a click, and a woman's voice.

"Inspector Kequahtooway is not on duty. Can someone else help you?"

"No," I said. "Do you have his home number?"

"We can't give out home numbers, ma'am."

"Right," I said, and I hung up and dialled Craig Evanson's number.

He answered, sounding breathless and excited. "We're on our way to the hospital, Jo. The baby's coming. Manda's contractions are five minutes apart."

"Craig, I won't keep you. I just need to get some directions. When you guys went hunting in the Vermilion Hills, you stayed in a cabin. I need to know how to get there."

As Craig gave me the directions, I sketched a quick map. My icy calm was starting to melt. I was scared, and I didn't want to leave anything to chance. I stuck the map in my purse, went up to my room, and changed out of my TV clothes into blue jeans, a sweater, and boots. I might have to move quickly, and I wanted to be ready. I walked down the hall to the family room. Taylor and the boys were watching *Blazing Saddles*. It was the beans-around-the-campfire scene, and Taylor was roaring.

"Pete, I need your car keys," I said.

"They're in my jacket pocket," he said. "Can I use your car?"

"No," I said. "Not tonight. Stick close to home, would you?"

Peter looked up from the screen. "You look kind of intense. Are you okay?"

"I'm fine," I said, and I hoped I sounded more certain than I felt.

I walked back upstairs and down the hall to the front door. Through the window, I could see the silver Audi parked down the street about half a block. It had started to rain, and the pavement looked slick. Peter's jacket was hanging on the coat-rack. I found the keys, then I looked again at the jacket. It was an Eddie Bauer, rainproof, with a hood I could pull over my head. I put the jacket on. When I pulled up the hood, it covered the sides of my face. Peter's book-bag was on the floor, and I picked it up and slung it over my shoulder. The empty book-bag gave me an idea. I went back up to my room, pulled the box of Jenny's mementoes out from under the bed and slipped it into the book-bag. Downstairs, I checked my reflection in the hall mirror. In the dark and with my head down, I could pass for Pete. At least that's what I was hoping.

There was no point in delaying. I opened the front door and ran towards Pete's car. I didn't look in the direction of the Audi until I got to the corner of Albert Street. When I checked my rear-view mirror, the Audi was right where I left it, and I sighed with relief.

Regina's streets were busy, but there weren't many cars on the Trans-Canada. It was 8:30 on a Saturday night, three weeks before Christmas. People had places to be; no one would be driving in this strange winter rain storm unless they had to.

The rain. If the temperature dropped five degrees, the highway would be lethal. But, as my grandmother used to say, there's no point jumping off a bridge till you come to it. I tested Veronica's brakes a couple of times. They held. For better or for worse, I was on my way, and I had to think about what I was going to do when I got there.

I tried to formulate a plan. The objective was clear enough: I had to get Jenny out. It was the obstacles that were shadowy. I didn't know what I'd be walking into. Jenny had been able to phone. That meant she was alone. But if she was alone, why hadn't she run away? I couldn't get the pieces to fit.

As I drove onto the overpass by Belle Plaine, the car started to make a gasping sound. I looked at the gas gauge, and uttered an expletive my grandmother would not have approved of. The needle was hovering a hair's breadth away from empty. I patted the dashboard. "Come on, Veronica," I said, "Pete says you're one hot car. You can do this. You can make it." She continued to climb, but she was coughing badly. I tried to visualize the highway ahead. Chubby's Café and Gas Station was along here somewhere, but where? The rain continued to fall. The car continued to cough. Then, from the top of the overpass, I could see a fuzz of light on the right-hand side of the road. "Please let that be Chubby's," I said as Veronica coasted down the overpass onto the highway.

I was in luck. The café was less than a kilometre down the road, and Veronica made it right to the tanks before she coughed her last. Chubby himself filled her up. When he'd finished, I gave him my credit card and showed him my map.

"I have to get down there tonight," I said. "Do you know of a shortcut I could take?"

He took the map between his thumb and forefinger and walked inside where there was light. I thought I had never seen a human being move so slowly. When he came back, he handed me my credit card and the map.

"No shortcut, not in this weather," he said. "Just stay on the highway till you see the sodium sulphate plant." He gave me my credit card. "Jeez, just a minute, I forgot something," he said, then he turned and lumbered heavily towards the bright lights of the café. When he came out, he reached through the window. "Merry Christmas," he said, and he handed me a candy cane.

"Same to you," I said. I finished the candy cane just as I came to the turnoff for the Vermilion Hills. As soon as I hit the grid road, I knew I was in trouble. The car started to fishtail on the wet gravel, and by the time I straightened it, I could feel the sweat running down my back.

There was no consolation when I looked up into the hills. In the spring, the Vermilion Hills are as beautiful as their name. In the summer, they're alive with wildflowers. But in the winter, stripped of the softness of grass and flower, they are primordial and terrifying. That night, as I followed the hairpin curves of the dark road that took me into their heart, I was engulfed by a fear that seemed as atavistic as it was intense. Then, out of nowhere, a deer leapt across the road ahead of me, and I felt the fear lift. I wasn't alone.

I held the map up to the light on the dashboard. I was almost there. A kilometre farther, I saw the yard-light of the cabin glowing dimly in the dark and the mist. I pulled onto the shoulder of the road, and began to walk. I wasn't sure who was in the cabin, but there didn't seem to be much point in announcing myself.

The rain was cool on my face, and the air was fresh. I took some deep breaths. "I'm coming, Jenny," I said, and I felt strong and clear-headed. I stood for a moment, getting my bearings. The cabin was set back about a hundred metres from the road. It was isolated. The last lights I'd seen had been fifteen kilometres back. This was short-grass country, and there weren't many trees around, but there was a wind-break of what looked like caraganas on the north side of the cabin. It would be a place to run if I needed one.

I could feel the adrenalin rush as I started for the cabin. The curtains were pulled tight, but as I moved closer I could hear music inside; it sounded like a radio or a TV. I told myself it was Lolita Temple's choir and that, if they were singing, nothing bad could happen to me.

I went to the front door and knocked. For a moment, the only sound was the music, then I heard someone coming towards me. When the door opened, I was facing Tess Malone.

"I knew you'd come for Jenny," she said.

"Where is she?" I asked.

"Dead," Tess said, and she turned away from me.

"But the phone call . . ."

Tess looked ghastly. Her hair, always so carefully sprayed in place, had come loose. In fact, it seemed as if everything about her had come loose. Behind the thick lenses of her glasses, Tess's blue eyes always seemed perceptive, but this night she wasn't wearing her glasses, and her eyes looked unfocussed. Even her body looked slack and shapeless.

"What happened to Jenny?" I said.

"She changed her mind," Tess said.

On the television, a child began to sing "The Little Drummer Boy." I glanced towards the set, hoping to see the familiar images of the Nationtv Christmas party, but the picture on the screen of the old black and white TV was so fuzzy, all I could make out was the shape of the singing child. It was a slender reed to cling to.

Tess went over and turned the sound down, then she started back towards the couch. She moved slowly. There was an open fireplace, with a roaring fire, and the room was stiflingly hot, but she pulled an afghan around herself.

"Tess, you've got to tell me what's going on here."

She lowered herself onto the couch. Beside it, there was a metal TV table. On it were the leftovers from a frozen dinner, an overflowing ashtray, and two packs of du Mauriers. Tess reached for a cigarette and lit it. I took the ashtray to the fireplace and dumped it, and came back to her.

"There's a bottle of rye over there," Tess said.

"Forget the rye," I said. "We have to get out of here."

She dragged deeply on her cigarette. "I'm in more danger out there than I am here. Get the rye, Jo. I'm tired of secrets. I want to talk."

"Tess, we have to go to the police. I don't think you understand everything that's happened."

When I told her about Julie's dark reference to a skeleton and the initials opposite the sixth Commandment on Kevin's list, Tess sagged, and when she spoke, her voice was small. "It isn't the way you think it is," she murmured.

"Then it's true."

"Yes, but . . . Jo, please let me tell you what happened."

"Tess, are we safe here?"

She laughed. It wasn't a nice laugh. "As safe as anyone is anywhere." She gestured towards the whisky. "Please, Jo."

I picked up the rye. There were no clean glasses. I took a dipper of water from the corner, rinsed two of the cleaner glasses, and poured rye into them.

I took a sip of my whisky. The warmth helped. "Okay," I said, "start talking."

Tess pulled her afghan tight around her. "How does Julie find out these things?"

I shook my head. "It doesn't matter. All that matters is that Julie's information was right. What happened to Jenny Rybchuk, Tess?"

"She died. It was six years ago, Jo, and it wasn't a murder – at least not the part we were involved in. It was an accident. A terrible, terrible accident."

"What are you talking about, 'the part we were involved in'?"

Tess went on as if she hadn't heard me. "It should never have happened," she said. "Everything was going so well. Jess was a perfect baby. Gary and Sylvie were there when he was born, did you know that?"

I shook my head.

"They were the most beautiful family. Jane and I went out to the airport when they brought the baby home. They were so happy. We thought Jenny was happy, too. It seemed as if everything had just fallen into place. Jenny had been writing to her father all summer. He hated having her away from him, but the plant had laid him off because of his drinking. He was having serious money problems, and he was relieved Jenny was paying her own way. Jess was born the first week in September, so Jenny was able to visit her father in Chaplin before she started university in Saskatoon. Everything went off like clockwork . . ." Her voice trailed off, and her eyes were remote.

"Except . . . ," I prompted.

Tess's voice was filled with pain. "Except Jenny couldn't forget her son. She started phoning Sylvie and Gary. At first, they didn't mind; in fact, I think they were pleased that she cared so deeply about his welfare. They told her about how much weight Jess was gaining and what he was doing, but no matter how much they told her, it was never enough. She hungered for her child, Joanne. It was that simple. Nothing could satisfy her but having him back. When the calls got truly desperate, Sylvie asked me to go to Saskatoon and talk to Jenny."

"And you went?" I asked.

"Of course I went, Jo. I was responsible." She spit out the last word with loathing.

"You tried to do the right thing," I said weakly.

"That doesn't exempt me from responsibility," she said, and, for the first time that evening, there was something of the old Tess in her voice. "Intention doesn't count, Jo. Just results. And the results of what I had done to Jenny Rybchuk were devastating. She wasn't the same girl I'd seen in Regina. She was thin and ill and driven. She said she had made a terrible mistake, and I had to help her get Jess back."

Tess lit a fresh cigarette off the stub of her first one. She dragged deeply and coughed till the tears came.

"Jo, I was so cruel to her. I told her she'd made an agreement, that life was about choices, and that Sylvie and Gary could give Jess a far better life than she could dream of. I said it was time for her to face facts, and walk away from the past.

"Until I die, I'll never forget the look of betrayal in that girl's eyes. Do you know what she said to me?" Tess's voice broke. "She said, 'You're the one who told me a baby isn't just a collection of cells a woman can walk away from.' After that, there was nothing more I could say except goodbye. I turned my back on her, Jo. It was a terrible abnegation of responsibility, and a fatal one."

I could hardly bring myself to say the words. "Tess, Jenny didn't commit suicide, did she?"

Tess's laugh was bitter. "No, she didn't commit suicide. God forgive me, maybe it would have been better if she had."

"What happened?"

"She went to the baby's father, and asked him to help her." Tess looked toward the fire. Finally, she said, "The father was Kevin Tarpley."

"Kevin Tarpley," I repeated stupidly. "I don't understand."

"There's nothing to understand. It was just one of those sad, stupid things. Maureen and her mother were visiting relatives for Christmas. Kevin was supposed to keep an eye on their house. You know, make sure the furnace was on and the pipes didn't burst. Apparently, one night during the holidays, Henry Rybchuk got drunk and started in on Jenny. She ran next door, and Kevin just happened to be there."

"But when Jenny found out she was pregnant, she didn't tell Kevin."

"No. She didn't tell him until I turned her away. That was at the end of November. A week later, Gary called. Someone had taken Jess from his carriage on the porch of their house. Sylvie was in Toronto making arrangements for a show. Gary said they put Jess in the same spot every afternoon because it was protected, and he thrived on all the fresh air and sunshine. That day he'd only been out for a few minutes. Gary was pretty sure Jenny must have been watching the house. She'd left a note, saying she knew that legally she still had time to change her mind, and she had. She wrote that she was sorry and she would be in touch.

"We didn't hear a word about Jess till the next day at noon. I wanted to call the police, but Gary was sure Jenny would come to her senses. We knew the baby was safe. There was that at least, but the wait was still terrible. Sylvie and Gary had wanted a child for so long. Gary and I sat in the living room and talked about Jess and all the plans they'd had for him . . . It was like a death . . . There was that sense of loss, and the feeling that nothing would ever be the same again.

"And then at noon, the phone rang . . ."

"Jenny kept her word," I said.

Tess picked up the bottle of rye and half filled her glass. "No," she said, "it wasn't Jenny. It was Maureen Gault."

CHAPTER

13

"I thought we'd been delivered from hell," Tess said. "Maureen Gault introduced herself as Jenny's best friend, and she said Jenny was ready to talk. You can imagine how desperate Gary was to get Jess back before Sylvie came home. From the time Sylvie and Gary realized it was unlikely they'd ever have a child, their marriage had pretty much been a disaster."

"Gary's promiscuity didn't help," I said, and I found it hard even to say his name.

"Sylvie wasn't blameless, Jo. She was so angry at Gary for failing her. People do strange things when they're hurting. But she was crazy about Jess, and Gary was counting on him to give them a new start."

"That's a pretty heavy burden for a baby."

Tess nodded her head in agreement. "It is, but Jess seemed to make everything right just by existing. Gary asked me to go with him when he met Jenny. I think he was afraid of dealing with her by himself. You know how Gary's always been about confrontation. I dreaded going, but I'd failed Jenny so badly in our last meeting that I felt I owed her some support. And, Jo, you have to believe me. When we drove out here, I was certain everything was going to work out."

"You came here?" I asked.

"Maureen said Jenny needed a private place to say goodbye to her son. Gary suggested his cabin. Hunting season had just opened, and Gary had been out to the cabin the week before. And since they'd be coming from Chaplin . . ."

"Why would they be coming from Chaplin?"

Tess sighed. "Because, according to Maureen, Jenny wanted to show Henry Rybchuk his grandson before she gave him up forever."

"But he didn't know Jenny had a baby."

Tess's voice was sharp with exasperation. "I know the story is full of holes, but don't forget, all this happened before we knew Maureen Gault. When she said Jenny had told her father about the baby, we had no reason to doubt her. The truth is we wanted to believe her. Anyway, the plan was that, after they'd seen old Mr. Rybchuk, Maureen and Jenny would drive back from Chaplin and meet us at the cabin."

I stood up to take off my jacket. The room was oppressively hot, and I could feel my shirt sticking to my back. "Tess, could I open a window? I'm dying in here."

She shivered, but she nodded. "I've had this flu."

I looked at her. Her skin had an unhealthy sheen, and her lips looked dry and cracked.

"I think I should drive you into Chaplin to the doctor," I said.

Her eyes grew wide with fear. "No doctors. No police, I told you."

"All right," I said, "but I'm going to stay here with you tonight. Just let me call and tell my family I'm okay."

I went to the phone and dialled our number. As the phone was ringing, I looked around the cabin. I'd asked Ian once what it was like. He'd laughed and said, "I think you have to

have a certain testosterone level to appreciate its charms."
The cabin was shabby, in fact, but comfortable looking. One
end of the large main room was obviously used as the living
area. In front of the old sectional couch where Tess huddled,
shivering beneath an incongruously cheerful afghan, there
was a coffee table scarred by cigarette burns and rings from
a score of drink glasses. The couch was on one side of a big
stone fireplace, and a couple of over-stuffed easy chairs were
on the other. The far end of the room was an eating area with
a small refrigerator, a stove, and a painted wooden table and
chairs. On the same side as the kitchen, there was a door to
what must have been a bedroom. The main room was pan-
elled in some dark wood. There were pictures of hunting
dogs on one wall, and a number of hunting rifles mounted
in racks on the wall by the door. I recognized one of them, a
small 30-30 bush gun. Peter had militated unsuccessfully for
a rifle like that the Christmas he was fifteen. I was remembering all the ads from hunting magazines that had littered
our house that year, when Pete answered the phone. He
sounded drowsy.

"It's me," I said. "Peter, did I wake you up?"

"It's okay, Mum. I was watching *Barbarella*. I must have
nodded off after Jane Fonda melted the cables on Duran
Duran's sex machine." He yawned. "What's going on?
Inspector Kequahtooway was here looking for you. He seemed
pretty worked up when I said you'd gone out."

"If he comes back, tell him I had to go out to the Vermilion
Hills."

"The Vermilion Hills. What's out there?"

"An old friend in trouble," I said. "Look. I'll explain when
I get home. Get the kids off to church tomorrow morning,
would you?"

"Does that mean I have to go with them?"

"Of course," I said. "How else would they get there? Goodnight, Pete, and thanks. I'm glad you're home."

I found a towel, poured some water from the dipper onto it, sat beside Tess, and wiped her face. "Do you have aspirin or anything here? You're burning up, Tess."

She shook her head. "I'm all right. Just let me finish. I can't hold on to this any more."

I opened the window on the other side of the room a crack, and took a breath. "Okay, Tess," I said. "I'm listening."

She pulled the afghan closer. "Maureen Gault had lied to everyone. Jenny had no intention of giving up that baby. She'd brought Jess to the cabin so Sylvie and Gary could say goodbye to him. She really was a very sweet girl."

"Was," I repeated numbly. It was hard to think of Jenny Rybchuk in the past tense. My chest tightened. I didn't want to hear the end of the story.

Oblivious, Tess went on. "That was the first time I met Maureen Gault. She was terrifying. She'd created all this confusion and misery, and she didn't care. Jo, it was as if the pain charged her up, filled her with energy. She couldn't sit still. She kept moving around the room with this little smile on her face. Gary and Jenny were over where you are, by the window, and I was sitting on a chair close to the fireplace. It was December; the cabin was chilly, and I'd moved the chair so the baby would be warm."

Tess covered her mouth with her hand as if she wanted physically to block the words she was about to say.

"It happened so fast. When he realized Jenny planned to keep Jess, Gary said something ugly to her. She looked so hurt. I remember thinking she looked like a child who'd been punished for no reason. Then she came towards me to get the baby. Gary pushed her. Jo, I know he didn't mean to hurt her. He was just trying to get to Jess, but Jenny lost her balance. There was a sheepskin rug on the hearth. She slipped on it and fell against the fireplace."

Tess pointed towards a long piece of fieldstone at the edge of the mantel. "That caught her in the temple. Gary went to help her up. I was furious with him. I said something like 'Now look you what you've done,' but, Jo, I thought she'd just fallen. Then Gary turned her over, and I saw her eyes." Tess's own eyes were dark with horror.

"The sheepskin underneath her head was soaked with blood. I couldn't move. Gary looked as if he was paralyzed, too. I guess we were both in shock. But Maureen Gault wasn't. She walked over to the fireplace and picked up a poker that was leaning against the hearth. Then she said, 'You shouldn't have fucked my guy, Jenny,' and she raised the poker and smashed it down on Jenny's head."

I closed my eyes. I knew what Jenny's head must have looked like after Maureen Gault was through with her.

Tess was crying now. "When she was done, Maureen went over and put her arm around Gary. She said, 'From now on, when you look at that sweet baby of yours, remember that if Little Mo hadn't taken charge, little Jess would be long gone.'

"All I could think of was getting the baby out of that room. I took him into the bedroom and closed the door. I stayed there all night. Gary came in once, for a sheet. They needed it to wrap Jenny's body. I remember I heard the door to the outside open, and a car drove out. When I was sure they were gone, I went into the living room and got Jess's baby bag. There was a bottle of formula in it, and I fed him. I was back in the bedroom when I heard them drive in. After a while, I smelled wool burning. I guess that was the sheepskin. Finally, it was over. Gary came in and we drove home."

Tess looked at me in wonder. "Jo, you won't believe this, but Maureen Gault stood on the porch and waved to us when we left."

I walked over to the counter, picked up the rye bottle, and poured some into my glass. When I turned to ask Tess if she wanted some whisky, I saw that she'd closed her eyes. She was either sleeping or pretending to sleep. It didn't matter. I'd heard enough.

I turned off the overhead light. The room was stifling. I pulled my chair back and opened the window an inch more. I could see Pete's book-bag by the door where I'd dropped it. The flap had fallen open, and I could see the corner of the box of mementoes I'd brought for Jenny. I breathed in the fresh night air and tried to think of nothing. After a few minutes, I heard the sound of Tess's breathing, deep and rhythmic.

I couldn't sleep. I stared at the fire for what seemed like hours, thinking about my husband and about the dancing ballerinas on the box that contained all that was left of Jenny Rybchuk's life. And I thought about Maureen Gault with her arm raised and her derisive smile. Finally, exhausted, I must have drifted off.

It was the cold air that awakened me. I'd been dreaming about the cabin, and the rifles on the wall, and a ballerina who came in and said Anton Chekhov believed that if there was a gun on the wall in Act I, it had to be fired by the end of Act III.

At first, when I opened my eyes and saw Gary Stephens standing in front of me, I thought I was still dreaming. He was wearing a wide-brimmed rancher's hat and a yellow slicker, and he looked like the kind of mythic figure who would appear in a dream. Then I saw the rifle in his hands, and I knew this was real. I looked at the place on the wall where the rifles were hanging. The rack where the small bush gun had been was empty. It took me a minute to put it all together, but when I did, I knew Act III had begun.

Gary was looking at me intently. "Sylvie said the cops were over tonight asking questions. I thought I'd better get out here and make sure Tess was all right."

"She's all right," I said. "Put down the gun, Gary. I don't think you're in much danger from two unarmed women."

He lay the gun on the window sill beside him. It was still in easy reach, but at least it wasn't pointed at me. Gary moved closer. "What did Tess tell you?"

"Everything," I said.

"You've got to hear my side of it, babe."

Suddenly I was furious. "I think I've already figured out your side of it . . . *babe*. I know what you've done. I just don't understand how you could do it."

His voice was both seductive and pleading. "Then listen to how it was for me. Please, Jo. Please." He paused. "For old times' sake."

"All right, Gary," I said. "I'll listen. For old times' sake."

He arranged his face into an expression of boyish sincerity. "I appreciate the chance, Jo. I really do." He took a deep breath. "None of it would have happened if Sylvie and I had been able to have kids. I know how you love your family, so you must understand it was a pretty hard thing for me to accept."

The narcissism grated. "So you coped," I said, "by having sex with every woman in sight, including your own sister-in-law, and by stealing a young woman's baby?"

He flinched. "All right, all right," he said. "I was a bastard, but Sylvie was no prize. She wouldn't stop talking about my problem – it was my problem, you know. Anyway, Sylvie wouldn't stop discussing it. It was the same thing every night. Finally, I just stopped coming home. Then, heartbroken but brave, my wife threw herself into her photography. She went down to Chaplin and shot *Prairiegirl*. That pretty well fucked up my political career. Then when she got tired of being the martyr, she decided our marriage was over, and she wanted a divorce."

"My God, if you hated Sylvie that much, why did you want to stay with her?" I asked.

"Because as lousy it was, it was the only life I had. Jo, what else was I supposed to do? When I was in politics, I'd pretty much let my law practice slide. After my wife's book came out, I didn't have much future in politics. Sylvie had all that money. It didn't make much sense to walk away from it." He shrugged. "I don't know. Maybe I just didn't think it through. But it seemed possible that, if Sylvie had a baby, we could go on the way we had for years, leading separate lives."

"But not lives paid for by separate cheques," I said.

"No," he said. "There were no separate cheques."

"So Jess was just an investment in your future."

He looked down at his hands. "Maybe, at first," he said softly. "But Jo, you've got to believe me. From the minute I saw Jess, everything changed. I held him when he was just seconds old. I think that was first moment in my life when I knew what people meant when they talked about loving someone. It was the best feeling I've ever known. But it didn't last." His beautiful blue eyes clouded with pain. "After Jenny passed away, it was hard for me even to be in the same room with Jess. I know how things look, Jo, but I'm not a monster. Every time I looked at my son, I could see Jenny's face. I'd try to block out the memories by getting drunk or by screwing some broad I hardly knew, but no matter what I did, I couldn't forget that night. I've suffered, too, Jo. I love Jess so much, but I can't hold him in my arms without remembering . . ."

As he always was when he talked about his son, Gary Stephens was transformed, and, for a moment, I felt myself responding to him. Then I remembered.

"Ian loved his children, too," I said.

He looked at me defiantly. "It wasn't my fault, Jo. Ian was the one who wouldn't leave it alone. That night at the party he told me he'd talked to Rybchuk, and he believed Rybchuk was telling the truth, that something had happened to Jenny. Ian said it didn't make sense that Jenny would say she was going to start a new life with her son, then disappear. I tried to tell him Jenny had probably just changed her mind, but he wouldn't listen. The old man had given him a picture of Jenny with Jess, and Ian was going to take it to the police." For a beat, Gary was silent. Then, in a voice full of wonder, he said, "Ian was always such a fucking boy scout."

"And the only way to stop the boy scout was to pay Maureen Gault to kill him," I said.

Gary recoiled as if I'd hit him. "For chrissakes, Jo. He was my friend. I would never have asked anyone to murder him. All I did was tell Maureen Gault that Ian was going to be a problem. What happened later wasn't my fault."

"The Becket defence," I said.

Gary's handsome face was blank. "I don't know what you're talking about."

"Didn't you ever study the Becket defence in law school, Gary? It was on the ethics course." I stood up and began moving towards him. "Since you seem to have forgotten anything you ever knew about ethics, I'll help you out.

"It's an old case, and it explores the question of culpability. A king is having trouble with a priest who was once his friend but who's begun meddling in things the king doesn't want meddled with. The king calls in four of his most loyal knights and says, 'Will no one rid me of that meddlesome priest?' You'll notice he's careful not to instruct them to do anything wrong, but the knights aren't stupid. They know what the king wants, so they kill the priest. The king, of course, is innocent. It's the knights who did the dirty work.

They're the guilty ones. Or are they?" I stepped closer to him. "What do you think, babe? Who's culpable here?"

Gary reached over and picked up his gun. "I'm not guilty of Ian's murder, Jo. The others were just a waste of skin. They deserved to die. But Ian was my, my friend."

On the couch, Tess was stirring.

I raised my voice to awaken her. "Gary, when you told Maureen Gault, 'Ian is going to be a problem,' you knew what you were doing. How much did you have to pay her to get her to kill him?"

He laughed. "You can't know much about Maureen Gault to ask a question like that. Killing was a pleasure for her. When I called her the night of the caucus party and told her Ian was going to the cops, she had a plan worked out before I hung up. All I had to do was drive her to Swift Current. She said she'd find Ian at the funeral, get a ride back to Regina with him, and talk him out of going to the police."

I could feel the rage rising. "Gary, you knew she wouldn't just talk to him. You were in this very room when Maureen Gault smashed her best friend's head in with a poker. You knew what she was capable of."

He looked at me miserably. "I didn't mean for her to kill him. Can't you believe me?"

"No," I said, and my voice was thin with fury.

He took a step towards me. "I loved Ian," he said. "You know that. I loved him."

"No," I said.

His face seemed to crumple. Finally, he whispered, "Can you forgive me, Jo? You can, can't you?"

In the firelight, I could see the tears in his eyes, but I didn't pity him, and, for what seemed like a long time, I didn't answer him. When the words did come, they seemed to tear themselves from a part of me that was beyond reason.

"No!" I shouted. "No! No! No!"

As the final *no!* hung in the air, a strange sort of calm filled the room. Gary's eyes stayed fixed on mine, then a smile started to form at the corners of his mouth. As slowly as a man moving in a dream, he swung the muzzle of the gun under his chin. For one crazed moment I wondered if the gun was loaded. Then Gary pulled the trigger, and the world exploded.

The next minutes are a jumble. Tess crawled towards the place where Gary had fallen, and I think I went to the phone to call for help. I'm not sure. What I remember are the smells: the hot metal smell of the gun and the smoky smell of the fire and the sweet, fetid smell of blood. And I remember looking down at the body to see if anything at all was left of Gary Stephens's perfect face.

Then the front door opened, and Alex Kequahtooway was there. So were a lot of other cops. The nightmare was over.

It was close to dawn when Alex and I left the cabin. Minutes after the police arrived, a squad car had taken Tess back to the city. Alex had asked if I wanted to go with her, but I hadn't. I'd waited six years, and I wanted to see this through to the end. The forensic specialists were there within an hour, and I sat by the window and watched as they measured and took photographs and put evidence into bags. When they were finished, they left, too. A few minutes later, an ambulance arrived to take Gary Stephens's body back to Regina. I stood at the door as the attendants lifted Gary's body onto the stretcher and carried him outside. As the ambulance pulled onto the grid road and started towards the highway, I turned to Alex. "Is it over now?" I asked.

He nodded and picked up my jacket. I put it on, grabbed Peter's book-bag, and stepped onto the front porch. It was the morning of December 6, but it felt like a spring day. The air, cleansed by the winter rain, was warm on my face, and I could smell the earth.

I looked up towards the road. "Where's Veronica?" I said.

"I had one of the guys drive her back," he said. "I thought maybe you'd rather be a passenger this time out."

"Fair enough," I said.

"If you think you can eat, Chubby's Café makes great bacon and eggs."

"I can eat," I said.

"My car's over there," he said, pointing towards the stand of caraganas that had been planted as a windbreak. "Pretty snazzy for a cop, I know, but I've driven reserve cars all my life, and this was a present to me from me on my fortieth birthday."

"I've always wanted to ride in a silver Audi," I said.

He grinned. "Now's your chance."

When we got to the highway, I touched Alex's arm. "Can we stop for a minute? There's something I want to leave at the place where my husband died."

Alex pulled onto the shoulder. I opened the box of Jenny's mementoes, took out the photograph of her with Jess, and got out of the car. The gravel along the side of the highway was still wet from the rain. I knelt down and picked up a stone. It was smooth and cool to the touch. On Hallowe'en night, Hilda McCourt had told me about a poet who said sudden death spatters all we know of dénouement across the expedient and wicked stones. I walked further down the shoulder of the highway, picking up stones as I went. When my jacket pockets were full, I walked back to the place where Ian died and began arranging the stones in a circle. When the circle was complete, I put Jenny's picture in the middle and anchored its corners with stones. I tried to think of a prayer, but my mind was empty. Finally, I said, "I did the best I could," and I stood up. Bits of gravel stuck to the knees of my jeans, but I couldn't summon the energy to brush them off. Lightheaded from exhaustion and hunger, I started back to the Audi.

Alex leaned across to open the car door. "Unfinished business?" he asked.

I shook my head. "Not any more," I said. I snapped on my seatbelt, and Inspector Alex Kequahtooway and I drove east towards the rising sun and Chubby's Café.

CHAPTER

14

By the time Alex and I got back to Regina, the kids were up, dressed, and eating breakfast. The sun was pouring through the kitchen window, and Angus was describing an amazing shot his friend, Camilo, had made at basketball practice the day before. Peter was arguing that nobody but Shaquille O'Neal could make a shot like that. Taylor, who knew nothing about basketball but who was second to none in her admiration for Camilo Rostoker, was saying that Camilo could do anything. They seemed so free of care, that I hesitated before I came into the room. I knew I was bringing ugliness with me.

As soon as they saw me, the kids fell silent. I didn't blame them. At Chubby's, I'd seen my reflection in the mirror behind the counter. My skin was ashen, and my eyes were red-rimmed and swollen. At the café I had looked like a woman teetering on the edge of shock. I doubted that my appearance had improved much since then.

I started to explain what had happened back at the cabin, but I didn't get far before the horror overwhelmed me. Alex touched my shoulder. "It's too soon," he said. "Go upstairs and get some sleep. I'll tell them."

Safe in my room, I peeled off my clothes and bundled them into the laundry hamper. When I stepped into the shower, I turned the water to hot, closed my eyes, and tried to forget. Ten minutes later, the bathroom was thick with steam, the water coming out of the faucet was cold, and I hadn't forgotten a thing. As I towelled off and headed for bed, I was sick with the fear that the memory of Gary Stephens's suicide would be an albatross I would always carry with me. When I opened the door to my bedroom, I saw that the drapes had been pulled, the phone on my bedside table had been unplugged, and the bedspread had been turned down. Alex was sitting on the windowseat.

"Are you going to be okay?" he asked.

I nodded.

"Good," he said. "There are some things I should take care of down at headquarters, but I'll let the kids know where I'm going to be, and I'll be back around supper. Try to get some sleep."

I tried. All that day, I lay in the dark, listening to the life of my house go on around me, hushed and alien. Late in the afternoon, I opened my eyes and saw Alex standing in the doorway, his silhouette dark against the bright light of the hall.

"Do you want to talk?" he said.

"Not yet. You don't mind, do you?"

"I don't mind. I have to go back downtown, but there's take-out from Bamboo Village in the kitchen. Taylor made some pretty serious inroads on the almond prawns, but there's plenty of everything else."

"Thanks," I said.

"My pleasure," he said and closed the door.

After he left, I fell asleep. When I woke up, it was midnight and I was hungry. I remembered the Chinese take-out and headed downstairs. Sadie and Rose were right on my heels. There had been too many upheavals in their old dog lives, and they were wary.

The cardboard containers from Bamboo Village were neatly stacked on the refrigerator shelf. I'd moved them to the counter and taken the lid off the carton that held the three almond prawns Taylor had left for me when I heard a knock at the front door.

It was Jane O'Keefe.

As soon as I opened the door, she stepped into the hall. She was still wearing her white hospital coat and her picture ID.

I touched her sleeve. "Are you making a house call?" I said.

Jane looked down at the white coat, bewildered. "I thought I'd taken this off and left it in my locker." Her shoulders slumped. "I'm sorry, Jo. I don't even know what I'm doing here. I was just driving around . . . I don't want to be alone tonight."

"Neither do I," I said. "Look, I was just going to have some Chinese food. There's plenty."

I opened two bottles of Great Western, and Jane and I filled our plates and sat down at the kitchen table. We ate in silence. When she was through, Jane said, "I don't think I've eaten since yesterday. There's been so much to deal with . . ."

"How's Jess?" I asked.

"Scared," she said. "Confused. Sad."

"And Sylvie?"

"She said her goodbyes to Gary a long time ago." Jane's voice went dead. "I wish I had. I was at the hospital this morning when they brought Gary and Tess in."

"Is Tess going to be all right?"

Jane shrugged. "Physically? She should be. It's pneumonia, but I think we got to her in time . . ."

"Did you see her?"

Jane shook her head. "No. But I saw Gary. I had a patient in emergency when they brought him in. It was just bad luck." She laughed. "Of course, when it came to Gary, if I hadn't had bad luck, I wouldn't have had any luck at all."

"I'm sorry," I said.

Jane picked up her fork and began tracing a pattern of interlocking circles on her empty plate. She seemed mesmerized. Finally, she said, "At least he didn't suffer."

Images of Gary in the last seconds of his life flashed through my mind: the pleading in his eyes as he asked if I understood, if I forgave; the curious resignation with which he positioned the rifle in the soft flesh beneath his chin.

"No," I said, "he didn't suffer."

Jane's fork hadn't stopped moving. Round and round, round and round it went. "Did he say anything at the end?" she asked softly.

"Let it go, Jane."

"I can't spend the rest of my life not knowing what happened." Her voice was thick with misery. "I loved him, Jo. I need to know why he killed himself."

She deserved the truth. "Gary killed himself because I wouldn't forgive him for killing Ian," I said.

Jane's head jerked up, and her eyes were bright with anger. "That's bullshit," she said. "Is that what he told you? That it was your fault?" She raked her fork across the plate. "That bastard. Trying to blame you. Trying to leave you with the guilt. Don't let him do it, Jo. Gary didn't die because you wouldn't forgive him. He died because . . ." She looked around wildly as if searching for an answer. Finally, she said, "He died because he'd backed himself into a corner, and there was no woman there to show him the way out." She threw the fork down and stood up with such violence that she knocked the table against me. "It wasn't your fault. And it wasn't mine. It was his fault." She was crying now. "If just once that son of a bitch hadn't taken the path of least resistance, he could have had a terrific life."

After Jane left, I couldn't get her epitaph for the man she had once loved out of my head. I don't know how long I sat at my kitchen table thinking about Gary Stephens. There were questions about him that would never be answered, but one fact was incontrovertible. Gary's weakness, his inability to withstand the lure of the easy way out, had altered the course of all our lives. It was hard not to think of what might have been, and for many hours in that endless night, I didn't even try.

During the next week, I did a pretty good imitation of a woman who was getting her life back to normal. I finished off my end-of-term marking on Wednesday. To celebrate, I went to the art gallery and bought a poster of a Harold Town self-portrait to put in Hilda's Christmas stocking. Thursday, Taylor and I made shortbread. Friday, I invited Alex to come over to meet Greg and Mieka and eat shrimp gumbo. I moved through all of this with the brisk assurance of someone who was putting the past behind her and getting on with her life. Then, on Saturday morning, Tess Malone phoned to say she wanted to see me, and I crumbled.

I drove down to Regina General just after lunch. The day was overcast and mild, and there were pools of standing water all over the parking lot. A young woman in a pink quilted housecoat was standing outside the entrance to the old wing. Her body had the soft shapelessness of a new mother. She was smoking.

When I passed her to go into the building, she grinned. "Unbelievable weather, eh?"

"Unbelievable," I agreed.

"Lucky, too," she added as she took a deep drag of her cigarette, "otherwise it'd either be give up these, or stand out here and freeze my buns off."

I climbed the back stairs up to Tess's room on the fourth floor. The stairwell smelled of hospital cooking and disinfectant. Things were better when I got up to the ward. Someone had made an effort to make the area festive. There was an artificial tree in the lounge, garlands of red and gold foil over the patients' doorways, and a huge pot of poinsettias at the nurses' station. It was cheerful, but as I walked down the corridor to Tess's room, I was far from merry.

Tess met me at the door to her room. She was wearing the blue cotton robe the hospital provides for its patients, and her feet were encased in blue paper slippers. She looked ten pounds thinner and twenty years older than she had looked the night of Howard's dinner. There was a package of cigarettes in her hand.

When she saw me, she smiled guiltily. "I was just going out for a smoke," she said.

"Tess, you're just getting over pneumonia."

"Don't lecture me, Jo. Please."

I embraced her. "Okay," I said. "I won't lecture. I'll even come with you. We can talk outside. But you have to wear your coat."

We took the elevator down, and I followed her to the steps where I'd seen the girl in the pink robe. As soon as she was out of the hospital, Tess lit up and inhaled deeply. Then she turned to me. "I can't stop thinking about them," she said.

"Them?" I asked.

She drew on her cigarette again. "All the ones who died."

"I can't stop thinking about them, either," I said.

"Maybe it'll be better after Gary's funeral."

"Maybe," I said. "When is it?"

"After the police are through with the body, I guess," she said, and her eyes filled with tears.

"Tess, perhaps you're not ready to talk about this yet."

"I thought there'd be things you'd want to know," she said.

"I guess by now I know most of it," I said. "The one thing I don't know is how Ian got involved in the first place."

Tess smiled sadly. "Ian got involved because Henry Rybchuk believed he was an honest man. That's what he told me the night of the caucus office party. He said 'the rest of you I wouldn't give a rat's turd for, but Kilbourn's different. He won't give a shit how many of you are involved in this. He'll help me find my daughter.'"

"And he was right," I said. Tess flinched, and I hurried on. "But that night at the party wasn't the first time you talked to Henry Rybchuk."

"No, it wasn't the first time," she said. "Henry Rybchuk came to Beating Heart the week before Christmas. He was already in a terrible state. Maureen had concocted some story about Jenny having to take the baby to Saskatoon for medical tests. That had put him off for a while, but when the days went by, and he still hadn't heard from Jenny, he called the place where she lived in Saskatoon. They told him she hadn't been there since early December. That's when he came to me."

"How did he know about you?"

"Jenny told him. When she told him about the baby, she told him everything. I guess she wanted him to know she'd acted responsibly about her pregnancy and Jess's birth."

"So Henry Rybchuk knew about Sylvie and Gary."

"He knew about them, all right. He'd gone to their house before he'd come to Beating Heart. He'd been trying to find somebody at home there for two days, but they were away. That empty house must have driven him over the edge. He was convinced Sylvie and Gary had taken Jenny and her baby away so he couldn't get to them."

"What did you do?"

"I lied. I told him I had no idea where Jenny was. I said I'd met Jenny once, when she'd come to Beating Heart in April, but I hadn't seen her since. He kept after me for a while, but I kept stonewalling. Finally, he seemed to realize he couldn't force an answer out of me, and he left."

"And you didn't see him again till that night at the party."

Tess shook her head. "No, I didn't. But Gary did. Henry Rybchuk came to their house Christmas night. Luckily, Sylvie was upstairs with the baby. Rybchuk was drunk. He had a picture of Jenny and her baby sitting on Santa's knee. Gary said he waved it in Gary's face and said, 'for the love of God, give me back my girl and her baby.' Gary was beside himself. He couldn't call the police, and it was only a matter of time before Sylvie came back downstairs. Then a woman walked by the house and asked Gary if she should call the police. Of course, that terrified Gary, but apparently it terrified Henry Rybchuk even more. He took off." Tess lit a fresh cigarette from the stub of her first. "The next day he was waiting when Ian came to his office."

"And the endgame began," I said.

Tess covered my hand with hers. "I've tried to make amends. After Jenny and Ian died, I knew I had to give my life to Beating Heart. Since then, I've saved a hundred lives, Jo."

I walked Tess back to the elevator. When it came, she shook off my offer to go back upstairs with her, and she stepped inside. Just as the elevator doors began to close, she said, "It wasn't enough, was it?"

I was lucky. The doors closed before I had to come up with an answer.

On Monday, when I walked into the kitchen and turned on the radio, the announcer said that Gary Stephens's funeral was taking place that morning. I thought of what Tess had said, and I hoped she was right. Maybe once Gary was laid to rest, we'd all find some peace.

I was having my first cup of coffee and savouring the quiet when Taylor came down to breakfast, carrying her cat. As she did every morning, she handed him to me while she got his food out of the cupboard and refilled his water dish. As he did every morning, the cat stiffened at my touch and stuck his claws through the material of my robe. Our time together was, it seemed, agony for both of us. Taylor was just about to shake the dry food into his bowl, when the phone rang. "Don't let him down till I get the food in the bowl," she said, and she scampered off to see who was calling.

I tried to shift the cat's position. "Bad luck for both of us, bub," I said, "but she won't be long." With my free hand, I pulled the morning paper closer. Gary Stephens's picture was on the bottom of the front page with the details of his funeral and a précis of the news that had been our breakfast fare all week.

When Taylor hung up, I turned the paper over so she wouldn't see the picture. She poured the food into the cat bowl.

"Who was that on the phone?" I asked.

She took the cat from me, and I could see his body go limp with joy. "Jess isn't going to school," Taylor said. "He's going to his dad's funeral." As she poured her juice and got her cereal, she was uncharacteristically quiet.

Finally, she asked, "Who goes to a funeral?"

"A person's family," I said. "His friends. The people who loved him."

"There were a lot of people at my mother's funeral," she said.

"A lot of people loved your mother," I said. "And a lot of people respected her work."

She rested her spoon against her cereal bowl thoughtfully. "Do you think there'll be a lot of people at Jess's dad's funeral?"

"No," I said, "I don't think there'll be many people there at all."

Taylor finished eating, then she got up from the table and put her bowl with the milk she always saved for her cat on the floor. "I was scared at my mother's funeral," she said.

"Of what?" I asked.

"Of what was going to happen next," she said. The cat licked up the milk. Taylor took her bowl to the sink and ran the hot water on it. "Jo, I think we should go to that funeral today."

"I don't think so, T," I said.

For a long time she didn't say anything. When she turned her face was strained and white. "If you died, I'd want Jess there," she said.

Three hours later. Taylor and I were walking up the centre aisle of Lakeview United Church. I'd been right about the crowd. I saw some familiar faces: Lorraine Bellegarde, Craig Evanson, a few people I knew from the Legislature, some members of the media, but most of the blond ash pews were empty. The band of mourners was small, too. Sylvie and Jane and, between them, Jess, looking small and sad in his new suit.

When I saw Jess, I thought of what Alex had told me about the police investigation. Everything they turned up had substantiated their theory that, for the last weeks of his life, Gary was a man possessed by his need to keep his son. The letter Kevin Tarpley had sent to Gary was in a box of unfiled correspondence Lorraine Bellegarde had packed when Gary had moved out of his office. Alex said the letter had been only three sentences long. Kevin had printed out Exodus 20:13 –

the sixth Commandment: "Thou shalt not commit murder."
He had promised Gary that, if he asked Jesus to forgive him,
he would gain eternal salvation. And then Kevin had written
a final and fatal sentence in which he told Gary he could no
longer let his son be raised by a man who had sinned as Gary
had sinned. There was a receipt from the private airline that
had flown Gary to Prince Albert on Hallowe'en and brought
him back to Nationtv in time to do the promotion for
Howard's dinner. There was a bank statement showing that
Gary had withdrawn all the cash in his business account the
day after Hallowe'en. The amount wasn't large. Certainly, it
was nowhere near the amount of money Maureen Gault had
been flashing when she'd made the offer to buy Ray-elle's
beauty salon.

It had taken the police a while to find the source of
Maureen's bonanza. When they questioned the people Gary
knew, a sad picture of Gary's activities in the days before
Maureen's death emerged. He had gone to everyone he knew
asking for money. He'd been so desperate he hadn't even
bothered to fabricate a story. He just said he was in trouble.
Most of the people Gary had gone to had already bailed him
out when he'd skimmed his legal accounts after Ian died, and
they turned him down flat.

Only one person was willing to help, and her identity was
no surprise to me. Lorraine Bellegarde owned a small house
on Wallace Street. She had been proud of the fact that it was
paid for "right down to the last nail," but she had mortgaged
it for Gary.

Alex had been the one to interview her, and her behaviour
had baffled him. "She seems like such a sensible woman,"
he'd said. "Do you think he just laid on the charm or what?"
I told him that Lorraine had been around Gary long enough
to be immune to his charm. Then I remembered the story of
how Gary hadn't let Lorraine get rid of the prostitutes who'd

been using his car as pick-up point. "I guess she decided he deserved a hassle-free zone," I'd said.

Alex had shaken his head in disgust. "What kind of guy would let a woman mortgage her house for him? He must have really been a piece of work."

"He was that, all right," I said. And we didn't talk of the matter again.

In the church, Jess laid his head against his mother's arm. The service was generic: the Lord's prayer, the twenty-third Psalm, a few mournful hymns. The young minister spoke obliquely about the mysteries of the human heart and seemed relieved when he was finished.

So was I. Gary had been cremated, and, despite everything, the cloth-covered urn on the altar was painful to contemplate. When the minister said the closing prayer and invited us all to join the family in a reception room at the back of the church, Taylor looked at me expectantly. I shook my head. I'd had enough. When we came into the vestibule, Sylvie and Jane were talking to a man from the funeral home. I headed for the door, hoping Taylor and I could slip out of the church unnoticed. But Sylvie spotted me and came over.

She seemed preternaturally calm, and I wondered if Jane had given her something. Then I remembered what Sylvie had endured in the last few days, and I knew there was nothing in the pharmacopoeia that could have even made a dint in her pain. Sylvie was a strong woman, and she was drawing on her strength.

She didn't waste time on preambles. "I need to talk to you, Jo," she said. She gestured toward an area down the corridor. "Come back and have a cup of coffee." Taylor and Jess ran on ahead, and I followed her down the hall.

If I'd needed anything to depress me further on that depressing day, the reception set out for Gary Stephens's funeral would have done it. There were plates of sandwiches and dainties, two big coffee urns, and cups and saucers for at least a hundred and fifty people. We were the only ones in the room.

Sylvie led me to the corner where four chairs had been grouped for conversation. When she sat down, she clasped her hands in front of her, like a schoolgirl. I noticed she wasn't wearing a wedding ring. For a moment, she seemed at a loss. Finally, she said, "I didn't know about Jenny's death, and I didn't know about Ian. I didn't know any of this, Jo. You have to believe me."

"I believe you," I said.

Sylvie pointed to Jess and Taylor sitting at another table. "I was afraid you wouldn't let Taylor play with Jess." When she said her son's name, her voice shook. "I don't want anything more to go wrong for him."

She looked away. "Do you remember how beautiful he was, Jo?"

I was confused. "How beautiful Jess was?"

"Not Jess," she said. "Gary."

"I remember," I said.

"I don't feel anything," she said. "He's dead and I don't feel anything. There was a time when I thought I couldn't live an hour without him."

For the first time that day, Sylvie's eyes filled with tears. "How is that possible, Jo? How can a person just stop loving?"

I didn't know what to say. At the same time, I knew Sylvie didn't need my words. At least not then. Mercifully, Taylor and Jess heard Sylvie and came over. I gave Jess a hug, then I stood and put my arm around Taylor. "Jess is welcome at our place anytime," I said. "So are you."

Sylvie nodded. "Thanks," she said. "And thanks for coming."

We started to leave, but Taylor grabbed my arm. "Jess says we're supposed to sign the book." Beside the door there was a small table with a guest book and a photograph of Gary. It was an outdoor shot. He was wearing an open-necked shirt, and he was squinting against the sun. Beside the portrait there was a vase with a single prairie lily. I signed my name in the book; under it, Taylor carefully printed hers. Ours were the only names on the page.

Craig Evanson was waiting outside the door. "I thought you and Sylvie might want some privacy," he said.

"Thanks," I said.

"How's the baby?" Taylor asked.

"Perfect," Craig said. "Would you like to see her?"

"You mean today?" Taylor said.

"Why not?" Craig said.

"Jo doesn't believe in kids skipping school for no reason."

"Seeing a new baby is a reason," Craig said.

Taylor looked glum. "It won't be a reason for Jo," she said.

"At the moment, I can't think of a better one," I said. I held my hand out to her. "Come on. Let's go."

When Manda Traynor-Evanson answered the door, she had the baby in her arms and the ginger cats, Mallory and Alex P. Kitten at her heels. Taylor didn't know who to grab first. Manda solved the problem. She asked us to take off our coats, then she turned to Taylor.

"Would you like to stay for lunch?"

"I would," Taylor said.

"So would I," I said.

"Great," said Manda. "But, Taylor, you'll have to give me a hand with the little one. Why don't you scoot into the family room and sit in the big brown chair. That's the official baby-holding chair."

When Taylor was settled, I stood behind her. Together, we looked down at the baby.

"She's beautiful, isn't she?" I said.

Taylor touched the baby's hand gently. "I didn't know babies were born with fingernails and eyelashes," she whispered. "I thought they grew those later, the way they grow teeth."

"No," I said, "they're pretty well perfect right from the start."

"She's perfect," Taylor said. Then she furrowed her brow. "Jo, what is this baby's name?"

"I don't know," I said. "There's been so much going on. I guess we just never asked."

"Ask," Taylor said.

"You ask," I said. "It won't sound so dumb coming from a kid."

Manda was standing in the doorway. "What won't sound so dumb?"

"That we don't know your baby's name," Taylor said.

Manda grinned. "Her name is Grace. After we'd bored everybody to death asking for advice and bought every book, we named her after Craig's mother."

I looked at the baby. Her hair was dark and silky, and her mouth was as delicate as a rosette on a Victorian Valentine. "Grace suits her," I said.

Lunch was fun. When Craig came home, he set up a table in the family room, so we could watch the birds at the bird-feeder while we ate. Manda had warmed up a casserole of tofu lasagna, so I was glad Taylor was distracted. When we'd had our fill of tofu, Craig and I cleared the dishes, and Taylor played with the cats while Manda fed Grace. Then we all drank camomile tea from thick blue mugs and talked about babies.

"If Grace had been a boy, what were you going to call him?" Taylor asked.

"Craig, Jr.," Manda said, shifting the baby on her hip. "We'll save it for the next one if that's okay with you."

"That's okay with me," Taylor said. "It's not a good name for a cat."

"Did I miss something here?" Craig asked.

"Taylor still hasn't named her kitten," I said.

Manda shrugged. "I've got a stack of baby name books over there, Taylor. If you like, you can take them with you when you go. We've already got a name for Kid Number Two, and when Number Three comes along, I'll get the books back."

Craig turned to Taylor. "You're welcome to the books," he said, "but I think I know a name that might work. It's the name of the man who's the patron saint of artists: 'Benet.'"

"Benet," Taylor repeated the name thoughtfully. "What do you think, Jo?"

"I like it," I said.

"So do I," Taylor said. "Because if my cat's name is Benet, I can call him Benny for short, and I really like the name Benny."

The wind was coming up as Taylor and I walked home. When we got to our corner, I saw that the boys had turned the outside Christmas lights on. The day had turned grey and cold, and the lights in front of our house were a welcoming sight. Even Jack O'Lantern looked good. During the long mild spell, his centre of gravity had shifted. From a distance, the lights inside him made him look like an exotic Central American pot.

Taylor ran ahead. She couldn't wait to tell Benny that, at long last, he had a name. Halfway up our walk, she wheeled around and waved her arms at me. "It's snowing," she yelled. "We're going to have snow for Christmas."

I looked up at the sky. Storm clouds were rolling in from the north, and with them the promise of a world that would soon be white and pure again.

A Killing Spring

CHAPTER

1

In the twenty-five years I had known Julie Evanson-Gallagher, I had wished many things on her. Still, I would never have wished that her new husband would be found in a rooming house on Scarth Street, dead, with a leather hood over his head, an electric cord around his neck, and a lacy garter belt straining to pull a pair of sheer black stockings over his muscular thighs.

I was on my way to my seminar in Politics and the Media when Inspector Alex Kequahtooway of the Regina Police Force called to tell me that the landlady of the Scarth Street house had found Reed Gallagher's body an hour earlier and that he wanted someone who knew Julie with him when he broke the news. Although my relationship with Reed Gallagher had not been a close one, I felt my nerves twang. Alex's description of Reed Gallagher's death scene was circumspect, but I didn't require graphics to understand why Julie would need shoring up when she heard about the manner in which her husband had gone to meet his Maker.

On the Day of Judgement, God's interest might lie in what is written in the human heart, but Julie's judgements had always been pretty firmly rooted in what was apparent to the human eye. Discovering she was the widow of a man who had left the world dressed like RuPaul was going to be a cruel blow. Alex was right; she'd need help. But when he pressed me for a name, I had a hard time thinking of anyone who'd be willing to sign on.

"Jo, I don't mean to rush you . . ." On the other end of the line, Alex's voice was insistent.

"I'm trying," I said. "But Julie isn't exactly overburdened with friends. She can be a viper. You saw that yourself when she paraded you around at her wedding reception."

"Mrs. Gallagher was being enlightened," he said tightly, "showing everyone she didn't mind that you'd brought an aboriginal to the party."

"I wanted to shove her face into the punch bowl."

"You'd never make a cop, Jo. Lesson one at the police college is 'learn to de-personalize.'"

"Can they really teach you how to do that?"

"Sure. If they couldn't, I'd have been back on Standing Buffalo Reserve after my first hour on the beat. Now, come on, give me a name. Mrs. Gallagher may be unenlightened but she's about thirty minutes away from the worst moment of her life."

"And she shouldn't be alone, but I honestly don't know who to call. I think the only family she has are her son and her ex-husband, and she's cut herself off from both of them."

"People come together in a crisis."

"They do, if they know there's a crisis. But Alex, I don't know how to get in touch with either Mark or Craig. Mark's studying at a Bible college in Texas, but I'm not sure where, and Craig called me last week to tell me he and his new family were on their way to Disney World."

I looked out my office window. It was March 17, and the campus, suspended between the bone-chilling beauty of winter and the promise of spring, was bleak. Except for the slush that had been shovelled off the roads and piled in soiled ribbons along the curbs, the snow was gone, and the brilliant cobalt skies of midwinter had dulled to gunmetal grey. To add to the misery, that morning the city had been hit by a wind-storm. Judging from the way the students outside my window were being blown across the parking lot as they ran for their cars, it appeared the rotten weather wasn't letting up.

"I wish I was in the Magic Kingdom," I said.

"I'm with you," Alex said. "I've never been a big fan of Minnie and Mickey, but they'd be better company than that poor guy in the room upstairs. Jo, that is one grotesque crime scene, but the media are going to love it. Once they get wind of how Reed Gallagher died, they're going to be on this rooming house like ducks on a June bug. I have to get to Julie Gallagher before one of them beats me to it."

"Do you want me to come with you?"

"I know you aren't crazy about Mrs. G.," he said, "but I've been through this scene with the next of kin enough times to know that she's going to need somebody with her who isn't a cop."

"I was just on my way to teach," I said. "I'll have to do something about my class." I looked at my watch. "I can meet you in front of Julie's place at twenty after three."

"Gallagher's identification says he lives at 3870 Lakeview Court," he said. "Those are the condos, right?"

"Right," I said.

After I hung up, I waited for the tone, then I dialled Tom Kelsoe's extension. This was the second year Tom and I had co-taught the Political Science 371 seminar. He was a man whose ambitions reached far beyond a Saskatchewan university, and whenever he heard opportunity knocking, I covered his classes for him. He owed me a favour; in fact, he owed me many favours, but as I listened to the phone ringing unanswered in his office, I remembered that this was the day Tom Kelsoe's new book was being launched. Today of all days, Tom was hardly likely to jump at the chance to pay back a colleague for past favours. It appeared that our students were out of luck. I grabbed my coat, stuffed a set of unmarked essays into my briefcase, made up a notice saying Political Science 371 was cancelled, and headed out the door.

When I turned the corner into the main hall, Kellee Savage was getting out of the elevator. She spotted me and waved, then she started limping down the hall towards me. Behind her, she was dragging the little cart she used to carry her books.

"Professor Kilbourn, I need to talk to you before class."

"Can you walk along with me, Kellee?" I asked. "I have to cancel the class, and I'm late."

"I know you're late. I've already been to the seminar room." She reached into her cart, pulled out a book and thrust it at me. "Look what was on the table at the place where I sit."

I glanced at the cover. "*Sleeping Beauty*," I said. "I don't understand."

"Read the note inside."

I opened the book. The letter, addressed to Kellee, detailed the sexual acts it would take to awaken her from her long sleep. The descriptions were as prosaic and predictable as the graffiti on the wall of a public washroom. But there was something both original and cruel in the parallel the writer had drawn between Kellee and Sleeping Beauty.

Shining fairies bringing gifts of comeliness, grace, and charm might have crowded one another out at Sleeping Beauty's christening, but they had been in short supply the day Kellee Savage was born. She was not more than five feet tall, and misshapen. One shoulder hunched higher than the other, and her neck was so short that her head seemed to be jammed against her collarbone. She didn't bother with eye makeup. She must have known that no mascara on earth could beautify her eyes, which goggled watery and blue behind the thick lenses of her glasses, but she took pains with her lipstick and with her hair, which she wore long and caught back by the kind of fussy barrettes little girls sometimes fancy.

She was a student at the School of Journalism, but she had been in my class twice: for an introductory course in Political Science and now in the seminar on Politics and the Media. Three times a week I passed her locker on the way to my first-year class; she was always lying in wait for me with a question or an opinion she wanted verified. She wasn't gifted, but she was more dogged than any student I'd ever known. At the beginning of term when she'd asked permission to tape my lectures, she'd been ingenuous: "I have to get good grades because that's all I've got going for me."

I held the book out to her. "Kellee, I think you should take this to the Student Union. There's an office there that deals with sexual-harassment cases."

"They don't believe me."

"You've been there already?"

"I've been there before. Many times." She steeled herself. "This isn't the first incident. They think I'm making the whole thing up. They're too smart to say that, but I know they think I'm crazy because . . ." She lowered her eyes.

"Because of what?" I asked.

"Because of the name of the person who's doing these things to me." She looked up defiantly. "It's Val Massey."

"Val?" I said incredulously.

Kellee caught my tone. "Yes, *Val*," she said, spitting his name out like an epithet. "I knew you wouldn't believe me."

This time it was my turn to look away. The truth was I *didn't* believe her. Val Massey was in the Politics and the Media seminar. He was good-looking and smart and focused. It seemed inconceivable that he would risk an assured future for a gratuitous attack on Kellee Savage.

Kellee's voice was thick with tears. "You're just like the people at the Harassment Office. You think I'm imagining this, that I wrote the letter myself because I'm . . ."

"Kellee, sometimes, the stress of university, especially at this time of year . . ."

"Forget it. Just forget it. I should have known that it was too good to last."

"That what was too good to last?"

She was crying now, and I reached out to her, but she shook me off. "Leave me alone," she said, and she clomped noisily down the hall. She stopped at the elevator and began jabbing at the call button. When the doors opened, she turned towards me.

"Today's my birthday," she sobbed. "I'm twenty-one. I'm supposed to be happy, but this is turning out to be the worst day of my life."

"Kellee, I . . ."

"Shut up," she said. "Just shut the hell up." Then she stepped into the elevator and disappeared from sight.

She hadn't taken *Sleeping Beauty* with her. I looked at the face of the fairy-tale girl on the cover. Every feature was flawless. I sighed, slid the book into my briefcase, and headed down the hall.

Class was supposed to start at 3:00, and it was 3:10 when I got to the seminar room. The unwritten rule of university life is that, after waiting ten minutes for an instructor, students can leave. I had made it just under the wire, and there were groans as I walked through the door. When he saw me, Val Massey gave me a small conspiratorial smile; I smiled back, then looked at the place across the table from him where Kellee Savage usually sat. It was empty.

"Sorry," I said. "Something's come up. No class today."

Jumbo Hryniuk, a young giant who was planning a career hosting "Monday Night Football" but who was saddled nonetheless with my class, pushed back his chair and roared with delight. "Hey, all right!" he said. "We can get an early start on the green beer at the Owl, and somebody told me Tom Kelsoe's publishers are picking up the tab for the drinks at that party for him tonight."

Val Massey stood and began putting his books into his backpack. He imbued even this mechanical gesture with an easy and appealing grace. "Tom's publishers know how to court students," he said quietly. He looked at me. "Are you going to be there?"

"Absolutely," I said. "Students aren't the only people Tom's publishers know how to court." Then I wrote a reading assignment on the board, told them I hoped I'd see them all at the launch, and headed for the parking lot.

There was a cold rain falling, and the wind from the north was so fierce that it seemed to pound the rain into me. My parking spot was close, and I ran all the way, but I was still soaked to the skin by the time I slid into the driver's seat. It was shaping up to be an ugly day.

As I waited for the traffic to slow on the parkway, I looked back towards the campus. In the more than twenty years the new campus of the university had existed, not many politicians had been able to resist a speech praising their role in transforming scrub grass and thin topsoil into a shining city on the plain. I had written a few of those rhetorical flourishes myself, but that day as I watched the thin wind-driven clouds scudding off the flatlands, I felt a chill. Set against the implacable menace of a prairie storm, the university seemed insubstantial and temporary, like a theatre set that could be

struck at any moment. I was glad when there was a break in
the traffic, and I was able to drive towards the city.

Wascana Park was deserted. The joggers and the walkers
and the young mums with strollers had been forced indoors
by the rain, and I had the road that wound through the park
to myself. There was nothing to keep me from thinking
about Julie and about how I was going to handle the next few
hours. But perversely, the more I tried to focus on the future,
the more my mind was flooded with images of the past.

Julie and I shared a quarter-century of memories, but I
would have been hard pressed to come up with one that
warmed my heart. C.S. Lewis once said that happy people
move towards happiness as unerringly as experienced travellers head for the best seat on the train. In the time I'd known
her, Julie had invariably headed straight for the misery, and
she had always made certain she had plenty of seatmates.

Craig Evanson and my late husband, Ian, had started in
provincial politics together in the seventies. In the way of
the time, Julie and I had been thrown together as wives and
mothers. From the first, I had found her brittle perfection
alienating, but I had liked and respected her husband. So did
everyone else. Craig wasn't the brightest light on the porch,
but he was principled and hardworking.

When we first knew the Evansons, Julie had just given birth
to her son, Mark, and she was wholly absorbed in motherhood. The passion with which she threw herself into making
her son the best and the brightest was unnerving, and when
the unthinkable happened and Mark turned out to be not just
average but somewhat below average, I was sure Julie's world
would shatter. She had surprised me. Without missing a beat,
she had cut her losses and regrouped. She withdrew from
Mark completely, and threw herself headlong into a campaign
to make Craig Evanson premier of the province. It was a fantastic effort, and it was doomed from the beginning, but Julie's

bitterness when her plans didn't work out came close to poisoning Craig's relationship with everyone he cared for. The Evansons' eventual divorce was a relief to everyone who loved Craig. At long last, we were free of Julie.

But it turned out that Julie had some unfinished business with us. Two months before that blustery March day, several of Craig's friends had found wedding invitations in our mailboxes. Julie was marrying Reed Gallagher, the new head of the School of Journalism, and the presence of our company was requested. For auld lang syne or for some more complicated reason, most of us had accepted.

Julie had been a triumphant bride. She had every right to be. She had married a successful man who appeared to be wild about her, and the wedding, every detail of which had been planned and executed by Julie, had been textbook perfect. But as I turned onto Lakeview Court and saw Alex's Audi parked in front of 3870, I felt a coldness in the pit of my stomach. Five weeks after her model wedding, Julie Evanson-Gallagher was about to discover the cruel truth of the verse cross-stitched on the sampler in my grandmother's sewing room: "Pride goeth before destruction, and an haughty spirit before a fall."

As soon as I pulled up behind the Audi, Alex leaped out, snapped open a black umbrella, and came over. He held the umbrella over me as I got out of the car, and together we raced towards Julie's porch and rang the doorbell. There was a frosted panel at the side of the door, and Julie's shape appeared behind it almost immediately, but she didn't hurry to open the door. When she finally did, she wasn't welcoming.

"This is a surprise," she said in a tone which suggested she was not a woman who welcomed surprises. "I was expecting the caterers. Some people are dropping in before Tom Kelsoe's book launch, and I'm on a tight schedule, so, of course, I've had nothing but interruptions." She smoothed her lacquered cap of silver-blond hair and looked levelly at Alex and me. She had given us our cue. It was up to us to pick it up and make our exit.

"Julie, can we come in out of the rain?" I asked.

"Sorry," she said, and she stepped aside. She gave us one of her quick, dimpled smiles. "Now, I'm warning you, I don't have much time to visit."

Alex's voice was gentle. "This isn't exactly a visit, Mrs. Gallagher. We have some bad news."

"It's about Reed," I said.

Her dark eyes darted from me to Alex. "What's he done?"

"Julie, he's dead." I said. "I'm so very sorry."

The words hung in the air between us, heavy and stupid. The colour drained from Julie's face; then, without a word, she disappeared into the living room.

Alex turned to me. "You'd better get out of that wet coat," he said. "It looks like we're going to be here for a while."

From the appearance of the living room, Julie's plans had gone well beyond some people dropping in. Half a dozen round tables covered with green-and-white checked cloths had been set up at the far end of the room. At the centre of each table was a pot of shamrocks in a white wicker basket with an emerald bow on its handle. It was all very festive, and it was all very sad. Less than an hour before, Kellee Savage had sobbed that her twenty-first birthday was turning out to be the worst day of her life. It was hard to think of two members of the sisterhood of women who had less in common than Reed Gallagher's new widow and the awkward and lonely Kellee Savage, but they shared something now: as long as they lived, they would both remember this St. Patrick's Day as a day edged in black.

Julie was standing near the front window, staring into an oversized aquarium. When I followed the line of her vision I spotted an angelfish, gold and lapis lazuli, gliding elegantly through a tiny reef of coral.

Julie was unnaturally still, and when I touched her hand, it was icy. "Can I get you a sweater?" I asked. "Or a cup of tea?"

She didn't acknowledge my presence. I was close enough to smell her perfume and hear her breathing, but Julie Evanson-Gallagher was as remote from me as the lost continent of Atlantis. Outside, storm clouds hurled themselves across the sky, wind pummelled the young trees on the lawn, and rain cankered the snow piled beside the walk. But in the silent and timeless world of the aquarium, all was serene. I understood why Julie was willing herself into the peace of that watery kingdom; what I didn't understand was how I could pull her back.

Alex was behind us. Suddenly, he leaned forward. "Look," he whispered. "There, coming out from the coral. Lionfish – a pair of them." For a few moments, the three of us were silent, watching. Then Alex said, "They're amazing, Julie."

They were amazing: large, regal, and as dazzlingly patterned as a bolt of cloth in a street market in Jakarta. They were also menacing. Spines radiated like sunbursts off their sleek bodies and, as they drifted towards us, I instinctively stepped back.

"They're my favourites," Julie said.

"Have you ever been stung?" Alex asked.

Julie dimpled. "Oh yes, but I don't care. They're so beautiful they're worth it. Reed doesn't like them. He wants a dog. Imagine," she said, "a dog." For a moment, she was silent. Then she said, "Was he alone?"

It seemed an odd first question, but Alex was unruffled. "He was when the landlady found him."

Julie flinched. "Where was he?"

"At a rooming house on Scarth Street."

"I want to see him," she said. Her voice was lifeless.

"If you want, I'll take you to him," Alex said. "But I need to know some things first. Could we sit down?"

Julie gestured to one of the tables that had been set up for the party. Alex took the chair across from her. He was silent for a moment, watching her face, then he said, "When did you last see your husband?"

Julie's answer was almost inaudible. "Last night. Around eight-thirty."

"Was it usual for you to spend the night apart."

She looked up defiantly. "Of course not. We'd just had a disagreement."

"What was the disagreement about?"

Julie shrugged. "I don't remember. It was just one of those foolish quarrels married people have."

"But it was serious enough that your husband didn't come home. Weren't you concerned?"

"No . . . Reed was angry. I thought he'd just gone somewhere to cool off. I went to bed."

"Did you try to locate him today?"

Suddenly Julie's eyes blazed. "Of course I did. I called his office, but he wasn't there."

"And that didn't surprise you?"

"He's an important man. He doesn't have a silly little job where he sits at a desk all day." She leaned forward and adjusted the green bow on the wicker basket. When the ribbon was straight, she looked up warily. "Why are you asking me all these questions?"

"The circumstances of your husband's death were unusual."

Alex's tone was matter-of-fact, but I could see Julie stiffen. "What are you talking about?"

"Well, for one thing, he was dressed oddly."

Julie's eyes widened. She was wearing a silk shirt, a cardigan, slacks, and sandals, all in carefully co-ordinated shades of taupe. She glanced reflexively at her own outfit as if to reassure herself that, whatever her husband's eccentricities, her own clothing was beyond reproach.

Alex leaned towards her. "Was your husband a transvestite?" he asked softly.

Julie leaped up so abruptly that her legs caught the edge of the table. The crystal wine goblet in front of her leaned crazily, then fell. "You don't know what you're talking about," she snapped. "I don't know why they'd send someone like you out here in the first place. What are you, some sort of special native constable?"

"I'm not a special anything, just a regular inspector who happens to be Ojibway."

"I don't care what kind of native you are," she said.

She disappeared down the hall, and when she came back she was wearing a trenchcoat and carrying an over-the-shoulder bag. "You can leave now," she said. "I'm going down to the police station to find someone who knows what he's doing."

As he zipped his windbreaker, Alex's face was impassive. "I'll give you a lift," he said. "I don't think you should be driving right now."

"I've got my car here," I said. "I can take her, Alex."

She shot me a venomous look. "So you can relay all the details to your friends? No thanks."

She headed back into the hall, and I followed her. There was a mirror near the front door and she stopped and checked her makeup.

"Julie, there has to be something I can do," I said.

Her mirror image looked at me coldly. "Always the girl guide, aren't you, Joanne? But since you're so eager to serve, why don't you phone my guests and tell them the party's cancelled. The list is by the phone in the kitchen." Beneath the mirror there was a small bureau. Julie opened its top drawer, took out a key and handed it to me. "Lock up before you leave," she said. "There was a break-in down the street last week. Put the key through the letter slot when you go."

"I'll make sure everything's safe," I said.

She laughed angrily. "You do that," she said. Then she opened the door and vanished into the rain.

Alex turned to me. "I'll call you," he said. "Right now I'd better get out there and unlock the car before Mrs. G. gets soaked."

I drew him towards me and kissed him. He smelled of cold rain and soap. "My grandmother used to say that every time we turn the other cheek, we get a new star in our crown in heaven."

Alex raised an eyebrow. "Let's hope she's right. I have a feeling that before Reed Gallagher is finally laid to rest, his widow is going to give us a chance to build up quite a collection."

CHAPTER

2

Julie's kitchen was the cleanest room I had ever seen. Everything in it was white and hard-scrubbed: the Italian tile on the floor, the Formica on the counters, the paint on the walls, the handsome Scandinavian furniture, and the appliances, which shone as brightly as they had the day they'd come out of their packing boxes. That morning my fifteen-year-old son had taped a sign above our sink: "Kitchen Staff No Longer Required to Wash Their Hands." Somehow I couldn't imagine Angus's sign eliciting any chuckles in Julie's kitchen.

The telephone was on a small desk in the corner. Beside it, in a gold oval frame, was Julie and Reed Gallagher's formal wedding portrait. They had been a handsome bridal couple. The week before the wedding, Reed had been invited to speak at a conference in Hilton Head. Judging from their tans, he and Julie had logged some major beach time in North Carolina. Against her white-blond hair and dark eyes, Julie's bronzed skin had looked both startling and flattering. She had worn an ivory silk suit at her wedding. She had made it herself, just as she had sewn the ivory shirt Reed wore, dried the flowers that decorated the church, tied the bows of ivory satin ribbon at the end of each pew, and smoked the salmon for the hors-d'oeuvres. She had been attentive to every detail, except, apparently, her new husband's appetite for unusual bedroom practices.

I picked up the photograph. Reed Gallagher didn't seem the type for kinky sex. He was a tall, heavy-set man, with an unapologetic fondness for hard liquor, red meat, and cigars. I'd met him only a few times, but I'd liked him. He took pleasure in being outrageous, and in the careful political climate of the university, his provocations had been refreshing. I tried to remember the last time I'd seen him. It had been in the Faculty Club at the beginning of the month. He'd been in the window room with Tom Kelsoe and my friend Jill Osiowy. They'd been celebrating Reed's birthday with a bottle of wine and, as people always do when they're celebrating, they had seemed immortal. I put down the photograph and started reading the names on Julie's list.

Twenty-four people had been invited to the party, and the first name was that of the guest of honour. I dialled Tom Kelsoe's office number. There was still no answer. There was no one at his home either. I hung up and dialled the next number. I drew a blank there, too, but there was an answering machine, and I left a message that was factual but not forthcoming. As the hour wore on, I had plenty of opportunities to refine my message. Out of the seven couples and ten singles on the list, I was able to talk to only three people.

One of those people was Jill Osiowy. She was an executive producer at Nationtv, but her concern when she heard the news of Reed's death was less with getting the story to air than with making certain that she found Tom Kelsoe so that he would hear the news from her rather than from a stranger. Her anxiety about Tom's reaction surprised me. In the years I'd known her, Jill had had many relationships, but none of them had ever reached the point where a blow to the man in her life was a blow to her.

Until she met Tom Kelsoe, Jill's romantic history could be summarized in one sentence: she had lousy taste in men, but she was smart enough to know it. The fact that the deepest thing about any of the men who paraded through her life was either their tan or the blue of their eyes never fazed her. When she came upon the term "himbo" in a magazine article about the joys of the shallow man, Jill had faxed it to me with a note: "Thomas Aquinas says, 'It's a privilege to be an angel and a merit to be a virgin,' but check this out – there are other options!"

For the past six months, it seemed Jill had decided that Tom Kelsoe was her only option. At the age of forty, she was as besotted as a schoolgirl. At long last, she had found Mr. Right, but as I hung up the phone I wondered why it was that Jill's Mr. Right, increasingly, seemed so wrong to me.

It was 4:30 when I crossed the last name off Julie's list. I could feel the first twinges of a headache, and I leaned back in the chair, closed my eyes, and ran my forefinger along my temple until I found the acupressure point I'd seen a doctor demonstrate on television the week before. I was so absorbed in my experiment with alternative medicine that I didn't hear the doorbell until whoever was ringing apparently decided to lean on it.

All I could see when I opened the door was someone in a yellow slicker hunched over a huge roasting pan, trying, it seemed, to keep the wind from tearing the lid off. I couldn't make out whether my visitor was a man or a woman. The hood of the slicker had fallen forward, masking individual features as effectively as a nun's wimple, but when the person at Julie's front door began to speak, it was apparent that I was not dealing with a Sister of Mercy.

"Holy crudmore," she said. "Are you all deaf? There's a monsoon going on out here in case you hadn't noticed."

She pushed past me into the house, and I glimpsed her profile: determined chin, snub nose, and skin rosy with cold and good health. She kicked off her shoes and headed for the kitchen.

"Just a minute," I said. "What's going on?"

"Catering's going on," she snapped. "At least it's supposed to be unless you've changed your mind again." She tossed her head, and her hood fell back. She glanced towards me and her mouth fell open. "Oh, my lord, you're not her. Sorry. I should have checked before I snarled."

"You may still want to snarl," I said. "I've got some bad news. There isn't going to be any party."

"You mean she gave into him after all?" She struck the palm of her hand against her forehead. "And what," she groaned, "am I supposed to do with that old-country trifle of hers with all those barfy kiwi shamrocks?"

"Mrs. Gallagher has had some bad news," I said. "She's just found out that her husband died. That's why I'm here. We just heard about what happened."

Her young face grew grave. "Bummer," she said, stretching out the last syllable in anguish. "Bummer for him, of course, but also for me." She looked thoughtful. "I guess I could make sandwiches out of the corned beef, and you can always do something with potatoes." She slumped. "But the Lunenburg cabbage! And the old-country trifle! No way I can hold that trifle over till tomorrow."

"You won't be out anything," I said. "Just send the bill to Mrs. Gallagher. She'll understand."

"She's not the understanding type." The girl's eyes filled with tears. "I'm sorry. It's just I've had such an awful week. Trying to please Mrs. Gallagher was about as easy as putting socks on a rooster. Then last night when she called to re-book, she told me that, if there were any extra costs, I'd have to swallow them because it was her party, and it was unprofessional of me to cancel the party without consulting her. I mean, wouldn't you figure that if a husband calls you and says 'Cancel the party,' you should cancel the party?"

"Yes," I said, "I would. Did Mr. Gallagher explain why he was changing their plans?"

"No, he just said the dinner was off, but at least he was nice about it. Told me he was sorry for the inconvenience and he'd pay the bill. Not like her. She'd squeeze a nickel till the Queen screamed. Trust me, this is going to cost me big time." She wiped her nose with the back of her hand. "Have you got a Kleenex?" she asked.

I opened my purse, found a tissue and handed it to her.

"Thanks," she said. "I never even told you who I am, did I? I'm Polly Abbey." She fumbled in the pocket of her slicker, pulled out a business card and handed it to me. "Abbey Road Caterers. Like you'd ever hire me after seeing me like this."

"I understand," I said. "My name's Joanne Kilbourn, and my daughter owns a catering business. I know what these last-minute cancellations do to her cash flow. Look, why don't I buy some of the meat. I haven't got anything started for dinner tonight, and my kids love corned beef."

Polly brightened. "You can have the Lunenburg cabbage too," she said. "I'll even throw in some potatoes. Now if I could only find a home for that stupid trifle."

I thought of Julie's poisonous dismissal of Alex. "Polly, do you know where the Indian-Métis Friendship Centre is?"

"Sure," she said. "It's on Dewdney. Actually, it's not far from my shop."

"Good," I said. "Why don't you drop the old-country trifle off there on your way back? Tell them it's a gift from an admirer."

Her eyes widened. "Not Mrs. Gallagher?"

I nodded.

"Cool," she said, and for the first time since she'd come in out of the rain, Polly Abbey smiled.

When I opened the front door to our house, Benny, my younger daughter's ginger cat, was waiting. He looked at me assessingly. As usual, I didn't pass muster, and he wandered off. Somewhere in the distance the Cranberries were singing, but theirs were the only human voices I heard.

"Hey," I shouted. "Anybody home?"

Taylor came running. She was wearing the current costume of choice for girls in her grade-one class: jeans, a plaid shirt, and a ponytail anchored by a scrunchy.

"Me. I'm home, and Angus and Leah are downstairs," she said, reaching her arms out for a hug. Benny, who had a sixth sense for the exact moment at which Taylor's affections wandered from him, reappeared and began rubbing against her leg. She picked him up, and he shot me a look of triumph.

"Guess what?" Taylor said. "I lost a tooth, and I'm going to draw a mural for the Kids Convention." She shifted Benny to the crook of her arm, and pulled her lip up with her thumb and forefinger. "Look!"

"The front one," I said. "That's a loonie tooth."

"Serious?"

"Serious," I said. "Now tell me about the Kids Convention."

"All I know is it's after Easter holidays and I'm making a mural about the Close-Your-Eyes Dance."

"The story Alex told you. He'll be pleased."

"I'm going to do it in panels. The first one's gonna be where that hungry guy . . ."

"Nanabush," I said.

". . . where he sees those ducks. Then I'm going to show him singing and drumming, so he can trick them. You really think Alex will like it?"

"I know he will," I said. "Now, come on, let's get cracking. We have to eat early because I'm going out."

Taylor's face fell. "I hate it when you go out."

I put my arms around her. "I know, T, but we've talked about this before. I'm never gone for long. And Leah and Angus are staying with you. If you like, you can invite Leah for supper."

Taylor's gaze was intense. "You promise you'll come back?"

"I promise," I said. "Now, I'm going to go change into something warm. Why don't you go find Leah and ask her if she likes corned beef and cabbage. If you guys play your cards right, I might even throw in green milkshakes."

Reassured, at least for the time being, Taylor ambled off towards the family room. In the past few months she'd become troubled when I left at night. Her fearfulness was something I'd been half-expecting since her mother died suddenly and Taylor had come to live with us. Even before her mother's death, Taylor's life had been tumultuous, and at first, when she had come to us, she had seemed relieved just to know that, when she woke up in the morning, the day ahead was going to be pretty much like the day before. But when her best friend's father died shortly before Christmas, Taylor had been shaken. As she watched Jess grieve for his father, she grieved too, and she grew anxious. At six and a half, the awareness that we are moored to our happiness by fragile threads had hit her hard. I was doing my best to reassure her, but some nights my best just wasn't good enough. As I changed into jeans and a sweatshirt, I was hoping this particular night wasn't one of them.

When I brought Polly Abbey's dinner in from the car, Taylor was sitting at the kitchen table, drawing. Benny was on her lap, and she looked so content I uncrossed my fingers. Maybe my going out wasn't going to be a problem after all.

When she heard me, Taylor glanced up. "I almost forgot. A lady called you," she said.

"Do you remember her name?"

Taylor's face pinched in concentration, then she lit up. "It's Kellee," she said. "Her name is Kellee and today's her birthday, and she's going to call back."

"Swell," I said. Then I took down the butcher knife and began slicing the corned beef. When I had the platter filled, the phone rang. I picked up the receiver without much enthusiasm, but I was in luck. It wasn't the birthday girl on the line; it was Alex.

"How are you doing?" he asked.

"Fine," I said. "I'm just slicing up the funeral baked meats."

"I don't get it."

"The caterer came when I was at Julie's, and I bought some of the corned beef they were going to have at the party. Any chance you can join us?"

"Nope. We're still searching this place for evidence, so I'm not going anywhere for a while. Anyway, there's something about a crime scene that takes away the appetite."

"At least you're free of Julie. Did she ever find her white knight?"

He laughed. "No. She decided to stick with me."

"Is she there now?"

"No, but she was. I tried to talk her out of coming. I thought it would be easier on her if she waited until they took her husband down to pathology at the hospital, but the lady was insistent."

"So she saw him there."

"Yeah, in all his glory."

"How did she take it?"

"Weirdly. Not that there's any rule about how to react when you see your dead husband decked out in leather and lace, but I would have thought it'd be a sight to grab a wife's attention."

"And it didn't grab Julie's?"

"Not for long. Jo, did you notice this afternoon how quickly she zeroed in on the question of whether Gallagher was alone when he died?"

"Yes."

"What did you make of it?"

"The obvious. I thought Julie was afraid Reed was having an affair."

"That seemed to be her focus while she was here, too. We'd already sealed the scene, so she couldn't get past the threshold, but she kept leaning in, looking around. One of the ident officers asked if he could help, but she just shook her head and kept on looking."

"What do you think she thought she'd find?"

"Given her concern this afternoon about whether Gallagher was alone when his body was discovered, I would guess that she thought she might find some evidence of his sexual partner."

"Poor Julie," I said. "She and Reed seemed so happy at the wedding, but apparently they really did have problems. The young woman they'd hired to cater their party told me Reed called her last night and said the dinner was cancelled."

Alex's voice was tight with interest. "Did she give you the time when he called?"

"No, but you can check. Her name is Polly Abbey and her company's called Abbey Road Catering – it's on Dewdney."

"Got it," he said. Then he paused. "Jo, am I missing something here? When we were at the Gallaghers' today, didn't you get the impression that the party was still on?"

"Yes, because it was. Polly Abbey said Julie called her last night to re-book. Maybe that's what Julie and Reed fought about."

"Maybe," he said wearily. "Or maybe they fought over the fact that she didn't share his sexual tastes. When it comes to domestic disputes, causes are never in short supply."

"Do you know anything more about what happened to Reed?"

"Splatter says that, judging from the condition of the body, Gallagher died last night."

"Who's Splatter?"

"Sorry, he's our M.E. – the medical examiner. His real name is Sherman Zimbardo. The guys call him Splatter because he's got this uncanny ability to interpret blood patterns at a crime scene."

"I'm sorry I asked."

"Actually, I think the guys see the nickname as a kind of compliment. Anyway, Zimbardo says he should have more solid information about how Reed Gallagher died after he's completed the autopsy. Till then, we're just calling it a suspicious death."

"Which means . . . ?"

"Which means that we don't know what happened, but there are enough loose ends to keep us interested for a while. Zimbardo says he's seen a couple of cases like this."

"You mean with the hood and the cord?"

"Yeah. Apparently, they indicate a particular type of auto-eroticism."

"Sex play on your own."

"Right. How did you know that?"

"I took Greek and Latin at school."

"Fair enough. Anyway, this particular variation of auto-eroticism is called . . . wait a minute, the name's in my notes . . . it's called hypoxyphilia. Did you cover that in class?"

"I don't think so."

"Good. It's a dangerous business. The people who practise it apparently find sex more interesting when they cut off their oxygen. Every so often the fun and games get out of hand, then we have to cut them down."

"That doesn't make sense to me."

"It doesn't appeal to me much either."

"I didn't mean the kinkiness. I meant that I don't understand why a man like Reed Gallagher would have a fight with his wife and decide that the next step was to hop in the car, drive downtown to a rooming house, and go through some sort of bizarre masturbation ritual."

"Zimbardo's done some reading on the subject. He says people who are into hypoxyphilia claim that it's a great stress-reliever."

"I think I'll stick to single-malt Scotch." I said. "And from what I'd seen of Reed Gallagher, I would have thought that would be his solution, too."

"The leather and lace doesn't sound to you like something he'd do?"

"No," I said, "Reed always struck me as a man who coped with life head-on."

"But you didn't know him well."

"No," I said. "Not well at all." Just then I heard the call-waiting signal. "Alex, could you hang on? I've got a beep."

At first, all I heard on the other line was music and party sounds. Then there was giggling, and Kellee Savage said, "Can you hear them singing? Well, they don't have as much reason to sing as I do." Her words were slurred. It was obvious that she'd been drinking, but I'd had enough. Birthday or no, Kellee Savage was going to have to find somebody else to play with.

"Kellee, I'll have to talk to you later. I have an important call on the other line."

"This is an important call," she said belligerently. "I've figured it all out. Exactly why he's after me all the time. Here's what's happening . . ."

"Kellee, I really have to go. If you want to talk to me, come to my office Monday morning." I clicked off, but not before I heard someone in the bar begin to sing "Danny Boy."

When I apologized for keeping him waiting, Alex's voice was easy. "It's okay," he said. "I was just remembering the Gallaghers' wedding."

"I would have thought you'd want to excise that from your memory."

"It wasn't that bad, Jo. At least nobody called me Chief. Anyway, the whole thing just seems so sad now. I keep thinking about those birds they had on the wedding cake."

"The doves," I said. "They were made of sugar. It's been years since I've seen any that weren't made of plastic."

"Julie Gallagher made them herself," Alex said. "She told me she couldn't find a store in town that sold them."

"That's Julie for you. Always gilding her own lily."

"I don't think it was that," Alex said softly. "Mrs. Gallagher told me there was an old wives' tale that every sugar dove on a wedding cake brought a year of happiness, and she wanted to make sure that she and her husband had a lifetime-full."

Despite my sad mood, dinner that night was fun. Angus's new girlfriend, Leah Drache, had a good head on her shoulders and a knack for smoothing over raw edges. Leah also had, according to Taylor, who had asked, thirteen separate body piercings. I'd seen the seven on Leah's ears, the two on her left eyebrow, the one through her right nostril, and the one in her navel. As we drank our green milkshakes and listened to Toad the Wet Sprocket, I tried not to think about the location of the other two.

When we started to clear off the table, Taylor stayed at her place, staring out into the night. I went back and sat beside her. "Penny for your thoughts, T," I said.

Her voice was small and sad. "I wish you didn't have to go out tonight."

"So do I. But a book launch is a special thing. It's a lot of work to write a book, and the man who wrote this one is Jill's boyfriend."

"Is he nice?"

I pointed towards the garage. "Look at the size of that branch the wind blew down. I'll bet Angus could cut it up and make a good scratching post for Benny."

Angus, who knew I didn't like Tom Kelsoe, turned from the sink where he was scraping his plate and gave me a side-long smile. "Nice feint, Mum."

"Thanks," I said. "That means a lot coming from the master-feinter." I gave Taylor a quick hug. "Okay, kiddo, it's time for me to grab a shower and get dressed. The sooner I get there, the sooner I get home."

The phone on my nightstand rang just as I'd finished undressing. I ignored it and continued into the bathroom. As soon as I turned on the shower, Angus hollered, "It's for you!" I grabbed a towel and swore. The law of averages that day pointed towards a bad-news phone call.

Kellee Savage didn't even bother to say hello. "I've got proof," she said. "I wasn't supposed to say anything till it was all checked, but I can't find him, so what's the point of waiting?" She enunciated each syllable carefully, confirming to herself and to the world that she was still sober. In the background I could hear laughter, but there was no mirth in Kellee's voice.

"Kellee, I don't understand what you're talking about. Who is it that you can't find?"

"That's confidential, and a good journalist honours confidences." For a beat she was silent, then she said sulkily, "And a good journalist knows when to get the story out. I don't care if he thinks I should wait. It's my story, and I'm getting it out. In fact, I'm coming to your house right now to tell you what's happening. You'll be sorry you didn't believe me."

"Kellee, it's a rotten night. You'll feel a lot better tomorrow if you just go back to your own place and go to bed."

"I don't wanna go to bed. It's my birthday. I'm s'posed to get my way. I have a birthday song. My mum made it up when I was little. 'Oh Kellee girl, today is your birthday and smiles and fun will last the whole day long.'" She fell silent. "I forget the rest."

"Kellee, please. Call a cab and go home."

"Can't," she said. "I'm a journalist. Got to get the story out. Besides I used up all my quarters phoning you."

"I'll call the taxi for you. Just tell me where you are."

She snorted. "Oh no, you don't. I know what you're trying to do. You're trying to stop me. He probably called and warned you that I'm dangerous." She giggled. "Well, I am dangerous. You know why? Because I'm a journalist, and if we're good, we're dangerous." There was a long silence, and I wondered if she'd passed out. But as luck would have it, she rallied. "Stay tuned," she slurred, then she slammed down the receiver so hard, it hurt my eardrum.

I walked back to the bathroom, stepped into the shower stall, lifted my face towards the shower head and turned the water on full force. It was going to take a real blast to wash away the last three hours.

CHAPTER

3

Tom Kelsoe's book launch was being held at the university Faculty Club on the second floor of College West. I'd been to some great parties there, but as I walked through the door that night, I knew this wasn't going to be one of them. Real shamrocks and shillelaghs that looked as if they could be real were everywhere, but the mood was sombre. The lounge to the right of the entrance area was jammed. Ordinarily, guests picked up their drinks at the bar and drifted into one of the larger rooms; that night, people weren't drifting. It was apparent from their pale and anxious faces that the news of Reed Gallagher's death had spread, and that the rumours were swirling.

Several of the people I'd left messages for that afternoon spotted me in the doorway and came over. They were full of questions, but I hid behind Alex's statement that, until the police had finished their investigations, Reed's death was being classified as accidental. It wasn't a satisfactory answer, but no one seemed to have the heart to press me.

I made my way through to the bar and ordered Glenfiddich on the rocks. When it came, I took a long sip; the warmth spreading through my veins felt so good, I took another.

"There are times when only single-malt Scotch will do." The voice behind me was throaty and familiar.

"And this is one of them," I said. "Care to join me?"

Jill Osiowy scrutinized my glass longingly. "Tom and I are off hard liquor," she said.

I turned to face her. There was no denying that the abstemious life agreed with her. I'd hedged when Taylor asked me about my feelings for Tom, but even I had to admit that the effect he was having on her lifestyle was a positive one. In the years I had known her, Jill had been a workaholic: routinely putting in fourteen-hour workdays, subsisting on junk food, too busy to exercise, and too tense at the end of the day to unwind without a couple of stiff drinks.

Tom Kelsoe had changed all that. He was into vegetarian-ism and weight training, and now so was she. She had never been heavy, but now she was very lean and muscular. Her auburn hair was cut in a fashionable new way that made her look ten years younger. She was wearing black lace-up boots, form-fitting black velvet pants, and an extravagantly beau-tiful jade jacket with a black mandarin collar and elaborate black fastenings.

"You look like about seven million dollars," I said.

"I feel like homemade shit."

"Where's Tom?"

"At the gym," she said. "He says he has a lot of stuff to get through. Reed was his first boss when he got out of J school. He was like a father to Tom."

"How much does Tom know about what happened?"

"Just what I told him, and I got that from you." She shook her head in a gesture of disbelief. "Jo, what did happen?"

I started to tell her what I knew. Then, over her shoulder, I saw Ed Mariani bobbing towards us. He was a portly and pleasant man, my favourite, by far, of the faculty at the School of Journalism. Earlier in the semester, I'd sat in on his lectures on the Politics of Image, and I'd understood why there were always waiting lists for the courses he taught. He was passionate about his subject, and while he was demanding with his students, he was genuinely excited about their response to what they were learning. In and out of class, Ed was fun, and, under normal circumstances, he would have been exactly the man I wanted to chat to at a party. But these were not normal circumstances.

I grabbed Jill's arm. "Come on," I said. "It'll be easier to talk in the hall."

Ed Mariani's face fell when he saw us leaving, but I didn't relent. Julie Evanson-Gallagher had leached me of charity. Jill and I walked to the end of the corridor and found an alcove where we wouldn't be spotted by latecomers. There, I told her everything I knew about Reed Gallagher's death.

Jill had worked in the media for twenty years; she had more than a nodding acquaintance with the tragic and the bizarre, but she stiffened as I described the scene the police had found in the room on Scarth Street. When I finished, she seemed dazed. Finally she said, "I have to get back inside. When Tom comes, he'll want me there."

"What about what you want?"

The harsh institutional light above her shone directly on her face, knifing in the years. "What I want doesn't matter. Tonight, Tom is all that matters. Jo, I've never been a very giving person, but I'm trying, and I've finally reached a point where Tom knows he can trust me absolutely. I can't let him down. There've been so many betrayals in his life."

"And I'll bet he's told you about every one."

"That was cruel."

"I'm sorry. It's just that I hate to see you acting like a Stepford wife, especially with Tom Kelsoe."

She moved towards me. "Tom has suffered so much, Jo. His father was a real horror show – bullying and abusive – but whenever Tom's mother threatened to leave, his father would force Tom to beg her to stay. You just don't know him. He is so vulnerable."

"And so manipulative. Jill, I do know Tom. I've worked with him for two years. I've seen him in action."

For one awful moment, I thought she was going to hit me; then, without a word, she turned and walked back down the hall. When she disappeared into the Faculty Club, I followed her. I couldn't afford to lose any more points with her by being late for Tom's party.

Inside the club, it looked as if the main event was finally about to begin. People were moving out of the lounge and finding places at tables which had been set up to face a lectern at the end of the room. On a table a discreet distance from the lectern, copies of Tom's new book were stacked beside a cloisonné vase of white freesia. Everything was ready for the reading, but the man behind the microphone wasn't Tom Kelsoe. It was Ed Mariani.

There was a certain logic in his being there. It was no secret that Ed had wanted to be head of the School of Journalism. In fact, his appointment had been considered a sure thing until Reed Gallagher applied, and Ed withdrew from the competition. His decision to take his name off the list of candidates had been as abrupt as it had been inexplicable, but whatever his reason for withdrawing, Ed had rapidly become Reed's staunchest ally. He had moved quickly to make sure that department members who had supported his own candidacy threw their support behind Reed, and he had spoken out against those who feared that Reed's plans for the school were too ambitious. That night, we had gathered to honour a member of the School of Journalism; with Reed gone, Ed Mariani was the one to take charge.

But as he adjusted the microphone, it was apparent there was no joy in it for him. Ed had features made for smiling, but his face was crumpled with sorrow. "This is an evening to be with friends," he said, and his voice broke. He took a handkerchief from his pocket, mopped his eyes, and began again. "As you have no doubt heard, Reed Gallagher died last night. We're only now beginning to comprehend the depth of our loss. He was our colleague, our friend, and, for those of us in the School of Journalism, he was our example of what a journalist should be. Rudyard Kipling called what we do 'the black art,' but as Reed Gallagher practised it, journalism was a shining thing – incisive, compelling, and humane. It's hard to know where we go from here, but I think those of us who counted Reed as a friend know that he would have wanted . . ."

Before Ed Mariani had a chance to finish, a door behind and to the left of the lectern flew open. Suddenly, all eyes were focused on the man in the doorway. Tom Kelsoe hesitated long enough to take in the situation, then he strode towards the podium and pushed Ed aside. It was a gesture so gratuitously rude that people gasped.

Tom didn't seem to notice or care. "Talking about what Reed would have wanted us to do is a waste of time," he said, and his voice was cutting. "And he despised wasting time as much as he despised anything that was fake or second-rate." He shot a furious look at Ed Mariani, who was standing by the window with his partner, Barry Levitt. Ed lowered his eyes, but Barry took a step forward. His face was flushed with anger, and Ed grabbed his arm and drew him back.

I moved to Jill. She didn't acknowledge my presence. Her attention was wholly focused on her man. I didn't blame her. As he stood gripping the edges of the podium, Tom Kelsoe was enough to grab anybody's attention. He wasn't a big man, no more than five-foot-ten, but that night, in a black stressed-leather jacket, black turtleneck, and jeans, his body had a kind of coiled spring tension that was almost palpable. There was always an admixture of woundedness and anger about Tom; grief seemed to have distilled the mix into an essence as potent as testosterone. As he leaned into the microphone, he looked, as Lady Caroline Lamb is reputed to have said of Byron, "mad, bad, and dangerous to know."

Without preamble, Tom picked up his book. "This is about the people who will never be in this room or even at this university. It's about the charter members of the permanent underclass in our country – the ones who've never read Hobbes but who don't need Philosophy 101 to know that life is nasty, brutish, and short.

"The title of this book is *Getting Even*. The words come from some advice a woman who's dead now gave her sons. The woman's name was Karen Keewatin, and I met her boys on the corner of Halifax and Fourteenth shortly after midnight on April Fool's Day last year. The date was appropriate. I *was* a fool to be in that area at night, but I was also more desperate than I can ever remember being."

At the table nearest Tom, a group of students from our class sat transfixed. Hearing your instructor publicly admit frailty is riveting stuff.

"I'd been given a substantial advance to write a book about life in the streets," Tom said. "The previous month I'd finished a manuscript and sent it to my publishers. I'd given it my best shot. I'd spent months researching life in the meanest areas of Vancouver, Toronto, and Winnipeg. I'd recorded and transcribed the stories of murderers, thieves, pimps, prostitutes, junkies, pushers, and street kids, but the book wasn't alive. I knew it, and my publishers knew it, but nobody knew how to fix it. Luckily for me, Reed Gallagher had just accepted the job here, and I called him and told him I needed help."

For a beat, Tom seemed overcome with the pain of his memory. Then he smiled ruefully. "Reed went through the manuscript that night, and he was brutal. He told me that what I'd given him was voyeurism not journalism and that I should throw out everything I'd written and start again. 'This time,' he said, 'get it right. Leave your tape-recorder at home. Give these people a chance to be something more than research subjects. Give them some dignity, and give your readers a chance to come to some sort of deeper understanding about what it feels like to be used and abused and choking with rage.'

"So that rainy April night when I was standing on the corner of Halifax and Fourteenth Street, I'd left my tape-recorder at home, which was just as well because, when those two kids jumped out from behind the bushes and started beating me with their baseball bats, I wouldn't have had time to push *record*. The next thing I remember is a nurse who looked like Demi Moore bending over me and asking me if I knew what day it was. Lovely as that nurse was, I didn't want to hang around Regina General. I wanted to find those kids with the bats and beat the shit out of them.

"Reed Gallagher had a better plan. He agreed that I should find the kids, but he said that, instead of killing them, I should try to win their trust. He said if I could get to a point where I understood what made two kids attack a person they'd never seen and from whom they took nothing, I might have something to write about." He shrugged. "So I did. It took a while, but I found them. I don't think I can read tonight. I just want to talk. I just want to tell you a story: the story of Karen Keewatin and her sons, Jason, who's eleven now, and Darrel, who just turned ten."

It was a brilliant performance. The room was filled with emotion, and Tom Kelsoe seemed to feed off it. It was as if he took the pain we were feeling and channelled it into his account of the pain that had fuelled the lives of Karen and her sons.

As he told their story, despite my distrust of Tom, I felt my throat burn. Karen was a reserve girl from the north who came to Regina in search of the good life. She had no plans beyond the next party, and she ended up on the street. She started working as a prostitute when she was fourteen; by the time she was nineteen, she had a significant police record and two babies. One frigid night, she got into the wrong car. The john took her down an alley, beat her, threw her out and left her for dead. When she regained consciousness, she crawled down the street till she found a girl she knew. Tom said Jason Keewatin told him his mother was afraid that if she went to the hospital, Social Services would take her boys away.

It took her six weeks to recover. Girls she knew from the street took turns caring for her and her children. Six weeks is a long time to stare at the ceiling and, for the first time in her life, Karen Keewatin started thinking about how she'd come into this world and how she was going to leave it. She made up her mind that, if she got better, she was going to change her life. And she did. She applied for social assistance and subsidized housing, and she enrolled in an upgrading program. School was agony. In the north, she had attended class sporadically, and the schooling she did receive was abysmal. In her upgrading placement exam, she tested at a grade-four level.

Karen Keewatin had a lot of catching up to do, but she was determined. Her boys told Tom Kelsoe that the most vivid memory they had of their mother was of her sitting at the kitchen table, trying furiously and often futilely to understand what was written in the books in front of her. But she never gave up. She told her sons, "You guys aren't gonna have to go through this, because if it's the last thing I do, I'm going to make sure you're even-Steven with everybody else right from the start."

It took her five years, but Karen finally graduated from high school and enrolled in a dental hygienists' program. After she got her diploma, she got a job, a "respectable job, with nice people." When she brought home her first paycheque she told her sons, "We're even now. You guys got nothing you have to prove." Six months later, she was diagnosed with AIDS. She was fired; she tried to find other "respectable" work, but her medical record followed her. Finally, she went back on the streets. Early one morning, she picked up a bad trick, and this time, after the beating, she didn't crawl back.

On the night Tom Kelsoe met them, Karen's boys were doing what they had done most nights since their mother's death. They were getting even with the men who lived in the world that killed their mother.

When he finished, Tom Kelsoe bowed his head. Then he picked up a copy of his book from the table beside him. "I'm proud of every page of this book," he said softly. "I'm proud because Darrel and Jason Keewatin have read their story and they tell me I've got it right. I'm proud because in here you'll discover what it feels like to live inside the skin of those who live without hope." His voice cracked. "And I'm proud because in the dedication I'm able to make a first payment on the immeasurable debt I owe to the man who was my teacher and my friend." He opened the book and read. "For Reed Gallagher, with respect and thanks."

There was silence; then Tom did a curious thing. He turned towards Ed Mariani, and held out his hand. After a moment that seemed to last forever, Ed walked over to Tom and shook his hand. It was a gesture as generous as it was characteristic. Everyone liked Ed, and the memory of Tom's rudeness to him was fresh. By his handshake, Ed made it possible for people to respond openly to Tom's reading, and they did. It was as if a breach had been made in the wall of emotion that had been held in check since we heard about Reed's death. People stood and applauded. More than a few of them wept; when I looked across the room, I was surprised to see the future Frank Gifford, Jumbo Hryniuk, crying lustily into his handkerchief. Beside him, dry-eyed but transfixed, was Val Massey. Even from where I was standing, I could see the glow of hero worship. At that moment, Tom Kelsoe was everything Val Massey dreamed of becoming.

A bookseller appeared and hustled Tom to the table of books. *Getting Even* was launched, and from the way people were jostling one another to get in line to buy a copy, it appeared that the evening was going to be a commercial triumph.

I walked to the end of the line to take my place, but as I queued up, a wave of tiredness washed over me. I had had enough. I looked around to see if I could find Jill, so I could apologize. I spotted her in the corner talking to Barry Levitt. There were reconciliations all around.

As I walked past the bar to get my coat, old Giv Mewhort spotted me. Giv was a professor emeritus of English and as much a fixture of the Faculty Club as the grand piano in the corner. Rumour had it that he raised his morning glass of Gilbey's when the Faculty Club staff were still laying out the breakfast buffet, but Giv was always a gentleman.

That night, as he came over to help me on with my coat, he was courtly. When I thanked him, he smiled puckishly. "My pleasure," he said. "In fact the whole evening has been a pleasure." He glanced towards the table where Tom Kelsoe was signing books. "I haven't enjoyed a performance this much since I saw the young Marlon Brando play Mark Antony in *Julius Caesar*." He waved his glass in Tom's direction. "That boy over there is good."

It was 9:00 when I pulled into my driveway. The wind had stopped, but it was still raining. It seemed to me I had been cold and wet the whole day. The dogs met me hopefully at the breezeway door.

"Not a chance," I said. "I promise we'll go for a walk first thing tomorrow. But right now, the best I can do for you is let you out for a pee."

When I came into the kitchen, Alex Kequahtooway was sitting at the kitchen table smearing mustard onto a corned beef sandwich. He looked up when he saw me. "I had an hour clear, so I took a chance that you'd be home early. Angus told me to help myself."

"Good for Angus," I said. "But I thought we were out of mustard."

"I carry my own."

"You're kidding."

"That's right," he said, "I'm kidding. I thought you looked like you could use a joke."

"Actually, I think what I could use is you."

He put down his sandwich, came over, and put his arms around me. His shirt was fresh and his hair was wet.

"You smell like lemons," I said.

"It's the shampoo," he said. "When you spend much time in the room with a body, the smell kind of soaks in. Lemon's the only thing I know that takes it out." He smiled. "Would you like me to change the subject?"

"Maybe just switch the focus. How's the investigation going?"

"Okay. The M.E.'s finished, and the landlady was co-operative. I bet she doesn't weigh eighty-five pounds, but she's a tough old bird. Most people would be pretty shaken if they'd walked in on the scene she walked in on, but her big gripe seems to be that Gallagher died in a room she was trying to rent. She'd just finished cleaning."

"The room was vacant?"

"Apparently. Come on. Let's sit down, and I'll tell you about it. Want some milk?"

"I think what I would like is a pot of Earl Grey tea."

"I'll put the kettle on," he said. "Anyway, the room was vacant, and at seven o'clock last night it was as presentable as a dump like that would ever be. Alma Stringer – that's the landlady – said she hauled the vacuum up herself because she'd shampooed the rug. Of course, with one thing and another, her shampoo job is pretty well shot now."

"Wasn't the door locked?"

"The doors on the main floor were. Alma has more locks on those doors than the government has on the Federal Mint, but she'd left the door to the room Reed Gallagher ended up in open; she wanted to give the rug a chance to dry. Anyway, the room's on the third floor, and there's a fire escape just a couple of steps down the hall. Alma says if she finds the tenant who left the door to the fire escape open, she'll kill him with her bare hands, and I believe her."

The kettle started to sing. I warmed the pot, then measured in the Earl Grey. "None of this makes sense, Alex. Reed Gallagher had money, and I'll bet he had a wallet full of credit cards. Why would he risk breaking into a rooming house when he could have just gone to a hotel?"

Alex poured the tea. "Zimbardo's theory is that with this kind of masochistic sex, the danger of the surroundings is part of the kick. You'll have to admit, Jo, it's not exactly the type of act you want to pull off at the Holiday Inn. And another thing, we found drugs at the scene. Street drugs. Gallagher might have been down there making a buy and just decided to stay in the neighbourhood."

"What kind of drugs?"

"Amyl nitrites. The street name is poppers. They dilate the blood vessels. They were originally used to treat angina."

"But you don't think Reed was using them for medicinal reasons."

"Not with the hood and the rest of the paraphernalia. Poppers are also supposed to prolong and intensify orgasm. Splatter figured that's what Gallagher was doing, but it was a bad choice. Amyl nitrites cause a sharp decrease in blood pressure. The current theory is that Gallagher blacked out, and wasn't able to extricate himself from his bondage."

"What an awful way to die."

"It's not the best, that's for sure." Alex studied the tea in his cup, then he looked up. "Jo, was Reed Gallagher bisexual by any chance?"

"I don't know. Why?"

"Because poppers are primarily used by gay men. It's odd to see a straight guy with them."

"The whole thing is odd," I said.

"It is that," he said. "And I think we've both had enough of it. Let's talk about something more pleasant. How was your evening?"

"Actually, not much better than yours." I started to tell him about the launch. I skipped the ugly exchange I'd had with Jill, but I did tell him about Tom Kelsoe's rudeness to Ed Mariani.

When I finished, Alex shook his head in disgust. "Why would a terrific woman like Jill put up with a prick like that?"

"She's in love," I said. "Or she thinks she is. But that was a pricky thing to do, wasn't it? I'm glad to have some objective corroboration. My instincts weren't very trustworthy tonight."

"You've got great instincts."

"When it comes to Tom Kelsoe, I'm not exactly impartial. You know, I'm embarrassed even to say this, but at the book launch I realized that, in addition to everything else, I'm jealous of him."

"Because of all the attention he's getting?"

"Partly, I guess. When my book came out, my publisher didn't lay on a launch. I just invited all my friends over for a barbecue and made them buy a copy."

"I didn't know you'd written a book."

"Neither did anybody else. It was a biography of Andy Boychuk. It's been almost five years since he died, but I still think how different this province, maybe even the country, would have been if he'd lived."

"Do you really believe one person can make a difference?"

"Sure. Don't you?"

"I used to. That's why I joined the force. I was going to show the public that a native cop could be as smart and as reliable as a white cop, and I was going to show the native community that the law was fair and impartial." He laughed. "In those days, I thought of myself as a force for change."

"And you don't think of yourself that way any more?"

He shook his head. "No," he said. "I don't."

I looked at him. Even in the softly diffused light from the telephone table, the acne scars of his adolescence were apparent. The first time we'd made love, he'd recoiled when I touched his face. The more I came to know Alex Kequahtooway, the more I believed the acne scars were just the beginning.

"We're wasting our hour talking," I said.

He came and put his arms around me. "So we are," he said. "So we are."

Angus's stage cough was discreet. "Sorry to interrupt, but Leah and I are going to 7-Eleven, and I wanted to make sure Alex was still going to give me a driving lesson tomorrow."

"I'll be here at nine a.m.," Alex said.

"With your Audi," Angus said.

"With my Audi."

"Was a driving lesson the price you paid for that corned beef sandwich?" I asked.

"I volunteered." He looked at his watch. "And I've got to get back."

Angus's eyes widened. "A break in a case?"

"Paperwork," Alex said, and he stood and zipped his jacket. "I'll see you tomorrow morning. Both of you."

I walked him to the door. Then the dogs and I headed for bed. I almost made it. I'd already checked on Taylor, brushed my teeth, and discovered that all my nightgowns were in the clean laundry in the basement when Angus yelled that there was a lady at the door who had to see me.

I pulled on my jogging clothes and sweatsocks and padded downstairs. Julie Evanson-Gallagher was standing in the hall. She was wearing the London Fog trenchcoat she'd put on to go down to police headquarters that afternoon, but she'd added gold hoop earrings, a paisley silk scarf, a tan leather bag and matching gloves. She was immaculate, but her careful grooming couldn't hide the tension in her body or the anguish in her eyes.

I stepped aside. "Won't you come in, Julie?" I said.

"No," she said. "I just wanted to give you the keys." She fumbled with her purse. When the clasp finally opened, she took out a set of keys.

"I'm leaving for the airport to catch a flight to Toronto. I'll need somebody to look after the house when I'm away. I don't know who else to ask."

I took the keys from her. "I'll be happy to help."

"I didn't mean you had to go over there. I thought I could pay one of your children. There's not much to do – just feed the fish and take in the mail. But someone should clean out the refrigerator. My cleaning lady quit last night." She shook her head in bewilderment. "Why does everything have to go wrong at once?"

"Julie, this has been a terrible day for you. Why don't you come in and have a drink, and when you're ready, I'll drive you to the airport."

"I can't take a chance on missing my plane," she said. "I don't want to be here when people find out how he died."

"Did you tell Alex you're going? The police should know."

"They know," she said dully. Then the implication of what I'd said seemed to dawn on her, and for a flash she was the old Julie. "Surely you're not suggesting that the police think I was connected with what went on in that room." Her voice rose dangerously. "How could they? How could anybody believe that, if I had a choice, I'd let the world see my husband like that?"

I touched her arm. "Julie, all I meant was that the police might need your signature for something."

"They can find me at my sister's," she said tightly. "She lives in Port Hope. The police have the address, and I've left it by the phone in my kitchen in case you need to get in touch with me. Everything's taken care of." Suddenly her composure cracked. "I don't deserve this," she said. "I did everything right, and I had such hopes."

As I watched her cab drive up my road towards the airport, I thought of Julie's epitaph for her marriage. The words were heartbreaking, but tonight wasn't the first time I'd heard her use them. Years before, I'd run into Julie outside our neighbourhood high school. It was late June, and she had just learned that her son, Mark, had failed every class in grade ten and the counsellor was recommending a non-academic program for him. She had been devastated. "He's never going to do anything that matters," she'd said, miserably. "And I don't understand. I did everything right, and I had such hopes." Then, having absolved herself of blame and purged herself of hope, Julie Evanson had closed the door on her only child forever.

CHAPTER

4

When I woke up Saturday morning, the sun was shining, the sky looked freshly washed, the birds were singing, and the phone was ringing. I picked up the receiver, heard Jill Osiowy's familiar contralto and felt my spirits rise.

It wasn't unusual for Jill to call on a Saturday morning. She produced Nationtv's political panel, and I was one of the regulars. The show was telecast live on Saturday nights, and if Jill spotted a provocative item in the morning paper, she'd often call to see how I felt about leading with it. But after my Stepford-wife crack the night before, I was anticipating a chill, and it was a relief to hear her sounding cordial.

"Jo, are you up for a whole change of topic for the call-in segment tonight? It seems there's been some major-league vandalism at the university."

"Where at the university?"

"I don't know. I haven't been to the campus yet, but one of our technicians, Gerry McIntyre, was out there for his morning run, and he saw squad cars over by the Education building. When he went over to ask what was going on, the cops told him the place had been vandalized."

"Jill, I hate to shoot down a story idea, but a certain amount of vandalism is one of the rites of spring at any university. It's ugly, but it doesn't usually amount to much beyond kids getting drunk and deciding to leave their mark on the world. Last year some Engineering students decided they weren't getting the respect they deserved, so they spray-painted 'Engineers Rule' on every blank wall they could find."

"This wasn't quite that sophomoric. Gerry says it looks like a hate crime."

"A hate crime?" I repeated. "Who was the target?"

"Homosexuals," Jill said. "Apparently, the graffiti the vandals left behind is homophobic, and, Jo, the reason I think this particular vandalism may be worth talking about is that it's not unique. I've been watching the wire services, and gay-bashing seems to be enjoying a certain cross-country vogue again. Anyway, what do you think about the change of topic?

"My stomach is already churning at the thought of the phone-ins."

"We'll screen the callers so we know everything about them but their blood type, and I'll keep my finger on the cut-off button . . ."

I laughed. "Okay. You're on."

"You're going to have to do some digging. There've been several rulings on sexual orientation lately, and you should have that stuff at your fingertips. Are you sure I'm not crowding you?"

"I'm sure. I try to keep up on the major rulings that come out of the Charter, and I have a file folder stuffed with articles on gay and lesbian rights."

Jill laughed. "Still clipping newspapers. Jo, you're a dinosaur."

"Maybe," I said. "But I like the way newspapers feel in my hands. Anyway, don't worry about giving me enough lead time. All I've got on today is taking Taylor to her class – oh, and feeding Julie's fish. She's going to her sister's in Port Hope till this blows over."

"When the going gets tough, the tough get going," Jill said mildly.

I laughed. "You know Julie. She's never liked a mess."

"I guess she's not alone in that," Jill said. "See you tonight."

She sounded more like her usual self than she had in months, and I felt the relief wash over me. "Jill, I'm so glad you called. And Springtime for Homophobes is a great topic."

"Thanks," she said, "but actually, it was Tom's idea."

After I hung up, I pulled out the telephone book, checked the university's listings, and dialled the number opposite the office of Physical Plant. I got a recorded message telling me when the regular office hours were and giving me a number to call if I deemed my concerns to be of an emergency nature. They weren't, but I *was* curious. I looked at my watch. If I hurried, I could drive up to the campus and be back before the demands of Saturday morning made themselves felt.

When I started for the bathroom, I caught a glimpse of myself in the mirror over my dresser and cringed. I'd slept in the clothes I'd greeted Julie in the night before. I was getting worse than Angus. I grabbed clean underwear and a fresh sweatshirt and jeans, then I went into the bathroom and splashed water on my face. As I began brushing my teeth, my mind drifted. The night before I had told Alex that Tom Kelsoe's new celebrity was only part of the reason for my jealousy. Most of the reason, although I hated to admit it, was Jill.

We had always been close. The day after she graduated from J school, she'd started working for my husband, Ian. He was the youngest attorney general in the history of our province, but he'd been in politics long enough to be both bemused and touched by Jill's fervent idealism. After he died, Jill kept working for the government, but she said the spark was gone. She moved to Ottawa, did a graduate degree in journalism, and started working for Nationtv. When she came back to Saskatchewan, one of the first things she did was hire me for the political panel. I'd never thought of doing television, but Jill had faith and patience; she shepherded me through the gaffes and panics of the early days, and it had worked out. Personally and professionally, Jill and I were a nice mix. Her relationship with Tom Kelsoe had changed all that, but as I rinsed my toothbrush I decided that, even if it meant holding my nose and learning to love Tom Kelsoe, I was going to change it back.

"Jo, look. I've started the drawings for my mural."

Taylor was standing in the bathroom door with her sketchpad under her arm.

I put my toothbrush back in the cup. "Okay," I said, "show me."

She pushed past me, flipped down the toilet seat and settled herself on top of it. After she had balanced her sketchpad on her knees, she began explaining. "Alex said nobody ever gets close enough to Nanabush to take his picture, but this is how I think he looks."

As Taylor's index finger danced across her sketchpad, pointing out details, lingering over problems, I was struck again by the gulf between the little girl perched on the toilet seat, legs dangling, and the gifted artist who had made the pictures of Nanabush on the pages in front of me. At the age of six, Taylor's talent was already undeniable. It was a question of nature not nurture. Taylor's mother had been a brilliant artist, and Taylor had inherited the gift.

When we'd looked at the last sketch, Taylor hopped off the toilet. "I'm hungry," she said.

"I wouldn't be surprised," I said. "You've already done a lot of work today. Why don't I get you some juice and cereal.

I have to go up to the university for a few minutes, but as soon as I get home, I'll make pancakes."

When I put the dogs on their leashes and led them to the garage, they looked dubious, and when I opened the back gate of the Volvo our aging golden retriever, Rose, sat down defiantly. "Come on, Rosie," I said. "Get in. We'll have our run out at the bird sanctuary. The paper says the bluebirds are back. It'll be an adventure." She cocked her head and looked at me sceptically. I moved behind her and pushed her until she finally lumbered into the car. Sadie, our collie, who was beautiful but easily led, bounded in after her.

By the time I pulled into the parking space at the university, the dogs had perked up, and they jumped out, eager to follow me, as I headed for the Education building. The red-white-and-blue police cars were still there, as was the vandals' handiwork. The long glassed-in walkway that linked College West and the Lab building was dripping with all the ugly anti-gay invective the wielder of the spray-paint canister could think of. I was cheered to see that the vandal had crossed out the extra *s* that had initially been in "cock-sucker." Maybe literacy was on the rise after all.

The dogs and I walked towards the Education building. A young police officer with a blond braid was standing by a squad car making notes.

"What's up?" I asked.

Her look was noncommittal. "Everything's under control," she said coolly. "Why don't you and your dogs finish your walk?"

"I'm not rubbernecking," I said. "I teach here."

"I hope for your sake that your office isn't in this building."

"Can I go in?"

"Not with your dogs."

I walked them back and put them in the car. First seduced and now abandoned, they began to bark, furious at the betrayal.

When I came back, the blond-braided police officer had been replaced by a young constable who looked as if he could bench-press two hundred kilograms without breaking a sweat. I flashed my faculty ID at him and said, "I teach here."

He waved me through. "Go ahead," he said. His voice was surprisingly high and sweet as a choirboy's. "Stay away from the areas marked by crime-scene tape, and if an officer asks you to leave, please obey."

I went into the building, turned left, and walked towards the cafeteria. It looked as it always did after hours: the accordion security gates were pulled across, the tables were wiped clean, and the chairs were stacked in piles against the far wall. Someone had suspended cutouts of Easter rabbits and of chicks in bonnets from the ceiling above the empty food-display cases, and by the cash register there was a sign announcing that Cadbury Easter Creme Eggs were back. Everything seemed reassuringly ordinary, but when I continued along the hall and pushed through the double doors that led to the audio-visual department of the School of Journalism, I stepped into chaos.

I was ankle-deep in paper: computer printouts, dumped files, books with pages torn and spines splayed. The walls around me were spray-painted with the same snappy patter I'd seen on the walkway between College West and the Lab building. It was slow going, but finally I made it past the photography department and turned down the hall that led to the Journalism offices.

As I walked towards Ed Mariani's office, I was reassured to see that whoever had done the trashing was an equal-opportunity vandal. The offices of straight and gay alike were destroyed. Through open doors, I could see books and pictures heaped on desks, plants overturned, keyboards ripped from their terminals. On Ed's door was a sign: "Of all life's passions, the strongest is the need to edit another's prose." Beside it somebody had spray-painted the words "Fairy-Loving-Bum-Fucker." I closed my eyes, but I could still see the words, and I knew Ed's sign was right: at that moment, I hungered for a paint canister of my own and a chance to do a little judicious editing.

Sick with disgust, I turned and doubled back towards the front door of the building. I wanted to be outside where my dogs were waiting; the air was sweet and the bluebirds had come home.

When I pulled up in front of our house, Taylor was sitting on the top step of the porch, with Benny on her knee. She was still wearing her nightie, but she'd added her windbreaker and her runners. "Winter's over," she said happily.

"It certainly feels like it," I said. "Now let's go inside and get something to eat. I'm starving." I made coffee and pancake batter. Taylor, who had already eaten a bowl of cereal and a banana poured batter in the shape of her initials onto the griddle; when she'd polished off her initials, she made Benny's initials. I was watching her devour these and waiting for my own pancakes when Alex came.

"I haven't even had a shower yet," I groaned.

"You look good to me," he said. "After yesterday, you deserve to laze around."

"I wish," I said. "I feel like I've already put in a full day." I took the pancakes off the griddle. "Do you want these?"

"You take them, but if there's plenty . . ."

I handed him the bowl and the ladle. "Taylor makes hers in the shape of her initials."

He smiled. "She's such a weird little kid." He went over to the griddle and poured. "Okay. Fill me in on your day."

I watched his face as I told him about the vandalism at the university. He listened, as he always did to whatever the kids and I told him, seriously and without interruption or comment.

"I guess it could have been worse," I said. "At least whoever did it vented their spleen in words. Nobody was hurt."

"Sticks and stones may break my bones but names will never hurt me," he said, and there was an edge of bitterness in his voice that surprised me. "Did Mrs. Gallagher get in touch with you last night?" he asked.

"She made a house call. She brought her keys over because she's going to her sister's in Port Hope."

"She told me she might do that."

"So she did talk to you."

"Of course. She's a good citizen. She wouldn't leave town without telling us where she'd be. Anyway, I was glad she called. I had some questions; she answered them."

"What kind of questions."

"Just tidying-up-loose-ends questions. I wanted her to go over again what she knew about where her husband was in the twenty-four hours before he died. She didn't have much to add except . . ."

"Except what?"

"Except I still don't think she's told us everything. For one thing, I have a feeling that yesterday wasn't the first time she'd been in that rooming house on Scarth Street. When I took her there, she started down the hall on the main floor as if she knew where she was going."

"But Reed's body wasn't on the main floor."

"No. It was upstairs, on the top floor. Actually, we have a witness who thinks he saw Gallagher going up the fire escape at the back at around quarter to nine."

"I don't understand how you can let Julie go when you think she might be holding something back."

"Jo, when someone dies suddenly, everybody who knew them holds things back. There are a hundred reasons why the living don't choose to disclose everything they know about the dead, but as long as those reasons don't have a direct bearing on our case, we don't push it."

"So Julie doesn't have to stay in Regina."

"There's no legal reason why she should. Her husband's dead, and human decency might suggest that she hang around till he's in the ground, but there's nothing to indicate that Gallagher's death was anything other than accidental. They're doing an autopsy this afternoon, but with the hood and the garter belt and all the other paraphernalia, I think we know what they'll find."

"Which is?"

"Which is that Reed Gallagher died of a fatal combination of bad judgement and bad luck."

"It still doesn't make sense to me."

"Jo, a lot of sexual practices don't have much to do with common sense, but that doesn't mean they don't happen. Sherman Zimbardo had coffee with a couple of doctors from the E.R. at the General last night; he says some of the stories those women had about what they've removed from there would curl your hair." Alex deftly slid his pancakes onto his plate and smiled at me. "And it's all in the name of love."

I passed him the butter. " '"Thank goodness we're all different," said Alice.' "

Alex looked quizzical. "Who's Alice?"

"Someone who stepped through the looking-glass," I said.

Alex picked up the maple syrup. "I know the feeling," he said. "Now, what's on your agenda today?"

"Nothing but good works," I said. "I'm going to take Taylor to her art class and get ready for tonight's program. How about you?"

"I'm taking Angus for his driving lesson."

I winced. "Talk about good works. Can I reward you by taking you to a movie after we do our show?"

"Sounds great, but I'll have to take a rain check."

I felt a sting of disappointment. "More paperwork?"

He looked away. "No, family matters." His voice was distant. "I've got a nephew out on the reserve who seems to be in need of a little guidance."

"How old?"

"Fifteen."

"Angus's age."

"Yeah, but he's not Angus." The edge was back in his voice, and I could feel the wall going up. Alex talked easily about his life on Standing Buffalo when he was young, but never about life there now, and I tried not to pry.

Angus appeared in the doorway. For once, his timing was impeccable, as was his appearance: slicked-back hair, earring in place, faded rock shirt, and jeans so badly torn I wondered how he kept them on. He went over and slapped Alex on the back. "So," he said, "are you ready to rip?"

It was only six blocks from our house to the Gallaghers' condo on Lakeview Court, but because we were going straight to Taylor's lesson after we were through at Julie's, we drove. When I opened the front door, Taylor slipped off her boots and ran inside to find the aquarium. Before I'd even hung my coat up, she was back in the hall, breathless.

"Oh, Jo, they're beautiful, especially the striped ones. We've got to get some. We could stop at the Golden Mile after my lesson. They've got fish in the pet shop – all kinds of them. And we'll need some of that pink stuff that looks like knobby fingers."

"Coral," I said.

"And a castle. These fish have a castle in the corner of their tank, and they swim right through the front door."

"Do you know who would really love it if we got some fish?" I asked her.

"Who?"

"Benny," I said.

Her eyes widened with horror. Then a smile played at the corner of her lips. "No fish, right?"

"No fish," I said.

After I showed Taylor how much food to put in the aquarium, I turned to the rest of my tasks. There wasn't much to do. The dishes and the checked cloths were off the rental tables, and the extra chairs had been stacked, ready for pickup. Julie had left the rental company's business card on the kitchen table with a note asking me to arrange a time when I could be there to let them in. The only hints of the evening before were the pots of shamrock that had been in the white wicker centrepieces. The plants were lined up neatly on a tray where they could catch the light from Julie's kitchen window. When I touched the soil, it was moist. She had taken care of everything, but those must have been bleak hours for her, alone in her house, dismantling the evening she'd planned with such care while her new husband lay dead in the morgue at Regina General.

The refrigerator didn't take long to clean. There were no nasty surprises mouldering in old yogurt containers, just perishables that had obviously been intended for the party: two quarts of whipping cream, unopened; two large plastic bags of crisp salad greens; three vegetable platters that looked as if they could still make the cover of Martha Stewart's *Living*. I boxed up everything for the Indian-Métis Friendship Centre. Julie was moving into contention for their award as Benefactor of the Year.

After I dropped Taylor off at her art lesson, I drove Julie's food donation to the Friendship Centre, and then headed downtown to check out the sales. Angus had been hinting about a new winter jacket, and Taylor needed rubber boots.

Cornwall Centre was in its spring mode. Hyacinth, daf-fodils, and tulips bloomed beside the water fountains, and winter clothes marked 60 per cent off bloomed on the racks in front of stores. At Work Warehouse, I discovered that the jacket Angus had admired loudly and frequently before Christmas had at last reached my price range, and I bought it. Then I went to Eaton's basement and found a pair of rubber boots in Taylor's favourite shade of hot pink. As the salesclerk was wrapping them up, I remembered my early-morning resolve to get back in Jill's good graces by cosying up to Tom Kelsoe. From what I'd seen of Tom, the surest way to his heart was through his ego. I went to City Books.

There was a single copy of *Getting Even* beside the cash register. When I handed it to the woman behind the counter, she groaned. "That's the last copy. I was going to buy it myself." She eyed the author picture on the back and sighed. "He is attractive, isn't he? He was on the radio yesterday morning. I didn't hear him, but people have been coming to the store in tears because of a story he told about a mother and her two sons – right here in Regina." She shrugged. "Well, I'll just have to order more. Cash or credit?"

I hadn't planned to drive by the rooming house where Reed Gallagher died, but as I headed along my usual route to pick Taylor up at her class on the old campus, I ran into a construction detour. The next street that would take me south was Scarth Street, and there was no way I could drive along Scarth without seeing number 317. It was a house straight out of an Edward Hopper painting: a Gothic spook with a mansard roof, a widow's walk, and a curved front porch. In summer, the porch was filled with vacant-eyed women in rockers and wiry men with wicked laughs who would taunt passers-by with insults and invitations; in winter, the tenants took to their rooms, and you could see their shadows, dark and shifting, behind the blinds that separated their blighted existence from the lives of the lucky.

A block past number 317, I yielded to impulse, pulled into a parking spot and started back towards the house. The porch was empty, but the blinds in every window were raised. Eyes that had seen it all were peering out to seek further proof, as if they needed it, that people were no damn good.

The spectacle in the front yard must have offered them proof aplenty. The rain had turned the grassless yard to gumbo, but it hadn't kept any of us away. The gawkers and misery-seekers were quite a group: media people with cameras; young couples with kids; teenagers with Big Gulps and cigarettes, and middle-aged, respectable people like me who should have known better but who came in response to stirrings as dark as they were ancient. As I walked towards the back of the building and the fire escape Alex had told me Reed used to get to the third floor, I heard snippets of conversation: "hookers with whips . . . ," "mirrors all around so he could watch himself . . . ," "wearing a dress and a Dolly Parton wig . . ."

After these fevered images of Sodom and Gomorrah, the actual fire escape seemed disappointingly mundane. It was a rickety metal affair that zigzagged from the back alley to the third floor, an eyesore that had been added on as a sop to some busybody at City Hall who took fire regulations seriously. Utilitarian as it was, it had done the job. It had taken Reed Gallagher where he wanted to go. I walked over to the foot of it, and for a few minutes I stood there looking up through the dizzying height of steps into the pale March sky. When I started back across the yard, I met an old man with a walker. He was moving with exquisite slowness, but as I passed him, he stopped and grabbed my arm. His voice was raspy whisper. "Did you hear what happened in there?"

"Yes," I said, "I heard."

He pulled me so close I could feel his breath on my face. "Men who don women's clothing are an abomination to God," he said, then he continued his methodical passage towards the site of the abomination.

After such a chilling insight into how a fellow being saw the heart of God, an afternoon reading the dry legal language of the Canadian Charter of Rights and Freedoms was a relief. When Angus came home at 4:00, I told him that, as a reward for babysitting on a Saturday night, he could choose the dinner menu. He decided on sandwiches from the Italian Star deli, an easy call for me, so after I picked up the mortadella and provolone, I had time for a quick nap before I showered and dressed. I was just fastening the turquoise and silver necklace Alex had given me for Christmas when Taylor came in and sat on my bed. Benny was in her arms, but her eyes were anxious.

I sat down beside her. "Taylor, in all the time since you came to live with us, have I ever not come home?"

"No," she said. "But what if . . . ?"

"What if what?" I asked.

She shook her head dolefully. "I don't know," she murmured.

I drew her close to me. "Taylor, life is full of what-ifs, but if you spend all your time being afraid of them, there's not much time left over for being happy, and I want you to be happy."

"I am happy," she whispered. "That's why I'm scared of what if . . ."

Twenty minutes later as I walked through Wascana Park towards the Nationtv studios, Taylor was still at the forefront of my thoughts. She'd come to the front door to wave to me when I left. She'd been hugging Benny to her, and doing her best. It was a worry, but it was a worry that was going to have to wait. I took a deep breath and started mentally running through the clauses relating to sexual orientation in the Charter. I was trying to remember the three key points of a bill on homosexual rights that had been defeated in the Ontario legislature when I realized I'd turned onto a path that had a degree of fame in our city.

The old campus of our university is on the northern edge of the park. It's a serene setting for the handsome pair of buildings that once housed our entire university, but which are now given over to the departments of Music, Drama, and Art. The path I walked along ran behind the buildings. By day, it was a place where students gravitated for a smoke, young mums wheeled strollers, dog-walkers walked dogs, and joggers jogged. But at night, the path changed character. After dark, it was a cruising park for gay men. The students at the university called it "the Fruit Loop." So, in my private thoughts, did I. More sticks and stones.

When I got to Nationtv, I went, as I always did, to makeup, where Tina, who had taught me that if I wanted a clean lip-line after the age of forty, I had to use lip-liner, and that I would be insane to buy any eye shadow more expensive than Maybelline, was waiting for me. As she swept blush along my cheeks, I looked at my reflection in the mirror. Despite my nightly slatherings of Oil of Olay, it was clear that Father Time was undefeated. I shrugged, turned away from the mirror, and asked Tina to tell me about her wedding. The week before, she'd been agonizing about how to tell her future mother-in-law that, since the wedding dinner was catered, she wouldn't need to bring the jellied salads in the colours of the bridesmaid's dresses that she had made for all of her other children's weddings. I was eager to hear if Tina had brought it off.

When Tina was done with me, I went, as I always did, to the green room to wait until Jill came out to talk me through the first question and walk me into the studio. But that night,

Jill didn't come. Five minutes before airtime, I took matters into my own hands. As I pushed the door into the studio open, a young man I'd never seen ran into me. He glanced at my face, then grabbed my arm and pulled me into the studio.

"They're waiting," he said.

"I've been here all along," I said.

He looked right past me. "Whatever," he said. "Let's just say there's been a screwup."

It wasn't the last one.

When she'd first set up the weekly panel, Jill had decided to cover the ideological spectrum rather than have representatives from specific political parties. From the outset, Keith Harris, who had once been my lover and was now my friend, spoke for the right, Senator Sam Spiegel articulated the view from the centre, and I was there for the left. Over the years, the images of Keith and Sam on the television monitor had become as familiar as my own. But that night as I glanced towards the screen, I saw a face I'd never seen before in my life. The woman on screen appeared to be in her mid-thirties; she had a head of frosted curls, cerulean eyes, and a dynamite smile.

The young man who'd dragged me into the studio was kneeling in front of me, trying to fasten my lapel mike. I touched his shoulder. "Who's that?" I asked.

He glanced quickly at the monitor. "Didn't anybody tell you? That's Glayne Axtell. She's the new voice for the right." He leaped out of camera range.

"What happened to Keith Harris?" I asked.

He looked irritated and moved his fingers to his lips in a silencing gesture. Through my earpiece, I heard the familiar "Stand by," and we were on the air.

By the time the last caller had been thanked and the moderator in Toronto was inviting people to join us next week, my back was soaked with sweat. It had been a rough evening. Keith's mysterious disappearance had been a blow. I had to admit that Glayne Axtell was good. She was far to the right of Keith, but she was witty and crisply professional. The problem wasn't with her; it was with me. I couldn't seem to adjust to the new rhythm, and for the first time, I let the callers on our phone-in segment of the program get to me. Usually, I dealt with the crazies by reminding myself that the law "every action has an equal and opposite reaction" governs physics not politics. In politics, most of the time, you got back pretty much what you handed out, and if you were lucky, reason would beget reason.

That night I seemed to be beyond both luck and reason. As the torrent of hate and fear poured through my earpiece, I couldn't seem to stop myself from lashing back. I kept wondering where Jill was with the cut-off button. But as the red light went black, and we were finally off the air, I had to admit that, as exhausting as it had been, the panel on homophobia had been good television.

Jill came down from the control booth almost immediately. She was wearing jeans, a black turtleneck, and a hounds-tooth jacket, and she didn't look happy.

I unclipped my mike and went over to her. "I thought you were going to keep the mad dogs at bay tonight. But maybe you were right to let them yelp and foam. It was an exciting show."

Jill gave me a tight smile. "Do you have time for a drink?"

"Sure," I said. "Angus is with Taylor. He has plans, but I've got time for a quick one. I wanted to ask you about Keith. Did he quit or what?"

"Let's talk about it later," Jill said.

It was a mild night, but when I told Jill I'd left my car at home and suggested we walk downtown to our old standby, the Hotel Saskatchewan, she said she'd rather drive to the

Chimney. It was an odd choice. The hotel bar was a place for grown-ups to unwind: elegant surroundings, deep soft chairs, and discreet bartenders. The Chimney was a family restaurant in a strip mall not far from where I lived. They made good pizza, and my kids liked the open fireplace, but it wasn't Jill's kind of place.

As we drove up College Avenue and turned onto Albert Street, she was uncharacteristically quiet. In fact, she didn't say anything until we'd found a table and ordered two bottles of Great Western.

When the waiter left, Jill glanced around the room as if she were seeing it for the first time. "This is nice, isn't it?" she said absently.

"I've always like it," I said. "But it must be thirty degrees in here tonight. Somebody should have told whoever's in charge of the roaring fire that spring has sprung." I leaned towards her. "But listen, I've been dying to know what happened with Keith. I know he's been busy since he moved back to Ottawa. Did he just have too much on his plate?"

"It was more of a mutual decision," Jill said. "We've been looking at the demographics – thinking we should try to hook a younger audience."

She wouldn't meet my eyes, and I knew the truth without asking. "And so you decided to replace Keith with Glayne Axtell."

"She did a good job tonight," Jill said defensively.

"Keith's done a good job ever since the show started," I said, and my voice was so loud the people at the next table turned and looked at us.

Jill winced. "Jo, please. Don't make this any worse than it already is."

The waiter brought our beer, and I took a long sip. The heat in the restaurant and the turn in the conversation were beginning to make my head spin.

Jill's voice was guarded. "I know Keith's done a good job, Jo. The panel just needed – I don't know – a fresh look."

"Spring cleaning?" I said. "Jill, we're not talking about a piece of furniture here. We're talking about a friend."

Suddenly, Jill looked furious. "Christ, Jo, it's never easy with you, is it? All right, here it is. We think it's time you considered other options, too."

I felt as if I'd been kicked in the stomach. "You mean I'm out as well? What about Sam?"

Jill was icy. "He's staying. Sam has an avuncular quality. We thought he'd be a nice mix with Glayne and . . . the other new panellist."

"Who is it?" I asked. And then, I knew. "Oh fuck, Jill. Is it Tom? Are you getting rid of me so you can hire your boyfriend?"

She didn't say anything. I stood up and grabbed my coat. As I pulled it on, I knocked my beer over. I was beyond caring. It had been a long time since I'd made a scene in a restaurant. I headed for the front door, but before I opened it, I turned and looked back at Jill. She was sitting, looking numbly at the mess I'd left behind.

The Chimney was less than four blocks from my house. Even in the state I was in that night, I was home in less than ten minutes. The Chimney's proximity to my house was, I suddenly realized, the reason Jill had chosen it in the first place. Once we had been as close as sisters. I guess she figured she owed me an easy exit. But I wasn't grateful; the thought of her planning the logistics of my firing made me sick to my stomach.

When I got home, Taylor was already in bed, and Angus was so full of news about an '85 Camaro he'd seen for sale up the street that he was oblivious to my mood. Leah, who was sensitive to emotional currents, looked at me with concern, but I told her it had been a tough show, and she said that she had tuned in for the phone-in segment and she understood.

When she and Angus finally left for the late movie, I felt the relief an actor must feel at the end of a bad performance. The audience was gone. I could wail, rend my clothing, or gnash my teeth to my heart's content. But as I walked into the living room and began searching aimlessly through my CDs, I was overwhelmed with self-pity.

I wanted to talk, but the three people I counted on most were busy with their own lives: Alex was out at Standing Buffalo; my friend Hilda McCourt was in Europe with her new beau; and, as the old saw had it, Jill was no longer part of the solution, she was part of the problem.

I selected a disc Keith Harris had once given me: Glenn Gould playing the Goldberg Variations. As I listened to the shimmering precision of Gould's performance, I felt my pulse slow, and, for the first time since I left the restaurant, I found myself able to think. Being fired from the show was not the end of the world. I still had family. I still had Alex. I still had friends and my job at the university. Summer was coming. Without the show, there would be no reason to be in town on Saturdays. We could rent a cottage and drive out there on weekends. Taylor could use the extra time with me. I could teach her to canoe. We could get Benny a life jacket. I had just convinced myself that it was all for the best, when the phone rang. I leaped to answer it. I was certain it was Jill, apologizing and making everything right again.

But the voice on the other end of the line wasn't Jill's. It was a man's.

"Is this Joanne Kilbourn?"

"Yes."

"Joanne, it's Ed Mariani. I just wanted to thank you for the things you said on your show. They were all the things I would have said, or I hope I would have said, if I'd been there. Barry and I were very moved."

"Your timing couldn't have been better," I said. "I just got fired."

"Not because of what you said tonight?" His voice was full of anger.

"I wish that were the reason," I said. "At least that would have a little dignity."

"What was it, then?"

"Ed, I'm sorry. I shouldn't have said anything. I'm just upset."

"Do you want to talk about it?"

"No. I'll handle it. I'm a big girl."

"Even big girls need a chance to vent once in a while."

"Thanks," I said. "I'll be okay."

"I know you will," he said. "But let's speed up the process. Come for dinner tomorrow night. Barry's making paella. It's his best dish, and he loves to show it off. You're welcome to bring whomever you like: significant other, kids, pets . . . Barry's paella is endless."

"All right," I said. "I accept. But there'll just be my youngest daughter and me. My son has a basketball game tomorrow night."

"We'll send you home with a doggy bag for him. Six-thirty?"

"Six-thirty would be great. And, Ed, thanks."

When I hung up, I felt better. Then I remembered the scene in the restaurant and I felt worse. I put some ice cubes in a glass, took down the Glenfiddich, poured myself a generous shot, and went back into the living room. Glenn Gould was still playing. I kicked off my shoes, collapsed on the couch, and took a long sip of my drink. It was terrific. As someone who had once been a good friend had told me not that long ago, there are times when nothing but single-malt Scotch will do.

CHAPTER

5

At church Sunday morning, we used the old Book of Common Prayer. When Angus pulled out a pencil and began drawing basketball strategies on the back of the bulletin, I opened the Prayer Book to the Service for Young People and pointed to the line "Lord, keep our thoughts from wandering." But my thoughts were wandering too: to Jill, to the end of my work on the political panel, to the scene I'd made the night before at the Chimney. When the rector read out, "Come unto me all that labour and are heavy laden, and I will refresh you," I knew it was the best invitation I'd had all week. An hour later, I left church, not yet in a state of love and charity with my neighbours, but at least in a state where I could contemplate the possibility.

The weather was so warm by noon that we took our egg-salad sandwiches and iced tea out to the deck. Angus, who was always quick to spot a mellow mood, asked if we could drive out to the valley after lunch, and I agreed. Alex had been letting him take the wheel for almost a month now, and it seemed churlish not to take my turn.

My son was already in the driver's seat when Taylor and I came out of the house.

"Hurry up," he yelled. "I want to open up this old junker and see how fast she can go."

"Don't even think about it," I said, as I buckled up.

I turned to make sure Taylor had her seatbelt on. She did, but she looked grim.

I tried to sound confident. "T, there's nothing to worry about. Alex says your brother's a good driver, and I know that Angus is going to be especially careful with you in the car." I looked hard at my son. "Aren't you?"

He gave me a mock salute. "Yes, ma'am," he said, and we were off.

He was as good as his word. I was boggled by the transformation that took place the minute the key was in the ignition. Angus drove through the city streets as prudently as the proverbial little old lady who only took a spin on alternate Sundays. Alex had obviously been an inspired teacher. It was as pleasant an uneventful a drive as a mother could expect from a fifteen-year-old with a learner's permit. Lulled by the absence of catastrophe, Taylor began to read aloud the roadside signs: "Big Valley Country"; "Stella's Pies, We-Bake-Our-Own"; "Langenegger's: All-Vegetarian/All-U-Can-Eat." As we turned off the highway and drove through the Qu'Appelle Valley, I felt my nerves beginning to unknot. In a month, the hills would be green, and the valley would be filled with birdsong. Other years, the demands of the political panel had kept us in town on weekends. A summer of freedom to enjoy these hills would not be hard to take.

We turned at the cutoff for Last Mountain Lake and drove till we came to Regina Beach, at the heart of cottage country. Regina Beach is one of those towns which spring to life on the May long weekend, rock all summer, and sink back into quiescence after Thanksgiving. That balmy March day, the town was still sleeping: the streets were empty, the playgrounds were forlorn, and the beach was deserted. Taylor ran down the hill to the playground, took a few desultory swings, then caught up with Angus and me. We walked out on the dock, and as we sat on the end, with our feet dangling over the edge, and watched the seagulls swooping towards the sun-splashed water, I tried to figure out how I could stretch our budget to include rent for a cottage. Then Angus took Taylor to the beach and showed her how to skip stones over the surface of the lake, and I knew that, even if I had to take in laundry, I'd find a way to get us all out here by summer.

When Taylor began skipping her stones farther than his, Angus realized he needed to rest his arm for basketball that night, and we walked back up into town. It was too early for Butler's Fish and Chips to be open for the season, but there was an ice-cream stand with waffle cones and a dazzling variety of flavours and toppings. We got cones and walked up one side of the town and down the other till we discovered a little shop that sold crafts and homemade jams and jellies. Angus zeroed in on a lethal-looking hunting knife in a hand-tooled leather sheath, but we settled on a basket of preserves: saskatoon berry, choke cherry, and northern blueberry for Taylor and me to take with us when we had dinner with Ed Mariani and Barry Levitt that night.

As we started up the hill, the Volvo's engine began to cough. I looked at the gas gauge. "Cruising on empty there, Angus," I said. "I hope you've got your credit card handy." He gave me a withering look. "I'm just trying to prepare you for the realities of life with an '85 Camaro." I said.

There was a station at the top of the hill, and we sputtered up beside the gas tank. The station was a low-slung Mom-and-Pop type of place with a garage on one side and a café on the other. What appeared to be fifty years' worth of hubcaps had been nailed into the wooden face of the garage, but except for two curled and faded cardboard photographs of ice-cream sundaes, the front of the restaurant was bare. It was not, however, without adornment. Suspended by chains from the frame of the café's front window was a jumbo-sized plaster wiener with the words "Foot Long" written in mustard-coloured script along its side.

Angus gave me the thumbs-up sign. "Check it out, Mum – wheels and weenies."

"You'd better hope wheels and weenies is open," I said. "Otherwise, you're going to have to haul out the gas can and walk."

Angus drew up next to the gas tank and turned off the ignition. "Relax, Mum. It'll be open. You always say I was born lucky."

It was true. When it came to the vagaries of day-to-day life, my youngest son always had seemed blessed. But as the minutes ticked by and no one who worked at the gas station appeared, I was beginning to wonder if Angus's run of luck was over. I was just about to remind him of the location of the gas can when Taylor pointed towards the station and said, "Look, here comes the gas boy."

His fine-chiselled features were grime-covered, and he was wearing greasy coveralls, not GAP, but there was no disguising the angular grace or the smile.

"What are you doing out here?" Val Massey asked.

"Looking for a summer cottage," I said. "At least, we're thinking about looking for one."

"We are?" Taylor asked.

"Yeah," I said, "we are." I turned to Val. "I didn't know you worked out here. Is it a weekend thing?"

He looked down at his feet. "Unfortunately, no. This job is permanent. It's the family business. I live back there." He gestured over his shoulder towards a small bungalow behind

the station. As if on cue, the door opened and a squat muscular man wearing the twin of Val's coverall stepped outside.
The man had a cigarette and an attitude.

"Step on it, Valentine," he shouted. "I don't pay you to
charm the customers."

Val flushed. "Yes, Dad," he said softly. He tried a smile.
"Well, Professor K., what'll it be?"

As Val filled the tank and wiped our window, his father
smoked and watched, alert to any possible transgression. It
was only after Val took my credit card inside that the older
man seemed to relax. When his son was out of sight, he
threw his cigarette down, ground it into the cinder path, and
headed back to the bungalow. Val's face was stony when he
came back to the car, and his hands trembled as he passed
me my receipt. "I apologize for my father," he said, and he
turned away.

Angus rolled up the window and started the engine. "I'd
go nuts if I had a father like that," he said. "Why does he put
up with it?"

"No option, I guess."

As we waited for a camper to pass, I glanced out the back
window. Val hadn't moved, but his father had come out of
the bungalow and started to walk towards him. When his
father got close, Val said something to him; then, without
breaking stride, the older man raised his hand and cuffed Val
across the side of the head.

I was the only one who saw. Angus was busy checking for
traffic on the road, and Taylor was back to looking for signs.
Suddenly, she crowed with delight. "Hey, there's one I
missed." The sign she'd spotted was handmade, an arrow
pointing back to the station from which we'd just come.
Taylor read the words on the arrow carefully. "Masluk &
Son, Gas, Food, Friendly Service."

We got home around 4:00. There were no messages on the machine, and given the chaotic state of my feelings about Jill, I was unsure whether that was good news or bad. Angus took the dogs out for a run, then went off to the 7-Eleven, pregame hangout of choice among the sportsmen in Angus's circle. Taylor got out her sketchpad and drew pictures of Regina Beach for a while, then she wandered off to choose her outfit for the dinner party. When she came up to my bedroom for inspection, I was stunned. Left to her own devices, Taylor was a whimsical dresser, but that night she was right on the money: a plaid ruffle skirt, a white pullover with a plaid diamond design, dark green leotards, and her best mary-janes. She'd even brushed her hair. It was obviously a rite-of-passage day.

Ed and Barry lived on a quiet crescent near the university. Their house overlooked the bird sanctuary and the campus, and it was clear when Ed shepherded us inside that they had designed their split-level to take full advantage of the view. The house was built into a rise so that you entered on one floor, but immediately moved up a short flight of stairs to the airy brightness of a large room that seemed to be made up entirely of floor-to-ceiling windows.

Ed led us down a short corridor to the kitchen. Barry Levitt was waiting for us. He was a small man with a receding hairline he made no effort to hide and a trim body he obviously worked hard to preserve. Ed had told me that he and Barry were the same age, forty, but Barry had the kind of charm that would be described as boyish until the day he moved into the seniors' complex. That night he was wearing an open-necked sports shirt the colour of a cut peach and a black denim bib apron. He didn't look up when we came in. All his attention was focused on the steaming pot of seafood he was dumping into a mixing bowl of rice.

When the pot that had held the seafood was empty, Barry stepped back and gestured for us to move closer so we could peer into the bowl.

Taylor stood on tiptoe and looked down. "Mussels," she said happily, "and shrimp and scallops and some things I don't know."

"Well, let's see," said Barry. "I remember throwing a squid in there, and some clams, and chicken, and a very succulent-looking lobster. I think that's the final tally."

"Paella," I said, inhaling deeply. "One of the great dishes of the world. If you can bottle that aroma, I'll be your first customer."

Barry grinned and waved his stirring spoon in the air. "Somebody get these discerning women a drink."

"We have a pitcher of sangria," Ed said, "and we have a cabinet of what Barry's father's bar book called 'the most notable potables.' "

"Sangria will be fine," I said.

He turned to Taylor. "And for you, we have all the ingredients for a Shirley Temple. Even the umbrella."

There is something ceremonial about a drink with an umbrella, and Taylor accepted her Shirley Temple gravely and waited till she was safely seated at the kitchen table before she took a sip. For a few moments, she basked in sophistication, then her eyes grew huge and she leaped up and grabbed my arm.

"Look at that," she said, pointing towards the living room, "they have a Fafard bronze horse! In their house! Jo, you told me real people could never afford to buy those horses because they cost fifteen thousand dollars."

Barry raised an eyebrow. "How old is Taylor?"

"Six, but she's pretty serious about art. Her mother was Sally Love."

Barry and Ed exchanged a quick glance. "We have a painting your mother did," Ed said gently. "Would you like to see it?"

Taylor put down her drink, then she went over to Ed and took his hand. "Let's go," she said.

The Sally Love painting Barry and Ed owned was an oil on canvas, about three feet by two and a half. It was a spring scene. Two men wearing gardening clothes and soft shapeless hats were working in a back yard incandescent with tulips, daffodils, and a drift of wild iris. The colours of the blossoms were heart-stoppingly vibrant, and the brushwork was so careful that you felt you could touch the petals, but it was the figures of the men that drew your eye. In painting them, Sally had used muted colours and lines that curved to suggest both age and absolute harmony. You couldn't look at the painting without knowing that the old gardeners were among the lucky few who get to live out a life of quiet joy.

"She was an amazing artist," Ed said.

"She was an amazing woman." I said.

Taylor turned to me. "I dream about her, but I can't remember her. Not really."

"Go up and touch the painting," Ed said.

"Jo says you're not supposed to . . . ," Taylor said.

"Jo's right," Ed agreed. "But this is a special circumstance. I think your mother would want you to touch her painting. After all, she touched it all the time when she was making it."

Taylor approached the painting slowly. For a few moments, she just looked up at it, taking it in. Finally, she reached out and traced the petals of an iris with her fingertips. When she turned back to Ed, there was a look on her face that I'd never seen before.

"Is it okay if I just stay here for a while?"

Ed bowed in her direction. "Of course," he said. "I'll bring your Shirley Temple." He gave me a quick look. "Why don't we grab our jackets and take our drinks outside. Taylor might enjoy some time alone, and it is a lovely night."

When Ed suggested that Barry join us, he waved us off. He was brushing focaccia with rosemary oil, and he said he'd enjoy our company more when everybody had finished eating and he could relax. So it was just Ed and me on the deck. We moved our chairs so we could look out at the university, and the view was worth the effort. The air was heavy with moisture, and in the late afternoon light the campus shimmered, as pastoral and idyllic as its picture in the university calendar.

For a few minutes we were silent, absorbed by our separate thoughts. Finally, Ed said, "Would you rather I hadn't suggested that Taylor look at her mother's painting?"

I shook my head. "No, I'm glad you did. Sally gave me a painting not long before she died. It's in my bedroom, but for the first year Taylor came to us, she refused to look at it. Lately, she's been spending quite a bit of time there."

"A way of being close to her mother."

"So it seems."

Ed nodded. "My father was killed in a car accident before I was born. He was a trumpet player. When I got old enough, I used to spend hours with his old trumpet. Holding something he had held was the only way I knew to bring him close."

"I hope Taylor can feel that connection," I said. "Her mother's death came at the wrong time for her."

Ed looked thoughtful. "Is there a right time to lose a parent?" he asked.

"I guess not," I said. "But the timing in Taylor's case was particularly savage. I think when Sally died, she had just begun to realize how good it could be to have a daughter."

"Motherhood didn't come easily to her?"

"I don't think Sally had a maternal bone in her body, but at the end, there was a bond." I sipped my sangria. "It had a lot to do with art. Taylor has real talent. When she saw that, Sally was determined to give Taylor the best beginning an artist could have."

"That sounds a little cold."

I shook my head. "It wasn't. It was the only way Sally had of loving. I guess love comes in all shapes and sizes."

Ed smiled. "Tell me about it."

"I don't think I have to," I said. "But it took Sally a long time to realize that there was room in her life for something besides her work. In a lot of ways, Taylor was her second chance."

Ed's face darkened, and he looked away. "That's the merciless aspect of death, isn't it? The taking away of all our second chances." He paused, then he turned to face me. "Reed Gallagher called me the night he died. I wouldn't talk to him."

"That doesn't sound like you."

"Oh, I can be a real prima donna, and a real ass. Just ask Barry. Anyway, that night I was both."

"What happened?"

"It was all so stupid. That morning Reed had come to my office with some terrific news. You know about our Co-op Internship Program, don't you?"

"Sure," I said. "The kids in the Politics and the Media class have been agonizing over where they're going to be placed for months."

Ed shrugged. "You can't blame them. It's a big step. They can't graduate until they've done their internship, and it's a great chance for them to make some connections. We have support from some pretty impressive potential employers. But that week we'd scored a real coup. The *Globe and Mail* had agreed to take one of our students."

"That was a coup," I said. "The grande dame."

"It was all Reed's doing. Of course, we knew as soon as we heard that we'd have to rearrange all our placements."

"You couldn't just bump everybody up a notch?"

Ed shook his head. "No. There are always personal con-
siderations: kids with family obligations, or just a gut feeling
that intern A and placement C might be a bad mix. Reed
suggested we meet at the Edgewater to hash it all out. He
said we needed privacy and perspective, so it was better to
meet off campus. We arranged to meet at three. When I got
there, the hostess said Reed had left a message that he had a
student to see, but he'd be there by quarter after. I waited till
four-thirty, but he never showed."

"So you were mad because he stood you up."

Ed winced. "It sounds so childish when you put it that way,
but that's about it. My only excuse is that I'd had a lousy day,
and by the time I got home, I was fuming. Reed called the
house just before dinner, and I told Barry to tell him to go to
hell. Of course, Barry just said I was unable to come to the
phone." Ed shook his head in disgust. "It was so petty.
Anyway, that was it. The next night I heard he was dead."

I walked over and stood beside him. Across the road, some
students ran out of the classroom building and began to
throw a ball around on the lawn. They were wearing shorts
and T-shirts. They must have been cold, but they were
Prairie kids and it had been a long winter. Exams were still
three weeks away, and spring and hormones were working
their magic. As I watched them, I felt a sharp pang of envy.

Ed Mariani seemed to read my mind. "Remember when
the biggest problem in our lives was Geology?"

"It was Physics for me." I touched his arm. "Don't be too
hard on yourself. It sounds to me as if Reed just wanted to
apologize for not showing up at the Edgewater."

"I hope you're right, Joanne. I'd hate to think I'd failed
him. He was always good to me." Ed balanced his glass carefully on the rail. "The first day he was here, he sought me

out. Of course, my ego was smarting, because he'd gotten the job I thought was going to be mine. Reed picked up on how wounded I was. He told me how much he admired my work, and how glad he was, for his own sake, that I'd withdrawn my name from consideration. Then you know what he did?" Ed smiled at the memory. "He said he thought it would be a good idea if we got drunk together."

"And you did?"

Ed shuddered. "Did we ever. I felt like the inside of a goat the next day, but it was worth it."

"That good, huh?"

"Yeah, it was fun, but it was useful too. There'd been some ugliness when I'd put my name into contention for the director's job."

"The kind of ugliness you could have taken to the Human Rights Commission?"

"No. I'm used to dealing with overt prejudice; this was more insidious, but from a couple of things Reed said that night, it was pretty apparent he hadn't anything to do with it. That was such a relief. And, to be fair, Reed really was a better choice for the job. The school needed somebody who had significant connections and strong administrative skills, and that wasn't me."

"Sounds like your boys' night out really cleared the air," I said.

Ed's expression was sombre. "It did. It was a good evening; unfortunately it wasn't the last one." He took a long swallow of his drink. "We spent some time together the Wednesday before Reed died. I must have replayed the evening a hundred times, wondering if there was something I could have said or done that might have changed what happened. But, at the time, it just seemed like an ordinary evening. We'd been working late on the budget for next year, and we went back to the Faculty Club for a drink. Reed was in a strange mood. He was always a serious drinker, but that night he was drinking to get drunk. I wouldn't have cared, except that whatever the problem was, the liquor wasn't helping. The more he drank, the more miserable he seemed to get. Finally, I asked Reed if he wanted to talk about whatever it was that was troubling him."

"And he didn't?"

"No . . . so, of course, I resorted to the usual bromides – told him that anytime he wanted to talk, I was there, and he could trust me not to betray his confidence." Ed looked perplexed. "It was just one of those things people say when they don't know what else to say, but Reed picked up on it. Joanne, he was so angry and so bitter. He said, 'I'll give you some advice: don't ever tell people they can trust you, and don't ever believe for a moment that you can trust them.'"

"I didn't know Reed well," I said, "but he never struck me as a cynic."

"He wasn't. Something had happened."

"Do you have any idea what?"

"My guess is it was his marriage."

"Did he say anything?"

"No. But he didn't have to – all that business about trust. Doesn't that sound as if there was a betrayal?"

I thought of Julie's wedding cake and of the sugar doves she'd made so that her new marriage would be blessed with years of happiness. She and Reed had only made it to a month and two days. What could have happened in so brief a time to turn hope to despair?

It was a question I didn't want to dwell on, and I was relieved when Barry Levitt opened the deck door, stuck out his head, and invited us to join Taylor and him for dinner.

The table was beautifully set: cobalt-blue depression ware and a woven cloth as brightly coloured as the Italian flag.

Barry had pulled the tables close to the window so we could watch the sunset. Taylor was uncharacteristically quiet, and when Ed asked her to light the candles, she performed the task without her usual brio. But she perked up when Barry brought in the paella dish and placed it in front of her.

"Did Jo tell you this is my favourite?" she asked.

"She didn't have to," Barry said. "Creative people love seafood. Everybody knows that."

For the next hour we sipped sangria, sopped up paella with the focaccia, and talked about summer plans as Puccini soared in the background. By the time we'd moved to Act III of *Turandot*, the paella dish was empty, and Ed brought out chocolate gelato and cappuccino.

Taylor was a great fan of gelato, and Ed's gelato was home-made. After she'd finished her dish, she turned to Barry. "This is really a nice party," she said. "I'm glad I wore my good clothes."

Barry raised his glass to her. "Whatever you choose to wear, you're always welcome at this table."

"Thank you," said Taylor.

"I'm afraid that has to be the last word, T," I said. "School tomorrow, and we're already past your bedtime."

As we stood at the doorway, saying our goodbyes, Taylor said, "Can I look at the painting one more time?"

"Sure," said Barry. "I'll come with you."

I turned to Ed. "It really was a lovely evening. Thanks for asking us. I needed some fun tonight."

"So did I," he said. "And I needed to talk about Reed. Barry doesn't want me to dwell on it, but I do. It was such a terrible ending to a good life. What's even more terrible is the possibility that the way Reed died will eclipse every-thing he accomplished – especially here at the university. He was so committed to the School of Journalism. Even on the night he died. Look at this." Ed reached into his inside jacket pocket, pulled out a single sheet of paper and handed it to me. "This was in the mailbox when I went out to get our paper Friday morning."

I unfolded the paper. On it, handwritten, were sixteen names. I recognized them as the students who were just completing the term before their placement. Opposite each name, Reed had written in the name of the media organization where the student would intern.

"Can you imagine what he must have been going through that night? But he still made sure the kids were taken care of. He must have dropped the list off after Barry and I had gone to the symphony." Ed swallowed hard. "Well, life goes on. I'll set up interviews with the students tomorrow to tell them the news."

"Would you like to use my office?" I said. "From the way yours looked yesterday morning, I think it'll be a while before you can even find your desk."

Ed frowned. "You should think carefully before you make an offer like that, Joanne. You know what Clare Boothe Luce said. 'No good deed goes unpunished.' "

"I'm not worried," I said. "I'll get a key made for you tomorrow morning. Consider it settled. But, Ed, there's one thing I don't understand . . ."

I never got to finish my sentence. Taylor was back, toting an armload of art books that Barry was lending her. As she showed her collection to Ed, I glanced again at Reed Gallagher's placement list. The class Tom Kelsoe and I taught was mandatory for Journalism students in their final year, so I was familiar with the work of the people Reed was assigning as interns. Most of the students on Reed's list were ranked just about where I would have placed them, but there was one surprise, and it was right at the top. The student Reed Gallagher had chosen for the plum internship with the *Globe and Mail* was Kellee Savage.

The clock in the hall began to chime. It was 9:00. I handed the list back to Ed. The mystery of Kellee Savage would have to wait.

"Okay, Taylor," I said, "now it really is past your bedtime. Say goodnight, Gracie."

"Goodnight, Gracie." Taylor said and roared with laughter the way her mother would roar when she made a joke. It had been quite an evening: paella, Puccini, and a reprise of an old Burns and Allen routine. I'd hardly thought about Jill at all.

Taylor didn't need a bedtime story. As she was telling me about how her mother swirled her brushstrokes, she fell asleep in mid-sentence. I tucked her in and started downstairs, but when I heard the ricochet of adolescent jokes and insults coming from the kitchen, I stopped and headed back up to my room. Angus and his buddies were in the kitchen, and his friend Camillo had just decided they should make nachos. Dinner with Ed and Barry had boosted my spirits but I knew my limits. I wasn't ready for a kitchen full of teenagers and the aroma of processed cheese warming in the microwave. I needed peace and I needed time to think, and one of the things I needed to think about was Kellee Savage.

She had been in two of my classes, but I had never seen anything in her work to indicate that someday she would be the one to catch the brass ring. My briefcase was on the window seat. I pulled out the folder of unmarked essays and sorted through till I found Kellee's. It was an analysis of how a councillor from the core area used the alternative press to get across his message that the city had to start listening to the concerns of the prostitutes who lived and worked in his ward. Like everything else Kellee had done for me, it was meticulously researched, adequately written, and absolutely without a spark. I curled up on the window seat and began leafing through some of the other essays. Jumbo Hryniuk had written about how J.C. Watts, the brilliant quarterback for the University of Oklahoma and the Ottawa Rough Riders, had parlayed fame on the football field into a seat in the U.S. House of Representatives and special status as one of Newt Gingrich's boys. As always, Jumbo was almost, but not quite, on topic. Linda Van Sickle, the young woman Reed had ranked second, had submitted a case study of a civic government that showed how the city council's political timidity was growing in direct proportion to the increasingly adversarial nature of local media outlets. It was a brilliant paper, good enough to be published. So, I discovered, was Val Massey's essay, "The Right to Be Wrong: The Press's Obligation to Protect Bigots and Bastards." Reed's decision simply didn't make sense. I skimmed through the rest of the essays. Of the sixteen people in our seminar, I would have ranked seven ahead of Kellee Savage.

When Alex called, I was still mystified, but the words on the page were starting to swim in front of me, and I knew it was time for bed. Alex sounded as tired as I felt.

"Glad you went home?" I asked.

"I don't know. I'm glad I was there, but I wish it hadn't been necessary."

"How's your nephew?"

"Immortal," he said. "Like all kids his age are. That's why they can drink and sniff and snort and speed and screw without protection."

"You sound as if you've had enough."

"That doesn't mean there's not more coming. Jo, sometimes I get so goddamn sick of these little pukes. I don't know. Maybe it's just that I'm sick of going to their funerals."

"Is it that bad with your nephew?"

"I hope not. Jo, I'd really rather not talk about this."

"Okay," I said. "Come over, and we don't have to say a word. That's the advantage real life has over telephones."

He laughed. "It's a tempting offer, but I'd better not. Even without words, I'd be lousy company tonight."

"Then come tomorrow morning," I said. "I don't have to teach till ten-thirty, and the kids leave for school at eight."

"I'll be there," he said. "Count on it."

CHAPTER

6

When I first met Alex Kequahtooway, there was nothing to suggest that he would be a terrific lover. He was knowledgeable and passionate about serious music, but he was guarded in his response to everything else. We went out for three months before we were intimate, and during that time of coming to know one another, he was kind but almost formally correct with me. After we became lovers, the kindness continued, but it was allied with an eroticism that awed and delighted me. Alice Munro differentiates between those who can go only a little way with the act of love and those "who can make a greater surrender, like the mystics." Alex was one of love's mystics, and that morning as I lay in bed beside him, breathing in the scent of the narcissi blooming in front of the open window, listening to Dennis Brain play the opening notes of a horn concerto on the radio, I was at peace.

He took my hand, leaned over and kissed me. "Mozart," he said. "The second-best way to start the day."

It was a little after 10:00 when I nosed into my parking spot at the university. The test I was about to give was on my desk, and I checked it to make sure it was typo- and jargon-free, then I went down to the Political Science office. I needed exam booklets, and I wanted to make copies of a hand-out for my senior class. As I counted out the exam booklets, I was still humming Mozart.

When Rosalie Norman, the departmental admin assistant, saw me at the copying machine, she hustled me out of the way. "I'll do that. Every time you faculty use it, something goes wrong, and I'm the one who has to call the company and then try to figure out whose secretary I can sweet-talk into doing your photocopying until the repairman decides to show up."

On the best of days, Rosalie was not a sunny person, but that morning, even the most casual observer would have seen that she had a right to be cranky. Over the weekend, she had got herself a new and very bad permanent. Her previously smooth salt-and-pepper pageboy was now tightly coiled into what my older daughter, Mieka, called a "Kurly Kate do," after the girl on the pot-scrubber box.

I tried not to stare. "Rosalie, if you have a spare minute later on, would you mind getting me an extra key for my office?"

Her blackberry eyes shone with suspicion. "What do you need an extra key for?"

"I'm going to be sharing with Professor Mariani until the Journalism offices are straightened around."

She sighed heavily. "I'm going to have to go over to Physical Plant in person, you know. They don't just give out those keys to anybody. More sweet-talking. I'll probably be there half the morning."

I considered the situation. Rosalie Norman had a choleric disposition, and for the foreseeable future, she was stuck with the permanent from hell. Chances that her day would ever begin as mine just had, with world-class love-making, were slim to nil.

I patted her hand. "I'll go over to Physical Plant," I said. "No use wasting your morning sucking up to an office full of sourpusses."

A smile flickered across her lips so quickly that I was left wondering if I'd just imagined it. "Thanks," she said, then she leaned over the copier, scooped up my copies and slid them into a file folder. "The next time you need copying done, put it on my desk in the tray marked 'copying.' We have a system around here, you know."

The phone was ringing when I got back to my office. It was Ed Mariani.

"I've told our admin assistant you're moving in," I said, "and I'm just about to phone Physical Plant for your key."

He laughed. "And I pride myself on being a Virgo. I really do appreciate your generosity, Joanne. I know it's not going to be easy having somebody else lumbering around your office. Now, I'm afraid I have another favour to ask."

"Ask away. You've already softened me up with your Clare Boothe Luce allusion."

"Thanks," he said. "It's about Kellee Savage. She wasn't in my class this morning. Normally, I wouldn't give it a second thought, but I want to get these interviews started, and Kellee's the logical person to start with. If she shows up for Politics and the Media, would you get her to give me a call at home?"

"Sure," I said. "And, Ed, don't worry about the lumbering. I'm looking forward to having you around." I hung up, called Physical Plant, arranged to pick up an extra office key later in the morning, and set out for class.

After I'd got my Poli Sci 100 students started on their test, I opened my briefcase to take out the senior class's papers. That's when I noticed I still had the copy of *Sleeping Beauty* that Kellee Savage had thrust into my hands on St. Patrick's Day. As it turned out, there had been more truth than poetry in the image of Kellee Savage as Sleeping Beauty. Her story might have lacked a handsome prince, but she had certainly nabbed the prize that would awaken all her possibilities. When Ed Mariani told her that she had been chosen to live happily ever after, or at least for a semester, in the big city, Kellee was going to be one triumphant young woman.

That afternoon, when I walked into the Politics and the Media seminar and saw that Kellee's place at the table was still empty, I felt a shiver of annoyance. Kellee had been made the recipient of a shining gift; the least she could do was stop pouting and show up to claim it.

As soon as class got under way, Kellee was banished from my thoughts. It was a spirited hour and a half, not because of the questions I'd prepared for discussion, but because of an item that had dominated the weekend news. Late Friday afternoon, an Ottawa reporter, faced with the choice of revealing the source of some politically damaging documents that had been leaked to her or of going to jail, had revealed her source. Early Sunday morning, the senior bureaucrat the reporter named had jumped off the balcony of a highrise on rue Jacques Cartier. The argument about whether a journalist ever had the right to put self-interest above principle was fervent. Even Jumbo Hryniuk, who usually cast a dim eye on the doings of the non-jock press, grappled vigorously with the ethics of the case. Only one student was not engaged. As the passions swirled about him, Val Massey remained preoccupied and remote. Remembering his father's casual act of brutality the day before, I was worried.

When the seminar was over, I handed back the essays I'd graded, and as always when papers were returned, I was soon surrounded by a knot of students with questions or complaints. Linda Van Sickle waited till the room had cleared before she came up to me. She was a sweet-faced young woman with honey hair and the glowing good looks that some women are blessed with in the last weeks of pregnancy. In her Birkenstocks, Levi's, and oversized GAP T-shirt, she was the symbol of hip fertility, a Demeter for the nineties.

I smiled at her. "If you're here to complain about your grade, you're out of luck," I said. "I think that's the highest mark I've ever given."

She blushed. "No, I'm very pleased with the mark. I just wanted to ask you about Kellee. I know I should have done something about this sooner, but I did try to call her a couple of times, and I was sure by now I would have run into her."

"Back up," I said. "You've lost me."

Linda shook her head in annoyance. "Sorry. I'm not usually this scattered." She smoothed her shirt over the curve of her stomach. "I'm a little distracted. This morning my doctor told me it's possible I'm carrying twins."

"Twins!" I repeated. "That would distract anybody."

She shrugged. "When we get used to the idea, we'll be cool with it, but the doctor wants me to have an ultrasound Friday, so I'm going to miss your class, which means it'll be another week before I can get Kellee's tape-recorder to her. She left it in the bar Friday night. I picked it up after she left. She was pretty . . . upset."

"I know she was in rough shape," I said. "She phoned me. Linda, I'm aware that Kellee was drinking pretty heavily that night."

"Then you know why she hasn't been coming to class or answering her phone."

"You think she's ashamed of her behaviour," I said.

"Yes, and she should be," Linda said flatly. "I like Kellee, but she wasn't just blitzed that night at the Owl; she was mean. She was sitting next to me, and I thought if I let her ramble on, she'd give it up after a while, but she never stopped. The worst thing was that the person she was accusing wasn't there to defend himself."

"Val Massey," I said.

"She told you!" Linda's normally melodic voice was sharp with exasperation. "That really was irresponsible. It's totally ludicrous, of course. Val could have any woman he wanted on this campus. He's not only terrific-looking; he's bright, and he's sensitive, and he's kind. There'd be no reason in the world for him to come on to Kellee Savage."

"That was pretty much my feeling too," I said. "When Kellee talked to me, I tried not to leap to Val's defence, but she knew I didn't believe her."

Linda looked at me levelly. "No rational person would believe her."

"That night at the Owl – didn't anybody realize Kellee needed help?"

"At first we all just thought it was sort of funny. That was the first time any of us ever remembered seeing her in the bar, and there she was, sucking back the Scotch." Linda wrinkled her nose in distaste. "I don't know anybody under the age of forty who drinks Scotch, but Kellee said she was drinking it because Professor Gallagher told her that once you acquire a taste for Scotch, you'll never want anything else. I don't know whether she acquired the taste that night, but she sure got hammered."

"Why didn't somebody take her home?"

"As a matter of fact, I'd just about talked her into letting me drive her back to her place, when Val walked in. That's when everything went nuts. Kellee ran over to him and started pounding him on the chest and saying these crazy things; then Meaghan Andrechuk discovered Kellee's tape-recorder whirring away on the seat in the booth where we'd been sitting. Can you believe it? Kellee had been recording the private conversations of people she was in class with the whole evening . . ."

"Did Kellee ever explain what she was doing?" I asked.

"She didn't get a chance." Linda gnawed her lip. "Did you ever read a story called 'The Lottery'?"

I nodded. "In school. As I remember, it's pretty chilling."

"Especially the ending," Linda agreed, "when everybody in town starts throwing stones at the woman who is the scapegoat. There were no stones Friday night, but there might as well have been. Everybody had had too much to drink, and Kellee didn't help matters. Instead of apologizing, she started shouting that she was the only one of us who was doing real journalism, and she was going to show us all. She was so loud the manager came over and threatened to throw her out."

I closed my eyes, trying to shut out the image. "It must have been awful."

Linda's gaze was steady. "It got worse. Kellee started arguing with the manager. He was really patient, but she kept pushing it. Finally, he gave up and asked one of the women who worked in the bar to help him get Kellee into a cab. They were trying to put Kellee's coat on her when Meaghan came back from the bathroom and said there'd been a bulletin on TV: Professor Gallagher was dead. Kellee went white and ran out of the bar. She left this." Linda opened her knapsack and took out the tape-recorder that I recognized from class as Kellee's. "You'll make sure she gets it, won't you?"

"Of course," I said. "And thanks for bringing it in. It'll give me an excuse to call her. I know Kellee's behaviour was pretty rotten, but it's so close to the end of term. I'd hate to see her lose her year."

"So would I," Linda said. "But, Professor Kilbourn, when you talk to Kellee, make sure she understands that she has to stop hounding Val. You saw what he was like in class today. That was Kellee's doing. I'm sorry that she's disturbed, but that doesn't give her licence to ruin Val Massey's life."

I thought of Val's face, pale and expressionless, and the words seemed to form themselves. "You're right," I said. "She has to be stopped."

On my way back to the department, I made a quick trip to Physical Plant and picked up the extra key I needed for Ed Mariani. The woman who handed it to me was friendly and obliging, and I wondered, not for the first time, whether Rosalie Norman would take it amiss if I suggested her life would be smoother if she weren't so prickly.

When I got back to my office, Val Massey was waiting outside. I was relieved to see him there. I unlocked my door and Val followed me inside. I was grateful that he was giving me a chance to confront the Kellee Savage quandary head on.

"I was just about to make coffee," I said. "Would you like some?"

"No, thanks," he murmured.

"Well, at least sit down," I said, gesturing to the chair across from mine.

He didn't seem to hear me. He walked over to the window and stood there, wordless and remote, until the silence between us grew awkward.

"You have to be department head before they give you a view of anything other than the parking lot," I said.

Val turned and looked at me uncomprehendingly.

"That was a joke," I said.

He smiled and moved towards my bulletin board. I'd filled it with campaign buttons from long-ago elections and with pictures of my kids.

"How many children do you have?" he asked.

"Four," I said. "The two you met when we came out to Regina Beach, a daughter who's married and running a catering business in Saskatoon, and a son who's at the vet college."

"Have any of your children ever got themselves into a real mess?" he asked.

"Of course," I said. "I've got into a few real messes myself. It seems to come with living a life."

He looked so miserable that I wanted to put my arms around him, but I knew that the most prudent course was simply to give him an opening. "Val, you don't need to be oblique with me," I said. "I know about Kellee Savage."

At the sound of her name he recoiled as if he'd taken a blow.

"It's all right," I said quickly. "I don't believe what she's saying about you. In fact, I've decided to talk to her about the damage she's doing, not just to you but to everybody, including herself."

"Don't!" he shouted. The word seemed to explode in the quiet room. Val winced with embarrassment. When he spoke again, his voice was barely a whisper. "Don't talk to her . . . please. Don't get involved." He raked his fingers through his hair. "I'm sorry," he said. Then he ran out of the room.

I went after him, but by the time I got to the door, he was already out of sight. The hall was empty. I was furious: furious at myself for handling the situation badly and furious at Kellee Savage for creating it in the first place.

Ten minutes later, when Ed Mariani stuck his head in, I was still upset.

"Ready for an office-mate?" he asked.

"Am I ever," I said. "Make yourself at home." I pointed to the bookshelf nearest the window. "There's the kettle and the Earl Grey, and, as you can see, the cups and saucers are right next to it."

"Since everything's so handy, why don't I make us some tea?" Ed said. He picked up the kettle and padded out of the office. When he came back, he plugged the kettle in and eased into the student chair across the desk from me. He was such a big man, it was a tight fit.

"Do you want to trade?" I asked.

As he raised himself out of his chair, he smiled at me gratefully. "I'll try not to be here when you are."

"Don't worry about it."

Ed put a bag in each cup, poured in boiling water, then settled happily into my chair.

"So was Kellee Savage in class today?" he asked.

I shook my head. "No."

Ed raised an eyebrow. "I think I'd better just go ahead and tell the students about their placements. They've waited long enough."

"Yes, they have," I said, and I was surprised at how acerbic I sounded. "Ed, do you understand why Kellee Savage was the one who got the internship with the *Globe*?"

"No," he said, "I don't, and believe me, ever since I saw her name heading up that list, I've wondered what Reed saw in her that I didn't."

"She works hard," I said.

He laughed. "No disputing that," he said. "But there's no imagination in her work, nothing that takes you into any deeper understanding of what she's writing about."

"How well do you know her?" I asked.

"The J school is small," he said, "so we're a lot tighter with our students than you are in Arts. By the time the kids graduate we've usually had them in a couple of classes, we've helped them with practical skills like interviewing, we've supervised their independent projects, and we've spent time with them socially. Not that Kellee has ever been exactly a party girl." He picked up my mug. "Weak or strong?" he asked.

"Strong."

"A woman after my own heart," he said. "What's that old Irish saying? 'When I makes tay, I makes tay, and when I makes water, I makes water.' Anyway, what I remember most about Kellee Savage is the obituary she wrote."

"Of whom?"

"Of herself. It's an exercise most J schools assign in Print Journalism I. It's partly to teach students how to make words count, and partly to help them focus on their goals. Most of the obits the kids write are depressingly Canadian. You know: 'his accomplishments were few, but he was always decent and caring.' Kellee's was different. The writing was predictably pedestrian, but she had such extravagant ambitions, and she did have one glorious line. 'Kellee Savage was a great journalist, because although no one ever noticed her, she was there.'"

I shuddered, "That's certainly gnomic."

"Isn't it?" he said. He put a spoon into my mug, pressed out the last of the tea and fished out the bag. "I believe your tea is ready, Madam."

After I picked Taylor up from her friend Jess Stephens's house, we drove to Lakeview Court to feed Julie's fish. For Taylor, most chores were obstacles to be dispatched speedily, so she could get on with the real business of her life, but Julie's fish intrigued her, and she gave her full attention to feeding them. She had developed a routine, and I watched as she pulled a needlepoint-covered bench close to the tank, kicked off her shoes, climbed up on the bench, and shook the fish food carefully over the surface of the water. When she was done, she jumped down, pressed her face against the glass, and watched as the minute particles drifted down through the water, driving the fish crazy.

We watched for a few minutes, then I said, "We have to boogie, T. I haven't even thought about dinner yet."

"I have," Taylor said. "Why don't we have paella?"

"Why don't we have fish and chips?" I said. "I think there's a coupon for Captain Jack's at home." I looked at my watch. "Angus has a practice at six-thirty, so I might as well call the Captain from here."

When I went into the kitchen to use the phone, the light from the answering machine on Julie's desk was blinking. I hit the button, and a woman's voice, pleasantly contralto, filled the quiet room. "Reed, it's Annalie. It's Sunday, ten p.m. my time, so that's nine yours. My husband and I were at our cabin for the weekend, so I just got your message. It was such a shock to hear your voice after all these years. It's funny, I thought I'd feel vindicated when you finally figured out the truth, but all I can manage is a sort of dull rage." She paused. When she spoke again, her voice was tight. "I guess Santayana was right: 'Those who cannot remember the past are condemned to repeat it.' But Reed, remembering isn't enough. Now that you know what happened, you have an obligation to make sure there are no more repetitions. If you want to talk, my number is area code 416 . . . ," she laughed. "Of course, you have my number, don't you?" There was a click and the line went dead.

I rewound the tape and played it again. It still didn't ring any bells for me, but while Annalie's message was perplexing, her voice was a pleasure to listen to: musical and theatrically precise in its pronunciations. It was a professionally trained voice, and as I archived her message, I found myself wondering what part the enigmatic Annalie had played in the past that Reed Gallagher had chosen not to remember.

When we got home, Alex was there. I asked him to stay for dinner, but he insisted on paying.

"If I'd known you were picking up the tab," I said, "I would have ordered Captain Jack's world-famous paella."

Taylor was placing knives and forks around the table in a pattern that a generous eye might have seen as a series of place settings. When she heard the word "paella," she swivelled around to face me. "We could still order some." She narrowed her eyes. "That was one of your jokes, wasn't it, Jo?"

"It was," I said, "and you fell for it."

After Taylor sailed off, I poured Alex a Coke, made myself a gin and tonic, and we sat down at the kitchen table to exchange the news of the day. When I told Alex about the message on the Gallaghers' answering machine, he tensed with interest.

"That was the whole thing?"

"I archived it, if you want to hear it yourself. What do you make of it?"

Alex centred his Coke glass carefully on the placemat. "It doesn't sound good. All that talk about dull rage and vindication and making sure there are no more repetitions of history sounds like Reed Gallagher was getting hit with some pretty heavy stuff from the past."

"I wonder if that's what he and Julie quarrelled about the night before he died."

He whistled softly. "Could be. Then to relieve tension after their fight, Gallagher went down to Scarth Street, broke into a rooming house, pulled on his pantyhose, opened the poppers, and tried his hand at erotic strangulation." He shook his head in a gesture of dismissal. "This still doesn't feel right to me, Jo. But we haven't got anything else. We've talked to everybody we can come up with. We've gone over that room on Scarth Street with the proverbial fine-tooth comb, and Splatter's spent so much time on Gallagher's body that we're telling him it must be love. Still, all we've got is what we started with – accidental death."

"So what's next?"

Alex shrugged. "Nothing. That's it. No leads. No evidence.

No case. They're ready to release the body, so we'll need a signature. I'll have to phone Mrs. G. – unless, of course, you want to volunteer."

"You're buying dinner," I said. "I'll call."

Alex raised an eyebrow. "I got the best of that deal."

"I know you did," I said. "But I'm keeping track."

After dinner, Angus talked Alex into letting him drive the Audi over to his basketball practice. As I watched the Audi lurch onto Albert Street, I decided if Alex could be heroic, I could too. I squared my shoulders, marched back inside, and dialled the number where Julie said she could be reached.

The listing was in Port Hope, a pretty town of turn-of-the-century elegance on Lake Ontario. I'd spent a summer there when I was young. Luckily, my memories were happy ones, because I had plenty of time to recollect summers past before Julie finally picked up the phone.

She did not sound happy to hear from me, and I didn't waste time on pleasantries. When I told her that the police were releasing Reed's body, she was curt. "I'll take care of it," she said. Then, mechanically, like a child remembering an etiquette lesson, she added, "Thank you for calling."

I thought of the last time I'd seen her. She had seemed so alone the night she dropped her keys by my house. "Julie, wait," I said. "Call me when you know your flight time. I'll pick you up at the airport."

Her tone was incredulous. "Why would I go back there? Hasn't he already humiliated me enough?"

"You can't just leave him," I said. "Somebody has to sign for the body and make funeral arrangements."

"There isn't going to be a funeral." She laughed bitterly. "What could people possibly say about the dear departed?"

The next morning, Ed Mariani and I had tea together in the office before class, and I told him about Julie's decision to bury Reed without any formal ceremony. Ed was furious.

"Damn it, Joanne, I never liked that woman, and it turns out I was right. Reed was a good man. He needs to be remembered, and the people who cared about him need to take stock of what they've lost."

"I suppose if Julie doesn't want to handle it, Reed's colleagues at the university could organize a memorial service."

Ed nodded agreement. "We could, and we should. But you and I aren't the colleagues who were closest to Reed."

"Tom Kelsoe," I said. "He's the one whose history with Reed goes back the farthest. He was Reed's student. Reed gave him his first job, and from what I heard at the time, Tom was the real mover and shaker in getting Reed appointed as director of Journalism."

Ed cocked an eyebrow. "So they say."

I felt my face go hot with embarrassment. "I'm sorry, Ed. You didn't need to be reminded of that."

"No," he said, "I didn't, but it wasn't your doing. Now come on. Let's get back to the memorial service."

"Somebody should call Tom, so we can get some people together and make the arrangements," I said.

Ed looked away. "Joanne, I'll help in any way I can, but I don't want to have anything to do with Kelsoe."

I waited, but Ed didn't elaborate, and I didn't ask him to. Instead, I reached for the phone and dialled Tom's office number. When an operator came on and told me the line was no longer in service, I remembered the chaos in the Journalism offices, and dialled Tom's apartment.

I had just about decided he wasn't there when Jill Osiowy picked up the phone. She sounded distracted, and for a beat I worried that I'd got her at a bad moment, then I remembered the scene at the Chimney Saturday night, and I hoped, childishly, that her morning had been filled with bad moments.

"How are you, Jill?"

"I'm okay," she said. "How are you?"

"Never better," I said. "But I need to speak to Tom. Is he there?"

"I'll see if he can come to the phone."

When Tom Kelsoe picked up the receiver, he barked his name in my ear, and I felt my gorge rise. But this wasn't about me. I tried to make my voice civil.

"Tom, Julie Gallagher has decided against a funeral for Reed, but some of us at the university have been talking about a memorial service. You and Reed were so close. I thought you'd want to be part of the planning."

He cut me off. "I don't get off on primitive group rituals, Joanne. I think the idea sucks. I won't help and I won't be there." He slammed the receiver down.

I turned to Ed Mariani. "Tom declines," I said. "And without regrets."

Ed put his hands on the arms of his chair and pushed himself up heavily. "Then I guess it's up to us," he said.

CHAPTER

7

Reed Gallagher's memorial service was held at the Faculty Club on Friday, March 24, a week to the day after his body had been discovered in the rooming house on Scarth Street. In every detail of the planning, Ed Mariani's watchword had been dignity; the service seemed to become his way of reclaiming for Reed the respect and regard which his bizarre death had stolen from him. The rooms I walked into that afternoon were an invitation to celebrate civility and the pleasures of the senses: simple bowls of spring flowers touched the tables with Japanese grace. At the grand piano in the bar, Barry Levitt, trim in a cream cable-knit sweater and matching slacks, was leafing through his sheet music, and in the club's window room, a buffet with hot and cold hors-d'oeuvres had been set up beside a well-stocked bar. Ed Mariani had done Reed Gallagher proud, but as I picked up a glass of champagne punch at the bar, I was edgy. I'd been tense all week, made restless by the deepening mysteries in the lives of two people I didn't really know. One of those people was Reed Gallagher.

Ed Mariani and Barry Levitt had volunteered to organize Reed's memorial service, but they had entrusted one job to me. Because I had keys to the Gallaghers' condominium, I was to find photographs and memorabilia for the display celebrating Reed's life. At first, I burrowed through the boxes of memorabilia I found in his closet as dispassionately as an archaeologist on a dig, but as the man Reed Gallagher had been began to emerge, Annalie's cryptic allusion to Santayana took on a haunting resonance. Try as I might, I could not reconcile Reed Gallagher's sad and tawdry death with the life that was emerging from the boxes and cartons that surrounded me. As Mr. Spock would say, it didn't compute. Nonetheless, the more I dug, the more I became convinced that the answer to the enigma of Reed Gallagher's last hours lay somewhere in his past.

By any standards, his life had been extraordinary. Before he had turned his hand to teaching, he had covered wars and political campaigns and natural disasters. He had been present at many of the events that had defined our history in the past quarter-century. He had known famous people, and he had, if one could judge from the affectionate inscriptions on plaques and photographs, been liked and respected by those who worked with him and knew him best. Everything I came up with reflected a life lived with gusto and commitment. Perhaps more significantly, my burrowing uncovered no evidence of the negligence Annalie's message had suggested, nor did it bring to light even a hint of an ache so ferocious that it would someday drive Reed Gallagher up a flimsy fire escape to his appointment in Samarra.

But, as I kept reminding myself, my job wasn't to analyse; it was to gather together what Barry Levitt called my Gallagher iconography, and that afternoon, as I stood in the Faculty Club looking at the graceful mahogany table that held

my handiwork, I was pleased with the job I had done. Reed
Gallagher had not been badly served by his iconographer.

Scattered among the awards and testimonials were
pictures of Reed flanked by two prime ministers, of Reed
gripping the hand of an American president, of Reed confer-
ring with media figures like Knowlton Nash, Barbara Frum,
Peter Newman, and Richard Gwyn, people who come as
close to being legendary as our country permits anyone to
be. But my real coup was a picture of Reed with a woman
who, in all likelihood, would be of no significance to anyone
in the room but me.

I had searched hard for a photograph of Annalie, but in the
end I had almost passed it by. My aim had been to balance
photos of the public Reed Gallagher with some that captured
his private moments, and I had found some lovely and evocative snapshots: Reed as a teenager, taking a chamois to a
shining convertible with fins while two middle-aged people
beamed with parental pride; Reed as a college boy in a
bathing suit, exulting in the pleasure of holding a sweetly
curved young woman in his arms; Reed as the very young
editor of a small-town newspaper, proudly showing off his
twin proofs of authority, a shining brass nameplate on
his desk and a brand-new moustache on his upper lip.

By the time I came upon the carton that Reed, in his large
and generous hand, had labelled RYERSON – DESK STUFF, I
thought I'd made all my choices. But remembering Reed's
affinity for the students at our J school, I decided to see if I
could ferret out something from his early days as an instructor. The yellowed newspaper clipping of the photograph of
Annalie and Reed was in an envelope with a clutch of odds
and ends: a dry cleaner's receipt, an old press pass from a PC
leadership convention, a ticket stub from a Leafs-Blackhawks
game. In the photo, Annalie, in her capacity as editor of
the *Ryersonian*, was presenting Reed with a bound copy

of the past year's issues. Both she and Reed were smiling.

Her full name was Annalie Brinkmann. On the phone, her voice had been filled with lilt and magic, but the picture showed a plain girl, heavy-set and wearing horn-rimmed glasses which had apparently failed to correct an outward-turning squint. Twenty years can change many things, and the girl of twenty is often barely discernible in the woman of forty, but I was hoping the picture might jog the memories of some of Reed's friends from the Ryerson days. There was even an outside chance that Annalie herself would appear. Ed had written an elegant obituary of Reed for the *Globe and Mail*, and placed a notice of Reed's death in the *Toronto Star*. Both had mentioned the time and place of the memorial service. If Annalie was a newspaper reader, chances were good she would know about what Ed Mariani had come to call Reed's last party. It was a slim straw to cling to, but if I was lucky, one way or another, the memorial service would link me and the woman who had left such a troubling message for Reed Gallagher three days after his death.

The newspaper clipping was unmounted, and I would need a frame. Fortunately, there was a small silver one at hand that was just the ticket. I didn't feel the smallest pang as I replaced the photograph of Tom Kelsoe with the one of Reed and Annalie Brinkmann. Tom had made it clear that he didn't want to be part of Reed's last party, and it was a pleasure to honour his request.

As the guests started arriving at the club, it seemed that Tom and Julie were the only people who had chosen not to come. Twenty minutes before the farewells were scheduled to begin, the room was packed, but newcomers were still appearing. I scanned the door eagerly, looking for two faces: one was Annalie's; the other was Kellee Savage's.

Kellee still hadn't shown up. As acting head of the School of Journalism, Ed had checked with all her instructors. Their reports had been the same: Kellee Savage hadn't been in class all week. Ed and I had taken turns calling the number Kellee listed as her home number, but we'd never connected. When I told Alex I was growing uneasy, he was reassuring. Kellee Savage was, he said, a white middle-class twenty-one-year-old who had got drunk and humiliated herself in front of her friends. Nothing in her life pointed to a fate worse than a bad case of embarrassment. In his opinion, when she screwed up her courage, she would be back.

Alex's logic was unassailable. Even I had to admit that Kellee's disappearance fell well within a pattern I knew. It was not uncommon for university kids to disappear from classes for a while, especially this close to the end of term. Sometimes the triple burden of a heavy workload, parental expectations, and immaturity was just too much, and the kids simply bailed out. Among themselves, the students called the syndrome "crashing and burning," but the image was hyperbolic. Most often, after a week or so, they came back to class with a stack of hastily completed term papers or a doctor's note citing stress and suggesting mercy.

The rational part of me knew that in a small Prairie city, a twenty-one-year-old woman should be able to drop out of sight for a week without setting off tremors of concern. But we are not ruled by reason alone, and that morning I'd made a decision. Ed had put a large announcement of Reed's memorial service in our local paper, and he'd posted notices all over campus, inviting students to come and pay their final respects. If Kellee Savage was in town, she would know about the service. Given her apparent closeness to Reed, if Kellee Savage had one decent bone in her body, she would be at the memorial service that afternoon. I had decided that, if she didn't put in an appearance, the time had come to find out why.

As the Faculty Club filled to overflowing, I began to circulate, looking for someone whose age suggested they might have known Reed in the Ryerson days. The group through which I made my way was an oddly festive one. Ed had let it be known that he didn't want to see anyone wearing a scrap of black at Reed's last party. The weather had continued mild and sunny, and both women and men had broken out their spring best. The swirl of pastel dresses and light suits made the rooms look like a garden party. When Barry Levitt sat down at the grand piano, and the bass player and the drummer took their places and began to play "Come Rain or Come Shine," the party took off. People had drinks, filled plates at the buffet, and visited. As the afternoon wore on, I exchanged pleasantries with many very pleasant people, but although a handful of them had known Reed Gallagher when he was at Ryerson, none of them displayed a shock of recognition when I mentioned Annalie Brinkmann's name.

There were more than a few famous faces in that room. For much of his career, Reed Gallagher had worked in the major media markets of New York and Toronto, and as I wandered, I saw some of our students in earnest conversation with people they could have known only by reputation. Success is a magnet, and our students were drawn to that small band of the elect who by anyone's criteria had succeeded: Americans who anchored television newsmagazines and supper-hour news; Canadians who wrote regular columns in Canadian newspapers that mattered or books that topped the best-seller list. But as had been the case since I was an undergraduate, the celebrities that no student could resist were the Canadians who had made it big in the U.S.A. When Ed Mariani went to the microphone to announce that the formal part of the afternoon was about to begin, he had to make his way through a group of J-school students jostling one another for a place in the circle that surrounded Peter Jennings. His manner held the implicit promise that, while the Holy Grail could only be found south of the border, it was waiting for their Canadian hands.

Ed didn't speak long, perhaps five minutes, but he touched on all the essentials: Reed Gallagher's integrity as a journalist, his commitment as a teacher, and his steadfastness as a friend. In closing, Ed said that perhaps the most fitting epitaph for Reed Gallagher could be found in H.L. Mencken's catalogue of the characteristics of the man he most admired: "a serene spirit, a steady freedom from moral indignation, and an all-embracing tolerance."

I glanced at the table near the windows where the Media class had congregated; from the rapt expressions on their faces, it was apparent that Mencken's words still had the power to inspire. It was an emotional afternoon for the J-school students. Ed concluded his remarks by inviting people to come up and share their memories. As Reed's friends and colleagues walked to the microphone, drinks in hand, to speak with tenderness about Reed Gallagher's passionate curiosity or his decency or his fearlessness, the students were visibly moved. They were young, and they had not had much experience of death; for many of them, the eulogies for a man who had been laughing with them the week before were an awakening to mortality. Linda Van Sickle was fighting tears, and when Val Massey put his arm around her, she buried her head gratefully in his chest. Then Jumbo Hryniuk, who was sitting next to Val, reached over and gently stroked Linda's hair, and I was struck again by the cohesion that existed among the students in that particular class.

As the afternoon wore on, I found myself tense with the effort to catch Annalie Brinkmann's characteristic lilt in the voice of one of the eulogists, but I never did, and by the time Ed Mariani joined me, I'd resigned myself to the prospect that Annalie was a no-show.

When the last speaker left the microphone and the jazz trio struck up "Lady Be Good," Ed leaned towards me. "Come on," he said, "there's someone I want you to meet. My one famous acquaintance. You'll like him – I promise." I followed Ed across the room, and he introduced me to a journalist from Washington, D.C., whom I recognized at once as a regular on the "Capitol Gang." Ed's friend had some rivetting stories and some even more rivetting gossip, and I was enjoying myself until I noticed that suddenly all the pleasure had vanished from Ed Mariani's face.

"What's the matter?" I asked.

Ed pointed towards the memorabilia table. "Look over there," he said.

Tom Kelsoe and Jill Osiowy were standing in front of the display. They had ignored Ed's edict about wearing black, and they were dressed in outfits that were almost identical: black lace-up boots; tight black pants; black shirts. Standing side by side, so close together that their bodies appeared fused, they seemed more like mythic twins than lovers. As soon as Tom Kelsoe saw me looking, he leaned down and whispered something to Jill. Then, in the blink of an eye, they were gone.

Beside me, Ed Mariani shuddered. "What do you make of that performance?"

"I don't know," I said, "but I'm glad it's over. I hate seeing Jill like that, and I'm not in the mood for a rerun of Tom as the suffering hero."

Ed's expression was bleak. "I'm never in the mood for Tom as anything." Then he shook himself. "I'd better get over and thank people for coming. Barry used to be a camp counsellor and he says you should always kill an event before it dies on you."

It didn't take long for the Faculty Club to clear. The painful ritual of saying goodbye was over, and people were anxious to get back to the concerns of the living. When the last guest had left, the Faculty Club staff began clearing off the buffet table and carrying dishes towards the kitchen, and I went over to the memorabilia table and began to pack up.

As I worked, I remembered the warmth of the eulogies, and the question that had been troubling me since I'd heard about Reed's death floated to the top of my consciousness: given the fulfilment and the promise of his life, how could Reed Gallagher have had such a death? It was a question for a philosopher, and as I closed the last carton, I knew that it would be a long time before I had an answer. I was just about to tape up the box when I realized that I didn't remember putting in the photograph of Annalie and Reed. I checked, but the mahogany table was bare. It was obvious I was mistaken, that I'd wrapped the photo and absent-mindedly stuck it in the box with the rest. The prospect of unwrapping everything and checking didn't thrill me, but the idea of losing the picture appealed to me even less. Reluctantly, I pulled everything out and began to search. The photograph wasn't there.

I was baffled. There had been signed pictures of celebrities that were rare enough that they might have tempted a light-fingered mourner, but an old newspaper picture of Reed Gallagher and a girl nobody knew hardly qualified as a collectible. The only logical possibility was that someone had picked up the photograph, wandered off, and put it down somewhere else. I went back to the Faculty Club office and asked the manager, Grace Lipinski, to ask the cleaning staff to keep an eye out for the photograph. Then I went back to my repacking.

I'd just about finished when old Giv Mewhort came out of the bar. He was wearing a vintage white suit that would have been the very thing for one of Gatsby's parties, and his face was pink with gin and emotion. He picked up one of Reed's photos and said, "'The noblest Roman of them all' – too famous doubtless to be cut." He smiled sardonically. "Although, from what I hear, Reed Gallagher hardly died a stoic's death. Still, he was the best of a sorry lot and a good man to drink with." He replaced the photograph carefully in the box. "I shall miss him."

The carton was unwieldy, and Barry and Ed offered to carry it down to the car for me. When we'd stowed it safely in the trunk, the three of us stood for a moment in the sunshine. I started to tell them about the missing photograph, but they both looked so weary I decided to give them a compliment instead.

"It was a terrific afternoon," I said. "I know how much work goes into making an event seem that effortless. You both did a great job."

Ed frowned. "I supposed you noticed that Kellee Savage wasn't there."

"I noticed," I said, "and I'm worried."

When I parked in front of our house, Angus was shooting hoops, and Leah was trying to teach Taylor how to skip rope. Benny, who, in repose, was beginning to look uncannily like a fox stole, was curled up on the step, watching.

When she saw me, Taylor held out her skipping rope. "Do you want a turn, Jo?"

"At the moment, I'd rather have my toenails ripped out one by one," I said, "but thanks for asking, and thank you, Leah, for giving T a hand with the womanly arts." Leah was wearing shorts, and I noticed she had a Haida tattoo of a fish on her calf.

I pointed to it. "Is that new?" I asked.

She smiled. "So new that even my parents haven't seen it."

"How do you think they'll take it?"

Leah grinned. "Oh, they'll probably want to rip my toe-nails out one by one, but my dad always says that as long as my grades are good, and my name doesn't end up on the police blotter, they'll adjust."

"Sounds like a wise father," I said, and I headed for the house. When I got to the porch, Taylor called out, "Don't forget. I've got a birthday party."

"Since when?" I said.

"Since Samantha gave me the invitation."

"I didn't see any invitation."

"It's been in my backpack all week." She squinted as if she was envisioning the missing invitation. "The party's from four-thirty till eight o'clock."

I looked at my watch. "Taylor, it's already twenty to five, you can't just . . ." I shrugged. "Never mind. Come on, let's drive out to Bi-rite. What does Samantha like?"

"Horses."

"Fine, we'll get her a flashlight."

Taylor ran to the porch, scooped up Benny, then came running after me. "Why are we getting her a flashlight?"

"Because they don't sell horses at Bi-rite. Now come on. Let's go."

Benny was not a happy passenger – he yowled all the way to the drugstore – but we did find a flashlight, a card that had a horse on it, and, on the clearance counter, a gift-wrap pack in what appeared to be the Old MacDonald motif. Close enough.

When we got back to the house, Taylor dumped our booty from the drugstore on the kitchen table and began wrapping. I pulled some turkey soup from the freezer, put it on to heat, and started to make dumplings. Within five minutes, Samantha's present was ready, dinner was under way, and the phone was ringing. It was Alex, and I invited him to join us for dinner. Half an hour later, Taylor was cleaned up and at the birthday party, and Angus and Alex and I were sitting in candlelight eating soup. Once in a while, I just have all the moves.

As soon as he'd finished his second bowl, Angus jumped up. "I've got to go down to the library. Can one of you drive down with me?"

"Take your bike," I said. "We'd like a chance to talk. Besides, I'm too old to jump up from the dinner table."

"You're not old," he purred.

"Thank you," I said, "but you're still taking your bicycle."

After Angus left, Alex and I carried the candles and our coffee into the living room, and traded our news for the day.

When I told Alex about Reed and Annalie's picture disappearing, he raised an eyebrow. "You think someone stole it?" he asked.

"I don't know," I said. "Probably not. It's just that I was already on edge when I discovered the photograph was missing."

"On edge about what?"

"About all the things that don't make sense about Reed's death. Alex, I wish you could have been there this afternoon. That memorial service would have given you a very different perspective on the Reed Gallagher case."

Alex's eyes were troubled. "There is no case, Joanne. Not any more. It's all wrapped up. The death certificate will read 'accidental death due to cerebral anoxia' – lack of oxygen to the brain."

"You sound as if you don't think that's what he died of."

Alex shook his head. "Oh, I know that's what he died of. Splatter Zimbardo worked this case hard, and he's as good as they come. The question marks aren't with the pathology reports; they're with our part of the investigation. It's not that we haven't done our stuff. We have, and the physical evidence is solid: we've got the bottle of Dewar's that Gallagher was drinking from that night; we've got the tumbler he was using; we've got the glass ampoules that held the amyl nitrite he inhaled; we've got the seduction outfit he was wearing, and the hood he had on and the electric cord that was around his neck. Gallagher's fingerprints are exactly where they should be on every single item, and there were no signs of a struggle. All the evidence points in one direction."

"Except you don't believe the direction it's pointing in."

"I believe it. I just don't understand it." He leaned forward. "You know, Jo, cops don't talk much about the role imagination plays in police work, but it's essential. When an investigation into a sudden death starts moving in the right direction, it's like watching a movie playing backwards. You can see what happened in those last hours and, crazy as it sounds, you can feel the emotion. We've put all the pieces of the puzzle together on this one, but I still can't see the pictures. And I can't feel whatever it was that Reed Gallagher was feeling when he tied that cord around his neck." Alex picked up his coffee, took a sip, and turned to me. "Tell me about the memorial service, Jo."

As I told Alex about the tributes Reed's friends and colleagues had paid him, and about the sense of loss that had been in the Faculty Club that afternoon, his dark eyes never left my face. When I finished, he said, "Not a stupid man."

"No," I said, surprised. "Not at all."

"And yet that's what Zimbardo says Gallagher died of. Stupidity. He says if Gallagher was into that scene, he should have known better than to use liquor with the amyl nitrite. The combination sends blood pressure through the floor. When Gallagher's blood pressure dropped, he must have blacked out. With the veins in his neck compressed from the cord, and the chemical stew from the poppers and the booze sludging his veins, and the hood, he was just too weak to fight for air. It was like drowning."

I felt my stomach lurch. At the Faculty Club that afternoon, Ed's graceful party had seemed to banish the ugliness of Reed's last hours in the rooming house on Scarth Street, but now the horror rushed back. All the show tunes and fond memories in the world couldn't negate the fact that Reed Gallagher had died a terrifying and humiliating death.

Alex put down his coffee cup. As if he'd read my mind, he said, "It's a hell of a way to die." Then he shrugged. "But that is the way it happened. Case closed."

"Alex, you just said this doesn't feel right to you. How can the case be closed?"

"I've told you, Jo. Because there's no evidence to suggest that Gallagher's death didn't happen exactly the way Zimbardo said it did, and the book says you can never prove a positive with negative evidence."

I thought of Kellee Savage. In police parlance, the fact that she hadn't shown up for Reed's memorial service would be negative evidence, but for me it was another piece in an increasingly unsettling puzzle.

"Alex, do you remember telling me that you were going to check out the last twenty-four hours in Reed Gallagher's life?"

"Sure. It's standard procedure. The report's in the file downtown."

"Would it be breaking any rules to let me see it?"

"No. The case is closed. There's public access, and you're part of the public." He raised an eyebrow. "Are you checking up on me?"

"No, I'm still trying to figure out what connection Kellee Savage, that student I told you about, had with all this. I was just curious about whether Reed Gallagher talked to her the day he died."

"Her name wasn't in the report, but Gallagher's secretary did say he had a meeting with a student that afternoon."

"Then the student's name should be in Reed's appointment book."

There was an edge of exasperation in Alex's voice. "Give me a little credit, Jo. I did ask. The secretary said Gallagher told her the meeting was private – the only reason he mentioned it at all was because he was leaving the office."

"Could I look at the report?"

He stretched lazily. "Sure, I'll make you a copy on Monday."

"Alex, could I get a copy tonight? I understand what you said about negative evidence, but there must be times when negative evidence points towards something being seriously wrong."

"You think this is one of those times . . . ?"

"I don't know. All I know is that the last time I saw her, Kellee was miserable, but she also said something like, 'I should have known it was too good to last.' When I tried to get her to tell me what she meant, she wouldn't, but I've found out since that Reed Gallagher chose her for the top internship the School of Journalism gives out. She's an ambitious young woman. If she knew she was in line for that placement, there's no way she'd be jeopardizing it by missing classes for a week. And there's no way she wouldn't have shown up at her benefactor's memorial service. Even if she didn't have feelings for him, there were a lot of important people there."

Alex looked hard at me. "Jo, why are you getting so involved in this now?"

"Maybe because I didn't get involved when I should have."

For a moment he was silent. Then he said wearily, "Bingo! Not getting involved when you should have is the one explanation I'm open to right now."

"Are things worse with your nephew?"

"Yeah," he said. He leaned forward and blew out the candles, but not before I saw the anger in his eyes.

The light was fading as Alex and I walked down towards the Albert Street bridge, but the night was mild, and the hot-shots who drive up and down Albert Street on weekend nights were out in force. When we got to the middle of the bridge, I leaned over the railing to check the ice on the lake. It hadn't started to break up yet, but there were dark patches, and the orange rectangles that warned of thin ice had been placed along the shoreline.

"Look," I said. "Signs of spring."

When Alex and I walked into the police station, some uni-formed cops greeted him, but he didn't introduce me, and as we walked down the hall together, I tried to look innocent or at least bailable. I'd been in Alex's office only twice before; both times I had been there on official business, and my mind had not been on the decor. That night as I looked around, I thought how much it was like his apartment: neat, spare, and impersonal. Among the standard-issue furnishings, there were only three personal items. Taped to the inside of the door was a computer-printed sign: "Don't Complain. Expect Nothing. Do Something." A CD player and a case filled with classical discs were within easy reach on the shelf behind the desk, and on the wall facing the desk was a medicine wheel. An elder told me once that the medicine wheel is a mirror that helps a person see what cannot be seen with the eyes. I remembered Alex's anger when he spoke about his nephew, and I wondered what he'd been seeing in this mirror lately.

It didn't take long for Alex to bring Reed Gallagher's file up on his computer. I stood behind him as he hit the print key, and when the machine began printing, I leaned over and embraced him.

Alex put his hands over mine. "One of the first things they teach us at police college is to build defences against the appeal of attractive women."

"You're not on duty right now, are you?"

"No," he said, "I'm not." He stood up and kissed me.
"And I'm glad I'm not."

While Alex checked through a stack of papers on his desk,
I looked through his CDs: Mozart, Beethoven chamber
music, Ravel, Bartok.

"I like your music," I said, "and I like your office. You
seem to have figured out how to hang on to what matters
and leave the rest behind."

Alex scrawled his initials on the last of the papers in the
pile, then he looked up at me. "You're not often wrong, Jo,
but you're wrong about this. I don't leave anything behind.
And I don't know what matters. All I know is that if I can
keep the externals of my life uncomplicated, I can function."
He walked over to the coat hook and handed me my jacket.
"Time to go," he said. Then he reached behind me and
flicked the wall switch.

The wind had come up, bringing with it one of those
sudden shifts in the weather that, despite precedent, always
seem to come as a surprise. By the time we had walked from
downtown to the Albert Street bridge, I was shivering.

"I'm always yelling at the kids about rushing the season,"
I said. "But I wish I'd worn a heavier jacket. I'm freezing."

Alex put his arm around me. "Better?"

"Much," I said. We were almost across the bridge when a
half-ton, travelling in the same direction as we were, slowed
down. The window was unrolled, and a beefy man in a ball
cap leaned out and shouted something at us.

I felt Alex's arm stiffen.

"Is that somebody you know?" I asked. "I didn't hear what
he said."

Alex didn't answer me, but when the light changed and
we started across the street, he tightened his grip on my
shoulder. The half-ton had stopped for the light, and as we
crossed in front of it, the driver yelled again. The words were

ugly and racist, but Alex wasn't his target. I was. "Hey, babe," he shouted, "when you're through fucking the chief, maybe you'd like to try it with a couple of white guys."

My reaction was immediate and atavistic. I broke away from Alex's hold and ran across to the sidewalk. In a heartbeat it was over. The light changed; the man in the truck cheered and yelled, "We'll be back for you, baby," and the truck drove off.

When Alex came to me, his eyes were filled with concern, but he didn't touch me. "Are you all right?" he asked.

"I'm fine." I laughed shakily. "Wow! As Mother Theresa would say, 'what a scumbag.'"

Alex didn't smile. I reached for his hand, but he drew away. "Alex, I'm sorry."

"Don't be," he said. "It was just a reflex. Getting out of the line of fire is instinctive."

"You wouldn't have done it."

He smiled sadly. "I couldn't have done it."

"Because you're not a coward."

"No," he said gently, "because I'm not white. That closes off a lot of options. Now, come on. You'd better get back."

He walked me to my door. "Come inside," I said. "I've got a few minutes before I have to get Taylor. I don't want to talk out here."

He came in and I closed the door and went to him.

"Alex, I'm sorry. I don't even know why I did that. I don't care what some idiot in a truck yells at me."

He took me in his arms and kissed me and, for a few moments, I thought I was home-free. Then he stepped away from me.

"That was just the first time," he said. "After a while, you'll care, Jo. Take my word for it. You'll care."

CHAPTER

8

My grandmother's maxim, "Morning is wiser than evening," has helped me through many troubled nights, but that Saturday morning daybreak didn't bring perspective. When the sun came up, I still didn't understand why I had run from Alex on the bridge, and I still had no idea how I was going to make things right between us again.

As the dogs and I started on our morning run, I ached with remorse and regret. The cold wind of the night before had disappeared as suddenly as it had come; the air was mild and the sky was luminous. Once, on a morning like this, Rose and Sadie would have been straining at the leash, but we were all growing older, less anxious to seize the day. As we started across Albert Street, I noticed shards of broken beer bottles at the spot where the half-ton had stopped the night before. I pulled the dogs out of the way, kicked the glass into the gutter, and headed for the lake. "Life's full of symbols," I said, and Rose, our golden retriever, looked up at me worriedly.

As we ran along the shoreline, I worked hard at thinking about nothing, but nature abhors a vacuum, and out of nowhere my mind was filled with images of my first-year

Greek class: chalk dust lambent in the late-afternoon sun, muted sounds of traffic on Bloor Street, and a professor's voice, infinitely sad, "Antitheses are always instructive. Take, for example, the pairing of 'symbol,' literally, 'to put together,' and 'diabol,' the root of our word 'diabolic,' 'to throw apart.' Symbol suggests the highest uses of our language and thought; diabol their uttermost degeneration."

The amazing thing was that the diabolical hadn't happened sooner. Alex and I had been going out together since late November; we lived in a city in which racism was a fact of life, and yet this was the first time that a stranger had felt compelled to hurl words at us. November to mid-March. We had, I suddenly realized, been saved by a northern winter. Most of our time together had been spent indoors: at my place, talking, watching movies or playing games with the kids; later, when we became lovers, at his apartment listening to music, making love. When we did go out, for a run with the dogs or to cross-country ski or toboggan with the kids, we were bundled in the layers of Canadian winter clothing that mask distinctions of race, gender, and faith.

Julie and Reed's wedding had been our first real event as a couple, and it had been, in my mind at least, a disaster. For reasons that I would never understand, Julie had decided to make Alex her trophy. She introduced him all around, stumbling over his name, dimpling in mock-confusion and laughter. "Well, it's one of those wonderful native names, but you'll just have to say it yourself, Alex." She'd paraded him through the wedding reception, telling everyone that he was on the police force, cooing over how commendable it was that he was giving his people a role model, someone to look up to. I had been livid, but Alex had been sanguine. "She has to start somewhere, Jo. Maybe knowing me can make the new Mrs. Gallagher more open to the possibilities in the future."

But it hadn't happened that way. In public, Julie may have fawned over an aboriginal police inspector, but in private, when she had needed the services of a cop, she had made it painfully obvious that her personal officer of the law had to be white.

With her smiles and her oh-so-subtle double standards, Julie was the poster girl for polite bigotry, but as comforting as it was to demonize her or dismiss the cretin who had yelled at me the night before as a bottom feeder, they weren't the problem, and I knew it. I had lived in Regina all of my adult life and, to paraphrase Pogo, I had seen the enemy and he was us. I knew the language, and I knew the code: a whisper about the problems in the city's "North Central" area meant native crime; "the people," said knowingly, meant native people. I'd never used the code; in fact, I had prided myself on doing all the right things. Years ago, when an aboriginal couple had wanted to buy a house in our area, a petition had been circulated to keep them out, and I'd gone door to door urging my neighbours not to sign; when racist jokes were told, I walked out of the room; when my kids came home from school talking about "wagonburners" and "skins," I sat them down and talked to them about how words can wound. But until the night before, I had been drawing from a shallow well of liberal decency. In my entire life, I had never once been on the receiving end of prejudice, and the experience had been as annihilating as a fist in the face from a stranger. Alex was forty-one years old. That morning, for the first time, I found myself trying to imagine how it felt to withstand forty-one years of such blows.

When I got back to the house, it was 6:25. I dialled Alex's number. There was no answer, and I didn't leave a message. There was nothing to do but take refuge in my Saturday ritual. I plugged in the coffee, showered, dressed, made pancake batter, brought in the morning paper, and tried to concentrate on the politics of the day. At 7:30, I tried Alex's number again. He picked up the phone on the first ring.

"I was just about to call you," he said.

"Synchronicity," I said. "That has to be a good sign, doesn't it?"

He didn't answer, so I hurtled on. "Alex, I'm sorry about last night. I'm more than sorry, I'm ashamed. I don't know what made me run like that."

I could hear fatigue in his voice. "You didn't do anything wrong. That's what I was trying to tell you last night. There's no reason to blame yourself. You were in a lousy spot, and you reacted."

"But I reacted badly."

"The point is, you wouldn't have been in that spot if you hadn't been with me."

"Alex, I wanted to be on the spot with you. I still do. Come over. Please. Let's talk about this."

"I don't think so. When we're together, it's just too easy to lose sight of the facts."

"What facts?"

"The ones we've been ignoring. Jo, that guy in the truck last night was not an aberration. That's the way it is."

"I know that's the way it is. I just wasn't prepared. Next time, I'll be ready."

"Nobody's ever ready for it. You're talking to an expert witness now. It doesn't matter how many times that kind of crap happens, it's always an ambush. And defending yourself against it changes you."

"Alex, you're one of the best people I know."

For a moment, he was silent. Then he said, "And you're one of the best people I know, but, Joanne, you don't know what you're getting into here. And you don't know what you're getting your kids into. Angus and Taylor are great kids, Jo – so confident, so sure that all the doors are open for them and that when they walk into a room people can't wait to welcome them. I don't think you want that to change."

As soon as he mentioned my children, I felt a coldness in the pit of my stomach. "It wouldn't have to change," I said, but even to my ears, my voice lacked conviction.

"Maybe we should step back for a while," Alex said. "Take a look at where we're headed."

I should have told him that the last thing I wanted to do was step back. I should have said that the direction in which we were headed was far less important to me than the fact that we were headed there together. But those were the words of a brave woman and, once again, I came up short. "Maybe that would be best," I said. And that was it. We told each other to take care, and we said goodbye.

I replaced the receiver slowly. My eyes were stinging. From the moment Alex had called to tell me about Reed's death, it seemed as if everything I'd done had been wrong: I'd failed a student who'd turned to me for help. I'd pushed my best friend so hard that I lost her. I'd been fired from a job that I liked. I'd made a scene in a restaurant. Worst of all, I'd betrayed a man I cared about deeply, and now I'd lost him. When I reached for a tissue to mop my eyes, I knocked over my coffee cup, and then, because I figured I'd earned it, I swore.

"I thought there was a major penalty for using that word." Angus was standing in the kitchen doorway. His face was swollen with sleep, and he was wearing the black silk shorts his sister, Mieka, had sent him for Valentine's Day. He yawned. "What's up?"

My first impulse was to protect him. Then, remembering how much he liked Alex, I decided it would be best to tell him the truth. I poured us each a glass of juice, then my son and I sat down at the kitchen table and I told him about the incident on the bridge, and that Alex and I weren't going to be seeing each other for a while.

He was furious. "That's totally stupid," he said.

"I think so too," I said, "but Alex is worried about us – not just me, but you and Taylor. Angus, has my relationship with Alex ever caused any problems for you?"

"No. Alex is a cool guy. Hey, he taught me how to drive, didn't he? And he lets me drive his Audi." He patted my hand. "C'mon, Mum. Lighten up. And tell Alex to lighten up. If other people are having a problem because you two are going out together, it's their problem."

"And Leah feels the same way you do?"

"She really likes Alex. They're both kind of independent."

"And no one's ever said anything?"

He shrugged. "Some of the guys sort of wondered, but you know me, Mum. I've never cared what people say."

It was true. Of my four children, Angus was the one who cared least about the opinion of others. "Inner-directed" was the term my college sociology book used to describe people like my youngest son. Ian had valued the trait more than I did. For me, Angus's indifference to praise or punishment meant he'd been a difficult kid to raise, but Ian saw it differently. "It means," he'd said, "that when Angus is older, he won't be blown off course by every wind." Ian had been right. Angus wasn't easily blown off course. But he didn't take after me in that, and I knew it.

I picked up our juice glasses and took them to the sink. Angus followed me over, and gave me an awkward one-armed hug. "Mum, don't worry about other people. Do what you want to do." He leaned forward and peered into the bowl of pancake batter on the counter beside the griddle. "Now, is this all for you? Or can I score some?"

In a few minutes, Taylor and Benny joined us for breakfast, and the conversation drifted to Samantha's birthday party. By the time I had scraped the plates and rinsed them for the dishwasher, Taylor's story was still crawling inexorably towards its climax. It was a tale with tragic possibilities. The flashlight had been a hit, but Samantha kept shining it in everybody's eyes, and she refused to relinquish it when her mother asked her to. Finally, Samantha's mother said there'd be no cake until Samantha started behaving, and Samantha said she didn't care. Events at the party had reached a *High Noon* standoff when our phone rang.

As I went to answer it, Taylor called out, "Don't worry, I won't tell any more about the party till you're back."

When I heard Rapti Lustig's voice, my first thought was that somehow I was back on the political panel. Rapti was an assistant producer on Jill's show, and usually she was unflappable, the calm at the eye of the storm, but that morning she sounded harried.

"Jo, I'm glad I got you. Listen, this is Tina in makeup's last show before the wedding, and we've just decided to have a little party for her after we wrap tonight. I know it's short notice, but we'd really like you to come." Then she added wheedlingly, "Please. For old time's sake."

"Rapti, it's only been a week."

"Maybe," she said, "but a lot of us here are already nostalgic for the good old days. Jill's new man is a royal pain. Anyway, say you'll come. Tina likes you so much, and we're ordering from Alfredo's. I'll get a double order of eggplant parmesan. I remember you like it."

I thought about Alex and about the empty evening ahead. I hated showers, but I did like Tina. "I'll be there," I said.

"Great," she said. "Now, people are bringing gifts, but don't get anything cutesy. One of the techs had a kind of neat idea. He suggested a tool box and tools. Tina and Bernie are buying that old wreck on Retallack Street. They're going to be fixing it up themselves. What do you think of the idea?"

"I think it's inspired," I said. "No bride can have too many hammers."

"We'll see you at six then."

"But the show starts at six."

"That's why it's our best time to get everything ready so we can surprise Tina. Makeup's through by six, so Bernie's going to take Tina out for a drink and bring her back as soon as the show's over. If you come early, you can help me decorate the green room and stick the food around."

It seemed my penance was taking shape already.

Rapti was buoyant. "We'll have fun," she said. "We can get started on the wine. I have a feeling we're going to have to be totally blitzed to endure Tom's TV debut."

"You don't think he's going to be good?"

Rapti chortled. "I have a premonition that Jill's boyfriend is going to be a twenty-two-karat, gold-plated, unmitigated disaster."

I was smiling when I turned back to Taylor and her narrative. "Okay," I said. "Did Samantha back down, or did her mother have to shoot the cake?"

Our day filled itself, as Saturdays always did, with the inevitable round of lessons and practices and errands. Twice during the day I told myself I should try Kellee's number again; both times, I drew back before I even picked up the receiver. I felt fragile, like someone whose energy has been sapped by a long illness, and I was grateful for the Saturday routine that carried me along in spite of myself. Whenever I thought of Alex and what he must be feeling, I wanted to be with him, but the best I could do was hope that his Saturday had its own pattern of mindless, sanity-saving errands.

In the afternoon, Taylor came with me when I went to Mullin's Hardware in search of something glamorous in a tool box. Then we came home and I made chili while T sat at the kitchen table and worked on her sketches of Nanabush and the Close-Your-Eyes Dance.

After she'd been drawing for about thirty minutes, she called me over. "It's not working," she said. "I'm trying to make it seem real but not real, like the story. But I don't know how to do it." I sat down and looked at her sketch. To my eye, it was amazing. The section Taylor was working on was the one in which the hungry Nanabush tries to convince a flock of plump ducks that if they join him in a Close-Your-Eyes Dance, they'll have the time of their lives.

"See, it's all too real," Taylor said. "Alex's story wasn't like that."

When I looked again, I saw what she meant. "I have something that I think can help," I said. I went into the living room and came back with a book on Marc Chagall that Taylor's mother had given me years ago. I flipped through till I came to an illustration of the painting "Flying Over Town"; in it, a man and a woman, young and obviously in love, float above a village. The village is very real, and so, despite their ability to defy gravity, are the young couple. But the world they inhabit is not a real world; it is a world in which love and joy can carry you, weightless, above the earth. In "Flying Over Town," Chagall had created a fantastic world that transcended physical facts; it was the same world that came to life when Alex told Nanabush stories.

Taylor leaned so close to the book that her nose was almost on the page. Finally, she said, "Nanabush and the birds don't have to be on the ground." Then, without missing a beat, she ripped up the sketches she'd been working on for days, and started again.

Taylor was still at the table when I left for Nationtv at 5:15. I kissed the top of her head. "Chili's on the stove," I said. "Angus promises to dish it up as soon as his movie's over, and I'll be home in time to tuck you in."

For the first time in months, Taylor didn't even turn a hair when I announced I was going out for the evening. "Good," she said absently, and she went back to her drawing. Finally, it seemed I had done something right.

It was strange to walk across the park towards Nationtv on a Saturday evening without feeling a knot of apprehension about the show, but I was grateful that there was no hurdle I had to leap that night. I'd had enough. All I wanted to do was take deep breaths and look around me. In the park, the signs of an early spring were everywhere: the breeze was gentle; the trees were already fat with buds; the air smelled of moisture and warming earth. As I walked, my mind drifted. Once I had heard a poet describe the eyes of Hawaiian men as "earth dark," and I had thought of Alex's eyes. When I told him, he had laughed and said I was a hopeless romantic. Maybe so, but I had still been right about his eyes.

The first person I ran into when I walked into Nationtv was Tom Kelsoe. He was wearing jeans, a black T-shirt, and a black leather jacket. Very hip. My first impulse was to pretend I hadn't seen him, but if I ever wanted to reconcile with Jill, I was going to have to bite the bullet.

I smiled at him. "Break a leg," I said.

Tom Kelsoe looked confused. "What?"

"Good luck with the show," I explained.

"What are you doing here?" he asked. For once, his tone wasn't rude. He seemed genuinely perplexed; somehow my presence had knocked him off balance.

"It's personal, not professional," I said. "There's a party for the woman who does makeup for the show. She's getting married."

"I guess Jill mentioned it," he said warily.

"Anyway," I said, "I'm glad I ran into you. I didn't get a chance to talk to you and Jill at the service for Reed yesterday."

I could see the pulse in his temple beating. "Who put that display by the door together?" he asked.

"I did," I said. "What did you think of it?"

He flinched. "It was fine." He checked his watch. "I'd better get down to the studio."

"Have you got another minute?" I said. "I need to ask you about Kellee Savage."

"What about her?"

"Apparently, Reed Gallagher had a very high opinion of her work. I wondered if you shared it."

Tom looked at me coldly. "She's a troublemaker," he said; then, without a syllable of elaboration, he headed for the elevators. Apparently I wasn't the only faculty member Kellee had gone to with her charges against Val Massey.

I was the first person at the party. The green room was empty, but somebody had brought in a clear plastic sack of balloons and made an effort to arrange the furniture in a party mode. Two tables had been pulled together to hold the food and drink, and the chairs had been rearranged into conversational groupings. The effect was bizarre rather than festive. All the furniture in the green room had been cadged from defunct television shows, so there was a mix of styles that went well beyond eclectic. I was trying to take it all in when Rapti Lustig came through the door.

Rapti was an extraordinarily beautiful young woman: whip-thin, with a sweep of ebony hair, huge lustrous eyes, and a dazzling smile. But as she looked around the room, she wasn't smiling.

"What do you think?" she said.

"I think it looks like the window of a second-hand furniture store," I said.

Rapti made a face. "A cheesy second-hand furniture store." She pulled a roll of tape out of her pocket and handed me a balloon. "Looks like we've got our work cut out for us."

It didn't take us long to get the balloons up, cover the tables with paper cloths, and set out the paper plates and glasses. Rapti had bought everything in primary colours and, despite its entrenched charmlessness, the room was soon as cheerful as a box of new crayons. At 6:00, Rapti gave the room a critical once-over, pronounced it not half bad, walked to the television set in the corner and turned on our show. When the theme music came up, and I heard the announcer's familiar introduction, I was grateful that I was sitting in the green room with Rapti. In less than a week, I had lost my job and my man. If I'd been sitting home alone, it would have been hard not to feel my life had become a country-and-western song.

Rapti handed me a glass of wine. "To good women and good men. May they find one another."

I pulled a chair closer to the television. "I'll drink to that," I said.

As I looked at the screen, the first thing I noticed was that Tom was still wearing his jacket. Black leather was perfect for Tom's "mad, bad, and dangerous to know" image, but before the show was five minutes old, it was apparent that Tom had given more thought to his outfit than to his homework. He made a lulu of a factual error about the powers possessed by the Senate, but when Sam Spiegel, who was a senator himself, nudged him gently towards the right answer, Tom was adamant. Glayne Axtell wasn't gentle. When Tom misrepresented what the leader of her party had said, Glayne said crisply, "It would help your case if you got at least one of your facts straight."

When the phone-in segment started, Tom's performance went from bad to worse. The callers, sniffing incompetence, made straight for Tom's jugular. As the show ended, and the screen went into its farewell configuration with the host in the centre and the panel members in their respective corners,

Sam Spiegel interrupted the host's wrap-up to announce that he wanted to say goodbye to two colleagues who had been on the panel with him from the beginning, and whom he was certain the audience would miss as much as he did. When Sam was through, Glayne Axtell sent what certainly appeared to be genuine good wishes for the future to both Keith and me. Tom Kelsoe, isolated in his box on the lower left of the screen, gave an odd little salute to the camera but remained silent. By the time the credits finally rolled, I almost felt sorry for him.

Rapti jumped up and turned off the set. "That," she said, "was the worst hour of television since 'The Mod Squad' got cancelled. Jill's going to be livid." She shuddered theatrically, "This is going to be one tense little party."

It turned out Rapti was wrong, at least about the party. It was a very merry prenuptial event. No one made a hat with ribbons for Tina, and no one decided to break the ice with games. The wine was plentiful and the take-out from Alfredo's was sensational. The only person happier than Tina was Rapti. As she pushed in the red wheelbarrow that was her gift, Rapti glowed with the effects of good Beaujolais and triumph.

Even I had fun. My improved spirits were, I had to admit, due in no small degree to Tom Kelsoe's pitiful debut. My pleasure might have been mean-spirited, but I was revelling in it until, almost an hour after the party had begun, Jill Osiowy walked in the door. She was pale and tense, and as she picked up a bottle of wine from the refreshments table and poured herself a glass, I saw that her hands were trembling. She drained her glass, refilled it, and walked over to join the group who had clustered around Tina.

I had known Jill for over twenty years, and as I watched her trying to blend in with that carefree crowd, my heart ached for her. I was familiar enough with the structure of Nationtv to know that Jill had spent at least part of the past hour on the telephone being castigated by someone who didn't have half her talent but who picked up a paycheque twice as hefty as hers. I also knew that the most punishing criticism Jill would be subjected to that night would come from herself. She was in a miserable spot. She was passionate about two things: her work and Tom Kelsoe. Tonight the show that she had created, lobbied for, and nursed along had sustained a heavy blow because she had been foolish enough to offer it up to the man she loved.

I had long since stopped trying to fathom the choices other people made in their relationships. Perhaps, as an old friend of Ian's once told me, it was all a matter of luck; if you were born under a benevolent star, your loins would twitch for the right one. In my opinion, Jill's star had led her astray. If that was the case, maybe the time had come for me to stop sulking and let her know she was still very dear to me.

I walked over and put my arm around her shoulder. "How would you like to curl up with a large tumbler of single-malt Scotch?"

She smiled weakly. "That beats my last offer. The vice-president of News and Current Affairs suggested hemlock." Suddenly her eyes filled with tears. In the years I'd known her, I'd seen Jill deal with deaths, betrayals, and disappointments, but until that moment, I'd never seen her cry. "Can I take a rain check?" she asked. "I think I just want to go home and go to bed."

"Of course," I said. "Any time."

Her voice was low. "Jo, I've missed you."

"Me too," I said.

The clock was striking nine when I walked in the front door. The kids were down in the family room. Taylor and Benny were curled up on the rug listening to the soundtrack from *The Lion King*, and Leah and Angus were huddled together on the couch, doing homework, or so Angus said.

"Fun's over, T," I said. "I'm back."

She rolled over and grinned.

"How's Nanabush?" I said.

"Better," she said, "but I don't want anybody to see it now until it's done."

"How was your party?" Angus asked.

"Good," I said.

"How good could it be if you're home by nine o'clock?" Then he grinned. "Alex called."

"And . . . ?"

"And he said he was heading out to Standing Buffalo for a couple of days. He said if we need him, we can get in touch through the band office." My son looked at me expectantly. "Aren't you going to call him?"

"Angus, I think he meant we could call if there was an emergency."

Angus rolled his eyes, but for once he held his tongue. Leah came over and handed me a piece of paper. "You had another call," she said. "I hope you can read my writing."

"Let's see," I said. "Grace from the Faculty Club called. She found the picture. She wouldn't have bothered me at home, except she thought I seemed worried about it the other night, and I can call her at the club until ten p.m." I held the neatly written note out to Angus, who had long been known as the black hole of messages. "This is how it's done, kiddo. Note the inclusion of all pertinent facts."

"Hey," he said. "I've got a life."

I kissed him. "And you're now free to lead it. Thanks for staying with Taylor, you guys. Angus, don't be too late. Church tomorrow. It's Palm Sunday."

He groaned, grabbed Leah's hand, and headed for the door.

I turned. "Okay, Miss, bath-time for you." When he heard my voice, Benny arched his back and hissed. I looked him in the eye. "T," I said, "why don't you throw Benny into the tub, too. I think he's starting to look a little scruffy."

While Taylor ran her bath, I called Grace at the Faculty Club. Her news was unsettling. The cleaners had found the photo of Reed and Annalie when they'd emptied out the receptacle for used paper towels in the men's washroom. Grace had been puzzled. "It was just an old newspaper clipping," she said. "Why would anybody go to all that trouble?"

I told her I didn't know, but as I hung up I thought it would be worth a couple of phone calls to try to find out. On her message to Reed Gallagher, Annalie Brinkmann had said her area code was 416 – that was Toronto. I dialled Information. There was only one "A. Brinkmann" listed and, as the phone rang, I felt my pulse quicken. But it wasn't Annalie who answered; it was her husband.

Cal Woodrow was a pleasant and helpful man. When he told me that Annalie was in Germany attending a family funeral, he must have heard the disappointment in my voice.

"If it's urgent, I can get her to call you," he said. "She'll be phoning here Wednesday night."

"It's not urgent," I said. "But maybe you can tell me something. Did your wife know that Reed Gallagher died?"

"No," he said. "She'd left for Dusseldorf by the time the obituary appeared in the *Globe and Mail*. I didn't see any point in breaking the news to her when she called to tell me she'd arrived safely. Isn't it strange that after all this time . . . ?" He didn't complete the sentence.

"After all this time what?" I asked.

"No," he said decisively. "That's Annalie's story to tell or not to tell."

"Could I leave my number?"

"Of course," he said. "Annalie will be most interested in talking to anyone who knew Reed Gallagher."

It was 9:45 when I tucked Taylor in. She'd brought the Marc Chagall book to bed with her, and she asked me whether her mother had given me the Marc Chagall book because Chagall was her favourite or because she thought he was mine. It was the first time Taylor had talked about her mother openly, and her healthy curiosity about Sally made me optimistic. Maybe Ed Mariani was right in believing that art was the answer.

When I turned out Taylor's light, I went downstairs, made myself a pot of tea, and picked up my briefcase. I was tired, but I was too edgy for sleep. There were a couple of journal articles I had to plough through before class Monday, and this seemed as good a time as any to get started. When I pulled the articles out, I saw Kellee Savage's unclaimed essay, and I felt a sting of irritation. Present or absent, Kellee was a problem that wouldn't go away. On impulse, I picked up the phone and dialled her number. No answer. It was a south-end number, and it suddenly occurred to me that I could stop by her place on the way to church. There were only two weeks of classes left. If Kellee was lying low, watching Oprah and eating Sara Lee, it was time she shaped up and came back to school.

I went over to my desk, took out my box of index cards, and pulled out the section marked Political Science 371 – the Politics and the Media seminar. I flipped through, stopping to smile at Jumbo Hryniuk's. The students filled out their own cards with name, address, and reason for taking the course. Jumbo had stated his reason succinctly: "Because in this day and age, nobody can afford to be just a jock." Fair enough. When I pulled out Kellee Savage's card and checked her address, I felt as if a piece had suddenly dropped into place in the puzzle. Two addresses were listed. One was her Regina address, and the other was the one she called her home address: 72 Church Street, Indian Head, SK.

She had gone home. The obvious answer to her whereabouts had been there all along. I reached for the phone and dialled the Indian Head number. The phone was picked up on the first ring. It was a man's voice. "Kellee?" he said.

"No," I said. "But I'm looking for her. My name's Joanne Kilbourn. I teach Political Science at the university. Kellee's one of my students, but she hasn't been in class for a week. I wanted to get in touch with her; I was afraid that there might be a problem."

"My name is Neil McCallum," the man said. "I'm Kellee's friend, and that's what I'm afraid of, too." He spoke slowly, and there was a slight distortion in his pronunciations, as if he had a speech impediment. He paused, as if giving careful consideration to what he was about to say. Then he cleared his throat and made me an offer I couldn't refuse. "Maybe," he said, "we could help each other."

CHAPTER

9

By 2:00 on the afternoon of Palm Sunday, I was on my way to meet Neil McCallum. After church, I had driven over to Gordon Road and stopped by Kellee's apartment. The building she lived in was called the Sharon Arms. It was a new and charmless building, but it was handy to the university and secure. In the outside lobby, there was an intercom with the usual panel of buzzers opposite the appropriate apartment numbers and name slots. On the information card she had filled out for the Politics and the Media seminar, Kellee had written that she lived in apartment 425. The name slot opposite the buzzer for 425 was empty, but that didn't surprise me. All of Kellee's actions on St. Patrick's Day suggested she was a woman who saw herself surrounded by outside threats; it made sense that she wouldn't advertise her whereabouts. I had pressed Kellee's buzzer long enough to let anyone inside know that I wasn't a casual caller, but there was no response.

By the time I got home, I'd made up my mind. I was going to Indian Head. I called Sylvie O'Keefe and we arranged a double-header for her son, Jess, and Taylor: lunch with me at McDonald's, then bowling with Sylvie at the lanes at the Golden Mile.

As I drove east along the Trans-Canada towards Indian Head, I saw that the fields were already bare of snow. It wouldn't be long before farmers were back on the land, and the cycle of risk and hope would begin again. It took self-discipline not to turn off onto the road that wound through the Qu'Appelle Hills towards the Standing Buffalo Reserve and Alex Kequahtooway. Alex had been a strong and passionate presence in my life for months, and I ached for him. I turned on the radio, hoping to shift my focus. Jussi Björling was singing "*M'appari tutt'amor*" from *Martha*. There had never been a time in my life when I hadn't thrilled to Björling, but as Lionel, his despair as he recalled his former happiness and hopes cut too close to the bone. I leaned forward and turned him off in mid-aria.

For twenty minutes I drove in silence, yearning like a schoolgirl. A few kilometres outside Indian Head, I realized that, before I met Neil McCallum, I had to get a grip on myself. I pulled over on the shoulder, turned off the ignition, got out and looked at the prairie. The sky was clear, and the air was sweet. In the ditch at the side of the road, the first pussy willows were growing, and I broke off some branches to take back to Taylor. The catkins were silky and soft, and the woody, wet smell of the willows filled the car, a foretaste of April, with its mingling of memory and desire. An omen, or so I hoped.

I hadn't hesitated about promising Neil McCallum that I'd drive seventy kilometres to talk to him. His recital of the reasons behind his growing concern about Kellee had been a Euclidean line of facts that pointed in only one direction: something was terribly wrong. Neil and Kellee were the same age; they had grown up next door to one another, and, according to him, they had always been close. The year

Kellee graduated from high school, her parents had been killed in a car accident, and she and Neil became even closer. When Kellee went off to university, he had helped pack her things; since then, he had been the one who had made sure her house was ready for her when she came home.

For three years, Kellee's routine, when she was at school, had not varied. She called Neil every Wednesday, she took the 6:20 bus back to Indian Head every other Friday, and she left on the 4:30 bus, Sunday afternoon. But on Friday, February 24, the pattern had changed. She had been home the weekend before; nonetheless, on the twenty-fourth she'd taken the bus back to Indian Head. She'd come home the next two weekends too; then on the weekend of March 17, her birthday, although she had told Neil to expect her, she hadn't shown up. He hadn't seen or heard from her since.

As I turned off the highway and drove over the railway tracks and down the tree-lined streets towards the centre of town, I found myself wondering about Kellee's best friend. The directions he'd given me were a model of clarity, but a certain thickness in his speech and a habit of hesitating before he answered a question and of waiting a beat between sentences made me curious.

Neil McCallum and his dog, a black bouvier who looked like a young bear, were waiting for me on the front lawn of his house. Neil was a little below medium height and stocky. He was wearing blue jeans, a green open-necked sweater, and a Saskatchewan Roughriders ball cap. Up close, I saw that the hair under his ball cap was brown and that he had the small almond-shaped eyes and distinctive mouth of a person with Down syndrome.

He watched as I got out of the car. Finally he took a step towards me. "You're Joanne," he said.

"And you're Neil." The bouvier was watching me intently. I walked over and held my hand out, palm up, for it to sniff. "What's your dog's name?" I asked.

"Chloe," Neil said. "A French name."

Chloe came over and nuzzled me, and I knelt down and stroked her back. "She's beautiful," I said.

For the first time since I'd arrived, Neil McCallum smiled. "I'm going to breed her pretty soon. I'll have puppies at the end of summer."

"Are you going to keep them?"

"Mum says one bouvier is enough. I'm going to sell them. To good homes."

"I always thought that breeding dogs would be a nice job."

He smiled mischievously. "If you breed dogs, you have to have another job. To pay for your dogs."

"I'll remember that," I said. "What's your other job?"

"I have three jobs," he said. "When it's winter, I help at the concession stand at the curling rink. I take care of the ice, too. When it's summer, I help at the concession stand at the ball diamond."

"Must keep you pretty busy."

"Busy's good," he said. "Let's look at Kellee's house."

Neil and Chloe started up the walk between his house and Kellee's, and I followed. The bungalows were almost identical: mid-sized, with white siding, shining windows, and well-kept grounds. On the face of each house were three wooden butterflies, poised as if for flight.

Neil pulled out a key-ring and opened Kellee's front door. The house had a slightly stale closed-up smell, but the living room was pleasant: uncluttered and filled with sunshine. There was a couch on the far wall, a couple of comfortable-looking chairs by the front window, and a television set in the corner. On top of the television were two framed pictures. Neil McCallum picked one up and handed it to me. "That's Kellee's parents."

The photograph had been professionally taken by one of those companies that set up in department stores and malls and offer great prices and your choice of three possible backgrounds. Kellee's parents had chosen spring in the Rockies. As they stood against the cardboard range of improbably pink-hued mountains, the Savages' smiles were open and their eyes were as grey and without illusion as a Saskatchewan winter sky. Good country people.

"Kellee's parents didn't have any other children?"

"Just her." Neil put the family photo back carefully in its place on the television, and handed me the other picture. "That's Kellee graduating from Indian Head High School. I went there too, but in a different class. I have Down syndrome."

"You seem to be having a pretty good life."

He shook his head. "Not any more. I'm too worried. My mum says Kellee's just busy. I don't think so. Something's wrong." Without explanation, he turned and walked away. After a second's hesitation, I followed him past the entrance-way and down a hall that seemed to lead to the bedrooms. Neil stopped in front of the only room with a closed door. The door had a lock, and he pulled out his key-ring and opened it. "Look," he said.

The room was unnaturally dark. When Neil turned on the light, I saw that thick drapes were pulled tightly across the only window. Someone had pushed an old oak filing cabinet and a heavy bookcase in front of the drapes. The result looked less like a decorating decision than a barricade. Flush against the wall to the left of me was the kind of computer table offices use; on top of it were a computer and a printer. Both were state-of-the-art, and both were pricey. To the right of the table was a small metal bookcase. It had three shelves of books, all with Library of Congress numbers on their spines. One shelf contained books I recognized as the reference texts Kellee had used in her essay on how the alternative press had been used to voice the concerns of prostitutes in our city's core area. A second shelf held books on the dynamics of groups, and the third held journals from the J-school library; all of them seemed to focus on the subject of journalistic ethics. Thinking of how old Giv Mewhort would have chortled at that oxymoron, I smiled to myself. I leafed through a couple of the J-school journals, hoping for a bonanza: a bus schedule or travel itinerary. All I could see were yellow Post-it notes marking various case studies and articles.

Neil was watching me with interest. "I don't like it here," he said.

"Neither do I."

Neil frowned. "It used to be nice."

"Before the window was blocked off."

He nodded. "I told her it wouldn't look good. But she said that's the way it had to be. So I put the furniture where she said."

"When did you and Kellee change the room?"

"The weekend she wasn't supposed to come home. That's when she bought the curtains too."

"To close out the light?"

"So nobody could see in." His brow furrowed. "Who would want to see in?"

I looked over at the barricade, and I felt a sense of oppression so overwhelming, I could barely breathe. Suddenly, I wanted to get out of that room. I turned to Neil. "Let's check Kellee's bedroom."

"For what?" Neil asked.

"I don't know," I said. "You might notice that something's out of place."

He looked puzzled. "How would I know? I never go in there."

Neil stayed in the hall while I went into Kellee's room. Everything seemed to be in order. A Care Bear and a Strawberry Shortcake doll rested side by side on a pink satin pillow at the head of the bed, and the girlish pink-and-white bedspread was smooth. A brush and comb were neatly aligned beside a wooden jewel box on the vanity. I opened the box. It was full of barrettes: butterflies, plastic ribbons, beaded sunbursts, feathery combs.

I closed the jewel box and turned back to Neil. "Did Kellee ever talk to you about friends she might want to visit?"

"I'm the only friend," he said gently.

"What about family?"

"She has an aunt."

"Here in town?"

"No, in B.C." Suddenly he smiled. "She sent Kellee a box of apples and I got half."

"Neil, do you think Kellee might have gone to visit her aunt?"

"She wouldn't go away," he said flatly.

I opened the closet door. Inside were clothes that I remembered Kellee wearing in class. Involuntarily, I stepped back.

Neil McCallum was watching my face. "You're scared too," he said.

"A little," I agreed. "But let's not panic. When I go back to Regina, I'll try Kellee's apartment again. I went there this morning, but she wasn't home."

"You should talk to Miss Stringer."

The name was familiar, but I couldn't place it. "Who's Miss Stringer?" I asked.

"Kellee's landlady."

"Neil, it's a brand-new apartment building. Those places don't have landladies."

Neil's voice rose with frustration. "It's not new. It's a dump. Kellee said so. And Miss Stringer lives there."

"On Gordon Road?" I said.

Neil shook his head impatiently. "You went to the wrong place," he said. "Gordon Road is where she lived before." He pulled a small black notebook from the pocket of his shirt, and thumbed through it. "This is where she lives now," he said. "She wrote it in herself. So it's right."

I took the book from him and read:

> Kellee Savage,
> 317 Scarth Street,
> Regina S4S 1S7

For a moment, I didn't grasp the significance of the address. When I did, my pulse began to race. It was the address of the house in which Reed Gallagher had died.

When I drove back to Regina, Kellee Savage's graduation portrait was in a Safeway bag on the seat beside me. I knew the picture would be helpful if I was going to make inquiries about Kellee's whereabouts, but Neil hadn't wanted to part with it. He told me that Kellee didn't like having her picture taken, and that he liked having a photograph of her where he could see it every day. I promised him that I would take good care of it, and he promised me that he wouldn't let anybody else into Kellee's house and that he'd be careful.

Neil and Chloe had walked out to the car with me. Before I left, Chloe gave me a final nuzzle, and Neil reached out as if to hug me, before he drew back and settled for a smile. "One more promise," he said. "No stopping looking until we find her."

"Okay," I said.

He looked at me intently. "You have to say it."

"All right," I said. "No stopping looking until we find her."

It was a little before five when I pulled up in front of the house on Scarth Street, picked up the Safeway bag with Kellee's photograph, and got out of the car. Alma Stringer was out on the porch, knocking down cobwebs with a broom. When Alex had interviewed her the day she found Reed Gallagher's body, he had characterized Alma as a tough old bird. As I watched her darting at the cobwebs with her broom, her arms and legs winter-white and pencil-thin, her scalp pink through her sparse and fading yellow hair, I thought there was something chicken-like about her. When she saw me, she raised her broom aggressively. Alma, it seemed, was more banty rooster than mother hen.

As I introduced myself, I tried to look pleasant and non-threatening. I must have succeeded, because before I had a chance to explain what I was doing on her grassless lawn, she had apparently made up her mind that I wasn't worth her while and gone back to her cobwebs.

I climbed the stairs and stepped in front of her. "I won't take much of your time," I said.

She gave the underside of an eavestrough an expert flick. "You won't take none of my time," she said.

I took the photograph of Kellee out of the bag and held it out to her. "I'm looking for this young woman. She's one of your tenants."

She looked at the portrait without interest. "Number six on the main floor."

"Is she there now?"

"No."

"Do you remember when it was that you saw her last?"

"What's it to you?"

"No one's seen her around for a while. I'm worried."

"You her mother?"

"Her teacher."

"That's a break for you. Popping a kid that ugly wouldn't give a mother much to be proud of." She chuckled at her witticism. Her laugh was a smoker's laugh, and its husky roughness seemed to act as a spur. She reached into her back pocket, pulled out a pack of du Mauriers, and lit up. As the smoke hit her lungs, she closed her eyes in satisfaction. I tried to take advantage of the new and mellow mood.

"Could you just give me a moment of your time, please? If you can't remember when you saw Kellee last, maybe you can remember a visitor she had. Anything, Miss Stringer. What you know may not seem important, but . . ."

She narrowed her eyes. "How did you know my name?"

"I'm a friend of one of the detectives who investigated the murder."

She inhaled deeply, then pivoted on her heel so she could be sure that the smoke she blew out hit me full in the face. "Why don't you get your friend, the detective, to answer your questions?"

"You've lived in the house all along. He doesn't have the perspective you have."

"Yeah, but he also don't have my problem." She looked at me expectantly.

"What is your problem?"

"My problem is that it's almost the end of the month. For your friend on the police force, that's not a problem. Cops can count on getting that monthly paycheque of theirs whether they've earned it or not. I can't count on dick. All I've got is those rents." Alma looked at me craftily. "Maybe you'd like to take care of number six's rent for her."

"No," I said.

Alma took a last deep suck on her cigarette, then, in a movement so effortlessly perfect that I knew she must have done it a thousand times, she drew her arm back and pitched her cigarette so that it sailed across her yard and hit the street beyond her property. "The next time you want to talk to me," she said, "make sure you got a rent cheque in one hand and a damage deposit in the other."

As I walked back to my car, I realized I hadn't eaten since breakfast. I was tired and hungry and discouraged, but Neil McCallum had extracted a promise from me. Police headquarters were on Osler Street, less than ten minutes away from Alma's; not far at all for a woman who had given her solemn word that there would be no stopping until she found Kellee Savage.

At the station, a downy-cheeked constable directed me to the office that dealt with reports of missing persons. As I turned down the corridor he'd indicated, I caught a glimpse of dark hair and a familiar grey jacket disappearing through an open door. It was Sunday night. Alex might have come back from Standing Buffalo early. Like an adolescent with a crush, I stood in the hallway, watching the door, knees weak with hope, while police and civilians walked by. Finally, the dark-haired man in the grey jacket emerged. I saw that he was a stranger, and I cursed Alex for not being there and myself for being so stupid that I believed he would be.

The name of the officer I talked to in Missing Persons was Kirszner. He was polite, but he pointed out the obvious: many people lived in the rooming house where Reed Gallagher had been found dead, and all of them were free to come and go as they wished. Then, echoing Alex, he suggested that the salient fact to consider about Kellee Savage was not that she lived on Scarth Street, but that she was a twenty-one-year-old student who was two weeks away from final exams.

As I walked along Osler Street to my parking place, I tried to buy the officer's explanation. What he had said was both reasoned and reassuring, but he hadn't felt the fear in that barricaded room in Indian Head. I had, and I knew in my bones that his explanation was wrong.

When I got home, Leah and Angus were in the kitchen making a meal that seemed to involve every pot and utensil we owned, but I didn't mind because I was ravenous and whatever they were making smelled terrific.

"What's on the menu?" I asked.

"Pot roast," Leah said. "And a salad and potato pudding and, for dessert, honey cake."

"I didn't know you could cook," I said.

She raised a double-pierced eyebrow. "Actually, what you're getting tonight is my entire repertoire. My grandmother says every woman should know how to cook one meal that will knock people's socks off. This is the one she guarantees."

"Does your grandmother live close by?"

"As close as you can get. She lives with us. So does my great-aunt Slava."

"Slava," Taylor said, rolling the word appreciatively on her tongue. "That's a nice name."

Leah wrinkled her nose. "I think it sounds kind of indentured myself, but the Russian meaning is nice – 'glory.' Slava's my grandmother's sister. Anyway, we all live together. It's like something out of Tolstoy."

"You're lucky," I said.

Leah looked thoughtful. "Most of the time, I guess I am."

We made an early evening of it. Leah's grandmother was obviously no slouch; the pot roast knocked our socks off. After we'd cleared away the dishes, Angus walked Leah home, and Taylor and Benny went to the family room to watch television. I poured myself a glass of Beaujolais, sat down at the kitchen table, and thought about the day.

I was deep in the puzzle of the barricaded room in Indian Head when Julie called. She asked about my family, her house, and her mail. Her questions were perfunctory, and her voice was flat and spiritless. Her lack of interest in my family didn't come as a surprise, but her listlessness about her own affairs was disturbing. Come rain or come shine, the one subject that had always engaged Julie's complete and fervent interest was Julie.

She seemed anxious to get off the phone, but I cut short her goodbyes. "Wait," I said. "There's something I need to know. Did Reed ever mention a student named Kellee Savage to you?"

Suddenly, the torpor was gone, and Julie was hissing, "You mean she was a student?"

I was taken aback. "Yes," I said. "As a matter of fact, she's in one of my classes. Then Reed did mention her."

"No," she said, and her voice was low with fury. "He didn't mention her, but I found out about her."

"What did you find out?"

"For God's sake, Joanne. I thought you were supposed to be so sensitive. You know the answers to these questions or you wouldn't be asking them. My husband was having an affair with that . . . *student*."

"With Kellee? What on earth made you think that?"

"The usual. We hadn't been married two weeks before he started going out nights – no explanations, of course, except when I pressed him, then my very original new husband gave me every cliché in the adulterer's handbook: he had to 'go back to the office' or he had 'a downtown appointment.' The Tuesday before he died, Reed's 'downtown appointment' called our home. We were having dinner, and I answered the phone in the kitchen. He ran down to our bedroom to take the call, but when he picked up the receiver, I didn't hang up. Joanne, I heard that woman telling my husband that she had to see him that night. And I heard him call her 'Kellee.' When he left the house, I followed him. Can you imagine how humiliating that was? Married three weeks and following my husband down back alleys, like some slut from a trailer court trying to get the goods on her lover. But I'm glad I did it. I needed to know the truth. I saw him go into that place on Scarth Street. After that, it was easy enough. I just checked the room numbers on the mailboxes in the front hall. The occupant of room six was 'Kellee Savage.' Isn't that just the dearest little name?" Julie's composure broke. "Kellee Savage," she sobbed. "She'd even stuck a goddamned happy-face sticker on her mailbox."

"Julie, listen to me. Please. I just can't believe Reed would have been having an affair with Kellee Savage."

Her voice was sulky. "Why not?"

"Because Kellee has . . . she has these physical problems. I think something must have happened before she was born. Whatever it was, she's terribly misshapen, and her face is . . . it's painful to look at."

"And you don't think Reed could have . . . ?"

"No," I said. "I don't. I don't think Reed could have been involved with Kellee."

"He kept saying he loved me," she said weakly. "I just didn't believe him."

She sounded bewildered, as, of course, she had every right to. In six weeks, fate had cast her in the roles of proud bride, betrayed wife, and embittered widow. It was hardly surprising that she had lost her sense of self.

"Julie, maybe it's time you thought about coming back here," I said. "When Ian died, it helped a lot being in a place where we'd been happy together."

My intention had been simply to give Julie an option, but she pounced on my suggestion. Five minutes later, it was all settled. Julie Evanson-Gallagher was coming home.

The next morning when I got to the university, Ed Mariani was already in my office. He was wearing a white turtleneck and a suede overshirt that I didn't remember seeing before.

"Nice threads," I said. "What do they call that colour."

"Edam," he said gloomily. He patted his belly. "You'll notice that I've graduated to a garment that's designed to cover a multitude of sins. On a brighter note, while I was shopping for my maternity top, I bought us a teapot." He held up a Brown Betty. "I know old Betty here isn't glamorous, but she does the job better than those pricey little beauties at the boutiques. I hope you don't mind."

"I don't mind," I said. "I could use a cup of tea."

"Kettle's plugged in," Ed said. He looked at me closely. "Joanne, is there something wrong?"

"I don't know," I said. "I just know that I'm starting to get scared."

I pulled the student chair closer to the desk and told him everything I'd learned the day before. When I finished, his expression was sombre. "Joanne, are you thinking what I'm thinking?"

"I'm not thinking anything," I said. "I'm absolutely in the dark about this."

Ed sighed heavily. "I wish I was, because what I've come up with isn't very appealing. But I don't know what else it could be. Look at the facts. In the weeks before he died, Reed lied to his wife fairly consistently about where he was. She followed him and discovered him going into Kellee Savage's room. The next thing we knew, Reed Gallagher chose Kellee for the prize internship, a position for which at least a half-dozen people are better qualified than she is."

"Surely, you're not suggesting an affair?"

"No," he said. "When Reed and I went to the Faculty Club the night before he died, he was not a man in love. He was confused and bitter and disillusioned." Ed paused, and when he spoke again, his voice was troubled. "Joanne, I think Kellee Savage was blackmailing Reed. I think she stumbled on something about him, and whatever it was gave her sufficient leverage to get the *Globe and Mail* internship."

"And made Reed so sloppy about his sexual practices that he died," I said.

"Or didn't care if he died. It makes sense, doesn't it?"

"I don't know," I said. "It's all so incredible." But the more I thought about it, the more credible Ed's theory seemed. As well as explaining why Kellee Savage had gone to the top of the internship list when other candidates were better qualified by far than she, it pointed to a logical motive for Kellee's decision to drop out of sight on the night of March 17. It also, I realized with a start, put my promise to Neil McCallum in a troubling new light. If Kellee Savage had dropped out of sight, not because she was embarrassed about getting drunk and making a fool of herself, but because she was a blackmailer who had pushed her victim so hard he hadn't cared whether he lived or died, she might not want to be found.

Ed poured boiling water into the Brown Betty. "Well," he asked, "what are we going to do?"

"I think this may be case of 'she's made her bed, now let her lie in it,'" I said. "Neil McCallum told me Kellee has an aunt in B.C. Kellee's probably out there right now, trying to figure out her next move. I don't think we should do anything."

And that's what I did. My conversation with Ed took place Monday morning. Kellee didn't show up for the Politics and the Media seminar at 3:00, and I had to admit I was relieved. It had been ten days since I'd last seen her, ten days of

remorse and anxiety. The possibility that Kellee was manipulator not victim was seductive, and I grabbed it.

I was late picking Julie up from the airport. She was on the
5:30 flight, but when I went to my car, I noticed someone had
left the side gate open, and the dogs had made a break for it.
Rose and Sadie were of an age where the delights of the larger
world had paled, but by the time I found them sunning themselves on the creek-bank and dragged them back to the house,
it was 5:35.

When I finally got to the airport, Julie's plane had landed,
and she was already at the luggage carousel. As soon as she
saw me, she threw her arms around me. The gesture was
uncharacteristic, but there was a lot that was uncharacteristic about Julie that day. For one thing, there was a stain on
her trenchcoat; for another, her roots were showing. The
veneer was chipping away, but, in an odd way, she was more
attractive than I had ever seen her. Her eyes were shining,
and her cheeks were flushed. It was as if she was feverish
with relief that Reed Gallagher hadn't been unfaithful to her
after all.

The graduation photograph of Kellee Savage that Neil
McCallum had let me take home was still in its Safeway bag
on the front seat of the car. Julie had to move it to the dashboard before she could slide into her seat. I told her to take
a look, and when she did, she became even more animated.
After she'd clucked pityingly over Kellee's deformities, she
started floating theories about why Reed might have been
visiting Kellee at the rooming house so late at night. All of
Julie's scripts cast her husband in the role of the caring and
humanitarian professional who was going the extra mile for
a needy student. I didn't say a word. Julie was obviously
delighted with her fantasies. It seemed cruel to suggest that,
asked to rank the possible reasons a forty-eight-year-old man
would visit a twenty-one-year-old woman late at night, most

sane people would put altruism at the bottom of the list.

When I dropped Julie at her condo on Lakeview Court, she invited me in for a drink. I declined. I was sick of other people's problems. As soon as I got home, I ordered pizza, took a hot shower, and got into my old terrycloth robe. It was Academy Awards night. I had seen three movies that year. Taylor had picked them all, and none of them featured flesh-and-blood actors. All the same, I knew that sitting in the family room with the dogs at my feet, Taylor and Benny sleeping beside me on the couch, and Angus braying loudly at the stupidity of the Academy's choices, beat my other options that night by a country mile.

On Wednesday night, Neil McCallum called. From the time I'd talked to Ed Mariani, I'd been filled with guilt every time I walked by a telephone and thought of Neil. The truth was I simply didn't know what to say, so I had taken the coward's way out and avoided making the call. Now Neil had taken matters out of my hands.

He waited until 6:01 to phone, but even at reduced rates, Neil didn't get his money's worth. As I always do when I'm flustered, I talked too much. I gave him a detailed account of my encounter with Alma Stringer. He laughed when I told him how much Alma reminded me of a cranky old chicken, but he became vehement when I told him about Alma's refusal to give us any information about Kellee unless we paid her.

"We can pay her," Neil said. "I've got money. I can send it on the bus. All you have to do is pick it up and take it to Alma. Then she'll tell us about Kellee. It's simple."

"It's not simple. You can't always trust people to do what they say they're going to do." Remembering the promise I had made to Neil, the words resonated painfully. He deserved to know the truth, or at least Ed Mariani's theory about what the truth might be.

"I need to talk to you about Kellee," I said. "There's a chance she's gone away because she's done something wrong."

"She wouldn't do anything wrong," Neil said angrily. "Kellee's my friend. I don't want to hear this."

For the first time since Neil called, I found myself wishing we were face to face. Over the telephone, it was impossible to tell if he was defending Kellee out of conviction or bravado. In the long run, I guess it didn't matter. Neil believed in Kellee; it seemed both pointless and cruel to disillusion him before disillusion became inevitable.

Before we said goodnight, Neil said he was sorry if he'd been rude and he thanked me for helping him look for Kellee. When I hung up the phone, I felt like hell. Neil's trust in me was absolute, but it seemed that, once again, he'd put his money on the wrong horse. He wasn't having much luck with the humans in his life. I was glad he had Chloe.

Life wasn't all grim that week. The next weekend was Easter, and my daughter Mieka, her husband, Greg, and my son Peter were coming home. Angus and I made up the beds, got out the new bath towels, and brought the leaves for the dining-room table in from the garage. Taylor and I drove out to the nursery and bought lilies and a pot of African violets the colour of heliotrope for Mieka and Greg's room. As I made up the list of food we'd need for the holiday, I could feel, despite everything, the darkness lift. It was Easter, the time, as the Prayer Book says, to be "inflamed with new hope."

When Alex called Thursday morning, I could feel the flames of new hope leaping. It was early when he called, so early, in fact, that I was still in bed. Hearing his voice in my bedroom brought back memories of other mornings: mornings after the kids had gone to school, when Alex would come over and we'd make love and lie in bed listening to the radio and feeling warm and blessed.

"I'm missing you," he said.

"I'm missing you, too," I said. "The room is full of sunlight, and the paperwhites in the window are blooming. If you give me five minutes, I can put on Mozart, slip into something erotic, and send the kids to school without any breakfast."

"I really do miss you, Jo," he said.

"Then come back."

"It wouldn't work the way I am now." I could hear his intake of breath. "Joanne, I called to tell you I'm going away for a while."

"Why?"

"I don't know. Partly because Eli – my nephew – needs more help than I can give him. There's an elder up at Loon Lake who helped me through a bad patch once. I think he might be able to help Eli." Alex paused, then he said quietly. "And I think he might be able to help me. I seem to have been making a lot of lousy decisions lately."

"Lousy decisions don't need to be carved in stone."

"Maybe Loon Lake will make me as sure of that as you seem to be."

"Alex, I'm glad you called."

"So am I," he said.

After I had showered and dressed, I felt so grateful that I thought it was time to get a few karmic waves going. As soon as I got to my office, I called Jill and invited her for Easter dinner. She said she and Tom had plans, but she sounded friendly, and when she heard Mieka and Peter would be there, she was wistful. "Don't let them go home without seeing me," she said. Jill had known Mieka and Peter almost all of their lives, and they had always enjoyed her as much as she enjoyed them. I promised they'd get in touch. Then I took a deep breath and dialled Julie Gallagher's number. To my surprise, she said she'd be delighted to join us. As I hung up, I sensed that we were, at long last, heading into the final act. If we were lucky, the play that had begun as a tragedy might end up like a Shakespearean comedy, with all past cruelties forgiven, all misunderstandings corrected, and all broken relationships mended.

When I got ready to leave the office late Thursday afternoon, I came upon the copy of *Sleeping Beauty* Kellee Savage had thrust into my hand a thousand years ago. Remembering Kellee's misery that afternoon, I felt a stab of remorse, but if Ed Mariani's reading of the situation was right, wherever Kellee was she should be feeling remorse, not evoking it. I flipped through the book in my hand, and noticed that it had been checked out of the Education library. I might not be able to exorcise Kellee from my consciousness, but at least I could get rid of a painful reminder of her.

The staff at the Education library were in the process of closing up. The next day was Good Friday, and with so many students out of town, there was little reason to stay open. I recognized the young woman on the desk as an old student of mine, Susan something-or-other. Not smart, but pleasant, and very cute: a mop of curly hair, big brown eyes, and a quick smile. She made a face when she saw me.

"You're not going to be long, are you? I'm hoping to get on the road before dark."

"Going home?" I asked.

"You got it," she said. "Three whole days with no texts, no assignments, and no research papers."

"I won't hold you up," I said. "I'm just returning a book." I slid the *Sleeping Beauty* across the desk to her.

She glanced at the cover. "I love fairy tales." She gave me a sidelong glance. "Do you still believe in happy endings?"

"Depends on which day you ask me," I said. "Today, I do."

"Me too," she said, and she took the book and started to place it on a trolley for re-shelving. Out of nowhere, Kellee's face flashed into my mind.

"Susan," I said. "That book wasn't mine. Actually, I'm not sure who did take it out. Could you check to see whose card it's on?"

She shrugged. "Sure," she said. "That's a real no-brainer – my specialty." She punched something into the computer, watched the screen, and then turned to me with a grin. "Maybe we women aren't the only ones who believe in happy endings. You're not going to believe who checked this book out."

"Who?"

"Marshall Hryniuk."

"Jumbo?" I said.

"The Guzzler himself," she said.

CHAPTER

10

That Easter weekend everything was eclipsed by my daughter Mieka's news that she was expecting a baby in September. She and Greg had planned a dramatic announcement; they even brought down a bottle of Mumms so we could drink a toast to the future. But Mieka had never been good at secrets. Friday night, Greg had scarcely turned off the ignition when Mieka raced up our front walk, burst through the door, threw her arms around me and whispered, "How do you feel about being a grandma?"

Her trenchcoat was open, her dark blond hair was flying out of its careful French braid, and she had a milk moustache from the Dairy Queen shake she was still holding in her hand, but I knew I had never seen my daughter so happy. She was twenty-two. She had dropped out of university in the middle of her first year, taken the money Ian and I had set aside for her education and opened her own catering business. I'd fought her decision hard, and in the way of nettled parents everywhere, predicted that she'd rue the day, but her catering business in Saskatoon was thriving, her marriage was a happy one, and now she was joyfully pregnant.

She had every right to say "I told you so." Luckily for both of us, Mieka had apparently decided to bite her tongue.

My son Peter was too thin and too pale, but I knew what the problem was, and I knew there was nothing I could do to help. From the time he was little, he had wanted to be a veterinarian, but he had no more aptitude for the sciences than his father or I had had. The genetic pool he needed to draw from to get a degree in vet medicine was shallow, but Peter was determined, and so year after year he soldiered away. I watched him grab a football and follow his brother outside for a game of pick-up and wished, not for the first time, that babies came with individual sets of instructions: "Teach this one to ease up on himself"; "Give this one the chance to find her own way."

I didn't need a set of instructions to understand Taylor's problem that weekend. As talk about the new baby and about a past that she hadn't been part of claimed our attention, Taylor became first clingy, then bratty. "Pay attention to me," Angus said witheringly as his little sister whirled giddily around the table where Mieka and I were poring through a book of baby names.

We all tried to reach Taylor. Mieka showed her the kiska and dyes she'd brought from Saskatoon and offered to teach her how to make Ukrainian Easter eggs. Peter admired her art and told her that in the summer he'd help her transform the sunroom into a studio where she could get some serious painting done. Angus told her to shape up or ship out. Nothing seemed to help. Saturday night I awoke to discover Benny on my pillow with his purr mechanism on full throttle, and Taylor beside him, eyes filled with tears, lower lip trembling.

I stroked her hair. "T, can you tell me what the problem is?"

She made a sound that was half sob, half hiccup. "No," she said, miserably.

I put my arms around her. "How about building a box and putting that problem in it till the morning?"

"It'll still be there."

"I know, but maybe spending a little time in a box will make it smaller."

"Jo, would it be okay if I stayed here tonight?"

I kissed the top of her head. "Absolutely," I said. "But you and I have a lot to do tomorrow, so you're going to have to ask Benny to put a silencer on that purr of his."

As it always does when life is at its best, the time went too quickly. Easter dinner was planned for mid-afternoon. Julie Gallagher arrived early with two mile-high lemon pies. She was wearing an outfit in jonquil silk, her hair was back in its careful coif, and her makeup was fresh. She looked like the old Julie, but there was uncertainty in her eyes, and as she followed me into the dining room her manner was diffident.

"I thought I'd come early, so I could give you a hand now and leave you and your family to visit after we're through eating."

"You're welcome to stay as long as you want to, Julie."

She set the pies carefully on the sideboard. "I know that, and I appreciate it, believe me. But this is a family occasion, and I'm not family. I'm not even a friend."

"You could be," I said.

"Could I?" she asked. "You'd have to forget an awful lot, Joanne."

"I'm fifty years old, Julie. My memory isn't nearly as sharp as it used to be."

She gave me a quick, dimpled smile. "Thank God for that," she said. "Now what can I do to help?"

Julie was quiet during dinner, but it was obvious she was enjoying herself. Besides, we'd already had our conversation. When she'd arrived, the big kids were in the park with

Taylor, throwing around Frisbees. Julie and I had had twenty minutes alone together; oddly enough, we had used them to talk about love. Our conversation was surprisingly light-hearted, but one of Julie's reminiscences was poignant. She told me that on their wedding night, Reed had said his greatest dream was to grow old with her. Then she had touched my arm and said how grateful she was to me for allowing her to believe again that when Reed died, that was still his greatest dream.

True to her word, Julie left early, but, as I watched her get into her car, for the first time since I'd known her I was sorry to see her go. Peter left early too. He had a lab test the next day, so he caught a ride back to Saskatoon with a friend as soon as we'd finished dessert. After Peter left, Greg started clearing the table.

"It's been great, Jo." he said. "But we'd better take off, too. Mieka's got a lunch for fifty oil guys tomorrow, and I've got a squash game with a client at seven a.m." He grimaced. "Sounds like a page out of Lifestyles of the Young and Upwardly Mobile, doesn't it?"

"Store up those golden memories," I said. "Come September, the oil guys and squash games are going to get nudged aside for a while." I turned to my daughter. "Mieka, I can help Greg get organized for the trip back. Why don't you drive over and tell Jill about the baby? I promised her you'd stop by. You don't have to stay – just a quick flying trip."

Jill's apartment was on Robinson and 12th, an easy five-minute drive from my house, but even so, I was surprised at how quickly Mieka was back, and at how downcast she seemed.

"Nobody home?" I said.

She shook her head. "No, they were home. It just wasn't a good time for a visit." She slipped her coat off and sat down at the kitchen table. "It was so weird. I knocked and knocked, but nobody answered. Finally, a man came to the door. He introduced himself as Tom Kelsoe, Jill's boyfriend, and said she was sleeping. I guess Jill must have heard our voices. Anyway, she came out of the bedroom. Mum, she was a mess. Her face was all bruised and she could hardly talk because her jaw was swollen. She'd been mugged."

"Mugged?" I repeated. "Is she all right?"

"You know Jill. She's tough. She kind of laughed it off – said the most-lasting damage had been to her vanity."

"But she *is* okay?"

"She says she is."

"Where did it happen?"

"In the parking lot behind Nationtv. Jill was working late. One of the men on her show had offered to walk her to her car, but she turned him down. She says the mugger just appeared out of nowhere. He grabbed her shoulder bag. Apparently, Jill put up a fight, and that's when she got hurt."

"That doesn't sound like Jill," I said. "She always said if somebody was willing to risk jail for a purse full of old Cheezie bags and maxed-out credit cards, she wouldn't stand in their way."

"I guess no one can predict what she'll do in a situation like that," Mieka said. "I'm just grateful it didn't happen to you, too. Tom Kelsoe said there've been several incidents in that parking lot lately. Apparently, there's some sort of a gang – they're after video equipment that they can pawn for drug money, but they'll take anything."

I was beginning to feel uneasy. "It's odd that I've never heard a word about any of this," I said.

Mieka gazed at me thoughtfully. "I guess all that matters is that Jill's going to be all right."

"Of course," I said. "That *is* all that matters." I started for the phone. "I'm going to call her."

"Why don't you wait?" Mieka said. "Tom wanted her to get some sleep. I volunteered your services, but he told me he had everything under control." She rolled her eyes. "He said he was going to find the man who did this to Jill and beat him to a pulp. I must have looked kind of shocked, because he backtracked pretty quickly. When Jill asked me to stay for tea, Tom suddenly became Mr. Sensitive and said he'd make a pot of souchong."

"Retribution and Chinese tea," I said. "He certainly is the Renaissance man."

The sterling flatware we'd used for dinner was on the kitchen table, clean and ready to be put back into the silver chest until what my old friend Hilda McCourt always called "the next high day or holy day." Mieka began sorting through it, placing the pieces back where they belonged. "You don't like Tom Kelsoe, do you?" she said finally.

"Not at all," I said. "And he doesn't like me. But I still think I should go over there."

"Jill seemed fine, Mum. Honestly. And they made it pretty clear they didn't want anybody else around." Mieka aligned the salad forks carefully and dropped them into their slot in the chest. Then she gave me a sidelong glance. "Aren't there times when you and Alex don't want other people around?"

"What do Alex and I have to do with this?"

Mieka reached over and squeezed my hand. "Nothing," she said. "But I'm leaving in ten minutes, and we haven't talked about him all weekend. What's going on there?"

"I told you," I said. "Alex went up north for a few days."

"But you two are still together?"

I didn't answer her. Instead, I turned so I could look out the window into the back yard. Sadie and Rose were lying in what would soon be the tulip bed, catching the last rays of spring sunlight. They were old dogs now, fifteen and sixteen respectively, and I felt a pang thinking about what inevitably lay ahead.

"Penny for your thoughts, Mum," Mieka said.

"You'd be wasting your money," I said.

Greg came in from outside. "No wasting money, Mieka. We've got to act like grown-ups now. Speaking of which, it's time we hit the road."

"Give me five minutes, would you? Mum and I have some unfinished business."

He shrugged. "Sure, I'll go in and say goodbye to the kids." He picked up the plate with the last of Julie's lemon meringue pie. "I might as well take this with me."

When he left, Mieka turned to me. "Are you and Alex having trouble, Mum?"

"Yes," I said. "We are. Something happened." I told my daughter about the incident on the Albert Street bridge. I didn't gloss over the ugliness of the words the driver of the half-ton had hurled at me, and I didn't hold back the fact that I'd run from Alex.

Mieka has the kind of translucent skin that colours with emotion, and by the time I'd finished her face was flushed. "That's just so sick," she said. "How can be people be like that?"

"I don't know," I said. "But I'd give anything to have handled what happened with a little more courage."

"Did Alex go up north because he was angry?"

"No," I said. "He was very understanding. He always is. I don't think what happened that night would have been a huge problem except it was so obviously a sign of things to come. Alex is afraid that having to deal with that kind of bigotry day after day would change me, change all of us."

"Is it that serious between you two?"

"I don't know how serious it is, Mieka. I think that's part of the problem. For a long time, Alex and I were just going along, enjoying each other's company, doing things with the kids. He's so good with them. When they talk, he really listens to them, and he tells Taylor all these terrific Trickster stories."

Mieka raised an eyebrow. "And, of course, he did teach Angus to drive. It must be love if he let a fifteen-year-old with a learner's permit drive his Audi."

"Alex would do that for any fifteen-year-old who wanted to get behind the wheel as much as Angus did. That's the kind of man he is – generous and decent. And he's an amazing lover."

Mieka reddened and looked away.

"Sorry," I said. "I forgot that mothers aren't supposed to have sex."

Mieka gave me a small smile. "They can have it; they're just not supposed to tell their daughters about it." Her face grew serious. "Alex isn't much like Daddy, is he?"

"Does that bother you?"

"Not as long as Alex makes you happy."

"He does. And I make him happy. But there are things that have to be considered."

"Such as . . . ?"

"Such as the fact that he's nine years younger than I am and his experience of life has been very different from mine."

"And those things matter?"

"I don't know, Mieka. In the long run they might. I guess that's what Alex and I have to figure out."

When Greg and Mieka left, Taylor and Benny and I walked out to the car with them. We watched the car drive towards the Lewvan Expressway; as it disappeared from sight, Taylor tugged at my sleeve.

"Are you going to love that new baby, Jo?"

"You bet," I said. "And I'm going to keep on loving you." I knelt beside her. "Taylor, when you first came to live with us, I didn't really know you, but I wanted you with us because I loved your mother. Now I know you, and I want you with us because every single day in this house is better because you're a part of it."

I didn't call Jill that night, but the next morning after I came in from my run with the dogs, I phoned her at home. There was no answer, but I left a message on her machine. When I got to work I called her office at Nationtv. Rapti Lustig answered and said Jill was working at her apartment that day.

"Isn't that kind of unusual?" I said.

Rapti sighed. "Tell me one thing that's usual around here these days."

Jill phoned me at the university around noon. I'd just come back from a particularly rancorous department meeting, but when I heard her voice, I forgot about my colleagues' crankiness.

"How are you?" I asked.

"I'm okay," she said.

"You don't sound okay," I said.

"My jaw's sore. It's hard to talk."

"Is there anything I can bring you?"

"I'm fine."

"Mieka said Tom was taking good care of you."

"He's right here," she said. "That's wonderful news about the baby, Jo. Congratulations."

"Thanks," I said. "Jill, are you really all right?"

She tried a laugh. "You should see the other guy."

"I'd like to do more than see him," I said. "But I guess that's why we have a legal system. Look, I don't have any classes around lunchtime tomorrow – why don't I bring you over a crème brulée? That's easy to eat, even with a hurt jaw."

"Good old Jo. Food for every occasion. But something sweet and soft does sound tempting, and it would be great to see you." Despite the painful jaw, Jill sounded warm and welcoming.

"I'll be there at noon," I said, and as I hung up, I felt as if I'd scored a major victory.

When Kellee didn't show up for the Politics and the Media seminar at 3:00, I knew the time had come to do what I should have done at the outset: find her and give her a chance to tell her side of the story. Neil McCallum had been vague about the name of Kellee's aunt, but if his family had lived next door to Kellee's all those years, his parents might remember hearing something about Kellee's relative in British Columbia. As soon as class was over, I'd call him, but first I had the seminar to get through.

It was no easy task. The tension in the room was palpable. Ed Mariani had told me once that everyone who taught this particular group had been struck by their cohesiveness. Kellee Savage hadn't been one of the elect, but her absence seemed to change the balance for the others. They were unusually quiet and uncharacteristically tentative in proffering their opinions. The minutes seemed to crawl by, and I was relieved when my watch finally indicated that it was time to go.

Val Massey and Jumbo Hryniuk were the last to leave. Beside Jumbo's cheerful bulk, Val looked both slight and vulnerable. As they passed me, I reached out and touched Jumbo's sleeve.

"I need to talk to you for a minute," I said.

Val looked at me questioningly. "Should I wait for him in the hall or is it going to take a while?"

"It might take a while," I said.

A flicker of concern pass across Val's face, but he didn't ask me anything else. He mumbled something to Jumbo about meeting him at the Owl, then he left.

Jumbo looked puzzled. "What's up?"

"It has to do with a book. Did you check out a copy of *Sleeping Beauty* from the Education library?"

He grinned. "One of the guys got you to ask me that, right? Very funny." He frowned. "Except I don't get it."

"It's not a joke," I said. "Actually, it might be pretty serious."

"Then seriously," he said, "I didn't check out *Sleeping Beauty*."

"Did you lend your library card to anybody?"

Jumbo was no poker player. It was clear from his expression that my question had hit a nerve. "Why would I do that?" he asked.

"I don't know," I said. "Why would you?"

For the first time, the gravity of the situation seemed to strike him. "Professor Kilbourn, can you tell me what this is about?"

"Of course," I said. "But why don't you sit down. I'm getting far too old to get a crick in my neck from looking up at a football player."

The joke seemed to relax him, but as I told him about Kellee and the book and the note that had been left in her place at the seminar table, Jumbo's amiability vanished, and he looked first confused, then frightened.

"I didn't write any note," he said. "I give you my word."

"I believe you, but there's still a problem. Jumbo, that book was taken out on your card. I know that because I had somebody at the Education library check it on the computer."

I could see him mulling over the possibilities. He was not what they call in football a thoughtful player; nonetheless, that afternoon, Jumbo Hryniuk called the right play. "I'll talk to the person involved," he said.

"Make sure the person knows how serious this is."

"I will," he said.

Neil McCallum was happy to hear from me. Chloe had been running in the fields and come home full of burrs. It had taken him all afternoon to get them out of her coat, and as he worked, he had worried about Kellee. As it turned out, Neil was way ahead of me. He'd already asked his mother if she remembered the name of Kellee's aunt. She didn't, but she knew someone who she thought might be able to help. Neil said his mother was doing her best, and he would call me as soon as he heard anything.

Tuesday morning when I got back from taking the dogs for their run, the phone was ringing. It was Margaret McCallum, Neil's mother. She was as affable as her son, but her news was disappointing. The woman she was counting on for help was a widow named Albertson who had spent the winter in Arizona. When Margaret had finally tracked down the woman's number in Tucson, she learned that Mrs. Albertson, like many other snowbirds at the beginning of April, was on her way home. Echoing her son, Margaret McCallum told me that as soon as she had any information, she'd let me know.

I thanked her, wrote her name next to Neil's in my address book, then went into the kitchen to hunt up my recipe for crême brulée. The kids were on Easter holidays, so I doubled the quantities and left a dish for them and put the one for Jill in a cooler and took it to the university with me. I had some newspaper articles I wanted to track down in the main library, so it was close to 11:30 when I got back to my office. Ed Mariani was sitting at the desk, marking papers.

"Finally," he said theatrically. "I was just about to send out the bloodhounds."

"Does this mean I'm grounded, Dad?" I said.

He grimaced. "Sorry, I guess that did sound a little paternalistic. It's just that Jill Osiowy called, and she wanted to make sure you got her message before you headed off to her place."

"What message?"

"Jill can't be there for lunch. She had to fly to Toronto – Nationtv business. They're apparently experiencing a crisis."

"They're always experiencing a crisis," I said. I thought of Jill having to fly to Toronto when she was feeling lousy and looking worse. In the days of cutbacks and takeovers, corporate hearts were hardening. I started to pack up to go home, then I remembered the cooler sitting in my car. "How do you feel about crème brulée, Ed?" I asked.

"Love it," he said.

"Good. Then let me snag us some bowls and spoons, and I'll buy you lunch."

Just as I was dishing up the dessert, Angus called. "Some of the guys are going over to play football on the lawn in front of the legislature," he said.

"Is one of those guys you?"

He laughed. "Well, yeah, Mum. Why else would I call? Anyway, Leah wants to know if it's okay for her to take Taylor over to her house to have tea with her Aunt Slava."

"I guess so," I said. "Have you met Leah's aunt?"

"Yeah. She's about a hundred years old, but she's cool."

"That's certainly a ringing endorsement."

"Whatever," said my son. "I'll be home at the usual time."

After we'd eaten, Ed started gathering his books together for his 12:30 class. "Dynamite crème brulée, Jo. Jill's loss is my gain."

"That'll teach her to go to Toronto," I said. "Actually, I'm just relieved she was well enough to go."

Ed looked at me anxiously. "Was she ill?"

"No, worse than that. She was mugged the other night. That's why I made the crème brulée. Her jaw was bothering her."

"My God, that's terrible. You never think of that happening to someone you know. Did the police catch the mugger?"

"I don't know any of the details. I haven't seen Jill. My daughter went over there Sunday night. Mieka said Jill was pretty banged up, but when I talked to her on the phone, she seemed to be in good spirits."

"So she *is* all right?"

"She must be if she's well enough to travel. Didn't she say anything when she called?"

"Just that she was in a rush." He leaned towards me, his moon face creased with concern. "Joanne, Jill's a kind of hero to me. The truth is she saved my life once – at least the part of my life that I value the most."

It was a line that cried out for elaboration. Ed didn't offer any, but his obvious affection for Jill gave me the opening I needed.

"Jill's a hero to a lot of people," I said. "This shouldn't be happening to her."

"You mean the mugging."

"If it was a mugging." I took a deep breath and plunged ahead. "Ed, I haven't said anything to anyone about this, but I'm not sure I buy the story that Jill was attacked by a stranger. Since I started doing the political panel, I've walked through that parking lot every Saturday night. It's a safe area: a lot of security lights and a lot of traffic. Nationtv vans are in and out of there all the time. Another thing – Jill would fight the good fight for a story, but I've never known anyone who's as indifferent about possessions as she is. If someone tried to take her purse, she wouldn't have turned a hair."

Ed gave me a searching look. "What do you think happened?"

"I think it was Tom," I said.

"You think he hit her?"

"I think it's possible," I said. "And as soon as Jill gets back, I'm going to talk to her. I won't let her put me off, Ed. Unless she can convince me that I'm way off base about this, and Tom is innocent, I'm going to go to the police."

Without a word, Ed picked up his books and moved heavily towards the door.

"Will you be in tomorrow?" I asked.

Ed looked at me oddly. "I don't know," he said. Then he was gone.

I thought about the afternoon ahead. Angus and Taylor were accounted for, so it was a good chance to get some marking done. I tried, but it was a profitless exercise. All I could think about was Jill. When I realized that I'd read an entire essay without retaining even the faintest hint of its content, I decided to go home. On my way out of the office I spotted the dishes I'd borrowed from the Faculty Club; I dropped them into a plastic grocery bag and headed out.

Grace Lipinski, the Faculty Club manager, was at the entrance to the bar arranging some dazzling branches of forsythia in a Chinese vase the colour of a new fern.

"I brought back the dishes," I said, "with thanks."

"Anytime," she said. "And while you're here, you can take back the picture that the cleaning people found. It was just in with the paper towels, but I wiped down the frame and glass with disinfectant to be on the safe side."

"You're a wonder," I said.

"Tell the board," she said. "I'll be right back. Enjoy the forsythia."

Grace disappeared, but I wasn't alone for long. Old Giv Mewhort was standing at the bar and, when he spotted me, he picked up his drink and started over. He moved with great precision, careful not to spill so much as a single drop of gin in the glass in his hand. It was mid-afternoon, but Giv had already reached the orotund stage of drunkenness.

"My dear," he said. "I haven't had a chance to tell you how distressed I was to see that young Cassius has taken your place on that political show. Did you step aside or were you pushed?"

"I was pushed," I said, "by young Cassius."

Giv sipped his drink and sighed. "'Such men as he be never at heart's ease/Whiles they behold a greater than themselves,/And therefore are they very dangerous.'"

I smiled at him. "Thanks for the warning," I said. "But I think Tom Kelsoe's done about all the damage to me that he can."

Giv leaned forward and whispered ginnily. "Don't bet the farm on it, Joanne." He pointed towards the back of the bar and roared dramatically. "'Yond Cassius has a lean and hungry look. . . .' See for yourself." I turned and glanced into the bar. On the couch in the far corner, two men were deep in conversation. They were so close together and so intent on their conversation that they seemed oblivious to everything around them. One of the men was Tom Kelsoe, the other was Ed Mariani. I felt the way I had in high school when I'd poured my heart out to my best friend and discovered her ten minutes later, laughing and intimate with the one girl in school I considered my enemy.

Grace came back with the photograph and handed it to me. "It's all yours," she said.

Giv Mewhort leaned across me and gave the picture of Reed Gallagher and Annalie Brinkmann the once-over. "So he gave it back," he said. "The Human Comedy never fails to surprise, does it? Although I must say that I never understood why he nicked that photo in the first place."

"You know who took this?" I asked.

Giv waved his glass towards the recesses of the bar. "Young Cassius." He laughed. "I warned you, my dear. 'He thinks too much: such men are dangerous.'"

When I slid behind the steering wheel of the Volvo, I realized how badly the scene in the Faculty Club had shaken me. Like Giv, I didn't understand why anyone would want to take an old newspaper photograph. But while the news that Tom Kelsoe was a thief was unnerving, it was the sight of Ed Mariani cosying up to him that had jolted me.

They were colleagues. There were a half-dozen innocent reasons for them to have a quick meeting in the Faculty Club. But in my heart, I knew there was nothing innocent about their meeting. For reasons I couldn't fathom, Ed had run to Tom as soon as I'd told him my suspicions. For a moment, I thought I was going to be sick to my stomach. It had never occurred to me not to trust Ed. I had told him everything: first about Kellee, and now about Jill.

I put my head down on the steering wheel and tried to think. At the moment, there was nothing I could do about the situation with Jill. She was in Toronto. I couldn't get to her, but neither could Tom Kelsoe. For the time being, she was safe. I didn't have that assurance about Kellee Savage. I'd already failed her twice, but there was still time to make amends. It was April 5. If Kellee Savage hadn't paid the rent for her room on Scarth Street, Alma Stringer might be interested in showing me the room.

When I got to Scarth Street, Alma was hammering a piece of laminated poster-board to the wall next to the mailboxes in the front hall. "I thought you and me did all the business we were going to do," she said.

I pulled a twenty-dollar bill from my wallet and held it up. "I want to see room six. I just want to look at it; I promise I won't touch anything. You can stand in the doorway and watch me if you like."

Alma's fingers took the twenty so quickly the act seemed like sleight-of-hand. Then, without a word, she turned and walked into the house. I followed along behind. She had an old-fashioned key-ring attached to the belt of her pedal pushers and she stopped in front of number 6 and leaned into the door to insert the key in the lock.

I don't know what Alma had expected to find on the other side of the door, but it was obvious from her shriek of fury that she hadn't anticipated being confronted by a room that seemed, quite literally, to have been torn apart. Whoever had destroyed Kellee's room had been as mindlessly destructive and as efficient as the vandals who had attacked the Journalism offices at the university. Bureau drawers were pulled out and overturned; the sheets had been ripped off the bed; the mattress had been dragged to the floor. The table had been upended and the drawer that held utensils had been flung across the room.

Alma looked at the mess, and said, "If shit was luck, I wouldn't get a sniff."

"Are you going to call the police?" I asked.

She laughed derisively. "Sure. That's what I'm gonna do. And have them all over the place, tracking in mud, leaving the door open, runnin' up my heating bill. No, little Miss Goody Two-Shoes, I'm not gonna call the police. I'm gonna hand the rummy in the front room a ten and get him to clean this up, so I can rent it." She started down the hall.

"Wait," I said. "When was the last time you were in here?"

"You know, that's quite a mess in there," she said innocently. "That rummy's probably gonna want at least twenty bucks."

I opened my wallet and pulled out my last twenty. Alma bagged it in a snap. "The last time I was in number six was the day she moved in, and that was January. As long as my tenants don't bother me, I don't bother them. We both like it like that."

"But Kellee hadn't paid her rent for April."

"I figured I'd let her use up her damage deposit." She smoothed her thin yellow hair. "I try to be decent. Now, unless you got the wherewithal to keep the meter running, get outa here. I got work to do."

When she left, I stood for a moment in front of the locked door of number 6. I hadn't had much time to look around, but even a quick glance had revealed there wasn't much in the room that was personal. There were a few items of lingerie near the overturned bureau drawers and a flowery plastic toilet kit had been flung into the corner, but there didn't seem to be nearly the quantity of personal effects you'd expect to find in a room someone actually lived in. It was apparent that Kellee had pretty well moved out by the time her intruder had trashed the room.

I walked back up the hall. Alma's laminated sheet was a bright square against the faded wallpaper. It was headed "Rules of This House," and a quick glance revealed that Alma had a an Old Testament gift for conjuring up activities that could be proscribed. Beside the list was the rack of mailboxes Julie had told me about. Sure enough, Kellee had placed a happy face sticker beside her name; I looked at her box more closely. There was no lock on it. I opened the lid and pulled out her mail. There wasn't much: what appeared to be a statement from the Credit Union, the May issue of *Flare* magazine; a couple of envelopes addressed to "Occupant," and the cardboard end flap from a cigarette package. On the flap, someone had pencilled a message. "I've moved. #3, 2245 Dahl. B."

I stuck the cigarette flap in my bag. It was a slender thread, but it was all I had. I walked back to the Volvo, slid into the driver's seat, and headed for Dahl Street.

CHAPTER

11

As I walked up the front path of 2245 Dahl Street, the building cast a shadow that seemed to race towards me, and I knew I'd had enough of sinister rooming houses with their emanations of despair and of hard-lived lives. This place was even worse than Alma's. The paint on the Scarth Street house might have been peeling and the porches might have been sagging, but it was still possible to spot vestiges of the building's former elegance and coquettish charm. There were no suggestions of past glory here. The apartment on Dahl Street had been a squat eyesore the day it was built, and sixty years of neglect hadn't improved it.

Someone had propped the front door open with a brick, and I thought I was in luck, but inside the vestibule there was a second door, and this one was locked tight. I pounded on the door, but when no one came I could feel the relief wash over me. I'd done my best, but my best hadn't been good enough. I was off the hook. As I turned to leave, a tortoise-shell kitten darted in from the street and ran between my legs. It was wet and dirty, but when I reached down to reassure it, it shot back out the door. My fingers were damp from where I had touched its fur and when I raised my hand to my nose, I could smell kerosene.

I hurried down the steps, eager to put some distance between me and this neighbourhood where horrors that should have been unimaginable were part of everyday life. I'd parked across the street, and before I opened the door of the Volvo, I took a last look at 2245 Dahl Street. The fire escape on the side of the building zigzagged up the wall like a scar. In case of fire, it would have been almost impossible to get down those metal steps. The life of the tenants had spilled out onto them, and the steps had become the final resting place of beer bottles, broken plant pots, and anything else small enough and useless enough to be abandoned. On the step outside number 3 someone had propped a statue of the Virgin Mary. According to the message on the cigarette flap, number 3 was B's flat. It seemed that Kellee's friend was a person with a faith life. I looked up the fire escape again. The door on the third floor was open a crack. It didn't look inviting, but it did look accessible. My time off the hook was over.

Climbing the fire escape was a nightmare. Picking my way through the litter meant watching my feet, and that involved peering through the metal-runged steps at the ground below. The effect was vertiginous, and by the time I'd reached the landing outside the door to number 3, my head was reeling, and I had to hold onto the Virgin's head to get my balance.

Inside, a television was playing; I could hear the strident accusing voices of people on one of the tabloid talk shows.

I leaned into the opening of the door. "Anybody home?" I asked.

There was no answer. I pushed, opening the door a little more. "Can you help me?" I called. "I'm looking for some-one who lives here."

On the television, a man was shouting, "you ruined my life . . . you ruined my life," as the studio audience cheered.

Nobody home but Ricki Lake. I turned to go back down, but when looked at through three flights of metal staircase, the ground seemed a dizzying distance away. It didn't take me long to decide that slipping into the house and leaving by the front door made more sense than plummeting to my death. I pushed the back door open and stepped inside. The kitchen was small and as clean as it would ever be. The linoleum had faded from red to brown, and it was curling in the area in front of the sink, but the floor was scrubbed, and the dishes on the drainboard were clean. The refrigerator door was covered with children's drawings and an impressive collection of the cards of doctors at walk-in medical clinics.

The curtains in the living room were drawn; the only illumination in the room came from the flickering light of the television. Still, it was easy enough to pick out the front door, and that's where I was headed when my toe caught on the edge of the carpet. As I stumbled, I caught hold of the back of the couch to break my fall. That's when I saw the woman. She was lying on the couch, covered with a blanket, but when our eyes met, she made a mewling sound and tried to raise herself up.

"I'm sorry," I said. "I was looking for someone."

She stared at me without comprehension. She was a native woman, and she seemed to be in her thirties. It was hard to see her clearly in the shadowy room, but it wasn't hard to hear her. As she grew more frantic, the sounds she made became high-pitched and ear-splittingly intense.

I tried to be reassuring. "It's okay," I said. "I'm leaving. I'm not going to hurt you." I reached the door, but as my hand grasped the knob, the door opened from the outside.

The woman who exploded through the door was on the shady side of forty, but she had apparently decided not to go gently into middle age. Her mane of shoulder-length blond hair was extravagantly teased, her mascara was black and thick, and her lipstick was a whiter shade of pale. She was wearing a fringed white leatherette jacket, a matching miniskirt, and the kind of boots Nancy Sinatra used to sing about.

She was not happy to see me. "Who the fuck are you?" she rasped. "And what the fuck are you doing in my living room?"

"My name's Joanne Kilbourn, and I'm trying to find Kellee Savage."

She reached beside her, flicked on the light switch and gave me the once-over. "Social worker or cop?" she asked.

"What?"

She narrowed her eyes. "I asked you if you were a social worker or a cop."

"Neither. I'm Kellee's teacher."

"Well, Teacher, as the song says, 'take the time to look around you.' This isn't a school. This is a private residence."

I reached into my pocket and pulled out the cigarette flap with the address. "I found this in Kellee's mailbox. It has your address on it. Are you B?"

She took a step towards me. Her perfume was heavy, but not unpleasant. "Teacher," she said, "let's see how good you are at learning. Listen carefully. This is my home, and I want you out of it."

"I just wanted to ask . . ."

She wagged her finger in my face. "You weren't listening," she said. She grabbed my arm and twisted it behind my back. As she propelled me through the door, she gave me a wicked smile and whispered, "Class dismissed."

It was almost 5:00 when I got home. The dogs came to greet me, but the house was silent. The kids would be barrelling through the front door any minute, but for the time being I was alone. I was also miserable and hungry and tired. I decided I would meet my needs one at a time. I poured myself a drink, took it upstairs, ran a bath, dropped a cassette of Kiri Te Kanawa singing Mozart's *"Exsultate, jubilate"* into my cassette player, and shut out the world. By the time I got out of the tub and towelled off, I wasn't quite ready to "rise up at last in gladness," but I had improved my chances of getting through the evening. As I pulled on fresh sweats and a T-shirt, I sang along with Kiri, but even Mozart couldn't block out the images of the kerosene-soaked kitten and the native woman's terrified face. The memories of that afternoon were a fresh bruise, but I was no closer to Kellee Savage. It seemed that, like the Bourbons, my destiny was to forget nothing and learn nothing.

When I went downstairs to start dinner, I discovered the cupboard was bare. I thought about take-out, but I'd given Alma my last twenty dollars. What I had on hand was half an onion, a bowl of boiled potatoes, a pound of bacon, and eleven eggs. Wolfgang Puck could have whipped these homely staples into something transcendent, but Wolfgang had never paid a visit to Dahl Street. I pulled out the frying pan and started cracking.

Angus had been outdoors all afternoon, and once again proving the adage that the best sauce is hunger, he inhaled everything I put in front of him. Taylor was finicky. Slava had spoiled her.

"She gave me tea with milk and sugar in a little cup that was so thin you could see through it, and cakes with pink icing, and we talked about art and her house when she was a little girl."

"Would you like to invite Slava for tea some day?"

Taylor's eyes lit up. "Do we have any of those little cups?"

"Of course," I said. "It'll take some digging to find them, but I distinctly remember getting some when I got married."

"When you got married," Taylor said dreamily. "Did you have a big dress?"

"The biggest," I said.

"I'd like to see that dress," Taylor said.

"I'm afraid the dress is long gone, T, but I do have some pictures. I'll hunt them up for you when I've got a bit more time."

"Good," she said, "because I'd like to draw a picture of you dressed as a bride."

Julie came just as I was clearing off the dishes. Before our sisterly reconciliation at Easter, I would have cringed if Julie had spotted yolk-smeared plates on our table at 6:00 p.m., but our relationship had entered a more equitable phase. I smiled at her. "One of those nights," I said.

She shrugged. "I ate the first two things I found in the freezer: a Lean Cuisine that I think was a pasta entrée and a pint of strawberry Haagen Dazs."

"Then we're both ready for coffee," I said. I poured, and Julie and I sat down at the kitchen table. She was wearing jeans and a sweatshirt and, for the first time since I'd known her, no makeup. She asked about my kids and about Alex and then finally she began to talk about Reed. As she remembered their life together, her brown eyes danced, and she smiled often. I recognized the syndrome. I'd felt that warmth, too, when someone let me talk about Ian in the months after he'd died.

Finally, the memories grew thin, and Julie returned to the present. "I've got to know what happened the night he died," she said simply. "When we were at the conference in Hilton Head, he gave the most wonderful speech, and he ended it with a quotation. He said it was just an old chestnut, but I can't get the words out of my mind. 'The journalist's job is to comfort the afflicted and afflict the comfortable.' That's what he said. Joanne, the more I think about it, the more I'm convinced that my husband's death was connected to his work."

"Do you mean at the university?"

She shook her head vehemently. "No, not there. Downtown. On Scarth Street. Joanne, I think Reed had discovered something in that house that someone didn't want brought to light."

"You think he was murdered?" I asked.

"It sounds so melodramatic when you say it out loud. But it's the only explanation that makes sense. Joanne, Reed and I hadn't been married long, but we'd been together since the first week he came here. I knew him. He was a healthy man. I don't mean just physically, but psychologically. He didn't have dark corners, and" – she smiled at the memory – "he was a very ordinary lover. Nothing kinky. Just lights-out, garden-variety sex. Don't you think I would have known if he had those tendencies? There was nothing, nothing in the man I knew that would connect him to that . . ." Her voice was breaking, but she carried on. "To that nightmare I walked in on."

"Did you tell the police this?"

"Not when he died. I wasn't thinking clearly. I was so humiliated. Seeing him like that. Try to put yourself in my place, Joanne. We'd been married five weeks. I loved him, and I thought he loved me. But after I followed him to Kellee Savage's room, anything seemed possible. Now . . . Jo, so many things don't add up, and I told the police that."

"You've talked to them recently?"

"Yesterday. They say the case is closed. They were civil enough, but I know they were thinking I was just a neurotic widow." She laughed ruefully. "They don't have your perspective, Joanne. If they did, they'd see that I'm less neurotic now than I've been in years. Not that that's saying much."

"You're doing all right," I said.

"Am I?" she asked, and her voice was thick with tears. "I can't even remember the last time I slept for more than two hours. And when I'm awake, all I do is think about everything I've done wrong in my life. Joanne, I've made so many mistakes. I set up expectations for everyone I loved, and when they didn't meet those expectations, I walked away. I've walked away from so many people: my first husband, my son, my daughter-in-law, my grandchildren." The tears were streaming down Julie's face, but she didn't seem to care. "And at the end, I walked away from Reed. But I'm not walking away any more. Reed was a good man, and I'm going to find out what happened to him."

"What are you going to do?"

She took out a tissue and wiped her eyes. "I thought I'd start by talking to the superintendent of the building where Reed died." She looked at me hopefully, seeking approval.

I thought of Alma Stringer saying that if shit were luck, she wouldn't have had a sniff. Finding another middle-aged matron in search of truth on her doorstep wasn't going to make Alma feel any luckier. I reached out and touched Julie's hand. "I've already talked to the landlady," I said. "So have the police. I don't think you're going to get very far there. But if you think Reed's death is connected with his work, why don't you go through his papers?"

She blew her nose. "I can't go through his papers," she said. "They're gone. I went up to the university the morning after I got back. I couldn't even get into his office. There was a work crew there. They said the office had been vandalized. Apparently, somebody from the School of

Journalism tried to retrieve what they could, but there wasn't much that was salvageable."

Julie ran her fingers through her hair in a gesture of frustration. "Everything Reed was working on was at the university. He didn't believe in bringing work home. He always said if you have to bring work home with you, your job needs redefining or you need retooling."

"Would the people in his department know that everything he was working on was at the university?"

Julie nodded. "Everybody knew."

The only association I'd made between the chaos in Kellee Savage's place on Scarth Street and the scene at the J school had been the fact that both places had been an unholy mess. The vandalism at the university had so obviously been the work of gay-bashers that I hadn't connected it with what I'd seen in Kellee's room.

Julie leaned towards me. She was frowning. "You look as if you're a million miles away," she said.

"Sorry," I said, "I guess I was wool-gathering. I'm back now." But I wasn't back, not really. I was still in room 6 of the house on Scarth Street, assessing the holes that were appearing in Ed Mariani's theory that Kellee Savage had been blackmailing Reed Gallagher. The possibility that whoever had wrecked Reed Gallagher's office had vandalized Kellee's room on Scarth Street had ceased to be a long shot.

I thought again about Reed's destroyed papers, and about Kellee's fortress in Indian Head. Another possibility was beginning to seem less remote; there was a strong chance that the vandalism I'd seen had been a smoke screen thrown up to camouflage two coolly deliberate missions of search and destroy. If that hypothesis were true, there was an adversary out there who was far more deadly than a pack of hate-filled kids.

But who was that adversary? No matter how much I wanted to turn from the thought, one name kept insinuating itself into my consciousness. From the beginning, Ed Mariani had been front and centre. He had been Reed's rival for the position of head of the School of Journalism. He had been with Reed the night before he died. Suddenly, there were troubling memories: of Alex, perplexed by the presence of amyl nitrite at Reed's death scene because amyl nitrite was most often used by gay men; of Ed seeking me out the night of Tom Kelsoe's book launch; of Ed, Johnny-on-the-spot with a dinner invitation the day I'd been at the J school and seen the vandalism. He'd been there all along, offering explanations, shaping my perception of Reed Gallagher, and, finally, conjuring up the blackmail scenario that I'd seized on with such alacrity.

I'd been wrong about the blackmail. I was convinced of that now. But if I'd been mistaken about the blackmail, it was possible that my perception of other events had been faulty, too. I had to go back to the beginning, try to look at everything afresh. If Julie was right about Reed Gallagher's sexual style, it was possible that the bizarre sexual scene the police had found when Reed Gallagher died was staged. And if Reed's death scene were bogus, where was the truth?

When Julie left, I told her to take care of herself, and it wasn't just a pleasantry. Something was very wrong. Remembering Kellee's room in the house in Indian Head, I decided Julie wasn't the only person who needed a reminder about being careful.

Neil McCallum answered the telephone on the first ring, and he sounded so sane and cheerful he seemed like a citizen of another planet. He and Chloe had been for a walk on the prairie, and they'd found crocuses.

"I wish I could see them," I said.

"You can," he said. "Just come out here. I'll show you where they are."

"It's not that easy," I said.

"Sure it is," he said. "People always make easy things hard. I don't get it."

I laughed. "Neither do I. But Neil, I didn't just call to talk. I wanted to ask you to keep a specially close watch on Kellee's house. Make sure the front door and the door to her office are always locked."

"I always do that." He paused. "Have you heard something bad about Kellee?"

"No," I said. "I haven't heard anything. Honestly. But Neil, you've got to promise me you'll be careful. If anyone you don't know comes around, make sure you've got Chloe with you, and don't tell them how sweet she is. Make them think she means business."

"Like on TV," he said.

"Yes," I said. "Like on TV."

For a moment, Neil was silent. Then he said, "But this isn't TV, and I'm getting scared."

That night I couldn't sleep. I was getting scared, too. For the first time since Alex had gone up north, I wanted him with me not because he was a man I cared about, but because he was a cop and he'd be able to put together the pieces. He had told me once that police investigations involved a lot of what he called mouse work. He'd pointed to the medicine wheel on his wall and talked about the Four Great Ways of Seeking Understanding. One of them was Brother Mouse's: sniffing things out with his nose, seeing what's up close, touching what he can with his whiskers. Alex had told me that when a police officer had a treasure trove of facts and information, it was time for him to stop seeing like a mouse and start seeing like an eagle. As I tossed and turned, mulling over my accumulation of fact and theory, only one thing was certain: as far as insights were concerned, I'd never been more earthbound in my life.

The next morning when I got to the university I went straight to Physical Plant. The cheerful woman who'd given me the extra key to the office for Ed Mariani was moving a tray of geranium slips in peat pots from a window on the west side of the office to a window on the east.

"Caught me," she said, and the lilt of her native Jamaica warmed the room. "There's so much light here, and I want my babies to get a good start. When spring comes, that garden of mine is my life. Now, don't tell me, let me guess. You lost your extra key."

"No," I said. "It's something else, but, in a way, it's connected to the key. The man who's sharing my office now is from the School of Journalism. I wondered if you'd heard how things were shaping up about that vandalism case."

She looked fondly at her sturdy little geranium plants, then she turned back to me. "I'm afraid you're going to have to be a Good Samaritan for a couple more weeks," she said. "The vandals really did a job on that place."

"Did the police catch them?"

She shook her head. "No. It's scary too, because it looks like it might have been an inside job. We've put a security officer in there all night now and a surveillance camera, but, if you ask me, we're closing the barn door after the pony's gone."

"What makes you think it's an inside job?"

"Whoever did it had to get through the outside doors somehow, and the lock wasn't forced. They must have had keys. There were no fingerprints, but that's hardly a surprise since they used gloves." She flexed her fingers. "Latex gloves. Ours. The gloves were traced to the Chemistry department, as were the lab coats."

"Lab coats?"

"To keep the paint off their clothes, I guess. Anyway, we got the gloves and the lab coats back, and the computer they took. It was a Pentium 90 – cost five thousand dollars. And they just pitched it in the garbage bin back of the Owl."

"When did you find it?"

"Last Friday. It hadn't been there long. Whoever took it must have decided it was too hot to keep around. Those Pentiums are great little machines. The one in the garbage was still functioning, but the memory on the hard drive had been reformatted."

"Who would go to all that trouble?"

She chuckled. "Somebody who had big plans, then got cold feet."

"Do you know who the machine belonged to?"

She went over to her computer, tapped in the serial number, and shook her head sadly. "Reed Gallagher. Well, I guess he won't be missing it now."

"No," I said, "I guess he won't."

When I went back to my office, Ed Mariani was there. The sight of him pouring boiling water into our Brown Betty disarmed me. How could I suspect such a gentle and giving man of . . . of what? I couldn't even articulate in my own mind what I suspected Ed of doing.

He opened his arms in welcome. "You must have smelled the tea," he said.

"I guess I did," I said. I took off my coat, sat down in the student chair, and buried myself in my lecture notes.

"Anything new on Kellee Savage?"

I shook my head. "Nothing significant."

Ed was watching me carefully. "Joanne, correct me if I'm wrong, but have I overstayed my welcome?"

"I just have to get ready for class, Ed." When I glanced up, he looked so wounded, I found myself thinking I must be

crazy. But I had to be careful, too. I'd never been good at sub-
terfuge. For the first time since we'd started sharing the office,
the atmosphere between Ed and me was strained, and I was
relieved when he finally picked up his books and headed out
the door.

Val Massey appeared so quickly after Ed left that it was
obvious he'd been waiting until I was alone. Like everyone
who teaches these days, I'm careful about leaving the door
open when a student is in the room, but when Val pulled the
door closed behind him, I didn't move to open it.

He looked terrible. He was pale, and there were deep
shadows under his eyes. It was apparent he'd been through
more than a few sleepless nights. I invited him to sit, but he
went over and stood at the window as he'd done the day he'd
come to my office and asked me if any of my children had
ever got into a real mess. I bit my lip, remembering how I
had jumped to what I believed was the heart of the problem,
and how quickly I had assured him that I didn't believe the
charges that Kellee Savage was levelling at him.

But I was through being impetuous. Like Freudian ana-
lysts and good interviewers, I was going to count on the
power of silence. It was an uncomfortable wait. If the silence
between Ed and me had been awkward, the tension as I
waited for Val Massey to talk was painful.

When he finally turned to face me, he didn't waste time
on a preamble.

"I was the one who borrowed Jumbo's library card," he
said. "And I was the one who left the book for Kellee." He
lowered his voice. "I wrote that letter inside the book, too."

It was news I was expecting, yet hearing the words was a
blow. "Whatever made you do it, Val?"

"I don't know," he said miserably.

Suddenly I felt my resolve harden. "That's not good

enough," I said. "You don't do something that cruel without a reason."

He flinched, but he didn't offer an explanation.

I got up from the desk and walked over to him. "Damn it, Val, I thought I knew you. I had a pretty good idea about what kind of person you were. For one thing, I thought you believed what you said in our seminar about the journalist's obligation to protect the powerless."

"She wasn't powerless," he said quietly. "She had her lies, and she was using them to destroy a decent human being."

"But, Val, you started it. You just said you were the one who wrote that letter, and Kellee said there were incidents before that."

Val laughed derisively. "Oh yes, there were other incidents, but I'll bet she didn't tell you about her part in them. Professor Kilbourn, whatever you may think, Kellee Savage is no victim. I know that what I did was wrong, but what she was threatening to do was worse. She was prepared to ruin someone's career, even their life. All I was trying to do was muddy the waters."

"Muddy the waters," I repeated. "I don't understand."

Val averted his eyes. "Kellee was threatening to make her charges against . . . against this other person public. The things she was saying were crazy, but you have no idea how terrible the consequences would have been if people had believed her. We had to make sure people wouldn't take what Kellee was saying seriously. It was like that story of the boy who cried wolf. We had to make certain that when Kellee talked, no one listened."

"It got a little out of hand, didn't it?" I said. "Kellee's disappeared, Val."

"And I've spent the last week trying to find her. I've tried to call her and I've talked to everybody who might have seen her. I feel sick about this whole thing. You've got to believe me. I didn't want Kellee to quit school. I just wanted to teach her a lesson. I couldn't just sit by and let her destroy a person's life, could I?"

"Whose life was she going to destroy?" I asked.

He shook his head vigorously. "No," he said. "I can't tell you that."

"Was it another student, or someone on faculty?"

"I've told you everything I can," he said. "If you have to take some sort of action against me, I understand, but please don't involve Jumbo in this any more. He really was just doing a favour for a friend."

"The way you were," I said.

"Yes," he said. "The way I was."

I came home to a crisis. Taylor had sliced her hand with a knife. The cut was a real bleeder, and she was wailing. Angus was holding a wad of paper towels against the wound with one hand and dialling my number at the university with the other.

I took a peek at the cut, reassured Taylor, and ran upstairs to the bathroom to get a sanitary napkin to act as a pressure bandage.

When I came back, I handed the napkin to Angus. "Wrap that tightly around the cut," I said.

He looked at me in horror.

"It'll stop the bleeding," I said. "And it's sterile." Suddenly I realized the problem. "Angus, nobody has ever died of humiliation from holding a Stayfree. Now do it."

An hour later, Taylor was wearing a button that declared, "Hospitals Are Full of Helpers," her wound was sewn up, and we were on our way to Kowloon Kitchen for Chinese take-out: Won-ton soup and a double order of Taylor's favourite almond shrimp. The cut had been nasty, but it had also been on Taylor's right hand, and as she was left-handed, the injury had already become an adventure rather than a catastrophe.

The phone was ringing when we got in the door. I picked it up, and heard a man's voice, not familiar. "Is this Joanne Kilbourn?"

"Yes," I said.

"Regina Police, Mrs. Kilbourn. You were in last week and talked to Constable Kirszner about a missing person."

"He didn't think there was cause for alarm," I said, but my heart was already starting to pound.

"He may still be right," the voice said. "However, we just picked up the body of an unidentified female. A farmer outside Balgonie found her in one of his fields. She's not carrying any identification, but the age and the general description seem to fit the woman you were concerned about."

At the kitchen table, my children were laughing, doling out the won-ton soup, sniping at each other about who would get the extra shrimp.

"How soon will you know?" I said.

"That depends on you. I wonder if you could come down to Regina General and have a look."

"Isn't there anyone else?" I said.

"If you'd rather not come down, we can go to the media."

I thought of Neil McCallum, having his supper, watching television and hearing about the discovery of a body that might be Kellee's.

"I'll be right there," I said.

"We'll have a uniformed officer meet you at the doors to the emergency room. Do you know the place I'm talking about?"

"Only too well," I said. "Only too well."

CHAPTER

12

The uniformed officer who met me was female, and she was good at her job: cool and perceptive. Angus would have said her energy was very smooth. She introduced herself as Constable Marissa Desjardin, and as she walked me to the elevator, she began to explain the identification process. All I had to do, she said, was look at the body long enough to make an identification, positive or negative, then I could be on my way. It was, she added briskly, important to keep my focus and not let my imagination run away with me. As I walked beside her through the maze of surgical-green corridors, I willed myself to heed her words; nonetheless, when we came to the double doors marked "Pathology," my heart began to pound.

Constable Desjardin gave me a reassuring smile and pointed to a room across the hall. "That's the staff room," she said. "Why don't you wait in there while I make sure they're ready for us inside?"

The staff room was small, with furnishings that were hearteningly ordinary: an old couch, a kitchen table and four chairs, a microwave oven, a small refrigerator, a sink with a drainboard on which mugs were drying. There was an acrid smell in the air; someone had left an almost empty pot on the burner of the coffee maker. I gulped in the familiar odour hungrily. Despite Constable Desjardin's sensible advice, my imagination was in overdrive. From the moment I'd seen the doors marked "Pathology," I was certain the air I was breathing carried with it a whiff of the charnel house.

I didn't have long to look around the coffee room before Marissa Desjardin was back. "All set," she said. "We might as well get it over with."

Hours of watching "Quincy" and other crime shows on television had prepared me for the harshly lit, sterile room behind the doors. I was even ready for the pathologist in the lab coat and for the gurney with its plastic-shrouded but unmistakable cargo. But nothing could have prepared me for the horror that was exposed when, at a signal from Constable Desjardin, the pathologist reached over and pulled back the heavy plastic sheeting. A quick glance, and I knew that the dead woman was Kellee. However, it wasn't Kellee as I had known her. Two weeks of exposure to weather had taken its toll. Her body was swollen and her skin had blistered and split; in places, her flesh looked as if it had been eaten away. Her green wool sweater had darkened and begun to rot as if it, too, was returning to its elemental state. Only the plastic shamrock barrettes in her hair remained unchanged. They were as sunnily cheerful as they had been on the morning when Kellee had chosen them, out of all the others, to anchor her hair on her twenty-first birthday.

I turned to Constable Desjardin. "That's her," I said. "What happened to her skin?"

Marissa Desjardin looked away. "Insects," she said tightly. "We've had an early spring."

I couldn't take my eyes off the ruin that had once been Kellee Savage's face. "She didn't live long enough to feel the insects doing that to her, did she?" I asked, and my voice was edged with hysteria.

"We won't know exactly what happened until we have the autopsy results," Constable Desjardin said quietly. Then she squared her shoulders. "Mrs. Kilbourn, I promise you that as soon as we know how Kellee Savage died, we'll tell you. Now, I really do think it's time we got out of here."

I didn't put up an argument. When Constable Desjardin went to get the forms I had to sign, I wandered back into the staff room. It hadn't been five minutes since I'd left, but everything about the room now seemed surreal. On the wall beside the sink was a poster, black with bubble-gum-pink lettering. I read and reread it numbly, trying to comprehend its message:

> No means NO. Not now means NO. I have a boy/ girlfriend means NO. Maybe later means NO. No thanks means NO. You're not my type means NO. $#@!!! off means NO. I'd rather be alone right now means NO. You've/I've been drinking means NO. Silence means NO. NO MEANS NO.

After I'd signed the forms, Constable Desjardin gave me a quick assessing look. "I don't think you should be driving," she said. "I'll take you home."

"I'm fine," I said, and I thought I was, but when I went to stand, my knees buckled. Marissa Desjardin leaned forward and slid a practised arm around me.

"Let's get you some air," she said. She steered me down another corridor and onto a ward. To our immediate left was a small room with some cleaning equipment and a window that Constable Desjardin cranked open. "Take some deep breaths," she said.

I did as she told me and immediately felt better. After the stale antiseptic air of the hospital, the oxygen was tonic. "I'm okay now," I said. "It was just a shock."

"It always is," she said.

"Even for you?"

She smiled. "How do you think I found out about this room?"

When we got to my car in the parking lot, I handed Marissa Desjardin the keys and slid gratefully into the passenger seat. We drove in silence. I was fresh out of words, and Constable Desjardin, mercifully, was not a person who saw silence as a vacuum waiting to be filled.

She pulled up expertly in front of my house. "There'll be a squad car picking me up here," she said. "It shouldn't be long." Then she added kindly, "You did fine."

"Do you know what happened to Kellee?" I asked.

She shook her head. "They'll be doing the autopsy tomorrow. If you'd like, I can call you when we have the report."

"Thanks, I'd appreciate that."

"Mrs. Kilbourn, there's something you might be able to help us with. You told Officer Kirszner that early in the evening of March 17, Kellee Savage called you several times from the Lazy Owl Bar at the university."

I nodded.

"Her body was found thirty-two kilometres east of the university. Do you have any idea what she was doing out in that field?"

I thought of Kellee's bedroom in Indian Head: the girlish pink-and-white bedspread, the Care Bear and the Strawberry Shortcake doll positioned so carefully on the pillows. "I think she was trying to go home," I said.

Constable Desjardin sighed. "You'd be amazed at how often they are," she said. She reached over and touched my hand. "If you don't mind my saying so, Kellee Savage was lucky to have a teacher like you."

I tried a smile. "Thanks," I said. "But you couldn't be more wrong about that."

After the squad car came for Marissa Desjardin, I sat in the Volvo, taking deep breaths and trying to shake off the existential horror that gripped me. It was an impossible task, and when the clock on the dashboard showed that ten minutes had elapsed, I gave it up as a bad job and headed for the house. Taylor met me at the front door. She was in her nightie, and I noticed she'd pinned her "Hospitals Are Full of Helpers" button to its yoke.

"How's your hand?" I asked.

"It's okay," she said. "I was brave, wasn't I?"

I put my arm around her. "Very brave."

She moved closer to me. "It was nice of them to give me the button, but I hate hospitals, Jo."

"Me too," I said. "Let's do what we can to stay away from them for a while."

When Taylor wandered off to find Benny and take care of his final needs of the day, I went into the kitchen. There was a note in Taylor's careful printing on the kitchen table. "Anna Lee called." It took me a minute to connect Anna Lee with Annalie Brinkmann, but when I did I started for the phone.

As I picked up the receiver, the memory of Kellee's ravaged face hit me like a slap, and a wave of dizziness engulfed me. I leaned against the wall. I wasn't hungry, but I knew I had to eat. I poured the last of the won-ton soup into a bowl and stuck it in the microwave. The soup was good, and after I ate it, I felt better. Still, I knew that all the won-ton soup in the Kowloon Kitchen couldn't make me strong enough for the task at hand. Annalie Brinkmann would have to wait. I rinsed my bowl and put it in the dishwasher, then, with limbs that felt like lead, I walked to the phone and dialled Neil McCallum's number.

Like many people confronted with brutal news, Neil's first refuge was disbelief. "You could have made a mistake," he said, "or the police could have. Everybody makes mistakes."

When, finally, I'd convinced Neil that there was no mistake, that Kellee Savage was the woman in the photographs I'd seen, he grew quiet. "I'm going to hang up now," he said. "I don't want you to hear me cry."

I didn't try to dissuade him. Neil had announced his decision with great dignity. He knew what he was doing; besides, I was fresh out of what Emily Dickinson called "those little anodynes that deaden suffering."

That night I couldn't sleep. For hours, I lay between the cool sheets, watching the shifting patterns of the moonlight on my ceiling, breathing in air scented by the narcissi growing in pots in front of my open window, and wondering what kind of fate could decree that a twenty-one-year-old woman should die before she had known a lifetime of nights like this. When, at last, I drifted into sleep, the room was dark and the air had grown cold, but I still didn't have an answer.

The first voice I heard the next morning came from my clock radio. The newsreader was intoning the final words of an all-too-familiar litany: "name withheld, pending notification of next of kin," she said, and I knew my day had begun.

When the dogs and I set off for our run, the city was thick with fog. As we started across Albert Street, there wasn't a car in sight. Obviously, most of Regina's citizens were smarter than I was. While we were waiting for the light to change, I reached down and rubbed my golden retriever's head. "Looks like we've got the world all to ourselves, Rosie," I said. She looked at me with disdain; apparently, that morning, she regarded the world with as little enthusiasm as I did.

Our progress through the park was slow. There were patches of muddy leaves on the path that curved around the shoreline. The leaves were slick and we had to travel carefully to avoid a misstep. As we rounded the lake, Sadie began to whimper with weariness. I reassured her and slowed our pace even more. And so we headed home: a woman in middle age and her two old dogs, trying to find their way through the fog. It was a metaphor I could have lived without.

By the time I'd taken the dogs' leashes off and fed them, I knew I was running on empty. It was time to shut down. I didn't have classes that day, and there was plenty of work on my desk at the university that could just as easily be done at home.

When I looked into my closet, the prospect of selecting something to wear to the university suddenly became as daunting as a run in the Boston Marathon. Anyone I ran into that day was just going to have to take me as they found me. Unfortunately, the first person I ran into was Rosalie Norman.

When I came into the Political Science offices, she looked at my jeans and sweatshirt assessingly. "Are we having Casual Friday on Thursday this week?" she asked.

"I've decided to work at home today."

Since the advent of her fatal perm, Rosalie had taken to wearing a series of hand-knitted tams. The tam *du jour* was the colour of powdered cheese and, as she framed her response to me, Rosalie tucked a wiry curl back under its protection.

"Must be nice to be able to work at home whenever you feel like it," she said.

"I'm hoping it'll be productive, too," I said.

"I suppose you'll want me to handle your calls."

"If you don't mind."

"What do you want me to tell them?"

"Tell them I'll call them tomorrow," I said. "Or tell them to go hell, whichever you prefer."

I walked out of the office, warmed by the pleasure of meanness. For the first time since I'd become a member of the Political Science department, I had rendered Rosalie Norman speechless.

One of the realities of university teaching is that mindless tasks are never in short supply, and it didn't take me long to fill a file folder with work that demanded less than my complete attention. I had my jacket zipped up and I was on my way out the door when I saw Kellee's tape-recorder on my shelf, waiting to be claimed. From the time she had asked permission to tape my lectures so she wouldn't miss anything, I had never seen her without it. The tape-recorder had seemed an extension of Kellee, ubiquitous and imbued with her plodding, mechanical determination to complete the task at hand.

When she'd telephoned me from the Owl on the last night of her life, Kellee had bragged about getting "proof." She hadn't mentioned the tape-recorder, but Linda Van Sickle had.

I went to my shelf and took down the tape-recorder. Linda had said there'd been some sort of blowup when Kellee's classmates had discovered she was taping their private conversations. I rewound the tape and pressed *play*, hoping, I guess, for some sort of revelation, but all I got were the sounds of a student bar on a Friday night: music; a burst of laughter; a drunken shout; more laughter. The first voice I was able to recognize belonged to a young woman named Jeannine who was in the Politics and the Media seminar, and who had told me on at least three separate occasions that I was her role model. As it turned out, she was talking about me again.

"If I'd known Kilbourn was such a bitch about not letting people express their own ideas I wouldn't have taken her fucking course. You know what she gave me on my last paper? Fifty-eight per cent! Just because I didn't use secondary sources! I showed that paper to my boyfriend and a lot of other people. Everybody says I should've got an A."

Unexpectedly, it was Jumbo Hryniuk who jumped to my defence. "Kilbourn's all right," he said. "She's kinda like my coach – tough, but generally pretty fair."

The conversation drifted to other subjects: exam schedules; a new coffee place downtown; the most recent movie at the public library. Then Jeannine was back, whispering sibilantly to Linda. "Doesn't it piss you off," she said, "that even though your marks are better, Val Massey's probably going to get that *Globe and Mail* placement? And he's only getting it because he sucked up to you-know-who. I know everybody brown-noses, but I hate the ones who get their nose right in there."

Linda's voice was mild. "Val's not a brown-noser," she said. "There's no reason he can't be friends with somebody on faculty."

"If you ask me, I think it's more than that," Jeannine hissed. "I'd have too much pride to do what he's doing, but it's going to pay off. Wait and see."

Someone whose voice I didn't recognize joined the group, and the topic changed. I listened until the tape ended, but there were no more references to the *Globe and Mail* placement, and there were no more references to Val Massey.

As I walked to my car, Jeannine's sour little discourse on brown-nosing was still on my mind. She had been wrong, at least in part. Not all students saw sucking up to professors as the surest route to academic success. Still, a surprising number did, and an equally surprising number of faculty members fell for student blandishments, hook, line, and sinker.

It was an old game, but Val Massey had never struck me as a player. The only faculty member Val had ever seemed close to was Tom Kelsoe, and that relationship was more complex than a simple friendship. At twenty-one, Val was a little old for hero worship and, to my mind at least, Tom didn't fit the job description, but there was no mistaking Val's unquestioning adoration. It had puzzled me until the day the kids and I had stopped at Masluk's Garage in Regina Beach. Given Val's father's performance the day we saw him, it wasn't surprising that Val had been desperate for someone to look up to.

All things considered I had a pretty good day. By mid-morning the fog had moved off and the sun was shining. I bundled up and took my work and my coffee out on the deck. Just before noon, Taylor called me into the house to show me her mural. Nanabush and the Close-Your-Eyes Dance was taking shape. Most of the time there wasn't much I could do to help Taylor with her art, but giving her the Chagall book had obviously been an inspiration. I'd hoped Chagall's "Flying Over Town," with its magical mix of reality and myth, would help Taylor paint the picture she wanted to paint, and it had. The world she'd created with her poster paints seemed to me to be very like the world Alex Kequahtooway had conjured up for us on those winter evenings when we listened to the wind howl and felt the darkness come alive with his tales of the Trickster.

Taylor was eyeing me anxiously. "Do you think it's any good?" she said finally.

"It's terrific," I said.

"Do you think Alex will like it?"

"I know he'll like it. As Angus would say, it's the smokingest."

She didn't smile. "Jo, when is Alex coming back?"

"Soon, I hope."

"But you don't know for sure."

"No," I said, "I don't know for sure."

After lunch, Taylor and I went to the mall to see the movie that was required viewing for everyone under the age of twelve that Easter. As I sat in the dark, smelling the wet-wool smell of little kids, watching the endless procession of parents and children moving up and down the aisles, slopping drinks, spilling popcorn, heading for washrooms, I felt my nerves unknot. The holiday matinee was familiar turf, and it was a relief, for once, just to sit back and watch the movie.

When we pulled up in front of the house after the movie, Angus and his friend Camillo were in the driveway, shooting hoops. I dropped Taylor off and went to pick up our dry cleaning.

Taylor was all smiles when I got back. "Guess who called?"

"I don't know. You're the one who was here. Why don't you tell me?"

"Alex. He said to tell you he's sorry he missed you and he'll call again Saturday night. He and Eli . . ." She scrunched her face. "Who's Eli?"

"Alex's nephew. He's the same age as Angus."

"Anyway, Alex and Eli are going to some island up there. He says he'll bring me a fish when he comes back."

"Did he say when that's going to be?"

"No, but guess what, Jo? I invited Alex to the Kids Convention to see the mural and he says wild horses couldn't keep him away. That's good, eh?"

"That's more than good," I said. "The Kids Convention is on the tenth – not long at all."

Angus and I were upstairs looking for the shorts to his basketball uniform when Annalie Brinkmann called. As soon as I heard her pleasant contralto, I felt a twinge. "I'm sorry," I said. "I meant to get back to you. But when I got your message, I'd just had some bad news. I teach at the university here, and one of our students died."

I could hear her intake of breath. "Not the one who was being harassed?" she said.

I felt as if I'd been kicked in the stomach. "How did you know about that?"

"Then it was her?"

"Yes," I said. "The student who died was Kellee Savage."

"Kellee Savage," she repeated dully. "Reed didn't tell me her name. And now he's dead too."

"Ms Brinkmann, how are you connected to this?"

"Through history," she said heavily, "and through Reed Gallagher. I have to know – did that young woman – did Kellee Savage commit suicide? Because if he drove her to that . . ." Her voice broke. When she spoke again, it was apparent she was fighting for control. "I'm not an hysterical person, Mrs. Kilbourn, but this case has a special resonance. Twenty years ago, what happened to Kellee Savage happened to me."

"Ms Brinkmann, you're going to have to . . ."

She cut me off. "I'm sorry," she said. "I know I'm being elliptical." Her pleasant voice had gone flat. "I was in J school here in Toronto. Reed Gallagher was my instructor. Charges were made." Unexpectedly, she sobbed. "Without ever seeing her, I can tell you what Kellee Savage was like. She worked hard. She took journalism seriously, and . . ." Annalie Brinkmann hesitated. "And she was ugly."

"What else did Reed tell you?"

"Not much. He just left a message on my machine – said he was having a problem with a student, that she was accusing another student of harassment, and he was afraid there might be some truth to her charges. Then he said he thought, because of my history, I might be able to help him get to the truth."

"Why would he drag you into this after twenty years? Did he just want your advice because what Kellee was going through was similar to what you'd gone through?"

Annalie laughed, not pleasantly. "It wasn't similar; it was identical. I was the prototype: the ugly girl who worked hard and came up with something the handsome young man wanted; the ugly girl who couldn't make anybody believe her when she said the handsome young man was pursuing her sexually. Mrs. Kilbourn, Reed Gallagher called me because he was suddenly facing the possibility that twenty years ago, when he believed the handsome young man instead of believing me, he'd put his money on the wrong horse."

I thought of Tom Kelsoe taking the picture of Reed and Annalie and shoving it into the paper-towel receptacle in the Faculty Club washroom. Suddenly, in the midst of all the questions, there was one answer. "The man who did that to you was Tom Kelsoe, wasn't it?" I said.

"Yes." Annalie's voice was low with anger. "It was Tom, and I'll tell you something else. Without knowing any of the circumstances of Kellee's death, I can assure you that when the facts come to light, you'll discover that that bastard Kelsoe might as well have been holding a pistol to her head."

After that, Annalie's account of her relationship with Tom Kelsoe tumbled out. Twenty years had passed, but the pain of what Tom Kelsoe had done to her was still acute.

Like so many tragedies, Annalie's grew out of an act of misplaced altruism. When Annalie left her home town and moved to Toronto to study journalism, she was lonely and homesick. Working on the premise that one way out of her misery might be to help someone whose problems were larger than her own, she became a volunteer at a private hospice for children with incurable diseases. The place was called Sunshine House, and it didn't take Annalie long to realize that it was an institution with serious problems:

administrative staff had thin credentials and fat expense accounts; the personnel charged with the care of the children were incompetent or indifferent; the children themselves were casually ignored or abused. Despite the conditions, Annalie stayed on for two and a half years – in part because she felt the children needed an ally, and in part because she was patiently building up a dossier on the mismanagement at Sunshine House.

By the time Annalie Brinkmann and Tom Kelsoe were thrown together in an investigative journalism class, two things had happened: the dossier on Sunshine House was bulging, and Annalie had been fired as a volunteer. She'd been caught in the director's office photocopying a particularly damning file. Sunshine House was about to launch a major fundraising campaign, and they had put together a series of heartbreaking pictures of dying children; the problem was the children had all been recruited from a modelling agency, and they were all healthy as horses. The director of Sunshine House had been brutal in his internal memorandum justifying the expense of hiring professionals: "a picture of any of the kids here would make Mr. and Mrs. John Q. Public throw up. We're not going to get our target group to write big cheques if they've got their eyes closed."

Even without the modelling-agency file, Annalie knew she had a story, but the director's letter was dynamite, and she wanted it. When a fellow student in the investigative journalism class confided that he hadn't come up with a subject for his major report, Annalie thought she'd found a perfect fit. No one at Sunshine House would suspect a connection between her and Tom Kelsoe. Tom could copy the relevant file and dig up whatever other dirt he could find. He would come out of the experience with enough material for a term paper, and she'd have a shining bauble to dangle in front of the Toronto media.

It was, in Annalie's mind, a fair exchange, but after agreeing to her plan, Tom Kelsoe decided not to trade. After he'd
photocopied the modelling-agency file, he told Annalie
he'd unearthed some material that was even more damaging, and that he needed time to bring it to light. When she
objected, he surprised her by making a crude but unmistakable pass.

The pattern continued. Every time she pressed him about
the file, he fondled her and murmured about their future
together. Annalie was, by her own assessment, both plain
and naive. She had never had a date in her life. A more experienced young woman would have seen through Tom
Kelsoe's ploy, but Annalie didn't. She believed the lies and
she enjoyed the sexual stirrings. She created a fantasy in
which she and Tom were journalists, travelling the world
together, famous and enviable. She knew the Sunshine
House story was their entrée into the glittering media world.
So complete was her belief in the fantasy that, on the day she
passed a newsstand and saw the Sunshine House exposé on
page one of the evening paper, her first thought was that
Tom had surprised her by getting their story published.
When she saw that the only name on the by-line was Tom
Kelsoe's, she fell apart.

By the time she pulled herself together enough to go to
Reed Gallagher, Tom Kelsoe had beaten her to the punch.
Tom's version of the story had enough basis in truth to be
credible. He acknowledged that Annalie had been a volunteer at Sunshine House, but he said she'd been fired before
she had anything more solid than suspicions. He acknowledged that Annalie had suggested that he volunteer his
services at Sunshine House, but he said the story he dug up
was all his own.

Then Tom Kelsoe made a pre-emptive strike. He confided
to Reed that he had a terrible personal problem. Annalie

had, Tom explained, become obsessed with him. She was phoning him at all hours of the night, following him on the street. He was, he told Reed, afraid for her sanity, but he was also afraid for himself.

Annalie said Reed had been very compassionate with her, very concerned. He heard her story, then he suggested she seek counselling. When she objected, he talked gently to Annalie about the importance of a journalist's good name. When that didn't work, he talked less gently about the possibility that, if she kept harassing him, Tom might be compelled to seek legal redress against her. By the time she left Reed's office, Annalie knew that Reed Gallagher hadn't believed a word she'd said. She also knew she had no alternative but to withdraw from J school.

She'd been lucky. She'd got a job at a small FM station that played classical music, and had been there ever since. She had married. Her husband didn't want children. He didn't like confusion. It had been, Annalie said, a very quiet life.

"But a good one," I said.

She laughed. "Yes," she said, "I've had a good life, but then so has Tom Kelsoe."

The first item on the 6:00 news was Constable Desjardin's announcement that the name of the woman whose body had been found in the farmer's field was Kellee Savage. When I made the identification of the body at the hospital, I had thought the worst was over, but the official announcement of Kellee's death hit me hard. There were no surprises in the way the television story unfolded; nonetheless, as Marissa's image was replaced by shots of the area in which the body had been found, and as the death scene faded into the inevitable interview with the finder of the body, I started to shake.

I turned off the television. I didn't need TV images to underscore a truth that seemed more and more unassailable:

Reed Gallagher's death hadn't been accidental. I didn't know who killed him, and I didn't know why, but I was sure of one thing: as soon as I knew what had happened to Kellee in the hours before she started her final, fatal walk home, a giant piece in the puzzle of Reed's death would slide into place. A theory was starting to gather at the edges of my mind, but a theory without substantiation wasn't enough. I needed proof. Annalie Brinkmann's story had been compelling, but if I was going to prove that Tom Kelsoe was behind Val Massey's harassment of Kellee, I had to have more to go on than a twenty-year-old story from a woman I didn't know. I needed to come up with some solid reasons why Kellee Savage had been worth attacking.

There was another reason I needed proof. If I was going to blow Tom Kelsoe out of the water, I had to make sure Jill was ready for the blast. She deserved to know the truth, and that meant waiting until I was absolutely certain what the truth was. I called Rapti Lustig to see if she knew when Jill would be back from Toronto. Rapti said Jill had called her to say she had a meeting Saturday morning, but she'd be back in time for the show. That meant she'd be on the late-afternoon flight. I started to ask Rapti for Jill's number in Toronto, but decided against it. If I phoned Jill to tell her I wanted to pick her up at the airport, she'd have questions, and, at the moment, I didn't have enough answers.

I ran through a mental list of what needed to be done before I confronted Jill with my suspicions. I had to go back to Dahl Street. I wanted to talk to Marissa Desjardin and I wanted to talk again to some of the people who'd been closest to Kellee in the Politics and the Media seminar. But the first piece in the puzzle was Val Massey's. I picked up the phone, called Information, got the number of Masluk's Garage and began to dial.

CHAPTER

13

There was no answer at Masluk's Garage the first time I called, and there was no answer any of the other times I dialled the Regina Beach number that night. The next morning, before I left for the university, I made a final stab at getting in touch with Val, but I came up empty again. It was puzzling. Val's father had struck me as the type who wouldn't shut his business for anything short of the Second Coming.

When I got to the university, Rosalie Norman was waiting for me. Today's knitted tam was a pretty shade of chestnut.

"That's a nice colour on you," I said. "It brings out your eyes."

She looked at me suspiciously. After my performance the previous day, I could hardly blame her. "I'm sorry about yesterday," I said. "The police had called me the night before to go downtown and identify Kellee Savage. I guess I was still pretty shaky when I came in here."

"Next time, if you're having personal problems, mention it," she said.

"I will," I promised meekly.

She handed me an envelope. "Professor Mariani asked me to give you this."

I looked inside the envelope. It was Ed's key to the office. "More coals upon my head," I said.

Rosalie's blackberry eyes were bright with interest. "Did you two have a fight? It's never a good idea to share a work space. That's what they told us at our ergonomics seminar."

"I guess they were right," I said, and my tone was so bleak that I startled myself. The sight that greeted me when I opened the door to my office didn't improve my spirits. On my desk were a florist's vase filled with irises and a gift beautifully wrapped in iris-covered wrapping paper. I opened the box. It was a paella pan with Barry Levitt's recipe, and a note in Ed's neat hand: "For Taylor and for you, with thanks and affection, E."

I called Ed's home to thank him, but there was no answer. I called Masluk's Garage. No answer there, either. Apparently, it was not my day to reach out and touch someone. Just as I was hanging up, Linda Van Sickle and Jumbo arrived.

Linda's glow had dimmed. Her face was pale and her eyes were dull. "I feel so awful," she said. "I can't stop thinking about Kellee. I keep replaying that evening, thinking about all the points where I could have acted differently."

"Me too," I said.

"There's no use retrospecting," Jumbo said sagely. "That's what my coach tells us and he's right. You've got to focus on what's ahead."

"What's ahead doesn't look all that terrific, either," I said. "But you're right. Going over what might have been is a pretty profitless exercise. Was there something special you two wanted to talk about?"

"The funeral," Linda said flatly. "Do you know when it's going to be? Jumbo and I think we should be there."

"I agree," I said. "You should be there. So should a lot of other people – Val, for instance. Have you seen him today?"

Jumbo and Linda glanced at one another quickly.

"No," Jumbo said. "We haven't seen Val. He wasn't in class yesterday and he wasn't at our eight-thirty seminar this morning."

Linda hugged herself as if she were cold. "I'm worried about him," she said. "The news about Kellee is going to devastate him."

Jumbo frowned. "Well, at least he's got nothing to feel guilty about. That night at the Owl when Kellee left, he was the only one who – "

Linda touched his arm, as if to hold him back.

Jumbo turned to her, perplexed. "Val tried to do the right thing. Why shouldn't I talk about it?"

Linda started to respond, but I cut her off. "Jumbo, what did Val do that night?"

"When Kellee left the bar, he went after her. I guess he knew she was in no shape to be out there alone."

"Why didn't he stay with her?"

Jumbo shrugged. "I don't know. I didn't see him again that night. Neither did anybody else. He never came back."

After Jumbo and Linda left, I went down to the library. The silent rows of books and journals were balm to my raw nerves. It was a relief to have concrete proof that ultimately all information and speculation can be catalogued neatly by the Library of Congress. By the time I got back to my office, the late-afternoon sun was pouring through my window. I put on my coat and packed up my books, then I caught sight of the telephone and decided to give Val's number one last try.

The voice that answered was male and as wintry as a Prairie January.

"I'm trying to get in touch with Val Massey," I said.

"He's not here."

"You're not Mr. Masluk, are you?"

"I'm the neighbour."

"Do you know when the Masluks are expected back? This really is important. I'm one of Val's teachers at the university, and there's something I have to talk to him about."

"They're at the hospital."

"What?"

The voice was kinder now, patient in the way of someone giving road directions. "Herman had to take young Val into the General this morning. I don't want to say any more than that. It's not my business."

"Is Val all right?"

"He's gonna be, but he gave everybody a scare. Now, I think you'd better save the rest of your questions for Herman or for Val when he's able."

I called Regina General and asked for Val's room number. The operator told me it was 517F – the psychiatric unit. The nurse at the charge desk told me that Val wasn't allowed visitors yet, but that his father was putting together a short list of people who could see Val the next day.

When I turned the Volvo onto the parkway, I was deep in the puzzle of Val Massey's connection with Kellee's death. I didn't see the city bus until it was almost upon me. I hit the brake, and the bus sped on. As it passed me, I saw Tom Kelsoe's picture on its side panel. He was wearing his stressed-leather jacket, his black hair was tousled, and his eyes burned with integrity. Under the photo, in block letters, was the word "KELSOE!" Then, in smaller letters, "Saturdays at 6:00, only on Nationtv." There were no pictures of Glayne Axtell or Senator Sam Spiegel. Just of Tom. He'd moved quickly. As I pulled up in front of our house, I knew it was time that I moved quickly, too.

When I walked into the living room, Taylor was kneeling at the coffee table drawing and Angus and Leah were sitting on the rug, drinking tea and playing Monopoly. Angus was in the middle of his usual Monopoly cash-flow problem, and he waved at me absently. "There's a message from Constable somebody-or-other, but it's nothing to worry about. You're just supposed to give her a call. Her number's on your desk."

Marissa Desjardin sounded weary. "There are no surprises in the pathology report," she said. "Death due to a combination of acute alcohol poisoning and exposure. In other words, Kellee Savage drank enough to shut down her major systems, and the weather did the rest."

I thought of the wicked storm we'd had on the night of March 17. It made sense and yet . . . "Constable Desjardin, if Kellee was that drunk, how did she get so far?"

"That occurred to us too, and we're looking into it. The most likely explanation is that once Kellee hit the highway, somebody picked her up and gave her a lift. I'll bet whoever picked her up regretted it. They'd probably have to fumigate their car. Even after two weeks in the open air, her clothes smelled like a brewery."

Something about what she said nagged at me. "You mean Kellee's clothes smelled of beer?"

"They were soaked in it. There was an empty beer bottle beside her when they found her, and a full bottle in her book bag. Do you have any other questions?"

"No," I said. "Thanks. That's all I needed to know."

As soon as I hung up, I realized why Marissa Desjardin's reference to the smell on Kellee's clothes had nagged at me. When Linda Van Sickle described Kellee's drinking that night, she said she'd been struck by the fact that Kellee had been drinking Scotch. The beer-soaked clothes were another puzzle piece that just didn't fit. I was more anxious than ever to talk to Val Massey.

It was close to 8:30 when I finally got through to Herman Masluk, and he was ready for me. It seemed that during his time at the hospital, Herman had figured out that the blame for everything that had gone wrong with his son could be laid on the doorstep of the university, and that night the closest he could get to the university was me.

Between the accusations and the invective, a few facts emerged. Sometime during the previous night, Val had tried to commit suicide. Herman Masluk had found his son parked in an old garage they sometimes used for storing vehicles. The door to the garage had been closed, and the motor of Val's Honda Civic had been running. Val had attached a length of hose to the exhaust and run it through the window on the passenger side into the car's interior. Mr. Masluk had been out looking for his son all night. It was just good luck that he noticed that the door to the garage hadn't been closed properly.

The ferocity of Herman Masluk's anger rocked me; so did the depth of his love for Val. It was apparent from what he said that he felt he'd been engaged in a battle for Val's soul. The university and all it stood for was anathema to this man who had worked for a lifetime to give his son a profitable business. Val's suicide attempt had terrified his father, but it had been proof that he was right, that nothing but trouble came from those alien buildings on the plain.

As he talked about Val, I found myself warming to Herman Masluk, and when it seemed his tirade had run its course, I told him about my daughter, Mieka, and the struggle we'd had when she decided to quit university. He listened intently, and soon the two of us moved into a discussion of that age-old topic: the struggle between a parent's experience and a child's hope. I told him that when I felt I was floundering with our kids, I'd often found my bearings by remembering C.P. Snow's line that the love between a parent and a child is the only love that must grow towards separation. He was silent for a moment, then he asked me to write out what I'd just said and bring it along with me to the hospital when I visited Val. Before he said goodbye, Herman Masluk told me that Val had never known his own mother, and that maybe what his son needed was a lady's perspective. I told him I'd do my best.

After I hung up, I dialled Ed Mariani's number. I knew Ed would want to know about Val; more selfishly, I welcomed any excuse that would allow me to get my relationship with him back on solid ground. There was no answer at Ed and Barry's, but I left a message on the machine, thanking them both for the paella dish and telling Ed I'd be in touch.

By the time I got to Taylor's room to tuck her in, she'd fallen asleep. In the crook of her right arm was the Marc Chagall book; in the crook of her left arm was Benny. When I reached down to move the book, he shot me a look filled with reproach.

"I've learned to live with your displeasure, Benny," I whispered, and I turned out the light and went downstairs. I made myself a pot of tea and put Wynton Marsalis's recording of Haydn's Concerto for Trumpet and Orchestra in E-flat Major on the CD player. I had plans to make, and I needed an infusion of clarity. As they did surprisingly often, Haydn and Marsalis did their stuff, and by the time I went to bed, I had the next day pretty well mapped out. The last thing I did before I turned out the light was drop Tom Kelsoe's book, *Getting Even*, into my bag.

If I had believed in omens, I would have found plenty to reassure me in the weather on Saturday morning. The sky was blue, the sun was bright, and I could feel the possibilities of birdsong and wildflowers in the air. Even the house on Dahl Street looked less grim.

As it had been on Tuesday, the front door was propped open with a brick, but this time when I pounded on the inside door, a girl about Taylor's age opened it and let me in. Flushed with good luck, I ran upstairs and knocked on the door to number 3. A good-looking native kid with a brushcut answered, and as he gave me the once-over, I was able to look past his shoulder and get a glimpse of life in apartment 3 on a Saturday morning. The television was blaring cartoons, and a boy, who judging from his looks was the older brother of the boy who had answered the door, was sitting on the couch. Beside him was the woman I had frightened so badly when I'd come in unannounced on Tuesday. Today, she had a pink ribbon tying back her long dark hair, and, as I watched, the boy reached up and smoothed it with a gesture of such tenderness that I felt my throat catch.

Across the room was the blonde who'd thrown me out. Today she was in blue jeans, a denim jacket, and her Nancy Sinatra boots. She was wholly engrossed in the television. Apparently, she'd been expecting a delivery, because when I came in, she gestured towards the door without looking up. "My purse is on the table, Darrel," she said. "Give the kid a nice tip."

"It's somebody else," Darrel said. As soon as she heard his words, the blonde woman's head swivelled towards me. She might have looked like a superannuated superstar Barbie, but she moved like the wind. Within seconds, she was so close to me that our noses were almost touching. "Teacher," she said in a voice heavy with exasperation. "This is Saturday. No school today. Go home."

I stood my ground. "I want you to listen to something," I said. "If you decide you don't want to hear what I'm saying, stop me. I'll leave and, I promise you, I won't bother you again."

Without waiting for her answer, I pulled *Getting Even* out of my purse and started to read the story of Karen Keewatin and her sons. I didn't get far before the blonde reached out and took the book from me.

"Let's go out in the hall," she said. "My name's Bernice Jacobs, and you and I got things to talk about."

Half an hour later, I was back on the sidewalk outside the apartment on Dahl Street. I was edgy but exhilarated; Bernice Jacobs had not only confirmed my theory about what had happened to Kellee Savage, she'd come up with some theories of her own.

When I saw the little girl who'd let me into the building throwing a ball against the side wall of the apartment, I called out and thanked her. What I had learned from Bernice Jacobs was terrible, but knowledge is a sturdier weapon than ignorance, and I was grateful I didn't have to go into the battle ahead unarmed.

I was halfway down the block when I heard the kitten's thin mewing. I almost kept walking. Taylor was the cat person in our family, and I had enough on my plate. But the image of the kerosene-soaked animal I'd seen the first time I'd come to Dahl Street was a powerful spur. I turned and retraced my steps.

The little tortoise-shell had crawled in between two garbage cans in the alley beside the apartment building where Bernice lived. When I moved one of the cans to get a closer look, the kitten struggled to get away. It didn't get very far. It was dragging its right front leg and, as I watched, it collapsed from the effort. I went back to my car and got the blanket we kept in the trunk in case we got stuck in a blizzard. After I'd wrapped the cat up, I went back to the building on Dahl Street. The little girl was still throwing her ball against the side wall. I could hear her voice, sing-songing through the same ball chant I'd used forty years earlier: "Ordinary, moving, laughing, talking, one hand, the other hand, one foot, the other foot." When she dropped the ball just before "clap in the front," I made my move. I pulled the blanket back so she could see the kitten's face.

"Do you know who this belongs to?" I asked.

She glanced at it without interest. "It don't belong to nobody."

"Are you sure?"

She sighed heavily. "It lives on the street," she said, and she turned away and threw her ball against the wall. "Ordinary, moving . . . ," she began. I covered the cat again and headed for the Volvo. It was 10:30; our vet stayed open till noon on Saturday mornings.

Dr. Roy Crawford had been our vet for more than twenty-five years. He was a gentle, unflappable man, but he winced when he looked at the cat I'd brought in.

"Can you do anything?" I asked.

He looked at me hard. "It depends."

"On what?"

"On whether this animal has a home to go to when I'm finished. That leg's going to need surgery. There's no point operating on this animal if it's going to be euthanized in a couple of weeks. Your decision, Mrs. K."

"It'll have a home," I said.

He raised an eyebrow. "With you?"

"Where else?" I said. "Incidentally, is it a male or a female?"

Roy Crawford leaned over and checked out the cat's equipment. "Male," he said. Then he smiled. "There's going to be hell to pay when Benny has to abdicate the throne."

"Benny won't abdicate," I said. "He believes he's there by divine right. But he is going to have to learn to share the crown."

By the time I'd signed the papers at Roy's, it was past 11:00. Herman Masluk had said that since the only two names on Val's visitors' list were his and mine, I could go to the hospital whenever it suited me. Eleven o'clock seemed as good a time as any.

I parked in the lot beside the General, made my way past the inevitable cluster of patients and practitioners huddled around the doorway smoking, and headed for the elevators. When I stepped out on the fifth floor, I was facing a desk and a nurse who looked like a defensive lineman. He had a lineman's professional warmth, too, but when I'd finally satisfied him that my name was on his list, he looked almost cordial. "Can't be too careful," he growled.

"You're telling me," I said, and I walked down the hall towards room 517.

It surprised me that Val was in his bed. At first, I thought he must be sleeping, but when I called his name, he turned. Then, reminding me of just how young twenty-one really is, he dived under the pillow.

I pulled a chair up and sat by the side of the bed. "We have to talk, Val," I said, "but I can wait till you're ready."

Waiting for Val to decide when to face the inevitable gave me far more time than I needed to check out his room. It was small and relentlessly functional; the only non-institutional touch was a soothing landscape of a pastel boat in which no one would ever sit, drifting serenely on a pastel lake which no ripple would ever disturb. Prozac art.

I'd just begun to wonder if I'd erred in letting Val take the initiative when he sat up, swung his legs over the side of the bed, and faced me. He was wearing a blue-striped hospital gown that seemed designed to strip the wearer of dignity, but Val managed to give even that shapeless garment a certain style.

"It's my fault she's dead," he said, and there was an edge of hysteria in his voice that frightened me. "I didn't mean for any of it to happen, but she's still dead, isn't she?" His face crumpled, and he buried it in his hands.

I reached out and touched his shoulder. "Yes," I said, "Kellee's dead. But, Val, if you can tell me what really happened between you and her, I think we can get at the truth."

"And the truth will set me free," he said bitterly.

"No," I said, "you'll never be free of this. But the truth might help you put what you did into perspective. Start at the beginning."

"You know the beginning," he said. "She was telling lies about . . ."

"About Tom Kelsoe," I said.

Val sighed with relief. "I'm so glad he finally decided to talk to somebody about it. Tom always puts other people first. Even when Kellee was trying to destroy him, he protected her. The night he called and told me that she was accusing him of sexual harassment, I said he should go to Professor Gallagher. But you know Tom. All he thinks about is his students. He said that Professor Gallagher would have to expel Kellee, and he didn't want that." Val's voice was filled with the fervour of the acolyte. "But Tom said that for Kellee's own good she had to learn that a journalist's reputation for truth must be beyond reproach."

"So he got you to put Kellee in a position where everyone would believe she was lying."

Val leapt up from the bed and began pacing. "She was lying about him. Can you imagine anybody lying about a man like Tom Kelsoe? You were at his book launch. You heard what he wrote about Karen Keewatin and her sons.

That's the kind of journalist he is. He sees the dignity in every one, and Kellee was going to destroy him." Val's voice broke with emotion. "All I was trying to do was protect the finest man I've ever known, but everything went wrong."

He was close to the edge, but I had to keep pushing. "Val, what happened at the Owl that night?"

He came back and sat on the bed. "It all happened so fast. I'd been over at Tom's office, so I was late getting to the Owl. When she saw me, Kellee went crazy. Somehow she'd figured out why I'd been . . . bothering her. She was very drunk and very hostile. She said she couldn't trust anybody at the university, so she was going to the media. She started hitting me, and then somebody – I think it was Meaghan Andrechuk – said Kellee had her tape-recorder going. By that time a lot of people had had too much to drink and there was a kind of scene. Then we heard that they'd just announced on TV that Reed Gallagher was dead. Kellee was standing in front of me. It was awful. All the blood just went out of her face. At first, I thought she was going to pass out, but she just grabbed her bag and left."

"Did she take any beer with her?"

Val looked at me curiously. "Beer? No. Why? Did somebody say she had?"

"No," I said. "I'm sorry. Go on."

"There's not much more to tell. I went after Kellee. She was over the edge. I was afraid she really was going to go to the media. When I got outside, I saw that she was walking in the direction of the J school, so I followed her." Val shook his head. "I watched until she went inside. Believe it or not, I thought the worst was over. I figured she'd just go into the cafeteria and drink coffee until she'd sobered up."

"And that was the last you saw of her."

"Yes, I was pretty much out of the party mood by then, so I just drove home."

"And people saw you there?"

"Friday's my Father's poker night. All the real men in town were sitting in his living room drinking rye and smoking Player's. I sat in the game until three in the morning."

"But you didn't go to bed after that, did you? You went back to the campus to make sure there was nothing on Reed Gallagher's computer that would incriminate Tom Kelsoe."

"Tom phoned me at home. He laid the situation out for me. No one knew what Kellee Savage had told Professor Gallagher. And now that he was dead, there was no way we could explain the truth to him. Tom said the last thing Professor Gallagher would have wanted to leave behind was a legacy of lies." Val raked his hands through his hair. "Dr. Kilbourn, I know it's hard to understand the vandalism, but Tom said that this was a case of doing the wrong deed for the right reason."

"And that made sense to you?"

"Yes," he said. "It did. I really screwed up, didn't I?"

"I guess the important thing right now is that you don't compound the error. Val, you do know that what you tried to do Thursday night didn't make anything better. You're not going to try that particular exit again, are you?"

He blushed. "No, that was stupid."

"Good, because you've got a great life ahead of you."

"Yeah, right."

I took his hand. "I am right, Val. Check it out. After I go, why don't you ask the nurse if you can take a little walk around the hospital. Try to find one person in this whole place who has as much going for him as you do."

I opened my purse, took out the paper with the C.P. Snow quote, and handed it to him. "Your father asked me to bring this for him," I said. "You can read it if you like."

He unfolded the paper. "'The love between parent and child is the only love that must grow towards separation.'"

Val looked at me uncomprehendingly. "Why would my father want this?"

I squeezed his hand. "Maybe because he knows you're not the only one who screwed things up."

Jill's plane wasn't coming in till 4:30, so after lunch I took Taylor and her friend Jess over to the Marina for ice cream. It was a bright, windy day, and on the lawn in front of the museum, people were flying kites. After the kids and I got our ice cream, we took it back to the museum lawn, found a bench in the sunshine, and gave ourselves over to the pleasures of banana splits and watching a sky splashed with diamonds as brilliantly hued as the colours in Taylor's first paint box. All in all, it was a four-star afternoon, and by the time I dropped the kids off at Jess's house I knew that, as difficult as it was going to be to tell Jill what I'd learned in the last forty-eight hours, I was ready to talk.

The problem was that Jill wasn't there to listen. My nerves were taut as I watched the passengers from the Toronto flight file into the reception area at the airport. A lot of travellers got off the plane, but I didn't spot Jill. My first thought was that, because she wasn't expecting me to pick her up, I'd simply missed her. I went over to the luggage carousel and watched as passengers grabbed their bags and headed for home. When the last bag was taken, I watched the carousel make its final revolution, then I went to the bank of phones by the doorway, dialled Nationtv, and asked for Rapti Lustig.

Rapti sounded tense, too, but it was only an hour and a half to airtime, so I wasn't surprised.

"I know you've got a million things to do," I said, "so I won't keep you, but I'm at the airport. I thought you said Jill was coming in from Toronto this afternoon. Did I get my wires crossed?"

There was a three-beat pause, then Rapti said, "Somebody's got their wires crossed. Jill called this morning to tell me I'd have to produce the show tonight because she was delayed. We talked for ages, trying to cover all the bases. As soon as I hung up, I realized I'd forgotten to ask her what she wanted to go with as a lead-in. I tried the hotel we all use when we're in Toronto, but she wasn't registered. Then I called our Toronto office. They didn't know anything about it, Jo. As far as they knew, Jill hadn't been in the city at all this week."

"Then where is she?"

"Your guess is as good as mine."

As I hung up, I felt the first stirrings of panic. I tried to tell myself I was overreacting. Rapti had talked to Jill that morning, and she'd been all right then. Obviously, there'd just been some sort of misunderstanding. Nonetheless, as I left the terminal, I was uneasy.

I was so preoccupied that I walked right by Ed Mariani. He called after me, and when I turned, I saw that he was carrying an overnight bag and was dressed for travel. I also saw that I'd hurt him.

"If you'd rather just keep on going, you can forget you saw me," he said. "But I did want you to know how pleased I was to hear your voice on the message-minder last night. I'm glad you liked our gift."

"I don't want to forget I saw you, Ed," I said. "It's just that I have a lot on my mind."

He put down his bag and came over to me. "Is something wrong?"

"I hope not," I said. "But there are some things I'd like to talk to you about. Do you have time for a drink before your plane?"

Ed shook his head. "As usual, I've left arriving at the airport till almost the last moment. But if it's an emergency, I can change my plans."

His generosity brought tears to my eyes. "Ed, I'm sorry if I've been cool to you lately."

I could see the relief on his face. "Don't give it a second thought. I know I can be a bit overwhelming in close quarters."

"It wasn't that. It had to do with Tom Kelsoe."

Ed's eyes were wary. "What about him?"

"I saw you with him in the Faculty Club on Tuesday. It was just after I'd told you that I suspected him of abusing Jill."

"And you thought I was warning him about your suspicions."

"Ed, what were you talking to him about?"

Ed picked up his bag. "I don't want to lie to you," he said.

"Then tell me the truth. I'm going around in circles here. First Reed, then Kellee, now Jill . . ."

He took a step towards me. "Jill! Nothing's happened to her, has it?"

"No, she's fine. It's just that Tom Kelsoe is the man in her life, and suddenly everything about Tom scares me."

"It should," Ed said quietly. "Tom Kelsoe is a violent man. That's what I was talking to him about at the Faculty Club when you saw us. After what you'd told me, I had to make certain that Jill really had been mugged."

At first, the implication of what he'd said didn't hit me. When it did, my knees turned to water. "What did Tom say?"

"He was very forthcoming. He gave me all the details of the mugging. Then he told me to call Jill and ask her myself."

"And you did?"

Ed nodded. "She gave me the same account, thanked me for my concern, and told me, very politely, to mind my own business."

"And that was the end of it?"

"Yes." Ed looked at his watch. "Joanne, I really do have to get in there. My flight is boarding."

I stepped in front of him. "Ed, what made you think Tom Kelsoe was capable of violence?"

I could see he wanted to bolt, but he stayed his ground. Then, unexpectedly, he smiled. "I guess the confessional moment has come. As it inevitably does." He took a deep breath. "Okay, here it is. Last year, Barry and I were having troubles: my mid-life crisis, I guess. I started cruising again, looking for younger men." Ed looked straight into my eyes. "I'm deeply ashamed of what I did, Joanne. It was stupid and dangerous and a terrible betrayal of Barry. Of course, this being Regina, my sin did not go undetected. Nationtv was doing an investigation of male prostitution in the downtown area, and I, apparently, stumbled into camera range. When Jill saw the tape, she killed it; she also phoned me and told me . . ." He winced at the memory. "She told me that I had a good career at the university, and a great relationship with Barry, and I 'should smarten the fuck up.'"

"But you didn't."

"No, I didn't. I don't know if you've ever been close to someone who's decided to self-destruct, but our instincts to be obtuse are quite breathtaking."

"So you kept on."

"Yes, I kept on, and this time it was Tom Kelsoe who saw me on Rose Street, cruising." Ed chewed his lower lip. "Tom didn't have Jill's scruples about protecting me from myself."

"And that's why you withdrew your name from the competition for head of the J school."

"And why I shook that bastard's hand the night of his book launch. I couldn't risk him telling Barry."

I was confused. "Ed, I'm missing something here. What's the connection between Tom blackmailing you and what you said about him being violent. Did he threaten you physically?"

Ed shook his head. "No. That's not where he gets his pleasure. Jo, during my walk on the wild side last year, I heard a few things, too. Tom Kelsoe is pretty well known to the prostitutes downtown."

"Male prostitutes?"

Ed smiled sadly. "No, at least we've been spared Tom Kelsoe. As they say on 'Seinfeld,' he doesn't play for our team. Tom's a red-blooded heterosexual, but I don't think that gives women much to celebrate. Rumour has it that he's into some pretty brutal sex."

My mind was racing, but I had to acknowledge Ed's trust. "Thanks for telling me," I said. "I know it wasn't easy."

"You were the easy one, Jo. In two hours, Barry's going to meet me at the Minneapolis airport. We've got tickets for *Turandot*. It's an anniversary celebration. We've been together eight years today. I hope after I tell him, we'll still have something to celebrate."

I leaned forward and kissed his cheek. "You will," I said.

I watched as Ed Mariani plodded heavily towards the terminal. When he reached the door, he turned back. "I'll call you from Minneapolis," he said. "In the meantime, tell Jill to be careful."

"I will," I said.

Fifteen minutes later, I pulled up in front of Jill's apartment on Robinson Street. There was a moving van parked outside, and as I ran up the front steps I almost collided with a burly young man who was carrying out a love seat. "Hope you get there," he yelled after me as I pushed past him and entered the building.

By the time I got to Jill's apartment on the third floor, the adrenaline was pumping. I was prepared, if necessary, to smash the door in, but Jill surprised me by answering after my first knock. She was wearing a jacket and dark glasses, and she'd tied a scarf around her head. She'd covered as much of herself as she could, but I could still see the bruises. Without a word, I reached over and lifted her dark glasses. One of her eyes was almost swollen shut, and the bruise under the other one was fresh. But there were other marks too: bruises that had faded and cuts that were healing.

"How long has Tom been beating you up, Jill?" I said.

Her voice was surprisingly strong. "Too long," she said. "But it's over. You'll notice that I'm dressed and on my way out."

"Are you going to the police?"

"Eventually," she said. "But first, I've got a television program to produce." She looked at her watch. "Twenty minutes to air."

I put my arm around her shoulder. "You'll make it," I said. "You always do."

CHAPTER

14

Tom Kelsoe had taken Jill's car, so we drove over to Nationtv in the Volvo. When I saw the pain on Jill's face as she climbed into the passenger seat, I was filled with rage. But anger had to wait. During the ten-minute drive to the studio, I told Jill everything. She listened in silence, but near the end of my account, when we stopped for a light, she pulled the cellular phone out of her briefcase and made a call.

"Rapti," she said. "It's me. I'm fine. Yes, Jo did find me. We haven't got much time, so you're going to have to take this one on faith. I want you to tell Sam and Glayne that we're changing the lead story tonight to a discussion of journalistic ethics. They're both pretty quick on the uptake, so they'll be okay with the change."

Jill paused. Rapti had asked her the obvious question. When she answered, Jill's voice was steely. "No," she said, "Tom isn't to know anything about this till we're on the air. You'll have to fill Toronto in on the change of focus, and you'll have to fax Cam a new intro: something about how journalists who use composite characters in their stories are violating the audience's trust. You'd better define what we mean by

'composite characters.' Nothing too technical – just something like 'composite characters are what you get when some
journalist who doesn't know his dick from a dildo rolls three
or four people together and presents the new creation as a
living, breathing human being.' Throw in the Janet Cooke
case. You remember that one from J school, don't you?"

As soon as Jill mentioned Janet Cooke's name, another
piece in the puzzle fell into place. An article about the Janet
Cooke case had been on Kellee Savage's bookshelf in Indian
Head. Cooke was a young journalist who had worked for the
Washington *Post* in 1981. She won a Pulitzer for a story
about child heroin addiction, but had to give the prize back
when her paper learned that Jimmy, the eight-year-old addict
Cooke had written about with such passion, didn't exist.
The story must have had a particular resonance for Kellee
after she discovered that Karen Keewatin, the heartbreakingly determined hooker and mother in *Getting Even*, didn't
exist, and that, like Janet Cooke, Tom Kelsoe had used the
lives and stories of a handful of people to create a character
who would tear at the reader's heartstrings and advance his
journalistic career.

That morning, when Bernice Jacobs began leafing through
my copy of *Getting Even*, it hadn't taken her long to figure
out that she was holding concrete proof that the story Kellee
Savage had been putting together when she died was true.
The tragedy of Bernice's friend, Audrey Nighttraveller, a
woman who'd been so severely beaten by a john that she was
incapable of caring for herself, had simply been material for
Tom Kelsoe. He had used Audrey's life and the life of her
sons as he had used the lives of countless unknown women
and their families to create a book that would enhance his
reputation. What he had done was, in Bernice Jacobs's words,
"worse than the worst thing the worst bloodsucker of a
pimp ever did to any of us."

And Kellee Savage was going to expose him. I thought of the Post-it notes in the journals stacked on the shelf in the barricaded office in Indian Head. Each one of them had signalled an article on a reporter's use of a composite character. Dogged to the end, Kellee Savage had been preparing the foundations for her story. Now it was up to Jill and me.

It was Saturday, so I didn't have any problem finding a parking place outside Nationtv. Kellee's graduation portrait was in its Safeway bag on the dashboard. After I'd helped Jill unsnap her seatbelt, I handed the picture to her. "This is Kellee Savage, the student who discovered what Tom did," I said.

Jill took the picture from me. "How old was she?"

"Twenty-one."

"Let's take this with us," she said. "I want him to see it."

Jill shook me off when I offered to help her get out of the car. She said she could do it on her own, but as she began her methodical, agony-filled ascent of the stairs outside Nationtv, I had to look away. I had watched her bound up those steps a hundred times; she had always seemed invincible.

Nationtv was deserted. Jill used her security card to get us in, and we didn't see a soul as we headed across the cavernous lobby. When we got to the elevator, Jill checked her watch and turned to me. "We have five minutes," she said. "I'm going to go to the control room. You'd better stay out of the way till we're on the air."

"But you *are* going to call the police, aren't you?"

"Of course I am, but not until every viewer who tunes in tonight has a chance to watch that bastard twist in the wind. Jo, if we hand Tom over to the police right now, the story will be page one here, but I have to make sure that what he did ends up on the front page of every newspaper in this country. I owe it to Reed , and I owe it to Kellee Savage."

"I'll wait in the green room," I said. "I can watch the show from the monitor in there."

"When it looks like the time's right, come into the studio," Jill said. "If you sit on that riser behind the cameras, he'll have to look at you. Be sure to bring the picture." She ran her fingers through her hair. It was a gesture she often made when she was on edge, but this time, as she touched the back of her skull, she winced. "Sonofabitch," she said softly.

I put my arm around her shoulder. "When the show's over, let's find ourselves a bottle of Glenfiddich and crawl in."

Jill gave me a grim smile. "Promises, promises." She pushed the elevator button, and we stepped in. "Let's go," she said. "It's showtime."

At some point within the past twenty-four hours, there had been a birthday party in the green room. Soggy paper plates, dirty coffee cups, and used plastic wine glasses littered the end tables and window sills, and on the coffee table in the middle of the room a big cardboard box leaked crumbs from the remains of a bakery birthday cake. I removed a plate full of half-eaten angelfood from the chair nearest the monitor and sat down.

The screen was already picking up images of the members of the political panel, taking their places, smoothing their clothes, adjusting their earpieces. Tonight, Glayne and Sam were both in Ottawa. Behind them I could see the shot of the Peace Tower Nationtv always used for its Ottawa segments. Usually, in the minutes leading up to airtime, there was laughter and nervous kibitzing, but tonight Glayne and Sam were all business. They might not have known exactly what was coming, but their tense silence was evidence that they foresaw trouble.

When Tom Kelsoe's face appeared on the screen, my pulse quickened. His microphone was turned on, and I could hear him chewing out the young woman who'd attached it to his jacket. She'd apparently caught the leather in the mike clip and he was berating her for her carelessness. The second hand of the clock on the wall behind the monitor was sweeping; in sixty seconds, the state of his leather jacket would be the least of Tom's worries. The young woman disappeared from the shot. Tom settled in his chair, caught his likeness in one of the monitors, and assumed his public face. "Canada Tonight" was on the air.

The host of the show, Cameron McFee, was an unflappable Scot with an easy manner and a ready wit that made him a natural for live television. He couldn't have had time to do much more than glance through the new introduction, but he read Rapti's lines about the immorality of journalists who pass hybrids off as truth with real conviction.

Until Cam began to describe the Janet Cooke case, Tom looked alert but not alarmed. However, when Cam started to give details about how Janet Cooke had entrapped herself with her lies, Tom's chest began to rise and fall rapidly, and sweat appeared on his upper lip. As the awareness hit him that Cam's homily about unethical journalists was a prelude to real trouble, I could see the panic rise sharply. Attentive as a lover, the camera moved in for a tight shot of Tom's face, found the desperation in his eyes, and moved closer.

At that moment, I could think of few activities more rewarding than watching Tom Kelsoe's persona crumble, but I had a part to play too. I picked up Kellee's photograph and started towards the studio. There were no police in the corridor, and I felt a tingling of apprehension. From what I'd seen on the monitor, Tom was close to the edge, and I would have welcomed the presence of some officers in blue. When I walked into the studio, Troy Prigotzke, a member of the crew on "Canada Tonight," was standing in the shadows near the door.

I moved close enough to him so I didn't have to raise my voice. "Troy, did anyone tell you that the police are supposed to show up here tonight?"

"Rapti did," he said. "That's why I'm here, but she didn't elaborate. She just told me that it was Jill's call, and that, when the cops arrived, I should make sure they got in."

"Well, as long as you're watching . . . ," I said, and I started towards the riser.

"Jo!" Troy's whisper was insistent, and I turned. "All the outside doors to the lobby are locked," he said. "Nobody can get in without a security card. Did Jill send somebody to let the cops in?"

"I don't know," I said.

"I'd better get up there and check," Troy said.

I went to the riser and sat down. When he saw me, Tom was in mid-sentence, but the sight of me seemed to derail his train of thought. He stumbled through a few more words, then fell silent. Our eyes locked. I pulled Kellee's photograph out of the Safeway bag. Then I leaned forward and held it out to him.

I'd expected that the sight of his victim's face would rock Tom. It demolished him. The photograph seemed to shatter whatever vestiges of ego were keeping him in front of the camera. I wasn't ready for what happened next. He bolted out of his chair and started to run off the set. In a moment straight out of a sitcom, the wire on the lapel mike Tom was still wearing jerked him back. He ripped it off, then darted past me towards the door that led out of the studio. My most fervent hope was that he would collide with Troy and the Regina City Police, but I couldn't take that chance.

I was on my feet in a split-second. By the time I got out of the studio, Tom had already made it past the green room and was heading towards the stairs. He spotted the two uni-formed police officers emerging from the stairwell before they caught sight of him. It took the police a moment to get their bearings, and by then Tom had doubled back and was running towards me. When he turned left at the corridor that led to the elevators, I was right behind him. So were the police and so was Troy Prigotzke. As I ran, I could hear their shouts and their footfalls behind me. On the wall facing us at the end of the hall was the same poster that I had seen the day before on the side of the city bus. Tom's likeness, poised, ironic, eyes burning with integrity, hovered over us all as we raced along. I caught up with him in front of the elevators. As he reached over to punch the button, I jumped in front of him. "Oh no, you don't," I said. "You're not going anywhere."

My intention was simply to block his way until Troy and the police reached us, but events spun out of control. It happened in a flash. I heard the mechanical groan of the elevator approaching; I felt the doors open behind me; then Tom Kelsoe pounded his outstretched hand against my collarbone and shoved me into the elevator. The police got there just as the doors were closing. My grandmother would have said they made it just after the nick of time. As the elevator started its ascent, Tom Kelsoe took a step towards me. He was panting with exertion, filling the small space with the smells of leather and fear.

I was breathing hard too. "Don't make it any worse for yourself," I said. "There are police all over this building."

Tom laughed and punched the stop button on the panel beside the doors. The elevator lurched to a halt. "There are no cops in here," he said.

For the first time since I'd fled the studio, I was afraid. I ran through my options. There weren't many. For a woman of fifty, I was in good shape, but Tom Kelsoe was forty, and he had spent a lot more hours in the gym than I had. In the close confines of an elevator, I wouldn't have a chance against him. I couldn't even appeal to Tom's highly developed sense of self-interest. He had already killed twice. He had nothing to lose by battering me. All I had going for me was the possibility that, like all egotists, Tom would be unable to resist the chance to tell his tale.

I tried to keep my voice steady. "I've always told my kids there are two sides to every story," I said. "Maybe it's time I got your perspective on everything that's happened."

His fist seemed to come out of nowhere. I jumped aside, and the punch he'd aimed at me landed on the elevator wall. The pain goaded him. He pulled his fist back and struck again. This time, he connected. My head snapped back, and my nose gushed blood. I cried out. As soon as he saw that he'd hurt me, Tom Kelsoe was transformed. The fear and confusion went out of his face. He looked like a man who had come to himself. "Don't patronize me, bitch," he said. "And don't you ever underestimate me."

"Is that what Reed Gallagher did?" I asked, and my voice sounded small and beseeching.

"He thought I needed help," Tom said, spitting out the word *help* as if it were unclean. "But Reed Gallagher was the one who was weak. When Kellee Savage came to him with her accusations, he should have thrown her out of his office. If he'd shown some balls then, the problem would have solved itself. But Reed said he had 'an obligation to the truth.'" Tom shook his head in wonder. "The truth. As if anybody gives a rat's ass about the truth any more. I tried to tell Reed that nobody cared if the characters in the book were composites. All people wanted was a chance to get their rocks off reading about a whore with a heart of gold. And they sure as hell didn't care if I used Kellee's interviews to give them their little catharsis."

I could taste the blood in the back of my mouth. I swallowed. If I didn't want to get hit again, I had to keep Tom talking. "But Reed didn't see it that way," I said.

"No," Tom said. "Reed didn't see it that way. Kellee Savage was useless, a total waste of skin, but Reed decided she needed an advocate. That's how I got him to come to Scarth Street that night. I told him I'd had a change of heart, that I was ready to accept the conditions he and that little toad had decided upon."

"What did they want?" I asked.

"Not much at all," he said bitterly. "Just a public admission that Karen Keewatin was a created character and that Kellee Savage had been an invaluable colleague in researching the book. Can you conceive of anybody obtuse enough to cave in to those conditions?"

Thinking the question was rhetorical, I remained silent, but silence seemed to be the wrong response. Tom took a step towards me. "Well?" he said.

"No," I said meekly, "I can't imagine anybody that obtuse."

Tom punched the air with his forefinger in a gesture of approbation. "Right," he said. "I know you've got a somewhat negative opinion of me, Joanne, but even you will have to admit that I'm not stupid."

"No," I said, "you're not stupid."

"Well, apparently Reed lost sight of the fact. When I told him I'd decided to apologize publicly for what I'd done, he fell for it. In fact, he was *thrilled*. He said that he knew all along that I'd do the right thing, and that he'd stand by me and help me salvage my career. As if there would have been any career left to salvage after I'd gone through that charade." Tom's eyes burned into me. "He didn't leave me any choice. I didn't enjoy what I had to do, but it had to be done."

My head was pounding. I thought of Reed Gallagher telling Julie that his greatest dream was to grow old with her. The words seemed to form themselves. "Why did you have to humiliate him like that?" I asked. "Why couldn't you just kill him?"

Tom looked at me incredulously. "Because I had a plan," he barked. "What the police found when they walked into that room on Scarth Street was a scene perfectly calibrated to divert their attention away from all the questions I didn't want asked."

"But Kellee would have asked the right questions."

Tom's tone was almost dreamy. "She would have, and from the moment I heard that they'd found Reed's body, I knew she'd be a problem. That's why I was in my office that night – trying to come up with a solution. I hadn't thought of a thing, then that stupid cow just came lumbering in." As he remembered the night of March 17, it was apparent that Tom's focus had drifted from the present. Wherever he was, he wasn't in the elevator with me. I calculated the distance between me and the panel beside the doors. The buttons that would restart the elevator were seductively near. I moved closer.

"What did Kellee want?" I asked.

"Justice," Tom said in a mockingly declamatory voice. "Revenge. Who the fuck knows? She was drunk, and she was half out of her mind because she'd just heard about Reed. It was so easy. There were some cases of beer in the Journalism lounge. I offered to get us a couple of bottles to drink while we talked things over. When Reed and I had had our meeting on Scarth Street, I'd added some secobarbital to the Dewar's I'd brought for him to sip while we discussed my rehabilitation. There was enough left over to make Kellee's beer a real powerhouse. It hit her like a bag of hammers. She started to cry. Then she asked me to take her home."

I backed along the wall of the elevator till the panel of buttons was within striking distance. "But you didn't take her to Indian Head," I said. "You dumped her in that farmer's field."

Tom shrugged. Suddenly he seemed bored by the turn the conversation had taken. When he dropped his glance, I shot my hand towards the panel of buttons. I thought Tom had lost interest in my movements, but I was wrong. As my finger touched the button for the mezzanine, Tom chopped my forearm with the edge of his hand in a gesture so violent it brought tears to my eyes.

"You knew Kellee would die if you left her there," I said.

He brought his face close to mine. "And I couldn't have cared less," he said. "Because I'm not like Reed Gallagher. I *do* have balls."

"And that's where you found the courage to kill a man who thought of you as a son and a twenty-one-year-old woman who was too drunk and too drugged to find her way home." I leaned toward him and whispered, "You really are piece of work, Tom." Then I raised my knee and caught him square in the crotch. He yelped in pain, and fell to the floor. I reached past him and hit *M* for mezzanine. This time Tom Kelsoe was too busy moaning to rip my finger from the button. All the same, it wasn't until the elevator began to move that I felt safe enough to cry.

My memories of the next few minutes are fragmented: sharp and separate vignettes as distinct as stills from a movie.

The elevator doors opened, and Jill and Rapti were there. So were five members of the police force, and a lot of people from the show. I was glad to see that one of those people was Troy Prigotzke who, in addition to being a nice guy, was a body builder. Beside me, Tom Kelsoe was struggling to his knees. When Troy saw him, he reached down, grabbed Tom's jacket collar and dragged him into the lobby. Then in a smooth and effortless move, he lifted Tom up and handed him to one of the cops. "I believe you have some interest in this piece of shit," he said.

Rapti had a sweatshirt tied around her waist; she took it off and draped it around my shoulders. Then she took the sleeve and mopped at the blood on my face. "Poor Jo," she said.

"I'm okay," I said, but my tongue felt thick, and my words didn't sound right.

As the police put the handcuffs on Tom Kelsoe, he shot Jill a pleading look. "You've got to help me, baby," he said. Jill gave him a glance that was beyond contempt, and turned to me. "Let's get out of here," she said.

Before the police left, they offered to radio for someone to take Jill and me to the hospital to get checked out and then bring us downtown to make our statements. I asked if Constable Marissa Desjardin was on duty, and they said they'd see.

While we were waiting, I went over to a pay phone and called Sylvie O'Keefe to ask if Taylor could stay the night. After Sylvie and I made our arrangements, Taylor came on the line. I started to ask what she'd been up to, but she cut me off. "You sound funny," she said.

"I have a nosebleed," I said.

"But you're okay." I could hear the anxiety in her voice.

"I'm fine," I said. "I'm just trying to be as brave as you were when you cut your hand. Now, you have fun, and I'll pick you up tomorrow morning."

Marissa Desjardin shuddered when she saw my face, but after the doctor in emergency had checked me over, he said nothing was broken and I'd live to fight another day. He said the same thing to Jill. When he went off to write a pre-scription for painkillers, Marissa Desjardin rolled her eyes and whispered "asshole" at his retreating back.

We were out of police headquarters in twenty minutes. Marissa Desjardin was a whiz at taking statements, and, as she said, she knew Jill and I were fading fast. It was a little after 8:00 when we walked through my front door.

After I'd helped Jill off with her coat, I said, "We can't combine painkillers and Glenfiddich. Which would you prefer?"

"The Scotch," she said. "And Carly Simon. Have you still got those old tapes of hers? The ones we used to listen to when we'd stay up and talk all night."

"Of course," I said. "I was just waiting for our next pyjama party."

While Jill went after the Scotch, I got out the glasses and ice and checked the messages. The first one was from the Parents' Committee at Taylor's school, wondering if I could bring a pan of squares to the Kids Convention Monday night. The second one was from Angus. He and Camillo had gone to Sharkey's to play pool, and he'd check in later. The third message was from Alex. It was a bad connection, and I could only catch snatches of what he said. But I heard enough to know that he had had car trouble somewhere outside of Meadow Lake and was waiting for parts. When I heard Alex's voice, I instinctively raised my fingers to my face, wondering what he would see when he looked at me.

Jill came into the room just as the tape played its final message. It was Dr. Roy Crawford. "Your new kitten came through the surgery with flying colours," he said. "You and Benny can pick him up on Monday."

Jill looked at me quizzically.

"Don't even ask," I said.

I dropped a tape in my cassette player. As Carly Simon began to sing "Two Hot Girls on a Hot Summer Night," Jill handed me a drink and raised her glass. "Life goes on," she said, but there was a bleakness in her tone that made me wonder whether she was wholly convinced that life going on was a good idea.

Jill and I listened to all my Carly Simon tapes twice that night, and we went through a fair amount of Glenfiddich. The combination seemed to help. Jill needed to talk, and I needed to hear what she had to say. The truth of the matter was I didn't get it. I didn't understand how a woman as smart and as competent as Jill could make herself believe she was in love with a manipulator like Tom Kelsoe, and I didn't understand how, once the beatings began, she didn't simply report him and walk away.

Every situation Jill described that night was a perfect fit for the pattern of abuse. Tom's father had been a batterer whose frequent absences only served to underline the horror of his presence. When Tom's father was away, the Kelsoe home was a happy one, but when he returned he was, by turns, demanding and cold. Tom could never measure up to the ever-shifting standards his father set for him, and he came to see his mother as his only anchor in a violent and unchartable sea of threats and violence. After enduring years of cruelty at her husband's hands, Tom's mother ran away with the first man who promised her safe haven. Tom was left with his father. He was devastated. As soon as he was old enough, he left home and began the search for his ideal: a woman who would never desert him, no matter what.

The first time Tom hit her, Jill had been dumfounded. She and Tom were, as Tom frequently asserted, the perfect match, complementary halves of a whole, logos and eros. Tom's remorse when he saw Jill's bruises the morning after the first beating had been so intense, Jill had feared he would harm himself. He'd come to her apartment that night with a bottle of expensive bath oil and a silk peignoir. As he bathed Jill's bruised body, he had tearfully offered up his excuse: he was obsessed by the fear that his new book would fail and that

Jill would abandon him the way his mother had, the way everybody he'd ever counted upon had. And so she had forgiven him.

As Jill told me about her relationship with Tom Kelsoe, I tried hard to make some sense of it. I couldn't. In my heart, I didn't believe Jill could either. That night, as we talked, she was filled with guilt. She felt that, if she had acted, Tom could have been stopped before two lives had been lost. Her anguish about what might have been allowed me to ask the question I'd been haunted by. "If you didn't want to involve the police," I said, "why didn't you come to me?"

She shook her head. "I don't know. I felt so cut off. It was as if I was living on the other side of a glass wall." Her eyes were miserable. "Jo, believe me, it's not easy to let people see that you've allowed yourself to be victimized."

After I showered the next morning, I flinched at the sight of my face in the bathroom mirror. When Angus and Taylor saw it, they were going to need a lot of reassuring. Before I took the dogs for their walk, I smoothed makeup over my bruises, swathed my head in a scarf, pulled up my jacket collar, and put on my largest dark glasses. As I gave my face a last anxious check before I left the house, the light began to dawn. Jill was right. It wasn't easy to face the world as a victim.

When it was time to pick up Taylor, I let Angus drive. Before she'd taken a cab home to her apartment, Jill had made me promise that I wouldn't get behind the wheel until I'd had a chance to recover. Besides, I didn't want to face Taylor alone. Angus had done exactly the right thing when he saw my bruises. He had put his arms around me without saying a word. When we got to Sylvie O'Keefe's house, Angus went to the door to get Taylor. As they walked towards the car, I could see him preparing her for what she was about to see. She looked scared, but she managed a smile when I told her there was nothing to worry about. As soon as we got home, I gave Taylor a short but honest account of what had happened. After I'd finished, she asked me two questions: the first was, did I hurt; the second was, did the doctor think my face would ever look the way it used to look. I told her the answer to both questions was yes.

I spent Sunday recuperating. The most vigorous activity I undertook was to find my old bridal picture so Taylor could draw a portrait of me in my big dress to cheer me up. Jill arrived at dinnertime with two pizzas from the Copper Kettle: spinach and feta for the grown-ups, and everything but the kitchen sink for the kids. By the time I slipped between the sheets, I felt I was on my way to recovery, but when the dogs and I set out on Monday morning, it soon became apparent that one day of rest hadn't been enough. I was bone-tired and we only made it part way around the lake before I gave it up as a bad job and came home. Rosalie Norman was sympathetic when I called in sick. She hadn't seen the political panel Saturday night, but she'd certainly heard about it. News travels fast on a university campus.

When I hung up, the day stretched before me. There were a hundred things that needed my attention, but only two jobs I had to do. I called Roy Crawford and told him the kids and I would be in after school to pick up the new kitten; then I got down my cookbooks and began searching for a recipe for Nanaimo bars.

I deep-sixed Taylor's plan to have Benny join us when we went to the vet's, but she was too excited to put up more than a token protest. From the moment she saw the tortoise-shell, Taylor was filled with plans. "He and Benny will be best friends," she said. "When I'm at school, they'll play all the time."

Angus rolled his eyes, but remained silent.

"Don't expect too much of Benny, T," I said. "His nose may be a little bit out of joint at first."

"Not Benny," she said confidently.

When we were leaving, the receptionist smiled at Taylor. "What are you going to call your kitten?"

Taylor didn't miss a beat. "Bruce," she said, and she headed for the car.

Benny's reaction to Bruce surprised me. Apparently, there were depths of feeling in Benny that had been unplumbed. From the moment Taylor undid the blanket and placed the new kitten in front of him, Benny was devoted to Bruce. It was clear that I had seriously underestimated Benny, and every glance he gave me let me know it.

It was still light when Taylor and I set out for the Kids Convention. As we walked towards Lakeview School, we spotted other parents with other kids and other pans of Nanaimo bars. Taylor was buoyant with the combined excitement of Bruce's arrival and of being out after supper on a school night. But as we crossed Cameron Street, she scrunched up her nose. "I wish Alex had got here in time for us to all go to school together."

"Taylor, I wish you wouldn't count on Alex making it tonight. Meadow Lake's a long way from here, and it takes time to get car parts."

Taylor's gaze was untroubled. "He'll be here," she said. "He promised."

The front hall of Lakeview School was hung with construction-paper stars. Inside each star was a student's picture. In case we didn't get the message, there was a sign in poster-paint script: "At Lakeview School, every student is a S*T*A*R!" After Taylor and I found her star, and Jess's and Samantha's and those of her seven other best friends, I said, "Let's go see your Nanabush mural."

"No," she said. "It wouldn't be fair. We have to wait for Alex. There's other stuff."

For the next half-hour, we looked at stuff: a fisherman's net filled with oddly coloured papier-mâché fish made by the grade ones; First Nations masks made by the grade threes; family crests made by the grade sixes; poems about death and despair written by the grade eights.

We ended up in front of a collage called "Mona and the Bulls"; in it, the Mona Lisa was wearing a Chicago Bulls uniform and looking enigmatic. "I can only take so many high points, Taylor," I said. "I think 'Mona and the Bulls' is going to have to be my last stop before the mural. I promise I'll enjoy it all over again when we look at it with Alex."

The Nanabush mural had been mounted in the resource room, and it had attracted quite a crowd. At the edge of the gathering, just as Taylor had predicted, was Alex Kequahtooway. When she spotted him, Taylor said, "There he is," and her tone was matter-of-fact.

She went over to him and tweaked his sleeve. He knelt down and talked to her for a moment, then he stood up and started towards me.

I put my hand up to cover my face. "I had an adventure," I said.

He reached over and took down my hand. "Marissa Desjardin left a message for me at the garage in Meadow Lake. I was on the next bus home." Alex reached out to embrace me; then he noticed, as I had, that we were attracting more than our share of sidelong glances. He stepped back.

I moved towards him. "Alex, I really could use someone to lean on right now."

He slid his arm around my shoulder. "Are you sure you're all right, Jo?"

I closed my eyes and lay my head on him. "No," I said,

"but for the first time since all of this happened, I think maybe I'm going to be."

It rained the morning of Kellee Savage's funeral, but by the time Jill and I were on the highway, the sky was clear and the sun was shining. Alex had offered to drive to Indian Head with me, but Jill had been anxious to go. "It's the least I can do for another journalist," she said simply.

The United Church was full, but the only people I recognized were Neil McCallum and Kellee's classmates from the J school. There were flowers everywhere. Ed Mariani, who'd come back from Minneapolis with a terrible cold and Barry's forgiveness, had sent the white roses that were on the table with the guest book, and the air of the church was sweet with the perfume of spring. The service had the special poignancy that the funeral of a young person always has. There were too many young faces in the pews, and the minister had the good sense to admit that the reasons for the death of a person who has just begun life were always as much a mystery to him as they were to any of us.

Afterwards, the congregation was invited down to the church hall for lunch. It was a pretty room: warm with pastel tablecloths and bowls of pussy willows splashed with afternoon light. Neil McCallum was surrounded by people, so I went over to the table where Linda Van Sickle and Jumbo Hryniuk were sitting. When he saw me, Jumbo leaped up and helped me with my chair.

"This is the first funeral I've ever been to," he said. "I almost lost it up there. Do they get any easier?"

"No," I said. "They don't. But I'm glad you're here." I turned to Linda Van Sickle. "I'm glad you came, too. I never had a chance to ask you the results of that ultrasound you had."

"I'm going to have twins," she said. "Two little boys."

"That must be so exciting," I said.

"It is," she agreed, but her voice was flat. Physically, Linda looked better than she had the last time I'd seen her, but she'd lost the serenity that had enveloped her during so much of her pregnancy. When she spoke again, I could hear the strain in her voice. "Is it true about Tom Kelsoe? That he killed Kellee and Professor Gallagher?"

"It's true," I said.

"The worst part," Jumbo said, "was the way he dumped Kellee in that field – just like she was an animal."

"Less than an animal," I said.

Linda chewed her lower lip. "What's going to happen to Val?" she asked.

"He's still in the hospital," I said. "I guess the first thing he's going to have to do is come to terms with what happened. His dad has a lawyer working on the legal questions."

Jumbo looked puzzled. "Val always thought his dad hated him."

"Val was wrong about a lot of things," I said.

Linda shook her head sadly. "I guess we all were."

I looked across the room. Neil McCallum was motioning to me to come over. I stood up, shook hands with Jumbo and gave Linda a hug. "There's someone over there I want to talk to," I said. "I'll see you in class on Friday."

Neil's eyes were red-rimmed and swollen, but he smiled when he saw me.

"How are you doing?" I asked.

"Not very good," he said. "I miss Kellee. I hate wearing a suit, but Mum says you have to for a funeral."

"Your mum's right."

"I know," he said. Then he brightened. "Are you ready to go?"

"Go where?" I asked.

"To see the crocuses," he said. "Don't you remember? When I told you Chloe and I saw the crocuses, you said you wanted to see them." He held out his hand to me. "So let's go."

I followed Neil outside, and we walked down the street to his house to get Chloe. As we headed for the edge of town, the dog bounded across the lawns and ran through every puddle on the street. When we hit the prairie, and started towards the hill where Neil had seen the crocuses, a breeze came up and I could smell moisture and warming earth. Neil and Chloe ran up the hill ahead of me.

Suddenly he yelled, "Here they are."

I followed him to the top of the hill and looked around me. For as far as I could see, the ground was purple and white. It was an amazing sight.

Neil bent down, picked a crocus and handed it to me. "They're nice, aren't they?" he said.

"They're beautiful," I said. "There's a story about where crocuses came from."

Neil sat down on the ground and began to take the burrs out of Chloe's coat. "Do you want to tell it?"

I sat down beside him. "Yes, I think I do," I said. "It's about a woman named Demeter who had a daughter named Persephone."

Chloe yelped, and Neil leaned over to reassure her.

"Persephone was a wonderful daughter," I continued. "Very sweet and thoughtful. Her mother loved her a lot. One day Persephone decided she had to go to the underworld to comfort the spirits of the people who had died."

"Like Kellee," Neil said.

"Yes," I said. "Like Kellee. But in the story, once Persephone was gone, her mother missed her so much that she decided that nothing would ever grow again." Chloe leaned over and put her muddy head on my lap.

"She likes you," Neil said.

"I like her too," I said. "Anyway, one morning when Demeter was missing Persephone so much she thought she herself might die, a ring of purple crocuses pushed their way through the soil. The flowers were all around her, and they were so beautiful Demeter knelt down on the earth so she could see them up close. Guess what she heard?"

Neil shrugged.

"She heard the crocuses whispering, 'Persephone returns! Persephone returns!' Demeter was so happy she began to dance, and she made a cape out of white crocuses to give to her daughter when she came back from comforting the spirits of the dead."

Neil lay down on the ground. For a while he just lay there, looking up at the sky with Chloe panting beside him. Finally, he turned to me and smiled. "I heard them," he said. "I heard the crocuses whisper."

Verdict in Blood

CHAPTER

1

When the phone on my bedside table shrilled in the early hours of Labour Day morning, I had the receiver pressed to my ear before the second ring. Eli Kequahtooway, the sixteen-year-old nephew of the man in my life, had been missing since 4:00 the previous afternoon. It wasn't the first time that Eli had taken off, but the fact that he'd disappeared before didn't ease my mind about the dangers waiting for him in a world that didn't welcome runaways, especially if they were aboriginal.

I was braced for the worst. I got it, but not from the quarter I was expecting.

My caller's voice was baritone rubbed by sandpaper. "This is Detective Robert Hallam of the Regina City Police," he said. "Am I speaking to Hilda McCourt?"

"No," I said. "I'm Joanne Kilbourn. Miss McCourt is staying with me for the weekend, but I'm sure she's asleep by now. Can't this wait until morning?"

Detective Hallam made no attempt to disguise his frustration. "Ms. Kilbourn, this is not a casual call. If I'd wanted to recruit a block captain for Neighbourhood Watch, I would have waited. Unfortunately for all of us, a woman's been murdered, and your friend seems to be our best bet for establishing the victim's identity. Now, why don't you do the sensible thing and bring Ms. McCourt to the phone. Then I can get the information I need, and you can go back to bed."

Hilda was eighty-three years old. I shrank from the prospect of waking her up to deal with a tragedy, but as I walked down the hall to the guest room, I could see the light under her door. When I knocked, she answered immediately. Even propped up in bed reading, Hilda was a striking figure. When the actress Claudette Colbert died, a graceful obituary noted that, among her many talents, Claudette Colbert wore pyjamas well. Hilda McCourt shared that gift. The pyjamas she was wearing were black silk, tailored in the clean masculine lines of women's fashions in the forties. With her brilliant auburn hair exploding like an aureole against the pillow behind her, there was no denying that, like Claudette Colbert, Hilda McCourt radiated star power.

She leaned forward. "I heard the phone," she said.

"It's for you, Hilda," I said. "It's the police. They need your help." I picked up her robe from the chair beside the window and held it out to her. "You can take the call in my room."

She slipped into her robe, a magnificent Chinese red silk shot through with gold, and straightened her shoulders. "Thank you, Joanne," she said. "I'll enlighten you when I'm enlightened."

After she left, I picked up the book she'd been reading. *Geriatric Psychiatry: A Handbook*. It was an uncharacteristic choice. Hilda was a realist about her age. She quoted Thomas Dekker approvingly, "Age is like love; it cannot be hid," but she never dwelled on growing old, and her mind was as sharp as her spirit was indomitable. While I waited for her, I glanced at the book's table of contents. The topics were weighty: "The Dementias"; "Delirium and Other Organic Mental Disorders"; "Psychoses"; "Anxiety and Related Personality Dysfunctions"; "Diagnosing Depression." Uneasy, I leafed through the book. Its pages were heavily annotated in a strong but erratic hand which I was relieved to see was not my old friend's. The writer had entered into a kind of running dialogue with the authors of the text, but the entries were personal, not scholarly. I stopped at a page listing the criteria for a diagnosis of dementia. The margins were black with what appeared to be self-assessments. I felt a pang of guilt as sharp as if I'd happened upon a stranger's diary.

Hilda wasn't gone long. When she came back, she pulled her robe around her as if she were cold and sank onto the edge of the bed.

"Let me get you some tea," I said.

"Tea's a good idea, but we'd better use the large pot," she said. "The detective I was speaking to is coming over."

"Hilda, what's going on?"

She adjusted the dragon's-head fastening at the neck of her gown. "The police were patrolling Wascana Park tonight, and they found a body sprawled over one of those limestone slabs at the Boy Scout memorial. There was nothing on the victim to identify her, but there was a slip of paper in her jacket pocket." Hilda's face was grim. "Joanne, the paper had my name on it and your telephone number."

"Then you know who she is," I said.

Hilda nodded. "I'm afraid I do," she said. "I think it must be Justine Blackwell."

"The judge," I said. "But you were just at her party tonight."

"I was," Hilda said, stroking the dragon's head thoughtfully. "That book you're holding belongs to her. There'd been some disturbing developments in her life, and she wanted my opinion on them. I left your number with her because she was going to call me later today."

"Come downstairs, and we'll have that tea," I said.

"I'd like to dress first," Hilda said. "I wouldn't be comfortable receiving a member of the police force in my robe."

I'd just plugged in the kettle when the phone rang again. It was Alex Kequahtooway. "Jo, I know it's late, but you said to call as soon as I heard from Eli."

"He called you?"

"He's back. He was here when I got home."

"Oh, Alex, I'm so glad. Is he okay?"

"I don't know. When I walked in, he'd just got out of the shower. He went into his room and started taking fresh clothes out of his drawers. Jo, he didn't say a word to me. It was as if I wasn't there. At first, I thought he was on something, but I've seen kids wasted on just about every substance there is, and this is different."

"Have you called Dr. Rayner?"

"I tried her earlier in the evening. I thought Eli might have got in touch with her, but there was no answer. Of course, it's a holiday weekend. I'm going to call again, but if I don't connect, I'm going to take Eli down to emergency. I hate to bring in another shrink, but I just don't know what to do for him, and I don't want to blow it."

"You won't," I said. "Eli's going to be fine. He's come a long way this summer. Most importantly, he has you."

"And you think that's enough?" Alex asked, and I could hear the ache.

"I know that's enough."

For a beat there was silence, then Alex, who was suspicious of words, said what he didn't often say. "I love you, Jo."

"I love you, too." I took a breath. "Alex, there's something else. About ten minutes ago, Hilda got a phone call from a colleague of yours. There was a murder in the park tonight. It looks like the victim was Hilda's friend Justine Blackwell. I'm afraid Detective Hallam – that's the officer who's coming over – is going to ask Hilda to identify the body. I don't want her to have to go through that."

"She shouldn't have to," Alex said. "There are a hundred people in this city who know Justice Blackwell. Someone else can make the ID – I'll take care of it. And, Jo, pass along a message to Hilda for me, would you? Tell her not to let Bob Hallam get under her skin. He can be a real jerk."

"I'll warn her," I said. "Alex, I'm so thankful that Eli's back."

"Me too," he said. "God, this has been a lousy night."

As I poured boiling water into the Brown Betty, Alex's words stayed with me. It had been a lousy night, which had come hard on the heels of a lousy day. The problem was, as it had been so often in the past few months, Eli.

He was a boy whose young life had been shadowed by trouble: a father who disappeared before he was born and a temperament composed of equal parts intelligence, anger, and raw sensitivity. Driven by furies he could neither understand nor control, Eli became a runaway who spattered his trail with spray-painted line drawings of horses, graffiti that identified him as definitively as a fingerprint. His capacity for self-destruction seemed limitless. He was also the most vulnerable human being I had ever met. Alex told me once that when he'd heard a biographer of Tchaikovsky say that the composer had been "a child of glass," he had thought of his nephew.

From the day he was born, the centre of Eli's life had been his mother. The previous May, Karen Kequahtooway was killed in a car accident. Eli had been sitting in the seat beside her. His physical injuries healed quickly, but the lacerations to his psyche had been devastating. The child of glass had shattered. For weeks, Eli's anguish translated itself into a kind of free-floating rage that exploded in graffiti and hurled itself against whoever was luckless enough to cross his path. On more than one occasion, that person was me. But as the summer days grew shorter, the grief and fury that had clouded Eli's life began to lift. For the first time since Karen's death, Eli appeared to be seeing a future for himself, and Alex and I had allowed ourselves the luxury of hope.

Then everything fell apart.

At first, it seemed as if the gods were smiling. When she arrived for the weekend, Hilda surprised Alex and Eli and my kids and me with tickets for the annual Labour Day game between the Saskatchewan Roughriders and the Winnipeg Blue Bombers. As we settled into our seats on the fifty-five-yard line, Alex and I grinned at each other. The seats were perfect. So was the weather, which was hot and still. And on the opening kickoff, the Riders' kick returner broke through the first wave of tacklers and scampered into the endzone for a touchdown. All signs pointed to a banner day.

From the beginning of our relationship, Alex and I had been careful not to use the fact that Eli and my son, Angus, were both sixteen as justification for asking them to move in lockstep. We had hoped for the best and left it to them to find each other. That Sunday, they were sitting a few seats away in the row behind us, and as their game patter and laughter drifted towards us, it seemed our strategy was working.

At the beginning of the third quarter, Angus announced that he and Eli were going to get nachos; they bought their food and started back, but somewhere between the concession stand and their seats, Eli disappeared. There were twenty-five thousand people at Taylor Field that day, so looking for Eli hadn't been easy, but we'd done our best. After the game, we checked the buses on the west side of the stadium. When we couldn't find Eli, we went back inside the stadium and waited until the stands emptied. There was always the possibility that he had simply lost track of where we were sitting. But we couldn't find him, and as we walked through the deserted parking lot it was clear that, as he had on many occasions, Eli had simply run away. The rest of the day was spent in the dismally familiar ritual of checking out Eli's haunts and calling the bus station and listening to a recorded voice announce the times when the buses that might have carried Eli away from his demons left the city. Now, without explanation, he was back, and it seemed that all we could do was hold our breath and wait until next time.

Detective Hallam arrived just as I was carrying the tray with the teapot and cups into the living room. On my way to the front door, I caught a glimpse of my reflection in the hall mirror and flinched. I was tanned from a summer at the lake, and the week before I'd had my hair cut in a style which I was relieved to see fell into place on its own, but after I'd talked to Alex, I only had time to splash my face, brush my teeth, and throw on the first two items I found in the clean laundry: an old pair of jogging shorts and a Duran Duran T-shirt from my oldest daughter's abandoned collection of rock memorabilia. I was dressed for comfort not company, but when I opened the door, I saw that Hilda's caller was dapper enough for both of us.

Robert Hallam appeared to be in his mid-sixties. He was a short, trim man with a steel-grey crewcut, a luxuriant bush of a moustache, and a thin, ironic smile. It was a hot night, but he was wearing meticulously pressed grey slacks, a black knit shirt, and a salt-and-pepper tweed jacket. He nodded when I introduced myself, then walked into the living room ahead of me, checked out the arrangement of the furniture, dragged a straight-backed chair across the carpet and positioned it next to the couch so he'd be able to look down at whoever sat next to him. He turned down my offer of tea, and when Hilda came into the room, he didn't rise. As far as I was concerned, Detective Hallam was off to a bad start.

He motioned Hilda to the place on the couch nearest him. "Sit down," he said. "Inspector Ke-quah-too-way has informed me that we don't need you to make the ID any more, so this may be a waste of time for both of us."

Hilda remained standing. From the set of her jaw as she looked down at the detective, I could see that she had missed neither Robert Hallam's derisive smile when he mentioned Alex's rank nor the exaggerated care with which he pronounced Alex's surname. She shot him a glance that would have curdled milk, then, with great deliberation, she walked to the end of the couch farthest from him and sat down.

The flush spread from Robert Hallam's neck to his face. He stood, grabbed his chair, and took it to where Hilda was sitting. Then he perched on the edge and pulled out a notepad.

"I'll need your full name, home address, and telephone number," he said tightly.

After Hilda gave him the information, he narrowed his eyes at her. "How old are you, Ms. McCourt?"

"It's *Miss* McCourt," Hilda said. "And I don't see that my age is germane."

"The issue is testimonial capacity," he snapped. "I have to decide whether I can trust your ability to make truthful and accurate statements."

Hilda stiffened. "I assure you that you can," she said. "Detective, if you have questions, I'm prepared to answer them, but if you wish to play games, you'll play alone."

Detective Hallam's face was scarlet. "How did Mrs. Kilbourn's phone number get in the dead woman's jacket pocket?" he rasped.

"Justine Blackwell put it there herself," Hilda said. "Yesterday I drove down from Saskatoon to attend a party celebrating her thirtieth year on the bench. Afterwards, at Justine's invitation, I went to the hotel bar and had a drink with her. Before we parted, she asked for a number where she could reach me. I gave her Mrs. Kilbourn's."

"How would you describe your relationship with Justine Blackwell?"

"Long-standing but not intimate," Hilda said. "She rented a room in my house in Saskatoon when she was in law school."

"And you've kept in touch all these years?"

"We exchanged holiday cards. When either of us visited the city in which the other lived, we had dinner together. But as I said, we were not intimate."

"Yet you drove 270 kilometres on a holiday weekend to come to her party. That's a long drive for a woman your age."

Hilda's spine stiffened with anger, but she didn't take the bait. "I came because Justine Blackwell telephoned and asked me to come," she said.

"How was Judge Blackwell's demeanour at her party?"

Hilda didn't answer immediately. Robert Hallam leaned towards her, and when he spoke his tone was condescending. "It's a simple question, Miss McCourt. Was the judge having the time of her life? Was she miserable? In a word, how did she *seem*?"

Hilda sipped her tea thoughtfully. "In a word, she seemed contumacious."

Detective Hallam's head shot up.

Hilda spelled the word slowly for him so he had time to write it in his notepad. "It means defiant," she added helpfully.

"She was defiant at a party celebrating her accomplishments?" Detective Hallam was sputtering now. "Isn't that a little peculiar?"

"It was a peculiar party," Hilda said. "For one thing, Justine Blackwell threw the party herself."

Robert Hallam cocked an eyebrow. "Wouldn't it have been more natural for the other judges to organize the tribute?"

"In the normal run of things, yes." Hilda said. "But Madame Justice Blackwell's thinking had taken a curious turn in the last year."

"Describe this 'curious turn.'"

"I can only tell you what Justice Blackwell told me herself."

"Shoot."

"Justice Blackwell had come to believe that her interpretation of the law had lacked charity."

"After thirty years, this just came upon her – a bolt from the blue?"

"No, she'd had an encounter with a prisoners' advocate named Wayne J. Waters."

Detective Hallam narrowed his eyes. "That man is lightning in a bottle. What's his connection here?"

"Justine told me he'd accosted her after a young man she'd sentenced to prison committed suicide. Mr. Waters told her that he held her personally responsible for the man's death."

"I suppose the lad was as innocent as a newborn babe."

Hilda shook her head. "No, apparently there was no doubt about his guilt. But it was a first offence and, in Mr. Waters' opinion, Justine was culpable because she had failed to take into account the effect the appalling conditions of prison would have upon a sensitive young person."

"Justice without mercy," I said.

My old friend looked at me gratefully. "Precisely. And according to Mr. Waters, that particular combination was Justine's specialty. He told her that her lack of compassion was so widely recognized that prisoners and their lawyers alike called her Madame Justice Blackheart."

"That's a little childish, isn't it?"

Hilda nodded. "Of course it is, and considering the source, the appellation didn't bother Justine. She'd been called worse. But she was woman who held herself to very rigorous standards, and she needed to prove to herself that the charge was unwarranted. She went back to her office and began rereading her old judgments. When she saw how uncompromising her rulings had been, she was shaken."

"Wayne J. had scored a bull's-eye?"

"He had indeed."

"Was Mr. Waters at the party last night?"

Hilda nodded. "Oh yes. He and Justine had an ugly confrontation."

Detective Hallam's eyes narrowed. "Describe it."

"It was at the end of the evening," Hilda said. "I'd gone to the cloakroom to pick up my wrap. By the time I got back, Justine and Mr. Waters were *in medias res.*"

"In the middle of things," Detective Hallam said.

This time it was Hilda's turn to look surprised. "Exactly. Mr. Waters was accusing Justine of failing to honour some sort of agreement. He stopped his diatribe when he saw me, so I'm not clear about the nature of the transaction. But his manner was truly frightening."

"Did Justice Blackwell seem afraid of him?"

"I don't know. The incident was over so quickly. But it was an unsettling moment in a very unsettling evening."

"Go on."

"Over the past year, Justine had made an effort to get in touch with everyone with whom she felt she had dealt unfairly. She'd sent some of them money and offered to do what she could to help them re-establish themselves. Last night was supposed to be the final reconciliation."

"Sounds like the judge got religion," Detective Hallam said.

Hilda ignored his irony. "Not religion, but there was an epiphany. Detective Hallam, in the past year, Justine's entire way of looking at the world had altered. She even looked different. She'd always been a woman of great style."

"A fashion plate," he said.

"Hardly," Hilda sniffed. "Fashion is ephemeral; style is enduring. Some of Justine's suits must have been twenty years old, but they were always beautifully cut, and her jewellery was always simple but elegant. I was quite startled when I saw her last night."

"She'd let herself go?" he asked.

"To my eyes, yes, but I don't imagine Justine saw it that way. She was wearing bluejeans that were quite badly faded and one of those oversized plaid shirts that teenagers wear. Her hair was different too. She's almost seventy years old, so for the last couple of decades I've suspected that lovely golden hair of hers was being kept bright by a beautician's hand; still, it was a shock to see her with white hair and done so casually."

"Was her hygiene less than adequate?"

Hilda shook her head impatiently. "Of course not. Justine was always fastidious – in her person and in her surroundings."

Detective Hallam's pen was flying. "Have you got the names of any of the other people at the party?"

Hilda looked thoughtful. "Well, Justine's children were there. She has three daughters, grown, of course. There was a man named Eric Fedoruk, whom Justine introduced as a friend of long standing. There were perhaps seventy-five other guests. None of the others was known to me."

"What time was it when you last saw Justine Blackwell? You can be approximate."

"I can be exact," Hilda said. "It was midnight outside the Hotel Saskatchewan. We'd had our drinks, and Madame Justice Blackwell came outside and waited with me until a cab pulled up."

"When you left her, did she give you any indication of her plans for the rest of the evening?"

Hilda shook her head. "She said she was tired, but she thought she should go back inside to say goodnight to a few people before she went home."

"And that was it?"

"That was it."

"Is there anything you'd care to add to what you've already told me?"

For a moment, Hilda seemed lost in thought. When she finally responded, her voice was steely. "No," she said. "There is nothing I would care to add."

Detective Robert Hallam snapped his notepad shut and placed it in the inside pocket of his jacket. "Thank you for your time, Miss McCourt. You've been very helpful." He bobbed his head in my direction and headed for the door.

After he left, I turned to Hilda. "You *were* helpful," I said. "Surprisingly so, after you two got off to such a rocky start."

Hilda shuddered. "The man's an egotist," she said. "But I couldn't let my distaste for him stand in the way of the investigation of Justine's murder. This news is so cruel. It's barbarous that Justine should die not knowing . . ." She fell silent.

I reached over and touched her hand. "What didn't Justine know?"

A wave of pain crossed Hilda's face. "Whether she was in the process of losing her mind or of finding a truth that would make sense of her life," she said.

"That book on geriatric psychiatry you were reading tonight was Justine's, wasn't it?"

Hilda nodded. "She gave it to me last night. Joanne, the information I gave Detective Hallam was accurate but not complete. Out of deference to Justine's reputation, I didn't divulge the nature of our final conversation. It was a deeply distressing one. Justine said she didn't know who to trust any more. Certain people, whom she did not name, were concerned about her mental competence. She wanted me to read through the diagnostic criteria for a number of conditions and, in light of what I'd learned, tell her if I believed she was in need of psychiatric help."

"She wanted you to reach a verdict about her sanity?" I asked.

"That's exactly what she wanted. And she wanted to make certain I had the evidence I needed to reach a just verdict." Hilda slipped a hand into her pocket and withdrew a cream-coloured envelope. She took out a single piece of paper and handed it to me. The letter was dated the preceding day, handwritten in the same bold, erratic hand I'd seen in the margins of the book on geriatric psychiatry.

> Dear Hilda McCourt:
>
> As you know, I have become increasingly concerned about my mental state. I require your assistance to determine whether I am still mentally competent. Therefore, I am concurrently executing a Power of Attorney appointing you as my attorney with all necessary powers to investigate and examine my past and current affairs, including the right to access and review all financial records, personal papers, and any and all other documents that you deem relevant in order to determine my mental competency. Further, should you determine that I am not mentally competent, then

I authorize you to apply to the court pursuant to the Dependant Adults Act to have me declared incapable of managing my personal affairs, and furthermore, to have you appointed as both my personal and property guardian. Incidentally, my trusted friend, I want to inform you that I have previously executed my will, appointing you as my Executrix.

The signature was Justine Blackwell's.

I felt a coldness in the pit of my stomach. "I can't think of many things more frightening than not knowing if I was losing touch with reality."

Hilda's voice was bleak. "In all the years I knew her, I never saw Justine unsure of herself until last night. When she handed me this letter, there was something in her eyes I can't describe – a kind of existential fear. From the moment I heard about her death, I haven't been able to get that image out of my mind. There's a story about Martin Heidegger."

"The philosopher," I said.

Hilda's nod was barely perceptible. "A policeman spotted him sitting alone on a park bench. He appeared so desperate that the officer went over to him and asked him who he was. Heidegger looked up at the man and said, 'I wish to God I knew.'" Hilda's eyes were bright with unshed tears. "Joanne, can you conceive of a fate crueller than dying without knowing who you are?"

I thought of Eli Kequahtooway, the child of glass. "Only one," I said. "Living without knowing who you are."

CHAPTER

2

When I awoke the next morning the sun was streaming through the window, and our golden retriever, Rose, was sitting beside the bed, looking at me accusingly. It was 7:00 a.m. Our collie, Sadie, had died in June, and Rose, in her grief and confusion at losing her lifelong companion, had become a stickler about adhering to the old routines. By this time, she and I were usually halfway round the lake. I rubbed her head. "Cut me a little slack, Rose," I said. "It was a long night, and I don't bounce back the way I used to."

Fifteen minutes later, we were on our familiar route. For the first time in weeks, Wascana Park wasn't throbbing with the drums and shouts of a team getting ready for the Dragon Boat Festival. The exuberant event had become a highlight of our city's celebration of the last weekend of summer, but now the paddlers had gone home, and the only sounds on the lake were the squawks of the geese and the shouts of the men loading the last of the big boats onto trailers.

The races had been held all day Saturday. A crew from "Canada Tonight," the TV show on which I appeared every weekend as a political panellist, had drawn a position in one of the first heats, and Alex and Eli and my kids and I had gone down to the lake to offer moral support. We found a clearing on the shore where we could see the finish line, and after the "Canada Tonight" team came in dead last, we cheered for whoever struck our fancy until we got hungry and decided to cruise the concession stands. After we'd sampled everything worth sampling, we came back to my house, dug out the old croquet set, and played until it was time to eat again, and Alex had barbecued burgers while I served up potato salad and slaw. When the sun started to fall in the sky, the five of us walked back to the lake and watched the final heats of the race.

The evening had been flawless. As the sun set, the lake glittered gold, transforming the dragon boats into sampans, those magical vessels that sailed through the China of fairy tales, a land of sandalwood, silk, and nightingales whose silence could break the heart of an emperor.

For the first time I could remember, the five of us seemed to be in a state of perfect harmony. On the way home, the boys talked about getting a team together to enter the race next year. My daughter, Taylor, who was two months shy of her seventh birthday, was adamant about being included.

Her brother winced, but Eli was gentle. "Sure we'll need you, Taylor. Somebody has to sit at the front of the boat and beat the drum. You'll have the whole winter to practise." When Taylor crowed, Eli looked at me anxiously. "That'll be okay, won't it?"

"Absolutely," I said. Then, tentatively, I'd let my hand rest on his shoulder. In all the time I'd known him, Eli had never permitted physical intimacy. When he smiled at me, I thought that, at long last, we might be home-free. Yet not even a day later, he'd run away again. It didn't make sense.

A cluster of dog-walkers had gathered along the shore. They were looking out at the lake. I joined them. A few metres out, police frogmen were diving.

"What's happening?" I asked.

A man with a black standard poodle half-turned towards me. "You heard about that murder last night?"

"Yes," I said. "I heard."

"Apparently, they're looking for the weapon."

I gazed out at the lake. It shimmered sun-dappled and inscrutable: a place for secrets.

"The woman was killed up there at the Boy Scout memorial," the man with the poodle continued, pointing towards the path that ran from the clearing where we were standing up towards the road. Between us and the road was the Boy Scout memorial. A handful of curious joggers were checking out the yellow crime-scene tape which roped off the area.

"You can take a look if you like," the man with the poodle said. "But there's not much to see."

"I think I'll give it a pass," I said. At the best of times, the monument gave me the creeps, and this was not the best of times. Both my sons had been Boy Scouts, so I knew that the memorial, a central stone circled by nine smaller stones, was a representation of the sign Scouts leave at a campsite to indicate to others that they've gone home. But these stones were as large as tombstones, and they were engraved. The chunk of marble in the middle was inscribed with the Boy Scout emblem and motto; each of the more modest stones encircling it was etched with one key word from the laws that stated what a Boy Scout should be: Obedient, Cheerful, Thrifty, Clean, Trustworthy, Helpful, Brotherly, Courteous, and Kind.

Tired of waiting, or perhaps responding to some atavistic urge the presence of death stirred in her, Rose began to whine.

I tightened the leash around my hand. "I'm way ahead of you, Rose," I said, and we headed for home.

When I came in, Alex and Taylor were sitting at the kitchen table reading the comics in the newspaper. It was a homey scene, but Alex's shoulders were slumped and his exhaustion was apparent. I said hello, and he looked up at me through eyes so deeply shadowed that I went over and put my arms around him.

Taylor looked at us happily. "This is nice," she said.

"I agree," I said. And for a while it was nice. We had breakfast, then Taylor took Alex and me out to the sunroom to look at the painting she was working on. She had started using oils that summer, and her talent, a gift from her birth mother, the artist Sally Love, was declaring itself with a sureness that filled me with awe. The picture on her easel was of Angus, Eli, and Taylor herself watching the dragon-boat races, and it throbbed with the energy of the contest. Spikes of light radiated from the sun, and as the dragon boats slashed through the water, they sent up a spray as effervescent as joy.

Alex gazed at the painting thoughtfully, then he took Taylor's hand in his. "Nice work," he said.

She scrutinized his face carefully. "You *really* think it's okay?"

"Yeah," Alex said, "I *really* think it's okay."

Content, my daughter picked up her brush and began shading the underside of a cloud.

I looked at Alex. "I don't think we're needed here," I said.

He grinned. "I think you're right."

I made us a pitcher of iced tea. We took it out to the deck and sat on the steps.

Alex closed his eyes and touched his cold glass against his forehead.

"Headache?" I asked.

"It's manageable," he said.

I turned to him. "Ready to talk about Eli?"

Alex shook his head. "There's not much to say. It's as if he's decided to shut down. He doesn't talk. His face is a mask. Even the way he moves is different – as if suddenly his body doesn't belong to him. The psychiatrist who's taking Dr. Rayner's emergencies is going to see him this morning. The new guy's name is Dan Kasperski, and he specializes in adolescents. I like his approach. When I started to tell him Eli's history, he asked me to wait and tell him later. Kasperski says it's best to start with a clean slate, no preconceptions; that way he can put himself into the patient's situation and pick up on what Eli thinks is important."

"It sounds as if Eli's in good hands," I said.

Alex sipped his tea. "Let's hope."

"I haven't thanked you for stepping in last night," l said. "Going downtown to identify her friend would have been very painful for Hilda."

"And unnecessary," Alex said. "Justine Blackwell had three daughters. They did their duty. Apparently it was quite a scene."

"The daughters made a scene?"

"No. From what I hear, they were quite businesslike. The problem was with the pathology staff. They were tripping all over one another to gawk at Lucy Blackwell."

"It's not every day you get a chance to gawk at a legend," I said. "When I was in my twenties, I was so proud that a Canadian girl was hanging out with Dylan and Joan Baez. I think I've got all of Lucy Blackwell's old albums. It's funny, I hadn't thought about her for ages, then I heard her interviewed on the radio this summer. She's just come out with a CD boxed set. It's called *The Sorcerer's Smile*. I've asked Angus to get the word out that's what I want for my birthday."

Alex laughed softly. "Angus has already got the word out. I might even be able to get you an autograph. Sherm Zimbardo is the M.E. on this one, and he said that Lucy Blackwell was very co-operative."

I shuddered. "Poor woman, having to go down to the morgue and see her mother like that."

"At least she was spared the crime scene." Alex's face was sombre. "Justine Blackwell did not die easily. She was bludgeoned to death. We haven't recovered the weapon yet, but Sherm thinks she was probably killed on that big flat stone at the centre of the monument." He looked at me questioningly. "Do you know the one I mean? It's got the Boy Scout motto on it."

"I know the one," I said.

"Sherm thinks that after the first couple of blows, Justine Blackwell fell back against the centre stone. The killer finished her off there, then dragged her over and propped her up where we found her."

"You mean the killer deliberately moved her to one of those stones with the Boy Scout virtues on them?" I said.

"Is that what they are?" he asked. "We didn't have a Boy Scout troop out at Standing Buffalo."

"Too bad," I said. "You would have looked mighty fetching in those short pants."

Alex's face was pensive. "I wonder what we're supposed to make of the stone Justine Blackwell was propped up against?"

"Which one was it?" I asked.

"'Trustworthy,'" Alex said drily.

It was almost 9:30 when Alex left. I walked him to the car and watched as his silver Audi disappeared down the street. Angus was waiting for me in the front hall when I went inside.

"Has anybody heard from Eli?" he asked.

"He's back," I said. "Too bad you didn't get up earlier. Alex was here. He could have filled you in."

Angus looked away. "I was waiting till he left."

"Waiting till Alex left? Why would you do that?"

"Because I need to talk to you alone."

"Okay." I put my arm around his waist. My son had shot up over the summer. He was close to six feet now, but he was still my baby. "Let's sit down in the kitchen so we can look each other in the eye."

As a rule, Angus met problems head on, but it took him a while to zero in on this one. He went to the fridge, poured himself a glass of juice, drained it, and then filled his glass again. Finally he said, "Something happened at the football game yesterday that I should have told you and Alex about."

"Go on," I said.

"You're not going to like it." He leaned forward. "Mum, when you asked me why Eli ran off at the game, I said I didn't know."

"But you did."

He nodded. "Remember those college kids who ran out on the field just before half-time?"

"Of course," I said. "I was surprised they didn't get thrown out. They were pretty drunk."

"But everybody thought they were funny," Angus said. "Those guys sitting behind Eli and me were really cheering them on."

"They weren't exactly sober themselves," I said.

Angus traced a line through the condensation on his glass. "When Eli and I were coming back with our nachos, another man ran out on the field. The guys in the row behind us started to cheer – the way they'd done for the college kids. Then one of them said, 'It's only a fucking Indian,' and everybody stopped cheering."

"And Eli heard them."

Angus nodded. "At first, I thought he was going to cry. Then he just went ballistic. Do you know what he said, Mum? He said, 'Sometimes I'd like to kill you all.'"

I felt a sudden heaviness in my limbs. "He didn't mean it, Angus. I've blown up like that when I was mad. So have you. It's just a figure of speech."

Angus shook his head dismissively. "I know he didn't mean it. Eli wouldn't *kill* anybody. What pissed me off was the way he just lumped me in with those jerks. I was ready to go up and pound those mouthy guys into the ground, but Eli didn't give me a chance. He acted as if we were all the same."

"Well, we're not," I said. "But Eli will never know that if you bail on him now."

After Angus went upstairs to shower, I poured myself another glass of iced tea and turned on the news. There was nothing there to cheer me up. The media had discovered Justine Blackwell's murder, and judging from the play it was getting on the radio, her death was going to be the biggest story to hit our city in a long time. A breathless account of the bizarre circumstances in which the body was discovered was followed by an obituary which moved smoothly from the highlights of Justine Blackwell's legal career to a synopsis of the life and loves of her celebrated daughter, Lucy. Finally, there were excerpts from a press conference with Detective Robert Hallam in which he announced that the police were following up a number of leads and asking for the public's help.

The saturation coverage of Justine Blackwell's death didn't leave much time for the other big news story, the heat. At mid-morning the temperature in Regina was 32 degrees Celsius and climbing. The last day of the holiday weekend was going to be a sizzler, and there was no relief in sight. I turned off the radio, called Taylor, and told her that if she wanted to hit the pool for her daily swimming lesson, now was the time.

When I'd been looking for a larger place after I adopted Taylor, one of the features that had made this house afford-able was its backyard swimming pool. By the mid-nineties, prudent people had filled in their energy-wasting pools, but the owners of this house hadn't been prudent, and I'd been able to snap it up at a bargain price. Angus and I had counted it a privilege to be able to swim whenever the fancy struck us, but no one took greater pleasure in the pool than Taylor. All summer, she had been working to transform her exu-berant dogpaddle into a smooth Australian crawl. She was no closer to her goal when we came home from the lake than she had been on Canada Day, and that morning she splashed so much that Rose, who was getting fretful with age, thought she was drowning and jumped into the pool to save her. After Taylor and I had helped Rose out of the water and praised her for her heroism, my daughter decided we'd logged enough pool time. She pulled a lawn chair into a shady spot, plunked herself down, and announced that she needed to rest. I grabbed a chair, sat down beside her, closed my eyes, and gave myself over to the rare pleasure of a silent moment with my little girl.

It wasn't long before her flutey voice broke the stillness.

"Was my mum a good swimmer?" she asked.

"Let me think," I said. "When your mum and I were growing up, we always spent summers at the same place, so all the holidays sort of blend together, but I think when she was your age your mum swam pretty much the way you do."

"Not great," Taylor said gloomily.

"Not bad," I said. "And she got better."

Taylor slid off her chair and came over and sat on my knee. She smelled of chlorine and sunblock and heat, good summer smells. "When Eli's mum was ten years old, she swam almost the whole way across Echo Lake."

"That's impressive," I said. "Echo Lake's big."

"And she could run," Taylor said. "Eli says she could have been in the Olympics."

"When did Eli talk to you about his mum?" I asked.

"That night at the lake when we had the corn roast. He told me his mum liked to cook her corn with the skin still on, then he just kept talking about her."

I pulled my daughter closer. "Do me a favour, Taylor. Do what you can to *keep* Eli talking about his mum. He misses her, and it helps him to talk."

"Sure. I like Eli."

Taylor wriggled off my knee. The subject was closed. "I'm going in now," she said. "I've got to find some shorts and a T-shirt to wear to school tomorrow. If I wear that back-to-school outfit we bought at the mall, I'll *boil to death*."

I lay back and closed my eyes again. I didn't intend to drift off, but the heat and the broken sleep the night before caught up with me. My dreams were surreal: Lucy Blackwell was there, singing with Bob Dylan, and Karen Kequahtooway was dancing to their music. Detective Hallam was trying to focus a spotlight on them, but he kept shining it on me by mistake. The glare hurt my eyes, but every time I tried to get out of the way, the spotlight followed me. Finally, someone tried to pull me out of the light's path, and I woke up.

The sun was full in my face and Hilda McCourt was bending over me with her hand on my shoulder. She was wearing a lime-green peasant skirt and a white cotton blouse with her monogram embroidered in lime green on the breast pocket. Her face was creased with concern.

"I hate to awaken you, Joanne, but I was afraid you were getting sunburned."

"I'm glad you did," I said thickly. "What time is it?"

Hilda looked at her watch. "It's a little after twelve," she said. "Why don't I make us all some lunch while you give yourself a chance to wake up?"

I stood up. "I feel like I've been hit with the proverbial ton of bricks," I said. "I think I need a shower."

"Before you hop in," Hilda said, "there was a telephone call for you from Jess's mother. She wondered if they could take Taylor to a movie with them this afternoon. Your daughter was at my elbow, militating for a positive answer, so I said yes, conditional upon your approval, of course."

"You've got it," I said. "I don't want Taylor racing around outside in this heat."

After I'd showered, I towelled off, spritzed myself with White Linen, slipped on my coolest sundress, and revelled in feeling fresh. The pleasure was short-lived. By the time I got to the kitchen, I could feel the rivulets of sweat starting. In ten minutes, my sundress would be sticking to my back. Hilda was sitting at the kitchen table, cutting salmon sandwiches.

I leaned over her shoulder. "Those look wonderful," I said.

"Angus thought so," she said. "These are my second attempt. He ate the first plateful. Incidentally, he's going to be gone this afternoon, too."

"Did he say where he was going?"

"No, but he did he say he'd be home for dinner."

"That's a good sign."

"Is something wrong with him, Joanne? He was uncharacteristically quiet when I saw him."

"He's worried about Eli," I said. "So am I. He ran away again yesterday. You'd already gone to Justine's party when we got back from looking for him, so I didn't have a chance to tell you. He showed up at Alex's late last night."

"Is he all right?"

"I don't know."

Hilda gave me a searching look. "I gather you'd prefer that I not press you for details."

"It's not that," I said. "I just don't know very much. At the moment, all we can do is be here if he needs us." I smiled at her. "Now, it looks like you and I are on our own this afternoon. Anything special you'd like to do?"

"I'm afraid we aren't quite on our own, Joanne. While you were sleeping, I checked the message manager on my phone in Saskatoon."

I couldn't help smiling. Hilda noticed. She lifted her hand in a halt gesture. "I know I said those machines were cold and impersonal and would erode even the small amount of civility we're still clinging to, but they really are handy, aren't they? Mine certainly proved useful today. I had a message from Eric Fedoruk. Do you remember my mentioning his name to Detective Hallam?"

"I remember," I said. The name had seemed familiar to me at the time, and it nagged at me still, but I couldn't place it.

"At any rate," said Hilda, "I returned Mr. Fedoruk's call. It turns out that he was Justine's lawyer as well as her friend. We had a very curious conversation." She frowned. "I'm still not quite sure what he wanted. He kept circling around the question of my relationship with Justine. For a man trained in the law, he was quite imprecise."

"Law schools aren't exactly breeding grounds for clear expression," I said.

Hilda gave me a wry smile. "True enough," she said. "But I had the sense that Mr. Fedoruk's obfuscations were deliberate. My reading of the situation is that he was less concerned with giving information than getting it."

"You think he was on a fishing expedition?"

"Exactly," she said. "And I don't like being baited. So, to stand your metaphor on its head, I reeled Mr. Fedoruk in. He's coming here at two o'clock. I hope you don't mind,

Joanne. I know it's a breach of etiquette to invite a stranger into a home in which one's a guest."

I picked up a sandwich. "Hilda, you're not a guest; you're family. Besides, you've made me curious."

Hilda handed me a napkin. "Wyclif thought 'curiouste indicated a disposition to inquire too minutely into a thing,'" she said, "but I have a premonition that it's going to be impossible to inquire too minutely into the circumstances of Justine Blackwell's death."

As soon as I opened the front door and saw Eric Fedoruk standing on the porch, I knew why his name had rung a bell. In the late seventies, Eric Fedoruk had played for the Toronto Maple Leafs. He was a prairie boy with a slapshot that could crack Plexiglas and a smile as wide and untroubled as a Saskatchewan summer sky. The man offering his hand to me was a boy no longer: his crewcut was greying and the athlete's body had thickened with middle age, but as we introduced ourselves, it was obvious Eric Fedoruk's smile hadn't lost its wattage. He was wearing black motorcycle boots and he had his helmet in his hand. Over his shoulder I could see the kind of sleek, lethal cycle that Angus lusted after. I thanked my lucky stars he wasn't home.

"I apologize for barging in on you like this," Eric Fedoruk said. "Holiday weekends should be off limits to everybody except family and friends. But Justine's death has thrown everything off balance, at least for me." His sentence trailed off, and he shook his head in disbelief.

"Come inside where it's cool," I said. "Or at least *cooler*. Isn't this heat unbelievable?"

"And getting worse, according to the last weather report I heard," he said. "Mrs. Kilbourn, could I trouble you for a glass of water? I've been out riding, and throwing a six-hundred-pound bike around in this heat really takes it out of you."

I led him into the living room where Hilda was waiting. When I came back with the water, I started to excuse myself, but Hilda motioned me to stay. "Joanne, if you have a moment, I'd like you to hear this."

Eric took the water and gulped it gratefully. "Thanks," he said. "I was just telling Miss McCourt that I've been on the phone all morning with Justine's colleagues. I think we're all just beginning to realize how completely we failed her."

I sat down beside Hilda. "In what way?" I asked.

"Isn't it obvious? Someone should have stepped in – faced the fact that Justine's mind was deteriorating and forced her to get some professional help. As people who work in the legal system, we were all aware of how dangerous that crowd she was associating with were." His gaze was level. "Mrs. Kilbourn, I know there are some ex-cons and gang members who turn their lives around but, believe me, they're in the minority. I don't know whether it's bad genes, bad breaks, or bad judgement, but many criminals simply lack the kind of control they need to keep their violence in check. Look at them sideways and they snap."

"And you think one of them snapped and killed Justine Blackwell."

"I've talked to the police. Justine was bludgeoned to death. Doesn't that sound like the murderer just went crazy? We blew it. We should have intervened. I guess we just didn't want to deal with what was happening to Justine. I know I didn't."

"Because you and she were so close," Hilda said.

A look of pain crossed Eric Fedoruk's face. "Not as close as I wanted to be. Justine didn't let anyone get too close. It's just that I can't remember a time in my life when she wasn't there. I grew up in the house next door to hers on Leopold Crescent; I articled with her old firm after I graduated from law school; I represented clients in her courtroom. She was

absolutely brilliant. That's why all this is so . . ." He fell
silent, fighting emotion.

In the course of her professional life as a teacher of high-
school English, Hilda had dealt with more than her share of
the agitated and the overwrought. When she spoke, her voice
was as crisp as her monogrammed blouse. "Mr. Fedoruk, I
understand that you've sustained a loss, but you don't strike
me as the kind of man who would come to a stranger's home
to vent his grief. What is it that you want from me?"

He flinched. "All right," he said. "Here it is. Miss McCourt,
last night at the party, Justine told me she was going to ask for
your help with a certain matter. Did she have time to talk
to you about it?"

"You'll have to be more explicit," Hilda said. "Justine and
I spoke about many matters last night."

Eric Fedoruk hesitated. I could see him calculating the
odds that, in divulging information to Hilda, he might lose
his advantage. Once he'd made his decision, he waded right
in. "What Justine said was that, as her lawyer, I should be
aware that she was about to ask you to assess her capacity
to handle her personal affairs. *Did* she ask you to make that
assessment?"

This time it was Hilda's turn to deliberate before answering. When she finally responded, her voice was firm. "Yes,"
she said. "Justine did ask me to intervene in her life. She gave
me a medical text on geriatric psychiatry and a handwritten
letter authorizing me to evaluate her mental competence."

"May I see the letter?"

"In due time," Hilda said. "Now, I have a question for you,
Mr. Fedoruk. What's your interest in this?"

"I'm Justine's lawyer. I need to know . . ." He was falter-
ing, and he knew it. He took a deep breath and began again.
"My interest is a friend's interest," he said. "In the past year,
Justine Blackwell was not the woman she'd always been.

Miss McCourt, you remember what she used to be like. She was so . . ." He shrugged, searching for the right word. Finally, he found it. "She was so *elegant* in everything she did: the way she wrote judgments; the way she dressed; the way she arranged her office; even the way she smoked a cigarette was stylish – the way actresses in those old black-and-white movies used to smoke." He smiled at something he saw in my face. "Oh yes, Mrs. Kilbourn, until last year Justine was a two-pack-a-day smoker. Quitting smoking was another of her changes."

"A positive one," Hilda said drily.

"Maybe," he said. "But if it was, it was the only one. Of course, Justine saw quitting smoking as just one of many positive changes she made in her life after she met Wayne J. Waters. Did she talk to you about him?"

Hilda nodded.

"Then you know what an impact he had on her. It was insane. Justine had always had a built-in radar for bull-shitters, but Wayne J. seemed to slide in under the beam. She told me that meeting him was her 'moment of revelation.' I tried to make her see how nuts that was. 'Like Paul on the road to Damascus,' I said. I was sure she'd laugh. Justine didn't have much use for religion."

"But she didn't laugh," I said.

He sighed. "No," he said. "She was very earnest. She said, 'If you consider the moment on the road to Damascus a metaphor for a life-altering experience, then your comparison couldn't be more apt.'"

To this point, Hilda had been silent, taking it all in. When she spoke, I could hear the edge in her voice. "So Justine *was* aware that her life had altered radically. She didn't just slide into this new pattern of behaviour."

"Oh no," he said. "She was fully aware that things were different."

"Then your assessment that Justine wasn't in complete possession of her faculties hinges solely on the fact that you found the choices she was making repellent."

Eric Fedoruk grinned sheepishly. "You would have made a dynamite lawyer, Miss McCourt." He got to his feet. "Now, I really have taken up enough of your time. I'm sorry to have cast a shadow over the last long weekend of summer, but I needed to know how things stood."

He started for the door, but Hilda laid her hand on his arm, restraining him. "I wonder if you could leave me your business card, Mr. Fedoruk."

He pulled his wallet out of his back pocket, took out a card and a pen. "I'll jot down my home phone number too. I'm not always the easiest guy in the world to get hold of." He scrawled his number on the card and handed it to Hilda.

She looked at it thoughtfully. "You'll be hearing from me," she said. "Last night, Justine Blackwell asked a favour of me. Her death doesn't nullify that request. She wanted me to look after her interests, and that's exactly what I intend to do."

Eric Fedoruk furrowed his brow. "We *are* on the same side in this matter. I hope you understand that."

"Allegiances are earned, not assumed," Hilda said. "I hope *you* understand that." She smiled her dismissal. "Thank you for coming by. Your visit was most instructive."

When the door closed behind Eric Fedoruk, I turned to Hilda. "Were you throwing down the gauntlet?" I asked.

She shook her head. "Just alerting Mr. Fedoruk to the fact that I'm a woman who takes her responsibilities seriously." She squared her shoulders. "If your afternoon's clear, Joanne, would you be willing to join me in paying a condolence call? I telephoned Justine's daughters while you were napping. They're expecting me at two-thirty. It would be good to have a companion with me whose judgement I trust."

CHAPTER

3

Half an hour later, we were on our way. Hilda had replaced her peasant skirt with a seersucker dress the colour of a ripe apricot and covered her fiery red hair with a summer hat, a straw boater with a striped band that matched her outfit. I was wearing a white linen shirt and slacks. When I came downstairs, Hilda nodded her approval. "Very nice. Thank heavens we've jettisoned that hoary rule about summer's colours being appropriate only during the weeks between May 24 and Labour Day." She picked up her clutch bag from the cedar chest in the hall. "Now, it's already two-fifteen, so I suppose we'd better step lively."

From my kitchen window I could see the creek that separated my neighbourhood, Old Lakeview, from Justine Blackwell's, an area of handsomely curved, pleasingly landscaped streets known, accurately if unimaginatively, as The Crescents. Justine Blackwell's home was almost at the end of Leopold Crescent. I had walked by her place a hundred times, and I'd never ceased to admire it. It was a heritage house and unique: cobalt-blue Spanish-tile roof, white stucco walls artfully studded with decorative tiles, and windows of styles so

varied and delightful that I'd once taken a book on turn-of-
the century architecture out of the public library just to
look them up. Their names had been as evocative as the
windows themselves: Oriel, Lancet, Mullioned, Œil-de-
bœuf, Catherine wheel.

The front door of 717 Leopold Crescent was oak, framed
at the top by a graceful semicircular window that my reading
had taught me was known as fanlight. The effect was, as Eric
Fedoruk would have said, elegant.

From the moment Hilda suggested paying a condolence
call on Justine's family, I had felt an adolescent thrill at the
prospect of meeting Lucy Blackwell face to face. Her name
summoned forth a kaleidoscope of images that were part
of the cultural history of every woman my age. In the
youthquake of the late sixties, Lucy had been a Mary Quant
girl in thigh-high clear plastic boots and leather mini, her
eyes doe-like behind the kohl eyeliner and fake eyelashes,
her hair ironed into smooth sheets the colour of pulled taffy.

She had been a ripe sixteen when she recorded the first song
that brought her recognition. The song was called "Lilacs,"
and she had written it herself. Its subject, the painful process
of losing a first love to a heartless rival, was an adolescent
cliché, but Lucy's treatment of the angst-ridden convention
rocked between low farce and elegy, and her voice was a husky
sensation.

In the seventies, shod in sandals hand-tooled in Berkeley
by people who'd got their priorities straight and wearing
granny gowns of hand-dyed batik, Lucy had woven flowers
in her hair and sung songs of misplaced faith and love gone
wrong that became anthems for a generation of middle-class
kids raised in the warm sunshine of Dr. Spock but yearning
for the storm of sexual adventure. We mined the lyrics of
each new song for autobiographical details. Was that "singin'
man" who left her on the beach, "cryin' and dyin' as the tide

washed in," James Taylor or Dylan? When she sang of "that small white room where I left behind a gift I could never retrieve," was she remembering the abortion clinic in which, it was whispered, she had gone to have Mick Jagger's baby cut away? It was heady stuff.

When the decade ended, she settled down somewhere on Saltspring Island with a man none of us had ever heard of and announced she was going to raise a family and write an opera for children. For a time she disappeared, and it seemed Lucy Blackwell was destined to become a candidate for a trivia-quiz answer. Then, in the early eighties, she surfaced again. She was alone and empty-handed: no man, no babies, no opera, but there was savage light in her eyes and a new and feral quality in her voice. Within a year, she'd written the score for a movie and the music for an off-Broadway show; both were hits. She was back, and with her beautiful hair permed into an explosion of Botticelli curls, her body hard-muscled from feel-the-burn exercise, and her voice knife-edged with danger, she was the very model of the eighties woman.

For three decades, Lucy Blackwell had been the first to catch the wave, but the woman who stood before me that Labour Day afternoon seemed to have left trendiness behind. She was barefoot, wearing bluejean cut-offs and a man's white shirt, with the sleeves rolled up to reveal a dynamite tan. Her eyes were extraordinary, so startlingly green-blue that they were almost turquoise, and her shoulder-length hair shone with the lustre of dark honey. Lucy was a Saskatchewan-born forty-five-year-old, but she had the long-limbed agelessness of the prototypical all-American girl.

"Thank you for coming," she said, extending her hand. She was holding an old-fashioned scrub brush, and when she noticed it, she laughed with embarrassment and lifted it in the air. "Trying to fix what can't be fixed," she said distractedly. "I'm Lucy Blackwell. Won't you come in?"

Hilda and I followed her through the entranceway and down the hall. The parquet floors along which we walked were scuffed and sticky underfoot, and the air was heavy with the rotting-fruit smell of forgotten garbage. "I hope you don't mind if we visit in the dining room," Lucy said. "My mother had some curious guests in the last year. The dining room's the only room in the house that doesn't look as if 2 Live Crew has been playing a concert in it."

The room was a damaged beauty. A wall broken by lancet windows looked out onto the yard. The shell-pink silk curtains that bracketed the view were coolly ethereal, but they were stained at child level. A rose Berber carpet that must have cost a king's ransom was discoloured by the kind of patches that are left by dog urine. Lucy motioned us to sit down at the mahogany dining table. The creamy needlepoint on the backs and seats of the chairs was soiled, but the wood gleamed and there was a scent of lemon oil in the air. A bucket of soapy water rested on a stool near the sideboard.

"I've been scouring away in here all day," Lucy said. "But no matter what I try, nothing seems to help." She pointed with her brush. "Look at them," she said, indicating walls covered in silk of a pink so delicate the colour seemed almost illusory. Figures were woven into the fabric: Rubenesque women, epicurean and lush. The wall-covering must have been a treasure once, but someone had desecrated the women's bodies. Crude breasts and genitalia were drawn in marker over the delicate lines in the fabric. Lucy had obviously been scrubbing at them; the places where she had worked were marked by ugly spoors of damp colour.

"When we were young, my mother wouldn't allow us to eat in this room. It was for adults only," she said. There was an intimate teasing quality in Lucy's voice that seemed to draw us into her orbit. "But if my parents had a dinner party," she continued, "my father would call us down to meet the guests. It was so exciting. Of course, my sisters and I would be all shined up for bed. I can still remember how soft the rug felt under my bare feet when we trooped in to be introduced. It was always so shadowy and scary in the hall, but the candles in here would be blazing."

"*'Three little girls in virgin's white, swimming through darkness, longing for light,*" I said.

Lucy shot me a radiant smile. "You remembered."

"'My Daddy's Party' is a pretty memorable song," I said.

"Thanks. That means a lot. Especially now." She looked around the room, and when she spoke again, her voice quivered with rage and hurt. "I haven't been in this room in years. Somehow, I'd hoped on this visit . . ." She swallowed hard. "Too late now. We'll never get things back the way they were. Metaphors aren't much fun in real life."

"Perhaps you should get professionals in to do this work," Hilda said gently. "As you're discovering, a home is a powerful symbol for those who live within it."

Lucy ran her fingers through her hair. "I guess that's why my sister Signe thinks trying to put things right in these rooms is good therapy for me. My other sister says it's a way of making up for my sins of omission."

"What do you think?" I asked.

"It doesn't matter what I think. The prodigal daughter doesn't get a vote." She laughed sadly. "I'm forgetting my manners. Can I get you a drink? The Waterford crystal my father bought my mother on their honeymoon is pretty much a write-off, but there must be a jam-jar or two around."

"We're fine," Hilda said. "Mrs. Kilbourn and I aren't planning to stay, but, Lucy, there is something I'd like to talk to you and your sisters about. Will they be able to join us?"

"Signe will. Tina isn't seeing people right now."

Lucy left to get her sister, and I walked over and looked out at the scene framed by the window. Zinnias, asters, and marigolds, prides of the late summer garden, shimmered in the gold September haze. A boy pushing a power-mower made lazy passes across the lawn. Heat hung in the air. Hilda came and stood beside me. The scene was idyllic, but I could feel my friend's fury.

"Why would anyone set that poor woman the Sisyphean task of cleaning up this disaster and tell her it was her way of making up for what she did or failed to do?" she asked.

"She does seem to be near the breaking point," I said.

"My sister doesn't break."

The voice, as huskily melodic as Lucy's, came from behind us. I turned, expecting to greet a stranger, but I knew the woman standing in the entrance to the dining room. Eli Kequahtooway had introduced us. She was his therapist.

"Hello, Dr. Rayner," I said.

She gazed at me, perplexed. "You'll have to forgive me," she said, "I don't remember . . ."

"There's no reason to," I said. "We only met once – at the Cornwall Centre. I'm Joanne Kilbourn, a friend of Eli Kequahtooway's."

"Of course," she said. "I remember thinking Eli must be fond of you to bring you over to me."

"I hope he is," I said. "I'm certainly fond of him. Dr. Rayner, this is my friend Hilda McCourt."

She took Hilda's hand. "It's Signe – please. My mother spoke of you often, Miss McCourt, and always with great respect."

"I'm flattered," Hilda said evenly. "Your mother was an extraordinary woman."

Signe Rayner gave Hilda an odd little smile. "There's no disputing that," she said drily. She gestured towards the dining-room table. "Shall we continue this conversation sitting down?"

Her offer seemed to be as much for her benefit as ours. She was a large woman, as tall as Lucy but much heavier, so heavy, in fact, that standing for any length of time must have been uncomfortable for her. She was wearing an ivory-and-black African-print gown which had affinities to both the muumuu and the caftan without being either. She had been wearing the garment's twin, in shades of coffee and taupe, the day Eli introduced her to me in the mall. Signe Rayner had impressed me then as a woman of self-confident authority, but it appeared her ability to dominate situations didn't extend to her family.

Lucy Blackwell came back into the room just as her sister pulled out a chair at the head of the table. As Signe settled in, Lucy's smile was wicked. "You'll notice how Signe chooses the seat of command. She's a psychiatrist, so watch your step."

Hilda's eyes widened. "A psychiatrist," she said, settling into the chair to Signe's right. "Your mother presented me with a book last night: a review of geriatric psychiatry. It was a medical text. Did you give it to her?"

Signe Rayner met Hilda's gaze. "I did. At her request."

"When did she ask you for it?"

Signe rubbed at a whorl in the mahogany table with her fingertip. "At the beginning of August. We have a family cottage up at Little Bear Lake. We take turns using it, but we always reserve the first weekend in August to be together – just the four of us. I'd been concerned about my mother's behaviour for months. I'd suggested she see a colleague of mine who specializes in geriatric patients, but my mother refused." Signe's brow furrowed. "She was quite vehement. She insisted that a change in the way one chose to live one's life was not necessarily an indicator of a progressive dementing disorder."

Hilda leaned forward with interest. "Did she use that term?"

"Oh yes," Signe said. "When it came to areas that touched her life, my mother believed in acquiring expert knowledge."

"Oedipus had great knowledge too," Hilda said gently. "He was even able to solve the riddle of the Sphinx, yet he never truly knew himself. That was the source of his tragedy."

Lucy twisted a hank of her hair around her finger. "Do you think my mother didn't know herself?"

Hilda smiled enigmatically, then she turned to Signe Rayner. "Perhaps you have an opinion?"

Signe shrugged. "I was trying to formulate one up at the lake. There are a number of standard tests that are used to determine mental status."

"And Justine agreed to be tested?" Hilda asked.

Signe Rayner looked rueful. "She wasn't supposed to notice. I was trying to be unobtrusive."

"Blending into the wallpaper isn't exactly your strong suit, Signe." Lucy Blackwell pushed back her chair and drew up one of her legs so that its heel rested on her other leg. Her legs were beautiful, long and shapely. The pose seemed deliberatively provocative. She was, I realized, one of those people whose every encounter is surrounded by an erotic haze. She gazed at her sister with interest. "To be fair, the time for subtlety did seem to be over. I hadn't seen Mummy since the summer before, but her life really had become quite bizarre."

"That's why Tina and I had been calling you for almost a year asking you to come back," Signe said.

"I had obligations."

"We hoped your obligation to your family might take priority."

"Families," Lucy said. She shot me a conspiratorial glance; then, in a voice that was thrillingly familiar, she sang, "'You *can slam the door and walk away, but you're still trapped in their photo albums.'"* She looked at me expectantly.

"'Picture Time,'" I said. "From the first album."

Signe glared at me. "Don't encourage her," she said sternly. She turned to Hilda. "Miss McCourt, you said Mother gave you my handbook on geriatric psychiatry. Did she explain why she wanted you to have it?"

"Justine wanted me to decide whether her mental faculties were intact."

"Isn't the fact that she dragged you into this proof that her mental faculties *weren't* intact?" Lucy's frustration was evident. "I mean no disrespect, Miss McCourt, but from what Signe tells me, you weren't that close to my mother. She had friends and family here. Doesn't it strike you as bizarre that she felt she couldn't go to the people who knew her best?"

"Not at all," Hilda said flatly. "It strikes me as eminently sensible. Your mother knew me as a person of probity who had no axe to grind. Now, let's deal with the situation at hand. When Eric Fedoruk came to see me this afternoon, we talked about the task your mother set me."

"*Eric* came to see you?" Lucy leaped to her feet. She seemed close to tears. "He hasn't even returned our calls."

Signe Rayner half-rose from her chair. "Lucy, don't."

"Why not? What did he tell you about us, Miss McCourt?"

"That's enough, Lucy." Signe's voice was commanding. "We can talk about this later."

Lucy walked over to Hilda. "Miss McCourt, don't believe everything you hear."

At close to five-foot-eleven, Lucy was almost a foot taller than my old friend, but Hilda took charge of the situation. "I've learned to make my own assessments of people, Lucy. Now, while I'm truly sorry for your loss, my purpose in coming here this afternoon is not simply to commiserate. Last night, when your mother gave me Signe's book, she also gave me a note authorizing me to do what I deemed necessary to protect her interests." Hilda turned to Signe. "I came here today to let all of you know that's exactly what I plan to do."

Lucy and Signe exchanged glances, then Signe thanked us, quite formally, for coming, and she and Lucy saw us out.

Silenced by the misery we had felt in Justine Blackwell's home, Hilda and I walked down the front path. Out of nowhere, another image from "Picture Time" flashed through my mind. "*Our last smiles frozen in Kodachrome.*" As we turned onto the sidewalk, I found myself thinking that there wasn't much about painful leave-takings that Lucy Blackwell didn't understand.

Hilda's musings had obviously been running parallel to mine. "Two very unhappy women," she said. "And I don't believe the genesis of their problems was their mother's death."

"No," I agreed. "Whatever's troubling the Blackwell sisters goes way back."

Hilda touched my arm. "And there's more trouble coming to them," she said. "Look over there."

A van painted in the style of comic-book high realism that Taylor's art teacher called jailhouse art had pulled up across the road. The vehicle was, by anyone's reckoning, a mean machine, and as its driver bounded out and started towards us, there was no denying that he was one tough customer. He was of middle height, with a shaved head, a full moustache, and the powerful physique of a bodybuilder.

As he brushed past us, I saw that the parts of his skin not hidden by his Levi's and white V-necked T-shirt were purpley-blue with tattoos. He vaulted up the front steps of the Blackwell house and knocked on the door.

"Another condolence call," I said.

"I wonder what the Blackwell sisters will make of this one?" Hilda said. She turned to me. "I assume you can guess at that man's identity, Joanne."

"Wayne J. Waters?"

"In the flesh," Hilda said.

Patient as a choirboy, Wayne J. waited for someone to respond to his knock on the door. When it was apparent that no answer was forthcoming, he pounded his closed fist into the open palm of his other hand and headed back down the walk.

As his van screeched back towards Albert Street, the words painted in red on the back of the vehicle leaped out at me: "Every Saint Has a Past. Every Sinner Has a Future." It seemed Lucy Blackwell hadn't cornered the market on folk wisdom.

That night, after Taylor's school clothes were laid out for the next day her backpack filled with her new school supplies, and she'd been bathed and tucked into bed with her cats, Bruce and Benny, and Hilda had been rung in to tell the next adventure in the ongoing saga of Sir Gawain and the Green Knight, I drove over to Alex's apartment on Lorne Street, and we made love.

When I was twenty, I had believed that the pleasures of sex were aesthetic and athletic. Then, the prospect of being physically intimate with a man when I was past fifty and my body was no longer a delight to look at or a joy to manoeuvre had filled me with alarm. I'd been wrong to worry. With Alex, I was enjoying the best sex of my life: by turns passionate, tender, funny, restoring, and transcendent. That September night, we managed four out of five. When we'd finished, our bodies were slick on the tangled sheets, and we were at peace.

It was good to be back in the apartment. Since his nephew
had come to live with him, Alex and I hadn't spent much
time there, but tonight we were alone. Declaring that Eli
was in need of chill-out time, Dr. Kasperski had decided to
keep him in the hospital overnight. As I looked at the lines
of worry etched in Alex's face, I thought the man I loved
could use a little chill-out time himself. The events of
the past twenty-four hours had taken their toll. Through the
open window of the bedroom, I could see the plaster owl a
previous tenant had anchored on the rail of the balcony to
scare off pigeons. Alex called the bird his sentinel, and we
had joked that as long as the bird was there, no intruder
could disturb our delight in one another. As I felt the tension
returning to Alex's body, I knew I had to face the fact that
even plaster owls had their limits.

I moved closer to him. "Talk to me about it," I said.

"There's not much to say. I had a quick visit with Dan
Kasperski after he saw Eli this afternoon. Considering Eli's his
patient only until Dr. Rayner gets back to her practice,
Kasperski's giving a lot of thought to the case. He says his first
task is to get Eli to see him as an ally who can help him find
a way to deal with all the things that are troubling him."

"That makes sense to me," I said.

Alex's dark eyes were serious. "Everything Dan Kasperski
says makes sense. The amazing thing is he looks like he's
about seventeen years old. Maybe that's why Eli's responding so well to him. This afternoon, when Kasperski came in,
I could see the relief on Eli's face."

"Maybe you should ask him to take Eli on as a patient. In
the next few weeks, Signe Rayner could have her hands full
just dealing with her own life."

"What do you mean?"

"Did you know she's Justine Blackwell's daughter?"

"You're kidding."

"No. Hilda and I went over to Justine's house today to pay a condolence call, and Signe Rayner was there. Alex, how does Eli get along with her? She seems so . . ."

"Forbidding? I know what you mean, but she came highly recommended, and she did get Eli to open up about the guilt he feels about Karen's death."

"Guilt? You never said anything about him feeling guilty."

"It was Eli's story to tell or not tell. Besides, he seemed to be dealing with it."

"Why would he feel guilty? Nobody can prevent a car accident, and from what you've said, Eli really loved Karen."

"He did love her, but he also caused her a lot of grief. I never could figure out why. Karen was about the best mother any kid could ask for: very devoted, very involved with the culture. But as great as Karen was, when Eli was about ten the graffiti started, and the running away to the city."

"Did something happen?"

"No. Eli just got mad at the world. I went through the same thing when I was his age."

"You straightened out," I said. "Can't get much straighter than a cop."

Alex drew me closer. "I was lucky," he said. "My mother didn't die when I was sixteen. By the time my mother died, I'd had time to show her I valued the things she'd taught me."

"But Eli never had that chance," I said.

"No," Alex said, "he didn't. And it's eating him up. Has he ever said anything to you about Karen?"

"Never," I said. "But he did talk to Taylor about her."

"To Taylor? She's the last person I'd have thought he'd open up to."

"There's a certain logic there, I guess. Taylor lost her mother too, and of course she's so young, Eli doesn't have to worry about being a tough guy in front of her. Just this morning, Taylor was telling me that she and Eli had talked about what a great swimmer Karen was."

In the moonlight, Alex's face grew soft. "She *was* a great swimmer. We used to tell her she was part otter. She loved that lake. We had this old canoe. When Karen was four, she went clear across the lake in it. She was so little, she could barely hold the paddle." His voice broke. "And could she ever run. Some of those hills we've got out at Standing Buffalo are steep, but that never stopped Karen. It seemed like every time my brother and I were supposed to be watching out for her, she'd take off on us. We always knew where to look for her – right at the top of the biggest hill she could find. As soon as she saw Perry and me, she'd start to run to us. We'd yell at her to slow down because we were afraid she'd break her neck, and then we'd catch hell. But she never slowed down. And she never fell."

For a long time, we were silent. Finally, Alex said, "The only thing that ever scared my sister was thinking about what could happen to Eli. When she died, I promised myself that I'd do everything I could to make sure he had a good life. Damn it, Jo, until yesterday, I thought Eli was going to be okay. What would make a kid take off like that, for no reason?"

I sat up. "He had a reason," I said.

As I told Alex about the incident at the Rider game, I could see the cords in his neck tighten, but he didn't say anything until I'd finished. Then, under his breath, he murmured a word I'd never heard him use before, and I could feel the barrier come between us. I went into the bathroom to get ready to go home. After I'd dressed, I looked out the bathroom window. On the balcony of the apartment across the alley, a man and a woman, who looked to be about my age, were having a late supper. There were candles on the table and fresh flowers. As I watched, the man leaned towards the woman and touched her cheek. When she felt his touch, the woman covered his hand with her own. That unknown couple might have had a hundred secret sorrows but, at that moment, I envied them their uncomplicated joy in one another. Moonlight and unspoken intimacies: that was the way love was supposed to be.

Alex walked me down to my car. I slid into the driver's seat. "Tell Eli the kids and I will come by and visit him tomorrow after school," I said.

"Considering the circumstances, maybe you'd better wait a while," Alex said.

"Whenever you think he's ready," I said.

I waited as Alex opened the front door of his building and walked inside. He didn't look back. His apartment was on the third floor at the corner. I knew exactly how long it took to reach it. I watched as the lights went out in his living room, and a few seconds later in his bedroom. Miserable at the thought of Alex sitting alone in the dark, his only protection against the vagaries of the world a plaster owl sitting sentry on a balcony railing, I took a deep breath and turned the key in the ignition.

CHAPTER

4

I slept deeply that night and awoke thinking about Alex Kequahtooway and Martin Heidegger and the question of whether any of us ever truly knows who we are. It was gloomy pondering for 5:00 a.m. on the first workday after a holiday weekend, and I was relieved when the phone rang and I heard my older daughter's voice. Mieka was twenty-four years old, and she had a great marriage, a career she loved, and a first child due any minute. To my mind, the only problem about Mieka's life was that it was being lived in Saskatoon, 250 kilometres away from me.

"I knew you'd be up," she said. "No baby news. I'm just calling to whine."

"Whine away," I said.

She took a deep breath. "Well, for starters, I don't think this baby is ever going to be born. My doctor says if I don't get cracking by next weekend, they're going to induce me. Is it just an old wives' tale that painting the kitchen ceiling gets baby moving along?"

"I don't know about kitchen ceilings," I said, "but I do

know that going out for Chinese food works. That's what your dad and I did the night before you were born."

Mieka laughed. "Tucking into a platter of Peking duck does sound more appealing than clambering up a ladder to slap on a coat of flat white." She sighed heavily. "Mummy, I'm so discouraged. I haven't slept through the night in eight months, I haven't seen my feet since Canada Day, and I've got a seductive line of black hair growing from my breast-bone to what used to be my organs of delight."

"It'll be over soon," I said. "I just wish I was there with you."

"But you will come when the baby's born?"

"Wild horses couldn't keep me away."

After we hung up, I reached under the bed and pulled out the cradle board that Alex had made for Mieka and Greg's baby. The hide bag stitched to the board was as soft as moss, and it smelled of woodsmoke. A newborn would feel safe in its snug confines. Later, the cradle board would hold the baby tight against its parent as it learned to keep a careful eye on the wonders and the terrors of the world.

I slid the cradle board back under the bed and walked downstairs. The heat and the humidity in the closed-up house were almost palpable, and I opened the front door to let in some fresh air. On the cedar chest in the front hall, Taylor's new tartan backpack bulged, waiting to be grabbed by its owner as she sped out the door, eager to seize all the learning and fun Grade 2 had to offer. Ordinarily, I loved fall days with their heady mix of elegy for the summer past and anticipation of adventures to come, but this September was different, and as Rose and I headed for our run around the lake, I wondered if the heat would ever stop pressing down on us, making our nerves jump and our spirits sink.

By the time we got back, my hair was curling damply, and my clothes were soaked with sweat. I grabbed the newspaper off the porch and went inside to get Rose a bowl of fresh water and to plug in the coffee maker. As I waited for the coffee to perk, I glanced at the front page. The story of Justine Blackwell's murder was above the fold. The picture the editors had chosen was a formal one of Justine robed for court. With her fair hair swept back into a smooth chignon and her coolly intelligent gaze, she seemed an unlikely candidate for grisly murder.

The story accompanying the photograph was circumspect and predictable: a dry but factual account of the murder, a review of Justine's legal career, a brief history of her personal life. No surprises, but the final sentence of the piece *was* unexpected: "Longtime friend Hilda McCourt announced that funeral plans for Madame Justice Blackwell were pending."

When Hilda came in, I held the paper out to her. It was 6:45, but she was already dressed for the day in a trim mint sheath, with a mandarin collar and neck-to-knee mother-of-pearl frog fastenings.

"You're famous," I said.

She took the paper, glimpsed at the story, and frowned. "I was afraid my name would be mentioned."

"How did the paper get hold of you?"

"Lucy Blackwell gave them my name and your number," Hilda said. "Joanne, I apologize for yet another intrusion in your home. This is becoming a distressing pattern."

"Don't give it a second thought," I said. "But I don't understand why Lucy would decide that you should be the one dealing with the press."

Hilda sighed. "Neither do I. But according to Lucy, I was the unanimous choice. Apparently, Tina Blackwell is having a difficult time accepting her mother's death. Her sisters think she's in no state for media scrutiny. They've concluded that since Justine asked me to protect her interests, I might as well act as an intermediary with the press."

I felt a rush of annoyance. Hilda was a wonder, but she was an eighty-three-year-old wonder, and she had just been handed an open-ended duty.

As always, Hilda was quick to read my face. "You're not convinced I'm the best choice."

I shook my head. "As far as I'm concerned, you're the best choice for any job you choose to undertake. I'm just not certain you should have been asked to undertake this one."

"It's been busy, I'll grant you that. Just after you left to meet Alex last night, I had a call from the journalist who is responsible for this." Hilda tapped the Blackwell story with a fingernail freshly painted in her favourite Love That Red. "Later, there were other members of the press. I'm afraid your house was photographed, Joanne."

I felt a stab of irritation, not at Hilda, but at the intrusion. "Don't worry about it," I said, but my voice lacked conviction.

Hilda leaned towards me. "Maybe it would be easier all around if I went back to Saskatoon. With facsimile machines and my message manager, I could handle everything from there, and you'd be spared the prospect of living in a circus."

"Don't be silly," I said. "In a day or two, there'll be another story for the media to chase. Besides I love having you here. You know that."

Taylor's ginger cat, Benny, padded into the room. As usual, her tortoiseshell, Bruce, followed meekly. My daughter wasn't far behind.

"I like it when you're here, too," Taylor said. She bent, grabbed Benny, hefted him under one arm, and scooped up Bruce. Then she twirled so Hilda could check out the back of her head. "Are my braids okay?" she asked.

Her braids were, in fact, okay. So was her face, which was clean, and her runners, which matched and were tied. What wasn't okay was the T-shirt she was wearing, which had a picture of a bull on it that bordered on the obscene, and an eyebrow-raising caption: "Bottlescrew Bill's Second Annual Testicle Festival – I Went Nuts."

I knelt down beside her. "T, you look great, but you're going to have to find another shirt."

"But this one's so funny. You laughed when Angus brought it home from the garage sale, and everybody at the cottage thought it was good."

"It was good for the cottage," I said, "but not for school."

"Why?"

"Because wearing that shirt to school would be like wearing tap shoes to church."

"Dumb," she said.

"Not dumb," I said. "Just not your best choice. Now come on, let's go upstairs and find a shirt that isn't going to get you thrown out of Grade 2 before the end of the day."

Taylor went off to school wearing a white cotton blouse and the intricately beaded barrettes Alex had bought the day we went to a powwow out at Standing Buffalo. They were reserved for special occasions, but she and I agreed this occasion was special enough. After she left, Bruce looked so miserable I gathered him up and began scratching his head. Benny came over, rubbed against my ankle and howled. Benny and I had never been close, but it was a day to put aside old enmities. I bent down to pick him up too. "She'll be back," I said. Benny shot me a look filled with contempt and streaked off; then Bruce, who was sweet but easily led, leaped out of my arms and dashed after him.

When I finally got around to showering and dressing, I was running late. I knew that if I didn't make tracks, I wouldn't be on time for the early-morning meeting the Political

Science department always held at the Faculty Club on the first day of classes. I decided to skip breakfast, grabbed my briefcase, hollered at Angus to get moving, called goodbye to Hilda, and raced out the front door and straight into the wall of muscles that was Wayne J. Waters.

At close range, he was even more intimidating than he had appeared at a distance. He was not a tall man; in fact, he wasn't much taller than I was, five-foot-six. But he was tattooed to terrify. On his arms, jungle beasts coupled ferociously; savage mastiffs chewed on hearts that dripped blood; buxom women straddled unidentifiable animals and embraced crucifixes. It was the Garden of Earthly Delights envisioned by a lifer. I couldn't stop staring, and Wayne J. Waters caught me.

"Better than an art gallery, eh?" His voice was deep and surprisingly pleasant. "Are you Hilda McCourt? That reporter who came to interview me did the usual half-assed job those media types always do – told me where to find Hilda but didn't give me a whiff about how to recognize her."

"I'm not Miss McCourt," I said. "But she is staying with me. I'm Joanne Kilbourn. Can I help you?"

"We'll give you a try. My name's Wayne J. Waters," he said. "I wanted to talk to Hilda about the funeral she's got pending." He shook his head and laughed. "The way we word things, eh?" he said. "Anyway, you get the drift." He stepped closer. His aftershave was familiar and distinctive. Old Spice. "So is Hilda around?"

My first thought was to lie, to simply say that Hilda had left town. In his sleeveless muscle shirt, Wayne J.'s upper arms were grenades, and Hilda's account of his nasty confrontation with Justine the night of the party leapt to my mind. But my friend was not a person who took kindly to having decisions made for her; besides, the rumble of Wayne J.'s laugh was reassuring, and there was something in his eyes which, against all logic, inspired trust. It was a tough call. Luckily, while I was vacillating, Hilda appeared and made the call for me.

As soon as he saw her, Wayne J. introduced himself and held out his hand. Hilda's response was icy. "Mr. Waters, when I've satisfied myself that you had nothing to do with Justine Blackwell's death, I'll take your hand. Until then . . ."

Hilda's blue eyes were boring into him, but Wayne J. Waters didn't flinch. "Fair enough," he said. "Do you want to talk out here, or can I come inside?"

Hilda shot me a questioning look.

"It'll be easier to talk where it's cool," I said.

As we walked back inside, Wayne J. glanced at the briefcase in my hand. "Decided to play hooky, Joanne?"

I shook my head. "Decided not to leave until you do, Wayne J."

He put his head back and roared. "Who could blame you?"

Wayne J. Waters might have had his troubles with the law, but somewhere along the line he had come up with some personal rules about how to treat a lady. He waited until Hilda and I were seated before he lowered himself into my grandmother's Morris chair. Once seated, he got right to the point.

"To set your mind at ease," he said, "I had nothing to do with Justine's death. If I have to give you specifics I will, but for now, I hope it's enough to say that she was the classiest woman I ever knew, and she was a good friend to me and to a lot of other people I could name."

Hilda adjusted the mother-of-pearl button fastening at the throat of her dress. "Yet you quarrelled with her bitterly the night of her party."

Wayne J. Waters put the palms of his hands on his knees and leaned forward. "Didn't you ever fight with a friend?" he asked softly.

Hilda wasn't drawn in. "Not one who was murdered a few hours after our dispute," she said.

Wayne J. reddened. "You were lucky. I'd serve ten years of hard time to see Justine walk into this room. But that isn't gonna happen. As they say, all we can do is honour her memory." He squared his shoulders. "That's why I'm here. Hilda, will the people who Justine helped out at the end be welcome at her funeral?"

Hilda's brow furrowed. "Provided it's not a private service, I see no reason why anyone who chooses to attend wouldn't be welcomed."

Wayne J. sighed heavily. "That's all I needed to know," he said, standing up.

"Wait," Hilda said. "I answered your question. Now please answer mine."

He turned and looked at her expectantly.

"What was the cause of your quarrel with Madame Justice Blackwell?" she asked.

The question could hardly have been a surprise, but as Hilda posed it, the pulse in Wayne J.'s neck began to beat so noticeably that the wings of the eagle tattooed on his neck appeared to flutter. I remembered Detective Hallam's one-phrase description of him: lightning in a bottle.

"Money," Wayne J. said, biting off the word.

"Can you elucidate?" Hilda asked.

He eased himself back into his chair. "Justine had promised to give some money to Culhane House – it's a prisoners' support group some of us started up for cons and ex-cons.

"Culhane House, as in Claire Culhane?" I asked.

He gave me a sidelong glance. "She was another classy lady," he said. "Justine suggested the name." He turned back to Hilda. "Prisoners' rights aren't exactly a hot ticket now. Most people seem to think the only choice society should give a con is permanent incarceration or the end of a rope."

"But Madame Justice Blackwell believed there were more humane alternatives," Hilda said.

Wayne J. shrugged. "You could say that, but I wouldn't. I think for Justine it was more a practical thing."

"Practical in what way?" asked Hilda.

"Like in the way that, most of the time, prisons just don't do what solid citizens want them to do. All prisons are good for is pissing away lives and pissing away money. You can make semi-good people bad in prison, and you can make bad people worse, but you never make anybody better. And I'll tell you another thing, Hilda. They may be hellholes, but I've never seen a prison yet that made anybody scared to come back. Every time I hear some expert running off at the mouth about that three strikes and you're out crap, I want to laugh. The only guy who's scared of going to prison is a guy who's never been there. Any ex-con knows that he might as well be in prison as anywhere else. Justine finally figured that there was a cheaper, better alternative to prison, and she was prepared to use her chequebook so that other people could figure it out too."

"But she withdrew her offer of financial support," Hilda said.

Wayne J. gripped the arms of his chair. Until that moment, I hadn't noticed how big his hands were. They were huge, and they were taut with the effort to maintain control. "God damn it, she didn't withdraw the offer," he said furiously. "She just decided to fucking reconsider."

The rage in his voice was a shock; so were his eyes, which had darkened terrifyingly. The Old Spice and the self-deprecating chuckle had lulled me, but there was no disputing the fact that only an act of will was preventing the man in front of me from springing out of my grandmother's chair and smashing everything in sight. My grandmother would have said I had been six kinds of fool to invite Wayne J. Waters into my house, and she would have been right. I began to run through strategies to get him out of the house. Just when I'd decided that none seemed workable, the storm passed.

Wayne J. hung his head in an attitude of abject apology. "Sorry about the language, ladies," he said. "It's just that there were so many people pushing Justine to 'withdraw' her offer. Miss McCourt, I don't know if she had a chance to tell you this the other night, but since Justine decided to support Culhane House, people have been lining up to tell her how crazy she is – *was*." He made a fist with one hand and pounded it repeatedly into the palm of his other hand. It was the same gesture he'd made when no one answered the door the day he went to Justine's house on Leopold Crescent. "They tried to tell her she was losing it because she was getting old, but she wasn't losing it, she was finding it." He looked at me. His eyes were black and mesmerizing. "Does that make sense?"

Almost against my will, I found myself agreeing. "Yes," I said. "It makes sense."

"Good," he said. "Because no matter what people said, Justine was with the people at Culhane House 110 per cent."

I narrowed my eyes at him. "Absolutely trustworthy," I said.

He didn't blink. "Except for that last night, absolutely."

When Wayne J. left, I followed him out. I'd decided to skip the meeting at the Faculty Club and concentrate my efforts on getting to the university in time for my first class. I backed the Volvo down the driveway, but as I turned onto the street, Wayne J. came over. I cranked down my window.

"I forgot to say thanks," he said.

"For what?"

"For letting me into your house. A lot of ladies wouldn't have had the balls." He realized what he'd said and grimaced. "Whoa," he said, "that didn't come out right."

"I took it as a compliment," I said.

He touched an imaginary cap. "That's how I meant it."

I got to the university just in time to run to the Political Science office to check my mail and pick up my class lists. Rosalie Norman, our departmental administrative assistant, was lying in wait. She was dressed in her inevitable twin sweater set, this time the colour of dried mustard. As it had been every morning since I'd come to work at the university, Rosalie's greeting was minatory.

"It helps to let me know ahead of time if you're not going to show up for a meeting. That way I don't order extra at the Faculty Club."

Wayne J. Waters might have seen me as a lady with balls, but dealing with Rosalie always unmanned me. "I'm sorry," I said. "Something came up at home. I hope you were able to find someone to eat my bran muffin." I looked down at my class list for Political Science 110. There were 212 students registered, twice as many as usual. I held it out to her. "Rosalie, something's wrong with this list."

She didn't even favour it with a glance. Instead, she tapped her watch. "Well, you're going to work it out yourself. When a person decides to come late, she can't expect the rest of us to pick up the pieces."

The day continued to run smoothly. My hope that the problem on my list was clerical rather than actual was dashed as soon as I walked into my classroom. More than two hundred students were jammed into a space with desks for a hundred. A computer glitch had timetabled two sections of Political Science 110 together, and by the time I had separated the classes, half the period was over. In the afternoon, my senior class informed me sulkily that their text wasn't in the bookstore. When I got back to my office, the telephone was ringing, but it rang its last as I unlocked the door. I checked my voice mail. My first two callers invited me to start-up meetings of organizations I had no intention of joining; my third caller was Alex, asking a favour. He had been phoning Eli's school all day, but hadn't been able to connect with Eli's teacher. Now he had a meeting that would run all afternoon, and he wondered if I could get in touch with the school and fill them in. I hung up the phone and grabbed my briefcase. Suddenly I had a legitimate excuse to get out of the office early, and I snatched it.

Gerry Acoose Collegiate was an inner-city experiment: an old secondary school that the community had convinced the Board of Education to give over to those who believed First Nations' kids might thrive on a curriculum that reflected their cultural history and an attendance policy that took into account the realities of adolescent life in the city's core. As I pulled up in front of the school, I thought about the new-model cars that lined the streets near my son Angus's south-end high school.

The students at Gerry Acoose weren't kids whose parents handed them the keys to a Nova on their sixteenth birthday. These young people had seen a lot more of life than the shining-eyed innocents who clutched Club Monaco book-bags in the back-to-school ads. Among other innovations, G.A.C. had a program for teen mothers, and as I waded through the students lounging on the front steps, I passed a number of girls, barely into puberty themselves, who were clutching babies. The only student who reacted to my presence was a whippet-thin boy with shoulder-length hair, worn in the traditional way. He gave me a half-smile, which encouraged me enough to ask him for directions to the principal's office.

The halls of the school were filled with student art: some good; some not so good. On the wall outside the gymnasium, there was a life-sized painting of a white buffalo that was absolutely breathtaking. I thought of Eli's spray-painted horses; this looked like a place where they might find a home. The principal wasn't in his office, but the school secretary, a motherly woman in a flowered dress, pink cardigan, and sensible shoes, checked the computer and directed me to Eli's homeroom.

At the back of Room 10C, a young woman in bluejeans and a T-shirt was stapling a poster of an aboriginal man in a white lab coat to the bulletin board. She didn't look old enough to be the one in charge of the staple-gun.

I coughed to get the woman's attention, but she didn't respond. Finally, I said, "I'm looking for the homeroom teacher."

"You're looking *at* the homeroom teacher," she said, without turning. "Hang on. I'll be right with you."

As I waited for her to finish, I glanced around. It was a pleasant room, filled with that gentle hazy light that comes when afternoon sun filters through chalk dust. There was a hint of sweetgrass in the air, a starblanket against the far wall, and a bank of computers in front of the windows. Posters brightened the other walls: a hockey player, a powwow dancer, an actor, a playwright, and an orchestra conductor – all aboriginal.

When Eli's teacher turned and saw me, her face was as impassive as those of the kids outside. "I'm Anita Greyeyes," she said, not smiling. "What can I do for you?"

"I wanted to tell you why Eli Kequahtooway wasn't in class today," I said.

Anita Greyeyes moved to the desk at the front of the room and motioned me to the chair opposite hers. "Are you his social worker?" she asked.

"No," I said. "I'm a friend. Of Eli and of his uncle." As

I explained the situation, Anita Greyeyes' gaze never left my face.

When I finished, she said, "What's Eli's prognosis?"

"I don't know," I said. "But, Ms. Greyeyes, he's very bright and he has a close relationship with his uncle. We're hopeful."

She looked at me thoughtfully. "I take it that your relationship with his uncle is also close."

"Yes," I said.

"Any chance that's the problem?"

"I don't know," I said. "I hope not."

Anita Greyeyes went to a table near the window that was loaded with texts. I watched as she chose a selection for Eli. She had small hands, blunt-fingered and efficient. As she recorded the titles in a record book, her precision-cut black hair fell forward against her cheekbones. She wrote assignments out in a small spiral notebook, put it on top of the books, and slid the stack to me. I noticed that one of the books was Eden Robinson's *Traplines*.

I picked it up. "Good choice," I said.

Anita Greyeyes didn't respond. "If it looks as if Eli's absence is going to be long-term, come back and we'll work something out."

"Thanks," I said.

I was just about out the door when she called to me. "Tell Eli that there's no shame in what he's going through."

"I will."

She was leaning forward, hands on the desk. "And tell him that it may be hard to believe right now, but life will get better." She paused. "I know because I've been there."

"I'll tell him." I offered a smile, but she didn't return it. Somehow, I wasn't surprised.

I was in the garden, making a desultory pass at propping up my tomato plants, when Taylor got home from school. She burst through the back door with Bruce and Benny in hot pursuit. She kissed me, bent to nuzzle her boys, as she had taken to calling them, and began her monologue. By the time I'd threaded the last yellowing leaf through the tomato cage, the salient facts had emerged: there were two new girls in the class and one new boy. The Grade 2 teacher's name was Ms. Jane Anweiler, and she had silver earrings that were shaped like dinosaurs. Ms. Anweiler also had a Polaroid camera with which she had taken pictures of everybody in the class. The pictures were mounted on a bulletin board outside the classroom, under a sign reading: WELCOME TO THE HOME OF THE GRADE 2 ALL-STARS!!! The letters were made out of baseball bats except for the O's, which were baseballs. Taylor would be allowed to sit beside her best friend, Jess, as long as she remembered not to talk. The Lakeview School year was, it seemed, off to a dazzling start.

Angus didn't get home from school till dinner time. I was making a salad when he came into the kitchen, poured himself a glass of juice, and started to leave.

"Hang on," I said. "Whatever happened to 'hello' and 'how are you'?"

"Sorry," he said. "Hello and how are you?"

"Fine," I said, "but you look a little down. Back-to-school blues?"

He shook his head. "No," he said. "School's okay. Actually more than okay. It looks like it's going to be a good year."

"So why the long face?"

"I went down to the hospital to see Eli."

"Was he still mad at you about what happened at the game."

My son's face was perplexed. "No. When I got there, Eli was the same as he'd been before. I thought he was just ignoring what happened, and for a while I went along with him. Then I decided it would be better if we talked about it."

Angus put his glass down and came over to me. "Mum, Eli doesn't remember what happened at the game. He doesn't remember anything from the time he took off till he saw his shrink yesterday."

"That's twenty-four hours."

"I know. So does Eli. He's really psyched about this. Mum, could you go see him?"

"Do you think it would help? Eli has never been exactly easy with me."

"It'd help. He likes you. I think he just kind of resented you."

"Because of my relationship with Alex?"

Angus frowned. "I never thought it was that. I always thought it was just that you were our mum and, every time he saw you, it reminded him of what he didn't have."

That night, after supper, Taylor and I drove to the hospital with the books and assignments Anita Greyeyes had given me. I was tense as we approached Eli's room, but he seemed genuinely pleased to see us. Physically, he was an immensely appealing boy: graceful, with the brooding good looks of a youth in an El Greco painting. He tried a smile of welcome, then stood aside so we could walk through the doorway. He was wearing brand-name sandals, khaki shorts, and a pressed white T-shirt, an absolutely normal sixteen-year-old boy, but one of his slender wrists was ringed with a hospital ID band, and his brown eyes were troubled.

Taylor immediately staked out one of the visitor's chairs for herself; Eli directed me to the other one and sat on the edge of his bed. For a moment, there was an awkward pause, then Taylor took charge. She amazed me. She didn't prattle about her cats or her school; instead, she asked Eli very seriously about what they did to help him at the hospital and whether he'd made any friends. Even more surprisingly, she waited for his answers, which came, at first haltingly, then with more assurance. When she told him a story about Bruce and Benny, Eli laughed aloud, and the melancholy that had hung in the air, heavy as the hospital smell, seemed to lift.

I wasn't as successful with Eli as Taylor had been, but I did my best. I told him about Gerry Acoose Collegiate and his homeroom. As I described the starblanket on the wall and the bank of computers by the window, Eli's eyes moved with interest towards the textbooks we'd brought. When it was time to leave, he gave Taylor an awkward one-armed hug, then he and I stood side by side in his doorway and watched as she wandered down the hall towards the elevators. It was a rare moment of connection for us.

Eli seemed to feel the closeness too. "Thanks for bringing the school stuff by," he said.

"It's a good school, Eli. You could be happy there."

For a moment he was silent. Then he said, "Do they know about me being in the hospital?"

"Your teacher does," I said. "She seems pretty decent. She said to tell you you're not the only person who's ever needed time to work things out."

"You mean this has happened to other kids in that class?"

"I don't know about the other kids," I said, "but I have a feeling Ms. Greyeyes has had some problems in her life. She asked me to give you a message."

His look mingled hostility and hope. "She doesn't even know me."

"Maybe not," I said, "but she says she understands what you're going through because she's been there."

"And she's all right now?" he asked. The question was barely a whisper, but I could hear the yearning.

"She's fine," I said. "And you're going to be fine, too. A lot of people care about you, Eli."

Riding down in the elevator, Taylor was quiet. As we

walked towards the parking lot, she said, "When's he getting out?"

"Soon, I hope," I said. "But I don't know."

"I'm almost finished that painting of us watching the dragon boats."

"Good."

"Do you think Eli would like it as a present?"

I smiled at her. "I know he would," I said.

When we got home, the dishes were done, the kitchen was shining, and the table was set for breakfast. I pointed Taylor towards bed, stuck my head into the family room where Angus was listening to a CD, and went out to the backyard. Hilda was sitting on the deck with a gin and tonic.

She raised her glass when she saw me. "I bought a bottle of Beefeater this afternoon. Will you join me?"

"Absolutely," I said. "But I don't think I've ever seen you drink gin before."

"It's been a gin kind of day," Hilda said.

I poured myself a drink and went back outside. It was a beautiful night. The air smelled of charcoal and heat, and from the park across the way we could hear the sounds of an early-evening ball game. I sipped my drink. "The house looks wonderful," I said. "I love it when you stay with us. Everything seems to run so smoothly."

"I don't do much myself, you know. Your children are very cheerful about pitching in."

"Only when you're here," I said. "The rest of the time, they pitch in, but I wouldn't characterize their attitude as cheerful." I smiled at her. "You're kind of like Mary Poppins."

Hilda winced.

"You don't like the comparison?" I said.

"Not much," she said. "But I am relieved to hear that you welcome my presence, because I'm going to ask if I can stay a few days longer."

"You can stay as long as you want to," I said. "You know that. Has something come up?"

She sighed wearily. "This business with Justine," she said. "I can't seem to extricate myself from it."

"Do you want out?"

"I don't know," she said. "I went to see Eric Fedoruk this morning. My intention was to tell him that, after giving the matter some thought, I'd concluded my responsibility to Justine Blackwell was discharged."

"That's an about-face, isn't it?"

Hilda turned towards me. "It is, but there are times when reversal is the only sensible course. Joanne, I went to Eric Fedoruk's because it seemed that my commitment to Justine was a problem for you."

"Hilda, you could never be . . ."

She made a gesture of dismissal. "I know what you're about to say, but I saw your face last night when I told you a TV crew had interviewed me at your house, and I saw you change your plans this morning when Wayne J. Waters turned up on your doorstep. This business with Justine has simply become too much of a burden on you, and that's what I intended to tell Eric Fedoruk."

"You were going to step aside?"

"I was. This morning after you went to the university, I sat down with Justine's letter. I read it many times, and as far as I could ascertain, I had honoured my commitment. The power of attorney she gave me ended with her death, and when I called Eric Fedoruk to ask if Justine had named me executrix of her will, he said she hadn't. He told me he had the will on the desk in front of him, and it named him executor. I went down to his office this morning fully intending to tell him that I'd satisfied myself there was nothing more I could do for Justine, and that I was going home to Saskatoon."

"But something made you change your mind," I said.

"Not something . . . someone. More accurately, several someones. Joanne, when I got to Eric Fedoruk's office, the Blackwell sisters were there. From what Tina let slip, I gathered they'd come about the will. They certainly had some agenda in mind. As soon as I came into the room, they began apologizing. Lucy said they were wrong to shirk their obligations to their mother. Signe said they should never have asked me to act as their intermediary with the press. Even Tina Blackwell chimed in; she said she was wrong to put her need for privacy ahead of my right to live my own life." Hilda frowned. "Although having finally met her, I can understand why Tina Blackwell wouldn't want to be photographed."

I was baffled. "Hilda why wouldn't she want to be photographed? She's on TV all the time. She's the anchor on the CJRG six o'clock news."

"With all that scarring?"

"What scarring? I don't watch that station much, but over the years I've caught their news a few times. Tina Blackwell's a very attractive woman."

"No one would describe the woman I saw this morning as attractive." Hilda's voice was thoughtful, then she added briskly, "But Tina Blackwell's appearance isn't the issue. The issue is whether my continuing to work on Justine's affairs is going to be a problem for you."

"It won't be a problem. But, Hilda, have I missed a step here? What did the Blackwell sisters do to make you change your mind about bowing out?"

"They nettled me." Hilda's blue eyes were dark with anger at the memory. "They treated me as if I were an old family retainer who was, oh so reluctantly, being relieved of her duties. Lucy offered the usual sweet female banalities: "It was too much to ask anyone outside the family to do." Signe Rayner wondered, *sotto voce*, whether the fact that I lived in Saskatoon would prevent me from acting effectively in a Regina-based case."

"I take it you countered their arguments," I said.

"I most assuredly did," Hilda said. I reminded the Blackwell women that their mother had asked me to protect her interests and that we lived in the age of technological wizardry. There was no disputing either argument. That's when Signe Rayner turned cruel."

"Towards whom?"

"Towards me and towards the memory of her mother. Dr. Rayner said that psychotic patients can often be quite charismatic, especially with elderly people. In her view, psychotics often infect those around them with their delusions. I asked her if she thought her mother had infected me. She said that, in her opinion, my determination to take on this commitment bordered on the obsessional."

"But she and her sisters asked you to handle the funeral arrangements."

"A decision they apparently regret," Hilda said tartly. "Dr. Rayner's attack on me was personal and it was vicious."

I shook my head. "All this from someone whose profession involves teaching other people to handle their anger."

Hilda sniffed. "Dr. Rayner didn't bring much honour to her profession today. At one point, Eric Fedoruk literally jumped between us. He was quite sensible. He said that things were being said that could not be unsaid, and that perhaps we should go to the restaurant on the main floor of his building and have a drink."

"Did you go?"

"No. At that point, I'd had enough. But when I started to say my goodbyes, Lucy Blackwell came over and put her arms around me. Joanne, it was the strangest thing. She was almost weeping, and she said, 'Hilda, don't be mad at us. It's for your own good. My mother left everything in such a mess, and my sisters and I would feel terrible if anything happened to you.' "

I looked across at her. In the dying light, a truth that I tried to banish was apparent. While Hilda's spirit was as robust as ever, there was no denying that physically she was becoming more fragile. I didn't want anything to happen to her either.

"Let's go inside," I said. "Even on a night like this, it's possible to get a chill."

CHAPTER

5

The next afternoon, when Taylor came home from school she grabbed an apple and her cats and headed out to her studio to work. She went back after dinner. She continued the pattern all week. "I want the painting to be ready for Eli as soon as he comes back," she said.

Taylor wasn't the only busy member of our household. As the first Friday after Labour Day approached, it was clear that the aimlessness and languor of summer was well and truly over. Angus's football team started practice, and his girlfriend, Leah, came back from theatre school in Toronto. I sorted my classes out and began to lecture in earnest. We all took turns visiting Eli.

Hilda spent Wednesday and Thursday downtown, continuing her investigation into Justine Blackwell's affairs. She described her movement back and forth between the courthouse on Victoria Avenue and the shabby storefront offices on Rose Street that harboured Culhane House as spider-like. In her attempt to connect the disparate strands in the complicated web of relationships that Justine had established in her life, Hilda talked to everyone she could find who had known the dead woman, from the small circle of colleagues, family, and friends who had watched with dismay as she metamorphosed from figure of judicial rectitude into eccentric advocate for prisoners' rights, to the ex-prisoners and their families and lawyers who exulted as Justine embraced their cause.

Often Hilda arrived hard on the heels of the police, whose frustration as they continued to come up empty-handed in their own investigations was growing. They weren't short on suspects. Justine Blackwell had spent the last night of her life in a room filled with people she had sent to prison. The final year of Justine's life might have been given over to making amends, but delayed charity can be cold comfort. Most of the guests at Justine's party would have known only too well the truth of the old saw that "a man that studieth revenge keeps his own wounds green." They would have known, too, that in the course of history few places have proven themselves more congenial to the study of revenge than the slammer.

The theory that Justine's death had been an act of prisoner vengeance was given credibility by the nature of the weapon the police now believed had been used to kill her. On the night of Justine's final party, Eric Fedoruk had presented her with handsomely engraved marble-based scales. The doorman at the hotel had seen Justine put the scales on the seat beside her when she stepped into her BMW, but they were nowhere in evidence when the police examined the car after Justine's body was found. The scales still hadn't been recovered, but the forensics unit, having examined both Justine's injuries and photographs of Eric Fedoruk's presentation at the banquet, had concluded that the marble base could have inflicted the fatal wounds. A healthy percentage of those who had watched the presentation had proven themselves adept at the art of assault with a deadly weapon.

An equally healthy percentage had no alibi whatsoever.

The police weren't alone in feeling disappointed that the truth about Justine was eluding them. Friday morning, when I came back from taking Rose around the lake, Hilda was sitting at the dining-room table surrounded by library books.

"What's up?" I asked.

"I'm trying to unearth a few appropriate passages for Justine's memorial service. It's tomorrow."

"I saw the notice in the paper." I sat down in the chair across from her. "Do you realize we haven't really talked about Justine all week?"

"You've had enough on your mind with Eli," Hilda said. "Besides, all I'd have had to contribute was a litany of failures. I can't even succeed at this." She picked up the letter Justine had written her and slipped it into the book she was reading.

I glanced at the book's title. "Montaigne's *Essays*," I said. "Searching for insights?"

"That's precisely what I'm doing. Lucy asked me to choose some readings that would sum up her mother's life."

"Another task," I said. "The Blackwell sisters must have decided you're too useful to alienate."

"That possibility has occurred to me as well," Hilda said. "But their motives don't interest me a whit. I've undertaken this assignment for Justine. I just wish I were making a better job of it. How can anyone sum up a life, if she's not certain what that life truly added up to?"

"You're no closer to understanding what Justine's state of mind was in the last year of her life?" I asked.

Hilda frowned. "It's as if I'm hearing about two separate and distinct human beings. Justine's legal colleagues speak of her with pity and anger. The people at Culhane House talk about her as if she were a saint." Hilda shook her head in a gesture of disbelief. "Joanne, I know that human beings contain multitudes, but as a rule one can reconcile the disparities."

I poured myself a cup of coffee and sat down opposite her. "What was Justine like when you knew her first, Hilda?"

"Bright, independent, ambitious." Hilda smiled. "I don't mind admitting that I saw a great deal of myself in her. She was, as my beloved L.M. Montgomery's Anne would have said, 'a kindred spirit.'"

"Then I would have liked her," I said.

Hilda took the compliment coolly. "Yes, you would have liked her. There was no reason not to. We met in 1946. I'd just bought my house on Temperance Street. It was a chaotic time, Joanne; the universities were jam-packed with returned soldiers. It was wonderful, but it was madness: students sitting atop radiators, on window-ledges, in the aisles, and still spilling out into the halls. Of course, housing was at a premium. That September, I decided that by offering room and board to a woman student, I could do a good deed *and* expedite the process of paying off my mortgage. I put a notice on the bulletin board in the administration building at the university. Within an hour, Justine, or Maisie, as she was known then, was standing on my doorstep."

"Justine changed her name?" I asked.

"Justine changed *both* her names," Hilda said. "She was born Maisie Wilson. Blackwell is her married name; Justine was her *nom de guerre*. The choice was a wise one. By the time I met her, it was plain that she saw her destiny as going far beyond that of a Saskatchewan farmgirl. For the future she had in mind, Justine was a much more suitable name than Maisie.

"I expect you can tell from the photographs in the paper that Justine was attractive, but in 1946 she was ravishing, no other word for it. Her hair was white blonde, and she wore it in a pageboy, as young women did in those days; it was immensely flattering. Her skin was flawless, and her eyes were the same colour as Lucy's. Since the advent of contact lenses, I've seen a number of young women with those aquamarine eyes, but the shade of Justine's was God-given. She had the same generous mouth Lucy has, and the same dazzling smile. When she asked me about the room, my first thought was that my house would be overrun with eager young men, so I asked her straight out how serious she was about her studies. She assured me there would be no late-night visitors, because her only goal in life was to graduate at the top of her class in law school."

"I take it she realized her goal."

"She did indeed. Top of her class. But she worked hard for it: left the house at seven sharp every morning; took one hour off for supper at five; then back to the library till it closed. It was a monastic life for such a handsome young woman."

Hilda seemed about to let the subject drop, but I wanted to hear more. "You *did* like her, though," I said.

Hilda seemed perplexed. "I'm not sure 'like' is the word I would use. I respected her. Justine knew what she wanted, and she went after it."

"Dedicated and persistent," I said. "She does sound like you."

Hilda laughed. "Justine made me look lackadaisical. There was an incident the first year she lived in my house on Temperance Street that revealed her measure. I owned a gramophone and an extensive library of recordings, and when Justine moved in I invited her to make use of them. She never did. Then one day, I came home and found her listening to *Manon Lescaut*. She was reading the libretto, taking notes. She didn't appear to be enjoying the music much, so I asked her if she liked Puccini. Justine said she didn't have an opinion one way or the other, but one of the men in her class told her that the senior partner in Blackwell, Dishaw and Boyle, the law firm with which she planned to article, was an opera lover, and she wanted to be prepared. Three years later, when she walked into Richard Blackwell's office, Justine Wilson could have won the Metropolitan Opera's Saturday-afternoon quiz."

"And she married the senior partner?"

"She did indeed – a month to the day after their first meeting. Richard Blackwell was twenty-five years older than Justine. He'd never married, and he was eager for a family. Justine complied. Signe was born in 1950, and the others followed. Justine never seemed very interested in motherhood. She was combative by nature, and she loved the rough and tumble of the courtroom. Richard retired to raise those children. He and his little girls became quite a well-known sight in Saskatoon."

"A wife with a high-powered career and a husband who stays home with the kids – the Blackwells were about forty years ahead of their time," I said.

Hilda's face grew sad. "From what I saw, Richard Blackwell relished every moment he spent with his daughters. It's too bad he didn't have longer with them."

"When did he die?"

"In 1967. I remember because he died at one of the banquets we had in Saskatoon that year for Canada's Centennial. The Blackwells had moved to Regina by then. Justine had already made a name for herself as a criminal lawyer, but she was ready for the next stage. She wanted to be noticed by those who influenced judicial appointments. Richard had come back to Saskatoon for the dinner. I was there. It was terrible. There were hundreds of people in the room. Everyone was rushing about, trying to summon help. But nothing could be done. It was a heart attack. Massive. The worst thing was that Lucy was with him. Richard had brought her over for a chat when they came in. She would have been about fifteen, I guess, and she was so proud of being at a grown-up event with her father. Then, in an instant, he was gone. I've often wondered if that trauma spawned the need to be surrounded by men which seems to have been so much a part of her life."

A line from one of Lucy's songs came back to me. *He painted a rainbow and took me along, then lightning split us, shattered my song.* I turned to Hilda. "I think that's probably a pretty solid observation."

Hilda's voice was thoughtful. "Justine didn't appear to suffer any permanent ill effects from her husband's death. Not long after Richard died, she was appointed to the bench. As I told that odious Detective Hallam, Justine and I lost touch except for the occasional lunch and holiday letters. Of course, Saskatchewan is a small province, so it was impossible not to hear news of her."

"From farmgirl to Justice on the Court of Queen's Bench," I said. "Justine put together quite a life for herself."

Hilda looked at me approvingly. "Thank you," she said. "It's amazing how often simply talking a problem through can help one solve it." She picked up the book of Montaigne essays and read aloud. " 'What? Have you not lived? That is not only the fundamental but the most illustrious of your occupations. . . . To compose our character is our duty. . . . Our great and glorious masterpiece is to live appropriately.' " She cocked an eyebrow. "Well, is that quotation equivocal enough?"

I smiled at her. "As equivocations go, I'd say it's almost perfect." I touched her hand. "Hilda, let this be the end of it. You've already done more than Justine would ever have asked of you."

Hilda shrugged. "Perhaps I have, but it's still not enough. Joanne, you know as well as I do that fine words butter no parsnips. Montaigne's *Essays* may get us through the funeral, but unless I discover the truth about Justine's state of mind in the last year, her enduring epitaph will be written in tabloid headlines. She deserves better."

"So do you," I said, and I was surprised at the emotion in my voice. "Hilda, don't let them draw you into this. Murder spawns a kind of ugliness that most people can't even imagine. It's like a terrible toxic spill. Once it splashes over you, you're changed forever. Believe me, I know. Don't let it touch you."

Hilda's expression was troubled. "It already has, my dear. Maybe that's why I can't just walk away. What kind of woman would I be if I just turned my back and let the darkness triumph?"

"There's nothing I can say that will dissuade you?"

"Nothing."

"Then at least promise me you'll be careful."

"I may be stubborn, but I'm not stupid," she said curtly. "I've been given a long and healthy life, Joanne. I'm not about to jeopardize what any sensible person would realize is a great blessing."

When Jill Osiowy, the producer of "Canada Tonight" and my friend, called my office later that afternoon, I was deep in weekend plans. Except for the usual round of Saturday chores, the next couple of days were clear, and I aimed to keep them that way. Our summer at the lake had been straight out of the fifties: canoeing, canasta, croquet, and a calm broken only by the chirping of crickets and the reedy voices of little kids calling on Taylor. I had come back from the lake with a tan and an overwhelming sense of peace. The tan was fading, and the events since Labour Day had made some major inroads on my tranquility, but in my estimation two days by the pool would go a long way to restoring both. If I was lucky, I'd be able to convince Hilda to join me.

"I hope you've got nothing more on your mind than chilled wine and serious gossip," I said.

Jill laughed. "We have a little task first. How would you like to look at some videos of men doing interesting things?"

"It depends on the men," I said. "And on the interesting things."

"These men are auditioning for the chance to replace Sam Spiegel on our political panel," she said. "I've tried to talk him into staying, but Sam says retirement means retirement from everything."

"I'm going to miss him," I said.

"Me too," Jill said, "but, ready or not, life goes on, and some of these new guys might work out. The network's narrowed it down, but I'd appreciate your input. Glayne's still in Wales but she says she trusts your judgement." Jill's voice rose to the wheedling singsong of the schoolyard. "I'll buy you a drink afterwards."

"Okay," I said. "And I'll take you up on that drink. You and I haven't had a chance to really talk all summer."

"Good. I'll meet you at the front door of Nationtv at two o'clock."

I'd barely hung up the phone when it rang again. It was Alex, and he sounded keyed up.

"Jo, I have another favour to ask. I just got back to the office and there was a message here from Dan Kasperski. He thinks Eli's ready to come home."

"That's good news, isn't it?"

"It is, except I have to go to Saskatoon. The cops there have a suspect they think I can help them nail. If I catch the seven-ten plane tonight, I can check out this creep and be back tomorrow afternoon. I hate to ask, but could Eli stay with you tonight?"

"Of course, as long as it's okay with Eli."

"It will be. Eli tells me he got pretty tight with you guys this week."

"We enjoyed being with him, too. Look, why don't you two come for an early supper? I could barbecue some of that pickerel we caught at the lake. A last taste of summer."

"Can we bring anything?"

"Just yourselves. And Alex, tell Eli I'm really looking forward to seeing him."

I hung up. I thought about my tan and my peace of mind. Both would have to wait. As Jill had said, ready or not, life goes on.

When Alex and Eli arrived, Eli was carrying his gymbag and a box of Dilly Bars from the Dairy Queen. He handed them to me. "Uncle Alex wanted to get an ice cream cake, but I thought these would be less trouble for you." He grinned shyly. "You know – no dishes?"

"Good move," I said. "And I love Dilly Bars."

Dinner was low-key and fun. Taylor's friend Jess joined us. He and Taylor were doing a school project on wildlife of the prairie, and in a burst of untypical enthusiasm, they'd decided to get started immediately. Hilda, who believed in rewarding zeal, however unlikely the source, had promised to take them to the Museum of Natural History after supper. It was a co-operative meal: I made cornbread; Taylor and Jess sliced up tomatoes and cucumbers from the garden; Hilda made potato salad; Alex barbecued the pickerel; Angus and Eli cleaned up. Afterwards, we ate Dilly Bars on the deck. Life as it is lived in TV commercials.

As soon as we'd finished dessert, Hilda took the little kids to the museum, and the big boys got out the croquet set and had a game with rules so bizarre even they couldn't follow them. Halfway through the game, Eli came running towards us, whirling his croquet mallet above his head. "You can play if you want to, Mrs. Kilbourn, but this is a take-no-prisoners game. Play at your own risk." Then he laughed the way a teenaged boy is supposed to laugh – wildly and uninhibitedly – and ran back to the game. I thought I had never seen him so happy.

Alex waited until the last minute to leave for the airport, and he looked at the yard regretfully before he went into the house. I slid my arm through his. I knew how he felt. After a troubling week, it seemed a shame to put a rent in the seamless perfection of the evening.

Before he picked up his overnight bag in the front hall, Alex pulled a notebook and pen out of his pocket and began to write. "Here's the number of headquarters in Saskatoon, and here's Dan Kasperski's number in case anything comes up."

"Nothing's going to come up," I said.

"Let's hope," Alex said. "Dan Kasperski says he can't figure this one out. Eli's doing a lot better, but he still has no memory of what he did in the time between the football game and his appointment with Kasperski."

"Does Dr. Kasperski think that overhearing what those drunks said caused all of these problems for Eli?"

Alex's jaw tightened. "He doesn't know. His theory is that Eli had been carrying around a lot of unresolved emotions and that asshole's remark just tipped the balance."

"The proverbial straw that broke the camel's back," I said.

"Something like that. Kasperski says it doesn't add up as far as he's concerned, but he's been a shrink long enough to know that there are a lot of times when things don't add up."

Alex held me a long time before he opened the door. "I'm glad Eli's going to be with you tonight."

"It's where he should be," I said.

I watched until Alex's Audi disappeared from my view. As I turned to go into the house, Sylvie O'Keefe drove up. She and I weren't close, but I liked and respected her. She was a photographer whose work had brought her a measure of fame and more than a measure of controversy. Surprisingly, for an artist so provocative, she was a very traditional parent, who was raising her only child with a mix of love, discipline, and routine that appeared to be just the ticket. Jess was a thoroughly pleasant and happy little boy.

"How did Hilda and the kids make out at the museum?" Sylvie asked, as she followed me into the house.

"They're not back yet, but I'm sure they triumphed. Things fall into place when Hilda's around."

She sighed. "I wish Jess and I had a Hilda in our life."

"I'm certainly glad she came into ours."

Sylvie furrowed her brow. "I always assumed you'd known her forever."

We went into the living room and sat down. "No, not forever," I said. "Just seven years. I met her when my friend Andy Boychuk died. She'd been his teacher. She and I became friends, and of course the kids loved her."

Sylvie gazed at me assessingly. "It looks to me as if Hilda's relationship with your family has been a good fit for everyone."

"It has," I said. "For a long time, I worried that it was pretty one-sided. Hilda always seemed to give us so much more of herself than we gave her."

"But something changed?"

"Hilda had a gentleman friend. His name was Frank, and he was the love of her life. When he died last spring, she was heartbroken. We went up for his funeral; then Hilda came down and stayed with us for a couple of weeks. I think she was glad not to be alone, and of course kids are always such a great distraction."

Sylvie grinned at me. "Aren't they just."

Right on cue, the front door opened, and the kids barrelled in, with Hilda behind them.

"How did it go?" Sylvie asked.

Jess went over to his mother. "You know those feathers owls have around their eyes?"

Sylvie nodded.

"They help owls hear," Jess said.

"How do they do that?" Sylvie asked.

Jess tweaked his own ear. "See this?" he said. "It catches the sounds and sends it inside our ears so we can hear. The owls' ears are right behind those feathers."

Taylor came over to me. "Could Jess stay over? It's not for fun," she said earnestly. "We need to work."

"Sorry, T," I said, "the owls will have to wait. We already have an overnight guest. Eli's staying here tonight, and he could use a little peace right now." I put my arm around her shoulder. "It gets pretty noisy around here when you and Jess are working on a project."

Sylvie smiled. "I don't mind a little excitement. If it's all right with you, Joanne, the kids can work at our house tonight."

Taylor's eyes were pleading. "Can I?"

"Sure," I said.

Taylor laid her head against my arm and lowered her voice. "After I go, make sure Eli goes to the studio to see the dragon-boat picture I made for him."

"He's right out back," I said. "Why don't you take him there now?"

She shook her head. "If I'm there, Eli won't be able to really look." She frowned. "Do you know what I mean?"

"Yes," I said, "I know what you mean, and I think you're right. I'll make sure Eli sees the painting."

After Sylvie left with the children, I fixed myself a gin and tonic and went up to my room to read. There was a new biography of the prime minister. The blurb on the jacket promised a Jungian exploration of the dark corners of his psyche. I had just about decided the PM was that rarest of beings, a man without a Shadow, when Hilda knocked on the door. She was wearing her dazzling poppy-red Chinese robe.

"I'm going to make an early night of it, Joanne," she said. "It's been a long day, and Justine's funeral is at ten." She leaned against the doorframe as if she were suddenly weary. "The last funeral I attended was for Frank," she said softly.

"Hilda, would you like me to go with you tomorrow morning?"

"But your Saturday mornings are so busy."

"There's nothing that can't be put off till later except for Taylor's lesson, and Angus can drive her to that."

"It would be good not to have to go alone," she said. "And not just because tomorrow's service will be painful. Joanne, you were right about the currents a murder sets loose. Sometimes this week, I've felt as if I were about to be swept away."

"Then let me be your anchor," I said. "You've been mine often enough."

In all the time I'd known her, Hilda had never made a physical display of affection, but she came over, bent down, and kissed the top of my head. "I hope you know how much I cherish your friendship," she said.

When I went downstairs to say goodnight to the boys, Eli was sitting at the kitchen doing a crossword puzzle. Angus was nowhere in sight.

I touched Eli's shoulder. "Where's your goofy friend?" I asked.

Eli gave me a small smile. "He went to Blockbuster to rent a movie."

"You didn't want to go with him?"

"No. I thought I'd just stay here."

I pulled out the chair next to his and sat down. "Feeling a little shaky?"

He gazed at me. His eyes were extraordinary – of a brown so dark they were almost black. "More than a little shaky."

"Taylor left a gift for you that might help," I said. "It's out in her studio."

"What is it?" he asked.

"A surprise," I said, "but in my opinion, a terrific one. Why don't you go out and have a look while I call Mieka and Greg and see if that baby of theirs is any closer to joining the world."

He started towards the door, then he stopped and turned. "Are you looking forward to being a *Kokom*?" he said.

"Yes," I said. "I really am. I like kids. It'll be fun to have a new one around."

"I hope everything works out okay," he said.

"Thanks, Eli, so do I."

My older daughter answered the phone in a voice that was uncharacteristically gloomy.

"I guess I don't need to ask you how it's going," I said.

"It's not going at all," she said. "I followed your advice about the Chinese food, and we've already scarfed our way through the whole menu at the Golden Dragon; I painted the kitchen ceiling; Greg's lost seven pounds from all the long walks we've been taking; and here I sit, still pregnant, barefoot, bored, and in the kitchen."

"Try to enjoy the moment," I said. "When the baby comes, all that peace and quiet is going to look pretty good."

As soon as I replaced the receiver, the day caught up with me. I decided to follow Hilda's lead and turn in early. I had an extra-long shower, dusted myself with last year's birthday bathpowder, put on a fresh nightie, and headed for bed. When I came out of the bathroom, Angus was sitting on my bed.

"Thanks for knocking."

"I did knock. You were in the shower, remember?"

"Sorry. I was just talking to your sister, and I guess I'm a little on edge."

"Still no baby?"

"No. It looks like your niece or nephew has decided to arrive on Mieka time."

My son grinned. "Late. Late for everything." He stood up. "Actually, what I came up for was to find out if you knew where Eli went."

"Isn't he downstairs?"

"Nope. I called and he didn't answer."

"He's probably still out in the studio. Taylor wanted me to give him the dragon-boat picture. She noticed he wasn't having a very easy time lately."

Angus shook his head in amazement. "Most of the time she's such a space-case, but every so often she tunes in."

"When T comes home tomorrow morning, I'll pass along your compliment."

I'd just crawled between the sheets and was reaching to turn out the light when I heard my son racing up the stairs. He burst into the room.

"Mum, something's the matter with Eli."

I sat up. "What do you mean?"

"Just come and see him, please." Angus's voice was tense. I grabbed my robe and followed my son downstairs.

"He's out in Taylor's studio," Angus said.

When I opened the door, the breath caught in my throat. On the easel in front of me was the painting Taylor had made as a gift for Eli. Once every centimetre of that canvas had danced with colour. Eli's painting of the black horse had obscured the brilliance. The lines of the animal's body were graceful, but the place where its head should have been was a jagged edge, clotted and sticky with paint bright as fresh blood. The animal's head was in the right lower quadrant of the canvas. Tongue lolling, eyes bulging, it was obvious the animal had died in terror. Eli himself lay in the far corner of the room; he was curled into the foetal position and moaning.

My son's voice was a whisper. "What's happening, Mum?"

"I don't know," I said. "Go upstairs and get my purse. There's a card inside with Eli's doctor's number on it. Call him and tell him we need to see him. Be sure he understands it's an emergency."

I took Eli in my arms and began to rock him like a baby. When Angus came back after making the call, I was still holding him.

"Dr. Kasperski's coming right over," Angus said. He bent closer to Eli and called his name.

When Eli didn't respond, I saw the panic in my son's eyes. "Why don't you go upstairs so you can watch for the doctor," I said. I tried to make my voice sound reassuring, but I was as scared as Angus was.

Less than ten minutes passed before I heard the doorbell, but it was a long ten minutes. Over the years, my own kids had had their share of broken bones, sprains, crises, and disappointments, and I had cradled them in my arms as I was cradling Eli. But after I had held them for a while, my kids had always responded. I had been able to feel them come back from the place of pain into which accident or misfortune had hurled them. Eli wasn't coming back. He didn't appear to be hurt physically, but his body was rigid. No matter what I did,

I couldn't reach him, and I was relieved beyond measure that someone who might be able to was on his way over.

When Angus came through the door, my first thought was that the young man with him was far too young to be a medical doctor. Dan Kasperski's body was as lithe as an adolescent's, and he was wearing the teenaged boy's uniform of choice that summer: cut-off jeans, a rock-and-roll shirt, and sandals. He was deeply tanned, and his hair was black, curly, and shiny. He seemed to radiate energy. Without preamble, he knelt beside me, and reached out and stroked Eli's forehead.

"Eli, it's Dan," he said firmly. "I need you to help me find out what went wrong here."

At the sound of Dan Kasperski's voice, Eli's body relaxed and he opened his eyes. Kasperski slid his arm under Eli's body and raised him to a sitting position. "Let's talk," he said.

"Would you like to go upstairs?" I said. "Eli's bed's already made up for him. He might be more comfortable."

Dan Kasperski leaned close to Eli's face. "What do you say, my friend?"

When Eli nodded, Dan Kasperski helped him to his feet, and I led them upstairs to my older son Peter's room. As I closed the door behind me, I could hear Dan Kasperski's voice, soft and persuasive. "It must have been a terrible thing to have made you so angry. Can you tell me about it?"

I decided not to call Alex until I'd had a chance to hear what Dr. Kasperski had to say. When I went back downstairs, Angus was sitting in the dark in the living room.

As soon as he heard my step, he jumped up. "What happened to him?"

I slid my arm around my son's waist. "That's what Dr. Kasperski's trying to find out."

"Did Eli say anything?"

"Not while I was there."

"Why would he wreck Taylor's painting, Mum? It was a present for him."

"I don't know. I guess he was just angry and confused."

"Is that what we're going to tell Taylor?"

I let my hand fall away from him. "Angus, I don't know what we're going to tell Taylor. And you might as well stop asking me questions because I don't have any answers."

"Mum, I don't mean to keep bugging you, but Eli isn't the only one who's confused."

"Angus, I'm sorry. It's just . . ." My voice broke. "Everything's too much."

For a moment, we stood together miserably. It was my son who broke the silence. "Do you want me to dig out the cards? We could play a game of crib while we're waiting." His voice sounded the way it had when he was little and wanted the reassurance of one more story before lights out.

"You're on," I said. "Loser has to walk Rose on the day of the first blizzard."

We were just starting what looked like the final hand when Dan Kasperski came downstairs. He leaned over and glanced assessingly at Angus's cards. "If your mother's playing for money, she'd better start collecting pop bottles." Then he looked at me. "I gave Eli something to help him sleep. He's down for the count, but you should get in touch with his uncle."

"I will," I said. "There's a flight back from Saskatoon in about half an hour. He can catch that."

"Good. Ask him to have Eli in my office by eight tomorrow morning. We need to get him working on this as soon as possible." For a moment he was silent, then he looked at my son and me. "Do either of you have any idea at all what went wrong here?"

Angus shook his head. "No, I thought everything was great."

"So did I," I said. "We had a pleasant dinner. Eli said he felt a little edgy, but he seemed fine. My daughter's an artist. She'd painted a picture for Eli – as a kind of welcome-home gift for him. She thought it would be easier for him to see the painting for the first time without the rest of us around. Anyway, Angus had gone to rent a movie, so I suggested to Eli that he might want to go out to the studio to have a look at Taylor's gift. When Angus got back, he found Eli the way he was when you saw him."

"Nothing happened . . ."

"Nothing ever *does* happen," I said, and I could hear the frustration in my voice. "At least not anything concrete. He just explodes. Dr. Kasperski, I know there's no magic bullet here, but surely you can do something to get to the source of Eli's problems."

Daniel Kasperski cocked an eyebrow. "Eli and I *are* doing something. We're talking, remembering, reconstructing. It takes time, Mrs. Kilbourn."

"But don't some doctors use sodium pentothol or hypnosis to help them home in on what went wrong in the first place?"

He shrugged. "Some do. I don't. Mrs. Kilbourn, think about it for a moment. Does it make sense to force a person as fragile as Eli to confront memories that are so powerful he's using every ounce of energy he has to suppress them? I know this way takes longer, but when Eli finally does face his demons, I want him to be strong enough to stare them down." He glanced at his watch. "I should be moving along," he said, "but before I go, could I have another look at that painting? When I was in your daughter's studio before, I was pretty much focused on Eli."

Angus shot me an anxious look. "Do I have to go out there again?"

"No," I said. "Why don't you try to grab some sleep?" I turned to Dan Kasperski. "Follow me, but there isn't much left to see."

Dan Kasperski's face was grim as he gazed at the canvas. "What did it used to be?" he asked finally.

"We were at the dragon-boat races Saturday," I said. "That was a picture of Eli and my kids watching the finish line."

"Does Eli like your daughter?"

"I thought he did."

Dan Kasperski continued to stare at the picture. Finally, he turned to me. "Can I take this with me? Signe Rayner might want to use it somehow in her therapy."

I felt a tremendous sense of letdown. "But I thought that you were Eli's doctor now," I said, and I was embarrassed at how forlorn I sounded.

He turned to me. "No matter how much I want to help Eli, Mrs. Kilbourn, he is not my patient. Signe Rayner is treating him. I'm just her surrogate."

I handed him the painting. "From the way Eli reacted to you tonight, I think he sees you as more than a surrogate."

Dan Kasperski frowned and looked away without responding.

"All right," I said, "I understand your position. Since you're not technically Eli's therapist, maybe you could answer a question for me. Is there any reason you know of why a patient who was doing as well as Eli seemed to be doing would suddenly fall apart like this?"

"Sure," he said. "He's a human being."

"Meaning?" I asked.

He laughed. "Meaning, as Albert Ellis once said, that Eli, like every human being who has ever lived, is 'fallible, fucked up and full of frailty.'"

CHAPTER

6

During the next few hours, if I'd been searching for insight into human behaviour, my own and that of those around me, I couldn't have picked a better guide than Albert Ellis. "Fallible, fucked up and full of frailty" pretty well covered it. Alex had taken the late plane back from Saskatoon. He arrived at my place at 10:30, keeping the taxi he'd ridden in from the airport waiting so he could take Eli home. Both of us were edgy with fatigue and fear, and our fight was as stupid as it was inevitable.

When he saw me, Alex didn't make any attempt to embrace me. From the moment he came through the door, his manner was distant and professional. "What happened this time?" he asked.

"I don't know," I said. "Angus and Eli were in the family room. Angus decided to go off to Blockbuster to rent a video . . ."

"Leaving Eli alone," Alex said.

I felt the first stirrings of anger. "Angus asked Eli to go with him. He didn't want to. Eli's sixteen years old, Alex. He doesn't need a babysitter."

"He'd just gotten out of the hospital, Jo. Angus knew that. So did you."

"So did you," I said. "But you weren't around."

"I had a job to do."

"So did I. And I have kids to raise. Alex, I know you're worried about Eli. I'm worried about him too, but your nephew's not the only one who's affected by what happened here tonight. What about my children? Tonight while you were in Saskatoon doing your job, Eli was out in Taylor's studio drawing this grotesque decapitated horse over the painting of the dragon-boat races she gave him."

Pain knifed across Alex's face. "He ruined her painting?"

"Yes, and that was *after* I'd told him Taylor wanted the painting to be a surprise for him. Alex, I'm going to have to explain this to her, but I don't even know where to begin."

I could see the pulse beating in Alex's neck, but his voice was impassive. "He shouldn't have been out there alone, Jo. If you knew he was going through some sort of crisis, you should have called me and stayed with him till I got here."

I took a step towards him. "Alex, there was no crisis. It was a perfectly ordinary Friday evening. As far as I could see, everything was fine."

"Maybe you only saw what you wanted to see, Jo."

"Meaning . . . ?"

"Meaning you might have looked the other way because you wanted a nice peaceful evening. You don't like problems, Jo."

"Alex, that's not fair. If I was afraid of problems, I would have bailed on you months ago. I did everything I could to help Eli. So did my kids. We did our best. It's not fair to blame us because our best wasn't good enough."

"You people are always beyond reproach, aren't you?"

I felt as if I'd been slapped. " 'You people' – Alex, you're talking about me and Angus and Taylor. We're not the bad guys." For a tense and miserable moment we faced one another in silence, like strangers whose lives had suddenly collided in some violent and permanent way.

When he finally spoke, Alex's voice was tight. "I'd better get Eli," he said. "Where is he?"

"In Peter's room."

Alex went upstairs. When he came back down, Eli was slumped against him. Dr. Kasperski's injection had relaxed Alex's nephew to the heavy-limbed state of a sleeping child.

Alex didn't stop to talk. When he reached the door, I opened it for him. "Let me know how Eli's doing," I said.

He didn't answer me. I watched as he and Eli made their awkward passage towards the taxi. Till the moment they got into the car, I expected Alex to turn and call out to me. He never did. As the cab pulled away, I felt a rush of pure anger. I slammed the door and started up the stairs. Alex hadn't once asked about Angus, nor had he expressed concern about Taylor. After months of doing everything we could to include Eli in our lives, my children and I had been shut out. We were an abstraction: "you people," an enemy not to be trusted.

Saturday morning, I awoke to the kind of thunderstorm that comes only at the end of a period of suffocating heat: lightning, thunder, and a downpour of rain that pounded the earth so viciously it seemed to assault it. I told Rose she was out of luck. There'd be no walk that morning. When I let her out in the backyard for a pee, I spotted the croquet set near the back gate where the boys had abandoned it after their ferocious game the night before. Eli had been happy that afternoon, grinning, waving the mallet over his head. "You can play if you want to, Mrs. Kilbourn, but this is a take-no-prisoners game." That had been a good time for all of us. As I ran across the backyard to drag the croquet set under the shelter of the deck, I wondered if we'd ever have a day of such mindless joy together again.

Sylvie dropped Taylor home at a little after 9:00. I didn't say anything about the painting, and miraculously my daughter didn't ask. She was filled with owl news, and as I made pancakes, I was grateful for the soothing rhythms of her prattle. After Angus came downstairs to take her to her lesson, I stood at the kitchen window and watched the rain. If it kept up, my tomato plants would be flattened by noon.

I was dressed and digging through my closet to find a raincoat to wear to the funeral when the phone rang. Certain it was Alex, my heart pounded as I picked up the receiver. But the call was for Angus.

I wrote down the number, hung up, and turned to go back to my closet. Hilda was standing in the door to my bedroom.

She was all in black: patent-leather pumps and handbag, a black suit in the timeless style of Chanel, and a pillbox hat that must have been thirty-five years old. Her outfit was both smart and appropriate, and I glanced assessingly at my black T-shirt and white cotton skirt.

Hilda read my mind. "You look fine, Joanne. This outfit was not of my choosing. I called and asked my next-door neighbour in Saskatoon to select something apropos from my closet. She's a dear soul, but she still lives her life according to *Emily Post's Etiquette*. Now, if I'm not rushing you, I'd like to get there early. Given our cast of characters, I'd like to be around to make certain this goes off without incident. Are you ready?"

I picked up my raincoat. "Ready as I'll ever be," I said.

The funeral was scheduled for 10:00 a.m. at St. Paul's Anglican Cathedral. The cathedral was not my church, but I'd been there on many occasions, happy and sad. One of the best had been the day my daughter Mieka had been married in its chapel.

The rain hadn't let up as we pulled up on McIntyre Street, so I dropped Hilda off and went to find a parking place. By the time I got back to the cathedral, Hilda was in an intense conversation with the Dean. I waved to them and made my way to the chapel. The last time I'd been there had been on Mieka and Greg's wedding day. It had been at 2:00 in the afternoon, and the late summer sun had poured through the stained-glass windows, suffusing my daughter and her new husband in a glow warm as a blessing. As she knelt at the altar, Mieka's profile, under the filmy circle of her bridal hat, had been a cameo. Today the shafts of light that split the chapel's gloom were murky, and as the rain drummed against the windows, I shivered with a nameless apprehension. I slid into a pew, pulled down a kneeler, and prayed that my daughter would come through childbirth safely and that the new baby would be whole and healthy. Then I prayed for my other children, and for Eli and Alex and for all of us.

When Hilda came and knelt beside me, I felt foolishly relieved. I was the mother of four, and soon I would be a grandmother; nonetheless, there were times when I was overwhelmed by the need to hand over all my problems to a grown-up. That morning was one of them.

As we walked back into the church, Hilda touched my arm. "Did you say a prayer for Mieka?" she asked.

"Among others," I said. "How about you?"

She gave me a wry smile. "I prayed for strength."

When the service got under way, I found myself hoping that Hilda's prayers would be answered. Justine Blackwell's funeral was a standing-room-only affair, but despite the crowding, the congregation had divided itself to reflect the two warring halves of Justine's life. On one side of the church sat men and women whose bearing and grooming suggested a privileged past and a promising future; on the other were people with wary eyes and faces which spoke of their hard lives. Hilda and

I took our places with those whose cause Justine had championed in the last year of her life. During the wait for the service to begin, the two camps regarded one another with mutual suspicion, but when the first chord of the opening hymn sounded, all eyes followed Justine Blackwell's daughters as Eric Fedoruk led them up the aisle.

The Blackwell women were a striking trio: Lucy, in a black scoop-necked, miniskirted, floral-print dress, seemed more seductress than mourner; Signe, her thick blonde hair braided into a Valkyrie's coronet, looked powerful enough to storm Valhalla; Tina, in black from head to toe, head covered by a lace mantilla, face hidden behind a black veil, suggested minor European royalty. When they took their place in the front pew, the church fell silent. Almost immediately, there was a second stir. Wayne J. Waters may have been wearing a cheap, ill-fitting suit, but he carried himself with the unmistakable air of a man who demanded respect. When he slid into the pew opposite the Blackwell sisters, it was obvious the show was about to begin.

For a while, it seemed Hilda had made all the right choices. The Mozart mass she had selected was pure beauty; the carefully barbered young men who had accompanied Justine's mahogany casket to the altar disappeared on cue; the Dean's prayers were comforting; and the eulogy by Eric Fedoruk was affectionate without being mawkish. He made no reference to the direction Justine's life had taken in the year before she died. When Eric Fedoruk went back to his seat, I glanced down at my program. All that was left was the closing prayer and the recessional. I picked up my purse and let my mind wander to thoughts of curling up on the couch with the Saturday paper and a pot of Earl Grey.

Suddenly, Hilda sat up ramrod straight, cutting short my reverie. Wayne J. Waters had slid out of his seat and started up the aisle towards the casket. As he reached it, he nodded, touched the lid affectionately, then turned to face the congregation. For a moment, I thought he was going to share one of those painful personal memories that have become the vogue at funerals. I was wrong.

"This one's for Justine," he said. "Not the judge Mr. Fedoruk was talking about, but the woman I knew. I learned this for her, because it was her favourite." In a deep and powerful voice he sang Blake's old hymn "Jerusalem," with its thrilling final verses about social justice:

> *Bring me my Bow of burning gold:*
> *Bring me my Arrows of desire:*
> *Bring me my Spear: O clouds unfold!*
> *Bring me my Chariot of fire!*
>
> *I will not cease from Mental Fight,*
> *Nor shall my Sword sleep in my hand,*
> *Till we have built Jerusalem*
> *In England's green and pleasant Land.*

When he finished, there was a smattering of applause, quickly muffled, from Wayne J.'s side of the church. Then he resumed his seat, and we were back on program. The discreet young men from the funeral home reappeared; the casket came back down the aisle and Eric Fedoruk and the Blackwell sisters followed it. Eric's arm was around Lucy's shoulder; she looked dazed, like the survivor of a disaster. Tina's emotions, hidden behind her black veil, were unreadable, but Signe Rayner was white with fury. When we came out of the church into the transept she was waiting for us. She grabbed Hilda's arm and took her aside.

"Whose decision was it to let that creature sing?"

Hilda tapped the program. "As you can see, Mr. Waters was not part of the Order of Service. He acted on his own initiative, and I, for one, am glad he did."

Signe's voice was low with fury. "Will you still be glad you let him sing when he's arrested for murdering my mother?" She turned on her heel and strode towards the mourners' limousine. One of the young men from the funeral home helped her in; the door slammed shut, and the car sped off.

"Wait." When I turned, I saw Lucy standing at the entrance to the church. "They left without me," she said. She looked at us beseechingly. "Can I go to the cemetery with you?"

"Of course," I said. "Hop in."

During the ten-minute drive to Crocus Hills Memorial Park, no one said a word. When we drove through the gates, Lucy, who was in the back seat, leaned forward and pointed. "It's just over there," she said. "It's past the place where all the soldiers are buried. You can't miss it. There's this incredible weeping willow."

Hilda turned towards her. "Your mother isn't being buried there, Lucy."

"Why not? That's our family plot. That's where my father is." There was an unsettling edge in Lucy's voice.

Hilda must have heard it too. Her answer was firm and factual. "When I talked to the people from Crocus Hills, they said the family plot was full. We had to purchase a new burial space for your mother. There was no alternative."

Lucy's teeth began to chatter. "That's crazy," she said. "That plot was for all of us." She opened the car door. "I'm going over there."

I glanced at Hilda. She nodded. "Maybe it's best if Lucy sees for herself," she said.

We drove past the area reserved for military burials. Under the gunmetal sky, it was a solemn sight: row upon row of identical grave markers, each with its own small red-and-white Canadian flag.

I pulled up in front of the area Lucy had indicated. Before I turned off the ignition, she was out of the car and running towards the weeping willow. She stopped in front of a low black marble headstone; then she gazed around her, as if she were trying to get her bearings.

Hilda and I walked over to her. The tombstone was engraved simply: RICHARD BLACKWELL: 1902-1967. The grave it marked was surrounded by other graves with small cheap markers. Lucy knelt on the wet grass and read out the names incredulously: WANDA SPETZ (1961-1997); KIM DUCHARME (1970-1997); DANIEL SOKWAYPNACE (1975-1997); MERV GEMMELL (1973-1997). When she looked up at us, her extraordinary turquoise eyes were blank with disbelief. "Who are these people?"

Hilda shook her head. "The man from Crocus Hills told me they're relatives of people your mother met in the last year."

"My mother let strangers be buried in the family plot? Sweet Jesus." Lucy laughed mirthlessly.

I touched her elbow. "Lucy, come back to the car. You can deal with this another time."

She stood up wearily. "Can I? Somehow I doubt that, Music Woman." She started back towards the car, then she turned to face us. "You understand that I don't give a good goddamn about the property. It's just that, after everything else she did to him, my mother shouldn't have done this to my father."

The three of us got back in the car and retraced our route to the cemetery entrance. Hilda pointed towards the new and treeless area where the limousines and hearse had stopped. A knot of mourners was already standing over the raw wound of a fresh grave, and the men from the funeral home were unloading their cargo.

Lucy put her hands up as if she were warding off a blow. "I'm not going over there," she said. "I want to go home."

I looked at Hilda. Her face was so pale and strained, I didn't even consult her. I just stepped on the gas.

As I started out through the cemetery gates, Eric Fedoruk was driving in. He slowed and rolled down his window.

His eyes were red-rimmed, but his voice was firm. "Is it over already?" he said. "I had an urgent call from a client."

Lucy leaned towards the window on the driver's side. "It isn't over," she said. "Eric, she gave away the burial plots around my father's grave. Did you know about it?"

He winced. "I knew."

"And you didn't tell us. Because you were protecting her. The way you always have."

As I drove down Albert Street, Lucy was silent, sunk into the corner of the back seat.

When I pulled up in front of the house on Leopold Crescent, Lucy mumbled her thanks. Before she went inside, she turned and gave us a small wave. I thought I had never seen anyone so alone.

"I guess if you needed proof that Justine's mind had deteriorated, you have it now," I said.

"I wonder," she said. "I was thinking of another possibility."

"What other possibility?"

Hilda's voice seemed to come from far away. "That Justine found her family so abhorrent that the idea of spending eternity with them was insupportable."

Hilda and I were met by the sounds of the Smashing Pumpkins when we got home. Normally, the Pumpkins were not my favourite group, but that day the pulsing rhythm of "Bullet with Butterfly Wings" was just the antidote I needed for the misery of our morning. Angus and his girlfriend, Leah, were in the kitchen making grilled cheese sandwiches.

Taylor was sitting at the kitchen table, pounding the bottom of the Heinz bottle she was holding over her plate. Just as we walked in, her efforts paid off and she flooded her sandwich with ketchup.

She glanced up at us, triumphant. "I didn't think this was going to work."

Hilda's face regained some of its colour during lunch. It seemed grilled cheese sandwiches and the company of young people was just the tonic she needed. At the end of the summer, Leah's theatre school in Toronto had performed a rock-opera version of Thornton Wilder's *Our Town*, and Hilda appeared genuinely absorbed by Leah's account of how she had played Emily. Hilda had taught high-school English for almost fifty years. *Our Town* couldn't have held many surprises for her; nonetheless, she appeared to find the prospect of an Emily with cropped hair, an eyebrow ring, and a tattoo of foxes chasing a lion around her upper arm as provocative as I did.

After lunch, I tried to get Hilda to take a nap, but she squared her shoulders and insisted on getting to work on Justine's papers.

"I don't mind telling you that business with the family plot has shaken me, Joanne. If there are other surprises, I'd like to know about them before Eric Fedoruk and I discuss the disposition of Justine's estate."

I was surprised. "But I thought Eric Fedoruk was the executor."

Hilda shrugged. "The situation is no longer that clear-cut . . ."

"Why am I not surprised?" I said.

Hilda's smile was wry. "Your point's well taken. For a woman who lived her life with such precision, Justine certainly left her affairs in a troubling state. A second will has just surfaced, Joanne."

"The one that names you executrix," I said.

Hilda nodded. "It was in a safety-deposit box at Justine's bank, and it's going to raise hackles. The original will was drawn up years ago, and it's pretty much what you'd expect of a woman like Justine. She makes contributions to some decent charities and arts organizations, and asks that the major part of the estate be divided equally among her daughters. This new will leaves *everything* to Culhane House, including the home on Leopold Crescent. It was dated three months before Justine's death."

"Then it would take precedence," I said. "Anyone who ever watched Perry Mason reruns knows that, but I wouldn't want to be in the room when Justine's daughters hear the news."

"Nor would I," said Hilda. "And Eric Fedoruk has suggested that we do a little investigating before he brings this explosive information to those most directly involved. He's staved them off until now, a tactic for which he deserves commendation. The Blackwell women have been nipping at his heels. But we were wise to wait. If there is a real possibility that Justine was *non compos mentis*, her daughters are in an excellent position to challenge the second will. You can imagine what the media would make of a legal wrangle between Justine's daughters and Wayne J. Waters and his crew."

I nodded. "That business with the family plot today would certainly make for engrossing reading."

Hilda's eyes were troubled. "Justine put her trust in me. As her friend I have an obligation to protect her reputation, but as her executrix I also have an obligation to see that her estate is settled fairly. I've decided the best route to honouring both obligations is to carry out the task she set me. If Justine was sane, she was entitled to do what she wanted with her money, including give it to Wayne J. Waters. If she was delusional, her money should go where she had intended it to go before her mind became clouded: to her daughters."

"And you have to decide," I said. "Damn it, Hilda, why does it always come back to you?"

Hilda gave me a small smile. "Because much as we wish it were, life isn't all meadows and groves." She stood up. "Now, I really had better get down to business. Luckily for all concerned, until the day she died Justine was a meticulous keeper of records. It's amazing how often one can find an answer to a big question by answering a number of smaller ones."

After Hilda went upstairs, I was restless. I threw a load of laundry in the machine, gave the living room a perfunctory dusting, and flipped through an academic journal that had arrived in Friday's mail. I couldn't shake the image of Lucy Blackwell, standing alone on the doorstep, her dark honey hair sleeked by the rain into the style that evoked the flower child she'd been when she made her first album. Curious, I went back down to the laundry room. The last time we'd cleaned the basement, I'd been merciless. I'd thrown out all our old cassettes. I'd deep-sixed Petula Clark and Jimmy Webb and a score of others, but I'd stashed the cassettes I couldn't part with in my old wicker sewing basket. With its cotton lining patterned in psychedelic swirls of orange, yellow, and red, the basket seemed an appropriate final resting place for old tunes and old memories. Lucy Blackwell's debut album was on the top of the pile. Almost thirty years had passed since she'd posed for the cover photo: a carefree girl on a garden swing, eyes closed in ecstasy, legs bared, shining hair flying. Almost thirty years had passed since Ian and I had embraced in the hush of the university library and whispered our plans for a perfect life.

I took the tape back upstairs, dropped it in the player on my bedside table, and turned down the bedspread. As I slipped between the cool sheets, Lucy was singing "My Daddy's Party." The lyrics were as poignantly beautiful as I had remembered them being, but for the first time I was struck by a curious omission. Lucy Blackwell's account of enchanted evenings in the lives of three little girls, mesmerized by candlelight and grown-up laughter, shimmered with detail, but nowhere in her remembrance of things past had she mentioned her mother's name.

When I woke up, Taylor was standing beside the bed, peering down at me. She was wearing the Testicle Festival T-shirt from Bottlescrew Bill's. "How can you sleep in the middle of the day?" she asked.

"It's easy," I said. "You just have to go to bed too late and get up too early."

She shrugged. "You don't let me do that." She ran her finger along the buttons of my tape player.

"Something on your mind?" I said.

She didn't look up. "You never said whether he liked it." When I looked at her quizzically, she frowned. "You never said whether Eli liked the dragon-boat painting." Her dark eyes were anxious.

"Who wouldn't love that painting?" I said. "Just looking at it made me feel happy."

Amazingly, the diversion worked. "Did you really like it that much?"

"I think it's the best work you've done," I said. "I hated to see it leave the house."

"I could do one for you," Taylor said. "Not the same. Maybe I could paint a dragon boat with all of us in it."

"Sounds good to me," I said.

"Sounds good to me, too," she said. She scrunched her nose. "How come you didn't say anything about my T-shirt?"

"It's Saturday," I said. "This house is a taste-free zone."

The rain had stopped by the time I pulled into the parking lot at Nationtv. When I got out of our Volvo, I noticed a spectacular rainbow arching over the east of the city. It seemed like such a good omen that when I got to Jill Osiowy's office I insisted she come to her window to have a look.

"Does this mean all our troubles are over?" asked Jill.

"Every last one," I said. "The rainbow never lies."

Jill had set up the VCR and TV in her office, and as she organized the tapes, I watched the colours of the rainbow fade, then disappear. I was so intent that I didn't notice Jill waiting for me.

She came over and tapped me on the shoulder. "Can we roll now, or do you want to check some pigeon entrails to see if this is an auspicious day for decision-making?

"We can roll," I said.

"Good," she said, then she leaned over and hit *play*.

Our first prospect was an Ottawa academic who was a Nationtv regular during federal elections. He was about my age, with a sonorous voice, a fifty-dollar haircut, and the perpetually aggrieved air of an elitist in an imperfect world.

When his commentary was finished, I looked at Jill. "I could never measure up," I said.

Jill ejected the tape. "I know what you mean. He always makes me feel as if I have spinach hanging out of my teeth." She dropped in the next tape.

"Now this one isn't empathy-challenged, but there is another teeny shortcoming," Jill said. The smiling face on the screen belonged to a premier who had been retired by the electorate in his province's last election. In the three minutes during which he spoke about welfare reform, the ex-premier dropped all his final *g*'s and made four factual errors.

"Thick as a two-bob plank," I said.

Jill nodded in agreement. "Wouldn't recognize an intelligent idea if it came with a side order of fries." She brightened. "But you have to admit he is folksy."

"Is that why he made the short list?"

Jill dropped the ex-premier's tape back in its case. "Nope. He made the short list because he's married to my boss's sister." She inserted a third tape. "Let's hope third time's lucky."

Jill's words were light, but I noticed she was watching my face with real interest. My reaction didn't disappoint her. Our third candidate was wearing bluejeans and a T-shirt and he had the kind of energy that made a viewer sit up and listen. He was young, in his late twenties, and as he described the recent convention of our official opposition party, he was smart and irreverent.

"He's good," I said. "What's his name?"

"Ken Leung," Jill said. "He teaches Canada–Pacific Rim Studies at Simon Fraser."

"I like him," I said.

"So do I," Jill said. "What do you think of the shirt?"

"Taylor was wearing one just like it when I left the house," I said.

"Serious?"

"Serious. Bottlescrew Bill's Festival obviously draws a varied clientele."

Jill laughed. "So, is the shirt omen enough for us to offer Ken Leung the job?"

"Sure," I said. "Especially when you factor in his intelligence, his presence on camera, and the fact that he will appeal to a whole new demographic. It'll be good for all of us to have somebody on the show who knows what the world feels like to people born after 1970.

"He speaks Cantonese, too," Jill said. "Do you think Glayne will like him?"

"She'll love him. He's a terrific find. If I were you, I'd offer him the job before somebody else grabs him."

Jill picked up the phone and dialled Ken Leung's home number. The person on the other end of the line said Ken was playing tennis, but he was expected back any moment. Jill said the matter was urgent and left her number. When she hung up, she screwed her face into an expression that was supposed to be beseeching. "Wait with me until he calls? It's so boring here on Saturdays; besides, it will give us a chance to get down and dirty about our lives without Angus flapping around."

"I'll stay," I said. "But at the moment, there's nothing in my life to get down and dirty about."

Jill frowned. "You and Alex *are* still together, aren't you?"

"I guess so, but it doesn't feel like we're together. His nephew's had a lot of problems lately, and Alex and I had a pretty nasty exchange about it last night."

"I didn't think you two ever fought."

"We don't," I said. "Maybe we'd be better off now if we had."

Jill frowned. "Is it that serious?"

"I don't know. There's just so much we never talk about. I think we're both afraid that if we ever really started talking about all the things we were worried about, we'd discover we had too many strikes against us."

"Is there anything I can do to help?"

"No," I said, "but thanks for asking."

Jill glanced at her phone. "Looks like we may be here for a while. Do you want a Coke?"

"Sure," I said.

Jill went to the apartment-sized fridge in the corner of her office. She took out two Cokes, snapped the caps, and handed me one.

I took a sip. "Jill, what do you know about Justine Blackwell and her family?"

Jill's eyes widened. "Where did that come from?"

"From my concern about Hilda," I said.

"I noticed she's become the family spokesperson," Jill said. "It struck me as a little bizarre."

"She's also the executrix of Justine's will," I said. "And I don't like it. I also don't like some of the people who've come with the package. Hilda offered to do an old friend a favour, then all of a sudden she's at the centre of all this hostility."

"Do you want me to do some digging?"

"Yeah," I said, "I do. What's your take on Justine's murder?"

"I haven't got one," Jill said. "If you watch our news or read the paper, you know as much as I know. There's the Wayne J. Waters and Co. angle, and there's the family angle."

"The family angle," I said.

"Surely you've cottoned to the fact that Justine wasn't exactly mother of the year."

"I have," I said. "But Justine's daughters aren't exactly children. They've all accomplished things in their lives. Besides, by the time they hit their forties, most people recognize that there's a statute of limitations on bad parenting."

"Sometimes there are fresh offences," Jill said mildly.

"That sounds as if you know something."

"I know about one specific problem. It was with Tina. About a year ago, Tina decided she needed plastic surgery."

"But she's so attractive."

"She's also forty-four."

"That's not old."

"It's old for television," Jill said. "By the time a woman's forty-four, the camera has stopped being her friend. Tina had been doing the supper-hour news on CJRG for twenty-one years. Anyway, some asshole over in their news division decided to trade her in for a newer model. Tina thought she might be able to hold on to her job if she got one of those bloodless facelifts.

I winced. "What on earth is a bloodless facelift?"

"We did a piece on it last fall. It's the hot new alternative to the surgeon's knife: laser surgery. It zaps wrinkles by literally burning away the skin on the face. Some of the people on the piece we did had great results."

"But Tina didn't."

Jill shook her head. "She tried to do it on the cheap. It's an expensive procedure. Twenty thousand U.S. Tina didn't have that kind of money. Regina's a pretty small market, and those local stations don't pay diddley."

"Why didn't she go to her mother?"

"That's what a lot of people wondered. Rumour had it that Madame Justice Blackwell was too busy dealing with the financial needs of her new friends to spend money on her daughter."

I sipped my Coke. "Do you believe that?"

Jill shrugged. "I don't know. People talk. Anyway, Tina pulled together what she could and went down to the some laser-surgery clinic in Tennessee. They botched it. Her skin looks like she's been burned and she's quite badly scarred. She came to me this summer to ask if we had anything for her in radio. She's good on air and experienced, but we're bringing along our own people. Our own *young* people."

The phone rang. "Speaking of young people," I said. "That must be our Generation X-er."

When Jill picked up the phone, I gathered up our Coke bottles and started out the door towards the recycle box. Jill shouted after me. "Hang on," she said. "It's for you."

Angus's voice was cracking with excitement. "I'm an uncle," he said. "Mieka finally had the baby. I talked to Greg. Everybody's all right. He says the baby weighs – just a minute, I wrote it down – nine pounds, eleven ounces. It could be a linebacker, Mum."

"Nine pounds, eleven ounces. Poor Mieka," I said.

"Greg said she was a little wiped," Angus conceded. "Anyway, I told her we'd come up to Saskatoon tonight. We can go up tonight, can't we?

"We'll leave as soon as I get home," I said. "Wow, I can't believe it! A grandson!"

"Where did you get that? It's a girl, Mum. Her name is – wait a minute, I wrote that down too – the baby's name is Madeleine Kilbourn Harris."

"But you said . . . Never mind. So the linebacker is a girl."

Angus laughed. "Greg said he's signing her up for the Powder Puff League first thing Monday morning."

When I got home, I called Mieka to tell her we were on our way. She sounded tired, but very happy. Then I dialled Alex's number. There was no answer, and he didn't have voice mail. I hung up the phone, reached under the bed, and pulled out the cradle board Alex had made for the new baby. Our relationship had hit a bad patch, but I still wanted him to be part of the next few hours.

I was throwing a nightie into my overnight bag when Hilda came in. Her hot-pink and apple-green outfit was as cheerful as a late summer orchard, and she was beaming. She came over and embraced me.

"Angus told me the good news," she said. "And he told me you're going to Saskatoon tonight. You're welcome to stay at my house, if that would help."

"Thanks," I said. "We'll be all right at Greg and Mieka's. It's only for one night. Hilda, should I call somebody to come in and walk Rose?"

She shook her head. "No need," she said. "I'll welcome the walk before bedtime. I have to finish going through Justine's private financial records, and that's bound to be unpleasant."

"Don't tell me Justine couldn't balance her chequebook," I said.

Hilda didn't smile at my joke. "No, Justine was meticulous. It's just troubling to see how much she gave and how little she seemed to get back." She shook herself. "Not one more word about Justine. This is a day for celebration."

I gave her a hug. "If you change your mind about Rose, there's a list of Angus's buddies by the phone. Any of them will be happy to walk her for the price of a Big Gulp."

Hilda smiled. "A reasonable fee. Now, off with you. Give Mieka and Greg my love, and kiss Madeleine for me." She drew me close. "Take care of yourself, Joanne. You're very dear to me."

"And you are to me," I said. "I'll call you when I get back from the hospital."

"I'll be waiting," Hilda said.

I zipped up my overnight bag, picked up a jacket, and grabbed the tape of Lucy Blackwell I'd been listening to that afternoon. Chances were good that Angus would howl at my choice of travel music, but there was always the possibility that Lucy had been around long enough to be retro.

Before I dropped the tape in my bag, I glanced at the photograph on the cover. Rumour had it that Bob Dylan had taken that photo of Lucy on the swing. Twenty-nine years ago, stuck with the coffee parties and the constituency lists while my new husband made a name for himself in politics, I had, on more than one occasion, envied that lovely girl her life of adventure and freedom. I didn't envy her now. Nothing in Lucy Blackwell's life, past or present, could hold a candle to the prospect of holding Madeleine Kilbourn Harris in my arms.

CHAPTER

7

Royal University Hospital in Saskatoon is a teaching hospital on the west side of the University of Saskatchewan campus. From our spot in the parking lot, I could see the riverbank above the South Saskatchewan River. The leaves of the willows and scrub birch were beginning to change colour. In a week, they'd be saffron; in three weeks, they'd be gone, and the long grey winter would be upon us. But that September evening, as the sun warmed the tindall stone of the campus's oldest buildings, we were in the timeless world of a university at the beginning of term, and the air was fresh with new beginnings.

Mieka's room was on the fourth floor. As Angus, Taylor, and I crowded into the elevator, I found myself hoping her roommates were a tolerant crew. We came bearing gifts. I'd stopped at a stand at the edge of town to buy gladioli, Mieka's favourites, and Taylor had picked out enough spectacular blooms for a Mafia funeral. Angus was carrying the cradle board Alex had made and an industrial-sized bag of Mieka's favourite gumdrops, and I had an armful of gifts from Jill, Hilda, and me, and a weathered package from my older son, Peter, who was working with a veterinarian in Whitehorse. One of Pete's friends from N.W.T. had dropped the parcel at our house the week before with strict instructions that we deliver it when the baby was born.

As soon as the elevator doors opened, Taylor hit the corridor at a dead run. Blinded by the gladioli, she missed by a hairsbreadth colliding with a young woman in a fuzzy pink housecoat who was moving with the painful steps of a patient recovering from a Caesarean section. My younger daughter was headed for trouble, but there was time to nip it in the bud.

"All right, T," I said, "that's enough."

She wheeled around and peered at me through the gladioli.

"Do we need to find a quiet place where we can talk?" I said.

Her lower lip shot out. "No," she said.

"Good," I said, "because you and I have been waiting a long time to meet Madeleine. I don't think either of us wants to waste time cooling our heels out here."

Mieka was in a semi-private room at the end of the hall. Greg met us at the door and, after a flurry of hugs, he ushered us in. Luckily, it appeared that there was no roommate. My daughter was sitting by the window, holding her daughter. I thought I was prepared for the moment, but as soon as I saw mother and child together, my throat closed. I walked over, kissed Mieka, and drew back the receiving blanket so I could see Madeleine. She was a beauty, with a mop of dark hair, a rosebud mouth, and fingers and toes impossibly small and perfect.

"Here," Mieka said, offering the baby to me. I took her. The first time I had held my own daughter, I had been exhausted from a too-long labour and terrified about whether I would be a good mother. The joy I felt when I looked down at my granddaughter that night was unalloyed by memories of past pain or fear of the future. I was simply and over-whelmingly happy.

"Hi, Madeleine," I said. The baby looked up at me intently.

Taylor stood on tiptoe to look into her new niece's face. "She knows who you are," she said softly. "I'm Taylor Love, Madeleine."

Angus leaned over for a closer look. "Pretty nice," he said. He turned to his big sister. "Good job, Mieka."

"Piece of cake," she said. "Now, come on, hand over those gumdrops, and let's open the presents."

The rest of the visit was etched in gold. We found containers for the glads, and I held the baby while Mieka and Greg opened the gifts. Jill had been shooting a series in B.C. over the summer and she'd brought back the tiniest siwash sweater I'd ever seen; Hilda's gift was a Beatrix Potter mug and porringer, and a cheque to start a bank account so the baby could see Beatrix Potter country some day; Peter's unwieldy package contained a handmade quilt in the spectacular colours of a northern sunset. My present was practical: a gift certificate for six months of visits from a cleaning service. We praised all the gifts extravagantly, but it was Alex's present that was the real hit. Greg, who was a weekend carpenter, gazed assessingly at the cradle board Alex had made.

"That's hand-done," he said. "It's a beautiful piece of woodworking."

I felt a rush of pride. "Alex will be glad you appreciated the work he put into it."

There was one final order of business. I called Taylor over. "There's a book in my bag. Could you get it?"

When Taylor pulled out the worn copy of Margaret Wise Brown's *Goodnight Moon*, she eyed it with interest. "You used to read that to me."

I nodded. "And before that, I read it to Angus and before Angus to Peter . . ."

"And before Peter to Mieka," she said. "And now you want to give it to Madeleine."

"I thought you might like to give it to her."

"I'll read it to her," Taylor said. And she did. In the flat cadences of the new reader, Taylor worked her methodical way through the story of the little rabbit saying goodnight to all the ordinary pleasures of his world. It was a stellar performance. Even Angus remained silent. When she'd finished, Taylor handed the book to Mieka.

It was a nice note to leave on. I kissed the baby and, reluctantly, placed her in her father's arms.

"I hate to see you go," Mieka said. "You'll come back first thing tomorrow, won't you?"

"As soon as they let us in," I said.

"Here," she said, handing me a Polaroid picture Greg had snapped of me holding the baby. "The first photograph of you as a grandmother."

Greg walked us to the elevator. It came almost immediately, and Greg surprised me by stepping in with us.

As the elevator doors closed, I turned to him. "Nothing's wrong, is it?"

He shook his head. "Everything's great, especially now that we have a cleaning service. That was an inspiration, Jo. And we'll be okay with Maddy. I've got a month's paternity leave."

"What an enlightened boss you have," I said.

"Actually I have a new boss. That's what I wanted to talk to you about. You know him."

"Who?"

"My Uncle Keith."

The elevator reached the lobby, and the doors opened. "I didn't even know he'd moved back to Saskatchewan," I said.

"It's pretty recent. He's the president of my company now. Started just after Labour Day."

"And the first thing he did was give you a month off?"

"No, the first thing he did was ask about you."

Amazingly, I found myself blushing.

Greg was too diplomatic to comment on my embarrassment. "Jo, I told Keith you were coming up to Saskatoon today. He didn't want to intrude the first night, but he said he hoped you wouldn't leave town without seeing him."

"I'll give him a call before we leave."

My son-in-law pulled out his cellphone. "No time like the present," he said. "You're not supposed to use these things in the hospital, so I'll walk you to your car. You can call Keith from there."

And so, an hour after I had seen my first grandchild, I was standing in the parking lot of the hospital where she'd been born, calling an old lover. It was a scene straight out of a telecommunications ad.

Keith answered on the first ring. Not that long ago, the sound of Keith's voice on the other end of a telephone was enough to make my heart pound. He had been my first lover after my husband's death, and our relationship had been good until geography separated us and Keith found someone else. The situation was hackneyed, but I had been wounded. It had taken Alex and the passage of time to put things in perspective. That day when I heard Keith's voice, I felt the easy uncomplicated pleasure you feel when you're reconnecting with an old friend.

"Jo, is that you? I made Greg promise, but I've been kicking myself ever since. Twenty-four hours isn't much time to discover all the wonders of Madeleine."

"I agree," I said. "Have you seen her?"

"I thought I'd give Mieka a chance to take a deep breath before she had to put up with the old bachelor uncle, but Greg says Madeleine's a beauty."

"And clever," I said. "Taylor's already read her her first story."

He laughed. "How is Taylor?"

"Thriving," I said. "So's Angus. He's in Grade 12 this year."

"Almost a college man." He paused. "And how is Jo?"

"Happy. Busy."

"Is there any chance we can get together tomorrow?"

"I don't think so," I said. "I want to spend as much time as I can at the hospital."

"Visiting hours don't start till eleven. I could buy you and the kids breakfast. If I remember correctly, you loved that decadent Sunday brunch at the Bessborough."

"You remember correctly," I said.

"Then it's a go?"

I hesitated, but I couldn't think of a single logical reason to refuse. "It's a go," I said. "We'll meet you in the lobby at eight."

I handed the phone back to Greg. "Satisfied?"

He grinned. "Absolutely. The rest of the day will be yours to do with as you please."

When we got to Greg and Mieka's, Taylor began to race up and down the stairs. I knew there would be tears before bedtime if she didn't get rid of some of her energy. As she peeled by me, I grabbed her hand. "Let's go check out the neighbourhood," I said.

In five minutes, we were on our way. My daughter and son-in-law lived in an old two-storey clapboard house in the Nutana section of Saskatoon. It was a neighbourhood that, in the past few years, had surprised itself by becoming trendy. That night, as the kids and I walked along Broadway Avenue, baskets of geraniums hung from replicas of turn-of-the-century lampposts, and upscale boutiques that sold imported cheese, antique clothing, and pricey toys stood

cheek by jowl with shops that still bore the names of original owners and sold homely necessities like hardware and
bread. We walked up to the intersection called the Five
Corners, and I showed Taylor the school Madeleine would
go to. All three of us agreed this was going to be a good
neighbourhood for her to grow up in.

Later, as I settled into my unfamiliar bed, a jumble of
images crowded my mind. The day just past had been
amazing: beginning with a funeral and ending with a birth. I
thought of Emily's poignant line from *Our Town* when, on the
day of her own funeral, she makes the mistake of revisiting a
day in her life. "Do any human beings," she asks, "ever realize
life while they live it? – every every minute?" As I looked at
the Polaroid photo of my new granddaughter and me, which
I'd propped up against the light on the nightstand, I knew that
I would hang on to this particular moment for a lifetime.

Keith Harris was waiting just inside the doors of the
Bessborough Hotel when we arrived. He was wearing light
tan slacks and a sea-green knit shirt that I'd once told him
was my favourite. He had the look of well-being golfers have
after a pleasant summer: tanned, fit, and at peace with the
world. Greg and he shared a family resemblance. They were
both men of medium build, with hazel eyes, substantial
noses, easy smiles, and faces that were agreeable rather than
handsome. Apart from age, the only significant difference
between them was their hair. Greg's was dark and thick;
Keith's had just about vanished.

When he spotted me, Keith took me in his arms. "It's good
to see you, Jo," he said.

"It's good to see you," I said, and I meant it.

We all ate far too much. Once, the Bessborough buffets
had featured butter sculptures and chefs in white hats
carving hams that glistened with clove-studded fat. The

menu had been scaled down and healthied up for the nineties, but the food was still good, and as we walked out of the hotel, Keith offered me his arm. "Care to undo the damage we just did to ourselves?"

It was a perfect early-fall day: cool enough for Angus to run along the jogging path that snakes beside the South Saskatchewan River, but mild enough for Taylor, bright as a butterfly in her red-and-orange sweater, to throw herself on the grass and roll down the hill towards the river. Keith and I sat on a bench near the fountain to watch, and as we watched, we talked about our lives.

Keith's had recently undergone some fairly dramatic changes. After years in Ottawa, he'd come back to Saskatchewan to manage a high-powered investment company. He was a lawyer by profession, but he'd spent much of his working life in the backrooms of Tory politics. I'd spent enough time in the backrooms to know that the political world is parochial, fevered, exhausting, nasty, and addictive. Keith said he was delighted with the change, but I couldn't imagine he would be happy away from the melee, and I said so.

He smiled ruefully. "You're the only who's seen through me. On paper, it's a great decision: it's secure; the money's unbelievable; people won't flee when they see me walk into a cocktail party. And I must admit, it will be nice not to have to listen to some snot-nosed neo-con explain the political process to me. All the same, I'm going to miss it."

"You can still be involved," I said.

"I've got too many enemies to be an *éminence grise*; besides I think my new company would prefer that I keep a low profile." He shrugged. "I'll work it out. One good thing: it's going to be great to be closer to you."

I didn't respond.

Keith touched my elbow. "Are you and Alex still together?"

"I don't know," I said.

"That doesn't sound like you."

"Maybe not," I said. "But it's the truth."

"Want me to change the subject?"

"Yeah," I said, "I do."

For a few minutes we sat in silence, enjoying the sunshine. When Keith turned to me, his smile was rueful. "We must be getting old, Jo: running out of conversational topics."

"I've got one," I said. "Justine Blackwell. Did you know her?"

Keith looked sombre. "That was a terrible thing."

"And close to home for us," I said. "Justine and Hilda McCourt were friends. Hilda was staying at our house the night Justine died. In fact, they were together just before she was killed."

"That must have been a nasty shock for Hilda," Keith said. "Is she handling it all right?"

"You know Hilda," I said. "She's rolled up her shirtsleeves and dug in to help sort out some problems with Justine's estate."

"Good," Keith said. He frowned. "What's that thing about being busy Hilda always says?"

"It's a quotation from Catharine Parr Traill," I said. "In cases of emergency, it's folly to throw your hands in the air and wail in terror – better to be up and doing."

Keith laughed. "Words to live by. Now, to answer your question. Over the years, Justine and I were at a lot of the same functions, but except for the usual pleasantries, I never really talked to her. I did know her husband, though. Dick Blackwell was a big contributor to the party, and he was a great guy – the best. I always thought he deserved a better personal life than the one he ended up with."

" 'Personal life' meaning his marriage?"

Keith sighed. "Yeah, 'personal life' meaning his marriage. One should be charitable about the dead, but Justine wasn't much of a wife. She was, however, one hell of a lawyer." He shook his head and smiled. "I saw her in action once. She was amazing. She had exactly the right temperament for criminal law: combative but cool. She was passionate when it suited her purpose, but every display of emotion was calculated: just enough outrage or fervent belief or shining-eyed hope to do the job, and not one iota more." Keith turned his head and glanced at me. "She never broke a sweat."

"Not with her marriage either," I said.

"No, not with her marriage, and not with her children. After Dick died, there was a rumour that Justine had been having an affair. I never believed it – not because she was such a dutiful wife, but because she didn't have that kind of passion."

"You didn't like her much, did you?"

Keith sat up. "Actually, I did like her. She was smart, she was beautiful, and, on the occasions we were together, she was good company. I just think Dick Blackwell would have had a happier life if he'd married someone else. Given the circumstances, that sounds harsh, but it's the truth – at least as I see it. If you want more details, you could talk to Dick's old law partner."

"No," I said, "your opinion's good enough for me."

"Hearing that was worth the price of breakfast."

His gaze was steady, and I was relieved when Taylor came peeling up the hill. She was sweaty and dirty and happy. "Is it time to see Madeleine yet?"

"After we scrub off six layers of dirt, it is. Let's find your brother and go back to Greg and Mieka's and hit the showers."

Angus found us, or rather, he found Keith. They walked ahead of us on the path talking about their common passion, football. By the time we hit the Bessborough parking lot, they had decided to get tickets for the Huskies game that afternoon. After Taylor climbed into the back and Angus slid into the driver's seat, Keith turned to me. "Should I get a ticket for Taylor? I don't think I'll have to twist Greg's arm too hard to get him to come. You and Mieka might enjoy some time alone."

"It's worth a try," I said. I bent down to the car window. "Taylor, Mr. Harris has an invitation for you . . ."

"I heard," she said. "And I want to go."

"Sounds like it's settled," Keith said.

When we said goodbye in the Bessborough parking lot, Keith held my hand a second longer than necessary, then he kissed me on the cheek. "Thanks for the morning, Jo. I hope it's the first of many."

Greg was waiting with the Polaroid when we came into Mieka's room. He wanted some pictures of the kids with Madeleine. Angus went first. He held her in one arm, tight against his body, the way his coach had made him hold a football for an entire weekend after a costly fumble. When he handed the baby off to Taylor, she was wildly enthusiastic. For ten minutes, she sat in the corner with Madeleine, crooning and chatting. When her eyes betrayed her restlessness, Greg said he'd buy the kids a burger before the game, and after a whirl of goodbyes, Mieka and I were left alone.

We pushed Madeleine's bassinet in front of the window, pulled our own chairs close, and gave ourselves over to the singular pleasures of two women wholly absorbed by a new baby. September sunshine pooled in a circle around us; air crisp with the smell of fall leaves and late gardens drifted through the open window, and my daughter and I swapped stories about childbirth and the primal pleasure of holding a child to the breast. In the larger world of the hospital, there was death and fear and pain and suffering, but in the safety of our small circle, there were only dreams and hopes and an unspoken thanksgiving that somehow the two of us had managed to navigate the risky shoals of the mother-daughter relationship and arrive at this moment together.

The drive back to Regina was pleasant and uneventful. All the way home, we saw farmers still out in the fields. It was an excellent crop, and nobody was taking any chances. In a little over a month it would be Thanksgiving. Maybe Greg and Mieka could bring Madeleine down. Keith could come too. If Alex and I could work things out, he and Eli could come. And, of course, Hilda and Leah. It was time for us to reap what we had sown, and it seemed the farmers weren't the only ones who'd be harvesting a bumper crop that year.

It was a little after 9:00 when we pulled up in front of our house. Taylor was sound asleep. As soon as I got out of the car, I could hear Rose barking inside.

Angus got out of the back seat. "What's up with Rose?" he asked.

"She's just glad to see us," I whispered. "Go in and let her out, would you? I'm going to try to carry Taylor up to bed without waking her." I leaned into the back seat and picked up my daughter. When I started up the walk, Angus was still fiddling with the front door.

He turned around and mouthed the words, "It's locked."

"Where's Hilda?"

He looked at me in exasperation. "Mum, I just got here too."

I handed Taylor to Angus, took my key out of my purse, and opened the front door. As soon as I stepped into the hall, I knew something was wrong. The area by the door was covered in dog faeces and urine.

Angus was behind me in the door; Taylor was in his arms, mercifully still sleeping. A wave of panic hit. "Take Taylor down to the family room and put her on the couch," I said.

My son stared at the mess in the front hall, but didn't say a word. He walked towards the family room. I took a deep breath and started up the stairs. My legs were leaden. There wasn't a doubt in my mind that something had happened to Hilda. I felt a dozen emotions, but the overwhelming one was guilt. Hilda was eighty-three years old. Unwilling to face her mortality, I had stood by as she had undertaken a task too onerous for a woman decades younger than she was; then I had left her alone.

The door to her bedroom was shut. My hand was shaking as I turned the knob. The image I'd conjured up of Hilda, dead in her bed, victim of a heart attack that carried her away in the night, was so vivid that, for a beat, I couldn't take in the reality. She wasn't there. Her bed was made up, the sheets and blanket pulled so tight under the chenille spread that a dime would have bounced off them. I ran down the hall to the bathroom. It was pristine: sink shining; towels lined up on the towel rack; fresh roll of toilet paper on the holder. For a foolish and relief-filled moment, I let myself think that everything was all right, that Hilda had just become so absorbed in her delvings into Justine Blackwell's affairs that she had lost track of time. Then, for the second time in forty-eight hours, I turned and saw my son behind me, white-faced and shaking.

"She's in the kitchen, Mum."

"Is she . . . ?"

He shook his head miserably. "I don't know." We started down the hall, but Angus turned into my room.

"Where are you going?" I asked.

"To call 911," said the son whom I'd accused more than once of lacking common sense.

"Good," I said. "After you get them, call Alex."

I ran downstairs. Hilda was sprawled by the back door. She was still in the outfit she'd changed into Saturday night before we left: sandals, apple-green pedal pushers, hot-pink-and-green striped shirt. It was as if the movie I'd been playing in my mind since I heard Rose barking had suddenly become real. There were, however, significant differences between the nightmare and the reality. Even in my worst imaginings, I hadn't seen Hilda's face. She was ashen and, for the first time since I'd known her, expressionless. Her mouth was slack, and her eyes unseeing. The other variation was a critical one. In those first, ghastly moments, I had assumed Hilda had been felled by a stroke or a heart attack, but the blood pooled behind her head, and the blood on the croquet mallet thrown to the floor beside her, told a different story. Hilda's body hadn't failed her; she had been attacked. When I put my fingers to her throat and felt a faint pulse, I thanked God.

Angus came into the kitchen. "They're on their way," he said. "I couldn't get Alex, so I called Jill. I thought I could go to the hospital with you." His voice trailed off. He was staring at Hilda. Suddenly, his face contorted in anger. "What the fuck did they think they were doing with that towel?"

I followed the direction of his gaze. One of our kitchen towels had been folded and placed under Hilda's head.

Angus's voice broke. "What kind of person would do that? Smash someone's skull in, then make a pillow for her head."

The next minutes had the jerky urgency of a movie made with a hand-held camera. As the paramedics fell to their work, they peppered me with questions: What was Hilda's name? Her age? Had I moved her? Had I placed the towel under her head? Did I know what had happened? Had she been conscious at all since I found her? As I answered, my voice was lifeless. I couldn't take my eyes off the activity surrounding my friend. It was purposeful but alien. An oxygen mask had been slapped on Hilda's face, and one of the paramedics, a young man, was kneeling beside her with state-of-the-art equipment that calibrated her pulse, respiration, blood pressure, and temperature. In a careful, calm voice, the young man called out numbers that I knew were related to Hilda's vital signs, but I was too ignorant to interpret them.

Two uniformed policemen arrived. They had their own questions, and I did my best to answer them, but I didn't have much information to give. When they were satisfied that I'd told them all I could, they began to check out my house, looking, they said, for signs of forcible entry or something the attacker might have left behind.

One of the paramedics bent and shone a pencil flashlight into Hilda's eyes, all the while calling her name, trying, I guess, to rouse her to consciousness. A medical collar was fixed around Hilda's neck, and an intravenous was started in her right arm. Finally, the paramedics slid her onto a kind of board. That's when I noticed the dark stain in the crotch of her pedal pushers. It was the final indignity: at some point, my proud friend had wet herself.

"No," I said.

The paramedic closest to me cast me a sidelong glance. "What?"

"She wouldn't want anyone to see her like that." I took off my sweater and placed it carefully so that it covered the stain. By the sink, the younger of the two policeman was wrapping our old croquet mallet in plastic; he, too, carried out his task with exquisite care.

The paramedics began to strap Hilda to the stretcher, and the questions started up again: Did she have any allergies? Any health problems? What medications was she on? Could I check her room and bring any prescription drugs with me to the hospital? When they lifted her and started for the front door, I turned to my son.

"You'll have to stay here," I said. "Jill must have been delayed, but she'll be along. I'll call you as soon as I know

anything." I kissed him on the cheek. "I love you," I said.
He nodded numbly.

The paramedics wouldn't let me ride with Hilda. I had to sit in the front seat. The sirens were wailing, and the driver didn't make any attempt to talk. It was a relief not to have to deal with another human being. As we sped across the Albert Street bridge, I was overwhelmed with guilt. I had promised Hilda I'd call from Saskatoon, but I'd forgotten. I had a clutch of good excuses: my excitement about the baby; Taylor's boundless enthusiasm; my reunion with Keith; my need to be with Mieka. All my rationalizations made perfect sense; none changed the fact that I hadn't picked up the phone.

As we pulled into the ambulance bay at Pasqua Hospital, I knew that I would live with that sin of omission for the rest of my life. I followed behind as Hilda was wheeled through the E.R. The medical people exchanged information. Most of it was indecipherable, but the fragments I understood were terrifying: estimated 30 per cent blood loss; thready pulse; pupils sluggish to light; extremities cold.

A nurse stopped me at the double doors that opened into the treatment rooms. Her words were diplomatic, but the message was clear: the experts were taking over; I would just be in the way. I turned back and, for the first time, I took in the scene in the waiting room.

It was Sunday night, and the place was filled with the pain of other people's lives: a filthy, wiry man with the crazed eyes of a prophet or a solvent-drinker; a terrified father with a feverish little boy; two uniformed police officers with a young woman who was very drunk and whose arm hung at an unnatural angle from her shoulder; a teenaged couple with a croupy baby; and a dozen other soldiers in the Army of the Sick and the Unlucky. I found a chair facing the doors behind which Hilda had disappeared. If she needed me, I'd be close at hand.

There was a pile of magazines, soft with age and use, on the table next to me. The magazine on top was titled *Southern Bed and Breakfast*. The prospect of losing myself in a world of magnolias, overhead fans, and silver filigreed holders for iced-tea glasses was seductive, but try as I might, I couldn't close the curtain on the human comedy playing itself out around me. An orderly was leading the wild-eyed man down the hallway; the feverish boy had begun to whimper and cry for his mother. The young woman with the hanging arm had turned against the police who had brought her in. All she was interested in now was getting patched up so she could leave. With her good arm, she was pounding on the chest of the younger of the cops, and saying, "What kind of fuckin' doctor are you, anyway?" He bore the assault with patience and grace.

Time passed at a snail's pace. Whenever the intercom crackled or a man or woman in medical gear appeared in the room, my heart leapt. But the name called was never mine, and as the minutes ticked by, panic threatened to overwhelm me. When Detective Robert Hallam came through the emergency-room door, my first thought was that he had arrived as backup for the police officers with the abusive woman, but although he nodded to them, he kept on coming until he got to me.

In his canary-yellow button-down shirt and Tilley slacks, he seemed an unlikely candidate for knight in shining armour, but, as it turned out, he was able to rescue me. He sat down in the chair next to mine.

"I'm sorry about Miss McCourt," he said.

My words came in a torrent. "Have you heard how she is? No one's said a word to me since I got here, and by now someone should know something."

He sighed heavily. "You're right," he said. "Someone should. Let me go over there and see what I can find out."

Detective Hallam walked over to the desk that separated the ones who feared and hoped from the ones who knew. When he showed the nurse his badge, she picked up the phone and made a call. Almost immediately a young man in surgical greens came through the door behind her. The three of them bent their heads together, then Detective Hallam came back to me.

"It's not good," he said. "They've done a CT scan. She has a bad concussion, but they're waiting for someone who specializes in head injuries to come in to see if she needs surgery. She's also seriously dehydrated, and she's lost a lot of blood. I don't think any of her conditions are life-threatening in themselves, it's the combination, and of course there's her age to consider." Unexpectedly, he smiled. "If you should happen to speak to her, don't tell Miss McCourt I mentioned her age."

"I won't," I said. Then out of nowhere, the tears came.

Robert Hallam waited out the storm. When I was finished, I blew my nose and turned back to him. "I'm sorry," I said.

"It's the not knowing that makes you crazy," he said simply. "But they have promised to let us know as soon as they decide about surgery." He gazed at me assessingly. "Are you up to a few questions?"

I shook my head. "I told the officers who came to the house everything I knew."

His voice was kind. "Well, sometimes people know more than they think they do."

At first, it seemed I was not among them, but when Detective Hallam asked me about the croquet mallet that Hilda's assailant had used, an image, disquieting as a frame in a rock video, flashed through my mind. It was of Eli, whirling his mallet high in the air on the day he and Angus had their crazy game. I didn't tell Detective Hallam about the memory. Stated baldly, it might have evoked a possibility that was unthinkable, and I banished it.

Detective Hallam had a few final questions. He had just snapped his notepad shut when a nurse came out to say that Hilda was being moved to intensive care, and I could see her briefly. I was on my feet in a split second. Finally, I was going to get to pass through the double doors.

Hilda was almost unrecognizable: a prisoner of tubes and of machines calibrating the vital signs of a no-longer-vital life. I bent to kiss her, but I was afraid I'd knock lose some critical piece of the apparatus, so I took her hand in mine. It was icy, and there were pinkish stains on her fingers. Whoever had taken off her favourite Love That Red nail polish had been in a hurry. A doctor came in to examine Hilda. The name on his identification card was Everett Beckles. I stepped back and watched. When he started to leave, I touched his arm. "Is she going to die?" I asked.

"I don't know," he said. "We've done a diagnostic workup, and we've decided against neurosurgical intervention."

"She doesn't need an operation," I said. "That's good news, isn't it?"

Dr. Beckles didn't answer me. He was a black man about my own age, and he looked as exhausted as I felt. "As you can see, we've closed the lacerations on your mother's skull and we're transfusing her. We've given her something to reduce the brain water, and we've started anticonvulsant therapy. In intensive care, they'll monitor her level of consciousness and her vital signs. Everything possible is being done," he said.

"Will it be enough?" I asked.

"We can only hope," he said. "You might as well go home and get some rest. Your mother's going to need you in the next few days."

I started to correct him, but the words died in my throat. My mouth felt rusty, and I ached. I covered Hilda's hand with my own. "I'll be back," I said.

As I waited for my cab, I looked up at the looming bulk of Pasqua Hospital. My second hospital of the day. Two hospitals, two cities: joy, sorrow; hope, fear. Somewhere in the distance, a dog howled. Its cry, feral, heartsick, and lonely, stirred something in me. Only my superior position on the evolutionary scale kept me from howling too.

CHAPTER

8

It was 1:00 a.m. when I got home. Jill had cleaned up the dog mess in the front hall, but Rose lowered her head in shame when she saw me. I bent down and put my arms around her neck. "It wasn't your fault, Rose," I murmured. "Don't blame yourself."

Jill came out to the hall when she heard my voice. She was carrying the Jungian biography of the prime minister I'd been reading. She had her place marked with her finger.

"How's Hilda doing?"

"She still isn't conscious," I said. "They sent me home. She has a concussion; she lost a lot of blood and she was dehydrated. The worst thing is that no one knows how long she was lying here. It could have been twenty-four hours."

Jill caught the edge in my voice. "Don't beat yourself up about this, Jo. Much as we want to, we can't always keep the people we love from harm. Sometimes terrible things just happen." She put her arm around my shoulder and led me into the family room. "Come on. Let's have a drink. One of the delights of this particular B and B is its well-stocked bar."

I sighed. "Scotch, but make it a light one. I have a nine-thirty class."

Jill frowned. "You're not planning to go to the university, are you?"

"I am. First-year students need some sense of continuity; besides, I'm afraid Rosalie will yell at me if I cancel out this early in the semester."

"The only rationalization I would accept," she said.

When Jill came back with our drinks, she handed me mine and took a long pull on hers. "What can I do to help?" she asked.

"You've already done it," I said. "I'm so grateful you could come over and be with the kids tonight. Did Taylor ever wake up?"

Jill shook her head. "Nope. She slept through the whole thing. Cops and all."

I winced. "Do the police have any theories about what happened here tonight?"

"If they do, they weren't telling me." Jill raised an eyebrow. "Of course, they couldn't keep me from listening when they were talking to each other."

"And?"

"And they didn't find any signs of forced entry."

Suddenly I felt cold. "You mean Hilda let her attacker in."

"It looks that way," Jill said grimly. "And it also looks as if this wasn't a robbery. The police asked me to check around and see if anything was missing. I couldn't spot any glaring aberrations. Your desk was a mess, but your desk is always a mess."

"I suppose you shared that little nugget with the police."

Jill nodded. "I did, but they didn't seem very interested. Actually, the one thing they seemed really interested in was some towel. From what they said, I gathered the paramedics must have taken it with them to the hospital."

"They did," I said. "It was one of my kitchen towels. Whoever attacked Hilda had folded it to make a little pillow under her head."

"That's sick." Jill's voice was icy.

"Sick or compassionate. I guess the folded towel could suggest remorse."

"A little late for that, wasn't it?" Jill drained her glass and headed for the liquor cabinet. "Care for a refill?"

"I'm okay," I said. "My stomach's doing nip-ups. Oh, Jill, I'm so glad Taylor didn't see Hilda. She really loves her. So does Angus."

"He gave me a pretty graphic description of the scene you walked into tonight."

"My son has had one hell of a weekend. So have we all, come to think of it." I stood up. "I'm going to grab a shower and get out of this dress. When Angus told me about Mieka, I was so excited, I forgot to pack anything but my toothbrush and a change of underwear. I've been wearing this outfit since Saturday afternoon."

"'Fashion File' says that once you get a look that works for you, you should stay with it."

"I think I've stayed with this one long enough. Jill, I really am grateful that Angus had you to talk to. Do you think he'll be okay?"

"Yeah, beneath all that hip-hop-happenin' attitude, he's a pretty sensible kid. He's worried, of course, but he's handling it." She looked at me hard. "How are you doing?"

"Not great," I said. "But I'm coping, and I'll cope even better when I get some sleep." I finished my drink. A thought hit me. "Jill, is the kitchen . . . ?"

"Taken care of," she said.

"Thanks," I said. "I couldn't have faced that." I stood up. My legs felt rubbery. "Would you mind staying here tonight?

If I have to go back to the hospital, I'd like somebody to be here with the kids."

Jill smiled. "I brought my toothbrush, just in case."

I slept fitfully, listening for the phone that, mercifully, did not ring and trying, without success, to banish the images of the night. The pictures of Hilda's suffering were sharp-edged, but the scene that made my heart pound was one that existed only in my imagination: my old friend, in her cheerful summer outfit, hearing the doorbell, putting down Justine's papers and walking down the hall to admit her attacker. But who had been on the other side of that door? In the week since Justine's murder, Hilda had travelled in circles I could only guess at, among men and women whose characters were a mystery to me. For hours, I moved between sleep and consciousness, trying to conjure up the face of her assailant, but it was a futile exercise. By the time my alarm went off, I knew there was no turning away from the truth: any one of a hundred people could have picked up that croquet mallet and tried to end my old friend's life.

I dialled the number of Pasqua Hospital. Hilda had made it through the night, but there was no change in her condition. For a few minutes I lay in bed, thinking about the day ahead. I wasn't looking forward to it.

Jill was at the sink filling the coffeepot when I got back from the park with Rose. She was wearing the same white shorts and black Nationtv sweatshirt she'd had on the night before, but her auburn hair was damp from the shower, and she looked fresh as the proverbial daisy. She glanced at me questioningly.

"No news," I said.

Taylor was sitting at the table with a bowl of cereal in front of her. Her spoon stopped in midair when she saw me.

"Wasn't yesterday the best day? Madeleine is so cute. I can't wait to tell Ms. Anweiler about her. I hope she's wearing her diplodocus earrings."

"Me too," I said. "Now, you'd better finish your breakfast. You don't want to be late. You're an aunt now, so you have to be responsible."

Taylor's eyes grew large. "I'm an aunt . . . really?"

"Sure," I said. "Mieka's your big sister, so that makes Madeleine your niece."

Taylor's spoon hit the bowl. "Now I really can't wait to get to school."

Angus came into the kitchen warily, and I caught his eye. "Come out on the deck for a minute, would you?"

He followed me out to the deck without a word. The air was hazy; the first brittle leaves from our cottonwood tree were floating on the surface of the water in the swimming pool, and the breeze was fresh with the piney coldness of the north.

Angus's voice was a whisper. "Did she die?"

I shook my head. "No, she's still alive but, Angus, I won't to lie to you. She may not make it much longer."

He turned from me. When he spoke, his voice broke. "It doesn't seem right," he said.

"What doesn't?"

He looked around him. "That it can be such a great day when such a lousy thing is happening."

When we went back in, the phone was ringing. Jill gave me a questioning look and then reached for it.

"It's okay," I said. Heart pounding, I picked up the receiver, but it wasn't the hospital calling with news; it was Eric Fedoruk.

"Hilda McCourt, please," he said.

"She's not available right now."

"Is this Mrs. Kilbourn?"

"Yes," I said, "it is."

"Mrs. Kilbourn, could you have Miss McCourt call me as soon as she gets back? She's supposed to come in today to discuss Justine's estate, but she didn't phone my secretary to arrange a time." There was an edge of irritation in his voice.

"She won't be coming in," I said.

"She has to," he said flatly.

"Mr. Fedoruk, Hilda doesn't have to do anything for you. She's in the intensive-care unit at Pasqua Hospital. Someone came into my house and attacked her."

"Is she going to be all right?" The concern in his voice seemed heartfelt, but I was beyond caring about Eric Fedoruk's feelings.

"I don't know if she's going to be all right," I snapped. "All I know is that I want you and everybody else connected with Justine Blackwell to stay away from Hilda. Leave her alone. No more making her the final arbiter; no more signing off on responsibilities; no more sending the press to my house. It's time everyone took responsibility for their own lives. Got it?"

Eric Fedoruk was stammering out his apology when I hung up. His words cut no ice with me. I was sick of justifications and explanations.

Jill made a face when I hung up. "Glad I wasn't on the other end of that," she said. "Jo, what's going on here?"

I gave her the bare bones: Justine's transformation in the past year; the request she'd made of Hilda; the will which named Hilda as executrix; the warring factions in Justine's life; the tensions that existed between Justine and all the people she was closest to.

"And you think what happened to Hilda is connected to Justine's death?"

"I don't know," I said. "Ever since you told me the police think Hilda must have known her attacker, I've been reeling. But, Jill, there has to be a connection. It's just too much of a stretch to believe that seven days after Justine's murder, somebody would take it into their head to try to kill Hilda."

Suddenly, Jill frowned. "Jo, is there some sort of guard on Hilda's hospital room?"

"I don't know." The penny dropped. "Oh God, what if . . . ?" I jumped up, went to the phone, and dialled police head-quarters. Detective Hallam was way ahead of me. In the early hours of the morning, he had sent a constable to Pasqua Hospital to monitor everyone who went in or out of Hilda's room.

I could feel the relief wash over me. I hung up and turned to Jill. "It's taken care of," I said.

Jill looked thoughtful. "Let's hope it is. Jo, I don't like any of this. I especially don't like the fact that we don't know who we're dealing with here." She picked up her coffee mug, walked to the sink, and rinsed it. Then she turned to face me. "When I get to the office, I'm going to see what I can pull together on the people in Justine's circle."

"You mean biographical stuff?"

"That and gossip. It's amazing how few secrets there are in a town this size. I'll call you tonight, and let you know what I come up with."

"Why don't you come for dinner? I'm going to have to tell Taylor about Hilda, and it would be good if she knew that some things in her world are still the same."

She gave me a weary smile. "That's my role in life," she said, "the permanent fixture. Six o'clock, okay?"

"Six o'clock's perfect," I said.

Before I left for the university, I made one more call. I hadn't left my office number at the hospital. I gave it to the nurse in intensive care and told her I'd come by later in the afternoon.

She said to make sure I had some identification; there was a young constable outside Hilda's door, and she was a tiger.

The lecture I gave to my first-year students wasn't the best I'd ever given, but it wasn't the worst either. When I finished, I went down to the Political Science office to pick up my mail. I was in luck. Rosalie was on the phone. I dropped a note on her desk, saying I could be reached at home for the rest of the day, and made my escape.

I stopped at the IGA and picked up a roasting chicken and some new potatoes. I was putting away groceries when my neighbour came over with two deliveries from the florist. One was addressed to Hilda, the other to me. I opened mine: an arrangement of bronze and yellow mums in an earthenware pitcher. The card read: "With the hope that you'll accept my most sincere apologies, Eric Fedoruk." I took the phone off the hook, set the alarm for 2:30 p.m., and went upstairs to bed. I was asleep before my head hit the pillow.

It was five to three when I drove into the parking lot at Pasqua Hospital. Angus had a football practice, so he wouldn't be back till supper time, but Taylor would be home at 3:30. My visit to Hilda would have to be a quick one. To the right of the glass doors of the main entrance, the usual contingent of smokers in blue hospital robes huddled, their intravenous poles looming over them like spectral chaperones. In the lobby, a gaunt young woman with a frighteningly yellow pallor looked on as a little boy showed her an apple he had cut out of red construction paper. The elevator was empty, and there was no one in the corridor as I walked into the intensive-care unit.

A fine-featured blond man, about the age of my daughter Mieka, sat at a desk in the centre of the nursing area. A small bank of TV monitors was suspended above the desk, and as he made notes on the chart in front of him, the young man kept glancing up to check the screens. The patients' rooms radiated in a semicircle off the area in which he was sitting. In one of those rooms, a radio was playing country music. The sound was incongruous but oddly reassuring. There was another reassuring note: in front of the room I presumed to be Hilda's, a uniformed police constable gazed out at the world, alert and ready.

I waited till the young man at the desk finished with his chart. "I'm here to see Hilda McCourt," I said.

"I'll have to ask for some identification," he said.

I took out my driver's licence and handed it to him. He glanced at it and handed back. "You can go in, Mrs. Kilbourn. Detective Hallam okayed you." He picked up another chart.

"Wait," I said. I leaned forward so I could read the name on his picture ID. "Mr. Wolfe, I wonder if you could tell me how Miss McCourt is doing?"

He shook his head. "No change. She's still scoring low on the Glasgow Coma Scale. That's the way we measure responses to things like light and speech and pain. The higher the score, the better the prognosis."

"And her prognosis isn't good?"

"You'll have to talk to her doctor about that." Nathan Wolfe flipped to Hilda's chart. "Miss McCourt's doctor is Everett Beckles. He'll be making his rounds in about an hour. You can talk to him then."

"I can't stay," I said. "Could you ask him to call me?"

Nathan Wolfe slid a notepad towards me. "Leave your number, but don't count on a call. Dr. Beckles is really busy."

"Thanks," I said. "Is there anything I should know before I go in there?"

"Nothing special. Just be sure to talk to her. Sometimes just hearing a human voice helps."

"Is that why the radio's on over there?"

Nathan nodded. "The guy in that room was in a motor-cycle accident. His wife says he's a big Garth Brooks fan, so she brought the radio so he'd hear some familiar voices when she couldn't be here."

When I started into Hilda's room, I remembered that I was carrying the flowers my neighbour had brought over. I handed them to Nathan. "These were sent to Miss McCourt. I know she can't have them in her room, but maybe you'd like them for the desk out here."

"This place could use some brightening," he agreed. He opened the floral paper carefully. Inside were at least three dozen creamy long-stem roses. Nathan whistled apprecia-tively. Then he reached into the folds of paper, took out the card, and handed it to me. "You'll want this," he said. "Whoever's paying the bill for those roses deserves a thank-you."

I glanced at the card. "For Hilda, with our love and best wishes, Signe, Tina, and Lucy." I ripped the card in two and handed the pieces back to Nathan. "Put this in the trash, would you? The people who are paying for those roses don't deserve diddley."

The constable who was on duty outside Hilda's room was a young woman I'd met before. Alex had introduced us at a dinner honouring outstanding police work. Her name was Linda Nilson, and she'd won an award for community service. She was coolly attractive: tall, slim, with a nicely chiselled profile, and dark hair cut in the kind of pixie style Audrey Hepburn made famous in *Roman Holiday*.

She smiled in recognition when she saw me, but still insisted on seeing a piece of ID, and I was relieved at her thoroughness.

Intubated and wired, Hilda looked impossibly small, but she'd lost the ashen look that had frightened me so much when I found her in the kitchen the night before. I bent to kiss her forehead, then opened my purse and took out a photograph I'd taken of her at the lake. She was sitting in our canoe, paddle poised. As always, she was dressed for the occasion, this time in white shorts, a navy-and-white striped gondolier's shirt, a bright orange lifejacket, and a straw boater to keep the sun off her extravagant red curls.

I taped the picture to the head of her bed. "This is so everyone will know what a knockout you are," I said. Then, heeding Nathan's advice, I began to talk. At first, I was self-conscious, then, despite the grim surroundings, I found myself relaxing into the easiness I always felt when I was with Hilda. I talked about everything that was on my mind: Mieka's baby; seeing Keith Harris again; my fears about the deterioration in my relationship with Alex; the dinner I was planning with Jill. I was careful to avoid any mention of Justine and her troubled family in my monologue. I was amazed when I looked at my watch and saw it was already 3:20. I kissed her forehead again. "I'll be back after supper," I said. "And this time I'll bring a book to read to you."

Taylor and I arrived at the house together. "Perfect timing," I said.

She beamed. She followed me into the kitchen and, as I prepared the chicken, she told me her about her day. It had been a good one. Ms. Anweiler had picked her to be the class monitor for the week ahead. Taylor was going to have a chance to show how responsible she was. I asked if she wanted a dress rehearsal in responsibility, and she agreed to set the table and wash the potatoes while I went out to the garden.

The herbs in our clay pots were flagging, but there was still tarragon, and the parsley was plentiful if drooping. Whatever the state of our parsley crop, my late husband, Ian, had always revelled in quoting his mother's aphorism: "Parsley thrives in a house where the wife dominates." As I snipped herbs for the chicken, I thought, not for the first time, how good it would be to have a husband to laugh with and to lean against. I was tired of dealing with problems alone, tired of having no one to pick up the baton when I dropped it, tired, to use an old friend's telling image, of being "always a driver, never a passenger."

Keith Harris and I had talked vaguely of marriage when we were together, and I think at some level I believed it was a likelihood. There were no impediments. He had never married. My kids liked him, and the fact that he was Greg's uncle was icing on the cake. We were the same age; in fact, we shared a birthday. Other people approved of us as a couple; I approved of us as a couple. Then he found someone else, and my fantasy that Keith and I would walk hand in hand through the golden years faded.

Alex and I had never talked of marriage. We had been content to enjoy the here and now, but lately even the here and now had been riddled with tensions. That day, as I bent to pick tomatoes for dinner, I wondered whether what we had had ever really been enough for either of us.

When the chicken was in the oven, I walked out to Taylor's studio and told her about Hilda. I was honest, but I didn't dwell on the worst possibilities. We would jump off that particular bridge when and if we came to it. Taylor's reaction surprised me. She loved Hilda, and she was a child whose emotions were close to the surface, but that afternoon she took the news calmly.

When I finished she said, "Is Hilda going to die?"

I shook my head. "I don't know."

Taylor looked at me steadily. "She talked to me about this."

"When?" I asked.

"At the cottage. I told her that next summer I'd be able to swim right across the lake, the way Eli's mum did. And I

said, 'Promise you'll be there,' and she said she couldn't
promise, because a promise was a serious thing and she
might not be able to keep it because she was old and nobody
lives forever."

"Did she say anything else?"

Taylor nodded. "She said she'd had more fun than
anybody."

I touched my daughter's cheek. "Let's hope there's more
fun ahead," I said. I left Taylor painting and went back in the
house. The next day in my senior class, we were dealing
with federal–provincial relations during the eighties. I'd
lived it, but I didn't remember it, so I had some serious
boning up to do.

The small room I used for an office was down the hall from
the kitchen. As soon as I saw my desk, I knew that Jill's
assessment had been right. It was a mess, but it wasn't a mess
I'd made. I started sifting through the chaos. Nothing
appeared to have been taken. Whoever had ransacked my
desk obviously had concerns larger than unmarked freshman
papers and academic articles. Before I'd left for Saskatoon,
Hilda had told me she was planning to spend Saturday night
working on Justine's personal financial records. But I hadn't
noticed any papers that might have belonged to Justine in our
house. I went upstairs to Hilda's room. It was pristine. The
only evidence that Hilda had stayed there was her library
books, which were neatly stacked on Mieka's old desk by the
window. There were no papers. I checked the family room,
and the dining room. There was nothing. I called Jill, but she
was gone for the day. Then I called the police. The officer I
spoke to took my information without comment, but she
seemed interested, and she made certain she got a number
where I could be reached that evening if the investigating
officers had further questions.

Perplexed, I went back to my office and picked up an article on the Romanow–Chrétien constitutional tour of 1981. The press had dubbed it the Uke and Tuque show; reading about it, even in the dry language of academe, brought back a lot of memories. I became so absorbed I almost forgot to get the squash ready. It was only after I'd prepared it with butter, brown sugar, and nutmeg, the way Hilda liked it, that I remembered Hilda wouldn't be at the dinner table to enjoy it.

By the time Jill arrived, the chicken and squash were ready, a casserole of new potatoes was waiting to be micro-waved, and I was slicing tomatoes to sauté with zucchini and onion and garlic. Jill was carrying a bottle of Chablis in one hand and a file folder in the other.

She handed me the folder. "Some interesting stuff in there, but it can wait." She waved the Chablis. "This, on the other hand, won't keep for a minute."

I poured us each a glass of wine.

Jill took hers and raised her glass. "To absent friends," she said solemnly.

"To absent friends," I said.

She pulled out one of the kitchen chairs and sat down. "So," she said, "what's shaking around here?"

"A mystery," I said. "That mess you saw on my desk wasn't of my making."

She narrowed her eyes. "You mean somebody tossed it?"

"Hilda was working on some financial records that belonged to Justine Blackwell. I think they must have been looking for those. Judging from the fact that the papers are nowhere in evidence, I'm guessing that whoever attacked Hilda found what they were looking for."

Jill sipped her wine thoughtfully. "This is beyond us, Nancy Drew."

"I know," I said. "I've already called the police. I've done everything I can. So have you. Let's take the night off."

"Good plan," she said. "We can start by refilling our glasses."

Dinner was less boisterous than usual, but we tried. Angus gave us a rundown on his team's chances for the coming season; Taylor talked about the trip to the Legislature Ms. Anweiler was taking her class on the next day. Jill had some funny behind-the-scenes stories about Nationtv. I recounted Ian's mother's parsley story. We all missed Hilda.

After supper, Jill and the kids drove to the Milky Way for ice cream and I went back to the hospital. It had taken a while to decide which book to bring to read to Hilda. There were three on her bedside table: Justine's *Geriatric Psychiatry: A Handbook*, A. S. Byatt's *Still Life*, and a translation of Bede's *Ecclesiastical History*. In my opinion, none quite fit the bill. I was casting about for something when I remembered Hilda's passion for L.M. Montgomery. So as I stepped into the elevator of the Pasqua Hospital, there was a copy of *Anne of Green Gables* in my hand.

I waved it at Nathan as I walked by the desk. "Ever read this?" I asked.

He looked up from his charts, "No, but I saw the TV series when I was fourteen, and I was hot for Megan Follows till I hit Grade 11."

There was a new police officer outside Hilda's door. He looked tougher than Mark Messier, and I didn't stop to chat. I showed him my driver's licence, went inside, pulled up my chair, and began to read: "Mrs. Rachel Lynde lived just where the Avonlea main road dipped down into a little hollow, fringed with alders and ladies' eardrops . . ." As the tubes attached to Hilda delivered their elixirs of antibiotics and nutrients and carried away her body's waste, and the machines recorded heartbeats and blood pressure, I kept on reading. I read until the intercom announced that all visitors must leave and Anne, holding the carpet-bag that contained all her worldly goods, entered Green Gables for the first time. When I bent to kiss my friend goodnight, I thought I detected a flicker in her eyelids. As I passed Hilda's police guard, he looked up at me. "Sorry to see you go," he said. "I was just getting interested."

Jill was still there when I got home. Angus and Leah were in the family room studying, and Taylor was in bed, but not asleep.

When she heard me come into her room, she propped herself up on one elbow. "How's Hilda?" she asked.

"The same," I said. "But no worse."

"Is that okay?"

"Yeah," I said, "that's okay, at least for now."

Taylor spotted the copy of *Anne of Green Gables* in the outside pocket of my bag. She leaned over and took it out. "Hilda told me a story from this," she said. "It was about this girl who dyes her hair green. Hilda said she'd read the whole thing to me at Christmas if I learned to sit still for a book with no pictures."

When I stood up after kissing my younger daughter goodnight, I was dizzy with exhaustion. The day had finally caught up with me. It took an act of will to force myself to go back downstairs. Jill was sitting at the kitchen table poring over the folder of information on Justine and her circle that she'd brought with her.

"Good stuff in here," she said. Then she caught sight of my face and frowned. "You look lousy, Jo."

"That only seems fitting," I said, "because I feel lousy. Jill, stay as long as you like, but I'm heading for bed."

Jill pushed her chair back and stretched lazily. "Nope, I'm out of here. I've had enough fun for one day too. But let's get together after you've had a chance to look through that folder.

For a figure of judicial rectitude, Justine Blackwell certainly surrounded herself with a compelling cast of characters."

"More compelling than the characters in *Anne of Green Gables*?"

Jill made a face. "Where did that come from?"

"It's a long story."

"Well," said Jill, "considering your state of mind, I won't press for the particulars. And, to answer your question, Justine's cast of characters may not be as compelling as Lucy Maud's, but they're a hell of a lot more dangerous."

CHAPTER

9

When I looked at the photo that dominated the front page of our local paper Tuesday morning, my heart began to pound. For a paralysing moment, I was certain that the young aboriginal man being pushed into the police squad car was Eli Kequahtooway. The man's face was half-turned from the camera, but his dark hair, worn loose except for a single traditional braid, was like Eli's, and his slender, long-legged body was the same.

Rose and I had just come back from our run around the lake, so I wasn't wearing my reading glasses. When I finally found them and looked at the picture more closely, I was relieved to see that the man being arrested was older than Eli, perhaps in his early twenties, and that his features were coarser. Still shaken, I glanced up at the headline. The man in the photograph had been charged with Justine Blackwell's murder.

The accompanying story was short on facts. The man's name was Terrence Ducharme. He was twenty-three years old, lived in the downtown core, and was employed as a busboy at the Hotel Saskatchewan, the hotel where Justine had celebrated her thirty years on the bench the night of her murder. I poured myself a cup of coffee, sat down at the kitchen table, and read through the item again. The journalist who had written it treated Ducharme's arrest as the end of the story, but to my mind there were still too many loose ends. It was entirely plausible that, given her activities in the last year of her life, Justine had encountered Terrence Ducharme. It was even conceivable that she and Ducharme had quarrelled. But where did Hilda fit in? What possible motive could Terrence Ducharme have had for assaulting her? The missing financial papers had to be the link, but what interest could a busboy at the Hotel Saskatchewan have in Justine Blackwell's banking?

I looked up at the kitchen clock. It was 6:45, not too early for a phone call, especially when I had a credible excuse like needing further information. Alex wasn't assigned to the case, but he might have facts that weren't in the papers. I poured myself another cup of coffee, picked up the phone, and dialled Alex's number.

Eli answered on the first ring. I tried to be matter-of-fact. "Eli, it's Joanne. How are you doing?"

"I'm okay," he said.

He didn't sound okay. His voice was dull, as if he'd been awakened from a deep sleep.

"Are you back at school yet?" I asked.

"No," he said. "I couldn't hack it. Dr. Rayner said I didn't have to."

"What happened to Dr. Kasperski?"

"I don't know," Eli said in his new dead voice. "I guess he quit."

He fell silent. It was apparent that holding up his end of a conversation, even a bare-bones one like ours, was painful for him. I didn't want to add to his misery. "Is your uncle there?" I asked.

"I'll get him," he said.

"Eli, wait. If you need me, you know how to get in touch with me."

"Yeah," he said, "I do." He paused. "Thanks."

Alex's greeting was terse. "Kequahtooway."

"Alex, it's Jo."

"Sorry, I thought it was headquarters." He paused. "How are you?"

"I'm okay," I said. I waited for him to ask about Hilda. I was certain that, by this point, he would have heard that she'd been assaulted, but he either hadn't heard or didn't want to bring up the subject. The dead air between us became awkward.

"Did Mieka have her baby?" he asked finally.

"She and Greg had a little girl. They're calling her Madeleine."

"Everybody okay?"

"Everybody's fine. Alex, I took the cradle board up to Saskatoon. Greg and Mieka thought it was terrific."

He didn't respond. This time it was my turn to pick up the conversational ball.

"Eli says he's back with Signe Rayner. Is he doing all right with her?"

"She started hypnosis with him yesterday. She's hoping to get to the source of whatever it is that's eating at him."

"But Dan Kasperski was so opposed to hypnosis. He said that forcing Eli to confront his memories before he's ready to deal with them could be devastating."

"Signe Rayner is his doctor, Joanne."

There was a warning in Alex's voice. I didn't heed it. Instead, I blundered on. "I just wonder if she has the feeling for Eli that Dan Kasperski has. For one thing, I thought it would be good for Eli to get back to school."

This time, there was no mistaking Alex's anger. "Drop it, Jo. Whether Eli goes to school or not isn't your concern any more. Friday night you made it pretty clear that you didn't give a damn about Eli's problems."

"I never said that."

"That's what I heard."

"I'm not responsible for what you think you heard." Suddenly, I felt an overwhelming sadness. "This is exactly what I didn't want to happen."

"Then unless you had a specific reason for calling, maybe we'd better just hang up. Take care of yourself, Jo."

"You too," I said, but he didn't hear me because the line had already gone dead.

Miserable, I walked into the bathroom. I hadn't learned a thing about Terrence Ducharme, and I had widened the breach between Alex and me. I stepped into the tub, adjusted the shower to its pounding cycle, and tried to wash away the last five minutes of my life.

It didn't work. As I towelled off, I knew that Alex and I had begun the ugly cycle of wounding each other with every word we spoke. Even the ordinary conversations we'd had in the past suddenly seemed heavy with meaning. I thought of an exchange we'd had the previous spring when we'd been in his office at the police station. Except for a medicine wheel, a CD player, and his collection of classical CDs, Alex's office was spartan and impersonal, and I'd paid him a half-rueful compliment about his ability to hang on to what mattered and leave the rest behind. His reply had been far from light-hearted. He said that he never left anything behind and that the only way he could function was to keep the externals of his life uncomplicated.

I flattened my hand against the bathroom mirror, cleaned a circle in the shower fog, and stared at my reflection. I didn't like what I saw: an almost fifty-one-year-old woman who had become extraneous, a complication in the life of the man she loved, or thought she loved.

When I walked into my bedroom to get dressed, Taylor was lying on my bed in her nightie, kicking her feet in the air and talking on the phone in the declamatory tones she reserved for adults.

"She's the same," my younger daughter said, "but Jo says that's okay for now. Jo says as soon as Hilda can have visitors, Angus and me can go see her." Taylor spotted me, jackknifed her legs in and swung her body around so she was sitting on the side of the bed. "Jo's finally out of the bathroom," she announced to the person on the telephone. "Do you want to talk to her? It's Mr. Harris," she said, handing me the phone. She gave me a little wave and skipped out of the room.

Keith's voice was warm and concerned. "I had no idea about Hilda. You should have called me, Jo."

"There was nothing you could do."

"I could have been there."

The simple logic unnerved me; my words tumbled out. "I'm so scared," I said. "I'm trying to keep a brave front up for the kids, but Hilda looks so frail, Keith, and there are all these tubes. The medical people try to be helpful, but half the time I don't understand what they're talking about. They have this chart called the Glasgow Coma Scale; it's supposed to measure Hilda's level of functioning. I try to take it all in, but I'm just too tired and too afraid of what's going to happen."

"I'll come down there," he said.

"No," I said. "I'm all right. You just got me at a bad moment. If I need anything, I've got Jill and the kids.'

"And Alex?"

"No," I said, "I don't think Alex and I will be seeing each other for a while." I took a deep breath. "I really am handling this, Keith. Don't worry about me."

"Easier said than done," he said, "but I'll give it my best shot. Now, are you ready for some good news?"

"The novelty might do me in."

Keith laughed. "I'll start small. I saw Madeleine last night."

"Tell me more," I said.

"Well, she is intelligent, charming, and very lovely – obviously a testament to the excellence of the Kilbourn–Harris genes."

"You're talking to Madeleine's grandmother," I said. "None of what you just said is news to me. All the same, it's nice to hear you say it."

"Any time," he said. "I'm always available, Jo."

When we hung up, it was together.

Keith's call buoyed me. By the time I got to the university, I thought it was possible that I might get through the day after all. The first omens at school were positive. When I got to the Political Science office, Detective Robert Hallam was inside chatting with Rosalie Norman. Even a fleeting look revealed that Rosalie had broken with tradition in two ways: she had replaced her inevitable twin sweater set with a smart black turtleneck, and for the first time in human memory, she was laughing.

The laughter died when I walked in, but Rosalie did manage to retain a smile. "Detective Hallam's here to see you," she said. "Why don't you have your calls forwarded to me, so that you can chat without being interrupted." Rosalie presented her offer as if mutual accommodation was an every-day occurrence for us; in fact, I couldn't have been more surprised if she'd proposed that we throw off our shackles and lead the people of the university in a revolution.

Nonetheless, it was a sensible suggestion, and I accepted it. As soon as Detective Hallam and I were settled in my office, I hit call-forwarding on my telephone and turned to my guest. "What's up?" I asked.

He shrugged. "More questions – what else? Did you see the morning paper?"

"Yes," I said. "I'm glad you made an arrest in the Justine Blackwell case."

"So are we," he said mildly, "but I thought this particular arrest might present you and me both with some questions."

"Such as . . . ?"

"Such as, who attacked Miss McCourt? We're back to square one there, Mrs. Kilbourn."

"You thought the incidents were connected?"

"That's why we put the guard outside her room."

"And now you're taking the guard off?"

"No way we can justify tying an officer up now," Detective Hallam said. "It looks like we're dealing with a routine break-and-enter that went sour. Miss McCourt was just in the wrong place at the wrong time."

"I don't believe that, Detective Hallam."

"I'm afraid you're going to have to," he said. "Terrence Ducharme was nowhere near your house last Saturday night. He was at his anger-management meeting from seven till ten; then he had one of the counsellors from Culhane House over to his place for a sleepover. Except for when Terry went to the can, he wasn't alone for a minute."

"So he's in the clear."

"Looks like . . ."

"But Justine Blackwell's death *was* connected with Culhane House."

Robert Hallam frowned. "You sound as if you're sorry to hear that."

"I *am* sorry to hear that," I said. "Culhane House is just the kind of project that appeals to bleeding-heart liberals like me."

"Pick your causes carefully, Mrs. Kilbourn. Justine Blackwell made a pet of Terrence Ducharme and lived to regret it."

"Did she meet him through Wayne J. Waters?"

"No, the judge and our boy, Terry, share some history. He appeared in her court after he had a nasty run-in with an old woman who hired him to paint her garage. Apparently, Terrence wasn't much of a lad with a paintbrush, so the old lady refused to pay him. Terry retaliated by burning her garage down. He had priors, so Justine gave him the maximum sentence. By the time their paths crossed again, Terrence was a proud graduate of every twelve-step program the correctional system has to offer, and he was Wayne J.'s protégé. Of course, the new and improved Justice Blackwell thought Terrence Ducharme was the greatest thing since suspended sentences. She got him enrolled in educational upgrading, arranged for him to do some casual work, and paid a year's rent for him at a rooming house on Winnipeg Street."

"That's not all she did," I said.

Detective Hallam shot me a questioning look.

"There's a Ducharme buried in Justine Blackwell's family plot," I said.

"In the *family* plot? Why the hell would she do that?" He shrugged. "Why the hell did she do anything? Anyway, I'll bet there was one thing she had second thoughts about."

With the timing of the born storyteller, Robert Hallam waited for me to prompt him. I complied. "What was that?"

"Getting Terrence Ducharme that job at the Hotel Saskatchewan. He was working the night she died. Apparently, he did his usual bang-up job. At one point in the evening, he dropped a plate of those fancy little what-chamacallits."

"*Canapés*," I said.

Detective Hallam gave me a mock bow. "Thank you. Justine caught him picking up the *canapés* and shoving them back on the plate. I guess she went ballistic. Apparently, she was quite fussy."

"*Fastidious* was the word Hilda always used."

"Whatever. Anyway, the judge tore a strip off Terry, and he followed her when she left. He told one of his buddies he was going to make her apologize."

"Justine's been dead for over a week. Why didn't all this surface before?"

"Terry's buddy ran afoul of the law yesterday and decided the story Terry had told him about the judge was a good bargaining chip."

"And your whole case rests on his story."

"Are you telling me how to do my job, Mrs. Kilbourn?"

"No," I said. "I just want to be sure you got the right person. Detective Hallam, I'm not trying to second-guess you. My only interest in any of this mess is Hilda. I want to be sure she's safe."

"None of us are safe, Mrs. Kilbourn. You should know that by now."

"Detective Hallam, I can't believe that what happened to Hilda was just bad luck. The night she was attacked, she was working on Justine Blackwell's financial papers. Doesn't that point to a connection?"

"Did you see the papers, Mrs. Kilbourn?"

"No, but Hilda told me she was going to work on them. My desk was ransacked, and now the papers are missing."

His face reddened with the effort to keep his temper in check. "Something you never saw is missing. You're a smart woman, Mrs. Kilbourn. You know that's not enough."

"Then what about the towel?" I asked. "If the person who attacked Hilda wasn't someone who knew her – even casually – why would they put that towel under her head?"

He flipped his notepad shut. "Just a sicko," he said. "I've seen worse things put in worse places."

There was a discreet knock, then Rosalie peeked around the door. "Just a friendly reminder," she said. "Ten minutes to class." Her radiant smile would have melted a harder heart than mine.

"Thank you," I said. It was an inadequate response to Rosalie's once-in-a-lifetime performance, but it was all I could muster. Detective Hallam pushed back his chair. I scooped up my books. "You'll keep in touch," I said.

"Count on it," he said.

As I left, Rosalie was dimpling at Robert Hallam. "I've just made some fresh coffee. It's a new blend. It'll put a spring in your step, I guarantee."

Class went well. It was early in the term, but my Political Science 110 class already showed signs of being an exceptional group: interested, talkative, and pleasant. Nevertheless, by the time I'd erased the boards, and reassured the last student, I had a knot of tension in my neck and a rawness in my nerves. I couldn't stop thinking about my conversation with Detective Hallam, and I couldn't shake the image of Hilda lying on our kitchen floor, white-faced on the blood-soaked towel.

As I walked out of the education building, the sun was full in my face. It was the second week in September, but students were lying on the grass, reading, tanning, smoking, and watching the scurrying of the colony of gophers that lived out their existence beneath the academic green. I gazed towards the concrete bulk of the classroom building. In my office on the third floor, there were a half-dozen tasks that could use my attention; all of them could wait. I turned right and followed the sidewalk that took me away from my office and towards the end of the lake that was set aside for birds who were nesting, migrating, or just hanging out. Most of the time, the birds at the sanctuary were familiar species: pelicans, mallards, Canada geese, ducks, pintails, snowgeese, loons, mudhens, grebes. But sometimes, during migration, amazing visitors presented themselves.

Often, when the weather was good, Alex and I met here at lunchtime to eat our sandwiches and split a Thermos of tea. One fall day, we came upon an explosion of gulls. The water was white with them. We sat at the water's edge and watched, and then we lay on the bank, hand in hand, looking up at the sky and listening.

Remembering that day, I felt a tug. I wanted Alex. All I had to do was dial his number and say . . . Say what? Say I remembered another September day? Say I wanted him back? Say I didn't care about the wall that seemed to spring up between us whenever the subject of race came up or about the way people looked at us when we walked into a room together? Say I was ready to try again with Eli, the child of glass, and with the shards that pierced all our lives every time his fragile psyche shattered? As I picked up my books and started back towards my office, I knew I wouldn't make the call. I was fifty-one years old, and, at the moment, I was shouldering all the burdens I could carry.

There were no messages on my voice mail; my e-mail was clear; my desk was empty. It wasn't quite noon. I stuck my head into the Political Science office to tell Rosalie I was leaving. She was arranging rusty-gold marigolds in an old-fashioned glass milk bottle. She looked up expectantly.

"I love marigolds," I said. "They always make me think of the September when my older daughter started school. Every morning she'd take her safety scissors out to the garden and snip a bouquet. She always cut the stems too short. I often wondered what her teacher did with all those stubby little flowers."

Rosalie laughed softly. "And marigolds last forever," she said.

"One of their charms," I said. "Anyway, there's nothing I need to stick around here for, and I have a friend in the hospital, so I'm off."

"Just a minute." Rosalie took a handful of the flowers, folded a piece of waxed paper expertly over the stems and handed the bouquet to me. "For your friend," she said.

As I walked along the hall towards Hilda's room, I had my copy of *Anne of Green Gables* in my bag and Rosalie's marigolds in my hand, prepared for anything. In the room where the young man was recovering from his motorcycle accident, Garth Brooks was singing "Ain't Going Down ('Til the Sun Comes Up)." Earlier in the week, I had brought in a radio for Hilda, and there was music in her room too. It was Callas singing "In questa reggia" from *Turandot*. Garth and Maria seemed like a compelling duet to me, yet the nursing station was empty. When I saw Nathan Wolfe leaning over Hilda's bed, I panicked, but as he turned to greet me, he was smiling. "Good news," he said. "She's coming out of it."

I looked at Hilda. Much as I longed to, I couldn't detect any sign of change. "Did she regain consciousness?" I asked.

"No," he said. "But remember me telling you about the Glasgow Coma Scale?"

"Yes, but I was so scared, I couldn't seem to take anything in."

"Got time for a quick lesson now?"

"Of course."

"Let's go out to the desk."

I followed Nathan to the nursing station. He picked up a pencil and a pad of paper. "Okay, this is how we monitor changes in the patient's level of consciousness. We look at three aspects of behaviour; the first is –" he printed the words "Eyes Open." "If the patient's eyes open spontaneously, that's a 4; if they open when you speak to them, that's a 3; if they open to a pinprick, a 2; not at all is a 1." As he spoke he wrote the numbers in a column opposite the responses. "The second is Motor Responses. If a patient can move what you ask them to move, that's a 6; if they respond to localized pain, that's a 5; if they withdraw, that's a 4; abnormal flexion – that's this," he said, demonstrating – "is a 3; extends is a 2; and nothing is a 1. The third thing we look at is Verbal Response. If a patient's conversation is oriented, they get a 5; if their conversation is confused, they get a 4; if they use inappropriate words, that's a 3; incomprehensible sounds get a 2; and nothing gets a 1." He added up the best responses in each category. "Highest possible score is 15; the lowest is 3. A score of 7 or less is generally accepted as coma. Miss McCourt's been scoring pretty low, but today when I pricked her arm, she opened her eyes and withdrew her arm."

I looked over Nathan's shoulder at the column of figures. "So those responses score 2 and 4," I said. "That's a 6."

"And," said Nathan in the tones of an enthusiastic nursery teacher, "she made some incomprehensible sounds. So 8 in total. She's moving up."

I stared at the column of figures. "What can I do to keep her moving up?" I asked.

Nathan smiled. "The problem with these figures is that they make recovery look like a neat and orderly process, and it isn't. A lot of what happens we can't explain."

"Then what should I do."

He shrugged. "If you're comfortable with it, just keep on doing what you've been doing."

I handed Nathan the marigolds. "Thanks," I said. I took *Anne of Green Gables* out of my bag and waved it. "If you need us, Hilda and I will be in Avonlea."

I read until Matthew and Marilla decided to let Anne stay, at least provisionally. Every time I turned a page, I glanced over at Hilda, watching for a sign of response. She seemed more restless than she had been, but she did nothing that would have counted on Nathan's Glasgow Coma Scale. When I finally closed the book, I was discouraged. "I'll be back tomorrow," I said. "Rest well."

As I opened our front door, I realized how much I was looking forward to an afternoon alone. I took a package of pork chops out of the freezer, set them on a plate on the counter to thaw, then picked up the phone and checked my messages. Eric Fedoruk had called twice; so had Wayne J. Waters. Signe Rayner, announcing that she was spokesperson for her sisters, expressed her deepest concern. All of my callers left numbers where they could be reached and implored me to get back to them. I deleted the messages without writing down a single phone number. Hilda and I were simplifying our lives.

I decided to begin my simplification by logging some pool time. The sun was high as I walked through the leaves to the swimming pool. The water was warm, and I didn't hesitate before I dove in and gave myself over to the mindless pleasure of swimming laps. If I'm lucky, I can lose myself in swimming, and that day I was lucky. When I finally noticed Keith standing by the edge of the pool, he was laughing.

"I was beginning to think I was going to have to jump in there to get your attention."

"What are you doing in Regina?"

"I came down to see you. Is this a private pool party, or can anybody join?"

"Got your suit?"

"As a matter of fact, I do," he said. "Now that I'm out of politics, I'm turning over a new leaf. This morning I bought the first bathing suit I've owned in twenty-five years. And I brought it with me, because I heard the weather in Regina was unbelievable, and I thought you and I might find time to do this very thing."

"I don't believe it."

"Believe it," he said. "Now, if you'll excuse me, I'm going to go in the house and jump into my new Speedo."

"The Speedo I don't believe."

"And you're wise not to. The only suits left on the clearance table were depressingly sombre and modest, but they *were* cheap."

For half an hour, Keith and I swam laps, silently and companionably. Then we collapsed on the lounge chairs and soaked up the sun. For the first time in days, I felt my nerves unknot completely. It was a nice sensation. Keith was telling me some unrepeatable gossip about our ex-premier, and we were both roaring with laughter when I glanced over and saw Alex standing by the side of the house.

"I rang the doorbell," he said. "I thought you might be back here."

I jumped up and started towards him. "Alex, I'm so glad to see you. Come in and sit down." My voice was all wrong – falsely hearty. "Keith just got here," I finished weakly.

Alex looked over at Keith, then back at me. "Then I won't intrude."

Keith was on his feet. "Why don't I go inside and give you two a chance to talk."

Alex's eyes never left my face. "Thanks," he said, "but I just came by to ask about Hilda. Bob Hallam mentioned her case today. I guess he assumed I knew about it. You should have said something, Jo."

"You never gave me a chance," I said.

For a beat, we gazed at each other in silence. I could see the anger in Alex's eyes, but when he spoke, his voice was steady. "It's pretty obvious you're moving along with your life. I'll let you get back to it." He nodded in Keith's direction, then disappeared through the side gate.

I didn't go after him. I stood frozen, listening till I heard the car door shut and the motor roar. Finally, Keith came over and put his arm around my shoulder. "I'm not making a pass," he said. "The sun's gone in. You've got goosebumps."

I leaned into him. "I'm glad you're here," I said.

"So am I."

He took my hand, and we walked into the house. As soon as we were inside, Keith took me in his arms and kissed me: a lover's kiss, not a friend's. It wouldn't have ended there, except that just as his hand slid over my breast, the front door slammed. Taylor was home. Keith smoothed my hair and smiled. "Does anyone on earth have lousier timing than me?" he asked.

"I don't think so," I said.

He shrugged. "Well, be warned. I'm going to keep trying till I get the timing right."

That night after dinner, Keith flew back to Saskatoon. Still shaken by the afternoon's events, I grabbed my bathing suit off the clothesline, changed into it, and headed for the pool again. As I knifed through the quiet water, I tried to focus on my grandmother's axiom for troubled times: forget the experience, remember the lesson. Lap after lap, I worked at bringing perspective to the day, but it was no use. Try as I might, I could neither forget nor remember. When I finally gave up and went to the house, I had found neither peace nor insight. The best I could hope for was distraction. I changed into my sweats, opened a bottle of Great Western beer, picked up the folder of material Jill had brought, and started reading.

I began with the guest list of Justine's last party. Jill had thoughtfully provided the rap sheets for a number of the merrymakers. The list of their offences against the Crown was impressive: break-and-enter, forgery, hit-and-run, counterfeiting, vehicular homicide, fraud, armed robbery, manslaughter, and assaults of every possible kind with every conceivable weapon.

Angus would have characterized the men and women among whom Justine Blackwell elected to spend the last hours of her life as a bad-ass group, but bad-ass or not, Justine had believed she owed them reparation. Much of the information Jill submitted was photocopied, but she had handwritten the notes from her phone calls and interviews, and the picture of Justine that emerged from these notes was of a woman prepared to use every resource she had to make amends.

According to Jill's sources, Justine had supplied the down payment for the building on Rose Street that became Culhane House, and she was making the mortgage payments. She'd promised a substantial renovation of the building to make it suitable as a kind of residential halfway house; she had guaranteed that any contractor who did the work would have to use ex-prisoners as part of their labour force. There had been more personal philanthropies: she had signed herself on as a guarantor of loans; she had paid instalments of tuition; she had written cheques to dentists and clothing stores and used-car rental agencies. But from Jill's information, one thing was clear. Justine might have been atoning, but she was atoning with a tight hand on the purse-strings. Except for small gifts, all Justine's bequests were conditional. With just a few well-placed calls, Justine could have put an end to Operation Reparation.

Wayne J. Waters' empire was a shaky one. And according to Jill's notes, Wayne J. was not a man to handle stress or reversal of fortune equably. He had started out as a kid doing break-and-enter, moved up through the ranks to robbery and armed robbery, and finished as a generalist, a jack of all illicit trades. He prided himself on never becoming involved with drugs or prostitution, but those seemed to be the only lines he refused to cross. He was immensely strong and enormously glib. No one Jill had talked to could say with any certainty whether Culhane House was a genuine attempt at altruism or just another scam. On one point, all Jill's sources were in agreement: despite his seeming conversion, Wayne J. Waters was a very dangerous man.

I was relieved to put his file aside and pick up Eric Fedoruk's. There was nothing in it to make the pulse race. An illustrated magazine article chronicled his smooth transition from hockey player to successful lawyer. There was a nice photo of him with Justine, whom the caption characterized as his childhood neighbour and enduring mentor. From Jill's notes, it appeared Eric Fedoruk was one of those lucky people who move from accomplishment to accomplishment. His two passions were the law and his Ducati Mostro, which Jill pointed out helpfully was a motorcycle. He had never married. "A possibility for me here," Jill had written in her large looping hand. "I've always longed to hop on one of those Eurobrutes and ride off into the sunset at 160 kph."

There wasn't much in the photocopied material about Lucy Blackwell's life that I didn't already know, but Jill's notes contained a surprise. After her father's death, Lucy had attempted suicide. She had been hospitalized briefly, and when she was released, she headed for San Francisco. Within months, she had a song on the charts and, apparently, she'd never looked back. Jill said her source was utterly reliable, but to my mind the story raised a number of questions, not the least of which was why Justine would allow a vulnerable sixteen-year-old to strike out on her own. It was puzzling, but when it came to Justine's life, it seemed there were many puzzles. I tried to remember if there were any suicide references in Lucy's famously autobiographical songs, but I came up blank. Like Wayne J. Waters, Lucy Blackwell had apparently decided there were areas where it was wise to draw the line.

There were other troubling revelations in Lucy's file. For one thing, Jill's source said that Lucy had been forced to finance *The Sorcerer's Smile* herself. The movers and shakers in the music industry had made it known that they saw Lucy as yesterday's singer, and that they had no interest in backing a CD boxed set that encapsulated her personal history in music. The rejection must have bruised Lucy's ego, but her decision to go ahead with the project had hit her in the pocketbook.

During the heady years of the eighties, Lucy had built a home in Nova Scotia. Jill had included a photo spread from *InStyle* magazine on Lucy at home in the oceanfront hideaway she had designed herself. The house was fanciful, idiosyncratic, and, to my mind, beautiful. In the article, Lucy had been lyrical about what her home on the ocean meant to her, but last year she had sold it, a sacrifice to her determination that her musical legacy would be preserved. The final photograph in the article was a close-up of Lucy exultant as the waves crashed behind her on the beach. Her smile was dazzling, but as I closed the folder, I found myself wondering about the pain behind the smile.

On the Post-it note she had stuck to the eight-by-ten glossy of Tina Blackwell, Jill had scrawled a three-word question: "See the problem?" I could. On the few occasions I'd caught Tina on TV, she'd struck me as the epitome of glazed perfection: flawless makeup, hair teased and sprayed to look casual, classic jewellery, sleekly fitted jackets. In the photograph in front of me, Tina Blackwell was still an attractive woman, but even the benevolent hand of the retoucher hadn't been able to erase the inevitable signs of aging: the softening of the jawline, the droop of the eyelid, the tiny lines around the corners of her eyes, the feathering of her lips. The printed material on Tina was minimal. Jill had included three items: a copy of the announcement CJRG had made when they fired Tina, or in their sly corporatespeak, "freed her to pursue other opportunities"; a copy of the c.v. Tina had submitted to Nationtv, and her cover letter to Jill offering to take "even a very junior position if one is available." CJRG had referred to Tina as "a longtime employee." In fact, she had been there for more than twenty years, her entire working life. With her surgically scarred face and her one-line résumé, it was hard to imagine what was ahead for her.

I almost put the material on Signe Rayner aside without reading it. So far, when it came to lousy lives, Justine Blackwell's daughters were two for two, and I wasn't eager for more sad revelations. But if I was going to resolve Hilda's unfinished business with Justine Blackwell, I had to be resolute. I opened the file, and as soon as I saw the first newspaper clipping, I was riveted. Dr. Signe Rayner was a woman with a past. The clippings were three years old, and they were from the Chicago papers. The parents of an adolescent boy Signe had been treating sued her after the boy committed suicide. According to trial transcripts, while the young man was under hypnosis Signe had returned him to an infantile state, and encouraged him to see her as his mother.

Signe's lawyers had earned their fees. They established that the dead boy's father, an architect, had recently declared bankruptcy, and that the mother had her own lengthy history of psychiatric problems. A clutch of Signe's professional colleagues had testified that, while her approach was unorthodox, it was not unethical. They supported Signe's contention that she was attempting to help the boy return to the genesis of his problems and that, in urging him to consider her as his mother, she was simply offering herself as an ally in his battle against his demons. The boy's parents lost their case. Signe Rayner was cleared of wrongdoing.

Despite her exoneration, she left Chicago, moved back to Regina, and began again. It was a puzzling coda to a court victory. A suspicious mind might have theorized that there had been some sort of prior agreement between Signe and her professional colleagues in Chicago, a kind of *quid pro quo* in which they agreed to support her in court if she agreed to remove herself from their jurisdiction.

I reread the account of Signe's bizarre relationship with the dead boy, then I picked up the telephone and dialled Alex's number. If Shakespeare was right about past being prologue, Alex needed to take another look at the doctor he was trusting to take his nephew to the brink and back again.

CHAPTER

10

I tried Alex's number until 11:00, when, exhausted, anxious, and furious at his refusal to have an answering machine, I turned out the lights and went to bed. Twice during the night, I woke up, rolled over, and dialled again. There was still no answer. The next morning I made a pact with myself; I wouldn't even attempt to call until after Rose and I had our walk and I'd showered and dressed for the day. Like most bargains with a fool, my compact got me nowhere. When Rose and I got back, I dialled Alex's apartment, and there was still no answer. Undeterred, I made another pact. The kids loved James Beard's pecan coffee cake, and I hadn't made one since the beginning of summer. I'd stay away from the phone until I'd made a coffee cake and put it in the oven.

My homage to James Beard paid off, but not with the dividend I'd expected. By the time Taylor and Angus straggled down to breakfast, the kitchen smelled the way a kitchen in a well-run home is supposed to smell in the morning, and I'd decided that calling Alex was a dumb idea. He was a man who operated on fact, not theory, and my concerns about

Signe Rayner were based on conjecture. Calling him would make me look hysterical. More seriously, it would make me look desperate. Whatever lay ahead for Alex and me, I didn't want him to remember me as a woman who grasped at any excuse to ring up her ex-lover.

After we'd eaten, I felt better. I'd made a world-class coffee cake, and I hadn't made a fool of myself. Not a bad record to rack up before 7:30 a.m. But praiseworthy as my restraint might be, it didn't change the fact that I still needed answers, not just about Signe Rayner, but about other members of Justine's circle of family, friends, and acquaintances. Detective Hallam might not have believed that Hilda had been attacked because someone Justine knew was desperate to get at her financial papers, but I did.

I was certain that Hilda's assailant was connected somehow to Justine, but most of the people in Justine's life were unknown quantities to me. Fortunately, as I'd been measuring out the cinnamon and butter for the coffee cake, I'd come up with a candidate who might be able to help me fill in the blanks. Eric Fedoruk had grown up next door to the Blackwells; he had considered Justine his mentor, and he had been her lawyer. If I was going to unearth the truth about Justine's life, he might just be my man.

For a successful lawyer, Eric Fedoruk was surprisingly accommodating. When I called his home number, he didn't miss a beat before offering to meet me at his office within the hour. The address he gave me was on the top floor of one of the twin towers at the end of Scarth Street Mall. I was early enough to get a parking spot a block away, but as I walked towards his building, the morning sun bounced off its glass face, blinding me. I hoped it wasn't an omen. There had been few occasions in my life when I'd been more aware of the need to see clearly.

Eric Fedoruk was waiting for me when I stepped off the elevator. His black motorcycle boots had been replaced by nutmeg calfskin loafers, his fawn suit looked like Armani, and his buttercup-yellow tie demanded attention. When he offered his hand, I was glad I wasn't being billed by the hour.

"I was relieved to get your call," he said, as he steered me smoothly past the firm's receptionist into his office. It was spacious and airy, filled with natural light from two walls of floor-to-ceiling windows. The other two walls were filled with photographs and hockey memorabilia. Eric Fedoruk led me past his desk and the client chairs which faced it to a trio of easy chairs that had been arranged around a low circular table in the corner of the room. He held out a chair for me.

"Can I get you anything before we begin?" he asked.

"Thanks," I said, "I'm fine." I leaned towards the window. "What a spectacular view of the city."

"It is, isn't it?" he said. "And it's beautiful in every season." He made a face. "I sound like I'm running for President of the Chamber of Commerce."

"You've got my vote," I said. "I think Regina's a great place to live."

He grinned. "It's nice to be having a civil conversation. You know, we *are* on the same side in this."

"Whose side is that?"

He didn't hesitate. "Justine's. In your case, Miss McCourt's, but she was on Justine's side. Now, since we are allies, can we graduate to first names?"

"That's fine with me, Eric," I said.

"Good." His eyes, the grey of an autumn sky before a storm, met mine. "Now, why don't you tell me what brought you here this morning."

"The attack on Hilda," I said. "I think the police are on the wrong track. Eric, I'm certain Hilda knew her assailant. Before I left the house that night, she told me she was going to spend the evening working on Justine's financial records. I think she was searching for something that would help her resolve the question of Justine's mental competence once and for all."

"And you believe she found it."

I nodded. "I do. I think that there was something in Justine's personal papers that tipped the scales, and that whoever came to my house that night knew it was there. That's why they tried to kill Hilda, and that's why they ransacked the house until they found what they were looking for."

Eric Fedoruk looked hard at me. "Where do I fit in?"

"I'm hoping you can help me understand some of the people in Justine's life. The problem is I don't know enough about any of them to ask the right questions." I leaned towards him. "I guess all I can do is ask you to tell me about Justine."

Pain crossed his face. "I don't know where to begin."

I gave him what I hoped was an encouraging smile.

He returned it; then he shrugged and glanced around his handsome office. "Well, for starters, I wouldn't have any of this if it hadn't been for her."

"She opened the right doors for you."

He shook his head. "She changed the course of my life," he said softly. "If it hadn't been for her, I never would have been a lawyer. Which means that, at this point, I would have been an aging jock, trying to get by with a smile, a handshake, and a basement full of game tapes nobody gave a damn about." He shuddered. "It's scary to look back and think how close I came. Anyway, thanks to Justine, it didn't happen."

"She was your mentor."

"She was more than that," he said. "When I was fifteen, all anybody saw when they looked at me was a kid with a great slapshot. My dad died a month after I was born, and I guess my mother was sort of overwhelmed by all the scouts knocking on her door telling her that, as soon as I turned sixteen, I should be in junior A. Of course, that was what I wanted too. My mother was just about to cave in, when – he smiled at the memory – "Justine took me out to dinner."

"Because she saw you as somebody who had more going for him than a slapshot."

"Right," he said. "She took me to the old Assiniboia Club, and she laid out a plan for my life. Get serious about my studies. Go to university. Play hockey for a while. Then go to law school. As we were talking, all these big-shot lawyers kept dropping by our table 'just to chat.'"

"Justine had invited them?"

"She never left anything to chance. Anyway, it was heady stuff for a fifteen-year-old: a glamorous successful older woman taking his life seriously, treating him like an adult."

"And you followed the plan?"

"To the letter. I finished high school, got a hockey scholarship to the University of Denver, graduated *cum laude*; went straight to the Maple Leafs, where, for six years, I had more fun than most people have in a lifetime, then came back to Saskatchewan and enrolled in law school."

"Right on track," I said.

"Yeah," he agreed. "But it was a good track to be on."

"Justine must have been an amazing woman."

"She was that," he agreed.

"All the same, what she did for you surprises me. It was so parental, and I got the impression she wasn't much of a mother."

"Given the daughters she had, Justine was as good a mother as she could be," he said tightly.

"Her children do seem to have had troubled lives," I agreed. "But, Eric, surely some of their troubles have to be rooted in their relationship with her. You may have every reason to be grateful to Justine, but from what I've heard she didn't find family life very congenial."

"If you got your information from her children, you should remember that there are two sides to every story."

"I know that," I said. "And I know that Justine's daughters aren't exactly poster girls for filial devotion, but they weren't my only source. Hilda got so involved with Justine and her circle that I had a friend do a little checking around. Some of what she came up with puts Justine in a pretty negative light."

"Such as?"

"Such as the fact that Lucy tried to kill herself after her father died. As soon as she recovered, she ran away and, apparently, Justine just let her go."

"There were reasons," he said coldly.

"What possible reason could any mother have for letting a distraught sixteen-year-old just take off?"

Eric Fedoruk's face was stony. "It was a complex situation, and Justine was the injured party." He got up, walked to the window and stood with his back to me.

"I take it the subject is closed," I said.

"It is," he said wearily. He turned to face me. "I want to co-operate with you, believe me. I want the truth to come out. Justine had nothing to hide, but that particular time in the family's life was painful for so many people. Can't we just drop it?"

"All right," I said. "We'll drop the subject of Lucy's running away. But, Eric, if Justine is the woman you say she is, wouldn't putting some of the other rumours to rest be the best way to honour her memory?"

"I was her lawyer, Joanne. There are matters I'm just not free to discuss."

"But there must be things you can talk about. Wayne J. Waters, for example. You and Justine must have discussed him."

"We *argued* about him. I don't think Justine and I were together once over the past year when his name didn't come up. I thought that he was pond-scum and that Culhane House was a scam." He looked away. "Justine didn't share my feelings about his character or his project."

"But Hilda told me Wayne J. and Justine quarrelled about money the night she died."

"I guess he was afraid she was reconsidering her commitment to Culhane House. She wasn't, of course. She'd just put her financial support on hold, the way she'd put everything else on hold until she'd found an answer to the question that was consuming her."

"Whether she was in full possession of her faculties."

Eric winced. "Exactly. By the night of her party, Justine had been so badly shaken by all the people, including me, who were questioning her behaviour that she did a very lawyerly thing: she decided to hold all her affairs in abeyance until she was certain she was sane."

"Then she hadn't rejected Wayne J."

"No. I wish she had. But on the night she died, Justine was still passionate about Culhane House, and she still trusted Wayne J. It makes me faintly queasy to say this, but in the last year of her life, Justine was closer to him than she was to anyone. She just wanted to make certain that when she signed a cheque, she was making a rational decision about the use of her money."

"Is that why she didn't loan Tina the money for the plastic surgery she needed?"

Eric Fedoruk looked genuinely puzzled. "Is that the story you heard? Because whoever told you that doesn't have the facts. Justine gave Tina the money she asked for. If we had the financial records, I'd be able to show you the cancelled cheque." He shrugged. "Unfortunately, we don't, so you'll just have to take my word for it."

"Eric, if Justine gave her the money, why did Tina get the surgery done on the cheap?"

"That's a question for Tina to answer, but if you want my opinion, somebody gave her a hard-luck story. Tina tries, but she's easily led."

"By men?"

"By everybody. But Tina's not the issue here; Justine is. And no matter what you hear, Justine was never selfish and she was never vindictive. At the end, she was just very confused." His voice was close to breaking.

I leaned towards him. "Eric, why didn't she get help? Her own daughter is a psychiatrist. She could have recommended someone."

"Signe was hardly a disinterested party."

"Because Justine was her mother?"

"No, because in the last year, there was a lot of tension there. Justine was doing everything in her power to get Signe to stop practising psychiatry."

I felt a chill. "Because of what she'd done to that boy in Chicago."

"Who told you about that?" Eric's tone was edgy.

"The news clippings were in my friend's research. But the papers said Signe was exonerated. Was she guilty? Is that why her mother didn't want her practising any more?"

Eric's eyes met mine. "I can't talk about this, Joanne."

"Were you involved in Signe's defence? I know you couldn't act for her in the States, but did you advise her? Is that why you can't talk about the case?"

Eric looked at his watch. "I have a nine o'clock appointment. I've already kept him waiting too long."

I stood up. "Thanks for seeing me," I said. "You've been a help."

"Have I? Maybe the more helpful thing would have been to tell you to get out while the getting's good."

"Meaning?"

He shrugged. "Nothing. Just be careful, Joanne. Now, if you'll excuse me, I really do have to see my client."

Waiting client or no, Eric Fedoruk was a gentleman. He walked me to the elevator and pressed the call button. As we listened to the elevator make its smooth ascent, I knew I was looking at my last chance. "I know you can't discuss what happened in Chicago," I said, "but can you answer a hypothetical question?"

He raised an eyebrow. "Depends on the question."

"Eric, if you had an adolescent child, would you let Signe treat him?"

For a beat, he didn't answer, and I thought I'd pushed too hard. But as the elevator doors opened, his eyes met mine. "I would move heaven and earth to keep Signe Rayner from getting anywhere near a child of mine." he said. Then he smiled. "Of course, that's just hypothetical."

As soon as I got to the university, I called Alex at the police station. He was in a meeting, but I gave the woman on the other end my name and told her it was an emergency. As I waited for Alex to come to the phone, my heart was pounding.

At first, he sounded like himself, warm and concerned. "Hilda's not worse, is she?"

"No," I said. "This isn't about Hilda. Alex, I have more information about Signe Rayner."

He made no attempt to conceal his irritation. "I thought we'd agreed Eli's treatment was no longer your concern."

"We didn't agree," I said. "You decided, but, Alex, you were wrong. You've got to hear me out. Even her own mother didn't think Signe should be practising medicine, and Eric Fedoruk says he wouldn't let her treat a child of his."

Alex's voice was coldly furious. "A woman who hangs out with felons and allows strangers to be buried in her family plot isn't exactly what I would consider a credible arbiter of someone else's competence. Damn it, Jo, are you so determined to prove that you're right that you've lost sight of the facts? At the end, Justine Blackwell's life had become so bizarre that even she wasn't sure of her sanity."

"Then what about Eric Fedoruk?"

"I couldn't care less what some lawyer with a six-figure income would do with his child. My only concern is Eli, and, Joanne, whether you like it or not, Dr. Rayner is giving my nephew something he hasn't had a lot of in his life: consistency. She's there, Jo. Every appointment, she's there waiting. She never decides Eli's too much trouble. She never abandons him. She never . . ."

I cut him off. "Sorry I bothered you," I said, and I slammed down the receiver. I was still shaking with anger when the phone rang. When I picked up the receiver and heard Keith Harris's voice, it seemed as if providence was taking a hand in the sorry mess of my life.

"Are you okay, Jo?" he asked. "You sound a little down."

"Nothing a few kind words won't fix."

"My pleasure," he said. "Now, listen. I have news."

As Keith gave me an account of the latest episode in his fortunate life, I felt my pulse slow and my spirits rise. The tenant who had sublet his father's Regina apartment was moving out at the end of September, and Keith saw the freeing up of the apartment as significant. "Everything's working out just the way it's supposed to," he said. "Part of a larger cosmic plan." As I hung up, I decided that maybe it was time to step aside and let the universe unfold as it should.

The rhythms of everyday life pushed us ahead. I talked to Mieka and Greg every night and we e-mailed each other every day. Their news was as miraculous as it was commonplace. Madeleine was eating and growing and discovering.

When I told them about the attack on Hilda, I tried to min-
imize her injuries, but as my daughter continued to press me
about coming up to Saskatoon again, I was forced to tell her
the truth. Mieka had always loved Hilda, and the anxiety in
her voice when she asked for details saddened me. Those
first days with Madeleine should have been a time of cloudless joy, but it seemed that days of cloudless joy were in
short supply that September.

I taught Taylor how to send messages to Madeleine on
e-mail, and she and Jesse got an A for their project on owls.
Even these accomplishments weren't enough to offset my
daughter's awareness that all was not right in her world.
My daily reports on Hilda's progress appeared to reassure
her, but Taylor continued to be perplexed about Alex and
Eli's absence from our lives. My explanation that Alex and I
had just decided to spend some time apart didn't satisfy her.
It didn't satisfy me either, but as unsatisfactory as the story
was, I didn't have a better one. Alex didn't call, and after a
few days I stopped expecting him to. As the third week of
school started, Anita Greyeyes, the woman who would have
been Eli's teacher, phoned to ask me what arrangements
had been made about Eli's schooling. I gave her Alex's work
and home numbers and told her that she should deal with
him directly. Another link had been severed.

My professional life was moving into high gear. My
classes were taking shape, the inevitable academic committee meetings had begun, and Jill and I had started to
mull over topics that might work on our first political
panel of the new season.

I visited Hilda at least once every day, and here the news
was good. Even my untutored eye could discern cause for
hope. Increasingly, as I read to her or as we listened to the
radio together, she became restless, as if she were wearying

of her long sleep. Even her stillness seemed closer to healthy consciousness. Nathan Wolfe was encouraged too. Hilda's numbers on the Glasgow Coma Scale were rising, and Nathan and I fussed over each incremental gain like new parents. Despite our hovering and hoping, when the breakthrough finally came it had the force of a surprise.

It was on a Friday afternoon, thirteen days after Hilda had been assaulted. I'd come to the hospital just after lunch. My morning had been busy, and Hilda's room was warm. From the moment I started to read, I could feel my eyelids grow heavy. After five minutes, I closed my book, turned up the radio, leaned back in my chair, and gave myself over to the considerable pleasures of Henry Purcell. When I woke up, "Rejoice in the Lord Alway" had been replaced by the news, and, for once, there was news worth noting.

Boys playing along the shoreline of Wascana Lake had discovered the marble-based scales that had been used to bludgeon Justine Blackwell to death. The scales, which had been presented to Justine with such fanfare at the dinner were half-buried in the gumbo of the lake bed. It was a case of *sic transit gloria mundi*, but it was also a piece of real evidence in an investigation which, if the media could be believed, was woefully short of concrete proof that Terrence Ducharme had murdered Justine. Reflexively, I glanced over at Hilda.

What I saw made my pulse race. She was conscious, but the woman before me was not the Hilda I knew. This woman's eyes were wild, and her mouth was contorted with rage and effort. She was trying to speak, but the sounds that came out of her mouth were guttural and unintelligible. When her eyes met mine, I almost wept. In that moment, I knew that she understood her circumstances and grasped the fact that we were both powerless to change them.

"It's all right," I said. "It's going to be all right."

She shook her head furiously and made a growling sound.

"What is it?" I asked. "Is there something you want me to get?"

For a beat, she stared at me. Then she lifted her head, and, in a voice rusty with disuse and hoarse with effort, she pronounced a single recognizable word. "Maisie," she said. "Maisie."

"She has to build new pathways," Nathan Wolfe said. It was mid-afternoon, and Nathan and I were sitting in the cafeteria of Pasqua Hospital. Twenty-four hours earlier, Hilda had entered a brief period of consciousness, and I had felt the darkness lift, but soon after she had articulated the single word "Maisie," my friend had lapsed back into her silent private world. Now Nathan and I were splitting a plate of fries, drinking Coke, and talking about what came next.

"She's almost there," Nathan said. "The restlessness and the fact that she actually talked are great signs, but it's going to take time. And learning how to say what she wants to say is going to take *a lot* of time. The communication pathways she used before are blocked, and until she builds some new ones, Miss McCourt has to use whatever's handy to get her message across.

"She could find the name 'Maisie,' but not 'Justine,'" I said.

Nathan speared a fry and dipped it in gravy. "She was lucky she made a connection you could understand," he said. "'Maisie' is at least in the ballpark. A lot of recovering coma patients come out with stuff like 'potato' when they mean 'water.'" He chewed his fry reflectively. "Makes it tough to meet their needs when they're thirsty."

"So how do I meet Hilda's needs?" I asked.

"Do anything you can to keep her from getting frustrated," Nathan said. "Listen hard to what she's trying to say, and translate. Play it by ear. You'll get the hang of it."

My chance came sooner than either Nathan or I antici-pated. When we went upstairs to intensive care, Hilda was lying on her back. Her eyes were open, but she didn't appear to be seeing anything. Nathan was quick to spot my fear, and he did his best to be reassuring. "Lethargy and stupor are part of the package, Mrs. K. Just do what you usually do, and don't panic if she gets agitated. That's part of the package too. In fact, a little flailing around is good exercise for the patient's arms and legs." He smiled.

I didn't smile back. "I hate this," I said. "I hate standing in this room, talking about Hilda as if she were a piece of wood."

Nathan pulled back Hilda's sheet, poured some skin-care lotion into his hand and began to rub it into her legs. "I know how you feel," he said, "but in these cases, there's a lot of behaviour that seems scary if you're not prepared for it."

I watched as Nathan massaged Hilda's legs and arms. As he rubbed her muscles, he talked to Hilda in a voice that was as soothing as his hands must have been.

"You're so good with her," I said.

"I like the work," he said. "Every so often, these patients come back. It's a real rush when you've got to know the physical part of a person so well, and all of a sudden the rest of them's there."

After Nathan left, I picked up *Anne of Green Gables* and began to read. As soon as she heard my voice, Hilda became uneasy. She shifted position, then drew her legs up.

"It's okay," I said. "I won't read any more. We can talk. Let's see . . . It's the third week in September, and it's Saturday – a real fall day. This morning, before her art lesson, Taylor and Jess decided they were going to earn money raking lawns. Taylor thought they'd get more people to sign on if we bought some of those Hallowe'en leaf bags.

She and Jess have about ten customers lined up. I hope this doesn't end up like Angus's pet-walking service. Remember that time we spent the whole weekend walking dogs and cats because he'd overbooked?"

Hilda's eyes were closed, but she seemed to be listening, so I rambled on about the latest batch of baby photos Keith had brought down from Saskatoon and about Angus's disgust at his football team's 0–2 record. I had just started describing the cormorants I had seen that morning in the park when Hilda's eyes flew open. "Maisie," she said, and her tone was pleading.

Remembering Nathan's advice, I translated and played it by ear. "I'm not sure how much you've been able to pick up about Justine's case from the radio," I said, "but there isn't much to report. Twelve days ago, the police arrested a man named Terrence Ducharme. He was one of the ex-convicts Justine got involved with in the last year. I'm sure the police are hoping they can connect him to those scales they found in the lake yesterday, but I haven't heard anything."

Hilda's eyes opened. As she took in her situation, there was the same bleak shock of recognition I'd seen the day before. I grasped her hand and leaned closer to her. "You're in the hospital here in Regina," I said. "You've had an accident, but you're going to be all right."

My explanation seemed to satisfy her. She squeezed my hand, then closed her eyes again. I leaned over and kissed her forehead. "I missed you," I said. "Don't leave me yet." Anxiously, I searched her face for a hint of response. There was none. I sat with her, listening to the opera on the radio until 3:00, when the shift changed, and a nurse I hadn't seen before came in to record Hilda's vital signs. I was in the way, and I knew it.

I kissed Hilda's forehead and promised to come back.

That night was our first political panel of the new season. Keith had come down the night before to lend moral support, but it was going to be a short weekend for us. He had business in Toronto, and he was taking the early flight out Sunday morning. When I got back from the hospital, he was in the backyard with Taylor and Jess, throwing around the yellow plastic football Eli had given me for safekeeping at the Labour Day game. Remembering, I felt a stab of guilt. Then I swallowed hard and tossed off the feeling. The football was, after all, only a cheap toy, and Alex had made it clear that Eli was no longer my concern.

Taylor threw me the ball. I had to dive, but I caught it.

"Good hands," Jess said appreciatively.

"Go deep." I threw him a pass and he made an effortless catch. "You're looking pretty sharp there yourself," I said. The four of us threw the ball around for a while, then Taylor and Jess went off to their lawn work.

Keith and I watched the kids until they had dragged their leaf bags and rakes around the corner onto Rae Street and disappeared from sight. "I envy them," I said. "I can't even remember when the biggest worry I had was filling a leaf bag."

Keith looked at me hard. "Let's grab Rose and take a walk. There won't be many more days like this."

"I should look at my notes for the show."

"I'll buy you an ice cream cone."

"Sold," I said. "These days, I come cheap."

We walked along the levee on the north side of Wascana Creek. It was an amazing day, and it seemed that literally everyone and his dog was out. Rose was a gregarious creature and as she greeted dog after dog, she seemed like her old self again. Keith and I bought cones and took them back to a quiet spot on the levee where we sat down, with Rose between us, and watched life in the creek.

When we'd finished eating, Keith leaned towards me. "You're looking a lot better. When you came back from the hospital, you looked pretty wiped. It worried me."

"Sorry," I said. "It's just that I'm so scared. And I feel so impotent. I just don't know what to do for Hilda. She asked about Maisie again today. Keith, I don't understand why she keeps going back to Justine's death. It has to be so upsetting for her."

"It's unfinished business, and you know as well as I do that once Hilda starts a job, she sees it through." He pointed towards the opposite shore. "Look," he said, "there's an otter over there on the bank."

"But not for long," I said, as the otter slipped into the creek and disappeared. "You're right, you know. Hilda prides herself on honouring her obligations. It must be so frustrating for her knowing that she never came to a final judgement about Justine." I stood up and brushed the dust off my slacks. "At one point, I thought I could finish the job, but as Hilda said, there are so many cross-currents in Justine's life. I didn't know who to believe, and I guess I just gave up trying."

"Want some help?"

"From you?"

"From me and from somebody with a little perspective. Jo, from what you've told me, everyone you've talked to has a vested interest in how that decision about Justine's sanity comes down. Maybe I can flush out a couple of impartial observers for you."

"Do you have anyone in mind?"

"I may," he said. "Dick Blackstone's old law partner is in a seniors' home down here. His daughter lives in town, and I ran into her last weekend. She said her dad's getting bored playing pinochle, and I should go see him. Let me give Garnet Dishaw a call and see if he's up for a visit."

"Do you think he'll be able to help?"

Keith shrugged. "I don't know, but at least we'll be a diversion from pinochle." He grabbed Rose's leash and stood up. "Ready to go?"

"You bet." I put my arm through his. "It's good to have somebody ready to share the load."

"Anything else I can do?"

I smiled up at him. "Sure. You can fill me in on all those provocative rumours I hear about dark plans to unseat your federal leader."

"I thought you hated backroom gossip."

"Not when it's about you guys," I said. "I love it, and the more stilettos the better."

By the time I walked into the TV studio that night, Keith had arranged for us to meet Garnet Dishaw at Palliser Place, the seniors' home in which he lived, as soon as the show was over. I'd been less successful with my second request. Despite my encouragement, Keith hadn't volunteered a single indiscreet insight into the machinations of his party. Luckily, the show that night didn't need inside information about dirty deeds.

Our topic was the proliferation of conservative parties in Canada. It was a red-meat topic, and Ken Leung made it sizzle. Glayne Axtell and I rose to the occasion. It was fun, and it was good television, but the real payoff came in the call-in segments. For the first time I could remember, we had callers who said they were under thirty years old. They were informed, witty, and iconoclastic; by the time the show ended, we all knew that it had generated more light than heat. It was a good feeling.

The glow endured. When I slid into the passenger seat of Keith's Mercedes, I was still buoyant.

"Ready to meet the prototypical curmudgeon?" Keith asked.

"Bring him on," I said. "Tonight I'm a match for anybody."

Palliser Place was a low-slung modern building with large windows and an air of being well kept. Its flower beds were already cleaned out for winter, and there wasn't an errant leaf on its spacious front lawns.

The young woman at the reception desk was reed-slim and carefully made-up. When we asked to see Garnet Dishaw, she rolled her eyes.

"He's in the hall outside his room, practising his golf shot," she said. She pointed with a well-shaped, French-manicured nail. "West wing."

Garnet Dishaw had set up a portable tee halfway up the hall. And he was indeed practising. The deep green broadloom of the hall was littered with balls from the shots he had missed. As we started down the hall, he was just getting into his swing. He connected with the ball, but he had an ugly slice and the ball ricocheted off a door a couple of metres away from us and bounced along until it came to rest at my feet. Keith bent down and picked it up.

"Good to see you again, Garnet," he said, extending the ball in his hand like a peace offering.

Garnet Dishaw had the patrician, silver-haired good looks of a lawyer in an old movie. He was dressed in the same casual manner as Keith: a golf shirt and casual slacks, but Garnet's clothes hung on him. It was obvious that not long before he had been a much larger man.

"Come inside, Keith," he said. "No use letting these senile old fools hear your business. Although your secrets would be safe enough; there isn't a person on this wing who's had a coherent thought since 1957."

When he bent to pick up the golf ball nearest him, I noticed he had trouble straightening. "Let me get those," I said. "Why don't you two go on in. I'll be along."

Garnet Dishaw and Keith disappeared into the last room in the hall. When I'd made the floor safe again, I joined them, or attempted to. Floor-to-ceiling bookshelves were pressed against every wall, and they were filled with books. In the corner, there was a single bed, covered with a piece of brightly patterned madras; next to it was a single chair and a TV table crowded with glasses and spoons and bottles of medications.

"You'll have to sit on the bed," Garnet Dishaw said. His voice was deep and assured, the voice of a man who, whatever his current circumstances, was accustomed to being listened to. "These residential rooms were designed for people who've decided to leave the past behind, but I am not among them. We inmates of Palliser Place are not allowed to screw anything into the walls without the written consent of the board of governors and of all the cherubim and seraphim, so we must make do with freestanding shelves." He squared his shoulders. "Now," he said, "may I offer you a drink? This institution subscribes to the principle of teetotalism, but most regulations can be subverted." He walked into the bathroom and returned with a bottle of Johnny Walker. "An old college trick," he said. "Not many people risk foraging through a man's laundry hamper, and even fewer sign on when the man is in his eighties. An old man's dirty laundry is not a pleasant thing," he said. Then he bowed to me. "I apologize for speaking of such matters before we've been formally introduced. May I offer you a drink, Ms. . . . ?"

"Kilbourn," I said. "And I'd love a drink. It's been a long day."

"Sensible woman," he said, approvingly. He poured whisky, no ice, no water, into glasses and handed them around. "All right," he said. "What's up?"

"Justine Blackwell," Keith said.

Garnet's shoulders sagged. "An awful thing," he said. "Death doesn't hold quite the terror for me that it does for you. Nonetheless, Justine deserved better; no one should die unprepared."

"Had you kept up with her at all?" Keith asked.

Garnet sipped his drink and settled back in his chair contentedly. "Good stuff. Something to be said for limiting one's intake. And yes, we had kept up, although I can take no credit for our association. *Palman qui meruit qui ferat.* Honour to whom honour is due. The praise goes to Justine, the Ice Queen, as she was known many years ago. She wasn't icy at all, of course. Just focused. That's never regarded as an admirable trait in a woman. I digress, a foible to be avoided at all costs when one is old. If I'm not careful, I could end up in a place even less forgiving than this.

"At any rate, Justine did keep in touch. And it surprised me. Before I retired, she was always good about Christmas gifts: the perfect cheese from Quebec or the best pecan fruit-cake from Texas. I knew I was merely a name on a list; nonetheless, it was a good list to be on. But when I was . . ." His face clouded. The pain of his memory was apparent, but he forced himself to go on. "When I was compelled to move down here, to my daughter's house, Justine stayed in touch. She was very faithful about visiting. I'll give her that . . ."

Keith leaned forward in his chair. "Somehow that surprises me."

Garnet Dishaw's bright eyes were piercing: "You thought she'd no longer have use for someone who was no longer of use to her?"

Keith's gaze didn't waver. "Something like that."

"To be honest, you weren't the only one who was surprised. The first time she came into my daughter's house, you could have blown me over with a fairy's fart, but she was sincere. And she didn't treat me like . . . Never mind. she treated me the way she always had. Even when my daughter moved me in here, Justine came."

"When did you move in here?" I asked.

He scowled in annoyance. "I don't know," he said, "last year sometime."

"Did you notice a change in Justine in the last year?"

"I'm not blind," he snapped. "When Justine visited me at my daughter's house, she looked the way she always looked, like she'd just stepped off a bandbox. In the last year, she looked like a goddamn tree-hugger."

I leaned forward in my chair. "But she was still Justine."

"Of course. She was trying to find answers to some big questions. That's what you do when you're old. I thought the answers she'd come up with were arrant nonsense, but they made sense for her."

"So you didn't think she'd lost her mind."

Garnet Dishaw sat back in his chair. "Why would I think that?"

"I'm not trying to meddle in Justine's personal affairs. These questions have to do with her estate."

"Are those girls of hers fighting over the lolly? Her death was a stroke of luck for them, no doubt about it." He drained his drink. "Poor Dick. Seeing his daughters like that would have been painful for him." Garnet Dishaw's voice took on a faraway quality. "Still, it wouldn't have been the first pain they caused him, nor would it have been the worst. He died of a broken heart, you know."

"Of a broken heart," I repeated.

Garnet Dishaw heard the doubt in my voice, and he turned on me angrily. "You heard me. If the great Howie Morenz could die of a broken heart because his leg shattered and ended his career, Richard Blackwell could certainly die of a broken heart after his whole life was shattered. I don't want to talk about this any more." Garnet pushed himself up from his chair and extended his hand to Keith. "It was good to see you again, my friend."

Keith took his hand and shook it. "Garnet, what the hell are you doing in a place like this?"

Garnet Dishaw made a moue of disgust. "I had a couple of falls," he said. "The first one was in the courthouse in Saskatoon. My feet got tangled up in my robe – a boffo Marx Brothers moment for my colleagues, but I ended up in hospital. My daughter brought me down here to recuperate and I slipped on the goddamn bathroom floor at her state-of-the-art house. We weren't getting along, and the fall gave her the chance she needed to get rid of me." His voice became a stage falsetto. " 'With my job and the children and all, I can't give you the care you need, Dad. You'll be better off where there's someone there to look after you twenty-four hours a day.' " When he spoke again, his voice had regained its normal tone. "It's not an easy thing to face the fact that you're extraneous."

Our eyes locked, and for a beat there was a powerful and wordless communication between us. "No," I said. "It's not easy at all."

"Will you come to see me again?"

I nodded. "I'll come again."

"Good." He looked puckish. "And bring something for the laundry hamper."

The drive home was a short one, and Keith and I were silent, absorbed in our own thoughts. When we pulled up in front of my house, I turned to him. "What did you make of Garnet's comment about Justine's death being a stroke of luck for her daughters?"

"That thought's never occurred to you?"

"I guess it has, but it just seemed too terrible to consider."

"That's where you and Garnet part company then, because I don't imagine there's much about human behaviour that he classifies as being 'too terrible to consider.' "

"I liked him," I said.

"I like him too." Keith touched my cheek. "It's not easy, is it?"

"You mean what's waiting for us in the years ahead?"

"That's exactly what I mean," he said. "It would be nice not to be alone."

"Yeah," I said. "It would be nice not to be alone."

He kissed me. "I'll phone you from Toronto."

It was a little after 9:00 when I walked through the front door. When I called hello, only Rose responded, but she led me to the others. Angus and Leah were on the back deck, curled up together in one of the lazy lounges.

"You two look cosy," I said.

"We are," Angus agreed. "But we're ready to move along, and a little coin for coffee at Roca Jack's would be appreciated."

"Is everything okay with Taylor?"

Leah stood up and stretched. "She's out in her studio painting. Mrs. Kilbourn, that new picture of hers is sensational."

"You're just saying that because you're in it," Angus said. My son gave my shoulder an avuncular squeeze. "Now, Mum, about that cash infusion."

I opened my bag and gave him a bill.

He waved it appreciatively. "Feeling generous tonight?"

"I'm investing in my old age," I said. "I want to make you so indebted to me that you wouldn't even consider making me spend my sunset years in Palliser Place."

CHAPTER

11

The first voice I heard Sunday morning was Detective Robert Hallam's. His gravelly baritone was uncharacteristically tentative. "I'm glad you're up and about, Mrs. Kilbourn. You are an early bird, aren't you?"

"It appears you are too."

"They say the early bird gets the worm."

"Exactly what worm are you after, Detective Hallam?"

He cleared his throat. "Actually, I'm after Rosalie Norman's telephone number." He coughed again. "It's not in the book, and I thought perhaps you might have it. You wouldn't be violating any privacy rights. Rosalie and I are planning to meet for lunch tomorrow."

"Couldn't wait, huh?"

"It's not that. It's . . ." He lowered his voice. "I thought Rosalie might like to go to the matinee of that play at the Globe."

"They're doing *Romeo and Juliet*, aren't they? I hear it's a very passionate production."

"Do you think Rosalie will feel I'm coming on too strong?"

I thought of the new kittenish Rosalie with her black turtleneck and laughter in her voice. "She'll love it," I said. "Hang on. I've got last year's university directory here. Her number will be in it."

After I gave him the number, he repeated it twice, then lowered his voice to a whisper. "Thank you, Mrs. Kilbourn. I appreciate your help."

"Any time. Detective Hallam, while I've got you on the line, have you made any progress on finding out who attacked Hilda McCourt?"

"No. We're back to interviewing people in your area about whether they spotted anyone suspicious that evening."

"Didn't you already do that?"

He sighed. "You bet we did. Twice. We're not exactly popular with your neighbours. But Inspector Kequahtooway is pretty determined about this one."

"I didn't think he was part of the investigation."

"He wasn't. But he followed up some leads on his own time, then asked to be assigned officially."

I remembered how I'd slammed the phone down the last time Alex and I spoke. More coals heaped upon my head. I took a deep breath. "Could you transfer me to Inspector Kequahtooway?" I said. "I'd like to let him know how grateful I am that he's involving himself in Hilda's case."

"No problem, and thanks again, Mrs. Kilbourn. I know I got off to a lousy start with you, but you're a peach."

"At the moment I'm feeling a little bruised."

"What?" he barked.

"It's a joke."

"I don't get it," he said. "Hang on, I'll transfer you."

For a few minutes, I languished in the silent land of *on hold*. Finally, Detective Hallam was back on the line, and his gravelly baritone was back to full volume. "Not on duty," he said. "Inspector Kequahtooway has booked off on personal business. One of the other aboriginal guys said he thought Inspector K. said something about going out to his reserve with his nephew."

"Thanks for trying," I said. "I hope you and Rosalie enjoy the play."

I took my coffee out to the backyard. It was another five-star day, perfect weather to be out at Standing Buffalo. The hills would be warm with the colours of autumn: silver sage, burnt umber, goldenrod. Echo Lake, free at last of its summer burden of Jet Skis and motorboats, would be serene. Karen Kequahtooway had loved those hills, that lake. I sipped my coffee and tried to imagine this woman I'd never met. As a child, she had, Alex said, been surefooted, confident, filled with life; as a mother, her love for her son had made her vulnerable. Her hopes and her fears for him ended in a twisted mass of glass and metal when the brakes on her car failed and she missed a hairpin turn on the road that winds through the Qu'Appelle Valley. Eli had been with her on that lonely road; he had seen everything, and now Signe Rayner was forcing him to unearth all the pain he had buried beneath his memory's surface.

When I spotted Eli's plastic football abandoned in our fading flower garden, the symbolism overwhelmed me. I didn't even try to hold back the tears. Eli was worth crying over; it had been a lousy month, and I was tired of being brave. After a few minutes of noisy crying, I felt better. I found a tissue in my jeans pocket that didn't look too disreputable, blew my nose, and walked down to the garden to pick up the football. When I turned to go back to the house, Taylor was running towards me. She was still wearing her nightie, her face was swollen with sleep, and her hair was a tangle. At that moment, I couldn't have conjured up a more beautiful sight.

I bent down and hugged her. "So," I said, "what's the plan for the day?"

"Come and see my new painting," she said. "Then we can decide."

I followed her out to her studio. One glance at the canvas on the easel and I knew Leah Drache had been right: the new picture was sensational. It was a fantasy, a picture of Taylor's dream dragon-boat team. The boat was pulled up on the shore, and the members of the crew were getting ready for the race. Taylor, wearing her orange lifejacket over her green Bottlescrew Bill T-shirt, was already seated in the prow, beating her drum. Mieka and Greg and Madeleine were in place behind her. Hilda was helping Leah climb into the seat behind them. Angus and Eli were still on the shore, handing out paddles. I was sitting at the back of the boat, alone.

I pointed to the empty place beside me. "Who's going to sit there?" I asked.

Taylor shrugged. "I don't know. Maybe just a made-up person."

"I'm glad you put Eli in," I said.

"I miss him," Taylor said.

"I miss him too," I said.

"I don't get it," my younger daughter said.

"What don't you get?"

"Why just because we lose Alex, we have to lose Eli too."

As I scrambled the eggs for breakfast, I thought about what Taylor had said. She was right. The fact that Alex and I hadn't been able to work things out didn't end my family's commitment to Eli. Whether Alex wanted me to be involved or not, Eli could use an advocate. I popped two English muffins into the toaster and poured the juice. Church was in an hour, and I had to get cracking because suddenly I had plans for the day.

During the service, I couldn't keep my mind from wandering. Twice, Angus had to turn the page in our shared prayer book; each time, he favoured me with the chilly raised eyebrow of the pious. But even my son's theatrical opprobrium couldn't prevent me from thinking of Eli and of Signe Rayner. By the time the choir and congregation had sung the recessional, I'd made up my mind. In the past month, Justine's daughters had burned up the wires calling to express their concern about Hilda; an impromptu visit would simply be a charitable way of responding to their interest, and if I had a chance to ask Signe Rayner one or two pointed questions, so much the better.

Taylor and I dropped Angus off at Leah's, grabbed a quick sandwich at home, then walked across the creek bridge to The Crescents. I'd considered calling Jess's mother to ask if I could leave Taylor with her, but my daughter loved to visit. There was a less altruistic reason to take Taylor along. She was an exuberant little girl, and I was counting on her enthusiasm to smooth over any uneasiness the Blackwell sisters might have about an unannounced social call.

As soon as we hit Leopold Crescent, Taylor found something worth looking at. A man at the house across the street from Justine's was out with his leaf-blower. Taylor watched with professional interest until he was finished, then she went over and asked him how his machine worked. He was an amiable, unhurried man who looked like the adviser in an ad for prudent long-term investments, and he explained the intricacies of his leaf-blower with the kind of loving attention to detail that characterizes the born teacher. Taylor was in luck. So was I. After he'd finished explaining, I held my hand out to him.

"Thanks," I said. "That was great. My daughter's just started a leaf-raking business, so you've given her something to aspire to."

"It was my pleasure, Mrs. . . . ?"

"Kilbourn," I said, "Joanne Kilbourn."

"Darryl Hovanak," he said. "And if your daughter wants a job working with me next fall, I might just take her on. These old trees are one of the beauties of this neighbourhood, but they do create work."

"This is such a beautiful street," I said. "Have you lived here long?"

"Twenty-eight years."

"Then you knew Justine Blackwell," I said.

His face clouded. "I did," he said. "Her death was a loss to us all. She was a good neighbour, and –" he gave me a small self-deprecating smile – "she was almost as house-proud as I am. Her place was always shipshape."

"Even with all her houseguests?" I said.

He frowned. "Did she have houseguests? I never saw anybody. Justine kept pretty much to herself."

"Even in the last year?"

Darryl Hovanak eyed me warily. "Mrs. Kilbourn, I hope you're not from the media."

"No," I said. "I teach at the university, but a close friend of mine is also an old friend of Justine's. My friend was concerned about . . ." I let the sentence drift.

Darryl Hovanak completed it for me. "About wild parties, that sort of thing? Tell your friend to put her mind at ease. From the day I moved in here till the day she died, Justine Blackwell was the best neighbour a man could ask for."

Taylor and I rang the doorbell of Justine's house, but there was no answer. I was just about to give up when Lucy Blackwell came around from the side of the house. She was wearing a flowing ankle-length skirt in swirls of russet and deep green, a loose-fitting deep-green blouse, and, wound around her neck, a scarf of the same flowing material as her skirt. With her tanned bare feet and her dark honey hair, she looked gypsyish. The effect was dazzling.

"This is a surprise," she said with a smile that was a beat too slow in coming.

"Surprises are good," Taylor said agreeably.

"Some are," Lucy said. She turned to me. "What can I do for you, Music Woman?"

"I need to talk to you," I said. "All of you. It won't take long."

She frowned and took a step towards me. "I don't think now's a good time to talk."

"It's as good a time as any," I said. "Are your sisters in the backyard too?" Then, without waiting for an answer, I pushed past her and headed for the garden.

It was obvious from the scene that greeted us that Taylor and I had interrupted a very elegant alfresco luncheon. On the fieldstone patio, three wrought-iron chairs had been arranged around a circular table covered by a snowy linen cloth so full it edges touched the ground. A graceful vase of yellow anemone was in the centre of the table, and at every place setting crystal glasses for water and wine blazed.

A woman carrying a tray came through the French doors that opened onto the patio. I had never met her, but there was no doubt about her identity. Tina Blackwell's hair was different than it had been in her TV days: the shellacked, platinum, anchorwoman 'do had been replaced by *faux sauvage* spikes in a becoming ash blonde, and her outfit was decidedly youthful: a tiny black mini, black lace-up boots, and retro op-art tights. It was a great look, but it was hard to get past the ruin of Tina Blackwell's face. The skin around her eyes was ridged with scar tissue and her cheeks looked as if they had been scraped raw. As soon as I saw her, I flashed a glance at Taylor, but she neither stared nor looked away. She kept walking until she was beside Tina.

"This is so pretty," she said, looking at the table appreciatively. "Is it somebody's birthday?"

"No, just a fancy lunch," Tina said, turning her face away in a gesture that seemed poignantly instinctive.

I walked over to her. "I'm Joanne Kilbourn, Hilda McCourt's friend. This is my daughter, Taylor."

Tina acknowledged Taylor's presence with a nod and a small smile. She raised her hand to her ravaged cheek. "I was sorry to hear about Miss McCourt's accident."

"It wasn't an accident," I said. "It was an assault, a vicious assault."

Tina Blackwell looked towards her sister. "I thought you said she had a fall."

Lucy shook her head. "Too much Prozac, Tina. You're going to have to cut back." She took a step towards me. "How's Hilda doing? We've called you, but you never return our calls, and that policewoman outside her door at the hospital is a dragon."

"You went to the hospital?" I said.

"You're not the only one who cares about Hilda."

"Sorry," I said. "To answer your question, she seems to be improving."

Signe Rayner came out through the French doors. She was wearing her signature muumuu-caftan; this one was magenta, and with her blonde hair swept into its Valkyrie braided coronet, she was a figure of such obvious rectitude that it seemed impossible to imagine her guilty of professional misconduct. But if I had mastered one lesson in my life, it was that appearances can be deceiving. Signe nodded to me. "Is Miss McCourt coherent?" she asked.

"She's improving," I said. There was an awkward pause.

Lucy and Signe exchanged glances. Suddenly, Lucy was all hostess. "We were just about to open a bottle of wine. Will you have a glass? Toast Hilda's recovery?"

"There's nothing I'd rather drink to," I said. As Lucy poured the wine, Tina disappeared into the house. When she came back, she was carrying a bottle of Snapple. She handed it to Taylor. "I hope this is all right," she said.

"I love Snapple," Taylor said. "Thank you." She pointed to a small pool at the bottom of the garden. "Is that a fishpond?"

Tina nodded. "And the fish are still in it. Do you want to go down and have a closer look?"

"Could we?"

Tina looked surprised. "You want me to come?" She picked up her glass of wine and shrugged. "Why not?" she said.

Lucy watched as her sister and my daughter walked to the end of the garden, then she turned to me and lifted her glass. "To Hilda."

"To Hilda," I said.

The wine was an excellent Liebfraumilch, but it was the glass that drew my attention. When I held it up to the light, the sun bounced off its beautifully cut surface and turned it to fire. I looked towards Signe Rayner. "And to Eli. Let's hope they're both back with us soon."

Signe Rayner flushed, but she didn't duck. "You were saying that Miss McCourt is improving. What's her prognosis?"

"Guarded," I said. "It's not easy to recover from the kind of blow Hilda sustained. Eli seems to be taking time to recover too. Dr. Rayner, I'm just a layperson and I know you can't talk about the specifics of Eli's case, but I wonder if you could explain to me why a psychiatrist would use hypnosis with a boy like Eli. It's obvious, even to me, that he hasn't got the strength to deal with his memories."

Signe Rayner looked at me coldly. "I couldn't explain Eli's treatment in terms that would make sense to you."

I leaned forward. "Fair enough," I said. "Then tell me if there are risks involved. Could a sensitive boy, like Eli, who was pushed too hard, get to the point where he might harm himself?"

Signe Rayner's eyes, the same extraordinary turquoise as her sister's, bored into me. "Mrs. Kilbourn, what's your agenda here?" she asked.

"I have no agenda," I said. "I'm on a fact-finding mission."

"Then may I suggest you use the university library. They have an adequate section on psychiatric practices."

"Thank you," I said, "I might just do that." I put down my glass and turned to Lucy. "You were lucky to find replacements for your mother's Waterford," I said. "This is an old pattern. I would have thought it would be impossible to match."

Lucy had the good grace to avert her eyes. I called Taylor, and she and Tina Blackwell came back. They had obviously enjoyed their time together and Tina looked stricken, when I said we had to leave. "So soon?" she said.

"You're just about to have lunch," I said.

Tina Blackwell looked quickly at Signe. Whatever she saw in her sister's face obviously made her decide not to press the invitation. "I'll walk you out," she said.

"Thanks," I said. "I wonder if I could use your bathroom before we leave."

"Of course," she said. This time Tina didn't seek her sister's approval. "Follow me," she said.

I held my hand out to Taylor. "Come on," I said. "You might as well go, too."

We walked in through the French doors. They opened into the living room, a coolly beautiful room with dove-grey walls, exquisite lace curtains that pooled on the floor, and furniture with the gleaming wood inlays and fine upholstery

of the Queen Anne period. A rosewood pier table between
the two floor-to-ceiling windows at the far side of the room
was covered in photographs. Taylor, who loved pictures, ran
over for a look. "Are these your kids?" she asked.

Tina smiled. "No, those photographs are of my sisters
and me."

They had been lovely girls, and the photographs of them
chronicled a happy life of Christmas stockings, Easter-egg
hunts, summers at the lake, and birthday parties. "My father
took all those," Tina said softly. "We stopped taking pictures
after he died." She took a deep breath. "Now, you wanted to
powder your nose. I'm afraid all the bathrooms are upstairs.
They're in the usual places. Just keep opening doors till you
find one."

"Thanks," I said. Walking up the curving staircase was a
sensual pleasure. The bisque-coloured carpeting under our
feet was deep, and the art on the walls was eye-catching.
The works were disparate in period and technique, but
all the pieces were linked by subject matter: justice and
those who dispensed it. There was a reproduction of a Ben
Shahn painting of Sacco and Venzetti, a wonderful contem-
porary painting of Portia by an artist named Kate Rafter,
whom I'd never heard of, but whom I was willing to bet my
bottom dollar I'd be hearing about again. There was also a
striking black-and-white photograph of LeCorbusier's High
Court Building in Chandigarh, and a kind of mosaic depict-
ing Solomon's encounter with the two mothers. Interspersed
with the art were formal photographs of actual judges in full
judicial rig-out.

I could have taken Tina at her word and opened every door
on the second floor, but by the time I got to the top of the
stairs, I didn't need further proof to validate the theory I'd been
forming since I talked to Justine's neighbour. Epiphanies be
damned: there was no way in the world the woman who had

assembled this house would have exposed its treasures to people who had the rap sheets I'd seen in Jill's report. I was now ready to bet the farm that the scene Hilda and I had walked in on the Monday after Justine's murder had been carefully arranged. The odour of garbage, the sticky floors, the desecration of the wallpaper in the dining room had all been part of an elaborate hoax. Clearly, the game had been to make us believe Justine's mind had disintegrated, but her daughters had lacked the time and the stomach to finish the job. I remembered how carefully we had been shepherded into the dining room, and led out again. Given the time constraints, the Blackwell sisters had put on the best show they could.

At least, two of the sisters had. Tina seemed to be in the clear. She hadn't been around the day Hilda and I had visited, and today she hadn't hesitated when I asked if we could use the bathroom. Nothing seemed certain in this house, but given her openness, it seemed reasonable that Tina Blackwell hadn't been part of the farce that had been prepared for Hilda and me.

I looked at the emblems of justice that decorated the wall beside Justine's staircase. Suddenly, all I wanted to do was get away from Leopold Crescent. I turned to Taylor. "Come on T, let's blow this pop stand."

"We didn't pee."

"Do you have to?"

"No, but you said . . ."

"I made a mistake. Let's go."

Tina looked wistful as she let us out the front door. "Thanks for coming over, Mrs. Kilbourn, and thank you, Taylor. It was good to forget for a while."

"It was fun," Taylor said.

"Maybe someday I could visit you," Tina said.

"Any time," I said. "By the way, I forgot to mention that I'm a friend of Jill Osiowy's. She tells me she admires your work."

For the first time that afternoon, Tina turned her face fully towards me. "Does she admire my work enough to ignore this?" she asked bleakly.

As we walked home, I tried to sort out the information I'd gleaned from our visit to the Blackwell sisters. It seemed that, like characters in a Pinter play, Justine's daughters' most significant communications were carried out through silence and subtext. While I puzzled over the line between illusion and reality, Taylor performed the useful work of planning the rest of our afternoon. As always, she proposed enough projects to fill a thirty-six-hour day, but we settled on a more modest agenda. We'd get the car, drive to the hospital to see Hilda, then take in the new show at the Mackenzie Gallery.

Our stay at the Pasqua was short. Hilda appeared to be sleeping comfortably, and we didn't want to disturb her. Taylor left her a drawing she'd made, then slipped away to sit with Nathan. When Taylor was out of earshot, I leaned over and kissed Hilda's forehead. "Justine's daughters lied to us, Hilda, but it won't happen again. Now that I know what we're dealing with, I won't be so gullible. We'll get to the bottom of this. I promise."

The new show at the Mackenzie was too cutting edge for Taylor and me. We hurried through, then headed outside to visit the Fafard cows; half-sized bronze sculptures of a bull, cow, and calf in front of the gallery. The animals' names were Potter, Valadon, and Teevo, and for me, the time we spent admiring their perfect lines and the gentleness of their expression had the restorative power of a romp in a meadow.

My sense of renewal was short-lived. When we got home, I could hear the phone ringing before I unlocked the front door. I raced to pick it up, heard the husky music of Lucy Blackwell's voice, and felt my spirits plummet.

"Music Woman, you've got to give me a chance to explain."

"Go for it."

"Not on the phone. Can we meet for a drink somewhere?"

"I have a family, Lucy. I have to make supper."

"I'll take you to a restaurant – all of you. Please, you have to listen to what really happened."

I almost hung up on her, then I remembered Signe Rayner. There was a chance that if I heard Lucy out, she might answer some of my questions about her sister. I took a deep breath. "Forget the restaurant," I said. "You can come over. But it's going to have to be a quick visit."

Lucy Blackwell was at our front door in ten minutes. She was still wearing the gypsy outfit, but there was nothing carefree in her manner. As she looked around the living room, she seemed both tense and unfocused. "This is so homey. That rocking chair is perfect."

"It was my grandmother's," I said.

Lucy laughed softly. "Somehow that doesn't surprise me. Can I sit in it?"

"Of course," I said. "Would you like a drink?"

She shook her head. "I had too much at lunch. After you left I was feeling a bit shaky."

"Because I'd caught you in a lie."

She flushed. "Yes. What Signe and I did was stupid, and childish, but it wasn't malicious. It was," she shrugged helplessly, "make-believe. We were just using make-believe to show you the truth. In the last year, my mother had fooled so many people." Lucy leapt to her feet and came over to where I was sitting. In a swift and graceful movement, she knelt on the rug in front of me. "Mrs. Kilbourn, you saw Tina's face today. That abomination was a direct result of my mother's enlightenment."

I almost cut her off. I had believed Eric Fedoruk when he told me that Justine had given Tina the money she asked for,

and I'd had my fill of make-believe. But there was a real possibility that, as she spun her latest fiction, Lucy would
reveal a truth that I needed to know. I sat back in my chair.
"Go on," I said.

Lucy's gaze was mesmerizing. "Tina was in a business
where you can't get old. When she asked for help to get the
surgery that might have saved her career, my mother didn't
even hear her out. Instead of cutting her a cheque, Justine
gave her a speech about how *privileged* we all were, and how
it was time we stopped taking and started giving. That job of
Tina's might not have looked like much to you or me,
Joanne, but it was her life. You should see her apartment. It's
filled with pictures of her doing all this demeaning public-
relations stuff for CJRG: riding the float in the Santa Claus
parade, flipping pancakes at the Buffalo Days breakfast,
running in the three-legged race with the sports guy on her
show. Total fluff, but it was her *identity*." Lucy raked
her fingers through her hair. "Tina's always been fragile,
emotionally. My mother knew that. She knew terrible
things might happen if Tina was hurt again."

"What kind of terrible things?"

Lucy looked away. "Forget I said that. I didn't come here
to talk about Tina."

"That's right," I said. "You came to explain why you and
Signe decided to produce that little vignette for Hilda
and me."

She winced, but she soldiered on. "I told you, it was just a
way of getting you to see the truth."

"How many lies do you think it's going to take before I see
the truth, Lucy?"

Her body tensed. "What do you mean?"

I moved closer to her. "I know Tina got that money from
your mother."

"How do you know?"

I remembered Eric Fedoruk's certainty. "There's a cancelled cheque," I said. It was a bluff, but it did the trick.

In a flash, Lucy was on her feet. "Tina must have lied to me," she said weakly and she started for the door.

"Wait," I said. I got up and followed her. "My turn now, and I haven't got time to figure out which of you is lying about what. Lucy, I have one question for you, and the answer you give me had better be truthful because I'm running out of patience."

Lucy gazed at me intently. "What's your question, Music Woman?"

"What happened between Signe and the boy in Chicago?"

Her face registered nothing. "I have to be going," she said.

"No, you don't," I said. "Not until you tell me if the story is true."

"Signe was found innocent."

"That wasn't what I asked."

Lucy walked to the window. "Is that your Volvo out there?"

"Yes."

"I've always wanted a Volvo wagon." Her back was to me, and her tone was flat. It was impossible to tell if her words were derisive or heartfelt.

"Lucy, you're running out of time here."

"Okay, I'll tell you the truth. I don't know what Signe did in Chicago, but she isn't using that treatment on Eli Kequahtooway. My sister doesn't make the same mistake twice."

"She talked to you about how she's treating Eli?"

Lucy shrugged. "She may have mentioned it." She whirled around and gave me her dazzling smile. "So, that's it, Music Woman. You've shaken out all the skeletons in our closet." She adjusted her scarf. "Now, I'd better be on my way, let you get on with making supper for your. kids." Lucy

Blackwell looked at me wistfully. "It must be nice to lead such an ordinary life."

As I stood in my garden in the late-afternoon sunshine, picking the last of the summer's tomatoes, I thought about Lucy. If the purpose of her visit had been to clear the air, she hadn't succeeded. As far as I was concerned, the Blackwell sisters were still, in Winston Churchill's famous phrase, "a riddle wrapped in a mystery inside an enigma."

All during dinner, I pondered the problem of where to find the pieces that would make sense of the puzzle. The possibility I came up with was born of desperation. After supper, I got Taylor bathed and in bed, pointed Angus towards his books, and drove downtown to Culhane House and the person who, according to Eric Fedoruk, had been Justine's closest companion in the final year of her life.

When I got out of my car on Rose Street, the chill of apprehension I felt wasn't wholly attributable to the fact that I was walking in an unfamiliar area on a moonless Sunday night. Detective Robert Hallam had characterized Wayne J. Waters as "lightning in a bottle"; it was impossible to predict how he'd react to an unexpected encounter. I checked the address I'd written down. Culhane House was only half a block away. I was almost there; it would be foolish to turn back now.

The building was an old three-storey house on a corner lot. In the first half of the century, this had been a fashionable downtown address, but the people who were on their way up in the world had long since abandoned the neighbourhood to those who were going nowhere. From the outside, Culhane House looked solid and serviceable. In selecting it as the site of an organization that would serve as both hostel and headquarters for ex-cons, someone had chosen wisely. The location was central; the upper storeys could be used as temporary living quarters, and the bottom floor appeared to be spacious.

The hand-lettered sign on the front door said "Enter," so I did. The room into which I walked was dark, acrid with cigarette smoke, and, except for the sounds coming from the television, silent. On the TV screen, the Sultan was plotting vengeance against Aladdin and Princess Jasmine; none of the half-dozen or so people watching his treachery even glanced my way.

"Do any of you know where I can find Wayne J. Waters?" I asked.

The blonde in leopardskin spandex draped over the chair closest to me gave me the once-over. "He's in the office," she said, "right through them double doors. But hang on to your pompoms, girlie, he's in a lousy mood."

The room in which I found Wayne J. appeared to have been the dining room in the house's earliest incarnation. The chandelier he was sitting under had long since shed its crystal teardrops, but the long oak table in front of him and the sideboard in the corner were battered beauties. When he saw me, Wayne J. jumped to his feet and surprised me with a smile. "I'd given you up for dead," he said. "How's Hilda?"

"Coming along," I said.

He made the thumbs-up sign. "Good, she's a classy broad."

"She is," I agreed.

"You got time for a coffee?" he asked.

"Sure," I said. "It's been a long day. Coffee sounds great."

When he went off to get the coffee, I looked around the office. There wasn't much to see: an old Tandy computer; a battered filing cabinet; a poster of a kittens rollicking with a roll of toilet paper under the words ". . . been up to any mischief lately?"; and a wall calendar for the month of September. The calendar had the kind of surface that can be written on with markers, and it was a crazy quilt of colour.

When I examined the entries more closely, I saw that they were a record of appointments, colour-coded to match the various names in the legend printed at the bottom of the calendar. Terrence Ducharme's name was in red marker, and his list of meetings would have kept him busier than most middle-class children: Anger Management; A.A.; Substance Abusers Anonymous; Interpersonal Skills. I was checking the entry for the night Hilda had been attacked when Wayne J. came back with the coffee.

"Terry didn't do her, you know." His tone was conversational.

I turned to face him. "I know," I said. "The police told me he had an alibi for the night Hilda was attacked."

"I'm not talking about Hilda," he said. "I'm talking about Justine."

"But he didn't have an alibi," I said.

"Maybe he lacked an alibi," Wayne J. said judiciously, "but he did have a disincentive."

"You're going to have to explain that."

"There's nothing to explain," Wayne J. said, setting our mugs of coffee carefully on the table. "Terry knew the same thing everybody here knew."

I slid into the chair nearest me and picked up my mug. "Which was?"

Wayne J. blew on top of his coffee to cool it. "Which was that I would have considered it my personal duty to kill anybody who touched a hair on Justine Blackwell's head."

Whatever his intention, Wayne J.'s words were a conversation-stopper. For a beat, we sipped our coffee, alone in our private thoughts. Wayne J. seemed content to be silent, but I wasn't. I hadn't come to Culhane House to reflect; I'd come to get answers.

"How are things going for you now?" I asked.

Wayne J. gave me a sardonic smile. "Fuckin' A." The table in front of him was littered with bills. He scooped up a stack in one of his meaty hands. "As you can see, our creditors grow impatient. Unfortunately, Culhane House lacks the wherewithal to meet their demands."

"And no prospects?" I asked.

He laughed his reassuring rumble. "None that are legally acceptable. And believe me I've explored my options. I even bit the bullet and went to Danger Boy's office."

I must have looked puzzled.

"Eric Fedoruk," he said. "Owner of one of the sweetest machines money can buy, and I'll bet he never takes it past 160 kph. What a waste! Anyway, Mr. Fedoruk gave me a rundown of the situation with Justine's money. He used a bunch of legal mumbo-jumbo, but I've spent enough time in courtrooms to cut through that crap. The bottom line is that I'm going to have fight like hell to get any of Justine's money."

"Are you going to do it?"

"No."

"That surprises me," I said.

Wayne J. leaned towards me; he was so close I could smell the Old Spice. "Why? Because I'm broke and because everything I care about is going down the toilet?"

"Something like that."

"Some things are worth more than money, Joanne."

I sipped my coffee. "What is it that's worth more than money to you, Wayne J.?"

"Not dragging Justine's name through the mud. If I got myself a lawyer and went to court about this, those daughters of hers would haul out all the dirty laundry. They don't have much regard for their mother."

Here was my opening. "What went wrong between Justine and her children?" I asked.

"They're losers, and Justine was a winner," he said judiciously. "And losers always hate winners. It's human nature. And you know what else is human nature? No matter what a winner does for a loser, it's never enough." Suddenly Wayne J. clenched his hands, raised his fists, and brought them down on the table so hard, I thought the wood might crack. "She fucking did everything for them," he said. "She gave Tina a bundle for that facelift or whatever the hell it was she wanted. And the singer was always there with her hand out too."

"Lucy asked Justine for money?"

Wayne J.'s tone was mocking. "It costs money to make records. Haven't you heard?" He was warming to his narrative now. "And the shrink had her own monetary needs – major ones. I know because I was involved in that one."

"What?"

He shook himself. "Look, I shouldn't be talking about any of this. It's violating a confidence."

"Justine's dead," I said. "Nothing she told you can hurt her any more."

Wayne J. furrowed his brow in contemplation. "What the hell," he said. "The good doctor never even thanked me. This couple in Chicago was shaking her down. Justine didn't want her daughter involved, so she asked me to deliver the money to them. It was the only time she ever asked me to do her a favour. I was proud to do it." Remembering, he looked away. "I was glad Justine didn't have to deal with those people. They were garbage. The architect was a peckerhead – totally pussy-whipped. His wife was crazy and mean as hell. She had this little dog, and she made it wear boots when it went outside. To keep it from tracking in mud, get it? No wonder her kid needed a shrink."

"Did you ever find out why these people were blackmailing Signe Rayner?"

"I never asked," he said. "I just delivered the money, and told them it was a one-shot deal. If they got greedy, they'd get sorry." His eyes bored into me. "Mrs. Kilbourn, I'd appreciate it if you kept this little story to yourself. I don't want anything floating around that will make Justine look bad."

"Then help me out with something else because, in my opinion, this *does* make Justine look bad."

He laughed mirthlessly. "That screw-up about the burial plots at the cemetery," he said. "I noticed you and Hilda didn't stick around."

"We had Lucy Blackwell with us," I said. "When she saw there were strangers buried in the family plot, she was devastated."

Something hard came into Wayne J.'s eyes. "Lucy's mother had her reasons for doing what she did."

"What possible reason *could* she have had? I know Justine had undergone some profound philosophical changes in the past year, and I know she wasn't close to her daughters, but didn't she have any feelings at all for her husband?"

"She respected him," Wayne J. said. "That's why she did what she did. She said he'd be better off spending eternity surrounded by the kind of people he'd spent a lifetime defending than with Goneril and Regan, whoever they are. I figured that was some kind of family joke, but Justine wasn't laughing when she said it. She was dead serious." He reached for my empty coffee cup. "Refill?"

"No thanks," I said. "I'd better be getting home."

He stood up. "Come on," he said, offering me his arm. "I'll walk you to your car. After dark, this neighbourhood is no place for a lady."

CHAPTER

12

I woke up the next morning with a sore throat, itchy eyes, and sniffles. By the time I'd showered, taken some echinacea, told Rose our walk was cancelled, and hustled the kids down for breakfast, I was ready to go back to bed. But the day ahead was mercifully short of demands: my first-year students had a quiz, and Howard Dowhanuik, our ex-premier and my friend since Ian's early days in politics, was coming in to talk to my senior class in the afternoon. It was a day to limit my aspirations and take comfort in Woody Allen's dictum that 99 per cent of life is just a matter of showing up. If I played my cards right, I could be home, curled up in bed with a hot toddy and a good novel, by 3:30 p.m.

When I walked into the Political Science offices, Rosalie was on the telephone. As soon as she heard my step, she blushed, whispered something into the receiver, and hung up.

"How was *Romeo and Juliet*?" I asked.

"Transcendent," she said. "Robert said he'd never realized Shakespeare was so s–e–x–y."

"I'm glad you had fun," I said, as I started towards the door.

"Wait," she said. She handed me a pink telephone-message slip. "Your calls are still getting transferred out here."

I glanced at the name. The message was from Alex.

Rosalie smiled shyly. "Maybe we'll both be lucky in love today," she said.

"Maybe," I said, but my voice lacked conviction.

Alex sounded as if he had a cold too, but even making allowances for the fact that he was unwell, his tone was more encouraging than it had been in days.

"Bob Hallam said you were looking for me," he said.

"I just wanted to thank you for getting involved in Hilda's case."

"Actually, Jo, I wonder if we could get together and talk about that."

"Has something happened?"

"Yes, but I'd rather talk to you about in person. Are you free for lunch?"

"Yes."

"It's raining, so I guess the bird sanctuary's out," he said.

His reference to our shared past touched me, but I was too taken aback to pick up on it. "There's a new restaurant in the University Centre," I said. "It's called Common Ground. If you can get past the symbolism, there's homemade soup and a piece of fresh bread for $2.49."

"Twelve o'clock okay?"

"Twelve o'clock's fine. Alex, I'm looking forward to seeing you again."

"Same here, Jo."

When I hung up, my heart was pounding. Alex had sounded like himself again. I had no idea what had brought about the change, and I didn't care. For the first time in days, we were talking, and in three and a half hours, we'd be talking face to face.

Garnet Dishaw's call came just as I was about to leave for class. Even over the phone, his voice seemed to fill the room. "I wondered if you could find a few moments this evening to come by and talk about Justine," he said.

I thought about the warm bed and the good novel I'd promised myself. "Of course, but could we make it earlier?"

"Later suits me better," he said. There was a silence. "Evenings are long around here."

"May I bring something for the laundry hamper?"

"I knew you were a perceptive woman?"

I laughed. "What's your preference?"

"Surprise me," he said. "But when you go to the liquor store, remember that extravagance is not numbered among the seven deadly sins."

The morning crawled by. For once, no students straggled behind after class to talk. Back in my office, there was a stack of papers to mark and a pile of minutes to read from a committee I'd agreed to join. But I knew my limits. Until I met Alex for lunch, any activity I undertook would get short shrift. Angus had been hinting at his desperate need for a new fall jacket, and the morning paper had announced a sale at Work Warehouse. The liquor store wasn't far from the Golden Mile shopping mall. If I took care of my errands in the morning, I could still grab some recuperative time in the afternoon.

Angus's jacket didn't cost me substantially more than the bottle of Johnny Walker Black I picked up for Garnet Dishaw. When I went into the mall bathroom to check my makeup before I drove back to the university, I knew how to spend the money I'd saved on the jacket. The clear lip gloss I'd chosen in June because it looked so great with a tan made me look sepulchral now that my tan had faded, and the circles under my eyes and the redness under my nose were not flattering. The cosmetics counter at Shoppers Drug Mart was beckoning, and I purchased with abandon: a new blush, a deeper lipstick, and a small tube of concealer. By the time I headed back to the university for lunch with Alex, I looked not great but better.

I was five minutes late getting to the University Centre. The noon-hour crush was on, and I had to battle my way through kids with wet slickers and sodden backpacks. Somehow, Alex had managed to find a table. It was in the corner, and as I pushed my way towards him, the opening notes of a Mozart horn concerto came over the sound system. Mozart was one of our mutual passions, and while I knew that the playing of classical music in the U.C. was a device to keep students who ached for heavy metal or grunge on the move, the fact that Dennis Brain began playing just as Alex and I were about to meet seemed like a good omen.

I slid into the chair opposite him. "I had some shopping to do. I hope you haven't been waiting long."

He shook his head and smiled. "I never minded waiting for you, Jo."

"Good," I said. "Shall we get our soup? I saw the sign. It's Louisiana gumbo, the real thing; they even use filé."

He frowned. "Sounds like you're getting the same cold I've got."

"I'm counting on the gumbo to be a pre-emptive strike."

We lined up with the students, ordered our soup and slices of dark pumpernickel, and went back to our table.

Alex sipped his soup gratefully. "I'm glad you suggested this place."

"Me too. So, what's up?"

He shrugged. "All hell's breaking loose. Terrence Ducharme's alibi turned out to be true. He's admitted all along that he jumped into the car with Justine Blackwell when she drove away from the hotel. But his story was that, after they drove to the park, Justine pulled into that little turnoff near the information centre and they talked until they made their peace with one another. According to Ducharme, she offered to drive him home, but he decided to walk because he was still pretty churned up."

I thought of the X's marking Terrence Ducharme's anger-management classes on the calendar in Culhane House. Seemingly, his efforts at behaviour modification were paying off. "Somebody's come forth who saw him walking home?" I asked.

"No, somebody's come forth who saw him back at his rooming house," Alex said. "Ducharme has always sworn that when he got back home, the old lady across the hall heard him, stuck her head out, recognized him, and went back into her room. Unfortunately for him and for us, by the time we started questioning Ducharme, the old lady had taken off. We did some checking, but the woman, whose name is Leota Trumble, hadn't told anyone in the building where she was going. Apparently, she's an odd bird, doesn't trust anybody to know her business." Alex buttered his bread and took a bite. "To be frank, we didn't exactly pursue the matter with vigour. The feeling was that Miss Trumble's absence was just something Ducharme had latched onto as an alibi."

"But he was telling the truth," I said.

Alex nodded. "Miss Trumble and a friend were on what she calls 'a musical motor tour of the American South.' They finished up at Graceland and came home."

"I guess after you see Graceland, everything else is anti-climactic."

Alex smiled. "Anyway, Miss Trumble corroborates Terrence Ducharme's story. He came home exactly when he said he did. More to the point, he was clean as a whistle. No blood on him, and whoever bludgeoned Justine Blackwell to death would have looked like they'd been in a bloodbath."

Instinctively, I winced at the ugliness of the image. Alex leaned towards me and covered my hand with his. "I'm sorry. That detail wasn't necessary."

"I'm all right," I said.

Alex left his hand on mine, and his dark eyes searched my face. "Are you really, Jo?"

I shook my head. "No," I said. "I'm confused and mad and hurt. How about you."

"The same," he said.

"Alex, what happened to us? I know we had more against us than most couples – the fact that I'm older and the difference in race – but I always thought the things we shared mattered more to us both than the things that divided us."

"I used to think that too."

A trio of students with baggy pants and sports caps turned backwards approached our table. They were laughing and horsing around, and as they started past us, one of them fell against me with enough force to tip my chair halfway over. His friends dragged him back quickly, but all three were full of apologies, and none of them would budge until I assured them no harm had been done.

When they'd finally moved along, I put my hand back in Alex's. "I guess when soup's only $2.49 a bowl, you have to accept the floor show."

"I can put up with the floor show as long as we're talking."

"So can I," I said. "Alex, why did you change your mind about us?"

"I didn't change my mind. Look, I won't explain this well, but I'm just starting to understand some things." He fell silent.

"What kinds of things?" I asked.

"Well, for starters, why I was such a jerk with you. After Eli came, all these problems I thought I'd dealt with began to surface again. I told you about how wild I was when I was a kid."

"I always found it hard to believe," I said. "You're so controlled now."

"Maybe that's part of the problem, because, when I look back, I honestly can't remember a day when I didn't wake up angry. If you're an aboriginal kid with a chip on your shoulder, there's always somebody willing to give you a reason to keep it there. My mother was a great woman, but even she couldn't seem to reach all that rage."

"But *you* found a way to reach it."

"I thought I had. Police work was a good fit for me. Part of being a cop is learning to depersonalize, tune out the insults, focus on the task at hand. By the time you and I met, I really believed I'd found the right formula: work, music, and no complications."

"And I was a complication."

He smiled. "You were. So were your kids."

"That's why you resisted so long."

Alex looked at me hard. "Resisting was a mistake, Jo. That was the best time of my life. I felt as if – this sounds like such a cliché – but I felt as if I'd found my place. Then Eli came. When I saw how angry he was and how much he was suffering, it was as if someone ripped my skin off. I was right back there. And I couldn't do anything to help him. I couldn't change anything. I just had to stand by and watch."

"Alex, why didn't you tell me all this before?"

"I don't know. At the time, you were part of the problem, and so were Angus and Taylor. They're great kids, Jo, and they brought me so much joy, but after Eli came, all I could see when I looked at them was how easy their lives were." He swallowed hard. "They're so confident, Jo. On his worst days, Angus has more confidence that life's going to work out than Eli will ever have – than *I* will ever have. And

Angus has reason to feel good about himself. Doors open when he knocks; people welcome him; he gets chosen for the ball team; he doesn't hear slurs every time he walks down the street. When I saw what Eli was going through, all the old wounds just opened again."

"I wish I'd known, Alex."

"I did everything I could to keep you from knowing, then I was furious when you didn't see that everything was going wrong. I felt the same way about the situation with Eli. I didn't want you to see all of his problems, then I was angry when you didn't understand what he was going through."

"At least I understand now," I said.

"When it's too late."

"Why is it too late?"

"Because you, very sensibly, have found someone else."

"But I haven't," I said. As soon as I said the words, I knew they were true. "Keith and I are just friends. Even if you and I can't work things out, my relationship with Keith isn't going to change." A student walking by looked at us curiously. I leaned across the table and lowered my voice. "Alex, I've had two loves in my life: the first one was my husband, and the other one is you. Neither relationship was very easy, but that doesn't mean I'm ready to settle for less."

I could see the tension leave his face. "Is there any place around here we can be alone?"

I shook my head. "Just my office, and Rosalie will be hovering. I'll walk you to your car." Alex's Audi was in the visitors' lot behind the University Centre. As soon as we got into the front seat, we were in each other's arms. Necking in a car parked in a public place was as awkward and as wonderful as it had been in high school. When Alex's cellphone rang, it seemed like an intrusion from another world. Unfortunately, it was an intrusion that demanded action. When he ended the call, Alex reached over and smoothed my hair. "Time to go," he said. "I'll come by the house tonight, but it'll probably be late. Is that okay?"

"It's more than okay. But if you can make it earlier, why don't you bring Eli?"

"I'll ask him, but I don't think he'll come. He doesn't like leaving the apartment." Alex sighed heavily. "Damn it, our first good moment in weeks, and we're already back talking about Eli."

"Eli's what we should be talking about," I said. "How bad are things there?"

"He seems to get worse every day, Jo. He's tight as a drum and he's started having these night terrors. He says they're like movies. Part of what he's seeing is Karen's death, but there's a lot of stuff that doesn't fit in. He says it's dark in his dream, and Karen was killed in the late afternoon. She'd just picked Eli up from school. And he keeps talking about all the blood. Jo, I saw Karen's body after the accident. There were all these internal injuries, but she just looked like she was sleeping. That's what made it so hard . . ." His voice broke. "Anyway, Dr. Rayner says I shouldn't talk to Eli about the night terrors, that the only one who can help him deal with what he's seeing is a professional."

"Meaning Dr. Rayner," I said.

"Yeah," Alex said wearily, "meaning Dr. Rayner. I'm beginning to think you're right about her."

"Then let's dump her," I said. "Alex, there are a number of very disturbing things in her history. I have news clippings about a case in Chicago. A boy's parents sued Signe Rayner because her therapy drove their son to suicide. They lost their lawsuit, but there's not much doubt in my mind that Signe Rayner was guilty."

I told him what I knew. When I finished, Alex shook his head. "That's good enough for me," he said. "I'll phone Signe as soon as I get back to the office. And I'll call Dan Kasperski to see if he can take Eli as a patient."

I sighed with relief. "Good," I said. "It's time Eli did better. It's time we all did better."

I got out of the car and started towards the University Centre. When Alex came after me, I thought that he just wanted to seize the moment to say something fond and foolish, but his words weren't about love; they were about danger. "Promise me you'll be careful," he said. "There's going to be a press conference this afternoon to announce that Ducharme's out of the picture, so all bets are off. We've got an officer outside Hilda's room again, so we're covered there. But until we make an arrest, don't rule anybody out, and don't take any chances."

"That's an easy promise to make," I said. "I've got a lot to stay safe for."

As soon as I got back to my office, I called the hospital. Nathan reassured me that indeed Constable Nilson was back in front of Hilda's door. Then in a voice edgy with excitement, he said, "I was going to call you. I wanted to be sure you came by when I was on duty. We've waited so long for good news about Miss McCourt."

"And there is good news?"

"The best."

I still had my coat on. I looked at my watch. Bang on 1:00. If I hit the lights right, I could see Hilda and be back in time to walk with Howard Dowhanuik to my senior class. "I'll be right over," I said.

As I drove down the freeway, I tested the rawness in my throat. It was still there, but it wasn't worse. Maybe the echinacea and the gumbo had lived up to their billing, and my cold had been vanquished. It was a comforting thought, because the day that had started out so free of demands was

getting complicated. Sick or well, I had a dance card that
was rapidly filling up.

Nathan was in his place at the nursing station. When I
called out to him, he picked up Hilda's chart from the desk.
"Look at that," he said, pointing to the latest figures on the
Glasgow Coma Scale. "If she keeps progressing at this rate,
we'll be able to move her out of intensive care."

"She's doing that well?"

Nathan gave me the thumbs-up sign. "The numbers never
lie."

As soon as I saw Hilda, I knew I didn't need the Glasgow
Coma Scale to tell me that she was better. The signs were
imperceptible but real. Everything about my old friend suggested that, sometime in the hours since I'd last seen her, she
had crossed the divide that separates the sick from the well.
I walked over to her bed, but, worried about germs, I didn't
bend to kiss her. It was enough just to know that she'd
decided to rejoin us.

I glanced at the photograph that I had taped to her bed
when she'd first been brought to intensive care. For the first
time, the picture of Hilda sitting in our canoe didn't make
my eyes sting. The day I'd snapped that picture, Hilda had
taken Taylor up to the top of a hill to pick wild strawberries.
They had returned with sun-pink cheeks, mosquito bites,
and mouths stained with fruit. Seeing them coming tri-
umphantly towards me with an ice cream pail half-full of
berries had been one of the best memories of the summer.
Now it seemed possible there would be other sun-filled days,
other memories.

"I knew you were indestructible," I said.

Hilda didn't open her eyes but she turned at the sound of
my voice. "For a while, I had my doubts," she whispered.
Then she smiled and went back to sleep.

My banner day continued. Howard Dowhanuik was a major hit with my senior class. Freed by retirement of the politician's need to weigh his words, our ex-premier was profane, indiscreet, knowledgeable, and funny, and the kids loved him.

When the last admiring student had wandered off, he turned to me. "I believe it's payback time. Does the Faculty Club still have that excellent bottle of fifteen-year-old Dalwhinnie tucked away?"

"They do, but, Howard, will you take a rain check? I've been promising myself a nap all day."

He was a big man, and he had the habit some big men in politics have of using their size as a tool to cajole. He draped an arm around my shoulders, dwarfing me. "Scotch would do you more good. Now that you're over fifty, why don't you let go of some of that caution? Open up a little. Embrace life."

I removed his arm from my shoulder. "I am planning to embrace life," I said. "That's why I need a nap."

As soon as I got home, I took some more echinacea and wrote the kids a note saying I was upstairs in bed. I slept for an hour and, when I woke up, I felt better. After I'd showered, I started to change into my sweats; when I remembered that Alex was coming over, I replaced the sweats with my new silk blouse and a pair of slacks. I was burrowing through my jewellery drawer for the mate to my best gold hoop earring when I thought about my meeting with Garnet Dishaw. I picked up the phone and dialled Alex's number to make sure he wouldn't come by while I was gone. Eli answered on the first ring. He sounded keyed-up and anxious.

"Who is it?" he asked.

"It's Jo, Eli. How are you doing?"

"I'm okay. Do you want my uncle? Because he's not here."

"Will you get him to call me when he comes in?"

"Is that all?"

"No," I said. "Your uncle and I had a long talk today. We're back together again, Eli, at least we're going to try to be, and we want you to be part of the picture. I've missed you – so have Angus and Taylor."

"They're not mad at me?"

"No."

"And they're not scared of me?

"Why would they be scared of you?"

He didn't answer. As the silence between us lengthened, I gave up. "If you ever want to talk, I'm a pretty good listener."

"Okay," he said.

"Eli, I mean it. Any time you need me, I'm here."

"I'll remember that," he said, then he hung up.

I was sitting at the kitchen table shuffling through take-out menus when Angus came downstairs. He'd obviously squeezed in a visit to the barber after school, and he was dressed for success: shined loafers; pressed slacks, and the jacket, shirt, and tie we'd bought for Madeleine's upcoming baptism.

"You're looking pretty *GQ* for dinner from Pizza Hut," I said.

He frowned at a piece of lint on his jacket sleeve. "Mum, I'm eating at the Draches tonight, remember? Mrs. Drache's brother is here from Toronto. He's a rabbi. Leah's even taking out all the rings from her body piercings."

"Talk about formal," I said. "What's Leah doing about that tattoo of the foxes chasing the lion?"

"Her mother bought her a long-sleeved dress. You should see it, Mum. She looks great, but she doesn't look like Leah. Anyway, I won't be late. Mrs. Drache says her brother needs his sleep."

"A man after my own heart," I said.

Angus looked quizzical. "What?"

"Nothing," I said. "Have fun, and say hi to the Draches for me."

Taylor and I passed up pizza in favour of won-ton soup, Chinese vegetables, and a double order of her favourite almond prawns from Kowloon Kitchen. As we ate, I filled her in on the visit we were going to pay Garnet Dishaw. As always, she was keen to extend the circle of her acquaintance, but when I mentioned that Garnet and I would need some time alone to talk, she looked thoughtful.

"I'll need some fresh books from the library to take with me," she said.

"Taylor, the library's downtown, and Mr. Dishaw lives out by the airport."

"I've already read the books I've got a hundred times."

Most of the time, Taylor was an accommodating child, but when she dug her heels in, there was no budging her. "Okay," I said, "we'll go to the library, but you'll have to promise me you'll tread easy with Mr. Dishaw. I'm not sure he's used to kids. Now come on, let's fill up the bookbag. The library's waiting."

As I walked by Hilda's room, I stopped and looked in. Everything was just as she'd left it, shining and ordered. Her bed was neatly made; her makeup kit, hairbrush, and comb were carefully arranged on the guest towel she always placed on the vanity to protect the finish; the books she had been reading the night before the attack were centred on her nightstand. Even the library books she had taken out when she'd been in search of an appropriate quote for Justine's funeral were still on Mieka's old desk, neatly aligned, and, it suddenly occurred to me, overdue.

The books were on my card, and Hilda would be mortified if she knew they hadn't been returned promptly. She had, I noticed, made quite a selection: Francis Bacon; Thomas Aquinas; Plutarch; and, the winner, Montaigne. I picked up the *Essays*. The envelope containing Justine's authorization was still where Hilda had slipped it to mark her place the morning before Justine's funeral. Events since then had given a painful resonance to the words Hilda had finally chosen: "What? Have you not lived? That is not only the fundamental but the most illustrious of your occupations. . . . To compose our character is our duty. . . . Our great and glorious masterpiece is to live appropriately."

I closed the book, but not before I'd removed the envelope. As far as I was concerned, if Hilda was going to live appropriately from now on, she had to be as far as possible from Justine and her troubled life. It would be a distinct pleasure to put a match to this document that had caused my old friend so much grief. I started to put the envelope in my pocket, but curiosity drove me to read Justine's final written instructions one last time.

When I took out Justine's letter, there was a surprise. Enclosed in the single folded sheet of expensive letterhead were two items that hadn't been there the morning Hilda and I had discussed Justine's life. The first was a slip of paper upon which were written two names, a Chicago address, and a telephone number with a 312 area code; the second was a cancelled cheque for thirty thousand dollars made out to Tina Blackwell and signed by Justine. The cheque was almost a year old. I turned it over. On the back were Tina's endorsement and the stamp of the branch of the bank that had cashed it. As I read the information, I felt my nerves twang. Justine's cheque had found its way halfway across the country to Lunenburg, Nova Scotia. Until her recent financial reversals, Lunenburg had been Lucy Blackwell's home town.

CHAPTER

13

It had started to rain by the time Taylor and I chose our library books and set out for Palliser Place. My younger daughter was full of plans. Buoyed by the news of Hilda's recovery, she'd checked out the video of *Anne of Green Gables* to watch when she and I got back from our visit. As our windshield wipers slapped rhythmically at the rain, the notion of losing myself in the blossom-heavy trees and azure skies of Prince Edward Island grew increasingly seductive, but the brutal realities of Justine's life made escape impossible.

The pieces of the puzzle were beginning to fall into place, and the picture that was emerging was a troubling one. There was no doubt in my mind that Larry and Paula Erle, the Chicago couple whose name and address had been in Justine's private papers, were the parents of the boy who had committed suicide because of Signe Rayner's treatment. Justine's reasons for keeping the Erles' address close at hand were less clear, but an unsettling possibility presented itself. If, as Eric Fedoruk had suggested, Justine had been determined to force her daughter to give up her psychiatric practice, the Erles would have been a useful weapon to have at the ready.

There was logic to my theory that Justine was prepared to use the Erles as a lever to pry Signe loose from her profession, but I was still grappling with the significance of the cancelled cheque. The reason for the cheque's journey from Regina to Lunenburg seemed clear enough. Somehow, Lucy had persuaded Tina to sign the money over to her. The endorsed cheque was certainly evidence that Lucy was a deeply flawed human being, but why had Hilda considered it important enough to remove from Justine's other records? By the time we pulled into the parking lot at Palliser Place, I still hadn't come up with a satisfactory answer.

Tonight, the pretty young woman behind the reception desk was wearing a lime-and-black-striped zipper-fronted Fortrel pantsuit. When I asked her where Garnet Dishaw was, she yawned and indicated the area behind her. "The place he always is when he's not in the hallway hitting balls around – in the dining room, watching the Golf Channel on the big-screen TV.

As soon as she turned her back, Taylor whispered, "I really like that girl's clothes."

"I used to have an outfit like that before Mieka was born," I said.

"Wear it again," Taylor said enthusiastically. "You'd look good with that zipper."

The tables in the dining room were set for breakfast, but the chalkboard inside the door still announced the evening meal. The menu was filled with exclamation marks: Beef Surprise!! Buttered Rice!! Garden Green Beans!! But the damp smell of food that had been held too long on steam tables revealed the unpalatable truth. The food at Palliser Place was not just institutional, it was lousy.

Garnet Dishaw had pulled a chair over in front of the biggest TV I'd ever seen. On the screen, two men were talking about a golf course, which was theatrically green and perfect.

"That's Old Head in Ireland," Garnet said. Painfully, he pushed himself to a standing position. "Isn't it a beauty?"

"It's nice," Taylor said. "But grass isn't really that colour."

Garnet looked at her severely. "Only a person born and bred on the short-grass prairie would be that suspicious. Are you a stubble-jumper?"

Taylor glanced up at me, questioningly.

"You were born in Saskatoon, and you've lived in Saskatchewan all your life," I said, "so I guess you qualify."

"Anyway," my daughter said with a shrug, "I'm Taylor Love."

Garnet made a courtly bow. "Garnet Dishaw," he said, "and I'm honoured to make your acquaintance." He turned to me. "Now, under other circumstances, my suggestion would be that we go back to my room and sample that excellent whisky peeking so seductively out of your bag. But I expect Ms. Love might like to eat some ice cream and watch TV."

"I *would* like that," Taylor said agreeably.

"Splendid," he said. "This institution has Dixie Cups by the truckload. Ice cream is their method of quelling potential insurrection from the inmates. And, Mrs. Kilbourn, we have coffee. A poor substitute for Johnny Walker, nonetheless . . ."

"Coffee would be fine," I said.

Despite our offers of help, Garnet Dishaw insisted on bringing the ice cream and coffee from the kitchen himself. The task wasn't easy for him, but he performed it gracefully. When, finally, he had Taylor settled with her ice cream in front of the giant TV, and he and I had found a table out of earshot, he turned to me.

"Let's begin by laying our cards on the table, Mrs. Kilbourn. In my opinion, Justine was as sane as you are. I saw her three days before she died. She was sound as a dollar. Now, where do you stand?"

"I don't know," I said, "but after yesterday, I think I'm moving towards your camp. For me, the piece of evidence that weighed most heavily against Justine was the fact that she'd let strangers be buried in her family's cemetery plot. It just seemed so crazy, but one of Justine's friends at Culhane House offered me a new perspective."

When I'd finished my précis of Wayne J.'s explanation, Garnet Dishaw chuckled. "So Justine thought Dick would be better off spending eternity with the usual suspects than with his nearest and dearest, eh? Still, it's no laughing matter deciding you don't want to buried next to your own children."

"Not much fun seeing yourself as Lear, either," I said.

"'How sharper than a serpent's tooth it is/To have a thankless child.'" Garnet Dishaw's face was grim. "Poor Justine. First that terrible business when Dick died, now this."

"What terrible business? When I was here with Keith, you said Richard Blackwell died of a broken heart. What broke his heart?"

Garnet sipped his coffee. "A lie," he said. "Someone told him Justine was having an affair. It wasn't true, of course, but Justine's accuser made a cruel choice in selecting the putative paramour. Sadly, Richard, who was usually the most perceptive of men, was blind to the motivations of the tale-bearer. By the time he arrived at my apartment with the story, he was a beaten man. He loved his family, and he made me promise never to tell a living soul. Forty-eight hours after Richard's midnight visit, he was dead." Garnet Dishaw's clever old face grew thoughtful. "There's nothing like death to give a casual promise the force of a blood oath."

"Who was Justine supposed to be having an affair with?"

Garnet Dishaw shuddered. "The boy next door."

"But there's only one house next door to Justine, and Eric Fedoruk said he'd lived there all his life."

"He had," Garnet said simply.

It took a moment before the penny dropped. "But Richard Blackwell died in 1967," I said. "Hilda told me he had his heart attack at a Centennial dinner. Eric Fedoruk couldn't have been more than . . ."

"Fifteen," Garnet Dishaw said. "Justine was forty and Richard was sixty-five."

"Who would make up something like that?"

Garnet's face closed in on itself. "No," he said, "that's one part of the story I won't tell. It may have been thirty years ago, but I have to honour my word to Richard there."

I sipped my coffee. "That's all right," I said. "I have a pretty good idea who told him. All I need to know is whether you're certain there was no truth to the accusation."

"I'm certain," Garnet said. "I've known Eric since he articled with our firm. There's not a chance in the world he would have had a sexual encounter with Justine. He had as little interest in physical intimacy as she did."

Taylor and I didn't stay long. After his revelation, Garnet Dishaw seemed somehow spent, and I was increasingly anxious to get in touch with Alex. Besides, we were no longer alone. The Saskatchewan–Toronto football game was being televised, and the residents of Palliser Place, decked out in the green and white, were arriving to cheer on the Roughriders.

We walked Garnet back to his room. Before he went inside, he shook hands with Taylor, then he took both my hands in his. "Be careful, Mrs. Kilbourn. We've already sacrificed one fine woman to this madness."

"I'll be careful," I said. I took the bottle of Johnny Walker out of my bag and passed it to him. "And I'll come back to help you make a dent in this."

His voice was firm. "Do I have your word on that?"

"You have my word," I said.

In the time we had been inside Palliser Place, the wind had picked up and the rain had grown heavier. Taylor and I had a soggy run to our car. As we drove home, Taylor, keyed-up by her visit and by the wildness of the night, prattled happily, but I was suddenly exhausted. It had been a long day, and the ache in my muscles and the soreness in my throat now made undeniable a fact I had spent the day denying: I was sick.

Spurred on by our agreement that she could watch half an hour of *Anne of Green Gables* after she'd had her bath, Taylor went straight upstairs. As soon as I heard the water running, I went into the family room to call Alex. When I picked up the phone, the beep indicating that I had a message was insistent. I tapped in our password. At first there was silence, and I thought the call was a prank. Then I heard Eli's voice, very agitated. "I'm a bad person," he said. "I've done bad things. It was her mother who died. I saw it on TV. I had to tell her about the blood. There was so much blood. It was everywhere." The line went dead. I replayed the message. Even when I was prepared for Eli's words, they chilled me. I dialled the number of the apartment. Alex answered on the first ring.

"It's me," I said. "Is Eli there with you?"

"I don't know where he is, Jo. When I came home the door to the apartment was open, but he was gone."

"He called us," I said. "There was a message on the machine when Taylor and I got home tonight." I relayed Eli's words.

"But he didn't say anything about where he was going?"

"No, but, Alex, I think I understand part of this. The six o'clock news showed that press conference announcing Terrence Ducharme's release. There was some file footage on Justine's murder. Eli must have seen it. I guess he hadn't realized till tonight that Justine was Signe's mother."

"And he called Signe Rayner to talk about it? God, Jo, I hope you're wrong. After I saw you today, I called her to tell her we thought it was time Eli tried another therapist. She went nuts. I'm no expert, Jo, but I would think that patients change therapists all the time. Signe Rayner acted as if I was betraying her. She told me I was ruining Eli's chances for recovery, then she started in about how Eli had done all these terrible things and how nothing he said could be believed."

"But she was his doctor. She was supposed to be on his side."

Alex's voice was tense. "I've got to find him, Jo."

"I'll come with you."

"No, stay there," he said. "Eli tried to get in touch with you once. He might try again."

I hung up. Tense and restless, I walked to the window. Even through the glass, I could hear the wind keening as it tossed leaves and litter through the air. Eli was out there somewhere, alone in the unforgiving night. Rose, who hated storms so much she never left my side until the weather calmed, whimpered. I reached down to rub her head. "It'll be over soon, Rose," I said, but as I gazed at the darkness, I wondered if the fear and the uncertainty ever truly would be over.

Miserable, I turned away. Propped on the mantel till it dried was Taylor's painting of the dragon-boat crew that would never be. It seemed that a hundred years had passed since that perfect night when Alex and the kids and I had walked home from the lake and made our plans for next year.

I repeated Eli's words aloud. "I've done bad things. There was so much blood." Two sentences, but they opened the floodgate. Details I'd been struggling to hold back since Labour Day overwhelmed me: Eli at the football game telling

Angus, "Sometimes I'd just like to kill you all." Alex's memory of Eli showering and changing into fresh clothes hours after Justine's murder. Eli's inability to remember anything that happened from the time he disappeared at the football game until he walked into Dan Kasperski's office. The crude brutality of the decapitated horse splashed over Taylor's dragon-boat painting. The recklessness with which Eli whirled our croquet mallet above his head, the same mallet that would be brought with such force against Hilda's skull that it would almost kill her.

Juxtaposed, the pictures formed a montage, dark with potential violence, but the composite was incomplete. There were other images of Eli, not the terrifying spectre of my worst imaginings, but the gentle boy with the shy smile who had worried about Mieka's unborn baby and looked at me with hopeful eyes the night I'd visited him in the hospital and talked about a school where he might feel safe. This Eli had worried that Taylor might feel left out and had brought Dilly Bars for dinner so I wouldn't have the bother of cleaning up. Something had gone terribly wrong Labour Day weekend. But remembering the Eli I knew, I was as certain as I could be of anything that, whatever Eli's connection was with those unknown events, he had been more sinned against than sinner.

I was still transfixed by the dragon-boat picture when Taylor ran into the room. Sweet-smelling and rosy from her bath, she came over, stood by me, and looked up at her painting. "Which one do you like better, this one or the one we gave Eli?"

"Well, I like the way Mieka and Greg and Madeleine and Hilda are in this one."

"You're in it, too," Taylor said.

"So I am. And guess what? I may have an idea about somebody to sit in that empty place next to me."

"Who?"

"Alex."

"Good," she said. "I miss him." She narrowed her eyes at the picture. "This one's okay, but I like the way the water looked in the other one."

"That's because the perspective was different. You painted the race the way it looked from higher up."

She gave me a look of exasperation. "I know," she said. "I was standing on that hill up by that Boy Scout thing."

I whirled to face her. "What?"

"That thing with the stones. From up there it looked like Angus and Eli had a wall of water in front of them. So that's what I painted, and I put me in too. Now, let's watch the movie." She slipped the video into the VCR and scrambled onto the couch. "Come on," she said. "It's starting."

From the time the opening credits rolled, Taylor was rapt, but my brain was racing as I ran through the sequence of events that fateful Labour Day weekend. Until that moment, I had seen the area in which we watched the races and the Boy Scout memorial where Justine was murdered as the focal points of two different tales. In fact, the places were separated from one another by less than fifty metres.

"There was so much blood." That's what Eli had said. What if . . . ? As *Anne of Green Gables* opened, I began to put together a hypothesis. Within half an hour, Taylor had fallen asleep in my arms, and I had a conjecture worth testing. All I had to do was wait for Eli to show up, so we could test it together.

At 9:30, I heard a car pull into the driveway. I leapt up and ran to the window, but it wasn't Eli and Alex, it was my son.

Angus was in an expansive mood. "It was the *best* evening. I didn't think it was going to be, but Rabbi Drache is a great guy. He knows everything. He's so smart, Mum, and he likes football. We watched the game."

"Who won?" I said.

"The Argos," Angus said. "But I didn't mind. Rabbi Drache was like a little kid. He was so wired." He stood up. "Anyway, I have a quiz in English tomorrow, so I should probably read the story."

"What's the story?" I asked.

"'The Painted Door,'" he said. "It's not bad. Do you want me to carry Taylor up to bed?"

"Oh, Angus, would you?" My voice sounded uncharacteristically plaintive.

For the first time since he'd walked into the room, my son really looked at me. "Is everything okay?"

"We don't know where Eli is," I said.

Angus's body tensed. "Should I go look for him?"

"No, stay here. If he calls, I might need to go and pick him up." I began coughing, and I couldn't seem to stop.

"Are you getting a cold, Mum?"

"I'm not getting a cold, Angus. I've *got* a cold, but at the moment, I'm not planning to do anything more strenuous than make myself some tea and sit around waiting for the phone to ring." I smiled at my son. "Don't look so worried, it'll take me back to my college days."

Rose stayed glued to me when I walked into the kitchen to fill the kettle. "You really are a major-league suck," I said. She looked wounded, but she didn't move. "Well, at least let's sit down while we wait for the water to boil." Rose started to follow me to the table, but suddenly she stopped, veered towards the back door, and began to bark. She and I had been together for a long time; as a rule, she trusted me to get the message after a couple of perfunctory woofs, but this time she was adamant. I went over to her, flicked on the yard lights, and opened the back door. The wind was still howling, and it blew a scattering of sodden leaves onto my kitchen floor. I nudged Rose with my toe. "Go on," I said. "If you have to go, go. The sooner you get out there, the sooner you can come back in."

My tone was sharp, but Rose, who was usually preternaturally sensitive, didn't budge; she just stood on the threshold, barking.

"There's nothing out there," I said, but as I started to shut the door, I saw that I was wrong. A slender figure in bluejeans and a white T-shirt was shinnying over the back fence. Even a quick glance was enough for me to recognize Eli's lithe grace. I walked out on the deck and called his name, but he'd already disappeared into the laneway. I ran down the deck stairs to the lawn. When I opened the back gate, the wind caught it and banged it against the fence. I stepped out into the alley. The creek was racing the way it did during spring run-off, and the wind was howling, but there wasn't a living creature in sight. I dashed back inside my yard, grabbed the gate with both hands and pulled it shut. It was only when I latched it that I felt the stickiness on my hands and smelled the paint. As I moved closer to the gate, I was able to see the outline of the black horse. Its message was as clear as a cry for help.

The Lavoline Taylor used to remove paint from her hands was in the carport. After I'd got off most of the black spray paint, I ran back inside, grabbed my coat, and called Angus. "Eli's out there," I said. "If Alex checks in, tell him I've gone out to look for him."

"Are you going to bring him back here?"

I shook my head. "I think when we've worked everything out, Eli will just want to go home."

When I pulled out onto Regina Avenue, I decided that, instead of heading directly for Albert Street, I'd double-back along the lane. Somehow, I couldn't believe that, having worked up the courage to come to our house, Eli would simply run away again. The decision was a good one. The gravel of our alley was spongy from the rain, and I had to keep the Volvo moving at a snail's pace. Nonetheless, it didn't take long to find Eli. As I'd anticipated, he hadn't gone far. My headlights picked him out, curled up between my neighbour's back fence and our communal garbage bin. I jumped out of the car and ran to him.

"Come on, Eli. You and I have things we need to talk about."

"Just leave me."

"I'm not going to leave you."

"You don't know what I've done."

"You didn't do anything."

"You don't know."

"But I do know. Get in the car with me, and I'll explain. If you'll give me a chance, I can show you that you didn't do anything wrong."

After a few seconds, he slowly got to his feet and headed for the car. Without a word, he slid into the passenger seat, closed the door, and sat, staring straight ahead. I glanced over at him. "Are you okay?"

Eli nodded. The light from the alley threw the carved beauty of his profile into sharp relief. Except for the trembling of his lower lip, he was absolutely still.

The road that winds through Wascana Park offers few places to pull over, so I drove straight to the cul-de-sac Justine had parked in the night of her death. It was behind an information booth that heralded the pleasures of Regina, the Queen City. The booth wasn't much: a Plexiglas-protected map of the area; a display case filled with posters of past and future events; a public telephone; and a clear view of both the Boy Scout memorial and the shoreline from which we'd watched the races.

I turned to Eli. "Look down there and tell me what happened that night after you decided you couldn't stay at the football game with us."

"Noooooo." The word ululated into a moan.

"Okay," I said quickly. "Let's go back to a better time. We're at the game. All of us. We were having fun. Then you and Angus went off for nachos."

"Just a fucking Indian," he said furiously.

I took his hand. "That's what the man said, and you were hurt and angry. Eli, tell me what happened next."

"I walked down Winnipeg Street – found some guys. They were doing solvent. They wanted me to do it too, but I wouldn't."

"Good for you," I said. "Then what happened?"

"I didn't know where to go." His voice broke. "I couldn't go home. I didn't want to disappoint my uncle again."

"He loves you, Eli. You couldn't disappoint him."

"Don't make me do this," he said miserably.

I stroked his hand. "We have to," I said. "Now, you decided you couldn't go home, so you came back here to where we watched the races."

"Not on purpose," he said. "At least I don't think so. I was just walking, and I ended up here." He smiled. "But it *was* nice to remember. I guess I fell asleep."

To this point, Eli's voice had been dreamy, the voice of someone whose mind was travelling through another time and place. Suddenly, his body grew rigid, and he began to breathe heavily. "When I woke up, the woman was screaming. I heard her. 'No. No. No. Don't do it. No, don't. Don't.' She sounded so scared. Just the way my mum did. . . . I went to help her. So much blood. There was so much blood." He had started to hyperventilate.

"Take a deep breath," I said. "You did everything right, Eli. Someone was hurt, and you went to help. That's the truth. All you did was try to help someone who needed you."

His body relaxed; his eyes met mine, and his question was urgent. "I didn't do anything wrong?"

"No," I said. "You didn't do anything wrong."

"I don't want to remember any more."

"That's all right," I said.

"Can we just go home now?"

"We can go home," I said.

He gave me a small smile and lay back against the seat.

I got a parking spot in front of the apartment building, which was a stroke of real luck because my adrenaline level had dropped dramatically. Even walking up the stairs to the third floor seemed to take every ounce of energy I could summon. Eli was tired too. When we got to the apartment, he reached into the old-fashioned milk chute to the left of the door, pulled out a key, and exhaled with relief. "I always forget my key, so my uncle leaves one in here for me." He looked at it curiously. "I think this one is his."

"We'll be here when he gets home," I said.

"I'm still scared," he said.

"Of what?" I asked.

"Of everything."

"We'll work on that," I said. "Now, let's go inside. I'm going to call our house so, when your uncle checks in, he'll know where we are."

"You're not going to leave me, are you?"

"No," I said. "I'm going to stay here till you boot me out. Now, why don't you have a shower and get into some dry clothes. Could I heat you up some soup or something?"

He shook his head. "I just want to go to bed."

I knew how he felt, but I still had miles to go before I slept. After Eli started his shower, I called home. Angus said that Alex had been checking in every half-hour or so from the cellphone in his car, and he was expecting a call any minute.

When I told Angus that Eli and I were safe at the apartment on Lorne Street, my son's relief was apparent.

After I hung up, I grabbed a quilt, sat down in an old easy chair Alex loved, closed my eyes, and listened to the reassuringly ordinary sounds of rainy night traffic and Eli's shower. When I heard the knock, I was so certain it was Alex that I opened the door without a second's hesitation.

She was in the apartment before I could even think of a strategy to stop her.

"Where's Eli?" she said.

"He's not here," I said.

She looked towards the bathroom. "Don't lie to me," she said. "I was waiting across the street. I saw you come in. Call him."

"No," I said.

"What's the point? I'm going to get him sooner or later." She shook her head sadly. "Music Woman, why did you have to get involved in this?"

"I don't know what you're talking about," I said. "I just came by tonight to stay with Eli. He wasn't feeling well."

Lucy Blackwell's turquoise eyes were cold. "I understand he's a very sick boy," she said. "My sister says he's delusional."

"That may be," I said carefully. "He's had a lot of trauma in his life. It's quite possible he's confused about many things." I took a step towards her. "Lucy, why don't you leave and let me take care of him."

"Has he said anything to you about me?"

"No," I said. "He's never once mentioned your name."

"I hear he's been talking about my mother's death."

"I wouldn't worry about that," I said. "As your sister pointed out, Eli is delusional. Nobody will put much credence in anything he says." I took a step closer to her. "If I were you, I'd walk out that door right now. At this point, there's no proof of anything. You can grab your passport and be on the first plane out of here."

She was wearing a silvery raincoat with a hood, and she pulled the hood down to reveal her dark honey hair. "I don't get it," she said. "Why are you offering me a way out, Music Woman?"

"I've loved your music for thirty years. Maybe I just want to see your life have a happy ending." My heart was pounding so loud, I was amazed she didn't hear it. "Just go, Lucy."

"You'd be on the phone to the police as soon as I started downstairs."

"There's nothing to tell them," I said. "It's all perfectly innocent: you knocked at the door; we talked; I asked you to leave; you left."

She looked at me thoughtfully. "You really would let this be our little secret?"

I nodded. "Just leave us alone," I said.

She pulled her hood up. "Okay," she said. "Maybe you're right. Maybe I can still get away." She smiled her wonderful dazzling smile. "Many thanks, Music Woman."

"No!" Eli's scream was atavistic. I whirled around to face him. He was wearing a white robe and his long black hair fell loosely to his shoulders. He looked like an acolyte in a religious order, but there was no peace in his face. His eyes were wide with terror, and his mouth was a rictus. "You did it," he said. "You killed her. I saw. I saw. She kept crying and asking you to stop." His voice grew higher. "'Lucy. Lucy, No. No.' There was so much blood," he screamed. "So much blood!"

Lucy's hands shot up, and she lunged at him. I stepped between them. In an instant, she changed her target. Suddenly, her hands were around my throat, and she was squeezing. I tried to call out, but the only sound that came from my throat was a strangled sob. When I reached up to unclasp her fingers, it was like grappling with steel. I kicked at her legs, but she didn't falter. Lucy Blackwell had the strength of someone engaged in mortal combat. Wildly, I looked around the room I knew so well, but there was nothing there to save me. My vision blurred. I saw red, then black. I felt the sensation of falling, and I knew I was dying.

Then, miraculously, it was over. The fingers loosened. I fell against a chair and gulped air thirstily. When I was able to focus, I saw what had happened. Eli had grabbed Lucy from behind. His arm was around her neck in a kind of stranglehold. Slowly but inexorably, he brought her to the floor and pinned her there.

A few seconds later, when Alex came through the door, everything was taken care of. He nodded at Eli. "Good job," he said.

Eli gave him a small smile. "Just the way you taught me." Then his face broke into misery. "She killed her Mum," he said. "She killed her own Mum."

"I know," Alex said. He went over to Lucy, pushed her arms behind her back, and handcuffed her. "Stay there," he said. "And don't move." He looked up at me. "Could you call headquarters, Jo? Get them to send some backup."

As the three of us waited, Lucy's eyes never left my face. It was obvious that, despite the events of the past few minutes, she still saw me as someone with the potential to be her advocate. "You shouldn't have got involved," she said in her low and thrilling voice. "Should have just stayed home with your rocking chair and your kids."

"Why did you do it, Lucy?" I said.

Lucy shifted position and groaned a little. She was obviously in pain. "Justine never invited us to the party. No matter how hard we tried or how perfect we looked or how much we accomplished, it was never enough. She never invited us to the party." Her voice was heartbreakingly sad. "*'Three little girls in virgin's white, swimming through darkness, longing for light.'* I killed my mother because she never once invited us to come in out of the dark. And do you know what? If I had the chance, I'd kill her again."

"And Hilda?" I asked. "Would you try to kill Hilda again?"

Confusion flickered across her face. "That was a mistake. Everybody makes mistakes, right?" She tried a gallant smile. "I just make more than most people."

For the next few minutes, Lucy rambled through her *apologia pro vita sua*. Much of the time she was incoherent, but two key points emerged. Lucy herself had been the one who went to Richard Blackwell with the lie about Justine's affair with Eric Fedoruk; nonetheless, she blamed Justine for her father's death. "He loved her too much," she said. "It didn't leave enough for me." Lucy held her mother responsible for Tina Blackwell's botched medical procedure, too. Although Justine had given Lucy a substantial amount of money to get *The Sorcerer's Smile* produced, when the boxed set of Lucy's musical legacy failed to take off, Justine refused to write the cheque that would have given her daughter the saturation ad campaign Lucy believed would salvage her dream.

"The only option she left me was Tina," Lucy said sulkily. "How do you think it makes me feel every time I have to look at my sister's face?"

The rest of Lucy's tale was equally ugly, equally filled with self-pity and bitterness. I was relieved when the sounds of a siren split the night. For three decades, I had loved Lucy Blackwell's voice, but I never wanted to hear it again. When the uniformed police arrived, it was over quickly. Two officers helped Lucy to her feet and led her towards the front door. As she walked by me, she gave me a sidelong smile. "So, are you still my number-one fan, Music Woman?"

"Not a chance, Lucy," I said. "Not a chance."

When the door closed behind her, Eli turned to me. "I want to watch them take her away," he said.

We walked out to the balcony together. The rain had stopped. The plaster owl which Alex and I had designated as our sentinel sat jauntily on his railing perch, and the air smelled fresh-washed. Down the street, the bells at the United Church were ringing. It was a good evening to be alive. Eli and I watched silently as Lucy was put into the squad car. Just before Alex got into the front seat, he called up to us. "I love you," he said.

Eli looked at me. "Did he mean me or you?"

"Both of us," I said. "Now, come on. Let's get inside. You and I have a lot to talk about."

"Like what?"

"Oh, like when you think you'll be ready to get together with Dan Kasperski and when you think you'd like to meet Ms. Greyeyes and get started at school."

"I'd like to come by your house some time again, to see the kids."

"That shouldn't be too difficult to arrange."

"I'll need to tell Taylor I'm sorry about what I did to her painting, won't I?"

"Yes," I said, "you will."

"Do you think she'll listen to me?"

"She'll listen. She's a good little kid."

I could see the relief in his face. For a moment he was silent, then he turned to me. "Do you know what I wish?" he said softly.

"What?"

"I wish we could have that dragon-boat team we talked about – the one with all of us."

"There's no reason we can't," I said. "But, Eli, do you really think Taylor's up to taking on all the obligations of being our drummer?"

Eli grinned. "Sure she is. We just have to let her know we think she can do it, and give her time."

* * *

A few days later, when Angus and I were helping Hilda move from the hospital to the Wascana Rehabilitation Centre, I remembered Eli's words about the importance of faith and time. Angus was wheeling Hilda out to our car, and we were talking about what she might need in her new home.

"A good poetry anthology," Hilda said. "Do you have one, Joanne?"

Angus screwed up his face with distaste. "Why would you want to read poetry? It's all about death."

Hilda touched his hand. "It's not about death, Angus. It's about time. All poetry is about time."

Therapy was about time, too. At least, that's what Dr. Dan Kasperski believed. There were no quick fixes for Eli. When Alex and I had gone to talk to him about Eli's prognosis, Dan Kasperski had been realistic. "He's got a lot going for him. He's smart and he's strong. He's come through far more than anyone should be expected to endure. The fact he acted heroically with Lucy Blackwell was a big move forward. But it's up to him. He has to decide what he's going to do with the time ahead. If he wants to give it up to anger and self-pity, he'll be screwed. If he uses his time wisely and bravely . . ." Dan Kasperski shrugged. "Who knows? Sky's the limit."

My horizons weren't sky-high. On our shared fifty-second birthday, Keith Harris and I went out for dinner, and I told him that Alex and I were going to try again. Keith didn't seem surprised, but he didn't offer congratulations. "I want what's best for you, Jo, but even if I can't be in the picture, I'm not sure if Alex is the right one. Somehow I can't see a future for you two."

"Maybe there isn't one," I said. "Alex and I may have to be content with the present."

Keith smiled. "Then let's drink to that." He raised his glass. "To the present. I hope it will be enough for you, Jo."

I raised my glass. "So do I," I said.

By Thanksgiving, Justine Blackwell's tragedy had reached its dénouement. Lucy Blackwell was awaiting trial; Eric Fedoruk had brokered an agreement between Culhane House and Tina Blackwell about Justine's estate; and the College of Physicians and Surgeons had set in motion procedures to revoke Dr. Signe Rayner's licence. There was, however, one piece of business still to be finished.

Thanksgiving Monday, I picked up Garnet Dishaw at Palliser Place, and together we drove to the Wascana Rehabilitation Centre to get Hilda. The day was grey and still, a day for remembering. As we made our way to the cemetery where Justine was buried, Garnet and Hilda traded memories of the woman they had known and cared for. When we turned onto the road that led to Justine's burial plot, I spotted Eric Fedoruk's Eurobrute pulled up beside Wayne J. Waters' elaborately painted van. As soon as we parked, the two men came over. Wayne J. reached into the back seat, pulled out Hilda's wheelchair, snapped it smartly into place, and helped her into it; Eric, after greeting Hilda warmly, helped Garnet Dishaw over the uneven ground to Justine's grave. Tina Blackwell, dressed in black, was waiting by the new headstone. She acknowledged us with a shy smile, then turned to Wayne J.

"Are we ready, Wayne?" she asked.

"Ready as we'll ever be," he said. The tombstone was covered with a beach towel. "I hope you don't think this is in bad taste," he pointed to the towel. "I should have thought ahead, found something appropriate. But I like the idea of an unveiling."

"I do too," Hilda said. "It gives the moment a sense of importance."

"Okay," Wayne J. said. "Here goes." He grabbed the corner of the towel between his thumb and forefinger. "This is a present from Tina and from all of us at Culhane House. Hilda chose the words. They're from Proverbs." He flicked aside the towel to reveal a creamy marble headstone. On it were chiselled Justine's full name and a simple inscription: THE MEMORY OF THE JUST IS BLESSED.

New from Gail Bowen

Fall 2004

THE LAST GOOD DAY

A Joanne Kilbourn Mystery

GAIL
BOWEN

A COLDER KIND OF DEATH

"A TERRIFIC STORY WITH A SLICK TWIST AT THE END."
– GLOBE AND MAIL

When the man convicted of killing her husband six years earlier is himself shot to death while exercising in a prison yard, Joanne Kilbourn is forced to relive the most horrible time of her life. And when the prisoner's menacing wife is found strangled by Joanne's scarf a few days later, Joanne is the prime suspect.

To clear her name, Joanne has to delve into some very murky party politics and tangled loyalties. Worse, she has to confront the most awful question – had her husband been cheating on her?

"A delightful blend of vicious murder, domestic interactions, and political infighting that is guaranteed to entertain." *– Quill & Quire*

"A classic Bowen, engrossing and finally, believable." *– The Mystery Review*

"A denouement filled with enough curves to satisfy any mystery fan."
– Saskatoon StarPhoenix

0-7710-1495-3 $9.99

A KILLING SPRING

"A COMPELLING NOVEL AS WELL AS A GRIPPING MYSTERY."
– PUBLISHERS WEEKLY

The fates just won't ignore Joanne Kilbourn – single mom, university professor, and Canada's favourite amateur sleuth. When the head of the School of Journalism is found dead – wearing women's lingerie – it falls to Joanne to tell his new wife. And that's only the beginning of Joanne's woes. A few days later the school is vandalized and then an unattractive and unpopular student in Joanne's class goes missing. When she sets out to investigate the student's disappearance, Joanne steps unknowingly into an on-campus world of fear, deceit – and murder.

"This is the best Kilbourn yet." *– Globe and Mail*

"*A Killing Spring* is a page-turner. More than a good mystery novel, it is a good novel, driving the reader deeper into a character who grows more interesting and alive with each book." *– LOOKwest Magazine*

"Fast paced . . . and almost pure action. . . . An excellent read."
– Saint John Telegraph-Journal

"*A Killing Spring* stands at the head of the class as one of the year's best."
– Edmonton Journal

0-7710-1486-4 $7.99

VERDICT IN BLOOD

It's a hot Labour Day weekend in Regina, Saskatchewan, which means the annual Dragon Boat races in Wascana Park, a CFL game, family barbecues, ice cream – and tragedy. A young man is missing. And Madam Justice Justine Blackwell has been bludgeoned to death.

This is Gail Bowen's sixth novel featuring Joanne Kilbourn, one of Canada's most beloved sleuths. Teacher, friend, lover, single mother, and now grandmother, Joanne's quick intelligence and boundless compassion repeatedly get her into – and out of – trouble.

"A deeply involving novel . . . Bowen has supplied such a convincing array of details about [Joanne's] family, friends and the landscape that we slip into her life as easily as knocking on a neighbor's door." – *Publishers Weekly*

"Bless Gail Bowen, she does it all: genuine human characters, terrific plots with coherent resolutions, and good, sturdy writing."
– Joan Barfoot in the *London Free Press*

"An author in full command of her metier. Like a master chef, Gail Bowen has taken disparate elements . . . and combined them seamlessly." – *Calgary Herald*

0-7710-1489-9 $8.99

BURYING ARIEL

Joanne Kilbourn is looking forward to a relaxing weekend at the lake with her children and her new grandchild when murder once more wreaks havoc in Regina, Saskatchewan. A young colleague at the university where Joanne teaches is found stabbed to death in the basement of the library. Ariel Warren was a popular lecturer among both students and staff, and her violent death shocks – and divides – Regina's small and fractious academic community. The militant feminists insist that this is a crime only a man could have committed. They are sure they know which man, and they are out for vengeance. But Joanne has good reason to believe that they have the wrong person in their sights.

"A study in human nature craftily woven into an intriguing whodunit by one of Canada's literary treasures." – *Ottawa Citizen*

"Excellent . . ." – *National Post*

"The answer to the mystery . . . remains tantalizingly up in the air until the entirely satisfying finale." – *Toronto Star*

0-7710-1498-8 $9.99

THE GLASS COFFIN

This chilling tale about the power of the ties that bind – and sometimes blind – us, is Gail Bowen's best novel yet. Set in the world of television and film, *The Glass Coffin* explores the depth of tragedy that a camera's neutral eye can capture – and cause.

Canada's favourite sleuth, Joanne Kilbourn, is dismayed to learn the identity of the man her best friend, Jill Osiowy, is about to marry. Evan MacLeish may be a celebrated documentary filmmaker, but he has also exploited the lives – and deaths – of the two wives he lost to suicide by making acclaimed films about them. It's obvious to Joanne that this is stony ground on which to found a marriage. What is not obvious is that this ground is about to get bloodsoaked.

"The end . . . is chilling and unexpected." – *Globe and Mail*

"[*A Glass Coffin*] takes the series into a deeper dimension." – *Times-Colonist*

"Part of Bowen's magic – and her work is just that – lies not only in her richness of characters but in her knack of lacing her stories with out-of-left-field descriptives." – *Ottawa Citizen*

0-7710-1477-5 $9.99